A BALLAD FOR THE BROKEN

CADENCE OF THE FALLEN
BOOK TWO

HAZEL S. WILKES

NOVA

A BALLAD FOR THE BROKEN

Cadence of the Fallen, Book Two

Hazel S. Wilkes

For the choices that both were and were not made;
For the blame which was and was not placed—
May they, at least, be understood.

Four hundred and eleven years ago, the continent was united under one ruler, one king. The king was an old man without any heirs. He was tired, senile, and a turned drunk, plunging the continent into disarray. Famine, illness, and poverty swept through the lands. Only the highest ranked nobles—those which hailed from the Great Houses—remained unscathed.

Desperate, many nobles took to the courts to devise strategies for which they could regain their wealth. Their dignity and livelihoods. Within the courts, it was decided the decrepit king would be overthrown, and the people would elect three new kings to three new kingdoms, inciting a new era of prosperity where the different needs of each region could be better met. A kingdom in the east, a central kingdom, and one in the west, each divided by a river border. Each kingdom would abide by its own governance, though all would agree to adhere to a small set of laws scribed in the Beginning, known as Tani law.

And thus, with this new order, the Three King System was born.

— EXCERPT FROM THE RECOVERED JOURNAL, *WE SANG THE DAWN.* AUTHOR REMAINS UNKNOWN.

PROLOGUE

LYRA

THREE DAYS AFTER THE ATTACK ON BATHARA....

I awake to screams.

Loud. Piercing. Sporadic.

For a moment, I am nothing more than a small girl again—tiny fists drumming against tiny patches of land, cruelty carving her skin like a blade.

The marks are permanent. There's nothing more we can do.

I hear someone say that.

Can they see the flames, too? Do they hear the screams? Have the wounds I carry finally manifested into nasty gashes along my body? I always figured they would someday.

Wait—who is that talking?

The screaming stops then. That's when I realize the sound was coming from me. A croakish, beaten thing. Like my vocal cords have been rubbed raw by sand and deprived of fluids for ages.

The memories return to me. Almost in a dream-like state, but not.

I see flashes of great power. See ribbons of skin twirling in the air. Black and crimson blood pours down onto rubble like splattered

1

pellets of rain. Strong arms anchor a hurricane; the waves are seafoam and blue.

I see Gray.

See his lifeless body sprawled across the ground as a bloodied blade glints against the moonlight.

Then there are endless bodies. Slain. Charred. Bleeding and broken.

I see a monster.

I see myself.

The screams return; the world goes black once more.

FIVE DAYS AFTER THE ATTACK ON BATHARA…

This time when I wake up, there are no screams or surrounding whispering voices. There is only the sharp smell of a bitter antiseptic mingling with floral undertones.

"Where am I?" I ask, pressing a hand against my head.

A figure appears behind light that is too bright. Too cheery and radiant. He bends down, handing me a flower.

"Exactly where you should be."

I take the flower and examine it, noting the strange coloring of the petals and the musky smell at odds with the odor of healing salves. I twirl the textured stem between my fingertips. While I do, a momentary peace settles within me. Until those crimson stained memories again crash into me, splitting me apart.

I scurry to a stand, the velvet petals slipping from my grip. I trample them as I approach Casimir with the grace of a fawn finding its legs. I shove his chest with as much force as my throbbing body can muster. He does not try to stop me. "*Murderer*," I seethe. "Monster." My vision flickers, snowflake flurries appearing at the corner of my sight.

I do not relent.

"You murdered Gray!"

2

"And you murdered my own people. Shall I refer to you as a murderer and monster as well?"

There is a blurriness attached to the haze of my memories. Some of it a distant dream, away from my grasp yet obtainable. Other parts are a void—a black hole where no light lives. I remember the slice of the blade as it went through Gray's neck. I remember the sheer eruption of anger from my veins. The explosion of power. I remember burning. Hearing screams. Until an anchor grounded me.

There was horror in his eyes.

Then there was utter darkness.

"I killed them," I rasp.

"Every last one of them," Casimir confirms. "Gone, by your hand. By your magic. By your lack of control and your ripe anger."

The guilt presses into me, suffocating and piercing, and my heart tightens. A strobing effect consumes my vision, the flurries multiplying.

"I—you—" I drop my eyes as the blood thrumming in my ears reaches an unbearable decibel. I am met by the sight of gnarled ugliness. By a permanent deformity forever reminding me of my unforgivable actions.

The marks are permanent. There's nothing more we can do.

So my sins are worn on my skin at last.

My chest clenches, and my vision blinks in and out, in and out. I wobble on my feet, wielding an accusatory finger pointed into Casimir's chest as though it is the tip of a blade.

You killed them, I want to say. *You murdered my best friend. Murdered Griff and left him to bleed out in Marcella's arms.*

Yet I don't say any of that because I can't. My jaw is locked, my tongue paralyzed. The only part of me that seems capable of moving are my swaying muscles. They move back and forth. Back and forth.

The world tilts.

Then goes black.

Nine days after the attack on Bathara...

Within the stars, a female voice hums. *Find me within the stars.*

Glittering images flicker in a quick sequence. A crimson river. A starry-eyed wolf. Ashen ribbon twirling over living blue fire. I hear the plucked strings of a breaking instrument. Hear the echoes of confessions, curses, and screams. I see a woman holding a small babe swaddled in cloth. A father's command to tell no one. I see two sides of different fires merging together. See a void of sharpened blackness as it swallows and consumes. Gold melts. Power explodes into the sky.

That's when it begins, the melodic voice warns. *That's when you must find me.*

In a world of mist and smoke, I am shown a burning kingdom and a blood-soaked battlefield. I am shown arrows, swords, and spears of magic lancing in front of a full, glowing moon. War drums drill their chilling heartbeat into my heels. It rattles my lungs and freezes my joints.

It is coming, the voice hums.

You must find me.

When I awake again, I am in a nondescript room wrapped in silk, my body aching and tight like unused hinges.

I sit up slowly, my head woozy and feeling two times its actual weight. There is a crystal glass filled with what I presume to be water resting on a table beside the large canopied bed cradling my sore muscles. A broad mahogany wardrobe rests against the wall facing me, and a small window exposes a thin streak of starlight.

Night time, then.

Perfect.

I throw the feather-soft covers from my body and slide off the plush mattress, my heels kissing cool stone while the pain from stiff, unused muscles kisses me. After my eyes adjust to the darkness, I

4

notice that nearest the window, there is a door, while another larger door fills the center of the opposite wall. I check the smaller door first, deciding it has the lesser chance of being the exit. I crack the wood open and peek inside. Through the silver moonlight washing in from a rectangular window at the back wall, I luckily find nothing more than an attached bathing chamber. Which means the other door must in fact be the exit as I suspected.

Great.

Now that that much is settled, I need to search this room top-to-bottom, looking for anything useful. Any clues. I would say any weapons as well, but... I am not foolish enough to believe Casimir would leave such a thing in my holding chambers.

Regardless, I have an escape plan to make.

I DO NOT SLEEP at all for the rest of the night.

Yet I do rest my eyes, feigning sleep. Once the sun blinks its golden eyes open, coating the room in gilded morning light, I lay upon the plush mattress and silky sheets. I keep my eyes shut and breathing steady as I hear footsteps come and go. I count two different sets of them—one whose movements are light and airy, almost like I imagine a dancer's to be. The other set is slow in their movements and nearly mute against the stone floor. They only visit my chamber once, and stay no longer than a minute or two.

The dancer's footsteps return around what I presume to be dinner time, something metal rattling in their hands. They lay what I suspect to be a tray down on the table beside me and position themselves at the very edge of the bed. The person takes my arm in their cold hands, and I say silent prayers in my mind that I can maintain this ruse effectively.

I do not.

They tap the crook of my elbow a few times, then I feel a sharp pinch as something cold pierces through my skin and into my vein. I jolt at the unexpected pain, which results in the person pausing their

5

movements. Even with my eyes closed, I can feel the weight of their stare as it crawls over every inch of me in close observation.

Deciding it best to play into the disturbed sleep a bit better, I nestle my head into the pillow and sharpen my breathing before letting it fall back to a steady, slow rhythm. Luckily for me, this seems to satisfy whoever the person is, and they continue with whatever the hell it is they're doing.

I hear the rustling of a bag, and then next thing I know a powerful wave of warmth floods my veins accompanied by a pleasant humming sensation blanketing over me. Healing magic, I think. The strange filling sensation finds every crevice—every inch of my body—before the hunger pangs previously torturing my stomach disappear, the need to chug five pitchers of water going along with it.

So that's how they've been keeping my body replenished.

I wonder what substance they're pumping into me? Perhaps an extract from piper's weed or longtails—both plants known to be filled with enough nutrients to sustain a body by itself.

When the person is finished, they pull what I now know to be a needle from my vein and pack up their belongings, small *tings* ringing into the air as they stack one object after the next back onto their metal tray. Then, they leave the room.

As I wait for the sky to fill with stars, I tally the time between each passing visit. Recount my approximations for how long they were in my room and what time of day they entered. It is only once night is well on its way and I am confident nobody is coming back into my chamber that I again throw the covers from my legs and revisit my ongoing escape plan. Tonight, I decide to daringly creak the main door open to glimpse what is on the other side. If it's a guard, I sign my own prison sentence. If it's an empty corridor, I may just sign my own freedom missive.

With a constricted throat and hammering heart, I pull back the door and brace myself for what may lie before me.

Blissful emptiness.

Nothing but a red-rugged corridor filled with guttering braziers and stone walls.

I look left. Then right.

Do I dare attempt to explore the corridor? Do I risk the consequences of being caught before I even have a real chance at escape?

I weigh the risks against the reward. If I am caught, they will know I am awake and probably change both my routine and surveillance, leaving me most likely without another escape window. I won't bother wasting my time imagining whatever the hell else Casimir may force me to do. The speculation isn't worth the worry it'll bring. But if I can successfully search the surrounding corridors, I'll be able to craft a much more informed plan. Will be able to strategize better, knowing potential escape routes and how many, if any at all, guards are posted.

Still, I've only been awake a day. What if someone is scheduled to check on me in the middle of the night? What if guards begin their rounds soon? *What if, what if, what if...*

With a quiet sigh and a made decision, I latch the door back into place.

Tomorrow.

THE NEXT DAY the routine is exactly the same. Two sets of footsteps appear on the exact hour they did the previous day. A cold needle is poked into my arm. Buzzing magic coats my skin. And most importantly, I am left alone through the night.

This time when the moon peaks in the midnight sky and I creak the hinges back to reveal a yet again blissfully empty corridor, I venture beyond the threshold previously containing me. I wander through the shadows, staying close to the stone walls as a means of precaution, and this time I do not shy away from the bold decisions, traversing to the end of the corridor to make a left then a right.

I am led into a sprawling room composed of nothing but floor-to-ceiling windows. Shimmering rays of a pressing moon spill over onto the marble flooring. The polished rock is ashen in color, vibrant blue veins extending like roots over the whole of it. There is no furniture. No items cluttering the space.

There is only what lies beyond it.

The night sky is filled with more stars than imaginable. As though the gods fisted handfuls of sand and tossed the grains upward, cementing them into the heavens themselves. Paired with the bright silver moon, I am able to catch formed images of the garden lying beyond the glass walls. It stuns me, the assortment of wildlife and vegetation. With such little light it's hard to be certain, but it almost seems like a garden oasis of sorts.

Which is a stroke of brilliant luck for me.

Within a blink, I am rerouting my escape plan. I begin accounting for the time it will take me to find useful items in the garden beyond the windows. I consider how long it might take me to concoct useful sleeping tonics. If perhaps I can even make a lethal poison. I decipher how I might do so without proper Gardner tools—wonder if there is a kitchen nearby where I can steal necessary supplies. I debate how to best use such items—if they are truly necessary, or if I am better off simply making a run for it.

I am swimming in the possibilities when a tired yet smooth voice sounds behind me.

"You're awake."

My muscles go rigid.

Slowly and against every screaming desire of my body, I turn around. Casimir stands tall only a few paces behind, his hands clasped and shoulders rolled back. I do my best to mirror the confidence.

"I am," I say.

"And how are you feeling?"

Like shit, obviously.

"As well as one could hope, I'd imagine," I say instead.

He tilts his head, his amber eyes seeming to glow against the midnight color pallet. He studies me for an unnerving amount of time. "Why are you wandering the halls in the middle of the night?"

"Why are you?" I counter pointedly.

Casimir remains silent, his movements eerily still. Eventually, he extends his hand to me and says, "Come. I will take you back to your room and send for you in the morning. Now that you are both awake and lucid, you and I can discuss why I have brought you here over breakfast."

The casual ease of that statement stings as if a direct slap to the face. "I'm not going anywhere with you," I hiss. "And I am certainly not having *breakfast* with the monster who murdered my best friend."

Pain digs into me with the force of a living beast. But I don't show a sliver of weakness to this vile creature standing before me. Instead, I lift my chin and hold my expression steady, allowing every ounce of defiance and loathing to show in my eyes.

Casimir again remains both silent and still. Though this time the look in his gaze appears to be one of consideration. Eventually, he sighs, those perfectly held shoulders slumping forward just slightly with the action. "He is not dead."

"What?" I breathe. Hope swells in my chest, but I clutch onto it, willing to keep it contained. "I saw him...saw *you* put a blade through his neck."

Casimir shakes his head. "What you saw was an illusion I wielded over you to make your power erupt."

Anger, relief, spent grief—it all slams into me with debilitating strength. My mouth flounders as I search for words, thinking I have a sentence but then realizing I have nothing more than stuttering words.

"So what I saw wasn't real?" I ask, daring to allow myself just a little hope. "It didn't actually happen, and Gray is alive?"

"Yes."

Tears swarm my eyes, hot and uncontrollable, but I pinch my teeth into my bottom lip to hold them at bay. "You swear it? By whatever god, whatever force you deign to actually believe in—you swear you're telling me the truth?"

"I swear it," he says.

The immediate relief the revelation brings me is enough to make me feel as though I can float away into the clouds. Until I am immediately shackled back into reality.

"Now, come," Casimir instructs. "I am taking you back to your room for the night."

I glare at him for a heartbeat, the wheels of my mind turning over. So be it, then. Plan B it is.

I nod my head and signal Casimir to lead the way, following him back down the path from which I came. When we reach my bedchamber, he opens the door for me and motions for me to enter.

"I will see you in the morning," he says.

Maintaining the disposition I normally would to prevent any red flags from raising, I hold his eyes with contempt in my own. Then, I stride off into my chambers, making a show of getting into bed and throwing the cover haughtily over me. I don't turn back to watch Casimir shut the door, but I do hear the familiar *click* of the latch.

To pass the time, I attempt to name every flower species containing poison my brain can conjure. Once I have, I pivot to every herb, plant, and flower that can cause paralysis. And when I have finished that, my mind can remain distracted no more, wandering to the memories of my inconsolable rage. Of my eruption of magic. Of Gray being alive—the joy and relief so overwhelming it feels tangible to my fingertips. A part of me knows Casimir may be lying, but I'd much rather believe he isn't.

I think of Draven.

The pain coating his face as he held onto me. The desperation I could feel pouring from him even in my state of delirium. The words that were distant yet near.

It's that you live, Lyra. You must live. And if you don't, then I'm coming with you, because I don't want to be in a world where I can't wake up and find you.

I don't want to live in such a world, either.

So fuck Casimir and his cruelty—I will not let him win by stealing me away. By robbing me of everything I worked toward to gain entry into Bathara. To start a new life. To feel and grow and heal.

As a reminder of all that I've overcome, I glance down at my finger, where a tiny blood droplet once was inked onto my skin. I noticed it was gone the second time I awoke from my long slumber. I also know what its disappearance means—the terms of the blood wager were fulfilled. And seeing as I am here—wherever the hell *here* is—and unable to provide King Alastair an heir, the only other option that would satisfy the terms of the wager are if I was Selected into an aggregate.

Deep in my heart, I know who is responsible for ensuring that happened.

With my resolve now steeled, I jump from the bed, deciding enough time has passed. If I am going to do this—if I am actually going to escape—it has to be tonight. It must be right now, in this moment.

There are no other options afforded to me.

I don't have time to formulate a plan. Don't have the luxury to scout and plot the best methods of escape.

So, in spite of knowing this is foolish recklessness, I throw the door open and sprint anyway.

THE AIR IS cool against my skin. Pleasant, even. It is a nice contrast to the pain plaguing every other part of my body.

My feet are stinging from all the surfaces they've trotted over. My lungs are screaming—*hissing*—at me to stop and take a proper breath. My muscles, not having been used for days upon days, are tight and angry, wounded with pain and on the precipice of giving out altogether.

Still, I don't stop.

Truthfully, I'm not even sure how I managed to get out from those lavish walls. I took turn after turn, and when they led to a dead end, I turned back and went the opposite way. I did my best to open as few doors as possible. Every time I did, I thought my pulse was going to hammer through my neck. Which meant running through those corridors was nothing more than a blurry maze of fervid determination and rapid desperation. Trial and error.

Until I got out. Escaped the maze.

Now, with my bare feet kissing grass and a pulsing scrape from where I tripped biting my knee, I am through the bulk of the wildlife and trees. I am marks away from those walls. I am staring out at a shadowy expanse veiled in moonlight, everything zipping past me in unintelligible imagery as I continue sprinting forward and doing my damn best not to trip on anything else.

A feat of which is made incredibly difficult, given my unfamiliarity with the landscape and the fact that it's the middle of the night.

At the adrenaline pumping into me, a manic laugh pours from my lips. I don't know where the hell I am, but I do know I am doing it. I am *actually* escaping. And each stride I continue to take is another one pushing me toward my own freedom.

The laugh comes too soon.

A glittering portal of silver, blue, and white sizzles into the air in front of me, and I skid to a halt. Casimir steps through it, his features perfectly placid. He does not look angry. He does not look surprised. In fact, he looks as though he has no feelings about finding me out here in the slightest.

"This is not your room," he says, the soft tiredness clinging to his voice.

Everything catches up with me. Somehow, stopping my sprint has made breathing harder, and my lungs catch fire while cement pours into my muscles and blinking stars twinkle in front of my eyes. My head becomes light as air, and I wobble.

Though I do not fall, planting my feet firmer into the ground.

Still, clearly it all gets to me, because my lip curls back at the sight of Casimir, and all that manages to spill from my lips is a hissed, *"Fuck you."*

He doesn't even react. "Let us go back."

"I'm not *going* back."

His head cocks, though his expression remains unchanged. "You speak as though I'm offering you a choice."

Now I know I'm feeling the full effects of everything—my pain, my exhaustion, my wooziness—because I take a step forward and grit through bared teeth, "You can try to keep me as your captive, but I will not make it easy for you. Do what you like to me, but I will not stop trying to escape. Will not give up until I'm back home, surrounded by the people I love."

"Ah," he muses, voice subtly sharpening with a tone screaming of danger. "Surrounded by the people you love." Now it is him who takes a step closer, swallowing any open space that was left between us. "Let me spell this out for you clearly this one time and one time only: you are here whether you like it or not because you have a purpose to serve. You will do as I ask when I ask it because the lives of my family are riding on your cooperation—on your being here. And if I am forced to choose between their lives or the lives of others, I will choose my family each and every time. And if I have to steal the lives of those people you *so* wish to be surrounded by to motivate you to cooperate, to force your submission, then so be it. I already have a mountain of blood stained on my hands, so what is another crimson seed in comparison?"

I swallow against the unbearable dryness overtaking my throat. I try to be brave—to find words to stand against this monster in front of me. But nothing comes.

The same is not true for Casimir. He tilts his chin to pierce my eyes with the glow of his and continues with his warning. "There is a reason I killed one friend while letting the other live. It is so you know I do not make hollow promises. So you know I have no quarrels with taking a life when necessary. So you have something you will be desperate to not lose again. So you now know the vivid taste of excruciating pain should that friend's life be lost once more."

I hate that fear hammers into my knees, making them tremble. Hate how my words are lodged deep into my throat, unwilling to risk flying free. All I can manage is to hold Casimir's cold gaze with a lifted chin, feeling on the verge of tears but knowing damn well I cannot show such weakness right now.

He glares into my eyes, and I swear I feel the look as sharply as a knife wound. "You are mine until I say so, and this place—my *home*— is where you will remain until I say otherwise. And if you are foolish enough to test my resolve, then I am not responsible for the bloodshed. It will be your own foolishness you'll have to thank when you are standing amongst the ruin of everything you feared losing."

"Monster," I whisper.

He takes another prowling step, dropping his voice lower. "I am glad you think so, darling. That way you will never think I'm bluffing when I tell you I *will* slit the throats of everyone you love if you try to leave my home."

I do not try to escape again.

PART I

THE OPENING STANZA

CHAPTER ONE

DRAVEN

"Tell me what you know."

Draven Dalmar digs the tip of his onyx dagger deeper into the fidgeting man's throat. Beads of chunky sweat form along the man's brow, trickling down into his amber-hued mustache, puddling along the hairs of it as densely as the puddle saturating the front of his pants.

"I've already told ya," he squeaks. "I don't know nothin.'"

"*Liar*," Draven accuses through clenched teeth, his breath hot against the mask covering the lower half of his face. He replaces the blade at the balding man's throat with his forearm, pushing down on his windpipe so forcefully, gargled choking sounds squeeze out the man's lips.

Holder Thistle is his name. A pudgy man whose rotten teeth perfectly match the condition of his conscience. Draven has been tailing him for the past three days, after a promising lead pointed him in his direction.

He repositions the dagger in his free hand and swipes the blade down the length of Holder's forearm. Without so much as blinking at the bloody gash, he pulls a small vial free from his pocket and pops the cork off. After, Draven returns his hollow stare back onto Holder, locking his eyes with his. Then, he empties the vial, pouring the black liquid directly onto the exposed, oozing vein.

Holder screams bloody murder; Draven lets him. They are marks away from the taverns lining these dirt-ridden streets, and Draven already scouted this particular alleyway. It is removed from any outpost lighting, any foot traffic, tucked even behind the trash heaps and opium houses and brothels. Not to mention, he's erected a dense wall around them with his dark magic, swallowing any noise or signs of life before they can escape.

So as Draven pours the venom into Holder's veins, he lets him scream and scream. And when he flicks his eyes down and catches the escaped blood bubbling and mutating to black tar, he growls with satisfaction. Over these past three days, he has witnessed Holder commit enough sins to condemn him to the noose three times over, and Draven holds no emotions over being this man's judge and executioner. He is the worst kind of scum, known around the Three Kingdoms as Skull Traders.

The title has two meanings. Skull Traders are in part called what they are because they trade in knowledge and information. At surface level, that's not such a terrible thing. Until one peels back the outermost layer and learns the truth of how their information is acquired— torture, sexual exploits, blackmail, and yes, even murder. Over time, Skull Traders somehow discovered their intel market overlapped nicely with trafficking, and as their reputations became more infamous and their activities more frequent, they needed a way to identify themselves. So they assumed their given nickname as a permanent title, tattooing skulls with some hidden mark within to denote the members of their criminal ring.

Draven relishes in watching the skull on the man's forearm bubble and bleed, and he hopes this ruins Holder's skin as viciously as the corrupted ruin Draven has felt living within himself.

Two months.

It's already been two months since Lyra's capture, and with every passing day, Draven feels the shadows growing thicker inside him as his desperation heightens.

That familiar stabbing sensation pierces his heart, and Draven digs his forearm deeper into Holder's throat. "Where the fuck is Casimir Vivaldri hiding," he seethes through his teeth, his already thin patience fraying.

Holder's face contorts, though not from his enduring pain. "The First Crowned Prince of Rivara?" he balks, anger seeming to overtake his fear. "What are ya doin' lookin' for a dead man? Better yet, why have ya senselessly targeted me over one?"

"You know something," Draven pushes. "I know you do." For emphasis, he turns the vial completely upside down, letting all the remaining drops trickle down like acidic rain onto his wound. "Now speak, Skull Trader. Before I find that vile tongue of yours so useless, I cut it from your mouth and feed it to the crows."

The man gulps, a small reprieve between his panicked pants. "Alright, alright," he says, winded. "I know a small somethin'. But I mean what I say when I tell ya I don't know nothin' about Casimir Vivaldri. And I'm not gonna ask why ya lookin' for a centuries dead prince anyhow."

Draven's stomach hollows, but he doesn't let it show. "Speak."

Holder glances left, then right. He drops his voice into a conspiratorial whisper. "In the weeds of the Kingdoms, snakes are leavin' their nests and movin' out the shadows."

Draven rolls his eyes and presses his thumb into Holder's open wound, letting tendrils of his dark magic fall into it and caress the damaged tissue like a cradle of tiny needle pricks. Holder gasps with shock before buckling in a near sob. The only thing keeping him from collapsing is the forearm Draven keeps wedged at his throat.

"What was *that* for?" Holder croaks.

"I did not tell you to give me cryptic stories or riddles. I told you to *speak*. Plainly, if that hasn't been made clear already."

Holder stares at Draven with the kind of hatred that would have made his father smile, and he flexes his jaw at the sight of it. Because this version of Draven? This is the version of him his father attempted to forge in the bowels of dungeons. The sort of ruthless machine Tynan Dalmar always hoped for his son to be.

It disgusts Draven down to his marrow to fulfill the aspirations his father always held for him. Especially after he was beginning to be someone better—a person more whole, worthy of wearing his mother's pendant once more.

But no matter the cost, he will do as he must to locate Lyra. To bring her back home. To attempt to right the many wrongs that have befallen her. And he will slice any man's skin or cut out any tongue until he can assure her safety. No matter how much it plunges him into the very shadows he swore to never dance with again.

Holder pauses for a moment too long, and Draven unfurls more of his magic from his fingertips, allowing wisps of his darkness to burrow like worms inside flesh and bone. A strangled sob rattles in Holder's throat as he attempts to cry out, but the noise is suffocated like a dying flame as Draven crushes his windpipe.

"I—I'll—talk." Each attempted word is nearly drowned out by the sound of his breathless, stuttering gasps.

Draven's reply comes only in the form of the small reprieve he gives Holder, removing just enough pressure from his throat to allow him to speak freely.

Holder sucks in air, coughing with the theatrics of a traveling troupe. Once his performance has finally ended, he resets his gaze to Draven. "Deep in the belly of the kingdoms, people gather. They gather and speak of the old ways."

Draven's brows twitch. "What do you mean, 'the old ways'?"

"I mean the ways before the Three Kings. Before the Great War and the Accords and before peace found its way to these here lands. A high bidder" —Holder stops, shooting him a pointed look— "and don't bother askin' who because I don't know, and I ain't tryna suffer more pain 'cause of it."

Draven nods his acceptance.

"A high bidder paid a pretty coin for us Skull Traders to find out all we can about the growin' movement. Made a bit complicated because the head of said movement also paid a bit of coin for information from us. But Skull Traders know no loyalty to no person. Our only loyalty is to our coin."

"What's this group's name?" Draven questions, ignoring his spineless commentary entirely.

"I don't know. I heard through the Trader grapevine once that they pull their ideas from some old-as-dust movement of the past, but that's all I know. I swear it."

Draven fights against his urge to hang his head in defeat. He can tell Holder is telling the truth, despite how much he wishes he were lying. Which means another fucking dead end.

His heart shrivels just a bit more.

"So to be clear," Draven bites out, his tone dry and expression sharp, "you don't have any information regarding Casimir Vivaldri's whereabouts, and what *trivial* information you do have, you don't even know the details surrounding it?" Draven drops the vial onto the ground and uses his now free hand to grip Holder's jaw. "What the fuck use are you to me, then?"

"I...do-don't..."

Draven squeezes Holder's jaw more tightly as his other arm remains firmly wedged against his throat, making it nearly impossible for him to speak. "You don't *what*, exactly?" Draven's frustration and anger spike, his self control slipping. He glances down and glimpses the black spiderwebs creeping along his forearm. One glance back at Holder's horrified stare also confirms to Draven that his darkness is seeping into the colors of his eyes.

Fuck.

He's been allowing this to happen far too often lately. But ever since that terrible fucking day—the day haunting his nightmares and living like poison in his veins, his mind replaying again and again all that he could have done differently to prevent Lyra's capture—Draven finds his ability to keep a lid on the ferocity of his magic increasingly difficult. It's as if dredging so deep into it during his fight with Casimir Vivaldri awakened a slumbering beast inside of him.

He has no desire to be swallowed into the belly of that monster.

Turmoil churns in his chest from another dead end as he grits his teeth and tries to bottle his humming magic. Yet his magic sings with glee as it cascades from his fingertips, burrowing into Holder's cut flesh, refusing to be jarred any longer. Draven slides him a quick glance before scowling and jerking his arm away from the Skull Trader's throat.

"*Stay,*" he growls at him like some stray pet he just found on the street.

Draven wraps his fingers around his wrist, squeezing tightly against the swell of magic overtaking his veins. As he does, he concentrates on reigning his dark magic back inside him. Somewhere along the way, the mask covering his face must have shifted, because he hears Holder audibly gasp with shock.

"You're the Dalmar Heir...." he accuses, slightly awestruck. "I—I knew somethin' was different about your magic."

Draven only spares him an irritated glance.

Holder keeps talking, licking his chapped lips. "Did you know all the Great House Heirs have a pretty price on their pretty heads?" In one swift motion, he reaches for a dagger strapped to his ankle and attempts to slice Draven's throat.

After sighing at the pathetic man, Draven presses two fingers together and flicks them forward, launching two spears of his magic directly into each of Holder's shoulders. Draven shakes out his hand after, wrangling his insatiable magic back into its cage. Once he's sure he's gotten himself under control again, he squares himself back to Holder. "I told you to stay."

"Fuck you." The Skull Trader spits at Draven's feet. "Go back to your pampered life on some cushy throne and leave us rats alone to play in the gutters, would ya?"

Draven grunts a laugh before mocking a dramatic sigh. "Alas, you've discovered my identity. I can't just go back to my plush throne with you knowing who I am, now can I?"

Glimpsing the intent simmering in Draven's eyes, Holder shakes his head, panic overtaking his features. "I won't say nothin'," he promises. "Not a peep. And I wasn't just about'ta actually harm ya. I was only goin' to—"

"—to what?" Draven presses with a cocked head, his cold smirk tipping his lips.

Holder's mouth flounders like a fish. Until he grits his teeth. "I won't say nothin'," he repeats, foregoing his declaration of innocence entirely.

Draven pretends to pick at his nails. When he hears a small choking noise slip past Holder's lips, he is sure Holder has finally seen what has been lurking in the shadows behind him. From his peripheral, Draven catches a glimpse of brightly glowing violet eyes as his shadow panther prowls forward.

"A Skull Trader's loyalty is only to their coin." His panther creeps another step forward, and then another. And another. Its large jaw unhinges, exposing sharp, inky teeth. Draven sets his expression with a savage indifference that, for once, is no mask. "I have no intention of opening my pockets tonight."

DRAVEN THROWS OPEN the door and drops himself into the chair resting in front of the burning hearth, hanging his head with a bitter mix of frustration and defeat.

"You look terrible." Kiran strolls over to him and outstretches his hand, offering him a crystal glass filled with a deep amber liquid. "But you smell even worse."

Wordlessly, Draven takes it and downs the whole thing in one gulp.

"I'll take that as a sign you had no luck this time, either?" Kiran sits down in the chair across from him and folds one leg over the other.

"If I had even an ounce of good fortune," Draven begins, his wary voice rough and pointed, "do you really think my face would look like this?"

Kiran opens his mouth, but after Draven shoots him a warning glare, he snaps it shut. "No," he replies, seeming to take a different path. "No, it would not."

Draven releases a frustrated sigh and leans back in his chair, raking both his stained hands through his unbrushed, mud-coated hair. "I was so sure someone in Zavir would know at least *something*."

He huffs a manic laugh. "But you know what, Kiran? It's fucking laughable how mad I sound, going around from taverns, to dens, to underground fighting rings and the sort asking about Casimir Vivaldri—a centuries-old prince thought to be dead—and his band of Abdites. During this particular journey, one drunken asshole laughed in my face and told me to get off the pipe."

"Well," Kiran coos neutrally, "it is all rather hard to believe."

Draven scrubs at his dirty face. "I know, Kiran. I fucking *know*. Still, I thought someone in Zavir—a city of thieves and criminals for the gods' sake—would be able to cough up something. *Anything*. But..." Draven trails off, leaning forward and balling his hand into a fist. "Nothing."

"How can you be sure they weren't lying to you?"

Draven only spares Kiran a quick glance, scoffing as his eyes drift to the fire. "If I ever suspected someone of lying, I bound them and injected venom into their veins. Their tongues loosened, but I was never given information that held any importance to me. I don't care about their underground criminal rings; I only care about finding *her*." A frustrated growl rattles in the back of his throat, and Draven rises, suddenly feeling restless. "You should know though, based on information I just received, we can probably expect to be dispatched with our aggregates soon. Sounds like there's some sort of uprising forming."

Kiran tugs his brows together. "What—in Zavir?"

Draven shrugs. "In all of Solaya. From what a Skull Trader told me, there's an underground movement taking shape, pulling their ideology from some centuries-old group."

"A Skull Trader, huh? Do you have a name?"

Draven shakes his head. "No. Whoever is pulling the strings has been careful with their movements."

Kiran is silent for a moment, his face pinched with thought. "I'll look into it," he says eventually.

Draven nods then heads for the door, in desperate need of a bath. But just as he reaches the mahogany wood, he stills, his hand hovering on the doorhandle. "How's she doing?" he asks in a low murmur.

Kiran unfolds his legs and sighs, bracing his weight forward on his elbows. "She is not eating, she is not attending her classes, and it is a stroke of luck when I see her at even one training session. It's safe to say she's still doing rather poorly."

"Should we intervene?"

He shakes his head, his unbound ruby hair spilling over into his face. "I have eyes on her, and they tell me Gray Nightenjoy is looking after her. Given everything, I'd say he's the best suited to help her."

"I'm glad they both chose Castaria—chose to have you as their captain."

Kiran doesn't reply, but instead gazes absently at the dancing flames in the hearth. The crackling noises from the burning wood swirl in the air and fill the stretching silence between them like escaped truths they can't bring themselves to voice.

Draven glances over his shoulder, his lips thinning as he watches his brother sink into the hollow spaces of his mind. "Kiran?"

He drags his gaze from the hearth, sucking in an absent breath. "Yes?"

"I miss him, too."

Kiran's eyes soften as sadness ripples in his expression, knowing immediately who Draven means. "My aggregate feels duller without Griff," he confesses. "And I have to bear the weight of that because I was his captain, and what did I do to keep him safe?" He tears his eyes from Draven. "Nothing," he bites out in a harsh whisper. "I did absolutely nothing. I failed him, and the price of my failure was his life."

Draven turns and strides for Kiran, resting a firm hand on his shoulder. "Look at me," he demands. When Kiran doesn't, he tightens his grip. "*Look. At. Me.*"

Kiran slowly pulls his eyes away from the hearth once more, locking them onto Draven.

"We *all* failed that day," he murmurs. "Every single one of us. The burden isn't yours alone to carry."

Kiran holds Draven's gaze, a subtle pointedness emerging within his sapphire eyes. "Burdens often aren't. Yet it's human nature to try and carry them alone anyway, isn't it?"

CHAPTER TWO

FINLAY

Finlay Fjolla leans back in his chair, fighting the urge to scrub at his face in both frustration and exhaustion.

This meeting with Bathara's council has been going on for nearly the entirety of the day, and still, they have yet to make even a *fraction* of progress.

"And what if Captain Dalmar does find her?" Cahlmon asks the assortment of faces seated at the lavish round table coated in gold, flailing his hands. "Then what? We just allow him to bring her back and let her train as if *nothing* happened?"

Tisara—a woman Finlay has always found to be quite beautiful and sharp—props her elbows on the table, her golden jewelry jingling from the gesture. She leans forward. "We all saw what happened, Cahlmon. The girl clearly possessed no knowledge of her powers, and those we interrogated unanimously corroborated that assumption. Not to mention, they all testified that she possesses no ill-will toward Solaya."

"She *murdered* over half our numbers! Bathara—hell the Jurafen in general—are in an unprecedented shortage of talent because of the girl's actions. She must pay for what she's done, and the only way to ensure she does is if *we* search for her ourselves."

26

Tisara tsks at him. "A waste of manpower and resources. Especially while Captain Dalmar searches for the girl. I mean, for the gods' sakes, who better could you ask for?"

"That boy is a wildcard and cannot be trusted," Cahlmon spits back. "He clearly has ulterior motives for finding her, and they are not in alignment with Bathara's in the slightest."

"Be that as it may," Tisara presses, "he is still useful. Not to mention, there is always the Tani to contend with. What if they choose to search for the girl and hold a trial? Will you attempt to move past them as well?"

Cahlmon's lips press into a flat line. "Discussing a matter that has not yet come to pass is outside the realm of my current interests."

Finlay balls his hands into fists beneath the table. "So what would you propose instead, Master Cahlmon?" He keeps his voice carefully indifferent.

"I'd like to appoint someone to discreetly search for the girl on our behalf."

Eyes of every color dart around the table as a chorus of whispers echo off the brazier-lit walls.

Cahlmon redirects his attention to Josiah—who, as the Keeper of Bathara, ultimately holds the most sway. "I know you must understand my reasoning, Josiah. That girl is dangerous, and she is now with a former prince who was supposed to have been dead for the past four hundred years—both of whom possess a magic that, until recently, we thought an impossibility."

Josiah remains silent, his thoughts concealed behind an impenetrable mask. As Finlay studies him, he can't help but notice Josiah looks as though he has aged a decade in only a couple months. The Abdite attack paired with learning of Casimir Vivaldri's existence has not been easy on any member of Bathara's council, but it has been especially rough on him, and Finlay has noticed considerable changes in his usual demeanor as a result.

Josiah releases a slow, measured sigh. "Very well." He lifts his hand. "I will support Cahlmon's motion."

The whispers return to the air like buzzing insects, and heads turn while men and women alike place hands over their mouths and murmur to their neighbors. Yet it is Nuha—the only other captain on the council besides Finlay— who speaks first.

"I second the motion," she says calmly while raising an idle hand into the air.

Finlay blows out his own quiet sigh. "I agree the girl needs to be found and interrogated—held accountable for what she's done. But I fear you underestimate Captain Dalmar's abilities. How do you intend to keep your search for the girl outside of his awareness?"

Cahlmon props his elbows onto the table and presses his fingertips together. "As it so happens, I was hoping you could help with that, Captain Fjolla."

"Me?"

Cahlmon nods. "Yes, you. You two were raised together, were you not?"

"We were."

"So it is safe to say you perhaps know him better than anyone else?"

"Outside of Captain Sulien, yes."

"Ah, Captain Sulien," Cahlmon mutters. "What a waste of talent, that one. He is even more unpredictable than Captain Dalmar." Cahlmon leans back in his chair and laces his fingers together over his chest. "You are our best chance at operating unseen. That is why I wish to charge you with the task of finding her. Discreetly, if you need that clarification."

Finlay's stomach drops, and flashes of red-stained memories float through Finlay's mind.

It was you.

I'm so sorry.

He buries the memories before they can take hold of him further.

"What would you have me do? Lie to Captain Dalmar? Deceive him?"

Cahlmon shakes his head. "You do not have to lie. Just see to it that he remains unaware of our mission. You will do whatever it is you must to ensure we operate inside of his blind spots."

"He has very few of those," Finlay mutters.

Cahlmon's answering smile is stiff. "Lucky for us, we only need one."

Master Asara Strithmore, a woman with long, silver hair that is always twisted into twin braids, raises her hand. "If Captain Fjolla heads this mission, I will also lend my support."

"As will I," says another council member.

Internally, Finlay imagines his shoulders hunching forward as he drops his head and heaves a ragged breath. Externally, however, Finlay rolls his shoulders back and lifts his chin. "Very well," he says. "I will do it."

Finlay catches Josiah studying him with a meticulous eye before he turns to scan the different faces of the council. "All those in support of Cahlmon's request?"

To Finlay's surprise, virtually every hand hangs idle in the air. All except Tisara and two others, whose eyes fill with disappointment. Though, why that is, Finlay can't be sure.

Cahlmon's proposal is logical. For the first time since the academy's founding, Bathara does not have enough students, and an unprecedented amount of Jurafen were wiped out from both the Abdite attack and the girl's explosion of power. Now that they know a threat like Casimir Vivaldri exists—not to mention that he is mobilizing Abdites—the need for swift action has never been so necessary. Plus, Finlay knows his brother well—even if it does feel like both he and Kiran have been slipping away from him more and more lately. Finlay could not say with total certainty that, should it come to it, Draven would make the necessary choice. Not when it comes to her. And should the girl and Casimir join together, it could very well collapse the Three Kingdoms as a result.

At the thought, a tinge of guilt stabs Finlay in the chest. For a brief moment, he shuts his eyes, and the prophecy plays in his mind.

Yet to all who hear these words, I beg—heed my warning. For it was whispered to me by the stars themselves.

Where one begins, the other must end, never meant to live beneath the same sky. For the two cannot wield the same power without breaking the spine of this world, and should the Chosen fall as the raven fell, the Cycle shall not turn again, but instead collapse beneath the weight of its own creation. And if such a fate unfolds, the skies shall fracture, the stars shall flicker and drown, and the gods, for the first time, shall know true fear.

Gray Nightenjoy had allowed both Finlay and Kiran to read the journal entries for themselves once the madness had settled down inside Bathara's walls. And while the Nightenjoy had given them a brief explanation of everything the day the Abdites attacked, it still wasn't enough to properly prepare them for all that they read.

His father's face flashes in his mind, a curl in his lip. He would berate Finlay if he knew what knowledge Finlay was harboring. Still, Draven made him swear not to tell anyone—practically begged him, even. So Finlay remains silent about what he knows, no matter how much it twists his insides, thinking he is straying from his honor in doing so.

"Finlay?"

Josiah's inquisitive tone has Finlay snapping his eyes toward the man. "I'm sorry?"

"I asked if there was anything you needed from the council to aid in your search for the girl."

Finlay clears his throat, cursing himself for letting his mind wander like that. "Have you questioned those two friends of hers?"

"We have," Cahlmon answers. "The Nightenjoy boy was remarkably unforthcoming in his answers, and the other one was practically mute for the duration of her questioning."

"She is grieving," Nuha says. Though her admonishing tone remains soft, Finlay does not miss the sharpness in her eyes.

"Plenty of students are grieving," Cahlmon counters. "Yet they have not gone mute and resorted to missing their classes." He pinches the bridge of his nose and sighs. "Though I digress. I do not believe either of them will be of any use to you, Captain Fjolla. They certainly were not to us. All we can offer you is the very information we have just discussed."

Finlay nods. "I will do preliminary investigations myself, then, and go from there."

Josiah dips his chin, seeming satisfied with the resolution. "Now, there is still the other urgent matter that must be addressed."

CHAPTER THREE

GRAY

Gray Nightenjoy approaches the arched bedchamber door. He releases a clipped breath, bracing himself for his new routine.

Balancing the tray of food in one hand, he knocks with the other. It's difficult, but he hears a small grunting noise from the other side of the wood. He takes that as his permission to enter, and he creaks the door open, the hinges squeaking as they move.

The room feels stuffy—heavy and shrouded in an invisible weight hard to explain with words. Sadness is a ghost, and it is haunting this room, coating the air in a film of grief. Still, Gray rolls his shoulders back, determined to be there for Marcella just as Lyra would want him to be. Simply because *he* wants to be. He has had his time to cry in his room already, sorting through his own devastation. His own anger and sadness, brought upon by so many different reasons. Because of so many failures to Lyra on his part.

Yet he can't dwell on that right now, allowing the weight of his own grief to accidentally slip onto tired shoulders. No. Right now, he needs to leave his own wreckage at the door so that he may be there for another, just as he decided to be.

He approaches the shell of a beautiful girl who sits frozen on a chair, overlooking the sun-coated hills. He sets the tray down on the wooden table beside her, and just like all the times before, he sits down on her bed, perching himself up against her headboard. Then, he pulls a book from his satchel—this one specifically on the rise and fall of Arellian trade—and he reads.

He does not attempt to speak. He does not attempt to pry. He just attempts to offer the only thing he can think of—a steady presence. A silent reminder that she isn't alone. For he learned long ago, as he watched the bearer of half his soul battle a grief far larger than anything Gray could ever comprehend, one cannot rationalize sadness. One can not fight it with logic nor can one wish it away. All a person can do is ride the storm, navigating the violent twists and turns of it.

Gray isn't sure how much time has passed, exactly, when he watches those cobalt eyes flick down toward the tray of food. All he knows is when he sees Marcella tear a small piece of bread from the loaf and dunk it into the stew, nibbling on it absently as she returns her hollow eyes to the window, his heart skips with a glimmer of hope.

THE NEXT DAY when Gray knocks on Marcella's door, he has more than a tray of food in his hands.

He hears a tiny *come in* from the other side of the wood, and a creeping curve forms at the corner of his mouth. Though he quickly smooths his lips into a neutral line as he opens the door. He knows she would hate for him to suddenly change his demeanor from the small advancement.

Like usual, Marcella is sitting in the same chair, her knee pressed against her chest as she stares out over the verdant hills and glittering waterfalls. Her copper hair is still a mess of curls, yet there is a sleekness to them that hasn't been there lately. She spares him a glance as he enters the room, and he nearly stills from finally seeing her look at him. Look at anything other than the view outside the window. And though it may only last a brief heartbeat before her eyes turn to gaze through the glass once more, it still fills Gray with hope that perhaps him silently being here is doing something for her, after all.

He steps forward and sets the tray of food down on the table beside her, this time paired with a book detailing the latest advancements in the ongoing study of static versus non-static wielder's marks. He still remembers how her eyes glittered when she explained it to Lyra, whether either of them realized it or not.

Then, as he has done for the past two months, he props himself up against her headboard and pulls out his own book. Only, as he cracks open the spine, this time, he finds his eyes cannot focus on the words filling the page. Instead, they keep roving to Marcella. To the small advancements he sees.

He decides perhaps now is the right moment to see if she'll finally talk about it.

"Marcella," he says, voice carefully neutral. "How are you feeling?"

She does not respond.

"Marcella?" he pushes.

Nothing.

Gray sighs, his chest tightening. "Please, Marcella. Talk to me."

She whips her eyes to him at those words, as if coming into herself temporarily. As if his provocation unleashed a creature that's been silently caged within her ribs all this time. "What do you want me to say, Gray? That I am hurting because I held Griff in my arms as he died by a sword's blade meant for me? Do you want to me say I'm angry because some fucking monster stole Lyra away from us? That despite all of Draven's searching, despite the aid both you and Kiran offer him, I'm frustrated because we still can't find any trace of her? Or would you like me to tell you about how it feels to be at this academy without a title or a famous surname? About how the only person who could possibly understand what it feels like to walk these corridors is gone?" Her jaw sets, and she wields the full weight of her emotion like a weapon. "What would you *like* me to say? To tell you?"

"I just wanted you to say something, and what you have just said is a great start." He pauses, eyes softening. "I want you to be angry. Or sad. I want you to cry if that's what you need. Or yell."

She scoffs, upper lip peeling back. "Cry," she admonishes. "Because crying is going to change things, right? Crying is going to bring Griff back from the grave and return Lyra home. Is going to change the whispers I hear outside my door as students pass by."

"No. It won't." He reaches for both her hands. He squeezes. "But you do not always have to be productive in your grief. Sometimes just letting it out is enough."

She tears her eyes away from him, returning them to the window, lips set in a thin, hard line.

She does not speak to Gray again that night.

THE NEXT TIME Gray is standing outside Marcella's door, he isn't quite sure what to expect.

He knocks. There is no soft voice telling him to come in. No glances spared his way when he opens the door anyway. Just a girl whose undereyes are pronounced by an extra smudge of purple and whose hair has tangled once more.

Gray sets the food down, noting the unmoved book.

He reads in silence.

THIS TIME GRAY is ready to enter Marcella's room with a new strategy.

He tossed and turned all night debating how to help her. He still wants to do something productive, but he also doesn't want to push her too far. Make her feel as though she must have a timeline on her grief or put her in a situation she isn't ready for yet. He still isn't sure if his previous attempt was or was not the right thing to do.

In his pondering, his brain snagged on a memory. One where they sat around a bonfire in preparation for their coming task during the second test of the entrance exam. She made a request, and he remembers the light in her eyes when he fulfilled it. Truthfully, Gray isn't sure why he's only just now thought about trying this. He knows more than anyone how powerful it can be.

He knocks.

"Enter."

He does.

This time when he sets the food down and positions himself on the bed, he does not reach for his book. Instead, he reaches for his double-flute and wets his lips in preparation. He brings the wooden tips to his mouth and begins to play, going through all the different Anatolian folk songs he has since learned after Marcella mentioned her hometown was filled with their tunes.

He does not try to force a happy song on her. Instead, he plays the saddest songs of all the ones he memorized. The ones whose melodies are slow and notes languid. The ones whose cries pierce the heart with something deeper than words ever can.

When it comes to climbing the mountain built on one's chest, Gray understands that sometimes a melancholy song is what's needed, if only to give reason to the sadness. To give it an exit to walk through, now having the sudden permission it didn't have before.

He wishes he had done this more for Lyra. Perhaps it would have helped her sooner.

Gray continues to play, shutting his eyes and losing himself to the music.

When he finishes his third song—a haunting ballad with swelling notes—Gray lowers the double-flute from his lips and opens his eyes. His plan was to merely take a sip of water before resuming his playing once more. Yet the sight of Marcella turned in her chair—glassy eyes latched onto him while silent tears streak down her cheeks—has him rethinking his next actions.

He sets his instrument to the side and leans forward, reaching out for her hands and positioning them between his own. "Tell me about it, Marcella."

Her bottom lip trembles, and she shakes her head. "I can't," she rasps. "I don't want to."

"Why?"

"Because it hurts."

He squeezes her hands. "Then share your pain with me and allow me to help you bear the weight of it."

"No." She shakes her head. "No, I deserve to carry it alone. Deserve to hurt."

"Why would you think that?"

"Because that blade was meant for me. I saw it right as Griff pushed me out of the way. And he—he still barely even knew me then. So why was it him who had to die when it should have been my heart ripped to shreds?" She pinches her teeth into her bottom lip, shaking her head. "And then Lyra... I should have never left her side. I can't help but to think things might have been different if I hadn't."

"You blame yourself?"

"I guess in a way, yeah, I do. For Griff. For Lyra. If I had just stayed with her, Griff probably wouldn't have died. Lyra may not have ever lost control. May not have been captured because of it. I said I would stay by her side, and then I didn't." The silent tears continue rolling down her reddened cheeks. Gray can't help but notice he sees little sadness in them, instead noticing other emotions like shame and regret. "Do you know how hard it is to realize someone died because of you? The guilt..." She trails off. "It should have been me. It really should have."

Gray's chest piles with an emotion so profound, he fears his sternum might burst. He can't bear hearing those words again. Can't watch as another light dims permanently behind eyes so beautiful and bright. He let Lyra suffer silently for far too long. Did nothing to help ease the ache of guilt wailing silently in her chest for over a decade. He had never felt like as much of a failure as he did when he watched Lyra battle her fears in the Feargate. As he saw her suffering, learned the truth of what happened to her mother, only then did he realize how deeply he had failed her all these years. He vowed to himself, then, to never again fail someone he cares for.

He just...won't.

Gray shifts forward and pulls Marcella into his chest, wrapping his arms around her and holding her with the conviction of a dying man. "Listen to me," he whispers against the top of her head. "You cannot torture yourself with the what-ifs. It is an endless path only leading you somewhere dark."

Gray does not say, *And had you stayed with Lyra, you most likely would have been the one to die.* Though, he does think it, feeling a tremor in his hand as he does.

"Griff made his choice," he continues. "And I know even in the afterlife he stands by it. Because though you say it should have been you, the reason Griff pushed you out of the way is because he knew it was the exact opposite—it *shouldn't* have been. And if you ever need to be reminded of that, I am here to wrench you free from any darkness, any trench. I will stand by you, reminding you again and again how deserving you are of the air residing in your lungs."

"There is so much darkness," she confesses into his shoulder, her hands squeezing at his tunic. "I feel it reaching for me, trying to swallow me whole."

He tightens his hold on her. "Then allow me to act as your light until the sun shines in your own horizon again."

She pulls away from him, wiping her eyes. "You've always been a light, Gray Nightenjoy." She chokes out a weak laugh. "You're practically the pure, beaming rays of a sunrise."

"Then you are the bleeding beauty of a sunset, Marcella Lynderful."

"Because the light is fading?" she asks, dry, self-depreciation punctuating the question.

"No," Gray answers. "Because it doesn't hide its proximity to the darkness. Because it is warm and brilliant and wild and soft. Because it knows its time to shine will come again." He holds her in his gaze. "Your sun will shine again, Marcella. Just hold on to let it happen."

CHAPTER FOUR

MARCELLA

Marcella goes through a torrent of highs and lows the next few days. Yet bit by tiny bit, with the help of Gray and through her own determination, color slowly bleeds into the world around her.

She has just finished the final twist in her freshly washed braid, her eyes skillfully latched onto the book she has propped open on her desk, when a knock sounds at the door. She strides across the room and pulls it back, revealing Gray mid-knock. His eyes temporarily widen before he smooths his expression over.

"Hi," he says.

"Hi."

"You answered the door."

"I did."

She can tell he tries to stifle it, but a small curve twitches at the corner of his mouth anyways. "Are you going somewhere?" He motions to the boots now on her feet, and Marcella glances down, blinking as if she had already forgotten she put them on.

"Uhm, no. I, uh…I just wanted to get dressed today." Marcella clears her throat and pulls the door back. "Do you want to come in?"

"I do, but…" He trails off, rubbing at the back of his neck.

Marcella frowns. "But what?"

He shifts on his feet. "Would you be willing to leave your bedchamber today?"

Would she?

"To go where?"

"Somewhere only very few know about." He smiles boyishly. "Kiran may or may not have told me about it."

Marcella's heart beats heavily for three breaths, her chest growing tight. She shakes out her now moist hands at her side, debating.

"If you're not ready yet, it's okay, Marcella. Move at whatever pace you're comfortable with."

Yet she only hears his other words as they echo through her. *Your sun will shine again, Marcella. Just hold on to let it happen.*

"No, I...I want to come."

He grins. "Then let's go."

OF ALL THE many ways Marcella thought today might go, she certainly never thought she would be sitting on a blanket at the very top of one of Bathara's many rolling hills, her skin hidden from the setting sun by the canopy of a beautiful weeping tree—whose white bark makes the tree appear in a constant state of winter—with a spread of homecooked Anatolian food around her.

From their position, the horizon is swallowed by the network of tiered waterfalls filling the Hills of Thanicka, making it feel as if they are in their own pocket of reality. Here, the academy and its occupants, all the grief and pain—it feels a world away.

Marcella takes a bite from her fluffy round bread. "Where did you get the recipes for all this food?"

"I asked Nuri."

A tiny chuckle—though still far different than her usual one—slips free of Marcella's lips. "And you cooked it yourself?"

"All of it," Gray says, taking a bite of his cured meat.

"Quite the chef," she attempts to joke. Yet in the silence, the heaviness lingers like a ghost waiting to haunt her once more. "Gray?"

"Yes?"

"Can I ask you something?"

"Of course."

"Why are you doing all of this for me?"

He does not answer right away, instead taking a moment of consideration as he draws his knees into his chest and watches the dimming sky. "Because it's what you need, and I want to be there for you." He pauses, brows lowering as he toys with a slice of bread. "I failed Lyra when she needed me, and I…" He trails off, biting down on his lip. Gray turns to look at her, soft eyes filled with raw determination. "I will not fail you too, Marcella."

She silently holds his stare, not sure of what to say or do. No one has ever cared about her in this way before. Has acted like a lifeline refusing to let her drown. And as Gray watches her, Marcella is surprised to find herself slowly feeling tethered to this world again. She isn't quite sure how to explain it, but there for a while, she felt like she was floating away—like she was fading. Whether from this world or her existence entirely, she didn't know. But there is something about the way Gray looks at her in this moment that makes her feel anchored. Makes her feel like she isn't a ghost. She doesn't feel better; she simply feels seen.

She threads her fingers through his and squeezes, knowing she doesn't need to say the words *thank you* for him to understand them.

He squeezes back, and emotion bloats in her chest.

"Maybe the next time we come to this hill, it'll be to watch the sunrise." He glances at her with a knowing look, and Marcella smiles.

"When Lyra returns," she says.

Gray's smile is poignant, yet optimistic. They both know the tedious bubble they currently reside in, unaware if Lyra is even alive, yet neither refusing to believe she isn't.

"Deal," he says.

They continue watching the bleeding sky, and as they do, the hollow spaces Marcella has carried within her fill with the chirps of birds and the bright notes of songs played on a double-flute.

Be happy, Marcella. Promise me.

I promise.

Perhaps after so many blurry days of mourning the new circumstances surrounding her, it's time she begins to try fulfilling her promise in the ways she can. She knows it's what Griff would want her to do. What would make Lyra smile, wherever she is.

So, she resolves to try.

CHAPTER FIVE

LYRA

My fingers glide along the seams of a velvety petal.

It is a shade of blue unlike all the others. Light and creamy with a distinct translucence, adding an ethereal flare to the flower. I bend down to inspect the peculiar color more closely, just before plucking it from its spindly stem, walking back to my work table and setting it down in the stone mortar after. Finding my previous spot on an amber-hued page from a large tome, I read about how to properly extract the medicinal properties from the flower.

I am just feeling confident enough to begin the process when *he* walks in, seizing my peace and quiet.

"Enjoying yourself?"

I grit my teeth, slowly setting down the jar of alcohol I had just picked up back onto the table. "I *was* enjoying myself."

Casimir Vivaldri hums, the sound a low rattle in his throat, and I hear him step toward me. "I just received the finalized list of all our dead. I'd like to have a ceremony for them tonight, and I'd like for you to attend."

I don't even spare him a passing glance. "No."

His soft, answering sigh is swift. "It is the perfect opportunity for you to meet the people here, and for them to finally meet you."

"Not interested."

I glimpse his moving shadow from my peripheral, allowing me to internalize my wince as his palm contacts the table next to me. "I'm not asking."

I still don't look at him. "Fine."

Casimir's hand remains planted onto the face of the wood as he lingers, watching me. "I have done everything you've asked." His voice is a sharp whisper. "I have given you space to acclimate to this new way of life. You were informed of the truth surrounding your friend's death when you awoke. I have allowed you to spend your days in this greenhouse, unbothered and without obligations. I have respected your wishes to not meet any of my family—a kindness to them, mind you. I have given you the choice of your room. Offered you books and supplies. What more can I *possibly* do to get you to open yourself up to this place and my people?"

I finally whip my eyes to him. "You can *give* me my *freedom*. You can let me go. Or, I don't know, you could have tried not kidnapping me in the first place."

Casimir is dressed in a black shirt lined with gold stitching—his usual attire, I've come to learn. His shoulder-length, raven-black hair is half-tied back by a leather band, and his glowing amber eyes are piercing. "I'm afraid that isn't possible."

I hold his stare with defiance in my own. "Then I'm afraid we will both remain disappointed in the other."

Despite my cold tone, I feel weakened by the mention of Gray's death—or rather, the illusion of his death. Even now, after demanding Casimir offer me proof of Gray's survival, given to me in the form of a memory shown through Caster magic, there are times I have to repeat the sentence in my head to remember it's true. *Gray is alive. Gray is alive. Gray is alive.*

I reach for a necklace no longer resting at my throat, now reduced to broken fragments discarded in the rubble and ashes I left behind at Bathara.

Casimir slides his hand from the table. "I've tried offering you the luxury of choice, but I'm afraid that will no longer be possible."

I snort, reverting my gaze back to the blue flower resting on my work table. "Please," I mutter under my breath, shaking my head at the absurdity of his words. "You haven't given me a choice—only the illusion of it."

He draws in a tired-sounding breath. "After tonight's ceremony, you will begin a new routine. One where you wake up and train with me. Where you open yourself to learning more about this place and its people in the afternoons. Where your evenings remain yours, with the exception of one evening a week, where you will be required to meet with me to begin entering the Veil."

I stiffen. "Why the Veil?"

"Because it is necessary." I hear the clack of his boots as he spins and walks toward the door—until the sound stops. "By the way, I've appointed a guard to keep watch over you. They will be responsible for escorting you around."

"Or in other words," I grumble back, not bothering to hide my disdain. "They will be responsible for making sure I'm doing as you've ordered me to do."

"However you want to frame it."

I shoot him a sharp look. "Can't wait to meet him," I mutter under my breath.

Casimir grunts a low laugh as he leaves the greenhouse, leaving me alone at last.

I FINISH with the final twist, resting my hands in my lap after, blinking at my reflection as I adjust to the girl staring back at me.

My frosty lilac hair now grazes just above my shoulders, and sometimes I swear the missing length is like a phantom limb—my fingers still reaching for long strands that no longer exist. I can't recall the last time my hair was short. In fact, I've found myself wondering lately if it has *ever* been short. King Alastair required me to keep it long, declaring he and his guests liked something to wrap their hands in—something to hold onto. Yet Casimir explained to me a few days after I woke up that this length was the best the healers could do.

I tuck the short strands behind my ear, and I lean forward, inspecting the next change in my appearance—my right eye. It never fully returned to its original color, instead maintaining a silvery hue while amethyst weaves like cracks in ice.

Casimir still has yet to explain that one to me.

Though I don't mind it. Because as twisted as it sounds, looking at it reminds me of Draven—of the way his eyes are mismatched, yet are the most beautiful pair of eyes I have ever seen; even if his dual-colored eye is like a washed gradient whereas mine is like a silver quilt threaded with purple stitching.

At the thought of Draven, a sudden pang appears in my chest. I wonder how he is doing—if he is alright and well and continuing forward. I've found myself thinking a lot about the words Kiran said to me the day he and I walked together between gilded hills as he escorted me to my training.

He has a lot of weight on his shoulders—weight that I fear he will never share. He takes responsibility for everything and everyone he cares about. I need you to understand that—it's important you know.

There was always something about the way Kiran said those words that stuck with me. Yet they never felt like as much of a warning as they did these past few weeks, leaving me to wonder…

Is Draven blaming himself? Is he driving himself mad, replaying all the ways things could have been different? Is he assuming the weight of my own failure—my own sins?

Every time I consider the possibility, I feel my heart splinter, losing another fragment of itself each and every time.

Still…

I miss him.

Gods how I miss him. What I wouldn't give to hear his voice. To feel his fingers sweeping along my skin like they did in that cave. To have him hold me, even if only more time, like he did in that greenhouse. To—

A knock rapping at the door interrupts my thoughts.

I suck in a sharp breath and steal another glance at myself in the mirror, my gaze lingering on the final change in my appearance. I rise from the vanity and stride over to the door, throwing it open as I prepare my tongue to be extra sharp toward the unlucky bastard who's been assigned to me.

My plan ends before it even begins when the hinges squeak and the wood swivels back, revealing a face younger than my own, dotted with freckles at the nose and complimented by a pair of gray-tinted eyes.

I blink. "Ah... who are you?"

"I'm Neilina. And you're late."

She reaches for my arm, but I sidestep her, cocking my head. "That's a beautiful name and all, but perhaps it's better if I ask *why* you're here."

She scrunches her brows together. "To escort you. I thought Master informed you of my coming?"

"Wait," I say, pinching the bridge of my nose. "Casimir assigned a *child* to watch over me?"

Neilina clicks her tongue. "I'll have you know I am seventeen and not a child whatsoever. I have spent the past three years training to be a member of his trusted guard. And now he's *finally* giving me a chance by making you my first official assignment, so I will not let you mess this up for me." She shoots me a very, very pointed look.

I study her. "Admitting you've never done this before probably isn't the best thing to tell the person you're guarding."

Neilina blinks. "Why not?" A silence stretches between us, and I am beginning to wonder if she actually expects a response to her question, but then she reaches for my arm and tugs it up toward her, leaning forward to inspect it. She lets out a low whistle. "Wow, so this is it, huh? The wielder's mark of a Binder?" She turns my arm over, raising it higher in the air.

And I'm so stunned at her carefree boldness, I just watch her, a slight crease between my brows.

"It's really quite pretty," Neilina muses. "Has Master explained any of it to you yet?"

"No. No, he has not. Though I really wish he would. At the least, I'd like to know why some flowers remain asleep while others are fully bloomed."

Neilina lets go of my right arm, her eyes gliding toward my left. She reaches for it, brushing her thumb across the skin. "Do they hurt?"

I resist the urge to wince, choosing to instead lift my chin. She's asking about the third and final change in my appearance.

The scars.

Not even the healers can get rid of them. To put it simply: My body was so wrecked that, despite piecing me back together, there was nothing more they could do about them. They run down my left arm like jagged seams stitched poorly together, rising up my neck and stretching over my jaw, into the lower portion of my cheek. For whatever reason, the right side of my body—the side where my wielder's mark resides—is perfectly unblemished.

"No," I answer, my voice soft. "I can't feel them at all."

Neilina smiles weakly at that, then resets her features. "Now then. Are you ready to go? Master is expecting you."

I snort. "Your Master expects a lot, it would seem."

Neilina tilts her head. "What do you mean?"

I wave her off. "Nothing."

CHAPTER SIX

LYRA

Neilina guides me away from my chambers, away from the area I have cooped myself up in all this time, along a winding outdoor path, through a garden, and to a large basin of water surrounded by nothing but the neighboring trees in the distance.

At first, my chest tightens at the overwhelming amount of people in attendance. Their eyes wander to me, lingering as they take me in. Based on what Casimir said this morning, I'm sure they all know about me.

Yet the fact remains I still know nothing about them.

I trail behind Neilina as she escorts us around the crowd, toward the north side of the water, where a large altar has been prepared. It is twined with angular flowers, their petals an ombre of white bleeding into a peculiar color much like misty moonlight. Extending from the center, the flower's pistil is a rich gold, and it practically glows against the rising twilight.

"What are those?" I whisper to Neilina.

She glances at the altar. "*Mortui.*"

My brows crease. "What language is that?"

Neilina shrugs. "An old one."

We walk in silence a beat longer, but my curiosity is too much for me to remain quiet. "And what does *Mortui* mean? Where do the flowers come from? What are they for?"

Neilina stops and turns around, holding up three fingers. "We use them for our death ceremonies." She puts a finger down. "I have no idea of their origin." Another finger goes down. "And it means heart of the dead. Now, please stop asking me questions."

I acknowledge her request with a nod, and Neilina spins on her heels, guiding me forward once more.

I last four seconds.

"But why do you use them for death ceremonies? What makes them so sacred?"

Neilina pinches the bridge of her nose and heaves a sigh. "You're a curious thing, aren't you?"

My lips stretch into a small smile. "My mother was a Gardner. I can't help it."

She angles her head to glance back at me, her face pinched. "What's a Gardner? Do you mean someone who attends to the garden's maintenance?"

I blink, my mouth popping open. "You don't know what Gardners are?"

Neilina shakes her head. "Whatever you speak of, we don't have those here."

I let that sentence linger before racing forward a few steps, falling in stride directly next to her. I offer her my best smile. "And where is 'here,' exactly?"

She snorts at me. "Nice try. But I'm under clear instructions not to discuss anything with you."

"We don't have to have a discussion," I point out. "I'll take a hint. Or even a quick, one word answer will do."

She eyes me sidelong before shaking her head, huffing a quiet laugh under her breath. "Oh look, what perfect timing."

I shift my eyes forward and find Casimir walking toward us. His hair is half-drawn, and he wears his crown of raven feathers atop his head. Though I've come to learn he always dresses nicely, his black tunic and breeches are exceptionally exquisite this evening—almost looking like silk, but seeming to be slightly different. The gold trimming accentuates his already bright, golden eyes, and though his skin is nearly gray-tinted, there is still a peculiar allure to it, despite the absence of warmth.

Upon reaching us, he inclines his head. "Ladies."

Neilina stands at attention and places the base of her fist against her chest. But instead of placing it over her heart like most soldiers, hers is placed on the right side of her chest.

Interesting.

"Master," she says. "I have brought the girl as requested."

I shoot Neilina a pointed look. "You know I'm your elder, right?"

To her credit, her attention remains on Casimir and Casimir only.

He smiles at her. "Thank you, Nellie. You've done well. I'll take over from here."

Neilina dips her chin.

When she turns to go, our eyes meet briefly, and I flash her a smile. "Thanks, *Nellie*."

Her answering groan and scrunch of her nose has me chuckling softly. Yet that chuckle soon dies in my throat as Neilina disappears into the crowd and Casimir offers me his arm. I flick my eyes down at the polite gesture and scowl. "No thanks."

"Please," he says, seeming to remain undaunted. "I understand your reservations. I do. But please join me for this."

I cross my arms. "If I agree, then I want answers. *Tonight.* I've been here for months, and you still haven't told me anything about why I'm here. Why you took me away from my home. From my friends. From —" I cut myself off, not wanting to give Casimir his name.

From Draven.

Casimir studies me. "From your lover," he surmises.

I lift my chin. "Yes."

Casimir nods, his eyes drifting as he seems to fade into a cold memory. But the moment is short lived, and he just as quickly resets himself. "You have my word. Join me tonight with an open mind and an open heart—observe my people, give them a chance—and as a result, I will give you all the answers I am able to at the first moment I can."

"Sounds like you've given yourself a loophole."

"No," he counters. "I just want there to be full transparency—I probably cannot answer all of your questions. Believe it or not, I am a man with some integrity."

I snort. "Could have fooled me."

"All the same," he replies, his voice remaining gentle. Casimir offers me his arm again.

I stare at it while an internal war rages inside me. In some way, accepting his gesture feels like I'd be betraying Solaya. Betraying all those who lost their lives in his attack. That accepting the arm of the man who single handedly slaughtered more lives than anyone else in the history of the Three Kingdoms would be an act of treason. Yet I need answers. I need to learn where I am—why I'm here. How to get home.

I loop my arm around his, accepting the offer. "You better hold up your end of the bargain."

"I will."

I purse my lips, and he chuckles as he guides me toward the large altar, keeping his arm at the perfect gentleman's bend.

"I see you wore what I laid out for you."

"I didn't think I had much of a choice."

When I had returned to my chambers after finishing with my studies in the greenhouse, there was a white linen dress laid out neatly across my bed, a note and a raven's feather resting atop it. I had half a mind to burn the dress and tell Casimir to go to the realms of hell, but when I slipped the dress on, I found it to be surprisingly comfortable. And while the open back annoyed me, even I had to admit the breeze licking my skin felt nice.

Casimir glances at me. "And why would you think that?"

My eyes narrow. "Well, surely it has nothing to do with me being your captive. And it certainly has nothing to do with the fact I've been forced to wear the clothes picked out for me for most of my life." I pause, making a show of thinking. "You're right. Assuming that was a *complete* stretch on my part."

He remains silent, guiding me closer to the altar. "Fair enough. But I didn't want you hiding it. Not tonight."

He doesn't need to elaborate. I know what he's referencing—the other piece to my wielder's mark. The elaborate design stretching across the entirety of my back while the silver, thread-like design twines up my arm and around the curve of my shoulder, down the length of my spine, where the twists spiral and extend to different geometric patterns. Some of which already have come alive with their own coloring and distinct markings.

Since I came out of the Feargate, the mark has hummed continuously. Like a constant reminder, as if to say, *I am here. Do not forget me.*

That day, the Abdite inside my Feargate told me it was a gift.

It feels far from it.

Casimir rests a gentle hand on top of mine. As if reading my thoughts, he says, "You have the most beautiful wielder's mark I have ever seen, and you should not feel any shame towards it. Be proud of what it represents. Proud of the power it signifies you carry." A pause. "Be proud of what you are, Lyra."

There is a sincerity to his words, and it is a trait which Casimir frequently exhibits that confuses the absolute hell out of me.

I do not offer him a response.

We reach the front of the sprawling stone altar, where an intricate wall built from wood towers high into the air. I inspect the carvings engraved into the timber, surprised to see how detailed and elaborate the markings are. My fingers graze a petal from the *Mortui* flower next, mesmerized by the subtle glint they carry.

"The markings are a mix of names and prayers for the dead," Casimir supplies. "And the flowers are part of our ceremony, acting as the guide to lead our dead to their next journey. It also acts as an offering to them —our final attempt to leave them with something beautiful."

"What makes the flowers so special?"

A soft laugh slips from Casimir's lips. "You'll see." He leads me to the far edge of the wall, near the end of the massive altar. With fluid movements, he points at a series of carved markings I can't decipher, paired with their own *Mortui* flower. "Do you see this section here?"

I nod.

Casimir turns to look at me, his expression oddly kind. He drops my arm, lowering his voice into a soft murmur. "I have taken the liberty of having your mother's name carved onto the pyre. I do not believe Rivara's ceremonial words have changed since I was there last, so I had them carved alongside it. I know you never had the chance to grieve her properly, so I thought tonight, as so many mourn and say their goodbyes, you might like the opportunity to do the same."

My throat runs dry as something heavy sinks in my chest. A wave of sadness rushes through me, and as the acute sting of it sinks its claws into me, I think of Draven. I think of the way he encouraged me to feel, to remember—to grieve. I know he would encourage me to accept Casimir's offer.

I miss him.

I miss my mother. I miss Marcella and Gray. I miss...

The thought strikes me, and it is an odd sensation—having anger and gratitude slam into each other. "Is there still time to add one more name? I'd... I'd like to say goodbye to someone else as well." Even if I'm sure Bathara held a ceremony for all their dead already. *I* want to say goodbye.

"Of course. Just tell me the name."

My bottom lip quivers, and I pinch my front teeth into the skin of it to hold it steady. "Griff. His name was Griff. He was an aether-wielder. Was someone who was pure and true and good." I pause, my eyes hardening. "And he was murdered. By you."

Casimir does not react to my words, his expression instead remaining steady. Without breaking his gaze from mine, he lifts a hand, flicks his wrist, and a red-gold light sizzles across the wood. Shortly after, a *Mortui* blooms next to it. "All finished," he murmurs.

I glance at the new carvings on the pyre. "Thank you," I croak, the swell in my chest intensifying.

"You are welcome." His tone remains gentle, despite the sharpness I speared at him. "Now, it is time we begin."

Casimir strides forward and addresses the sea of sad eyes spread before us. "My brothers. My sisters. Tonight, we honor our dead. Those who valiantly gave their lives to our cause. To our future. Knowing the pain they would suffer, they opened themselves to the madness. Allowed corruption to burn through their veins. But their sacrifices were not hollow." He swivels his chin, scanning the faces in the crowd. "A new dawn is rising," he declares, his powerful voice dripping with passion. "And with it, the long night will finally bleed. Justice will weep. The world will be remade."

Casimir turns and finds my gaze, stretching his hand out for me to take. At the gesture, my heart picks up speed in my chest. What the hell is he doing?

With a subtle nod, Casimir beckons me toward him. There is something magnetic about the gesture, pulling me into his orbit. I slip my hand into his, and he guides me forward. Presents me to his people, who watch with a mix of tears and curiosity in their eyes.

He leans down and whispers into my ear, "I'm going to draw on magic. All I want you to do is allow yourself to feel what you recognize—let it enter your veins." Before I agree, he pulls back from me, keeping my hand in his.

Casimir continues addressing the crowd.

"A light—brighter and more powerful than any other—has finally appeared, and we have brought her home. Brothers, sisters.... lend me your hearts, and allow me to carry your pain tonight as we grieve as one. And as we light the sacred flame and the names of those passed rise to the heavens, do not let despair weigh on you. For in their ashes, hope has returned."

Casimir lifts my hand above our heads, and a warm sensation rushes my veins. Doing as he asked, I allow the trails of magic that feel familiar—that I know with utter certainty I have touched before—course through me. At the decision, my skin heats, rising in temperature at an alarming rate. When the crowd erupts in murmurs, I glance up at my right arm. At the arm Casimir holds in the air like a prize.

My wielder's mark is glowing.

Along the thread-like marks—all the way from the tips of my fingers, into the arcs cresting at the base of my shoulder—iridescent light glows brilliantly like a coursing river. It flows into the flowers that blossomed from sleeping buds into fully-bloomed, unfurled petals, where the light glitters and pulses like living seams.

A man near the front of the crowd places the back of his fist over the right side of his chest. Again, away from the heart. Just like Neilina. "*Sithraki,*" he begins chanting. "*Sithraki.*"

A chorus of voices join him, and within seconds, the entirety of the crowd has placed the back of their fists over the right side of their chests and are chanting the word *Sithraki* over and over again.

I look up at Casimir. "What are they saying?"

He watches the crowd, tired eyes glittering. "They're saying... *Savior.*"

A sharp pang twists in my heart. "I am not a savior." Flashes of my unchecked power rip through me similar to how it ripped through flesh, staining my conscience. The guilt is like lead in my stomach; a living creature whose merciless claws have forever marred something within me.

Casimir drops my arm and faces me. There is a keen sharpness waiting in his gaze. "You could be." Then, without warning, he steps toward me and grips my shoulders, spinning me around. It puts my back on full display for the crowd. The mark I have spent hours upon hours staring at, trying to understand it, warms against my skin.

"*Sithraki!*" Casimir bellows, his fingers remaining clasped to my shoulders.

The crowd chants louder; I grit my teeth.

Being put on display like this...

It dredges up shadows of a past I clawed tooth and nail to escape. One where a cruel king forced me to dance and wear ridiculous outfits while hungry eyes devoured me like I was their property to claim.

Anger courses through me. My skin burns hotter. The colors

zipping along my wielder's mark shift from iridescent to a deep maroon.

"This was *not* part of our deal."

Casimir slides his eyes to me, his gaze landing on the new color saturating my skin. He swiftly turns me back around and steps in front of me. Then, he lifts a hand, and the crowd falls silent. "Brothers. Sisters. It is time we say goodbye." Casimir doesn't so much as look at me when he faces the altar.

Three female singers with markings painted across their bodies and kohl lining their eyes step forward, kneeling into the dirt a few paces away from the pyre. One of the girls with flowers twined into her braid slides the drum strapped to her back forward, and she begins beating against the head of it.

Within seconds, the three girls are humming in tune to the rhythm of the drum, filling the air with an ethereal melody bleeding with sorrow, equal parts haunting and beautiful. The girl with cascading white hair opens her mouth and sings in a language I don't recognize, and suddenly, I find the edges of this world melting away. As if I am falling under some spell.

A flicker of light flashes in my peripheral, and I turn back to find Casimir wielding a bow and arrow forged entirely in flames. Magic, I realize. He is wielding fire magic to create the weapon, the glowing tendrils pinched between two fingers as he draws tension on the conjured string, ready to send the burning arrow soaring.

There is a stir in my chest at the sight of it.

Still not looking at me, but instead with his eyes glued to the altar, where a pyre climbs up and up into the sky, Casimir asks, "Would you like to say the ceremonial words for your mother and friend before I release my arrow?"

My breath stutters in my throat. Still, I nod, squaring my shoulders and lifting my chin. I close my eyes and allow the haunting voices pouring into the sky to swirl around me, filling the hollows of my bones and fueling the beats of my heart. I picture my mother's face. I remember her mauve eyes, her warm hugs, and the love I felt when she'd call out to me. *Come, my sweet flower*, she would always say.

I remember Griff and his goofy smiles. The way he dropped himself atop of Marcella and me that day in the hills, laughing alongside us. I remember his nervousness as he stood outside my door, smiling as he fell helplessly for a fiery girl. I allow myself to see it all—to remember. I dig the details from the shadows and hold them up to the light.

I reopen my eyes. "In Death you walk. In Life I remain. Bound together, yet neither the same. Safe travels, weary souls, for I shall see you soon. But until that day, I'll give you life by remembering you."

Casimir releases his burning arrow, and it soars through the air in a flash of brilliant, golden light. The pyre goes up in flames, swallowed immediately by a swell of heat. As the tongues of vermillion climb higher, the *Mortui* flowers begin to glow—the delicate traces of their petals not crumbling to ash, but instead fluttering into the sky like a trail of endless iridescent fireflies.

So, as dusk officially bows to the night—as three voices mingle together in harmonies that lasso around the heart of this world—a million fluttering pieces glow brilliantly as they scatter across the horizon, rising up to the heavens alongside the smoke, making the world appear as if the night sky has fallen, and we are surrounded by living stars.

"Beautiful, isn't it?" Casimir says from behind me.

"Breathtaking," I whisper, my neck craned back as my eyes hungrily sweep across the sky, watching the petals ascend like remnants of living souls.

Though I don't look at him, I feel Casimir's eyes on me. "It helps my people say their goodbyes. It is like getting to watch those we have lost travel on to their next journeys." A pause. "Do you feel like you have gotten to say goodbye?"

I watch a petal float through the sky, rising higher and higher into the night. Its blue core is bright, but the gleam of white cast around its edges makes it stand out against the rest, the light both soft and radiant.

"Yes," I answer after a passing silence, my eyes glued to that glowing piece. "I finally do."

CHAPTER SEVEN

LYRA

After the ceremony is finished, Casimir offers me a wordless parting, and Neilina finds me to escort me back to my chambers.

As we walk in stride, the people part for us like a receding sea, and they bow their heads in deference as we pass. It makes my chest ache. I am not what these people believe me to be. I am not a Savior. I am not a person who has done acts worthy of such respect.

No.

I have blood on my hands. Have flashes of dreams where I cocoon myself in a swirl of insatiable power, devouring skin and bone mercilessly. And while I do now understand that what happened with my mother, with Delroy, the kind stablemaster, isn't my fault—I was the product of circumstance; the desperate action taken in a divided world; the result of King Alastair's own blackened heart and choices—there is no justifying the power I unleashed that day. I know I cannot blame myself and hold the weight of another's sins, but I cannot rationalize nor minimize the destruction I caused.

All the lives I took.

It is a guilt I will be forced to forever bear. One I *deserve* to carry.

Near the end of the line, there is an older man with long white hair

59

and bushy white eyebrows who bends a knee and drapes his left arm across his chest, bowing his head. For a moment, shock rattles through me like a jolt of lightning because I think I've just seen a ghost.

He looks just like Delroy.

I stop in front of him and lower myself to my knees. I reach for his hand and drop my head, attempting to catch his gaze. "Please, do not kneel for me."

He slowly lifts his eyes from the ground. They are a rich brown and warm. "You are *Sithraki*," he says with an accent I've never quite heard before. "We owe you our lives."

"You owe me nothing," I murmur, confusion and more squeezing in my chest.

As I focus on the man, I notice more details about him. The way his eyes are ringed by a thin gray circle. The way his wielder's mark rests at his neck, an inverted wave cascading downward instead of up. I notice the subtle gray tint resting beneath his skin, running through his veins, and the scars resembling scratch marks scattered across his wrists.

It hits me then, and I marvel at how I could have missed it.

He's an Abdite.

He seems so...normal. So sane. His speech patterns are regular, thoughts coherent. He is nothing like the Abdites I've encountered.

As if sensing my thoughts, the old man smiles. "There is always more to the story."

And there's something about the way he says it—a quiet knowingness. My lips part to ask him to elaborate, but before I get the chance, Neilina is pulling me up by my arm and dragging me forward.

"Come on," she says in a hurried whisper. "It's time we go."

As if coming out of some daze, I finally become aware of my surroundings. Of the hundreds of people who have circled around us, watching. Being so close to them, I now see all the markings painted down their bodies. Some with clay, others with charcoal and kohl. Some marks I recognize to be associated with mourning, others I don't recognize at all.

I glance back at the man a final time. He remains kneeling, his arm still draped across his chest. "*Sithraki*," he chants. "*Sithraki*."

In a low hum, the word travels to the lips of hundreds. They continue parting for Neilina and me as we pass, but they observe us as we go, chanting lowly.

"*Sithraki. Sithraki. Sithraki.*"

The word swirls through the wind like a promise of hope; they cling to it like a prayer.

"*Sithraki. Sithraki. Sithraki.*"

The word follows me all the way back to my bedchamber.

I PACE in front of my canopy bed, restless.

I was expecting Casimir to find me shortly after the ceremony ended, finally allowing me to ask my questions and receive answers, but he has not. My guess is he figures if he waits long enough, I'll simply fall asleep. Then again, he knows I was a night attendant and am used to being up all hours of the night. So maybe he's done no figuring at all. Maybe he just doesn't give a shit about the bargain we made. Maybe he never even planned on actually answering my questions.

Like hell I'm going to let that happen.

I storm toward the door and throw it open. To be truthful, I half-expected to find Neilina standing guard outside the door, watching me like some dangerous prisoner in need of monitoring. Yet to my pleasant surprise, it seems Casimir didn't instruct her to keep watch over me through the night. No one stands outside my door, and, as far as I can see, there is no one standing watch in the brazier-lit corridors, stretching east to west.

I make the executive decision to go left, realizing after only a few stomps I haven't the slightest idea where I'm going or how to find Casimir. I've never been to his personal chambers, and I certainly haven't had the motivation to walk around this place and explore. The only areas I can navigate with full confidence are the gardens, the greenhouse which now acts as my own personal workspace, and then back to my chambers from either of those two locations.

I halt in the corridor, pinch the bridge of my nose, and heave a sigh. What is the best way to find someone when I haven't the slightest clue where I'm going? When I don't even know a general location for where the person might be?

On the verge of resigning to the bitter fact I may have to go back and wait in my chambers, the thought dawns on me.

Laktî can sense other laktî. At least, that's what Draven told me time and time again. And Casimir just funneled magic into my veins mere hours ago. Which means...

I close my eyes and draw on everything I've learned about sensing magic. Truthfully, it makes me grateful for the first test in Bathara's entrance exam, where Gray and Marcella—the ever dynamic pair—sat in a circle with me, explaining how detecting one's magic works.

I open myself up, looking for that tugging thread. Casimir and I share the same magic type, and with the touch of his laktî fresh in my veins, I imagine sensing his laktî must feel similar to how sensing my essence flower in the Whispering Grove felt.

I'm right.

A tug pulls at me like some magnetic draw, and I follow the guiding feeling. It leads me down a series of winding corridors, up a flight of stairs, and to a large, decadent door approximately three times the size of the one leading into my chamber. An odd sensation happens once I'm standing at the threshold. The feeling that's guided me here intensifies then disappears. As if to declare Casimir is, in fact, behind this door, and I no longer need a tour guide to show me the way.

For a moment, I simply stand in front of the stained wood, my fist frozen in midair as I wonder whether or not I should knock. But then I remember he kidnapped me, and frankly, I don't think kidnappers deserve to have privacy when their victim quite literally arrives at their doorstep.

I creak the door open and step inside unannounced. The room is lavish, but not quite as decadent as I thought it would be based on the colossal door guarding it. A large canopy bed with black, silky sheets is pressed against a wall on the north side of the room—an artistically crafted stone hearth roaring with a fire directly across from the bed—and three floor-to-ceiling windows compose the adjacent wall beside it. In front of the windows, an oak writing desk sits with papers scattered across the top of it, ink stains pressed into the wood like scars. A large, feather-tipped quill rests at an angle in the inkwell, as if Casimir was scribbling something on parchment and stopped suddenly. The smell of said ink mingles with bergamot and burning wood.

I creep forward, losing a bit of my nerve. I'm in his personal chambers, and something about it feels intimate. My plan was to track him down and demand answers, and while a person being in their bedchamber in the middle of the night is completely logical, it is a thought that evaded me entirely in my heated moment. I don't know where I thought he would be, but… it wasn't here.

I turn on my heels to leave. A voice stops me. "Going so soon?"

I freeze, my eyes finding the ceiling. I blow out a sigh.

Well, since I've been spotted, I might as well do what I came here to do.

When I turn back around, my expression is hardened, and I find Casimir now standing in the middle of the room, a glass filled with deep amber liquid in his hand. His hair is unbound and falling into his face, and though he still has on the same clothes from earlier, they look ruffled—messy. It's the first time I've seen him look even the slightest bit disheveled.

I don't bother mincing words. "You never came to my chamber tonight. You broke your end of the bargain."

"No," he says calmly. "I did not."

"You promised me answers if I did something for you; you didn't give me answers after I completed what was asked of me. That's called breaking a bargain."

Casimir spins the liquid in his glass before taking a sip from it. After, he walks over to the hearth and sets the glass down on the mantle, his eyes lingering on the crackling flames. "I did not say I would give those answers tonight."

My blood boils. "Yes, you did. You—"

"—No," Casimir counters with an admirable level of calmness. "*You* said tonight, but I did not agree to give any answers to you at such a time. Think back on what I said."

With frustration burning through me, I do.

You have my word. Join me tonight with an open mind and an open heart —observe my people, give them a chance—and as a result, I will give you all the answers I am able to at the first moment I can.

He watches me while arching a dark brow. "I said I will give you answers the first moment I am *capable* of it. After the ceremony, I did not feel capable."

I'm not sure if I'm angry with him for using such tricky word play or at myself for getting lured into such foolish semantics.

As if sensing my thoughts, Casimir shrugs. "You don't live four hundred years and not learn a thing or two."

My mouth opens, but I just as quickly snap it shut. At those words, even more questions pelt me, demanding to be answered. How *is* it possible he's alive? How has he lived this long? And what the hell do I have to do with any of it?

"I want answers," I say, voice stern.

Casimir sighs, raking a hand through his soot-black hair. "I don't suppose that desire can wait until morning?"

"Not unless you want the hassle of dealing with a very uncooperative captive."

He studies me through inscrutable eyes. "You know I could call for a guard and have you escorted back to your room within minutes, correct?"

I brace my hands on my hips. "And *you* know you desperately need me for some undisclosed reason, and if I refuse to cooperate, I can make things very, very difficult for you."

"And I can make you very, very dead," Casimir counters.

I shrug. "Do it."

Casimir lifts a brow, but says nothing. Eventually, he motions for me to sit in one of the two lounging chairs resting in front of the burning hearth. I mock a pointed curtsy, then waltz over to the chair.

Once I'm seated and comfortable, Casimir asks, "Would you like a drink?" As if for emphasis, he reaches for his glass on the mantle.

I scrunch my nose at the offer. "Right. Like I would drink anything you give me."

Casimir sips from his glass. "You eat and drink the food and water provided to you just fine."

"Not willingly," I grumble under my breath.

Casimir only glances at me. With deft movements, he rests himself gently into the chair across from me and folds one leg over the other. "What is it you'd like to ask?"

A lot of things. More than a lot. So many things, simply finding a starting point feels difficult.

Still, I try. "Why am I here? Why did you take me away from a place that, for the first time in a long time, was finally starting to feel like a home to me?" Emotion clogs my throat as their faces flash through my mind. Gray. Marcella. Griff. Kiran.

Draven.

Casimir stares at the crystal glass as he swirls the liquid inside. "I can answer that question. But only to a certain extent. At least for now."

I rub between my brows, already frustrated. If this is any indication of how this conversation is going to go, I'm in for a long, trying night. Still, I gesture for him to continue.

Casimir sips from his glass. "You are here because I need you. My people need you. You are here because this place and all it's founded on is where you belong."

"And why is that?"

"Because it is filled with those rejected by the world of nobility. Those persecuted, spat on, made less than, and forced to suffer because of a broken system that cares more for its one percent than it does the other ninety-nine percent of living and breathing souls." Casimir leans forward and sets the glass down on the small, rounded table between us. "You are here because you are going to help me destroy that system."

My heart picks up in my chest. "How?"

"By destroying the Cycle."

I fight against the urge to bark a laugh. Surely he can't be serious.

Yet as his eyes remain glued to me, they are alarmingly resolute. I lean forward, dropping my voice. "You're joking, right? One cannot simply *destroy* the Cycle. It's...it's..."

"A force beyond reckoning?" Casimir offers in lieu of my stammering.

"*Yes*," I breathe. "Not to mention, even if you were somehow successful, who knows what would happen to the order of this world?"

"I do," Casimir states simply. "Magic would no longer be distributed. It would just...disappear."

A chill caresses my spine. "And what about the people who already have magic?"

Casimir steeples his fingers in front of him. "I am still working that part out. All things in this world have a frequency; that is an indisputable fact. Magic is no exception, and as such, the laktî in our veins is already attuned. But once the Cycle collapses, the structure sustaining that resonance will shatter. I suspect it is logical to assume once the force giving magic is taken away, the essence of magic itself will disappear with it."

I study Casimir. His face is calm—so indifferent. I shake my head. "Okay, so you destroy magic—then what? What does that even accomplish?"

"It resets the hierarchy," Casimir says. "It severs the root feeding the Great Houses. Bloodlines won't matter without their gifts. Power becomes a question of merit, not magic. It will be chaos—for a time. But by leveling the foundation, something better can be built."

I stare at him, unable to make sense of what he's suggesting. "You're talking about collapsing the fundamental root of Solaya's civilization."

"No." Casimir's voice is quieter now. "I'm talking about rebuilding it."

"But the implications of that..." I stop, my face scrunching as I try to grasp the sheer magnitude of what he's saying. "The world would lose its healers. Its Gardners. The Jurafen. And what of the creatures lurking within our borders? Who would be able to protect the people from them? Not to mention the rebellions sure to rise from the power imbalances you're proposing. You wouldn't just be plunging our continent into structural chaos, you'd be damning the next generation to *war*."

"Drastic change requires drastic action." Casimir stares off into the distance, silent for three heartbeats before returning his eyes to me. "Provide me with a better alternative," he murmurs. "Show me a better option for cleansing the filth of this world."

My lips part as I will persuasive words to form on my tongue, but...nothing comes. I have nothing to offer him.

And the way Casimir watches me shows me he recognizes I've come up empty-handed. "If it's any consolation," he says. "In destroying the Cycle, I would not just be taking. I would be giving as well."

My voice is sharp. "And how is that?"

"My people would be free at last."

His people. The Abdites.

"Free from what, exactly?"

"The madness that was never theirs to claim. The cruel reminder that, at one point, society deemed them completely expendable."

I press a hand against my reeling head, feeling suddenly exhausted. "And how is it I am supposed to help you accomplish this? What about me is so special, you felt the need to extract me from my home? Leave a journal for me to find?" I pause, perking up and lifting my hand. "Actually, before you answer that question, I'd like you to answer this one instead: why the hell *did* you leave me your journal?"

This is a question I've pondered a lot lately. Why Casimir felt the need for me to read his most personal thoughts. His own account of history. I've had a gnawing feeling about it—one telling me it surpasses a simple desire for me to learn the truth of my magic. Odds are I would have discovered the truth eventually, so...why?

Casimir's voice is soft. "Because I wanted you to understand how I arrived at my conclusion. To know evil deeds don't simply exist from nothing; they are born from necessity."

I think of his journal entries. Of the faith he had once placed in humanity. In his early entries, he always seemed so good and optimistic. An idealist over a pragmatist. He advocated for peace and diplomacy. Reached for something which would mend instead of break.

How far removed that person is from the broken man who sits before me now.

I realize then that I could continue asking him why. Continue to demand answers which could potentially help me understand how it is he arrived at his conclusion. Yet we would simply go round and round in circles. I'm not ever going to understand—ever going to agree with him nor his methods. So, for now, I might as well save myself the headache and move on.

"And how do I fit into all this? What is it you're expecting me to do?"

"For now, all I want you to do is train your magic. Discover the depths of your abilities. Explore the Veil. And get to know my people."

I lift a brow. "That's it?"

Casimir leans back in his chair. "For now."

"And when can I go home?"

He doesn't answer, instead only observing me.

"When. Can. I. Go. *Home?*" I ask again, not bothering to pull any of the bite from my voice.

Another moment of silence. And then—

"It depends."

I grit my teeth. "That's not good enough."

Casimir shrugs. "It doesn't have to be."

"And if I refuse your request?"

He pulls his eyes away from me, now looking at the glowing hearth. "You seem to have forgotten my words to you the night of your attempted escape." Casimir sighs, mussing a hand through his hair. "Make no mistake—I wish for civility between you and me, but I am not asking you for any favors. You *will* do this, like it or not.

Because if you don't, the cost of your resistance is the lives of those you love most."

Thorned vines twist in my stomach, rising up to pierce the skin of my throat. An immense weight sits heavy on my chest, and I know I've hit my capacity for one evening. I rise from the chair and make for the door. "I've had enough answers for one night."

"Good." Casimir's voice has grown cold. "You can see yourself back to your chambers, then."

I throw the door closed behind me and walk at a quickened pace down the stairs, through the corridors and back to my bedchamber. Once inside, I slam the door shut and press my back against it, heaving shallow, jagged breaths. It isn't until I've again become the master over my own breathing that I strip the clothes from my body and crawl into bed. Yet sleep does not find me like I had hoped—even if I figured it wouldn't.

No.

Instead I lay tossing and turning in silky sheets that bind around me like a blanket of guilt, mulling over all Casimir said tonight. And as his words echo in my head like a resounding war drum, what unnerves me most is not the repercussions of his decision.

It's that I see the logic in it.

CHAPTER EIGHT

DRAVEN

"What do you think this urgent announcement Bathara is summoning us for will be?" a man from the Iradine aggregate whispers to his friend as they pass by Draven unknowingly, who remains in the back of the room, draped in shadow.

"I don't know," the friend answers. "But I heard Bathara has not only gathered all the aggregates for it, but emissaries from the Three Kingdoms as well."

"That's odd, right?"

"Very."

Draven is inclined to agree. Truthfully, he was equally as surprised when he noticed emissaries for both Rivara and Erandor Kingdom sitting in the crowd. He hasn't the slightest idea why they're here. Still, noticing their presence means Draven has chosen to remain as far away as possible, leaning his shoulder absentmindedly against a back wall with one ankle crossed in front of the other.

Master Cahlmon's classroom is virtually a smaller version of the Arena, featuring a circular tier of seats with extended tables instead of benches. The sprawling floor below—crafted with a mosaic collection featuring the different aggregate emblems—acts as Cahlmon's lecture area, but it also acts as a large-scale fighting pit for students once the floor is pulled back by magic.

Draven glances across the room and finds Arden—captain over the Iradine aggregate—watching him. Ever since he revealed just what he is capable of, with his veins turning black and his eyes glazing into dense obsidian orbs, both Arden and Nuha have maintained their distance from him. Not like he cares—even if he's always liked Nuha. Besides, having Arden keep her distance from him makes his life a hell of a lot easier.

Draven rolls his head languidly in the other direction and sighs. He dreamt of Lyra last night, once his frustration from being unable to leave Bathara recently to search for her simmered down enough for sleep to even find him. It was such a vivid dream.

She was crouched down in a field of flowers. Her lilac hair was loose and wild, and she waltzed through the field barefoot while clutching a wicker basket to her side, where she gently—reverently—placed an assortment of flowers, plants, and weeds to rest. She rose, spotting Draven, who stood behind her, admiring her in all her grandeur—the descending sun casting the most perfect golden glow behind her.

Gods, even in his dreams she was breathtaking.

After Draven woke up that morning, he was forced to sit dazed in his bed, piecing together the images of Lyra's face from his memory, attempting to savor every beautiful detail. But he couldn't. Because how does one give an amateur a brush and expect him to suddenly paint a masterpiece? Nothing his mind conjured could do the real thing justice.

For just a brief moment, Draven rests his eyes and allows himself to drift back into that dream.

With the basket still wedged between her forearm and her hip, Lyra strutted between the rows of colorful flowers toward him. When she reached him, she looked up at him and smiled. The gesture made her eyes crinkle slightly, and as wisps of hair blew into Lyra's face, Draven knew he could spend eternity drowning in a lilac sea.

With her free hand, Lyra teasingly crawled her fingers up Draven's chest. "It's not polite to stare," she teased.

Draven wrapped his arms around her waist. The gesture was automatic—without a sliver of thought. It was an action he marveled at, once believing he would never be capable of showing such affections and emotion. "And who said I ever claimed to be polite?"

"Would you say that makes you an unmannered brute, then?"

He pulled her more tightly against him, until he could feel her against his pelvis. Against the part of him that incessantly ached for her. "Oh," he said, his voice low and thick with unchecked desire. "I can be very, very uncivilized."

Lyra gazed at him through lowered lashes. "Is that so?" she hummed.

"It is."

"Show me," she demanded in a husky voice. "Show me just how indecent you can be."

Draven moved. He didn't need to hear anything else. He plunged his fingers into her hair and tugged on the strands, exposing her neck to him. He dragged his lips over her skin, sucking, kissing, and biting every inch between the crook of her shoulder and her jaw. Then he kissed her. Devoured her. Lost himself entirely in the taste of her lips.

A frenzy of desire rushed through Draven, and though the bulge in his pants was nearing the point of pain, he didn't care. He wanted to savor her. Take his time with her. Devotedly worship every single inch of her.

"Well?" she challenged once Draven relinquished control over her lips. "I'm waiting to experience the depravity of these manners I've heard so much about."

Draven practically growled like a wild animal. He hooked his arm around her waist and laid her gently on her back.

But nothing about what Draven did next was gentle.

Now on top of her, he ripped her shirt clean in half, tearing it from her body and exposing her perfectly rounded breasts. He wasted no time bringing his mouth to them and letting his tongue—

"Draven? Stars to Draven?"

Draven squints an eye open and finds Kiran watching him with a smirk on his face and a small notch in his brow.

"What?" he practically growls.

Kiran's smile widens. "You wouldn't happen to be having inappropriate thoughts about a certain someone, now would you? I mean, not when a very mysterious yet important announcement is about to take place." He flicks his eyes down toward the bulge Draven feels pressing against the seam of his trousers.

Draven lets a low hum rattle in the back of his throat and resists the urge to adjust himself. Even he can admit letting himself fall so deep into last night's dream probably hadn't been the best idea.

Kiran laughs at him.

Draven turns his attention away from his brother just in time to catch a glimpse of Marcella and Gray as they enter through the double doors and descend down the stairs toward an empty table. The corner of his mouth tugs up at seeing Marcella back in her classes. She was absent for months, and Draven knows the Masters were beginning to lose their patience. He slides his eyes to Nightenjoy next, noting the way his arm hovers just so behind her, fingertips grazing across the small of her back.

Draven chuckles quietly to himself, refolding his arms and shaking his head.

He watches them a heartbeat more, imagining Lyra wedged between the two of them, her arm looped through Marcella's as her head tips back with laughter. It makes his heart both swell and ache.

Gods he has to find her soon. He *must*. Even if it means renouncing his position as Captain and facing his father's wrath so he can wander all of Solaya without restraint.

Yet just as quickly as the thought comes, it is overturned with another. One where his father holds his favorite bargaining chip over Draven's head, using it to make him submit to his will. And as long as his father has that, Draven will never be able to fully do as he pleases, which includes leaving the academy behind to dedicate all his time and resources to his search for Lyra—a fact which has nurtured a constant, bitter anger inside him.

Kiran snaps Draven from his thoughts once more. "How unfortunate," he drawls through a frown, crossing his arms. "A blizzard just blew in."

Draven rolls his eyes at the theatrics just before Finlay reaches the two of them. "We need to talk."

"Well hello to you, too, dear brother." Kiran's sweetened tone is wrapped in thorns.

Finlay shoots him an admonishing look before squaring his shoulders to Draven. "Listen, there's something you need to know about the upcoming announcement. And before I tell you and you threaten to murder me, yes, I knew the action was happening, but no, I had *no* idea they were planning to conscript—"

A resounding *boom* clamors off the walls, followed by a three-pitched harmonic chime signaling everyone to be silent and in their seats. Master Cahlmon struts out from the door leading to the center of the platform, followed by Josiah, Master Strithmore, and of all people, his fucking father, Tynan Dalmar.

Draven feels both Kiran's and Finlay's stares on him. Yet he glances only at Finlay, his focus snagged on a particular word. "What do you mean they were planning to *conscript* someone?" His eyes narrow. "And conscript *who*, exactly?"

Finlay slides his eyes to Kiran, pleading lines creasing around his gaze. "This is not going to be good…"

Master Cahlmon addresses the room. "Students. Emissaries. Thank you for joining us. To discuss why we have gathered you here today, I will be turning my classroom over to the Keeper. Please, give him your undivided attention and listen with an open mind."

Josiah steps forward, and Master Cahlmon inclines his head to him, receding back a few steps to stand in line with Tynan and Master Strithmore.

"Thank you, Master Cahlmon," Josiah begins. "It will come as no surprise to you when I say, in light of the recent attack, Bathara finds itself with an unprecedented shortage of numbers, both in students and active Jurafen. It has long been Bathara's tradition to allow our Jurafen and other military personnel from across the Three Kingdoms to observe our third and final test in our esteemed entrance exams. And it is that very tradition which resulted in so many of our numbers being clustered together in one place, creating the perfect target for our attackers. Because of this, difficult questions had to be asked, demanding difficult answers."

Josiah pauses, and Draven can see the visible tension his shoulders carry.

"Firstly, Bathara will have to amend its policy on student participation. Whereas only third-year students were previously allowed to participate in active duty, when aggregates are now dispatched to handle altercations, creature reportings—anything of the sort—both first-years and second-years will now be required to join."

Slight murmurs fill the room, but they seem to teeter on the edge of excitement. To the first and second years, this is something thrilling. A chance to prove themselves. They do not yet see it for what it truly is.

A death sentence for most.

Bathara's entrance exam is child's play compared to the vast assortment of tasks and assignments given to a Jurafen, ranging from arresting rogue wielders, neutralizing Abdites, stopping creature attacks, and more. The second-years will have a better chance, sure, but there is a reason Bathara has kept a strict rule on only allowing third-year participation in official Jurafen assignments.

"Furthermore," Josiah continues, "for the first time in our long, prestigious history, due to the shortage of students, and thus candidates for replacement Jurafen, Bathara has made the decision to conscript any necessary, high-caliber wielders, regardless of rank, status, or previous ties to any kings and kingdoms."

The news moves like a wave through the crowd. It is an unparalleled decision. One of the founding principles of Jurafen was they *elected* to dedicate their magic to protect the Three Kingdoms. It was part of the design meant to protect the realm—use wielders who are willing to die honorably for their cause. And while Draven could spend hours naming reasons why that original design has since broken—with only noble blood seeming to be deemed worthy of dedicating themselves—the fundamental principle of it has remained throughout the years.

Draven glances at Finlay, quickly noting that Kiran looks equally as surprised as Draven feels beside him. "Who did they conscript, Finlay?" The clipped question grates between his teeth.

Finlay remains expressionless, resorting to the baseline he's created for himself, standing with a slightly lifted chin and curl in his lip. No doubt he fears he's being watched at this point, which again indicates he knows far more than either Draven or Kiran does.

A crawling spider starts tracking fire up Draven's stomach and into his chest as he considers answers he does not like.

The room is a mess of heated whispers, sounding like a den of snakes hissing at one another, and Josiah lifts his hand to silence the voices. "I know, I know." He remains admirably calm. "Please understand we did not arrive at this conclusion lightly. Yet it was the only viable decision remaining." A pause. "I will now invite Supreme Commander Dalmar to speak. There are a few words he'd like to share with you regarding the matter."

Draven scowls.

Well, that at least explains why the hell he's here.

Tynan steps forward, his attire without a single wrinkle and tied-back hair without so much as a loose strand. "When Bathara's council approached me with their proposal to conscript not only wielders, but wielders in service to kings, I must admit, I—like you—was rather shocked. However, I come here today to speak to you as not the man known as the Supreme Commander, but as the man known as the Master Strategist."

Draven wants to gag at the words.

"What Bathara is proposing makes sense. In fact, given the current situation, it is perhaps the only choice with an advantageous outcome that maintains a minimized set of negative repercussions. Yes, our kings and noble houses will lose some of their most cherished wielders, but it is a small price to pay when considering both the safety and longevity of the Three Kingdoms."

Tynan finds Draven, and a taunt only Draven could read swims in his eyes. "So, I am here as a show of good faith on behalf of both the King of Erandor and the King of Rivara to bring you the first of many wielders who will find themselves conscripted to the academy. It is with our greatest hopes this will help ease any rising friction within the noble houses. Though make no mistake—there is no choice regarding the matter, considering this is endorsed by Tani Law. Yet the choice you all *do* have is to make this an amicable process."

A loud echo fills the room as two hands slam down against the table, and a girl with black, twisted braids adorned with golden jewelry rises. Draven recognizes her. She was assigned to Lyra's team during the second test. The healer—Nuri Calhart.

"Why is it only Erandor and Rivara who are here to show their *good faith?*" She bites the words out, her Anatolian accent notable. "What about the Anatolé Kingdom?"

Unfazed, Tynan only frowns at her, wearing a mask of regret. "I'm afraid Anatolé did not offer a response when asked to show support for Bathara's cause. Unfortunately, since the conscription has yet to formally begin and Bathara did not make an official request for any of their wielders, there was nothing that could be done to force their hand."

"*Lies,*" Nuri seethes. "Anatolé would never do such a thing."

Tynan mocks sympathy. "I can tell from your accent you must hail from the Anatolé Kingdom, so please know it brings me no joy to inform you what I say is entirely true." He draws in a deep breath that sways his shoulders. "Now, please do not disrupt again."

Clearly unsatisfied and silently raging, Nuri sits back down. Draven studies her for a moment longer, noting he should make it a point to have a conversation with her to see what she knows.

"As I was saying," Tynan begins again. "As a show of good faith, I'd like to formally offer you the first two wielders who have been conscripted by Bathara, each given away willingly and without force by both King Erasmus and King Alastair."

He glides his arm back toward the door leading to the platform. It groans open, and two figures emerge. One Draven instantly recognizes as the aether-wielder who does King Alastair's biddings, transporting his courtiers and emissaries however instructed. He also just so happens to be the man he saw flirting with Lyra when Bathara hosted Rivara and Erandor emissaries.

That is certainly something that *will not* be happening again once Draven finds Lyra and brings her home. If he so much as gazes at her for too long, Draven will see to it personally that the man loses his ability to see at all.

The second figure is a woman with raven-black hair marked with silver stre—

Draven's heart both drops and erupts with a rage so sharp, he scarcely has control over himself for a beat.

His simmering glare whips to Finlay, who winces. For the first time since they were teenagers, Finlay looks openly afraid of what Draven might do. He quickly glances at Kiran next, whose face has gone pale and looks equally as horrified as Finlay's.

"I tried to warn you," Finlay mutters, rubbing between his brows.

Tynan returns his eyes to Draven, where a small, satisfied smirk tugs at his lips. He knows Draven didn't see this coming, and he is relishing in ruffling every single feather Draven possibly has.

But Draven doesn't even gaze back at Tynan. He instead stares at the girl, hair black as the night, made distinct by two silver pieces framing her face—complimenting the paleness of her skin and the blue of her eyes, always sparkling like a lapis lazuli stone.

A cold, merciless rage settles in Draven. "I'll *kill* him."

CHAPTER NINE

RHEA

Rhea Brooksley stands with her chin held high next to a man she's only just met—Klytis Hilthrop—and she watches silently as Tynan displays the two of them like some sacrificial offering to the Three Kingdoms.

Fuck the Three Kingdoms.

Fuck Tynan Dalmar.

And fuck anyone who thinks differently.

The older man with aged white hair and soft blue eyes steps forward and stands beside Tynan once more. He addresses the room, his voice a calm melody oozing with quiet power. "The next recourse, as some of you might have already begun to ponder, is how these newly conscripted wielders will be assigned an aggregate. As most of you are already aware, once wielders pass our entrance exams, they are then personally Selected by a captain and extended an offer to join that captain's aggregate. This is a pivotal decision for our examinees—once they join an aggregate, even after they graduate, they remain a member of that unit even when acting as fully-trained Jurafen. Naturally, there were many considerations when deciding the best course of action. By allowing wielders to simply choose, we risk a power imbalance. But having the captains Select wielders they've not yet spent time assessing poses risks as well."

Rhea actively suppresses the urge to roll her eyes. Men just *love* talking about how they arrived at their decisions. They turn it into such a spectacle—making grand speeches which make it seem as though the fates of the world rely on what sentences spew from their mouths.

Oh, Tynan most certainly made a grave error when deciding to bring her here. Before, she had to remain silent and subservient. If she didn't, she would have been crucified in as cruelly of a way as Tynan's twisted mind could imagine. But now, it's like she's been handed the key to unlock the jail cell she's been shoved into for a decade. And now that she's loosened her shackles—now that she will *finally* be able to operate outside of Tynan's watchful gaze—she can dedicate her every fiber to achieving what it is she wants most.

Draven's freedom. And her revenge.

Her eyes rove toward the shadows—toward *him*. She locates him instantly. His lip is curled like it always is, his features lined by a mask of cool indifference.

The fucking coward.

She hates him. Hates everything he stands for. Hates what he took away from her—all that he cost her. And the thing about hatred is it doesn't fade. It remains in the shadows, growing—festering. They say time forgives all, but hatred does not operate within the bounds of time. So as the years passed and Rhea served under Tynan's thumb, her hatred only deepened. Twisted over itself like gnarled roots sinking into rotten soil, sowing soured weeds that clotted in her veins. Now, her starving hatred is only ready to be fed.

A wave of something almost pleasurable sweeps through her as she imagines it: the blade, the look in his eyes, the finality of steel plunging through his icy chest.

Yes, no matter how long it takes—no matter how much she must plot and scheme—she will get her revenge.

She will see the one who stole everything from her murdered by her hand.

CHAPTER TEN

FINLAY

She glares at Finlay like she's already buried him in an early grave.

He knows Rhea hates him. He knows she would do nearly anything to see his head on a platter—a blade protruding from his chest. He knows and doesn't care. Not even a little.

He hates her, too.

Hates her mixed blood. Hates her low status. Hates what he sees when he looks at her.

A low growl rattles in his throat before he glances at Draven, who is seething in a silent fury, making him entirely too unpredictable. Entirely too dangerous.

All bets are off when it comes to Rhea. It's always been that way, and Finlay suspects it always will be.

"Did you know?" Draven asks, his eyes remaining glued to his father.

"I already told you," Finlay mutters pointedly. "Yes, I knew Bathara was going to begin conscripting wielders, but I had *no* idea they were conscripting her. Frankly, I don't even know how they became aware of her or her magic."

"I do," Draven murmurs with such bitter resentment, it even takes

Finlay aback. He watches as Draven wraps his fingers around the railing enclosing their corner, his knuckles going white. Black stains slowly splotch his skin, creeping along his veins.

Finlay puffs out his cheeks and looks to Kiran, hoping he'll say something to calm Draven down. Yet Kiran's face remains pale, as if he's just seen a ghost. His unblinking eyes watch Rhea as worry carves itself into wrinkles on his face.

Finlay rubs at his forehead. Draven is fiercely protective over Rhea and goes into instant fighting mode the moment he suspects anything awry. But Kiran? Kiran has always been a nurturer, not wanting to fight, instead protecting in other sly ways. For as much as Draven loves Rhea, Kiran loves her similarly, if not more softly.

Finlay resists the urge to heave a loud, drawn out sigh.

And this is why both his brothers are fools for allowing such useless affections to infect them.

Oh, but gods be damned Finlay knows he's fucked. He knows what's coming next, and honestly, he won't be surprised if they both gut him right here and now once they find out. Yet Finlay has a duty to see through. He has obligations as both a captain and a member of Bathara's council—not to mention his duty as the Fjolla Heir. A member of the Archbloods. Obligations that both his brothers are always far too content turning their backs on, leaving the weight to rest heavier on his shoulders.

"The conclusion we've reached is simple," Josiah continues, drawing Finlay's attention forward once more. "Each conscripted wielder will duel the Skyborne aggregate's captain while Master Cahlmon, Master Strithmore, and myself observe. Based on their performance, we will decide which aggregate the wielder is best suited for, basing it on where their skills are currently most needed."

He paces slowly as he speaks, letting the weight of it settle. Finlay glances sidelong at Draven, who still hasn't released his death grip on the railing. Black spiderwebs slowly creep up his forearms, and Finlay flexes his jaw at the sight.

Not good.

Josiah glances up at the corner housing Finlay and his brothers.

"Captain Fjolla, would you be so kind as to offer a live demonstration?"

Finlay dips his chin, his voice perfectly poised when he answers. "Of course, Master. Which wielder should I—"

Before Finlay can finish his question, Rhea steps forward. "I'll offer myself as his opponent."

Josiah seems to internalize a sigh while Finlay catches the slight twitch in Tynan's lips, who undoubtedly had a hand in Rhea being here right now. Finlay has no doubts everything unfolding is going exactly as Tynan planned it—though why this plan is necessary, Finlay hasn't a clue.

What game *is* Tynan playing at?

Finlay keeps his features carefully neutral as he turns away from the railing to head down the nearby staircase. Yet a strong hand clutches his shoulder, halting his movements. He turns and finds Draven glaring at him, the promise of something bloody and painful burning violently in his eyes.

"I swear to the gods, Finlay. You better not leave a single fucking mark on her."

He wrenches himself free of Draven's grip. "If I don't fight her as I would any one else," Finlay hisses under his breath, "you know *he* won't let me stop until I do." Finlay flicks his eyes to Tynan, glaring back at Draven after.

Finlay makes to move past him, but Draven tightens his hold, snarling something inaudible under his breath. Kiran steps between them and shoves Draven's arm back down to his side, flashing him a sobering look.

"Go," Kiran instructs softly, only sparing Finlay a glance. "I've got him."

Finlay works his jaw before setting it into something immovable. Then, with a slight lift of his chin, he glides down the stairs, stopping when he reaches Josiah, who motions for Rhea to join him at his side. She obliges, stopping only a few feet in front of Finlay.

She does not avert her eyes from him for a single moment, her gaze filled with a scorn so tangible, it almost stings Finlay's skin like a living flame.

Josiah glances between them, as if sensing the current of loathing streaming between them. He cocks a brow, eyeing both of them pointedly after. "Your rules are as follows: no dirty shots and no fatal blows. Past that, you are free to duel using whatever means you'd like."

Without averting her gaze from Finlay, Rhea asks, "Daggers?"

"Perfectly acceptable," Josiah answers.

Rhea smiles a tight-lipped grin, more mocking than it is anything else. "Fantastic."

Josiah glances at them both a final time, appearing a bit weary. Ultimately, however, he lifts his hands, and he uses his magic to slide the floor panels back, exposing the large fighting pits filled with sand. Finlay kneels down and unties his combat boots, removing one after the other. When he rises, Tynan stands before him, his arm hooked loosely around Rhea's waist.

It is an act of sheer will not to glance back at Draven, who must be beside himself with a honed rage hotter than Illithious Lake and sharper than an Arellian steel blade.

"Finlay," Tynan drawls diplomatically. "I'm sure you are well aware how crucial it is that you do not go easy on Rhea here. She must be treated as anyone else. Do not let your..." He pauses, lip curling slightly. "...*attachments* affect your judgment or diminish your combat abilities."

Finlay keeps his expression level. "Never, Commander."

Tynan smiles, the gesture entirely insincere. "Excellent." He pushes Rhea forward, and anger flashes in and out of her expression within a blink, so savage and wild, she looks like she wants to snarl in his face. Yet her training sends her mask snapping back into place just as quick.

Tynan rejoins Josiah, who is whispering something to Master Strithmore.

In his absence, Rhea cocks her head, her grin now devilish. "Long time no see, asshole."

"An eternity could have passed, and it still wouldn't have been long enough," he quips back, his mild tone carrying an air of disgust.

Her lips flatten into a saccharine smile, and she tugs them up at Finlay. "Cute," she mocks, bending down to remove her combat boots. When she stands, she motions toward the exposed sand pit. "Well, what are you waiting for, *Captain*? Are you going to fight me or not?"

Finlay's lips twist, yet he catches his scowl before it tugs at too much of his expression. "Of all the fucking people," he mutters under his breath, stripping his tunic from his body, exposing his bare chest to the world—including his wielder's mark, which curves along his back. Not that he minds. Finlay works hard for his body, and he has no problem displaying his wielder's mark for all to see. He is a Fjolla, after all. Power is expected of him.

Rhea drags her eyes along the length of his chest, down his torso, all the way to his toes—an arch wedged deep in her brow.

Finlay cocks his head, his smile nothing short of taunting. "What? I go away for a few years, and suddenly you like what you see? Want a touch?"

"I'd sooner fuck myself with my dagger than have your body come even close to touching mine." Without another word, she pads into the pits, assuming the south end as her base.

Finlay grits his teeth and follows, standing on the north side. He studies Rhea carefully. Her soot black hair is half drawn back with a silver hairpin wedged through her bun, revealing a section of silver hair that she dyed to match the two front pieces. She wears a pair of black pants that are loose in the legs and taper at the ankles—not too far off from Bathara's standard uniform. Her cropped black shirt is tight against her chest, swooping at her neckline, exposing the sweeping lines of some tattoo plunging beneath her shirt. Her softly angulated blue eyes are ringed by lines of dark kohl. His eyes snag on the three silver piercings lining her left ear first, and then her wielder's mark inked on her right arm next.

She smirks at him, the gesture anything but warm. "Like what you see?"

He snorts a hollow laugh before dropping his voice into a harsh whisper. "Why are you here, Rhea?"

She doesn't answer, instead choosing to glare at him in silence.

"Do you know what your presence here is going to do to him? Do you even understand how complicated you just made things? How—"

"I *know*," she snaps quietly, so no one else can hear her but Finlay. Her voice drops into a harsh whisper, as if she's speaking more to herself now. "I fucking know."

"Captain Fjolla," Tynan calls out. "Is something the matter?"

Finlay glances at the Commander. "No. I was just briefing the girl on Bathara's—"

"There will be time for that at a later point," Tynan interjects, not even allowing Finlay the respect to finish his sentence. "We don't want to waste anyone's precious time, so let's begin, shall we?"

With a slight wrinkle in his brow, Finlay glances at Josiah, wondering why the hell he is allowing Tynan to even voice opinions on the matter when Bathara is strictly meant to remain politically neutral. Sure, Bathara seeks stratagem advice from him from time to time, but that is always behind closed doors, and asking for battle advice from a Master Strategist is an entirely different matter than allowing him to appear as though he wields even a semblance of power within Bathara's walls. What the hell is Josiah thinking?

Finlay ensures all of those thoughts stay outside of his expression though, instead dipping his chin. "Of course." He redirects his eyes to Rhea and assumes his stance. "You're lucky Draven's here. It means I'll have to hold back considerably."

She snorts, inspecting her nail beds. After an irritating handful of passing seconds, she glances back up at Finlay. "Well?"

Finlay's jaw clenches at her tone. The disrespect dripping from that single word makes the pit in his stomach burst to life with wildfire. She purposely increased the volume of her voice so it would echo throughout the high, brazier-lit walls. So people would hear her challenging him.

Finlay's anger boils.

"Careful," Rhea croons in a low voice. "People are watching,

Captain. And I'd hate for your public tantrum to get back to your precious father. Just imagine what he might do should he find out his golden son lost his temper." She mocks a pout. "In front of another Head of a Great House, no less. Why, he may even do something as extreme as disowning you." She makes a show of gasping, clapping a hand to her mouth. "Oh, wait—that's already a touchy subject, huh?"

Finlay sees red. He moves without another thought, charging to engage her in hand-to-hand. She's not even worth using his magic on. He won't need to.

Rhea's lip tilts with a smirk as she effortlessly dodges his punch, slipping sideways as she pivots on the ball of her foot. His fist cuts nothing but air, and he draws his arm back, a deep scowl now wedged permanently into the lines of his lips. He scans her, and he nearly balks with anger when he realizes her hands are clasped behind her back, her head cocked sweetly to the side while a cloying smile curves her lips.

"You lowborn trash," he mutters.

"If I'm trash," she counters, still mocking innocence, "then it should be easy for the great Fjolla Heir to take me out." Her eyes harden. "Come on, Finlay. Hit me. Or better yet, use that *oh so* talked about ice magic of yours. Surely my muddied blood couldn't possibly stand against it." Whatever she sees in Finlay's expression makes her smirk deepen. "Thought you'd be able to win this fight without drawing on it, right?" Her upper lip curls into a sneer. "No chance."

She charges, and her moves are fluid and precise, like a snake striking its prey. She rounds, sending a powerful kick at Finlay's throat. He raises his forearms and absorbs the blow, pushing back forcefully against her shin. Finlay charges at her, jabbing at her side first and moving for her throat next.

She evades his attack effortlessly. Like she's moving half a speed faster than him.

His eyes narrow on her. He attempts a series of strikes again— moves ingrained deep into his muscles—and she simply lifts a hand and redirects them as though they are nothing but soft leaves floating in the wind.

"Did you know Tynan fired the tutor most involved in your combat training years ago? Something about her not being competent any longer." She mocks a shrug. "I trained with her for a year or so before she left. Yet now seeing you in action, I'm starting to wonder if Tynan was right." Rhea takes a step back and pouts at Finlay. "I mean really, must you be *so* predictable?"

Finlay's chest tightens at the mention of Matris, and his anger spills over his skin, unleashing itself in the same way heat curls from a flame. Magic tingles at his fingertips, sharp and biting. "If I were you," he warns in a low voice, "I would really watch what you say next."

With hatred brimming in her eyes—so cold it's nearly scalding—Rhea leans forward. "And if *I* were *you*, I'd watch my back from now on, *Murderer.*"

Finlay snaps.

He slams his palms down into the sand and freezes the ground at their feet, the ice shooting for her ankles like a rapid creature. Yet she presses two fingers together and lightly taps them to the ground, halting the ice before it ever reaches her. It shatters slowly, until it disappears into the air like glittering flakes.

She huffs a humorless laugh. "Not going to cut it."

Finlay's breathing turns jagged in his chest as anger bubbles higher and higher into his throat. Without thinking, he flicks his wrists, and an army of dagger-sharp ice shards rises into the air around him. He sends them flying toward her. She presses the heels of her palms together, pushing her hands outward. A small glimmer materializes around her, and the ice shards disappear once they reach that warp of energy.

Finlay grits his teeth. He already knows Rhea is a Nullifier—meaning her magic is virtually being able to cancel out all magic—but the catch to wielding nullifying magic and being an effective magic breaker is the wielder has to be able to overpower the opposing wielder. Which means their laktî has to be more potent—more abundant—than their counterpart's. Because if the opponent's laktî can overwhelm the Nullifier, then the Nullifier is virtually useless. It is a rare and powerful magic to have, yes, but one which requires *extensive* training, demanding the wielder be masterful in hand-to-hand combat and magical control. Finlay is confident Tynan ensured Rhea excelled in both areas, but...

There is no gods-damn way her laktî should be able to overwhelm his, nullifying his magic.

He is the Fjolla Heir. An Archblood. Noble by birth.

She is merely the daughter born from a disgraced noble house. A lowborn raised in a ragged bookshop in a backwater town before she arrived at House Dalmar.

And there is no fucking way Finlay will lose to someone so far beneath him. Because if his father ever caught wind of it...

If Audwin Fjolla somehow ever found out this girl was able to nullify his magic, Finlay doesn't need a strong imagination to know what the scornful expression burning in his father's disgusted gaze would look like. To know what venomous words would leak from his lips, dripping poison beneath his skin in an attempt to cut him down and paralyze him with the reminders of his incompetence.

It would hurt far more than any dagger ever could.

Finlay conjures more of his magic, and he begins to lose himself to the rage coiling around his spine. The faces, the voices—they all slowly fade away as his attention becomes wholly focused on defeating Rhea. Ice roars from his palms as he shoots it straight for Rhea's heart. Her lips tilt with a smirk before she spins, throwing out a lazy hand and dispelling all the ice with ease.

Then she charges at him.

Finlay meets her challenge with savage hunger, striding toward her in turn. He will put her in her place. He will retain the honor his father demands of him.

They clash in the center of the fighting pits, a resounding *BOOM* echoing off the towering stone walls as her magic crashes against his. Finlay performs a series of movements, baiting her with a feint, then reaching for her wrist and swinging her over his shoulder. Her back slams into the sand, the breath whooshing from her lips. She coughs in wheezing breaths.

Finlay settles himself on top of Rhea, wrenching her arms above her head and pinning them into place with one hand. He leans forward, bringing him nose-to-nose with her. "Concede," he growls.

"No," she bites back.

Finlay flexes his jaw. "Don't be prideful, Rhea. *Concede.*"

Rhea's upper lip curls with anger as she nearly bares her teeth to him. "*Fuck. You.*" She spits in Finlay's face, the warm saliva dripping down his cheek like a damning mark. She swings her leg up and wraps the crook of her knee around Finlay's neck, swiping him to the ground and propelling herself on top of him with the momentum. She reaches back and pulls out the hairpin wedged into her half-drawn bun. Only, it's not a hairpin at all, but instead a small dagger made to look like one.

She goes straight for Finlay's throat, attempting to slice his skin with one quick movement.

But he catches her wrist—the dagger hovering just above his neck —before extending her arm out and rolling them over so he is again on top of her. He snaps her wrist back, forcing her to release her grip on the hairpin dagger. Rhea lets out a grunt of pain, but still she bucks against his hold, kicking out immediately after, breaking them apart.

She rises, reaching for two more daggers sheathed at her thighs. With a hilt in each hand, she crosses them in front of her chest, her gaze filled with nothing but murderous intent.

Fine. If she wants to take it there, then he will match her every step of the way. Because fuck her and the disrespectful way she keeps looking at him. The way she's *always* looked at him since they met.

The red-stained memories flash through Finlay's mind in quick succession, replaying snippets of that terrible night. Guilt starts to crawl from the pit he casts those memories into, and he has to actively throw them back into the shadowy recesses, not allowing them to see the light. He can't afford to feel guilty. He *can't.*

Rhea narrows her eyes on him as if she was able to read the entirety of what just passed inside him. She shakes her head at him, her sneer even more prominent than it was before. "You are such a coward," she mutters under her breath.

Finlay has to temporarily look away from her, not able to glimpse the pain surfacing in her eyes.

But then a soaring metal tip forces him to revert his attention forward as a dagger races for his throat. He erects a wall of ice just as the blade is about to pierce through his skin, and the dagger clinks off it, clattering onto the ground. Finlay's eyes are wide and wild as he looks back to Rhea.

That would have killed him. If he hadn't thrown up his wall at the last second, her dagger would have absolutely pierced the artery in his throat. Not to mention, she was aiming to slice his throat open just moments before.

Finlay isn't sure why, but the bitter realization she is *actually* trying to murder him right now slams into him like a lethal blow, causing his unchecked anger to corrupt him like poison. He knows she hates him. He knows she wants to watch him rot in an early grave somewhere. But Finlay never thought she would *actually* try to be the one to send him there.

The air around them plunges into a bone-chattering cold as Finlay surpasses mere rage. A terrifying sort of calm settles inside him, and he allows his magic to flow freely through his veins, calling on it in the same way he did when battling the Abdites. His breath becomes visible as he heaves in clipped bouts of air, his neck prickling from the sudden surge of magic he's allowed to escape.

Finlay raises both of his hands and opens his palms, facing them toward Rhea. Then he unleashes a razor-edged ice storm, sending the ferocious flurry hurtling at her. Simultaneously, he sends a sheet of ice racing toward her feet, attempting to lick her skin as it seeks to wrap itself around her legs, freezing her into place. Yet despite him tugging on even more of his magic, the ice continues to die as it meets the small bubble-like shield she's cocooned around herself. As she pushes that energy further outward, the ice melting midair, Finlay grits his teeth and pushes more magic at her. And more. And more. Until the tips of his fingers are tingling from the surge of magic he unleashes upon her.

He is so lost in his frenzy, he doesn't even realize Rhea has buckled, the edges of the razor-sharp ice nicking her skin, leaving oozing red slices up and down her body. Yet her expression remains undaunted, set in an infuriating mix of anger and determination. Her hands stay in front of her as she attempts to retain any remaining bits of her nullifying magic.

For whatever reason, it makes Finlay push harder. Throw more magic at her as his father's voice swirls around in his head. *Show her the true power of the Fjolla line. Make her respect you, even if it means breaking her in the process. Show her your worth. Show her no mercy.*

Wisps of her hair fall into her face, a sharp contrast against her ivory skin as the silver and black mingle together. Blood seeps from her arms like a tattered doll whose seams have come undone. Yet she remains upright, attempting to fight against the force of Finlay's magic. Her blue eyes remain locked on his, not pulling away for even a second as she defends herself against Finlay's onslaught with every last dreg of magic she can conjure.

She battles him until she can fight no more, his magic finally overpowering her.

Rhea tumbles backwards from the force, and Finlay—still lost in a sea of rage—lifts his hands before slamming them down, sending his sky of glittering icicles plummeting at her. Something scratches violently in his chest as he watches the frozen shards race toward her body, threatening to impale every infuriating inch of her.

It isn't until Finlay realizes he is seconds away from killing Rhea that he finally snaps free from whatever daze just overtook him. A small tinge of horror washes through him as he comes to, as if only just now becoming aware of what he's doing. But before Finlay has a chance to pull back his magic, the ice crashes into the location he sent it, the damning sound mirroring that of shattering glass.

Finlay blinks at the destruction he created, his heart pounding wildly in his chest. Yet relief floods his veins when he glimpses an impenetrable black wall coated in blue flames hovering over the place Rhea went down. His shoulders sag, and just as he banishes his father's voice back into the shadows, the wall drops, revealing Draven and Kiran standing shoulder-to-shoulder in front of Rhea as she attempts to rise to her knees. Her clothes are practically tattered rags now, blood dripping in the sand, leaking from her skin like she's a busted pipe—her hair a disheveled mess and her cheeks splattered with oozing scarlett slashes.

Finlay's stomach twists, and it seems like the whole world stills for a moment. Her eyes drag to his, and where he expects to see defeat, he sees only a stronger resolve. She braces a hand to her lifted knee, and she stands, her chest rising and falling as she gasps for air, her eyes never looking away from him as she cements the scowl back to her lips.

Draven's low growl snaps Finlay's attention from her. "That is *enough.*" His arms are laced with black spiderwebs as his dark magic spills into his veins, creeping up into his neck.

Finlay slides his gaze to Kiran, who assumes every inch of his height in this moment, blue flames burning in his hand as he watches Finlay with a measured gaze. Kiran's fire only turns blue when he's dug deep into his magic, pulling at it with merciless fury, and Draven's veins only bleed black when he's ready to burn the world to the ground.

Finlay realizes with visceral intensity he just royally fucked up. He allowed himself to get lost in the rage he keeps bottled deep inside himself—let his father's voice echo too loudly in his head this time. But that's what happens every time he sees Rhea. She spews hatred his way, and everything from that night surfaces.

Gods, he fucking hates her.

Josiah claps his hands, drawing the attention of them all. When he looks at him, Finlay suddenly remembers he's had an audience this whole time. Honestly, the room had been so quiet, he'd forgotten they weren't alone.

Finlay scans the room and finds a mix of gazes filled with either horror or approval. His eyes snag on Gray Nightenjoy and Marcella Lynderful. Sitting in the far corner, Gray leans forward, observing the scene with keen interest, while Marcella remains slumped in her chair, her arms folded over her chest while she watches with cool indifference.

"Captain Fjolla," Josiah says, drawing Finlay's attention back to him. "Thank you for that engaging demonstration. You and Ms. Brooksley valiantly demonstrated both the raw power of a Captain, and how valuable a capable Nullifier can be." He turns to Rhea and inclines his head to her. "Ms. Brooksley, you will be a valuable asset to Bathara, indeed. You showed great resilience and admirable combat abilities just now. We welcome you with open arms."

Finlay glances at Rhea and watches as she silently dips her chin at him. Her only form of acknowledgment to what he just said.

"Master Cahlmon. Master Strithmore," Josiah calls out. "Will you please join me for a moment of deliberation?"

The two Masters step forward and meet Josiah in the center of the platform, where they huddle together and begin discussing the fate of Rhea's temporary aggregate. As they do, Draven and Kiran march over to Finlay, their faces lined in a cold rage. For some reason he can't explain, Finlay glances past them and to Rhea. She catches his wandering eye, and her upper lip curls before she puts her back to him, strutting out of the sand pit and over to her combat boots, kneeling down and shoving her feet back into them. His eyes linger on her. Until a forceful blow to his chest pulls his attention away.

"What the *fuck* is wrong with you?" Draven hisses under his breath.

Finlay slides his eyes to Tynan Dalmar, who remains a few steps behind the conspiring Masters, his hands clasped behind his back, a neutral expression plastered onto his face. He watches Finlay and his brothers with an unnerving sharpness to his gaze.

"You know I couldn't take it easy on her, Draven," Finlay argues, keeping his voice low. "I don't know why she's here, but now that she is, it doesn't matter what she is to you—you know we can't give her special treatment."

"Like fucking hell I can't," he bites back.

Finlay resists the urge to sigh, instead glancing at Kiran, hoping he'll interject with logic like he normally does. Yet Kiran only watches Finlay with cold disdain in his eyes, his signature smirk nowhere in sight.

Draven points a finger into Finlay's chest—*hard*. "You took it too far. *Way* too fucking far."

Finlay scowls, his defensive walls erecting into place despite knowing he agrees with Draven on some level. He lifts his chin. "You wouldn't be saying that if she were anyone else."

"I would be saying that even if it was a second-year part of your own gods-damn aggregate. Have you forgotten I can *feel* your magic? I know how much you unleashed on her, Finlay. And I swear to the gods, if *you* were anyone else, I would have already ripped your throat out. So, maybe you should be more grateful for that preferential treatment you seem to be so against right now."

Though his head is telling him Draven's right, Finlay's stubborn pride takes over, and he feels the words bubbling in his throat, his defensive nature forcing them from his tongue as if blown away on a gust of strong wind. "You act as though you and I aren't on equal footing. You could try to rip my throat out, but perhaps you've forgotten that my magic and combat abilities rival your own, *brother*."

Draven's eyes flicker with darkness. "Would you like to make a wager on that?"

Finlay steps forward, opening his mouth, but the sound of Josiah's voice has Finlay snapping his mouth shut, his jaw clenching with frustration. He turns away from Draven, instead choosing to give Josiah his full attention.

"It has been decided. Ms. Brooksley," he says, his gaze roving to her. "Your aggregate has been chosen. After the incredible display you and Captain Fjolla just shared, you will join Skyborne, where you will continue to work with him to see if you can reach a level of magical power allowing you to nullify his magic completely." Josiah turns his keen-eyed stare onto Finlay. "Captain Fjolla, the three of us request you continue working with her personally, pushing her magic to its limits safely. We have a rare opportunity here with Ms. Brooksley, and if we can hone her nullifying magic to its full potential, we may find ourselves at a considerable advantage against the Abdites, should they attack again."

At the mention of the Abdites, the room erupts in whispers.

Master Cahlmon wastes no time silencing them. "If you are meant to be in my class at this present moment, remain in your seats and we will begin shortly. If you are not, you have every bit of information we can offer at this time, and so you are dismissed from this room. Please get out immediately." Without so much as another word, he turns his back on those watching in their seats, joining Master Strithmore, Josiah, and Tynan in their forming circle.

Finlay returns his attention to Draven, who remains inches from his face. He looks as though he's going to say something else, but ultimately, he clenches down on his jaw and jerks his chin away from Finlay, as if he'd been slapped by him.

Honestly, that perhaps hurts Finlay more than anything Draven could have possibly said.

Draven storms off without so much as another word. He approaches Rhea, and the moment he nears her, Finlay watches as the rage and all the venomous hatred she carried in her eyes fades away. Her entire expression slackens, her eyes rounding, and her bottom lip quivers as Draven gets closer. He stills at the sight, scanning Rhea with softened eyes, his mouth tightening at all the marks Finlay left on her body. Draven reaches for Rhea and tugs her into his chest, his arms practically swallowing her as he wraps them around her. He plants a kiss to the top of her head, squeezing her tightly.

"Did it make you feel good?" Kiran asks softly, continuing to watch Draven and Rhea, his words coated in an ice as cold as Finlay's.

Feeling suddenly more exhausted than he has in a long time, Finlay replies, "Did what make me feel good?"

"Acting just like your father. Performing in a way that would have made Audwin Fjolla proud. Pushing the boundaries of necessity until they bled into cruelty." Kiran still doesn't look at him. "In that moment, you were everything your father hoped you could be."

He does not say it as a compliment.

The words are like a dagger to his heart—though he will never show it. "That's not fair," Finlay counters. "You know what my father might have done if Tynan—or anyone else for that matter—told him Rhea could nullify my magic."

"And why does it still matter so much to you? We're not teenagers anymore, Fin." For the first time in years, Kiran's voice turns slightly pleading. Like what just happened is his final straw. He looks at Finlay, the lines encasing his normally bright eyes filled with pain. "Give up trying to please your father. Stop with this pretentious, noble bullshit. You look down your nose at everyone and everything —spit on those you deem lesser in his name. And for what? Audwin's cruel affections? You don't *need* him. You have us."

Finlay clenches down on his jaw. "I'm trying to regain my honor. Trying to be a man worthy of his title. Worthy of the Fjolla name. Something *you* will never understand, *Prince of Flames*." Finlay spews Kiran's nickname at him with an air of disgust. "You get to float through life without a care in the world, fucking and drinking and laughing. *I* am not so fortunate to be born into such a forgiving House."

Kiran watches Finlay for a long, silent moment. "If you keep walking down this path, you are going to tread too far, turning around one day and realizing you've stumbled into a place where no one will follow you."

Finlay remains silent, and Kiran takes that as his cue to walk away, striding toward Draven and Rhea. Once Rhea spots him, her face brightens, and those distinctly blue eyes widen with joy. She pulls away from Draven and practically flings herself into Kiran's arms. When she pulls back, he watches as laughter bubbles over her lips and Kiran's signature grin returns. They start chatting, and Finlay takes that as his cue to excuse himself.

As he strides out of the corridor—as he wanders back to his aggregate's wing alone—he curses the Masters for placing Rhea in his aggregate. For asking him to continue working with her to enhance her magic. Curses the way that girl has always put a wedge between him and his brothers.

Really, he just curses her and everything she represents.

Everything she forces Finlay to remember.

CHAPTER ELEVEN

DRAVEN

Draven paces in front of a sprawling oak bookshelf littered with dusty spines.

After his far too brief reunion with Rhea, Master Cahlmon approached him before his class began and informed him his father would like "a word" with him before he departs back for Talderine. Draven nearly snarled in the aging man's face at the information, but he knew that would get him nowhere. Plus, as it so happens, Draven has *many* words he wishes to have with his poor excuse of a father.

Starting with what the fuck Rhea is doing here. Her presence at Bathara... Him *daring* to jeopardize her safety like this... It goes against every fundamental principle of their arrangement. And by the gods, Draven is going to make sure the man knows it. Though he needs to get his anger in check before his father arrives. If he doesn't, he'll get nowhere. There is nothing his father loathes more than an emotional argument. Hell, emotions at all, really.

The door swings open—cobwebs and dust flurries stirring in the air from the conjured brush of wind—and his father strolls in, his jet-black hair neatly tied back and that skin-crawling, placid expression painted on his face.

On the outside, Tynan Dalmar is a civilized, sharp-minded, high-class member of society. But on the inside, a dirty-blooded, sinister monster lurks. A beast who relishes in feasting on human elements—on how far one must go before the animal overrides the man.

"Draven." His father hums his name like the opening notes to a song.

Draven hates the fucking melody.

"Tynan." He keeps his voice carefully neutral, not wanting to lose the battle before it has even begun.

With measured steps, Tynan strides deeper into the room and pulls out the tufted gray chair resting at the base of a decadently crafted walnut desk. He rests himself gently in the heart of it, swiping a finger against the rich, deep-brown wood, gathering dust to his fingertip. "Really," he says through a frown. "You think Bathara would have better upkeep."

Draven fights the urge to roll his eyes. Instead, he musters the most uninterested voice he can manage, keeping his face a perfect mask of indifference. "This is an abandoned study in a nearly abandoned area of the Main Hall."

Tynan inspects his now gray-tinted fingertip. "And why is it abandoned?"

"Because the academy expanded and now has better classrooms and study areas than when originally built." Draven feels his patience thinning already.

"And what about all the priceless knowledge resting within the rooms? Was it merely forgotten?"

Draven counts to three in his head before answering, giving himself a small buffer to check his tone. "A question far better suited for the captain over the Philator aggregate, seeing as they are the ones who typically deal in knowledge and are the keepers of our Grand Library."

"You make a valid point." He drops his hand, reorienting himself. "I imagine you have questions for me. A few words you'd like to remove from your chest, perhaps?" He props his elbows on the desk, interlocking his fingers in front of his chin. "I'll give you one minute to say whatever it is you'd like to say, however you'd like to say it."

Without wasting a second, Draven strides straight for the desk, slamming his palms down onto the surface. "What the *fuck* is Rhea doing here? Our arrangement is for you to keep Rhea safe and cared for, which keeps me on your gods-damn leash. Her being here right now goes against *everything*. Especially now that first-years can be dispatched on missions with their aggregates." With each word spewing from his lips, Draven feels his anger elevating—as if some unseen force is holding a burning matchstick to his blood. "And how could you let her reveal the strength of her magic like that? You know kings *kill* for magic breakers with even a *fraction* of her power. Not to mention, you did a damn good job of making her one of the best combat fighters I've seen in a long gods-damn time. Which was made very fucking clear as she sparred against Finlay."

"So what is your problem, exactly?" The polish in his smooth voice makes Draven curl his upper lip. "While at Bathara, kings cannot reach her. And from my vantage point, all I am seeing is someone perfectly capable of becoming quite a formidable Jurafen, who shows great promise with their abilities. I certainly am not seeing a wielder in need of protection or coddling."

"It's not about that," Draven snarls. "I know Rhea doesn't need my protection in a fight. I *know* she is powerful and capable. But—"

Tynan cocks his head with interest. "But what?"

"But this life isn't *meant* for her. It never was." A sudden tightness appears in Draven's chest, and he presses his lips into a thin line to keep the emotion from showing on his face.

There is so much more he could add to those words. So many dreams and aspirations he could stand here and throw in his father's face, making sure he remembers that *he* is the one who stole those lights from her sky. Yet his father doesn't deserve to know those parts of her. He isn't worthy of being offered a glimpse into the materials comprising Rhea's heart—the wishes fueling the beats of it. Plus, he would only be giving Tynan another toy to play with should he offer up that information.

Draven rubs his fingers across his forehead and drops his voice. "How did she end up here, Tynan? Did she choose this, or did you force her? And don't you dare insult me by attempting to insinuate this happened because of the new conscription; I know enough to be certain you could have shielded her from being conscripted if you tried."

Tynan's expression remains unchanged. "Perhaps you should simply ask her that question yourself."

Draven's eyes flash with rage. "And would she even be capable of giving me her honest answer?"

With a fully-formed smile now present on his lips, Tynan leans back in the tufted chair, keeping his fingers clasped together and resting them on his chest. He remains like that, watching Draven with quiet amusement in his eyes.

And Draven waits. Five seconds. Ten seconds. Thirty. Still, Tynan provides him with no answer.

He jerks his chin away and scoffs.

"Is it so hard to believe she may have wanted this?" Tynan challenges, his voice a hollow attempt at sincerity. "The girl has spent a decade at House Dalmar, isolated and scrutinized. Finlay, Kiran, and yourself have been gone for many years now. Has the thought never occurred to you that she may have grown lonely? It's not easy, constantly wearing a mask in a world you know you do not belong in. Sure, the mask covers you from the outside. But what about what remains within? Those pesky, intrinsic feelings can never truly be concealed—all things surface eventually. You know that."

"And whose fault is it that she has been subjected to such a life?" Draven growls between clenched teeth.

"Fault bears no meaning on the topic. Though, I find it worth mentioning that the burden of fault tends to change when the scope of time is broadened." Tynan lifts a hand, rubbing his thumb in a circle against his index finger. "Gaze one day into the past, perhaps the fault is my own. Gaze six months into the past, perhaps the fault isn't mine in the slightest. Interesting, isn't it? The way human nature determines where faults lie."

"Do not spew your nonsense to me right now. I have no patience for it."

Tynan chuckles, leaning forward to creak a wooden desk drawer open to peer inside. "That's quite alright. Besides, I'm done speaking on the matter anyways. I've already given you more time to speak than I offered."

"Then get to the real reason you summoned me here," Draven demands, piecing his mask back together and attempting to dull the sharpness in his words.

"You know, Draven," Tynan drawls with a measured smirk tipping his lips, ignoring his request completely as he continues rummaging through another drawer. "Even though offers are given, they shouldn't always be accepted. For example, I offered you a test to speak freely, and you took it. As a result, you've shown the entirety of your hand, and now you have no leverage." He releases a dramatic sigh. "I'd have thought I taught you better, but evidently not."

"I don't care about your sick perversions with human behavior right now. In fact, I don't care much about anything you have to say unless it's telling me what the hell you've summoned me for, or informing me of the concrete security measures in place for Rhea's safety. Otherwise, that fucking collar you've relished in having around my neck all this time? It's gone. And you can curl your lip at me and make all the snide remarks you want, but at the end of the day, without Rhea holding me back, you know as well as I do that a storm even *you* can't stop will be unleashed. I don't *need* leverage; I have power."

Tynan watches him with a soft smile painted on his lips. "And what is *true* power? Is it a display of might? Is it the magic I passed along to you, running through your veins?" He straightens in his chair, his eyes sharpening as they slowly come alive with intrigue. "See, boy, I think information is true power. Not magic. Not skill with weaponry or all the strength in the world. But knowledge. With it, the bearer of such facts needn't even lift a finger; those who seek what they know will do all the work for them. Destroying your enemies and conquering your goals without having to lift a finger by lever-aging the contents of your mind—*that* is the superior power."

Draven balls his hands at his side, trying to keep his anger in check. "What good is knowledge if you're dead? The information dies with you, and it cannot protect you in a fight."

Tynan's smirk grows tenfold at that, and Draven's skin crawls as a true laugh escapes from his lips. "I thought I raised you better than to think like that; how wrong I was." He slides his tongue along his bottom lip, wetting his skin as if with anticipation. "Knowledge, infor-mation, facts—they are the greatest protection there is. Would you like me to demonstrate?"

Draven doesn't answer. Instead, he watches with an indent wedged between his brows as his father slowly—methodically—pulls out an ornate dagger, forged with an onyx blade and adorned with anthracite embedded into the hilt, from a sheath strapped at his ankle and gently rests it on the desk, sliding it across the surface so that it's closer to Draven.

"Let's play a quick game," Tynan coos, joy wrapping around his words, licking through the air in poisonous streaks.

Distant screams echo in Draven's mind. He smells the tangy scent of blood first. Then the scent of burnt flesh next. His throat constricts, yet he rolls his shoulders back, not willing to let his scars show. "Fuck you. Fuck your games. I'm not playing."

"Oh," Tynan drawls with a small pout, "I think you'll want to play this one. After all, you did just inspire the rules. Let's allow the game to determine what the greater power truly is, hm?"

Draven glares at him, remaining silent.

Tynan lifts a finger and begins explaining. "The rules of this game are simple: you may either take that dagger and plunge it through my chest without me fighting back, or you relinquish that opportunity in light of me giving you life or death information."

Without hesitation, Draven reaches for the dagger and positions the hilt in his palm. He approaches his father, prowling toward him like a predator. Yet instead of pointing the tip of the blade to his chest, he positions the serrated edge against his father's throat. "Information regarding my life is worthless to me so long as your stain of existence is removed from this world."

Tynan holds Draven's murderous gaze, his smirk creeping up and up. "And what of the girl you've grown to care for so dearly? Is the same true for her life?"

Draven stiffens, his face paling. Suddenly, his chest tightens, and he finds his breathing has become ensnared in his lungs like an animal caught in a hunting trap. "If you attempt to lay even a *single* finger on her," he seethes in a rough whisper. "I swear to the gods, there is no force in existence powerful enough to stop me from taking your life as repayment." Yet Draven finds himself dropping the dagger from his father's throat without so much as another thought, receding a step.

His father smirks like a snake at the sight, then shrugs cooly. "Even if I wanted to, how could I? She's missing, after all. Perhaps even dead." He plucks a black strand of hair from his opulent shirt, embroidered lavishly with both silver and gold threads. "Now, make your choice: would you like to know what I know, or would you like to plunge that dagger through my chest? Whichever choice you make, it must be stated aloud."

Draven clenches his jaw and glares at him, chucking the dagger back onto the dusty desk, the noise of defeat clattering loudly in the air. "Tell me what you know."

Tynan watches Draven through sparkling eyes, not commenting on his decision. He doesn't need to—Tynan knows his point has been thoroughly made. It leaves Draven with the sneaking suspicion this was a trap laid out for him from the very beginning, and he unknowingly played right into it.

Tynan holds the room in silence a few heartbeats longer, visibly noting the tension coiling in Draven's shoulders with each passing beat. Finally, he repositions himself in the chair and peaks his fingers together, pressing them to the underside of his chin. "Bathara's council wishes to hold a trial in front of the Tani for the girl's crimes should she ever return in one piece."

"*Crimes?*" Draven spits. "What crimes? Destroying the Abdites during an unprecedented attack on Bathara? Sacrificing her body—potentially her *life*—for her fellow wielders?"

"For indiscriminately murdering over half of Bathara's numbers in a cataclysmic display of power she clearly had no control over."

"She is *learning*."

"She is a threat."

Draven shakes his head against the words. "That isn't right. She should have clemency. All she did, everything she sacrificed, it was for the greater good of the Three Kingdoms. To *protect*."

"Was it?"

"*Yes*," Draven answers in a stern hiss.

Tynan makes a show of sighing. "Well, unfortunately for her, it won't matter what you believe—only what the Tani does." He summons the Dalmar's signature dark magic—the very magic he cursed Draven to carry in his veins—and weaves the nimble tendrils through his fingers. As he does, Draven catches flickers of the crimson living in the heart of his magic. Though, it seems different than Draven remembers. Then again, he could be mistaken, seeing as his father doesn't wield their magic often. It's an odd power play of his, always claiming he doesn't need to. "To put it bluntly: should this girl you carry useless affections for somehow return, she will be put on trial, and she will lose. The Tani will see her magic as too much of a threat, and the girl too much of a wildcard. They will find her guilty, but they will not execute her. No, someday they may *need* her. So instead, they will condemn her to a life sentence in Toellor prison, and you will never see her again."

The mere thought of it uproots the world from Draven's feet, and it is a sheer act of will he doesn't buckle to his knees. He can't believe he is standing here having to entertain a reality where this could happen. Where Lyra returns—because she *will* return—and Bathara's council drags her to a trial in front of the Tani. Where the highest order of magical governance condemns her to a life in Toellor. The same fucking prison housing all the sentenced Abdites. She would be forced to drink the elixir created by Gardners, disconnecting her from her laktî. She would be bound. Gagged. Kept in the dark.

Draven shakes his head, squeezing his eyes shut against the images of Lyra suffering as they run rampant through his mind. "I won't let that happen." He pinches the bridge of his nose in an attempt to tamper his rage and push the images away. "I *won't*."

With every fiber of his being, he means it. He will kill who he has to, beg who he has to, make allegiances, pledge fealty—he will do whatever it takes to ensure when Lyra comes home, there is nothing but the warmth of his embrace waiting for her.

"Ah," Tynan coos, drawing back the wisps of darkness into his palm. "That is precisely the look I expected to see in your eyes." He smiles, the gesture more mocking than it is sincere. "You always have been the protective type. Even as a child."

Draven narrows his gaze at him, watching—waiting. He's shown far too much of himself already during this conversation, and he needs to reel in his brimming emotions. But that is so gods-damn difficult after learning Rhea's been conscripted to Bathara and Lyra has an unjust death sentence straight to Toellor.

"I have a proposition for you, Draven," Tynan drawls in his smoothest voice, propping his elbows up on the desk and clasping his fingers once more. "A proposition I think you'll find serves both our interests."

The increasing chill in Draven's bones rises to overtake the heat from his skin. No matter what his father proposes, he knows it won't be good.

His heart sinks into his stomach, and he is convinced the room is now three times smaller and the air four times thicker. "What is it you're proposing?"

The corner of Tynan's lip twitches. "I find myself in a position where, should the girl…" He trails off, brows furrowed. "Remind me her name again?"

Draven's upper lip curls, and he makes no attempts to hide it. His father knows. He fucking *knows* her name. He just wants to make Draven say it.

"Lyra," he rasps, the sound of her name on his lips reminding him even damnation can taste sweet.

"Ah, yes. That's it." Tynan smiles. "I remember her, you know. From that time in Rivara all those years ago. Tell me, have you told her about that encounter?" At Draven's notable silence and clenched jaw, his father hums. "You haven't? Hm...how fascinating. Nevertheless, what *was* her surname again? Lyra....?"

"Izacalli."

Tynan snaps his fingers. "Yes, that's it. Izacalli. I remember now. Such an odd surname, don't you think?"

Draven glares at him, not deigning to answer.

"As I was saying," he drawls. "I find myself in a position where, should Lyra Izacalli somehow return, I can prevent her from going to trial and secure her a proclamation of innocence throughout the Three Kingdoms."

"*How?*" Draven growls. "Bathara answers only to the Tani, and the Tani does not answer to anyone but themselves. You may be powerful in court politics and diplomacy, but not even you, Supreme Commander, hold sway with the Tani."

Tynan lifts a lazy shoulder. "Have you ever known me not to fulfill my end of a deal? You would just have to trust me to follow through with what I say."

Draven flexes his jaw. "And what must I give you in return for guaranteeing Lyra's freedom?"

"You must marry Arden Larking."

For a heartbeat, it's like he has been slapped—too stunned or dazed to respond.

"No. *No.* There is—I won't do that."

"Then I'm afraid Lyra's future is sealed. She either remains where she is, living or dead. Or she returns and is incarcerated for the rest of her life. There are no other options." He tilts his head, as if reconsidering that last part. "Well, I suppose she *could* go on the run and have both the Jurafen and the Shadows chasing her until she's caught, providing her a few more years of freedom at best—if you consider such a thing to be freedom at all."

Draven's lungs struggle for air as his chest practically caves in on itself. "There must be something else I can offer you," he murmurs, feeling desperate but doing his damn best not to show it.

"There is nothing else I want from you."

Draven rakes a hand through his overgrown dark locks of hair. This is not the first time his father has attempted to arrange this marriage with Arden. Of all the marriage proposals thrown his way, House Larking is the only one his father has ever entertained. For what reason, he doesn't know—most arrangements are strategic, and House Larking's powerful bloodline of light wielders is entirely at odds with House Dalmar's dark magic. Which means Lord Larking must possess something his father wants. Still, Draven was able to escape all his father's previous attempts to arrange their marriage in a way that never jeopardized Rhea. Once upon a time, he even talked to Arden directly about it—though, the circumstances leading up to that conversation were a bit messy, to say the least.

Fucking wine.

But now....

Now he doesn't see another option. He either refuses this offer outright, preserving the integrity of the choice his heart has already made, damning the girl his heart yearns for to a life of miserable captivity as a result. Or he accepts, securing the safety of the girl who stirs his soul, and damns his heart to a life where it will forever yearn to bleed the color lilac once more.

In the conversations between their training sessions—amongst a sea of questions Draven couldn't stop asking, desperate to know anything Lyra would offer him—she once told him that the thing she wants above all else is her freedom. Her right to choose her own path for herself. And during a brewing storm where chaos consumed the air—Abdites banging on obsidian walls and screams echoing in the distance—Draven once attempted to wordlessly show her through his gaze that all he desires is a life with her. That his thoughts, emotions, flesh—it all belongs to her, for reasons far deeper than she is even aware.

But now the very things they each want the most cannot be realized simultaneously. He cannot have her while she has her freedom;

she cannot have her freedom while he has his life with her. It is the exact sort of twisted thing his father relishes in—accepting one fate and forsaking another.

Draven releases a sigh from deep within his chest. As much as it hurts—as much as it will *always* hurt—he will do as he must to preserve a future for the girl who deserves to experience the world in the shades she chooses.

For Lyra, he will do this. For her dreams of freedom, he will submit—will shackle himself.

For her, he will burn. Just as he said he would.

Draven lifts his chin. "I have terms to this agreement."

Tynan leans back in his chair, his small smile a portrait of unconscionable delight. "I'm listening."

IN FEAR OF PRYING EYES, Draven stays to the shadows as he walks down the corridor.

He takes a hard right when he reaches the opening with an arched, stain-glassed window. There, a door leading to the back entrance of the gardens awaits.

Throwing a veil of darkness around him just in case, he slips through the threshold, taking care to shut the wood gently, not wanting the underused hinges to squeak. The crisp breeze is a balm to his battered senses, and he rests his head gently against the stone, pressing his palms into the rough surface, desperate to feel something other than the slashing sensation overtaking his chest.

He shuts his eyes, and he takes a long, shuddering breath. "I'm so sorry," he murmurs.

The broken sound of his voice is enough to make his lips quiver.

He grits his teeth and pinches his brows together in... grief?...pain?...heartbreak? He can't even isolate a feeling. It's all bitter. All broken.

He squeezes his eyes tighter, flashes of a long ago memory playing in his head. A guard. Swollen bruises and dribbling blood. An eruption of chaotic power. A small yet brave girl—far braver than Draven ever was, even at such a young age.

You are not a monster.

She has no idea how that simple sentence carried him through the years. How hard it was for him when he saw her again—their bodies matured and faces aged—not to immediately approach her and tell her how tightly he clung onto that seemingly inconsequential sentence. How, alongside a list of other things, it saved him from being lost to the darkness entirely. Simple words from a stranger— from a girl he thought he would never see again.

Only, he did.

"I at least did right by you this time," he whispers, letting all the emotion slip out of him in this temporary moment of isolation.

He concentrates on the forming colors in his head, seeing himself standing in a corridor with cracked paint and chipped walls, nothing more than a young boy who was still helpless to the cruel whims of his father. His chest clenches with guilt for not fighting harder for a lilac-haired girl who was about to have her memories of their first encounter stolen away from her.

Draven reopens his eyes and looks up to the dimming sky. He stares at it absently for a long, long time.

Would he ever even get the chance to tell her? Why *hadn't* he told her sooner? Why had he always just dodged her questions with the same answer?

A story for another day.

He has no justifications to offer himself.

Draven's eyes fall from the sky, instead grabbing onto a swirl of twirling leaves swept up in the wind. There is a rogue petal tangled up in the mix. It reminds Draven of something, and he slides his hand into his pocket, tugging free a sea glass pendant. He stares at the smooth, glistening surface as it lays heavy in his palm.

Not yet, Draven thinks.

He slides the pendant back into his pocket, his hand finding its way to his chest after. Draven clutches at his heart, digging his finger-

A BALLAD FOR THE BROKEN

tips into his skin as he rests his head against the stone wall. "I miss you, Lyra," he whispers. "Everything feels dull again."

A sound rustles in the distance, and Draven drops his hand from his chest and stands at attention, waiting with still movements as he sends his magic to sense if anyone is coming. Once he's sure no one is, he decides he needs two things: a drink and someplace better to consume it.

CHAPTER TWELVE

GRAY

Gray wanders down the long corridor, out the door and through the courtyard, heading for the greenhouse to search for some herbs to put into a tea for Marcella. His chin is pinched between two fingers as he drowns in his thoughts, attempting to unpack the day's events—which he knows are more nuanced than meets the eye.

Why was Tynan Dalmar in attendance at the briefing today? Better yet, why was he stirring up thoughts of conflict while operating under the guise of peace? Gray had spotted the gleam in that man's eyes when he was lecturing the emissaries on amicability. The speech was nothing more than smoke and mirrors. A plea to look left, while everyone should really be looking right.

His father made damn sure he would always be capable of spotting motives like that, and Gray would have been nothing short of a blind fool to have missed it then. He is certain Tynan is up to something, but…

Gray hasn't the slightest clue what it is he's trying to accomplish.

Then there is everything else.

First years are going to be dispatched on missions with their aggregates. Bathara is going to conscript wielders for the first time in history because of the wielder shortage. And then there is the matter of that girl, who is perhaps the most powerful Nullifier Gray has ever seen. For a while, she was nullifying Captain Fjolla's magic like it was no impressive feat whatsoever—not to mention the way she was going blow-for-blow with him in combat.

Normally, Gray would feel comforted in knowing Bathara has gained such an asset. Yet his stomach sours as the image of Draven Dalmar squeezing that girl in his arms like she was the center of his gravity burns through him.

Gray has never been one to jump to conclusions, but it is a well known fact that Draven is the only offspring Tynan Dalmar has. So, it's not like Gray can rationalize the sight by simply chalking it up to her being his sister.

He feels a dark flicker in his magic as he is forced to imagine the agony sure to destroy Lyra if Draven ever turned his back on her like that. As he imagines what he would do if Lyra is left to experience such a betrayal after opening her scarred heart, finally dropping the walls she built so high around herself. Gray has to clench his jaw against the mere thought of it, balling his hands into fists at his sides. If he finds out Draven has truly acted so selfishly, by the gods, he will make it his life's mission to discover what illusion he can cast upon Draven to make him suffer most. To make him bleed from an internal wound cutting far deeper than any wound his actions would cause Lyra.

Gray approaches the greenhouse doors and blows out a sigh. He flattens his palms against the cool glass and bows his head for a heart-beat, allowing the chilled breeze to sweep through his hair as browning leaves rustle behind him. Since knowing her, he has never been away from Lyra for this long, and he misses her to the point of physical pain. He worries for her. He longs to embrace her and hear her laugh. He wants to know if she's okay—alive and breathing and fed. If the nightmares have stayed away, or if they cling to her more viciously wherever she is. If Casimir has upheld his promise and allowed her to keep his shirt. Has she worn it? Has it brought her even the smallest sense of comfort?

Has she found what he hid within it...

With an ache now throbbing in his chest, Gray pushes the doors open and steps inside. He rounds the corner and freezes. Laying on the ground, leaning up against one of the glass panes, he spots a body.

Draven Dalmar rests with his head tipped back against the arched window, one leg outstretched while his arm drapes loosely over his other leg, bent at the knee, a jug of wine clutched loosely in his fingers. His eyes are closed, and though one would think he must surely be at peace in this moment, his pinched expression instead tells a story of pain. Gray waits a few seconds, and when Draven still doesn't acknowledge him, he clears his throat.

"I already know you're there," Draven says without opening his eyes, sounding exhausted.

Gray folds his arms over his chest. "Be that as it may, I think the better question is why *you're* sitting *there*." He nods in his direction for emphasis, even if Draven can't see the gesture—his eyes remaining closed.

"Because it smells like her," he murmurs so gently, it catches Gray off guard. Draven brings the jug of wine to his lips and takes a long, hearty pull.

Gray furrows his brows, unable to reconcile what he's witnessing. "What?"

Draven inhales sharply through his nose and finally opens his eyes, that strangely colored gaze of his finding him with ease. "I'm not fond of repeating myself, Nightenjoy, so you shouldn't make a habit of asking me to."

Gray glides his tongue along the grooves of his teeth, a flicker of irritation passing through him. "Fair enough," he mutters. It feels odd talking to Draven while towering over him—hell, it feels odd talking to Draven like this at all. Still, Gray plops himself down on the ground, folding his legs beneath him. "Are you talking about Lyra?"

Draven glances at him, rolling his head in the opposite direction as his gaze shifts onto something in the distance. "I am."

Gray's lips twitch with a smile. Though he, himself, hasn't exactly thought about it, this greenhouse *does* smell a lot like Lyra's normal scent. One glance at the corner across the room tells Gray why. There are rows and rows of sage growing upright in terracotta clay pots.

A bit of sage. A note of something earthy as it mingles with subtle floral undertones. A hundred percent Lyra.

"You're right," Gray agrees through a helpless smile. "It does." He looks back to the Dalmar Heir, studying him closely. His eyes snag on the endless black lines snaking up Draven's arm and into his neck, looking like an elaborate tattoo. After seeing the markings up close the day Draven and Kiran sparred in the hills, Gray has always suspected the entirety of the design is his wielder's mark. And if Gray is guessing correctly, he'd wager Draven paid someone to ink over certain parts of it to make it look more like a tattoo in some areas, confusing wielders as to what belongs to his mark and what doesn't. Which, if that is true, would mean Draven Dalmar possesses a well of magic far greater and more terrifying than the average wielder can even fathom.

Gray still isn't sure if he feels comforted or unnerved by such a man having his eyes set on Lyra.

"You know," Gray begins, "you could always take a bundle of sage and keep it in your chambers. Maybe even clip some flowers and plant them in a pot of soil. You'd basically get the same smell."

Draven's eyes are hollow as he continues staring off into the distance. "I know."

Feeling protective over Lyra and needing to carve out an opening to discuss that girl Draven held in his arms, Gray pushes further. "So why rest in the greenhouse? Unless you're hiding from—"

"I'm not hiding from anything," he refutes in a lifeless tone wrapped in thorns. Draven cuts him a sharp look, and Gray notices the debate weighing in his eyes as he stares at him. Whatever conclusion he arrives at, however, has him banishing the threat in his gaze back to the shadows and releasing a deep sigh after. "I'm having a really bad fucking day and I'm buzzed, so that is the only reason I am going to say this to you, Nightenjoy. And if you were anyone else—if you weren't so damn important to Lyra—I would have already blackened your eye for disturbing me."

Though on some level Gray feels his male ego rise in protest at the challenge, he silences it. Draven can say and do as he pleases in this moment. Because fuck his own pride and ego. For Lyra, Gray will cast them both aside so he can make sure Draven Dalmar is actually someone worthy of having her. Of receiving her love and being offered the gift of her heart. Because that girl is scarred and bruised and battered, but she is also resilient and beautiful and deserves the entirety of the night sky strewn together on a string.

And Gray is going to make damn sure that is something Draven can offer her.

The sky bleeds crimson as the sun descends behind rolling hills stretching outside the greenhouse windows. Gray notices the copper tones in the dimming horizon first.

He glances back at Draven, setting his jaw. "Well then, I'm all ears."

Draven's lips twitch before setting in a thin, hard line. He lets his head fall back against the glass panes once more, and he closes his eyes. "I come to this greenhouse every evening, at every sunset, and I lay in this exact spot and rest my eyes, allowing the smell of her to envelop me so I can pretend she's still here, in my arms, just like she was before I let her go. I try to imagine her warmth and how good it felt when it seeped into my skin. I picture her smile. Remember the spark of her touch." When he reopens his eyes, his gaze has darkened into something cold and distant. "I come here—where she first kissed me—and pretend like I didn't fail her. That I was enough to save her."

Gray is stunned into silence, and all he can do is blink at the sight of Draven Dalmar sprawled across the greenhouse floor, his shoulders slackened by sadness and his face pinched with unmasked pain. This version of the Dalmar Heir is so far removed from the image painted throughout the entire Three Kingdoms—so different from the rumored insouciant and barbaric captain over the infamous Elefet aggregate. Gray struggles to remedy the two opposing identities into one. To view this version of Draven as the formidable, ruthless weapon known as Tynan Dalmar's son.

With something now lodged in his throat, Gray presses on. "Those are strong words for someone who's barely known her for a full season. How can you know you mean them?"

Gray braces himself to be met with a loaded threat or a dagger stare, yet Draven gives him none of that. Instead, his tired eyes remain fixed on something in the distance, and Gray finally traces his line of sight, curious to know what he's been staring at.

"Nox's Caelum," he muses, surprised to find Lyra's favorite flower amongst the sea of color filling the greenhouse.

"Nox's Caelum," Draven repeats with a rasp. "I thought she might like to return home to them." He releases a sigh and finally pulls his gaze away from the flower, meeting Gray's eyes. "Have you ever had your soul scream at you before? Not your heart. Not your cock. I mean your *soul*. A piece of you that is beyond comprehension."

At first Gray isn't sure if he is looking for an actual answer, but as Draven's intense gaze bores into him, he realizes he is. "No," Gray admits. "Not in the way you are describing. At least, not yet I haven't."

"From the very first moment I ever laid eyes on Lyra," Draven begins, his eyes hazing over, seeming filled with a poignance Gray can't place, "my soul shouted at me. Tugged at some invisible thread in my chest, as though sensing this rare, precious recognition in her." He pauses, a deep wedge forming between his brows. "I'm fully aware of all that's left for us to learn about each other—all the layers left uncovered. But I promise you, Nightenjoy, once your soul has decided it's found its other half, there is no turning back. Time does not exist for a soul—only feeling does."

Gray studies Draven, looking for any signs of deception.

He finds none.

And Gray suddenly sees what happened those few minutes after Lyra came through her Feargate—unconscious, unresponsive, and with gash marks all along her singed throat—in an entirely new light.

Wordlessly, Gray uncurls his fingers from his palm, and golden light pools in the center of his hand, the snake on his arm illuminating with a richly golden tone. Gray casts his magic outward, recreating the moment. He puts it on display for both him and Draven to watch.

Lyra's back fell to the ground with a heart-wrenching thud, her chest rising with jagged pants of breath.

Gray strode forward to go to her—to hold her, help her, apologize for all the shadows he missed swimming inside her. But before he made it a step, Draven rushed forward, pushing the crowd that formed around Lyra back with his magic, whispers of horror swirling in the air. He immediately dropped to his knees, and he gingerly—tenderly—pulled Lyra into his lap. His fingers traced her marred skin, and Gray couldn't help but feel like the touch looked nothing short of reverent. His face was filled with so much pain. Like he, too, was feeling what Lyra had just felt. Yet he also possessed the calmness of a person who had experience with similar tragedy.

"I've got you," he whispered so low, Gray nearly missed it. "I'm here."

Another emotion rested within his downturned eyes, and Gray blinked against what he saw, convinced he was mistaken.

Pride.

That was pride swimming in his eyes as he gazed down at Lyra—like he couldn't even begin to mask how proud of her he was for facing her demons. For walking away from the Abdite. For facing her greatest fears and still having the courage to fight back against them.

And that pride clung to another emotion. Something uninhibited, unadulterated, and entirely unmistakable.

Gray curls his fingers into his palm, killing the illusion. "I wasn't convinced of what I saw that day," he offers in way of an explanation for what he's shown Draven. "But you may have just convinced me."

Draven stares at the space where the illusion had just resided, his brows knitted together. He redirects his gaze to Gray. "Neat trick," he mutters.

Gray huffs a laugh, the corner of his lip tugging up. "You have no idea."

Draven grunts, as if the tiniest bit amused, and a flicker of satisfaction flares in Gray's chest. He enjoys feeling like he is perhaps starting to bond with the man Lyra has chosen to give her heart to. Though he must contain the feeling—his work here still isn't finished. Not yet. Especially when considering he may never get another opportunity to speak so openly with Draven again.

"So who was that girl from earlier, then? You two seemed…famil- iar. I saw the way you pulled her into you. That wasn't nothing." Gray is careful not to let his words get bitey, despite the current of anger seeping through him as the mere thought of Draven doing something like that to Lyra bites at him once more.

The corner of Draven's lip kicks up in a near smile, as if he was expecting that question. "Who is Lyra to you?"

Gray frowns. "What does that have to do with anything?"

"It has everything to do with it."

He sighs, glancing around the greenhouse, barely any light remaining as the final flickers of sunlight bow to the prowess of night. "Lyra is my heart given flesh," he answers simply. "And if something were to happen to her…" Gray trails off, his jaw clenching as the shadows inside him stir. "Well, let's just say there are parts of myself that she would forever take with her."

Draven's answer arrives softer than he is expecting. "Rhea means exactly the same to me."

Gray studies him, hesitant. "I didn't think I needed to specify this, but I am speaking platonically."

"As am I."

Gray narrows his eyes on Draven; Draven raises his brows in chal- lenge right back.

"Okay," Gray drawls, trying to put the pieces together. "Care to elaborate on that?"

"Not particularly. You're lucky I've even told you as much as I have already."

Gray stretches his hands behind him and shifts his weight back, tilting his chin up and heaving a quiet groan. "You know," he grum- bles. "Lyra has never been one to be very forthcoming, either. If this is what you two's conversations look like, I'm not sure how long your relationship is going to last."

For the first time, Draven cracks an *actual* smile. And honestly? The sight of it makes Gray feel a tad uneasy. Yet he can't help but notice there is something melancholy about his smile; though Gray knows it isn't his place to comment on that.

"Why are you smiling?" he semi-jokes instead. "It's...unnerving."

Draven drops his eyes to the ground, shaking his head as his mouth remains punctuated by soft curves. "I liked hearing you say Lyra and I were in a relationship." He takes another swig of wine.

Gray regards him for a while. "So to be clear," he presses, not wanting to have to revisit this conversation ever again. "You and that girl, Rhea, have no romantic feelings, no romantic connections, and what I saw in that classroom was nothing more than a platonic display of dedication?"

Draven's lips twitch. "Does it deepen your appreciation for how accepting I am of your and Lyra's relationship?"

"Please. That's not even close to the same thing."

"Isn't it?" Draven counters, his tone lighthearted. Another odd sight. He laughs under his breath, cocking his head at Gray. "You know, in Foreigner's Valley, I thought the two of you were lovers."

Gray huffs an amused laugh at the admission, rubbing at the back of his neck. "We tried fooling around once after having too much wine," he confesses. "But it felt wrong, was severely awkward, and we both vowed *never* again."

"So I was told," Draven deadpans, his lips flattening into a tight line, as if the mere mention of someone else touching Lyra has ruined his entire mood.

Gray fights against the growing laugh in his throat, shifting his weight forward and peaking his fingers in front of his lips before directing them toward Draven. "And so you and Rhea have a similar dynamic? Does Lyra know about her?"

"Rhea is my little sister for all intents and purposes, and she and I have *never* crossed those boundaries. She is far too much like my own blood to even entertain the thought." He shoots Gray a very sharp, very passive look. Actually, scratch the passive part. "And no," he continues. "Lyra doesn't know about her. I almost told her after she explained your relationship to me, but..." He trails off, and Gray glimpses ghosts awakening, dancing cruelly in the lines of his eyes. "For reasons I'm not going to discuss, all I managed to tell her was that I understood the two of you's relationship completely."

Gray isn't sure what to say to him; he doesn't know the Dalmar Heir well enough to offer him anything of worth. Not while shadows he could probably never understand haunt his downturned gaze. Plus, Gray's father made certain he understood no words were better than hollow ones. So, he offers Draven what he can—a comfortable silence.

And it seems like those few seconds of offered quiet is all the Dalmar Heir needs. He shakes the ghosts away, reorienting his attention back onto Gray. "Speaking of romantic affiliations, what's going on with you and the flora-wielder?"

Gray nearly chokes at the shift in questioning. The skin at his neck turns scorching, and he stiffens. "What the hell are you talking about?"

Draven shrugs lazily, his expression entirely too indifferent for the sort of conversation they are approaching. "Look," he begins, his voice now carrying a hint of amusement. "Let me save us both some time by reminding you I *am* the son of Tynan Dalmar, as unfortunate as that is. I was bred to identify the things in a person they'd most like to hide. I know what I saw. I know what it means. But what I don't know is what you're doing about it?"

Gray's brows pinch together as he folds his arms over his chest. "And I don't know why the Dalmar Heir is suddenly so interested in the status of my love life."

Draven grunts a laugh, the corner of his lip hooked up. "You two are the most important people in Lyra's life."

Gray waits, expecting him to elaborate.

He doesn't.

Gray heaves a sigh, rolling his eyes up to the glass ceiling. This is certainly *not* a conversation he was expecting to have tonight. *Especially* not with Draven Dalmar.

Still, it has been weighing on Gray's chest for so long, he can hardly remember what life was like before the weight started pressing against him. Ever since the night he wandered into the room Lyra and Marcella shared, waiting to make sure Lyra was okay after Klytis found him to relay the news about Delroy. Ever since they stayed up all night talking. Since their skin accidentally brushed against each other and Gray felt like his heart was jolted by an electric shock.

Ever since she looked at him that way, if only for a moment…

Truthfully, his head has been a mess of confusion, and with Lyra gone, he has had no one to unravel the messiness with. So, maybe that's why he actually feels enticed to take Draven up on his offer to talk about Marcella. Why he speaks so openly to him, a near stranger for all intents and purposes.

Gray sucks in a breath and nods in the direction of the wine jug. "May I?"

Draven's knowing smirk is his only answer, extending out the wine jug for him to take. Gray brings the tip of it to his lips and gulps, hoping to catch a quick buzz for this. Luckily for him, once he finishes drinking and hands the jug back to Draven, the taste of luxury on his tongue tells him the wine is indeed far from common-er's wine, and a euphoric warmth coats him in a blanket within a blink.

"I've grown to care for Marcella." His words come out slow and tentative. "She is….well, she is a force of nature. Is sharp-witted and brave. And though she wouldn't want people knowing it, she is soft and caring. Not to mention, she loves magic like I do. Not invested in it for power, but fascinated by the knowledge surrounding it. And gods she is beautiful. When she looks at me, I—"

At Draven's raised eyebrows and smug *I told you so* smile, Gray cuts himself off, scrubbing at his face and groaning.

"Please," Draven drawls wryly, "don't stop on my account."

"I'm not going to keep talking if you insist on looking at me like that."

Draven exposes his palms to him in surrender; Gray fights against the growl growing in his chest.

"Anyway," Gray continues. "I can admit I feel those things, but none of it matters."

Draven frowns. "Why not?"

"Because I'm not going to act on them while Lyra is gods-only-know where, kidnapped and forced to do gods-only-know what." Gray pauses, clenching his jaw. "Look, I'm not going to argue what I say next is logical or rational; I'm just simply going to tell you it's how I feel, and there is no changing it."

Draven offers a silent nod to acknowledge the words.

"To pursue the only female friend Lyra has ever had while she's being held captive somewhere feels like the most selfish decision I could ever make. She may be fighting for her life every second of every day where she is, and I would be the world's most selfish asshole if all I did during that time was pine for her best friend." He attempts to quell the emotion bubbling in his chest. "And Marcella is hurting, grieving the loss of Griff. She needs someone right now, and for whatever reason, she has allowed me to be the one she leans on. I could never betray that sort of trust." Gray reaches for the wine from Draven, taking another pull and staring at the ground for a long moment after. "To act on my feelings would be like I'm dismissing every terrible thing that has happened, and I won't do that. So, every day when I wake up and see Marcella, I swallow the rise of feelings in my chest, and I simply show up for her as I hope a friend would show up for me."

Draven's eyes darken, and he drops his voice, swallowing thickly against whatever emotion has risen in his throat. "Convenient timing is a myth. There will always be reasons to not do something; your time would be better spent focusing on the reasons you should. You never know what you might miss out on by stunting your life."

"But that's the thing," Gray counters. "I'm not stunting my life on account of timing; I am merely respecting the relationship my life has to theirs." He pauses, opening his hands to expose his palms to himself. "Besides, I don't think Marcella feels as I do anyways, so none of this really matters."

Gray continues staring at his palms while Draven lets the silence stretch between them, seeming to chew on his next words. "Well," he finally says, "you can find out whether or not she does when Lyra returns. I find myself able to search for her more freely now with Rhea here, and I am going to bring her home, Nightenjoy. I swear it."

Gray's heart slams against his chest as his dizzying mind turns everything over. He realizes then he has been a fool for not telling

Draven about what he and Marcella had done that blood-stained day, mere moments before Casimir Vivaldri strode off with Lyra. About the tiniest seed of hope they were able to plant, offering a sliver of a chance at finding her. He hadn't told anyone in fear of there being a secret mole amongst them. Given everything that happened during the Abdite attack, Gray is certain there is someone feeding insider information to *somebody*. And seeing Gray hasn't the slightest clue who it is or who it could be, he hasn't known who he can trust. But if this conversation has shown anything to Gray, it's that he can be certain he can trust Draven. At least when it comes to Lyra and her safety.

"There is something I need to share with you," Gray says, finally tearing his eyes away from his hands and locking them onto Draven. "About Lyra. About what Marcella and I managed to accomplish just before she was taken."

Draven's gaze shifts into something lethal, and Gray realizes he is now looking at the version of the Dalmar Heir people know him to be. Ruthless. Sharp. Intense. "Tell me."

Gray does. He tells him everything. As he finishes explaining the smallest glimmer of opportunity they were able to create for themselves—Draven's features zipping through a spectrum of emotions—Gray realizes they are both left with the bittersweet caress of hope as it sinks its teeth into their skin. It wraps around the two of them, humming promises that may never come to be in pretty melodies.

Gray looks at Draven, and he knows with utter certainty they are thinking the same thought—

If Lyra is able to realize what was done, it could change everything.

CHAPTER THIRTEEN

LYRA

Sweat drips down my neck, and I hunch over my knees, gasping for breath.

Neilina rests a hand on her popped hip, frowning at me. "Your combat skills truly are terrible."

I look up just long enough to shoot her a sharp glare. "I already told you," I pant. "I came into my magic late, and I haven't received a lot of training because of it."

Her frown deepens. "I thought you were being modest. You possess a strong ability to sense my attacks and maintain your center of balance while countering them. You do not let your eyes lie to you —something that normally implies someone has at least…*some* level of competence. You are toned. Quick to decide." Her brows pucker with thought. "You possess every signal that would imply you are skilled in the art of combat, yet you aren't in the slightest." She scratches at her temple. "It is very confusing."

I stand upright and swipe the sweat from my forehead with the back of my hand. "Yeah, well, I had to be trained in a hurry, and I had a damn good mentor who ensured I was given the correct foundation to build on."

My heart aches as flashes of Draven and me training together between sun-coated hills race through me. I miss him. Not even just as the man who makes my heart pound and causes butterflies to stir in my stomach. I miss training with him. Miss his instruction. His company.

Training with Casimir and Neilina over this past week has made me realize how good of a mentor Draven truly was. How skilled and competent his every instruction had been. Honestly, somehow, it's made my attraction for him grow all the more—something I didn't think possible considering my chest always feels like it's at max capacity when I think about him.

"Hm," Neilina hums, walking to the edge of their fighting ring to reach for her waterskin. "Your mentor must truly be something special then."

"He is."

I feel Neilina's lingering stare on my skin like a physical touch. I imagine she's probably curious at the sudden tenderness I let seep into my voice—a feature she has not seen from me often. Yet I just lift my chin and sweep the hair from my face, pressing my hands into my lower back as I stretch out my muscles before turning around to face her.

Whatever thoughts she may or may not have about my display of softness, she doesn't comment. Instead, she finishes drinking her water and sets her waterskin back down on the fluffy grass. "You are meeting with Master to enter the Veil tonight, yes?"

"I am."

She nods. "Master has instructed me to stay behind and wait for you in your bedchamber. He says you will most likely need my assistance once you've finished with your work tonight, but that you are to meet with him alone."

A slight wrinkle forms in my brow. "Alright," I say. "That's fine."

Neilina watches me a moment longer, her gray eyes a beautiful contrast against her stark white hair. "I just wanted to let you know so you weren't waiting for me to escort you tonight."

"Thank you."

She waves me off. "You are to meet with Master in the Astral

Chamber come sunset. Don't be late." She begins to stride off in the other direction, but I call out to her, halting her movements.

"Uhm, where is the Astral Chamber, exactly?"

Neilina glances at me over her shoulder, smirking. "I was told to let you figure that out for yourself. Master says it will encourage you to explore our lands and speak with our people."

I open my mouth to protest, despite knowing full well it is a good plan to make me branch out, but before I can utter a word, Neilina is already five paces in the other direction.

As if sensing my gaze, she throws a lazy hand over her shoulder. "Good luck."

I bite down on my scowl, secretly thinking I wish I was half as cool as her when I was seventeen. Perhaps I would have found my way out of King Alastair's iron grip faster. Would have faced my demons sooner.

A sigh blows past my lips, and I shove more strands of loosened hair from my face. What I should *really* be doing right now is going to the bathing chambers and scrubbing all the sweat and dirt from my body. But some defiant part of me doesn't want to. If Casimir is going to make me explore his lands, meet his people, and enter the Veil for him after, then I will do it on my terms, my way, rendering control over the situation however I can.

So with a disheveled braid, grass-stained clothes, and dirt-coated skin, I do as Casimir asks and finally explore wherever the hell it is I am.

———

THE MARK of true maturity is being able to admit when one is wrong —whether from being stubborn-headed, prideful, or whatever other congestive emotion rises to the surface and takes control of sensibility. My maturity must have grown tenfold, because as I stroll along an arched stone bridge hovering above aquamarine water flowing between dusty-colored mosaic walkways, I am forced to admit to myself I have been *extremely* wrong for not exploring this place sooner.

God's veins, it is beautiful.

More trees than I can count tower overhead, creating a canopy of bright green foliage as leaves of different sizes cast dancing shadows across the running stream of water, glistening like a sheet of crystal. Rough vines twist around thick trunks of bark, and patches of moss and ivory cling to nearly every surface imaginable. Along the open spaces, where the stretch of tree limbs fail to consume open air, circular stone buildings overflowing with soft, luminescent light hum. The pillars are carved from iridescent moonstone, and the domed glass roofs house numerous stringed lanterns cascading along the exposed panes. From a few open doorways, music escapes; the sound of a fiddle's strings a heartbeat through the mosaic streets. The smell of mint leaves, no doubt growing within the lush foliage, sweeps along the breeze. It mingles with the woody notes from the trees, fusing with moss and lily to make the scent tiptoeing through the air intoxicating.

I even catch a glimpse of a tavern through one of the open doors. There's a large barrel beside the threshold, and a wooden sign hangs over the entrance, though I can't make out the words. A woman with long silver hair and a loose white dress frolics through the small crowd inside, her fiddle resting against her shoulder while her bow masterfully manipulates the strings in her other hand. She looks ethereal. Happy, even.

I want to follow those signs of life. I want to feel the melodies etch into my skin and leak into my bones. To feel something good in my chest instead of the hollow aching sensation I've felt since being here. Yet flashes of the Abdites murdering innocent wielders at Bathara pelt me. Memories of what they did to Meiji haunt me. The image of Casimir plunging his blade through Griff's chest destroys me. I hear their lunatic rantings. Remember the way Lexamon stroked me in Foreigner's Valley. And even though I recognize—for reasons I still don't understand—the Abdites are different in this unknown place, I still can't bring myself to attempt to have any sort of relationship with them, despite Casimir's many requests for me to do so. I just.... can't.

So, I turn and walk away, putting the soul-stirring sounds of joyful strings and echoes of laughter to my back.

As I wander deeper into the grounds, following the path of oblong stones, the trees give way to exposed buildings resembling old bathhouses, the pillars supporting the open structures carved from varying hues of marble. At every center, a large rectangular pool rests, rich in its lightness and clear as glass. Beyond those structures, a breathtaking garden sprawls for what has to be miles. On and on the green expands, bursting with a riot of colors so vibrant, it nearly steals the air from my lungs. It is a garden oasis to rival that of any other—including the one I woke up in when I first arrived here. As beautiful and legendary as I imagine the Hanging Gardens to be.

At the thought of the Hanging Gardens, a smile tugs at my lips. "Hi, mom," I murmur to the wind, conjuring an image in my mind of her standing in the middle of the trickling stream, an assortment of herbs and flowers collected into her dirt-smudged hands. I picture her dress hiked up, precariously pinned in place by its muddied hem. Imagine wisps of her hair blowing in her face as her mauve eyes crinkle with joy. My heart squeezes and aches from the longing and grief the conjured image pours into me. But I do not turn away from it. I instead relish the feeling, accepting that the flashes of pain are reminders of all the harbored love between us.

You'd be proud of me, Draven. I'm finally doing it—feeling the grief and honoring the pain.

I am so lost in the emotion of it all, I don't notice the person sneaking up behind me. Not until a rough, calloused hand claps me on the shoulder and whirls me around to face them.

Silver, bloodshot eyes stare at me, black veins branching along the woman's temples like streaks of jagged lightning. Her cascading hair perfectly matches the shade of her irises, and as I blink at her, I find myself unable to place her age but recognize her as the woman I had just seen playing the fiddle. She is marked with an upside down eye centered on her forehead, and her gaze skips with a manic glint—

forcing me to realize that for the first time since arriving here, I am face-to-face with the version of an Abdite I know most intimately. A version that is deranged and dangerous and entirely unpredictable.

"A game will soon be played," she croaks. "Where winning is not and losers are flayed. For the strings of death are not meant to be tugged, yet a Master of fraught will find the plug." A shimmering white light swallows the entirety of the woman's eyes, and her words grow more erratic, her voice shifting into a shrill song. "Dark. Light. A jagged mark. To you, dear girl, a good place to start. Restore. Reborn. Reignite. Relight. Remember, child, there is joy in the Night. A father. A king. A murderer. A son. The two who walk now will never run."

I rear back, but the woman grips me with her other hand, digging her nails into both my shoulders, drawing blood.

"What are you saying?" Pain sparks down my spine from her puncture marks, and I clutch her wrist and attempt to pry her off me. Yet her fingers dig deeper into my flesh, refusing to let go.

"My tongue is tied not to my Master, but to... to..." A groan gargles in her throat. "Dispel. Attacker. Lord. Master. Actor. Restore." The glowing dims in her eyes, the silver flickering before fully saturating her irises once more. She pants in wheezing breaths, and her gaze widens as if she has only just now realized where she is—like she has suddenly come through a hazy fog of some sort.

Her eyes dart wildly around the area before settling on me. The lines of fear wrinkle her expression. She digs her nails deeper into my skin, and I suck air between my teeth from the shooting pain. As the tips of her fingers saturate with crimson, her stare drifts farther and farther away—like she is viewing something miles in the distance.

"My curse is I See free but speak in chains." She whispers the sentence, a sudden sadness clinging to her manic words. "And bound I have been, which has made me insane. I have Seen it all, yet am spelled by silence; it is not who you think perpetuating violence." Her features scrunch together, as though pained yet defiant. "Your blood has now stained my skin; I told you more which is my sin." Clicking noises echo in her throat, and she begins gasping for air. "Begin in a room where illusions lie. Preferably an item that has gotten you by.

There the clock will begin to tick down. In the heart of darkness, you will be found."

The black veins framing her eyes suddenly crawl forward, until they spill over into her scleras, overtaking the bloodshot stain as darkness leaks from ruptured blood vessels, pooling her gaze into an obsidian slate. She pulls a dagger from somewhere beneath her dress, and without a sliver of hesitation, she cuts her tongue from her mouth and drops the spongy pink muscle to the ground as if it is nothing more than a discarded piece of trash.

Black blood spews from her lips at an alarming rate, and shock rears through my muscles, paralyzing them like a poison. I shake my head violently as I attempt to grasp the situation in front of me, but my shaky hands aren't sure what to do. As I watch her body overflow with black veins and collapse onto the ground—her limbs freezing mid-movement as an inhuman stillness falls over her—all I can do is stare at her corrupted wielder's mark.

"TELL me again what the woman said to you before she cut out her tongue." Casimir paces in front of me, anger pouring from his body like rain from a stormcloud.

Once the woman passed, everything sort of happened in a blur. Casimir appeared seemingly out of nowhere, his eyes lined with a terrifying rage and marked by a wild gleam. He told me he sensed magic that didn't belong in his home, and given the elaborate protection spells supposedly in place, he informed me that should have been an impossibility.

The sequence of events following his arrival all seemed to have happened within a blink. Guards staggering in. The body being inspected. Casimir escorting me to some atrium nearby so he can interrogate me. I've barely been able to process a thing.

I huff a sigh and strategically repeat my conversation, only offering him bits and pieces. "A game will soon be played," I repeat. "Where winning is not and losers are flayed. For the strings of death are not meant to be tugged, yet a Master of fraught will find the plug." Casimir's pacing quickens, and my eyes glide back and forth, following his movements as I continue. "My curse is I See free but speak in chains. And bound I have been, which has made me insane. I have Seen it all, yet am spelled by silence; it is not who you think perpetuating violence."

He halts, squaring his shoulders to me. "And that is all? You are being truthful?"

I dip my chin. "That's all she said."

Casimir drags a hand down his face. "So many questions," he mutters under his breath, seeming to be talking to himself. "So much to unravel."

"Tell me about it," I grumble pointedly. "In fact..." I kick off the wall I was leaning against and stride for Casimir, plunging my finger into his chest the moment I'm close enough to touch him. "Now would be a *great* time for you to explain this place and its people to me."

Casimir tilts his chin to stare at me, his amber eyes bright and piercing as flecks of gold swirl through the rich color. "You mean for me to explain the place and the people you so begrudgingly look down upon?" His voice bites like an animal as his gaze screams with silent exhaustion. "You wish for me to divulge their history because now that someone has sacrificed their life to help you, *now* you wish to understand them?"

My brows twitch at his choice of words. *To help me?* Still, I don't comment on that further. "No," I argue instead, caught off guard by his sharp, abrasive tone. "It's not like that. I just—"

"You just *what?* Suddenly have an entirely unrelated interest in the people I have been asking you to speak with?" His chest rises and falls as he glares at me. "Only when we bleed do we think to stop cutting. Only when the world is choking does it take a moment to breathe." Casimir shakes his head, his upper lip curling. "Irreplaceable is the price, and a sacrificed life always seems to be the currency."

"You spew words against humanity as if you are so far above us all. But you're no different. You have kidnapped me. Held me captive against my will. Murdered my friends. Committed unspeakable atrocities. You even betrayed Sitara, the woman you claimed to love so dearly in that damn journal of yours. Stole her happiness away by sabotaging her love for another." Anger roars to life in my chest. "You are the worst parts of humanity given flesh. Why would I do *anything* you ask?"

Casimir's expression is unreadable as he studies me. Without averting his gaze, he takes a slow, prowling step toward me. Then another. And another. He pinches my jaw roughly between his fingers and jerks it up toward him, leaning down until I can feel his breath against my cheek. Still, I do not balk, nor do I let the fear slowly crawling up my spine reveal itself on my face.

I will not cower. I will not yield. I will not falter.

And I certainly will not let him win.

"I have plenty of demons within me," he says in a low voice, his fingers tightening their grip on my jawbone. "But I assure you, there are far worse demons out there than the ones living inside me."

Unsure of how to respond to his words—a nagging feeling in my chest telling me he isn't wrong—I hold his eyes in silent defiance while a scowl creeps over my lips.

We remain gridlocked like that until our heartbeats fall out of rhythm. He uncurls his fingers from my skin, dropping his hand back down to his side. Casimir recedes a step, running a hand through his dark hair and jerking his chin away from me. "You look at me like some monster who needs to be caged."

"Sometimes you behave like a monster in need of caging."

He only glances at me, his eyes softening into their normal tired expression once more. "I am no threat to you."

"But does that mean you're a threat to everyone else?"

His silence sings the song of the guilty.

Finally, after our anger has melted away and nothing but hunched shoulders remain, Casimir lifts his gaze from the floor. "Let's be on our way," he says, his voice settling back into its gentle, regal sound. "You still have to enter the Veil this evening."

"Why are you so determined I enter the Veil for you?" It is a question I've been wondering since he first told me I would be entering the Veil once a week. A question made more prominent over this past week as he continuously dropped reminders and comments about it in passing.

He offers me his hand, but I reject the gesture by merely staring pointedly at it. He drops it back down to his side with a sigh. "There are many reasons you must enter the Veil. Some are for my own selfish purposes; others are not. You will learn them all in due time."

"Allegedly," I grumble.

"You will," he reaffirms. "The Veil is an incredibly powerful place that abides by laws transcending our own. There is a reason Veilreaders are highly sought after by kings and upper noble houses. Though the art of it can be more fickle than visions given by Seers or Diviners, Veilreaders can see matters of the past, present, and future if they are skilled enough. But the mark of an especially gifted Veilreader is one who can bend the Veil to *their* will. It is a once-in-every-century gift."

"Do you have that ability?"

"No," he answers. "But you do. I've already seen it; the Veil responding to you in uncommon ways."

I remember the second time I encountered that voice in the Veil. The voice ultimately belonging to Casimir. The Blue-Horned Adder's venom was seeping into my veins, spinning my mind into a haze of delirium. As I wandered deeper into the world of smoke and mist, I remember images emerging like light through a cloud. *The Veil responds to you*, he had said to me at the sight of it.

I tug my bottom lip between my teeth, not sure what to make of that. "Is it...does it have anything to do with the magic you and I possess?"

He shakes his head. "We can manipulate our magic in such a way that allows us to enter the Veil, but that does not guarantee the Veil will show us anything. Does not mean we can make its colors intelligible. It *especially* does not imply it will respond to either one of us."

"Yet it does to me..."

"It does. So, I will make sure you know how to use that gift. Are properly trained, so that one day you might use it to your benefit."

"Why?"

"Because it is what I've decided."

I suck on my tooth. Why must conversations with him always be so cryptic?

"How is it you know so much about the Veil?" I ask, pivoting. "I thought Veilreaders kept the art mostly secret, passing knowledge down only to those who show signs of the ability."

"Once upon a time, I became close with a woman from the Izavarda bloodline, and she provided me with extensive knowledge. She…" His eyes soften. "She was a remarkable woman, and one of the greatest Veilreaders this world will ever know."

"A legacy bloodline," I point out, despite being sure he is well aware of the bloodline's status. Still, the tender sincerity of his voice forces me to pause. "What happened to her?"

The poignant curves of his smile grow more prominent. "I'm not sure," he murmurs. "But whatever it was, I hope it was gentle and quick."

I study him, finding myself filled with more questions, far different than the ones I've been overflowing with. "How long ago was this?" My voice escapes in a whisper for some reason.

He slides his amber eyes to me; they are filled with quiet torment. "Over four-hundred years ago."

The shock of hearing how long he has lived still jolts my system. "*How*? How are you still alive? And immortalized as a twenty-some-thing-year old man at that?"

He tips his chin into the air, glancing out the glass domed roof above our heads. "Because a scorned heart does not wither," he answers, a contradicting softness coating his words. "It burns."

CHAPTER FOURTEEN

LYRA

Artificial stars glitter in an inky expanse curving down and outward, swallowing the snowy marble floors beneath its cupped embrace.

With my mouth hanging ajar, I wander deeper into the Astral Chamber, a keen sense of wonderment filling me as I marvel at the ethereal blues and sparkling silvers fusing together, bleeding from the sphere like rain bleeds from a stormy sky. The swirling white floors seem suspended in midair as the innumerable dots glowing all around me cascade from the peak of the walls and disappear beneath the marble at my feet. Portraits of different moon phases line the space, and at the very center of the room is a circular platform where beams of iridescent light shoot downward, enclosing the platform in a circle.

"I've never seen anything like this before," I marvel with my chin pointed up into the air. "You must truly love the stars to have created such a wonder."

Casimir steps out of the shadows and closer to me. "Actually, I loathe them quite viscerally."

I whirl around to face him. "You loathe the stars yet have an entire chamber *dedicated* to them? A chamber that makes you feel as though you're floating amongst them, no less."

"I assure you," he replies, his flat tone echoing as he steps past me and toward the circular platform encased by beams of light. "This was not my doing."

I blink at him, entirely confused.

He glances back at me with secrets dancing in his eyes before tugging his chin, beckoning me. "Come along," he instructs. "We'll be entering the Veil in here."

I arch my brow at it. "It looks like some creepy sacrificial altar."

Casimir huffs a laugh, old smile lines revealing themselves. "It isn't," he assures me. "There will be no sacrifices today."

"Except maybe my dignity," I mumble under my breath, trudging forward and accepting his hand as he escorts me up the steps, through the light beams, and to the center of the circle.

The platform is elevated and forged from bronze. Intricate marks branch from the very center, swirling out and around in swirls resembling threads. There is a bedroll sprawled out in the middle, and directly above it, a small glass case filled with what appears to be swirling colored smoke hangs in place.

I glance at Casimir. "I feel like I've entered another world."

"In some ways," he begins, holding my gaze, "you have."

"I don't understand any of this," I whisper, feeling at once desperate to understand and so exhausted with being kept in the dark. I'm tired of feeling ignorant. Tired of feeling three steps behind, grasping at a rope that is pulled away before I can ever grab onto it.

"You may understand more shortly, depending on what you do with your time in the Veil." He watches me, seeming to debate something. "Tomorrow," he offers, voice softening. "Tomorrow, during our training session, I will finally begin providing you with the answers you seek." He turns, heading toward the bedroll, where a small golden goblet I didn't previously notice awaits. Casimir bends down and plucks it from the ground, putting the stem between his fingers as he cups the simply designed bowl. He motions for me to lie down.

Not wanting to seem subservient, I count to five in my head before doing as he asks. Then I sit down on the roll, cross my legs, and puff out my cheeks. When he hands the goblet off to me, I take it cautiously, smelling the liquid inside and swirling it around to note both the consistency and reaction it potentially has with the gold. The smell is slightly bitter with a woodsy undertone, and the liquid has a reddish hue to it.

"Murmuring Mirage," I guess, swirling around the drink some more.

"You are correct."

I hum, a small bit of pride swelling behind my chest. "When my mother would enter the Veil, she always had a close confidant forge her elixir. Naturally, this was because her confidant was a fellow Gardner." I eye him pointedly. "Only Gardners have the required knowledge to make the elixir needed to guarantee a safe passage to and from the Veil. Neilina has already told me you do not have Gardners here nor do your people even know what they are, so how is it you know how to make the elixir?"

Casimir chews on his words, seeming to consider how he would like to answer my question. "I have been alive for four centuries," he begins slowly, clasping his hands behind his back. "Do not underestimate the knowledge one can acquire during such a long lifespan."

It really never gets less shocking—hearing him say his age.

How. How. How.

Gods I have so many questions. About his declining faith in humanity. What happened to forge him into the tired looking man before me. About his connection to the Abdites. Why they call him Master and serve him with such unabated loyalty.

"It's time we enter the Veil. Drink."

I glance back down at the goblet in my hand, chewing on my bottom lip. There are as many reasons as there are stars in this room regarding why I should absolutely not trust him nor enter the Veil for him. Reasons that scream at me not to drink the elixir from this goblet. Yet some small part of myself *wants* to. I want to discover more about my Veilreading gifts. I want to know what my mother experienced when she intentionally walked through the Veil. I want to know what I'm capable of. Just how far my power stretches.

I bring the cool metal to my lips and drink.

A nearly instant rush of warmth floods beneath my skin, heating me from the inside out. A euphoric buzzing sensation hums within my bones, pressing pleasurable kisses to every inch of my body. Oddly, it feels similar to a climax, and the blurred line of what my body is feeling while staring at Casimir is too confusing for me to process.

Casimir crouches down and pushes hair from my forehead; I lick my lips.

He laughs silently while feeling my skin with the back of his hand. "Good. It's working. Which means you need to lie flat on your back."

My head feels light while my vision undulates like a rolling wave in an uncharted sea. I know my mind is already beginning to feel woozy, but....

Did he just say he wants to put me on my back?

Though I can admit Casimir has an undeniable appeal, being at once mysterious, regal, ungodly handsome, and eerily magnetic, the thought of me lying down for him draws on a sad song within me. In my mind's eye—so vivid and clear I'm convinced I really see it—a gradient of blues and greens crash together, mingling in the heart of a seafoam wave. Then those colors wrap around a body covered in whorling black marks. Those marks rise until they kiss a face with shaggy hair like a starless night sky.

I see Draven.

I lurch for him, wanting so badly to press his chest against mine and collapse in his arms. I want to be shielded in his embrace. To feel like, even just for a moment, I do not need to be brave and strong and unbreakable. In his arms, I can just be a girl who doesn't have to brace herself against the harsh realities of this world. I can just be as I am, no walls, no defenses.

Yet something stops me from reaching him. Two hands gripping me back, holding me in place. "It isn't real." It's Casimir's voice, coming from directly next to my ear. It is calm and assuring, but... wrong.

It isn't Draven.

"Lyra," Casimir says, "you need to lie down."

Lie down like a good girl.

Lie down and take it.

Lie down and spread your legs.

Suddenly, images from my past emerge like projections in the air around me, voices whispering and shouting as I see a mirage of the past nobles I was forced to entertain while being King Alastair's prized pet. In every single image, I am forced to lie down—most times on my stomach, sometimes on my back.

Lie down. Lie down. Lie down.

Fuck I hate those words. I am so through with just lying down. I am not going to lie down; I am going to rise. Higher and further, until everyone is beneath my feet. Until I look down my nose at *them*. Until it is I who is forcing them to kneel before me. *Fuck* lying down.

Yet the more determined I become, the more the voices hiss and scream. I attempt to ignore them. To not allow them any space inside my head. But just as Draven said of emotions, the voices demand to be felt.

My breathing hitches in my chest, and the pool of oxygen in my lungs grows shallow. Suddenly, everything around me feels encased by dark outlines, and it presses into me with the force of a hurricane. I can't breathe. Can't think. I—

Strong hands cup my face as two thumbs rub soothing arcs across my cheeks. "Breathe," the calm voice says. "Breathe and look at the lights."

I listen, drawing in steady breaths as I lose myself in the shimmering, iridescent lights circling around me. The visuals that were pelting me melt away, leaving space for the new ones to take shape. Stars soar through the beams like a coursing river. A kaleidoscope of glimmering petals sweep along an invisible wind, passing from light to light. I see a stark white wolf chasing a black, unruly one. It is mesmerizing.

Someone tips me back. My head falls to rest in a warm lap. Strong hands hold onto me, bracketing my shoulders.

I stare at the glass encasing of colored smoke, the world around me slowly ebbing away as I watch the colors float and dance. As if hypnotized, it becomes all I see. I feel drawn to it. Then, next thing I know, I am moving toward it, as if being called to enter the smoke. While rising, images emerge all around me, each calling out for me to come to them. There are images of King Alastair sitting on his throne. Images of the entertaining chamber. There are images of Bathara. Of Sterling and Azalea. Gray, Draven, and Marcella. I attempt to go to their images, but the light beams morph into a solid wall, not allowing me to escape its bounds as I rise toward the smoke.

Then there are images I can't make sense of. Of a burning arrow. Of a land on fire. Oddly, I see King Yarum looking at me with awe and something else in his striking eyes. His lips move as he voices something to me, yet no sound enters where I am.

As I slam into a place of smoke and mist, where the light is not bright and up and down make no sense, I am simply left wondering what it is King Yarum was trying to tell me. Why I saw an image of him at all.

My FEET TOUCH a water-like ground that is firm yet possesses no real shape. A mixture of fog and smoke sits waiting in the formless void. As I step closer to it, colored light materializes behind the hanging veil.

That voice I once knew yet didn't know sounds behind a colored cloud of misty smoke. *"I'm afraid this is as far as I can go in the Veil. The rest is up to you."*

Feeling like my mind is finally my own again, I glance at where the voice sounds from, then back to the endless expanse of smoke, fog, and mist. "What am I supposed to do?"

"Ask the Veil to show you something and see if it will respond to you. Start with something of the past. It will be more straightforward since it has already come to be, and it will require little interpretation on your part."

I clench then unclench my hands, staring at the sprawling void before me. I want to know more about my mother. About her past, who she was before she had me. Yet I know that is not what is most pressing. I should try to see what happened four hundred years ago. The true events surrounding the Great Clamaté War. *What happened to Casimir.*

The thought comes before I can stop it.

A song hums, filling the space of everywhere and nowhere. The tune is familiar, even if I can't make out the words. The smoke and mist shift, brightening and glowing with a spectrum of color. It crawls toward my ankles, rising like a tidal wave until it crashes over me, swallowing me whole.

A hand slams down onto the walnut table. "War is here, damnit! It is banging at our door, practically splintering the wood to get in. How much longer are you going to cling to these deluded ideals of yours, Casimir?"

My gaze glides toward the moving figure, whose kind eyes and clasped hands are the portrait of what a prince should be. I glance down and look around, realizing I am nothing but a ghost in this memory of the past, being forced along like a loose, brittle leaf swept on a breeze.

"I recognize your concerns as valid, Magaius. I truly do." Casimir paces *back and forth in a lavish room composed of floor-to-ceiling windows, overlooking the crystal channels flowing through a glittering white city.*

Keziah, I realize. My home city. The capital of Rivara Kingdom. It is so similar, yet so different. I'm also able to place the name after considerable thought. Magaius—Casimir's best friend, according to his journal.

"If you recognize them as valid, then why are you not heeding their warning?" Magaius rubs soothing circles against his temple, dropping his eyes and sighing loudly. "You cannot play peacemaker for eternity, brother. There are times where brute force is an unavoidable necessity. To incite peace is at times to ignite violence. Unfortunate yes, but a truth of this world nonetheless."

Casimir halts in the middle of the room, squaring his shoulders to the brown-haired man. "I choose differently," he says simply, as if it could truly be that easy. "The Restorationists seek a war, but a war I will not give them."

"One does not merely get to choose when war arrives at their doorstep," Magaius counters, his words sounding sad and tired.

"I will find a way. There must be a solution that will allow us to avoid conflict. A solution that will allow my men to bed their wives and laugh with their children. And until then, I will continue to work for my people, feeding the hungry and offering aid to the poor."

"You already house too many peasants and beggars in the estate already." Magaius rubs his forehead, pinching the bridge of his nose after. *"Our staff is overworked and our resources stretched far too thin from the excess numbers. We cannot afford any more mouths to feed or bodies to clothe."*

Casimir cocks his head at Magaius, like he didn't understand a single word he just said. "I am a Prince, am I not?"

"You are," Magaius answers through a sigh.

"Then what good is the title if I cannot expend my resources as I please and act as I wish?"

Magaius kicks his brows up in concession, leaning back in his chair and shrugging.

"They are families, Mag. Children that have no say in their present fates. They do not deserve to sleep in lice-infested streets with empty bellies."

"Not all people can eat like a king; not all kings can feed their people. It is the way of things. The natural order of the world."

"I will believe in no such order."

Magaius opens his mouth to speak, but a knock comes at the door, and the wood swings open a second after. A breathtaking woman strides inside, her ethereal beauty complimented by her blue eyes and ash-colored hair. She wears a silver tulle dress that hugs her waist and spills at her feet.

Casimir stiffens and Magaius jumps to his feet, knocking the chair back. In unison, they both incline their heads to her.

"Sitara," Casimir drawls, his eyes seeming suddenly brighter. "To what do we owe the pleasure of your unexpected company?"

She bounces her gaze between Casimir and Magaius, a wry smirk tugging at her lips.

The scene ebbs aways, and I am pulled immediately into another.

Casimir's cheeks are speckled with blood, both old and new alike, and he leans over the edge of a river, the bright blue sky reflecting down upon the waters in a peaceful portrait.

He plunges his hands beneath the surface, disturbing the peace, and he scrubs at his skin like it is tainted by some infectious disease. His eyes are panicked, and he heaves in hiccuped breaths. There is a sword discarded a few paces behind him, the blade covered in crimson and mud. When he pulls his trembling hands from the water, he inspects them. They are spotless, yet he plunges them deep beneath the water once more, the feel of the filth still clinging to him.

He repeats the process again and again. Until finally he falls back, still and silent for long enough to let a bird's song play. Then, without warning, he leans over onto his hands and knees and vomits.

The vomiting lasts only for a couple of minutes, and once he has swiped the leftover spit from the corner of his mouth with the back of his pruned hand, he threads his fingers into his hair, tugging at the strands as he tucks his knees into his chest.

"Why did it have to come to this..." he whimpers under his breath. "Why."

I am again pulled out of that moment and thrust into a different one.

Humming fills a modest room while the woman with hair like ash tends to a wounded man sprawled out unconscious on a bed.

Sitara cleans the grime and dried blood from Casimir's body, only a pair of linen pants covering him. An oozing gash stretches across the length of his muscular chest, and his skin is slicked with sweat. He groans in his sleep, his brows knit together.

Sitara stills, gazing at him with worry and something else in her eyes. A knock on the door startles her, but she quickly resets her features, smoothing out her pained expression and rising from Casimir's bedside.

"Enter," she says with all the grace and finality of a true noble.

The door opens, and a woman who shares Sitara's exact eyes yet possesses hair as black as a raven's feather enters. "You called for me?"

"Yes," Sitara says, lifting her chin. Her voice sounds strong, but the slight quiver in it betrays her. "I need a Diviner."

The woman with raven hair wrinkles her brows. "Why? What are you planning?"

Sitara glances back at Casimir with tender eyes, a fever clearly wrecking his body as puss seeps from his wounds. When she looks back to the woman, her gaze is set with determination, and she opens her mouth to speak—

I am ripped from the memory with so much force, my mind swims in a twirling sea as dizziness overtakes me. I reach out, trying to grip it between my fingers and return to it, certain I need to see more of what happens next. I'm not sure why, but I just know that moment is important—feel it deep within my chest. Yet the Veil does not listen to my request, instead dropping me into a different moment entirely.

A jeering crowd throws stones and rotting food at the carriage as it passes through the streets.

Casimir sits across from Magaius, his head dropped into his hands, his shoulders hunched forward. When he lifts it, revealing dark smudges beneath his downturned eyes, he locks his gaze to a worried-looking Magaius.

"I have done everything I can to help them," he murmurs. There is such defeat in his voice. "I have sheltered them. Fed them. Listened to them. Aided them in every way I feasibly could. Why have they turned on me so easily?"

"Peace demands sacrifice," Magaius supplies gently, his brown hair falling into his face. "And unfortunately, brother, despite your many contributions, they have made you their offering."

Casimir remains still, seeming to absorb his words. Until his eyes ignite with a quiet rage, and he jerks back, shouting at the coachman. "Stop! Stop the carriage at once!"

The carriage jerks to a halt. Magaius's expression grows wild. "Cas, whatever you are thinking right now, unthink it."

But Casimir just stares at him a second longer before exiting the carriage. He swivels his gaze left, then right. The streets are crowded with lowborns whose hands are all filled with expendable items they can launch at the passing carriage. Upon seeing him, the shouts grow louder and more erratic. Casimir's lips thin at the sight.

He splays his arms out, facing the crowd head on. "What do you want from me?" he bellows. Thunder crackles behind gray clouds, and the sky cracks open, thick drops of rain pouring out. "I have offered you all I can. I have bled for you. I have advocated for you. I am at war to protect a new system that benefits you." His chest rises and falls as raindrops streak down his face, his black hair sticking to his skin. "I have not only given you my resources, but my flesh and blood. What more can I give you to appease this restlessness? What weight do I need to shoulder?"

"Abdicate!" someone shouts from the back of the crowd.

Hissing murmurs of agreement sweep across lips. "Abdicate! Abdicate! Abdicate!" the crowd chants.

The first stone thrown hits him the hardest, knocking him on his cheekbone. Then comes rotten food, dirtying his clothes and staining his soul with a permanent mark which never managed to wash away.

Magaius sticks his head from the carriage. "Guards! Guards!" He points at the child who threw the first stone.

Guards charge forward and apprehend the boy who can be no more than twelve or thirteen. They shove him to his knees at Casimir's feet, mud splashing up and splattering onto his face. "Your order, Prince," one of the guards says, glancing between Casimir and the boy.

"Execute him!" Magaius hisses through clenched teeth, striding toward them. "He assaulted the Crowned Prince, gods-damn it."

Simultaneously, the crowd erupts with a jarring mix of pleas for mercy and curses. A mother steps forward, her shrill voice piercing as her thrashing body is held back. "Please. Please," she cries. "Spare my son. He does not understand. He only knows what he is told."

"Weapons at the ready!" Magaius bellows.

The guards shift on their feet, looking back to Casimir, who remains silent, staring at the child with an entirely unreadable expression. Shouts echo and mingle, orders are given, yet all that can be heard is the sound of the rain pattering against cobblestone streets.

"Why did you throw that stone?" Casimir murmurs to the child.

The boy wrinkles his nose. "Because my Pa says you and your father have brought war, sir. He says your hunger for power has blinded you to the hungry. Says the Restorationists have offered their compromise—you and your father abdicate the throne—yet you do not accept and leave us to die like infected rats on the street."

Casimir lowers himself to his knees, his drenched clothes clinging to him like a second skin. "Have any of my actions truly supported that claim?"

"What you've done doesn't matter; it's what you won't do."

Casimir winces at the words, his brows furrowing deeply. He slowly reaches his hand out, cupping the boy's cheek and bringing his face closer to his. *"I want nothing but the best for my people. For all of humanity. Every-thing I have done—all I* continue *to do—it is for the good of the people."*

"My little sister died yellow and a bag of bones. What's good about that?" The boy's upper lip curls, and he rears back, spitting in Casimir's face. *"Abdicate the throne! Down with the Vivaldri rule!"*

"GUARDS!" Magaius snarls. "I gave you an order! Or does your Crowned Prince need to be assaulted yet again before you obey it?"

Two guards jerk Casimir back, shielding him with their bodies. One guard straightens the boy's shoulders while another unsheathes his sword. Lightning breaks across the gray sky, and a loud crack of thunder booms. The rain falls harder, as if the sky has already decided to weep.

"Sword at the ready," Magaius barks.

"NO!" The boy's mother screams in horror. "No, I beg you! Let him go. Do not take my boy away from me. Please. I already lost my daughter. I can't lose my boy, too. Please!"

"Restrain her!" Magaius orders.

Casimir pushes forward against his guards. "Stop this," he says, his brows furrowed like he can't make sense of what's happening. "Stop this madness."

A thunderclap rattles the ground at their feet, drowning out his voice. A guard turns his chin over his shoulder, glancing at him hurriedly. "Stay back, Highness. It isn't safe." Right on cue, an assault of flying rocks pelts the guards.

Casimir shakes his head. "Stop," he tries again. "Let me through."

Through gritted teeth and with a trail of blood streaking down from his temple, the guard says, "Sorry, Highness. But we have strict orders from the King to keep you protected at all costs. We cannot let you pass."

"Just let me speak with them. Nobody needs to die. I cannot take anymore bloodshed. It was only spit for the gods' sakes." He looks past the guards' shoulders, through the rain to where Magaius and the other guards hold the strings of a young mortal life in their hands. "Stop!" he shouts again.

But the sound of his voice is muffled by the roar of the angry crowd, the timbre chords of the storm, a sobbing mother, and Magaius's booming instructions.

The next three words tumble simultaneously from different lips, each mouth only spewing one word. Yet the noises fuse together to form a single discordant sound.

"Release!"

"NO!"

"Stop!"

Lightning reflects off the shiny blade as it comes crashing down against skin. The boy's eyes remain open, the look of defiance giving way to shock frozen in his unmoving expression. His head rolls across the muddied ground, halting only once it reaches Casimir's feet. He stares blankly at it, his eyes finally moving to trace the trail of blood already being swept away from the torrent of rain. Casimir buckles, his weight seeming to cave in on itself.

The crowd erupts.

"Murderer!" they accuse. "Murderer! Murderer! Murderer!"

They come together and attempt to push past the line of guards, flinging every item they hold hostage in their hands at Casimir. Though the guards shielding him try to stop it, rocks still pelt him from all sides, rotten food making a disgusting splat sound once it contacts his skin.

He doesn't attempt to shield himself against a single thrown item.

"Protect the Prince!" Magaius instructs, covering his head and making for Casimir, wrapping his hand around his arm and yanking him back toward the carriage.

A man snarls and lunges for a guard. The guard reacts instantly, plunging his sword directly through the man's chest. Crimson bubbles from his lips, and the guard jerks his sword free from the man's body, stumbling back three steps.

The crowd grows angrier—hatred burning through all of them with a palpable intensity. Casimir shakes his head against what he sees, fighting against Magaius's hold.

"Stop this! All of you—stop!" His voice goes nowhere, swallowed entirely by the sounds of conflict.

Yet no matter how hard Casimir tries to soothe the situation, it only gets worse. Until a full-scale bloody battle begins against the royal guards and the lowborns.

Magaius finally manages to wrangle Casimir back into the carriage, slamming the door closed behind them. A hollowness fills Casimir's gaze that *hadn't been there previously. "This is all my fault," he whispers, his eyes fixed to the floor. "I should have never left the carriage."*

Magaius says nothing.

Casimir's lips thin, and he finally drags his eyes up to look at Magaius. "Did the boy truly have to die? Is it really fair to kill a child who acts on nothing more than what they are told by their parents? We claim they are too young to care for themselves yet condone murdering them for actions they don't even understand. He...." Casimir pauses, emotion seeming to clog his throat. He flexes his jaw against it. "He was a child, for fuck's sake."

"The price of order and peace is blood," Magaius mutters, pushing his sopping hair back and sprawling out across his seat, tipping his head against the carriage wall. "It is and will always be blood. The only question that ever exists is whose blood it'll be."

I am ripped from the seams of smoke and mist, immediately plunged into a new sea of fog.

Casimir strides through a brazier-lit corridor, his hollow eyes matching the emptiness in his expression.

He clutches a limp body in his arms. She is dressed in a beautiful sparkling gown that compliments the ashen color of her hair. I imagine that if her eyes were open, the blue undertone of the fabric would accentuate the hue of her irises. I notice that Casimir himself is dressed decadently, making him look exceptionally handsome with his drawn-back hair and piercing amber eyes.

He walks on, the noise of his shoes clacking against the floor the only sound. Until Magaius comes sprinting from the other end of the corridor.

"I came...as soon...as I heard," he says through winded breaths.

Casimir ignores him entirely, continuing to walk forward mindlessly—numbly.

"Cas," Magaius whispers, skipping a few steps to stay next to him. "Cas, is she...." He flicks his pained eyes down to Sitara, who remains unconscious and limp in Casimir's arms. "Did he do this to her?"

Casimir still does not answer him.

"Where are you taking her?" Magaius questions, the panic beginning to settle in his tone. "The healer's quarters are in the opposite direction."

Wordlessly, Casimir continues forward, as lifeless as the unconscious girl hanging limp in his arms.

"CAS!" Magaius shouts.

The image washes away like smoke swept up in a breeze. Distant yet near, a voice of ages hisses in my ear. *"Last one."*

I am dropped out in front of a beautiful white temple that glitters beneath the moonlight. I cock my head and blink at it, feeling as if it's familiar, somehow. I glance around, taking in my surroundings, and then it hits me square in the face.

I am standing at the foot of the Temple of Rhylia. A quick dip into my memory, and I recall Casimir's journal entry where he recorded following Magaius here.

I watch the past unfold.

One by one, men, women, and some children dressed in dirty rags with gaunt cheeks stagger out of the temple. There are enough of them to form a small army. They scratch at their skin as if plagued by a drug. Like tiny snakes, their wielder's marks shift and slither across their flesh, changing in real time as their veins slowly evolve to black lines. Words hum in the air.

Erhé akta maht.

"You've corrupted them," Casimir accuses Magaius, their bodies illuminated by nothing but stray beams of moonlight.

"I've unshackled them."

"You've damned them."

Magaius jerks his chin away. "A decision had to be made, and I chose. I'm sorry, Cas. I am. But I could see no other way."

Casimir stares at Magaius like he doesn't recognize him. "You've infected these people with generations of corruption. As far along as they already are, it'll be centuries before their bloodlines are cleansed. You can truly live with that?"

"They knew the price," he mutters, his eyes never meeting Casimir's. "And yet they volunteered anyway. You know why? Because war demands sacrifice. A truth I have tried to help you see. I cannot help it if you chose to ignorantly remain blind. And now? Now we have the edge we need to finally end this accursed conflict."

"What would Sitara think?"

A chilling quiet fills the air. "Sitara is gone. And a god has already come to claim her soul."

Magaius opens his mouth to say something else, but rustling in the distance has both of them whipping their heads in the direction of the sound. A giant wolf with glowing eyes emerges from the shadows, and the moonlight suddenly disappears, taking all the stars with it, leaving nothing but a pit of darkness between them.

"Magaius," Casimir breathes in horror. "What have you done?"

I am forcefully ripped out of the mirage, soaring away from the world of smoke and fog and mist. I am falling down, down, down—that familiar song humming around me—until I slam into a surface. My eyes jolt open and I gasp in a loud breath, pressing my hands to my chest.

I sit upright, and the world spins. I groan, feeling drunk and horribly disoriented. Pressing my palms into my eyes, I try to shake the feeling away. Yet all that happens is residual images of what I just witnessed surface back to the forefront of my mind, becoming clear like a painting once more.

My body becomes too heavy to move. Like rocks have invaded my bones, weighing me down and threatening to pin me in place. The weight of my stiff muscles coupled with my swimming head has me falling back to the ground. Yet I do not land on a hard, cold surface like I'm expecting. I return to the warmth of a lap.

"I've got you," Casimir soothes. "This is the after effects of the elixir—of reading the Veil."

All I can do is groan; my tongue is lead in my mouth.

"I know," he agrees, as if replying to intelligible words. "It is quite unpleasant, indeed." He shifts, gently removing himself from beneath me and resting my head back down. "I am going to open a portal back to your room. Think you can manage until then?"

I squeeze my eyes closed in the world's longest blink. "I....feel... drunk," I slur.

While I can't be certain—my mind too hazy to process anything—I think I hear a quiet laugh whisk into the air. A circle of glittering color appears before me. It is so alluring, calling to me like an insect being lured into a trap. I want to fall into its beauty—drown in its light.

I receive my wish.

I am suspended into the sky, and I travel through the glowing silvers, whites, and blues. When I emerge on the other side, I blink, recognizing the space as mine, though not mine in the slightest. Neilina jerks up from the bed, standing at attention.

Has she always been able to move so quickly?

"Master," she says.

Casimir makes for my bed, and I only then realize he is carrying me, my arms slung around his neck. He lays me down onto the mattress, pressing his hand to my forehead. His lips thin at whatever he feels.

He glances over his shoulder at Neilina. "Fetch a bucket of cool water and a rag. She needs her body temperature brought down."

Neilina dips her chin. "Yes, Master."

She scurries from my chamber, and Casimir turns back to face me. "Neilina will take good care of you. I will leave her detailed instructions on what to watch for. Though your fever is higher than I'd like it to be, you should recover fine, without the intervention of magic." He recedes a step, making to turn away from the bed and exit the room. "I'll come check on you in the morning. We can discuss things then."

He heads for the door, but I reach my clumsy hand out and catch his wrist before he can leave. "Stay with me," I whisper.

His brows furrow. "You....want me to stay? Why?"

Why, indeed?

My mind is currently a cloudy maze I can't navigate, but for whatever reason, it chooses to continue showing me the images of Casimir I just saw in the Veil. Images of him allowing the penniless to stay in his estate. Of him fighting for diplomacy and peace. Of him outstretching his arms, baring it all to his people.

What more can I give you to appease this restlessness? What weight do I need to shoulder?

Perhaps what I saw is no more than a way to better understand him. A small trail of bread crumbs to piece him together. I can't be certain what to make of it all yet. But what I do know is—in this delirious version of myself—I want him to stay. Because…because…

"I don't want to be alone," I voice aloud, my words tumbling awkwardly from my tongue. My fingers squeeze his wrist tighter. "Stay."

When I glance up at him, I find him staring at me like some puzzle in need of figuring out. Finally, after a handful of silent seconds, with his brows still pinched together, Casimir blows out a soft sigh and nods. "Alright," he murmurs. "If that is what you wish." He jerks his chin in the direction of the lounging chair across the room. "I'll go sit over there."

"No," I retort, shaking my head. "Don't walk away. Just… lay with me."

"You're comfortable with that?" He sounds tentative. "You trust me to lay in your bed?"

"I do."

And fuck I *must* be some kind of drunk to feel like I mean it. Yet something about all I witnessed in the Veil has forced a sudden shift within me. I can't be certain because of these debilitating side effects, but… I don't think I'm as angry with him anymore. If anything, I feel like I sort of understand him. Or perhaps I should say I better understand the circumstances which forged him.

"Alright," he says softly.

I release his wrist, and he walks to the other side of the bed, lying down and propping himself up against the headboard, crossing his feet at the ankles. There is a few inches of space between us, and I shimmy further down the plush mattress—far more comfortable than anything I ever slept on back in Solaya—and nestle into the pillows and blankets.

Casimir glances over at me and huffs, pulling back the blankets from my body and moving them off to the side. "You have a fever," he reminds me. "You can't cover your body with more heat."

"Oh," I mutter. "Right."

We lay in silence, both of us staring up at the silk canopy hovering above our heads. Time feels odd to me right now; I'm both inhumanly aware of it while simultaneously having no concept of it. So, I'm not sure how much time has passed when I speak again, voicing the thought running through my swirling mind, brought on by the flashes of images from the Veil where his expression brightens upon seeing ash-colored hair and glowing blue eyes.

"You loved her," I muse.

His eyes remain on the canopy. "Loved?" he repeats, an air of disbelief coating the word. "I still do."

His answer makes me smile. "I might love someone, too," I admit.

He readjusts, lowering himself from the headboard and shimmying down the bed until our heads are both laying flat against soft pillows, our shoulders level with each other. "I know."

A brief silence, and then—

"Did you mean what you said the day you attacked Bathara? About love?"

This is the fate of humanity. The curse of our existence. You love? You hurt. You do not love? You still hurt.

He doesn't ask me to elaborate, seeming to know what I mean. "Yes."

"What happened to her? Sitara?"

He glances at me sidelong. "The Veil didn't show you?"

"Didn't you see for yourself what it showed me?"

"No. As I told you, I am able to follow you into the Veil, but I do not have the gift of reading it. Which means, all I can see are unintelligible flashes of color behind the smoke and mist."

"So you have no idea what it showed me?"

"None whatsoever." A pause. "Though, based on the shift in your behavior, I have some guesses on the subject matter."

I huff a laugh, intertwining my fingers and resting them on my chest. "I saw her, too." I tell him. "Sitara. I saw her, and she was as breathtaking as the stories describe."

"No," he disagrees, his voice wistful and his smile sad. "The stories do not do her nearly enough justice."

My eyes become weighted, and I feel my body being pulled into a heavy sort of sleep. Yet I have one final question I want to ask before I fade. "Casimir?"

"Yes?"

"How can someone once filled with so much good commit so much evil?"

I may have now seen glimpses of him before he deteriorated into the man he currently is, but the fact remains. He admitted to committing mass genocide. He plunged a blade through Griff. He ordered Abdites to invade Bathara—to slaughter and take and destroy. A good beginning does not erase a bad ending.

"Perhaps if you read the entirety of the story from my perspective, you would be asking me that question under different pretenses. But..." He sighs. "To provide you with some form of an answer, monsters are seldom born, darling. They are forged in the pits of darkness. Their faces are sprung from the masks of vengeance, discovered in the rubbles of peace and sharpened by shadows. I did not wish to become what I am; yet here I am all the same. I will let you decide what to make of that for yourself."

My blinking slows, and it becomes increasingly difficult to reopen my eyes. "I think," I say through a yawn. "I would have chosen differently."

Casimir lets out a quiet laugh, not seeming at all offended. "We all think that. Until the time comes where we are forced to tear off our masks and glimpse the reflections of the ugly monsters lying beneath them."

Now basically asleep, I curl onto my side, tucking my hands underneath my cheek. Though still not touching him, I am close enough to Casimir to feel his warmth. It feels nice, not being in an empty bed for once. "Impossible," I drag out, sleep clinging to my words as notably as it does my body. "I don't think your face could ever be considered ugly. Not even if you tried."

Through my final moments of consciousness, I hear Casimir chuckling. "Neither could yours, Lyra Izacalli."

CHAPTER FIFTEEN

LYRA

Light crawls into my fluttering eyelids, clobbering me upside the head with the force of a thrown stone.

I groan in pain, draping my arm over my face.

The door swings open, and Neilina's voice fills the room. "Neilina to the rescue," she declares in half-song, her sweet melody like a shrill shriek to my senses.

I wince at the piercing sound. "Please," I whine, peaking out beneath my arm and attempting to squint an eye open. "Make it stop."

She plops herself down on the edge of the bed, extending a small pewter mug to me. "As it so happens," she says, her cheery tone nauseating, "I am here to do exactly that."

I drop my arm from my face and shift a fraction upright. "What is it?"

"A tonic," she chirps.

"What kind of tonic?"

"The kind of tonic that's going to help ease the pounding in your head and ringing in your ears. But if you don't want it because you are too scared of—"

I don't even let her finish her sentence before I pry the mug from her hands and chug.

I'm that desperate.

The rich taste of peppermint coats my tongue, and I find myself inspecting the empty cup, looking for any signs of what I just drank. Finding absolutely nothing, I inhale deeply, the air now coated with a minty taste, and fall back onto the pillows. As I wait for the effects to kick in while staring blankly at the canopy swaying subtly above my head, a wrinkle forms in my brow as I try to recall the details of last night.

Of course, I remember the woman and her eerie words. I remember entering the Astral Chamber and drinking the elixir from the goblet. But everything after feels...distant. I know something exists in my mind, but the moment I reach for it, it dodges me in a cruel game of hide and seek. Still, I feel the memories humming in the seams, remaining just beyond my grasp, dancing on the tip of my tongue.

"Annnd that should just about do it," Neilina says, getting up from the bed and watching me with mirth in her eyes.

I blink, tearing free of my daze. She's right. The throbbing in my head has stopped, and my body doesn't feel like it's carrying boulders any longer. I sit up, pushing hair back from my face and pressing my palm against my forehead. "Whoever made that tonic would have made one hell of a Gardner. Who should I thank for their services?"

"Master."

"Casimir made me the tonic? Why?"

She shrugs. "Probably because he knew you were going to need it. I didn't see the two of you long before you both fell asleep, but you looked pretty out of it from what I did—"

I lift a hand to stop her mid-sentence. "Woah, woah, woah. Wait a second. What do you mean, 'before you *both* fell asleep'?"

"I mean when Master carried you into your chambers, you were swimming in la la land. I was instructed to go fetch some cool water and a rag to help bring down your fever. After I returned, you were sound asleep. He still aided you, though, and once you were in the clear, he asked me for a favor, and by the time I returned from that, the two of you were *both* sound asleep in your bed." She smiles.

"Between you and me, the personal guards like to talk amongst themselves, and they say Master doesn't sleep well. That he is often up through the nights." She huffs an amused laugh, turning away from me and heading toward the wardrobe housing all the clothes provided to me. "You should have seen him lying next to you; he was the epitome of sleep."

My brows scrunch together, locked memories pressing more sharply against my mind. "We weren't…. He wasn't…."

She glances back at me, a knowingness in her expression. "He was on his side of the bed, as you were on yours. Both fully clothed, neither touching." She returns her attention to sorting through the wardrobe, clearly looking for something. "Though it was sort of cute, the way you were facing him in your sleep, practically wedged into his side. Even unconscious, it was like his body attempted to morph around you."

"I—"

All at once, the memories slam against me. The different visions of Casimir I saw in the Veil. The disorienting, severely debilitating effects I felt when coming back into my body. Being carried into my room. Asking him to stay with me. Telling him his face could never be considered ugly.

My cheeks heat with embarrassment at that particular memory. I groan, once again falling backward onto the bed as my reeling mind spins and spins. "I am not leaving this bed today," I mutter like a pouting child, feeling unable to face Casimir yet. I need to let the embarrassment wear off a little first.

"Great," Neilina replies. She spins around, putting the wardrobe to her back and facing me, a wad of clothes clutched in her fist. She chucks them at me, and they fall perfectly into my lap. One glance down at them has me groaning again.

Training clothes.

Neilina braces her hand on her hip and smirks. "You have training with Master in precisely one hour."

As instructed, I trudge into the flower-filled courtyard where Casimir and I have been training exactly one hour later.

He sits on a stone bench in front of a rose bush, his ankle resting on his knee as a crisp leather journal rests in his lap. His hair falls freely into his face as he scribbles words on the pages—a rare sight, seeing as he normally has it tied back in a leather band. He is wearing a breezy white shirt made from a material I'm not sure I'm familiar with. The neckline has a deep v-shape that exposes the panes of his chest, and the hem of it rests just above the waistband of his black, similarly stitched trousers.

I make a mental note to ask him what material his clothes are made from later—it looks wonderfully comfortable.

Still. He looks so....peaceful. At ease, even. Like he was able to lock the demons whispering in his ear away in a cage, if only temporarily. Freedom looks good on him. It makes him look young and alive.

I roll my shoulders back and head straight toward him. As I approach, Casimir glances up from his writing and offers me a small grin. "Good afternoon."

"It would be a better one if I was allowed to stay in bed." I stop short a few paces away and fold my arms across my chest. I nod in the direction of his journal, my brow lifted. "I would have thought you had your fill of journaling."

He huffs a quiet laugh, shutting the journal gently and unfolding his legs. "The practice rather grew on me," he offers by way of explanation. "I never really did stop writing."

"I'm sure those pages are riveting," I grumble.

He rises from the bench and flicks his wrist, a half-formed smirk tipping his lips. A tiny silver and blue portal opens, and Casimir places the journal through it, retracting his hand after. The swirling colors disappear as the portal blinks from existence, the journal with it.

"Nifty."

"Convenient is more like it," he counters, stepping toward me. "How are you feeling?"

"As good as one can after entering the Veil, I'd imagine." I rake my fingers through my hair, reaching for a phantom length that no longer exists. "I see now why my mother always had me stay with the Night-enjoys on the nights she knew she was going to enter."

"You handled it admirably," he offers, his soft words sounding just a tad more jubilant than usual. "Do you remember the visions the Veil showed you?"

I meet his eyes. "I do."

"Good," he says with the dip of his chin. "You can tell me about them on the way."

My brows wrinkle together. "On the way to where?"

"Our training location for the day." At my pointedly inquisitive expression, he elaborates. "I promised to provide you with more answers today." He pulls his gaze from mine, looking out at something in the distance and making to stride toward it. "I intend to keep that promise."

"I've heard that before," I mutter under my breath.

I turn on my heels and follow him.

Two-hundred stairs in, and I am gasping for air—sweat coating my body like morning dew coats grass—convinced I will keel over like overworked cattle at any moment.

To get here, Casimir guided me over bridges, along a stream, and through beautiful paths lined by fruit-filled trees, until we reached the base of a glittering building, towering high in the clouds. Along the way, I told him the details of what I saw in the Veil. Described the people and events that were brought to life through the trails of colored fog and mist. He remained silent the entire time, only giving his emotions away once, when the vision of Sitara caring for him was mentioned. His eyes softened and his shoulders slackened, his mouth teetering somewhere between a smile and a frown.

Whatever happened between them, he loved her deeply. That much I am sure of.

I heave in a stinging sigh and pry my eyes up from the staggering white limestone stairs to glare at Casimir's backside. "Couldn't you have just brought us here using the aether-magic you so *clearly* can wield?"

"Where's the victory in that?" he throws over his shoulder. His voice is annoyingly steady. "Besides, this is the first part of today's training."

"Conditioning?" I scowl. "*Seriously?*"

"Not quite."

After what feels like an eternity longer, my feet finally land on flat ground. I hunch over, bracing my hands on my knees as I attempt to soothe the burning ache inside my chest, making yet another mental note to thank Draven for his training. I know my lungs and muscles would be a hell of a lot more angry at me right now without it.

When the heat is finally sated, I stand upright once more, attempting to take in my surroundings. Yet before I get the chance to glimpse a single thing, a stream of water splashes me straight in the face, cooling the warmth from my skin but fanning the flames inside me. "What the *hell* was that for?"

With one hand bent behind his back, Casimir twirls nimbly on his heel, pacing back and forth in front of some mosaic artwork carved into the ground. "Attack me or defend yourself. Whichever you choose, you must always do one of those things. Remember that."

"What?" I question, swiping water droplets from my narrowed eyes. "What are you even—"

Before I can finish my sentence, Casimir sends a sheet of ice shooting for my ankles, locking me into place. "Stop it!"

How is he doing that so effortlessly, anyways? I don't see any wielders around whose laktî he can Bind to. Just how far a distance can he reach for someone's magic?

"If you want me to stop," he drawls, "then *make* me stop."

"I don't know *how.*"

"Wield the magic in your veins." He says it so simply; like it's just that easy.

"There are no wielders around," I point out.

"Call the magic to you," he counters.

"I—"

The ice gripping my ankles melts, and a blast of wind knocks me down before I get the chance to argue further. I whip my blazing gaze to him. He just clasps his hands behind his back and shrugs indifferently. And what's pissing me off all the more is that he looks so gods-damn casual while doing all this, with his unbound hair and loose clothes. Like this is all just *so easy* for him.

I will not let them win.

That still includes him.

I grit my teeth and rise. Wiping the dirt from my training clothes, I open my palms skyward and attempt to draw in magic. The only issue is, I just climbed hundreds of stairs and have about as much energy as a pebble.

"Dig deep," Casimir urges.

"Yes, because saying that always helps."

Thunder rumbles over my head as small, gray-tinted storm clouds form directly above me. They sway on an invisible breeze, hovering. Within seconds, they open their gates, and rain pours down, drenching me.

"Try harder."

I brace my hands on my hips and resist the urge to do something completely childish like stick my tongue out at him. "Joke's on you," I bite out bitterly. "I love the rain."

The corner of his lip kicks up. He lifts two fingers, twirling them in the air. Lightning cracks across the contained storm above me, and a bright blue bolt snakes down from the cloud and bites my skin.

"Fuck!" I wince, shooting Casimir a sharp look. "That *hurt*."

"It was supposed to." He again clasps his hands behind his back. "And it's only going to get worse from here." Another bolt of lightning strikes for me, but I dodge it, rolling out to the side. Casimir continues talking. "I taught you a lot this week. Tell me what you've learned about your magic."

"What—right now?"

Another lightning bolt, this one three times faster and four times hotter, strikes right at my feet. I blink at the intensity of it, a little horrified.

"Please do not ask me ignorant questions," Casimir says through a sigh. "They waste both our time."

I arch a brow, glancing up at him. "Noted." I rise, circling him as I watch his hands carefully. "A Binder's laktî is like a muscle," I begin, recalling all that Casimir has taught me about our magic thus far. "It needs to be worked and strengthened to be capable of attuning properly to other wielders' magics. If done correctly, a Binder can wield the magic they've connected to with the same strength and potency as the originating wielder themself."

Casimir remains standing straight-backed, his fingers still clasped together. Only his chin moves as he follows my movements. "And if a wielder's laktî is weaker than yours?"

"Though difficult," I answer, "I can still filter my own magic through it, increasing its strength."

"And what are the risks?"

"Two which are most pressing." I pace in front of him, keeping my palms turned up as I attempt to call on magic. Thus far, I've received no answer, so I recite what he's taught me and bide my time. "The first is my own burnout. If I draw on too much magic at once, I can eviscerate myself mind, body, and soul."

"A painful feat which you've already experienced."

Crimson pools in my mind. Shouts echo quietly. *Lyra, you have to let go of your magic.*

I shake my head against the memories. "The second risk is I can cause another's burnout if I pull on too much of their magical resources at once."

"And the final thing you've learned?"

"You suspect Binders can have a primary magic."

"Meaning?"

"Meaning a magic source they can always call on. One which will always answer."

"But?"

I sigh. "But you also theorize the wielder must accept the magic—another peculiarity of Binding. If the wielder chooses right, it will feel like silk in their veins, allowing them immense mastery over the magic type. If they choose wrong..."

"It'll be like poison," Casimir supplies, studying me. "And have you yet decided on what you believe yours should be?"

I curl my fingers into my palms. "No."

My reward for that is being swept up in a small hurricane filled with bone-chilling water, a gust of wind again knocking me down.

"You need to. You may unlock another level of power once you do."

Casimir continues speaking about our magic, yet I don't protest. My veins are finally warming, a humming sensation awakening beneath my skin.

My call for magic is finally being answered.

"Since we are the only ones of our kind," he says, seeming completely engrossed in what he's telling me, "there isn't much research on the matter, but I have a theory when—"

I don't let him finish his sentence.

Someone's laktî clicks into place with mine, and I throw my hand out, a giddy stream of fire roaring from my palm, barreling toward his head.

With fluid movements—and one arm still annoyingly bent behind his back—Casimir redirects the flames, moving his hand and spinning them into a tight circle. He keeps them hovering next to him, the bright orange tendrils continuing to turn over themselves. "Oh now see, that is rather interesting." He observes me. "I did not expect fire to answer you first."

I rise from the ground, sliding my foot back as I assume my fighting stance. "Why not?' I ask defiantly, despite the answer being quite obvious.

"Because you fear the flames. You fear the risk of being burned."

My chest squeezes as my heart stills from beating for two whole seconds. Two sentences echo like a sweeping ballad inside me.

I'm scared something like this will end in flames.

Then I will burn, Lyra, so long as it's by your flame.

I shake my head at him. "You know nothing." Another answer to my call arrives, and a different laktî clicks into place with mine. This laktî against my own feels warm and familiar.

Roots spring from the ground, twisting over Casimir's calves, charging up to twirl around his limbs. Black flowers unfurl their venomous petals, a ghostly vapor streaming from their center.

He glances at it, a look of approval on his face. "Clever," he admits. "But not good enough." Casimir releases the spinning flames and uses them to burn the roots and flowers to a crisp, the remnants disintegrating to ash and crumbling to the ground much like my ego. "You were better off with fire."

With a flick of his wrist, he sends a quick succession of water streams spearing toward me. I manage to dodge the first two, but I am caught in both the face and the chest with the rest.

With anger tearing through me, I erect a network of thorn-coated vines and send them soaring straight for his heart. Yet with fluid movements, he forms a wall of ice to enclose himself. The moment the vines kiss the glittering surface, the ice stretches out, freezing them in place. Within seconds, they shatter into a million scattered pieces while a noise which resembles shattering glass pierces the air. He watches me, and I can tell he wants me to wield fire again. Yet I refuse, feeling angered by his earlier words and defiant toward his wishes.

I drop my hands back down to my sides, not willing to fight him any longer.

Casimir sighs. "It would seem your natural affinity is for flora and fire. I suspect those are your two best options for your primary magic."

I tilt my head at him, suddenly curious. "What's yours?"

The corner of his lip curves up, yet he remains silent. When enough time has passed for me to recognize he isn't going to tell me, he jerks his chin in the direction of a staggeringly giant arched door, hewn from bronze and encased in gold. "Come," he says. "There is much for me to show you."

Casimir turns and heads for the entrance. I follow, finally afforded the chance to take in my surroundings. The first thing I notice is how high up we truly are. We are towering above the oasis below, as if propped up on a small mountain, hovering suspended in the clouds. The second thing I notice is the lavish courtyard Casimir and I had just been battling within. Gold railings encase the entirety of the courtyard, and a white, beige, and blue pebble mosaic design sprawls across the ground. I notice the smooth, sprawling building carved from white marble and adorned with gold last.

It looks like a palace of dreams.

As we near the door, I realize various panels depict different scenes. There is a large wolf whose eyes are stars. A deity resting her hand upon a kneeling man's shoulder. There is an illustration of a fire, and one showing two people dancing together at a ball. I glide my fingers over the panel depicting a nondescript woman playing a lyre.

"Are you ready?"

I glance at him pointedly. "If this door is any indication of what's waiting for us beyond the threshold, I have a feeling I could never truly be ready for what I'm about to see."

"Your feeling would be correct."

He guides me inside.

CHAPTER SIXTEEN

LYRA

The gods live here.

Obviously, not the *real* gods, but golden statues larger than anything my eyes have ever beheld. They tower in a circle, stretching far up the horizon, disappearing behind a small haze. Each member of the Canamae is represented. Adhara. Algol. Araceli. Astralis. Raffir. Saffi. Their parents, Ahlai and Merikh, are not amongst them.

There is no roof above our heads; only blue sky and candied clouds. It compliments the white marble and the shiny floors washed in a gold gradient, adorned by arctic marble columns with golden ornaments, towering in between the statues.

My mouth hangs agape as I drink it all in, wandering to the center of the lavish room. As I walk, I spin in circles, my eyes attempting to grasp the grandeur of all that lies before me while the sweet scent of jasmine stuffs itself into my nose.

"This is the source of my home's protection and power."

I whip my gaze to Casimir, shocked at his admission. He has a hand stuffed into one of his pockets, and despite what he's just said, he looks at the statues disapprovingly.

"How?" I ask.

"Centuries ago, after the outcome of the Great Clamaté War had been decided, a few gods themselves erected this place and their statues within it. Here, they slumber within, their magic flowing through the gold as a conduit that casts a dome over our oasis. It is how our land survives. How my people are shielded from their madness. Why magic moves differently here."

"Wait... these statues." I point for emphasis. "These gold things right here. They contain the *gods?*"

"Well, not all of them, as you can see. Only the Canamae."

My jaw drops. "So all this time—while everyone has been saying prayers and burning altars in temples for the Canamae's aid or favor —we've actually been living in a world without the gods?"

"More or less."

Okay. Alright. Like that isn't a world altering revelation.

I stop at the foot of one of the mountainous statues. There is a crack climbing from the foot of the god, up its calf, halting near its thigh. I study the statue's face, frowning. "Who is this?"

"Astralis," Casimir answers, a weight dragging his tone. He strides over, tilting his chin to gaze up at the statue's face alongside me. "And he is awakening."

"What do you mean by 'awakening'?"

"I mean as I say. The gods slumber within these gold confines, and Astralis is awakening. He is attempting to break free."

Yeah...okay. My head is officially reeling.

I pinch the bridge of my nose, trying to make sense of what he's telling me. "How is it the gods ended up here, in these statues, in the first place? How is that even *possible?*"

"Because I put them there." He watches me sidelong before looking back to Astralis. "This is no ordinary gold, and with the help of a deity, it was decided that to stop the few, all the Canamae needed to be put to rest. Most came voluntarily, others by force. It was the only way to end the Great War." He puts Astralis to his back and struts to the center of the room, where he glances up at the exposed sky. "The thing the history books have right is the gods' involvement in the war —that much was true. They interjected themselves, divided, as some aligned with their father, Merikh, while others with their mother, Ahlai. Merikh backed his favorite mortals—his champion—gifting them kernels of his magic, providing wielders with access to knowledge they should have never received."

My stomach hollows. "Are you talking about forbidden magic? About Magaius?"

Casimir does not turn around to meet my eye. "Yes. Magaius was chosen to be Merikh's champion, gifted with forbidden magic and the knowledge to help others access it as well."

I think of the worn book Nuha showed me that night in Philator's library, *We Sang the Dawn*. Her words drift into my mind.

It belonged to the one the story calls Prince. Also known as the Wielder of All. In this story, he was bestowed with a great gift to wield all magic from the Mother Goddess herself, after the Commander, known in the story as the Wielder of the Forbidden, received access to forbidden magic without consequence.

Glimmers of the final vision the Veil showed me play in my mind next.

"Because war demands sacrifice. A truth I have tried to help you see. I cannot help it if you chose to ignorantly remain blind. And now? Now we have the edge we need to finally end this accursed conflict."

"Magaius," Casimir breathes. "What have you done?"

I study Casimir as if for the first time, my mind spinning. "And so you were the Mother Goddess's champion," I muse aloud. "Chosen to be the one who would stand against your best friend and Merikh. Is that how you're able to wield all magic? Did she gift you the ability?"

He is silent a long moment, and then—

"Yes."

The beginning of the prophecy from his journal—words that are permanently seared into my brain—rattle around in my mind, turning over each other.

Beneath the gaze of a gripping white moon, where a lone, starry-eyed wolf waits, a raven will be made, forged in the weight of his sins. Cursed by another and rejected by the threads sewn into his withering heart, the raven will no longer be shackled by the weight of time, but rather a servant to the whims of it—destined to forever fly, no matter how many times it clips its wings to fall.

Images I saw in the Veil flicker in my mind. Ones of the wolf with glowing eyes prowling toward Casimir. It is met with humming. The humming from the vision I couldn't discern. Except, it loudens in my head, the song morphing from a faint echo to something like a haunting lullaby. I finally recognize the tune.

I hear Nuri's ethereal voice; the song she sang during the second test while firelight flickered across her skin.

A wolf that lurks in the blackest of nights, his glowing eyes are a stream. Alone, he wanders lost in this life, awaiting sweet release. A child, a child, he finds deep in the trees, washed in mud and weeds. A child, a child, a knife deep in his skin, awaiting sweet release.

Chills sweep down my body as realization dawns on me.

Holy shit.

I sing the next words aloud, and Casimir stiffens at the sound of them. *"The voices, they crow, in the moonlight. Until the child believes. The wolf will keep him locked in this life, awaiting sweet release."*

I remember Casimir's words the day he came for me. The answer he fed me as I was aching and confused, attempting to understand what he was trying to accomplish.

I hope to bring you back with me; I hope to teach you the nature of our magic. I hope to provide you with a home and a family—with my own family a home. But most of all, I hope to die.

I hope to die.

When I pry my eyes from the angelic marble floors, Casimir is watching me with a quiet sadness brimming in his gaze. "You're the boy from the song."

Casimir nods, the action slow. "I created it during my first century of life. I was...struggling. Wandering from place to place aimlessly. I sang it on the road, in front of fires and in taverns. I always sang it like a lament for myself, but..." His brows furrow, and he shakes his head, his hair shifting into his eyes. "I am not sure how the song caught on. It was a very dark time for me, and there is so much I do not remember. I must have sung it in front of a bard or in some farming town whose people kept the melody alive. Though, some of the lyrics have changed through the centuries. I never have been able to figure out where the child line came from."

Despite everything, I arch a pointed brow at him. "So you mean to tell me one of the most famous folk songs in all of Solaya is nothing more than a song you made up in your self-loathing?"

He shoots me a look. "Your compassion is extensive." And for a moment, in his plunging shirt, loose pants, and tousled hair, he appears so normal.

I shrug. "You kidnapped me."

"So you like pointing out."

"Apologies—how annoying of me to keep bringing that up." Yet I soften when I glimpse the awakened shadows in his eyes. "The raven will no longer be shackled by the weight of time, but rather a servant to the whims of it—destined to forever fly, no matter how many times it clips its wings to fall." I allow the words to settle. "Your immortal life is not a gift—it's a curse, isn't it?"

His jaw flexes, and for the first time, I see unbridled emotion surfacing on his features. "It is the cruelest curse that could have ever befallen me."

"So you truly cannot die?"

He tucks stray hair behind his ear, eyes falling to the ground. "It's just as the prophecy says: destined to forever fly, no matter how many times it clips its wings to fall."

A sudden sadness overtakes me, clogging my throat and piling inside my chest. "How many times have you tried?" I murmur. "To... die."

"More times than you could count in your lifetime."

His pain—so tangible in this moment—temporarily becomes my own. "Did you feel..." I swallow, steadying my voice and ensuring pity does not seep into my words. Nobody needs pity; just someone to hear their experience. "Did it hurt?"

"Every single time."

I cannot explain why I do what happens next. Only that I see the layers in his emotions so clearly in this moment. I see the pain haunting him, cutting him from the inside out, leaving him to bleed. I see his determination to rise above that pain—to not be a prisoner to it. But that brings conflict, and I know that better than anyone. He is a conglomeration of hurt, anger, numbness, pity, regret, and perhaps the most confusing of all...hope. And while I don't think he would ever confess to harboring such an emotion, the quiet moments—the underlying melody fueling his lament for humanity—assure me of the truth.

As odd as it is to think, this version of him? It makes sense to me. I understand it.

Perhaps that is the driving force behind my actions.

I reach for his free hand and lace my fingers through his, squeezing tightly, wrapping my other hand around the base of his wrist. Then, when his eyes snap to mine, an indent wedged deep between his brows, I quietly hold his gaze and attempt to remind him of the brighter things humanity can offer—our connectedness. Our ability to stand with another, holding their hand and sharing their pain without words.

We remain frozen like that for a few heartbeats. Until I release his hand and recede a step, the moment washing away as if it never happened.

I refocus on the information at hand. "Who or what is the wolf with glowing eyes, and why did they curse you with immortality?"

"I..." He stops, biting down forcefully and flexing his jaw, seeming to debate something as he glances at Astralis's golden statue. "The gods are bitter and childish," he mutters finally, appearing to take his answer in a different direction. "And all you need to know is they revel in their twisted sense of justice."

"So you've seen the gods?"

Casimir scoffs a bitter laugh. "Seen them. Spoke with them. Fought them. They are like jealous mortal children who've been given immeasurable power."

"They sound lovely."

He glances at me, the corner of his mouth tugging up into a smirk. "They are positively dreadful."

I huff a quiet laugh, reaching for the phantom length of my hair. One would think I would have gotten used to the change by now, but my mindless fingers still reach for it, just as they constantly reach for an ice necklace that is no longer there. Though, the shortened length *has* grown on me. Easier to wash. Less weight. Lower maintenance.

The thought of my new look has me turning over my forearms, inspecting the scars littering my left arm. I study my wielder's mark twining beautifully along my right arm next. Then, I press my fingertips gently to the scars marring the side of my jaw where my eye is now permanently weaved with silver. Ghosts of my own atrocity flash through my mind, haunting me, reminding me that we need not fear monsters; most already live within us.

"Casimir…" My voice a near-silent whisper as the final words of the prophecy echo through me like a death sentence.

But a promise, I can give: another shall come.

One who is defined by a name both two and one, born from the ashes of what the raven desired most, yet never found. And when they awaken— chosen by the Cycle to harbor the greatest power of all—the ashes of one great war will stir, giving way to another, and the Chosen will decide the fate of kingdoms, just as the raven himself had.

"Yes, Lyra?" His soft voice is so at odds with the cruelty I frequently have to remind myself he has displayed.

"What does the prophecy mean?" I glance up and meet his questioning gaze, only then realizing my fingers are still touching the scars on my cheek. "I mean" —I drop my fingers from my face— "what is my part in all this? What does the Cycle want with me? Why did it choose *me* to harbor this power?" Emotion betrays me, forcing a tremor into my voice.

He is silent for a long moment, his eyes remaining glued to mine as he seems to truly give my question considerable thought. "Truthfully, there are some factors at play that not even I am aware of. Though I can tell you this: what has been bestowed upon you will come with considerable weight, difficult choices, and a chance to change this world. I cannot tell you what those choices will be—if only prophecies were so specific—but I can say you have a pivotal role to play in what's coming, Lyra, and there is no running from it nor hiding from what the Cycle has imparted on you. And while I also cannot say why *you* specifically were chosen, I can ask you an equally important question, which is: why not you?"

I glide my jaw side-to-side. "Because I am no one of importance. I am nothing special. Have no remarkable qualities. I'm just... a former servant girl looking for a free life. That's all."

"You are a fighter who has been given a gift far greater than she can even imagine at this moment." He takes a step toward me. "It's time you discover your worth, Lyra."

My bottom lip quivers. I pinch it between my teeth to steady it, ignoring his last sentence and choosing to unpack the hollow ache I feel at his words later, when I am alone. "It doesn't feel like a gift," I counter instead, the words soft in my throat. "If that prophecy is true, I am to decide the fate of kingdoms while some cryptic, great war erupts within them. And I—I..."

Casimir takes another step and gently wraps his fingers around my elbows. "I am not going to let another great war plague the lands." He says the words so sternly, I almost want to believe him. "One great war is enough, and I will not see another in my lifetime. Not as long as I have a family to protect."

"How?" I ask. "What can be done?"

He releases my arms and recedes a step. "I've already told you my plan."

I furrow my brows, the night I let myself into his room replaying through my memory. "Destroying the Cycle? *That* is your plan? What does—what does that even truly accomplish?"

"To be clear," he muses, his spine straightening into its tighter posture and his shoulders rolling back. He clasps his hands behind his back. "My plan is not *only* to destroy the Cycle; that is merely a component of it."

"Oh, well I apologize for not understanding the full scope of your grand plan. Especially while you have been so forthcoming with everything."

He watches me for a few, silent seconds. "Alright, Lyra. You want to know the entirety of my plan? Well, here it is: I will destroy the Cycle, thus eradicating magic and freeing my people from their madness, abolishing the root of the classist system that has infected the heart of this world. Then, to ensure an era of *true* peace can flourish after magic has disappeared—to cement the rise of a new system based on merit, inherent talents, hard work, and dedication—I will then eliminate the entire class of people that stomped their boots on the necks of the hungry to ensure their grips on power were never questioned. After that, I will murder a god. And then, hopefully, after that, I will finally die."

My tongue is immobile in my mouth. My brain spins with so many different thoughts, I'm unable to simply pull on one. I think of Draven. Think of Kiran. Hell, even Finlay—they all flash through my mind, their Houses erupting in flames as Casimir spears his magic through their chests.

Nausea roils in my stomach at the thought. Because perhaps the most frightening, looming fact of all is that he has the power to do it—to simply eradicate an entire class of people if he wanted to. And even if I have full faith in Draven's ability to defend himself and hold his own against Casimir, not even he could defend so many at once.

"What you're proposing is not going to soothe war from these lands—it is going to incite it." A ball of twisting emotions tangles in my chest. "Not to mention, mass genocide of an entire class is *never* the answer, and it's not going to prevent the prophesied war from happening. How does eliminating an entire noble class carve a path for this new, better age you speak of? Your new world is built on bones and painted with blood."

"As is all change." Casimir retreats a step from me. Then another. And another. Until he is again at the center of the sprawling room, temple—whatever the hell this place should actually be called—and returns his gaze to the sky. "Were you there for the first Great War?"

Both the alarming calmness in his tone and the question itself take me aback. "No," I answer, my brows wrinkled. "Obviously not."

"Exactly. You know nothing of war. Of the vile, repugnant evil it brings out in humanity. I was not only a Crowned Prince during the

Great War; I was a commander on the battlefield. I do not fault you for never experiencing the savagery of a war-torn land—in fact, I celebrate it—but do not stand here and speak to me like I do not know what I am talking about whilst you do."

"Murder is not the answer," I push. "And your sense of revenge, justice—whatever you want to call it. It should not cost hundreds— *thousands*—of lives. What good is change if the cost of it is the very evil you claim to fight against?"

He whirls around, anger clouding his eyes. "Yet murder is justified under the terms of war every *single* time. Those lives lost are nothing more than a necessary means to an end, right? A catalyst for the desired change of kingdoms. How is what I'm proposing any different?" He scoffs, his upper lip curling. "The murders of hundreds— thousands, as you say—are suddenly digestible when it is in the name of kings. Done under the guise of sovereignty. Stolen under the protection of Her Majesty, Justice herself."

"No," I argue, shaking my head against what he's saying. "That isn't... I...I..." I struggle for words—for an argument. Nothing comes to my aid.

He studies me, his stone face hardened as his voice somehow remains soft, despite the chill of it. "Do you know what the first lie of this world was? I will give you a hint: it was not that bloodlines are sacred. Or that kingdoms bring peace. Or that heroes are born from light. No. The first lie was justice." His amber eyes do not waver, boring into me with the intensity of a lightning strike. "They taught us to believe in it the way children believe the stars are gods. But justice is not divine, Lyra; it is inherited. Handed down from generation to generation like bloodstained heirlooms. Chiseled into law by the last man standing." He takes a step toward me, his low voice sharp as a blade's edge.

I swallow against the lump forming in my throat, an unsettling chill crawling up my spine while unease pools in my stomach. I don't disagree with him, and that in itself is terrifying, yet...

I faced the consequences of those truths for nearly the entirety of my life.

"You know how we reset the cycle of justice? By wiping it clean, exterminating those who have been preposterously given their *justice* through inheritance—through blood that bleeds the same color yet is deemed more pure than another's." He threads his fingers into his hair, pushing it away from his pinched face, dropping his eyes. "The stain of what I intend to do will be so great, it will live on in the souls of men, and the future generations will be forced to forever remember the moment humanity finally looked at its reflection and wretched. Finally stood in front of a mirror and asked themselves, *what have we become?*" His gaze finds mine, and despite the shaking in my knees, I can't look away from him. Can't focus on anything else but his words. "You think my objective is revenge or simply out of hatred, when, in fact, quite the opposite is true. War is not the cost of what I intend to do; war is the cost of forgetting. So I will make sure they never forget again."

The silence stretches between us like weighted lead, and Casimir turns away from me, keeping his clasped hands behind his back as his shoulders hunch slightly forward.

Despite everything, my brain still can't help but notice how odd it is to see him slip into his normal, weary demeanor while looking so casual—so different from his normal crisp tunic and breeches and drawn-back hair. It's like I'm seeing the exterior version Casimir was before circumstances shaped him into the interior version I'm dealing with now—the two seeming at war quietly with the other.

"Once I've accomplished these tasks," he continues, his fatigued tone officially returned and hollowed. "The world will need a new leader. One who understands both sides of the coin and will rule with a level gaze. One who understands that what its predecessor saw as weakness is no such thing, just as what was seen as strength never was." He pauses. "I'd like for that person to be the heir to my magic." Another pause. "I'd like for that ruler to be you, Lyra."

My brows slam together, and I shake my head, backing away from him. "What? No. I.... I have no desire to rule. I have no desire for power; there is no freedom in power."

"Powerful men would say otherwise."

"Powerful men are *fools* who are blind to their own ambitions," I spit.

He takes his time before speaking again. "Which is why you are perfect to lead this new age. You will not condemn my people but instead give them an opportunity at the life that was robbed from them. You will not pass judgment on blood but on action. The hungry will starve from their actions and not from their birth." He squares his shoulders to me, his gaze meeting mine with an intensity that nearly steals the breath from my chest. "You are *perfect*, Lyra. It is why I have brought you here—to prepare you for your role in my plans."

"I am nobody's puppet to cast in their plays," I bite out. "Besides, despite whether or not you are inherently correct, you speak of uprooting an entire civilization and committing mass genocide against the noble class. I will not just stand pretty by your side and watch those atrocities play out. Not all nobles are bad and deserve to die."

"I agree with you," he answers gently. "But it is the only way to forge a new dawn. Even leaving one could topple the delicate new order we are trying to create; could result in an uprising or a person grasping at power, using their 'legitimacy' as a claim to it."

"*We?*" I balk, incredulous laughter spilling from my lips. "Do not lump me in with your plans. Just because I've gained a better understanding of you and your motivations these past few days doesn't mean I'm suddenly with you." I pace, my anger seeming to have a delayed reaction but finally spilling over, molten and sharp. "You want to destroy magic. You want to indiscriminately murder every noble, highborn, and king inside the Three Kingdoms. Oh right," I scoff. "And you want to kill a god. A fucking *god*. Then you want to sit me, your 'heir', on some bloodied throne while you lie cold in a grave somewhere, not dealing for one second with the ramifications of your actions. Well you know what? *Fuck. You.*"

He watches me, remaining silent, seeming to allow me space to process my thoughts.

It makes me at once angrier while also forcing me to grasp at fleeting words. "Why do you want to kill a god anyway? And which god? Better yet, *how?*" The incredulous disbelief, the boiling anger—it all clings to me like a second skin, making my vision blur and the magic heat my veins. "Nevermind. Don't answer that. I've had enough answers for one day."

I don't voice my following thought: that my reeling mind doesn't feel like it has the capacity to handle anymore. I know I have been pushing for answers—I know I have been the one who has *insisted* on being told everything, but... I could have never imagined the information would be as heavy as what I've just learned.

Not to mention, when I wanted answers, I was thinking more like:

Where am I?: Oh, you are being hidden in some remote jungle located just off of Glass Water Bay, coordinates blah, blah, blah.

Why did you take me?: Easy, because I want your help in ruling this remote jungle.

Will you please let me go?: You know what? Sure, Lyra.

Alright, I concede it was definitely wishful thinking on my part, but... just even a fraction of gods-damn simplicity would have been nice. Not this complicated mess of morals and ethics which now sit heavy in both my head and my heart.

Casimir reaches a hand out, seeming to sense my inner turmoil. I jerk back as if on reflex. The corner of his lip pulls into a frown before he resets, again rolling his shoulders back and reclasping his hands. "I think you are right—this has certainly been enough for one day. I'll walk you down."

"No," I say, waving a hand at him. "I'll..." I pause, sighing heavily. "I'll see myself back to my chambers."

The dip of his chin is his only reply.

I feel him watching me as I turn around and make for the staircase that is most definitely going to cause my calves to scream at me in the morning. Right before I descend the first step, however, I turn back and glance at him, finally caving into asking the gnawing question that has been burrowing in the front of my mind ever since it floated through it.

"The prophecy says I was born from the ashes of what the raven desired most yet never found." My heart skips like a rock over a glassy river. "What is it you wanted most but were never able to have?" I don't say my echoing question aloud to him, not wanting him to glimpse any of the emotion resting within its syllables.

What ashes was I born from?

He observes me for a long, silent moment. Until he again glances up at the sky, as if searching for something—someone, even. He releases a quiet breath, the sound filled with so many untold stories. "A great love."

CHAPTER SEVENTEEN

LYRA

hat ashes was I born from?

A great love.

The words follow me like a shadow as I wander back to my bedchamber, the world a blur around me as my mind spins.

If what Casimir said is true, if I am truly born from the ashes of a great love, then that would mean my mother truly loved my father. No, actually—they were madly in love with *each other*. A great love, as Casimir said. Which makes me wonder what happened to them. Why weren't they together in the end?

I think about the one time I asked my mother about my father. Remember the pain and longing on her face, so palpable I swore to myself I would never ask again. All these years, I had thought it was because perhaps her relationship with my father was a mistake. Maybe he didn't want me. Maybe he no longer wanted my mother, or he did, but my mother didn't want him because of some tragic circumstance or trait. I don't know—when left to its own devices, the mind can conjure innumerable theories, each one more distressing than the last. Yet in my wonderings, I never considered they *truly* loved each other. I guess I just decided that if they had, they would have been together.

My heart sinks as I now consider the other possibilities. What if he died? What if something terrible happened to him, and my mother was left to grieve? Had I ever met him, too young to remember his face? Most of all, who *was* he?

The thoughts fill me with an even deeper sense of curiosity—bordering on the edge of desperation—to know what the other line from the prophecy could mean. *One who is defined by a name both two and one.* Perhaps it is meant philosophically; I am defined by both my name Lyra, and my name in its entirety, Lyra Izacalli. I mean, when I think about it, my name does mean lyre, and the story Draven told me of Sitara and Astralis—two figures who I can now reasonably assume played pivotal roles in the past Great War—is punctuated by a constellation in the shape of a lyre. That couldn't just be a coincidence...right?

I groan and scrub at my face, puffing out my cheeks right as I reach my door. Neilina is nowhere to be seen, so this must be one of those nights where Casimir told her her services weren't needed.

I enter my room and immediately head straight for the bathing chambers. In the center of the small room rests a lavish, clawed foot bathtub, and I shut my eyes, calling for water magic to see if it will answer. It takes a hell of a lot longer than I like, but eventually, I feel that increasingly familiar sensation of another's laktî clicking into place with mine, and water streams from my palm as I fill up the porcelain-coated tub. Once the level is adequate, I call on fire next, the accompanying answer arriving so quickly, I blink in shock as the glowing tendrils curl around my fingertips lovingly, as if they belong there. I stare at them a moment, noticing the hypnotic lure of the flames.

Still. I chalk it up neatly to a fire-wielder being closer by than any water-wielder was. Because when Casimir asks for my formal answer on what my core magic will be, I will choose flora magic. The element that brought me happiness, a sense of security, and pleasure. I certainly will *not* choose the element that haunted my nightmares for years upon years, plaguing me with a debilitating sense of guilt and an overwhelming feeling of terror. No matter how strong my natural affinity is for it. I will no longer pull at the bad like I did during the first test when my magic instinctively reached for the soporis plant. I will pull at something good—something which has filled me with happiness. And that something is flora magic. *Not* fire magic.

To prove that point, I uncurl my hand and again shut my eyes, calling out for my happiness. When it answers, I open my eyes and catch the remnants of glittering silver light as lavender flourishes in my palm. With a content smirk tugging at my lips, I toss it into the water, pride caressing me like a validating hug.

I strip the dirty clothes from my body and sink into the steaming water after, a groan of pure ecstasy escaping from my lips as I relish in scrubbing my skin clean with a bar of soap while cleansing my mind from the stain of today's revelations. The warm water is like a cradle against my skin. When it chills, I reheat it—twice—knowing I just need to sit and decompress. When I finally get out of the tub, my skin is deliciously pruned, and I am reminded of how sometimes a good bath can feel like a purification ritual.

Before wrapping myself in a towel, I shut my eyes and try to call out for wind magic. I give it a few minutes, and when it never answers, I decide there must be no wielders of its kind nearby. Or I just can't wield wind magic at will yet. Who knows.

I stride out of the bathing chamber and glance around the room, my upper lip curling when I glance at the wardrobe sitting across from my bed. I don't want to wear those clothes tonight; I want to wear *my* clothes. Clothes I am familiar with—that bring me comfort.

I remember something then, and I strut toward the small, rectangular trunk resting at the foot of my canopy bed. I fling it open, the object of my desires resting right at the top of a pile of miscellaneous items which don't belong to me.

Yet this item—this dirty, ragged, stained article of clothing—does.

I gingerly pluck Gray's tunic from the trunk and clutch it against my chest, the ruined fabric gripped tightly in my fist. Though faint, I catch a whiff of cedarwood and amber, and my bottom lip quivers as tears sting my eyes. An unexpected wave of emotion crashes into me then, making me feel like I have whiplash from my sudden mood shift. I wrap my arms around the tunic, bringing it to my chest, and hold it against me as if Gray were actually in it.

I miss you, Gray.

The thought is like sea salt in a healing wound. I collapse into myself, scratchy fabric irritating my clean skin. Then, I cry, hot tears streaming down my cheeks like broken promises. In all my life since knowing him, I have never been away from Gray for this long, and I didn't realize my chest has been slowly splitting apart this whole time without him near until the smell of him wrapping around me once more forced me to recognize the cracks. What I wouldn't give to see him—to be free of all this madness and just go *home.*

To fall back into Draven's arms—to have him kiss me, hold me, tell me everything is going to be okay.

I squeeze Gray's tunic tighter, the object a physical representation of everything I was stolen away from—everything I miss. Spending time with Gray. Laughing and gossiping with Marcella. Being held by Draven. I even miss Kiran. Miss Bathara. Miss the life I was slowly beginning to watch unfold in front me while hope—for the first time in so long—started to bloom in my chest.

I press the tattered tunic deeper into my skin, as if I can somehow use it to mend my fractured soul. Yet I push it so forcefully against my chest, something sharp pokes me, and I quickly jerk it back, my brows scrunching together. Pulling the fabric in all sorts of directions, I inspect the seams and find nothing hiding within. Confused, I plop it in my lap and wipe the tears from my eyes, resetting my emotions and expression. I stare down at it, a feeling stirring in my chest.

Slowly, I glide my hand along every single stitch in the fabric, taking care not to miss a single spot. I suck air between my teeth when my fingers land on something slender and solid. Yet when I glance at the space they're hovering over, I see nothing. Feeling both frustrated and challenged, I wrap my fingers around the invisible object then yank.

"Holy shit," I breathe, gaping at what I know to be Gray's Ever-Know Quill now resting in my palm, his personally selected red and golden feather giving it away. It is the magical quill which allows wielders to communicate with whomever they need to by imbuing their laktî into the tip of it as it writes. Based on what Casimir told me of how he came to have Gray's tunic, Gray must have stitched it into the fabric somehow and cast an illusion over it before giving it to Casimir.

His words to me the night he told me he was leaving for Bathara play in my mind.

Since you possess no magic, the Ever-Know Quill isn't an option.

Then I shall write you letters the magic-less way.

Only, I have magic now. And a powerful one at that. Which means....

I jerk up from the bed, my heart pounding to an erratic rhythm. I scour the room, throwing open every drawer in sight until I stumble upon a loose piece of parchment. It is old and crinkled and stained, tucked into the back of my vanity's desk drawer, forgotten. But the parchment is not what matters; the ability to use the quill is. And now that I can—

I can write to Gray.

The quill is magical, so it doesn't need an inkwell for me to begin scribbling like a mad man. I drop the nib to the parchment, my pulse hammering against my throat. My tongue pops out and hooks up the corner of my mouth as I write.

Gray? Are you there? Please tell me I'm not wrong about this. Please tell me you left your Ever-Know Quill in your shirt for me to find.

I wait and wait and wait. But no answer comes. I pace about the room, suddenly realizing I am still wrapped in a towel instead of clothes. Just to be sure, I steal a glance at the parchment to see if a reply has come before changing, and when I glimpse one hasn't, I make for the wardrobe and throw on a loose-fitting night gown. After, I hurry back to the bed, where I've rested the parchment and quill, and defeat sinks deep into my chest when I see I still haven't received a reply.

I swish my lips side-to-side, glancing around the room. While I wait, I guess I could do some of the exercises Neilina has instructed me to do, toning both my body and precision with magic. I wander to an area where there is enough open space for me to complete the movements, yet I find myself only making it through one or two reps before I stop to again peek at the parchment.

Nothing.

A low growl rattles in my throat, but I am determined to distract myself while I wait. I play with my magic, calling on different elements—the easier magic-types to wield, according to Casimir—and attempt to make shapes from them. Then I braid and unravel my hair. Twice. I straighten up the bathing chamber—not that there was really anything for me to actually tidy—and I even attempt to write my own song, thinking if Casimir did it, how hard could it really be?

I glide around the room, my night gown billowing behind me, and sing my forming lyrics aloud. *"A girl who was forged in the brightest of fires, her eyes now silver and weaved. For a time, she wandered lost in her life, a victim to her grief."*

I lift my brows in surprise, pride pulling on my lips. Honestly, not bad—even if I'm stealing the melody from Casimir's song.

I keep going. *"A man, a man, she let into her heart. His... His..."* I pinch my chin between my fingers, halting near the bed as I think. Okay, maybe this is harder than I thought.

A flash of curling ink catches my eye, and I practically trip over myself as I scurry toward it. I grip the parchment between my shaking fingers, relief, shock, hope, and many more emotions clamoring through me as I scan the sheet.

Lyra? By the gods, is that really you? I need to be sure.

An odd noise which sounds part sob, part laugh breaks from my throat. I blink back tears entirely different from the ones I just shed a moment ago and scribble my reply.

Ask me anything. Something only I would know.

A brief pause, and then—

Who was the name of my first kiss, and what happened?

I laugh, tears spilling over my eyes.

Her name was Margaret Dupret, and she started sneezing while you two were kissing, resulting in her biting down on your bottom lip so forcefully, she punctured a small hole through it.

More laughter pours from my lips as I remember Azalea and Sterling standing over a young Gray with furrowed brows to observe his wound, his bloodied lip filling his mouth while utter disappointment filled his eyes. Though it sounds tragic, after the healers mended the hole in his skin, he explained Margaret informed him she already was having some allergic reaction to his scent or something, and when they were kissing, his hair tickled her nose and set off her sneezing.

He tied his hair back for a week straight after that, and I laughed about it every single day.

God's veins, it's really you. You're alive—well enough to write. Tell me where you are, Lyra. Are you safe? Has Casimir Vivaldri been decent to you? Are you fed and clothed? Gods, Lyra, I... I am so sorry we couldn't do more to stop him. Sorry we haven't been able to do more to save you. To find you sooner.

I stare at the parchment, disbelief swelling in my chest as the realization that I'm *actually* writing with Gray right now sends a tremor through me. Flashes of the illusion Casimir cruelly conjured flicker in my mind's eye, and I see Gray's head tumbling from his body. See his body cold and bloodied and ruined.

My throat closes, and my heart stutters for a beat. Even after Casimir told me the truth, there has always been a small voice whispering in the back of my head, attempting to convince me it was all just a lie to make me more docile. Though I never gave into it, refusing to listen to those hissing voices.

I don't know where I am. All I know is, wherever it's located, it is far from our home. Things feel... different here. Magic moves more freely, and the sun shines in strange ways—piercing and red-tinted. The place itself is a sprawling oasis, and it is filled with flora I have never seen in Solaya. Yet I think I am as safe as one could hope to be as a captive. I am fed. I am clothed. Most importantly, I am okay. It's strange, really—being treated better here than I ever was in Rivara Kingdom.
I know this will sound strange, but I've been learning a lot about my magic—how to refine and wield it like a true master would. I have so much to tell you, Gray... You wouldn't believe all the things I've seen and learned.

I pause my writing, breathing against the heaviness piling in my stomach as I consider all my conversations with Casimir. Consider telling him about my time in the Veil—simply about my Veilreading gift in general, a talent I have yet to discuss with him or anyone else outside of Casimir. Yet for the sake of time—so scared this connection to home will somehow end—I choose not to discuss those things.

But I don't want to focus on that yet; I want to hear about you. How are you? How are things at Bathara? What aggregate did you choose? Did you and Marcella join the same one? How is she doing? Is she coping okay after losing Griff? Is Kiran? Draven? Are you taking care of her—being there for her at whatever distance she needs? You know I'd lecture you if you weren't.
By the Mother, I have so many questions for you, Gray. So much I'd like to know. One of those many things being how the hell you managed to pull off hiding an Ever-Know Quill in your shirt?

I finish that final sentence and blow out a sigh, as if the rotting weight I've been carrying since being here is purging itself from my body right alongside the magical ink spitting onto the page. Writing with Gray makes all the wrongs of the world feel right again. Like I'm no longer sinking beneath the ocean's surface, grasping at a fading light I can't ever seem to reach, screaming and hollering as water floods my lungs. No—it's like I have finally risen to the surface, a revitalizing, crisp bout of oxygen swirling beneath my ribcage instead.

A sizzling, red-golden light appears as I watch Gray's reply curve onto the parchment.

> *During the battle, it became clear the direction everything was heading. To make a long story short, my quill was stuffed into my boot, and while Casimir was distracted, Marcella weaved small vines around the quill, sewing it into the underside of my shirt. I cast an illusion over it after that, using the barest minimum of magic I could so the quill and my magic would remain undetected. Though I did weave the very essence of my lakti itself into it, praying to the gods the illusion would hold.*
> *Truthfully, even as I write this I am shaking my head with disbelief that it actually worked. But by the gods am I glad it did.*

Gray's letter then goes on to tell me about Draven. He tells me Draven fought for me until the very end. That he only stopped because his father attempted to force him to stand down against the fight. He says Draven wasn't going to do it, but then Captain Fjolla knocked him unconscious, allowing Casimir to take me. Supposedly, that's when Gray draped his shirt over my body, begging Casimir to let me keep it.

My heart both flutters and pounds as I continue reading.

> *You know I will never lie to you, Lyra. So I will just tell you Draven blames himself for your capture, and he searches for you tirelessly. I heard from Kiran that his father forces him to show face at the academy, not allowing him to neglect his duties as the Captain of Elefet. I suspect that is the only reason why he is still here.*

Marcella is alright. She grieves, but I am with her. (And yes, I'm well aware of the lecture I'd receive if I weren't; not that I need that as a reason. I care for her, and so I want to be there for her anyhow.) We both chose Castaria as our aggregate.

Now it's your turn to provide some answers. What happened to make you erupt with magic like that? What did you see, or hear, or feel? And before you think otherwise, you know you can tell me anything, and I will never judge you.

I love you, Lyra. I'm sorry I didn't say that to you more. Gods, there is actually so much I'm sorry for. I'm sorry for not noticing how deep the pain you held quietly inside you ran sooner. I'm sorry I didn't push you harder to tell me about your nightmares; perhaps if I had, I could have helped you more. I'm sorry for what happened to your mother—that I never knew. I'm sorry for everything you suffered and that I was blissfully ignorant to it all. But perhaps most of all, I'm sorry I was never there for you in the ways you needed me to be—that I was too blind to realize you were drowning and needed a hand to help pull you free.

P.S: I am also sorry for my long reply, I just.... since the day you were taken, so much has sat heavy on my chest, and I didn't know if I would ever get to say these words to you. So, please forgive my eruption of words.

P.P.S: I love you.

P.P.P.S: Kiran is still Kiran, in all his glorious smirks and humor.

Tears stream steadily from my eyes as I read and re-read the parchment. For the life of me, I can't distinguish if the tears are falling from joy or in sadness or from relief. It's as if all my emotions have mixed together like muddied paint, no longer shining with their own individuality.

I write Gray back, describing to him the illusion Casimir weaved over me. How broken and desolate I felt on the inside at thinking he was gone. I describe to him the way the sadness gave way to nothing but pure rage. The rage I felt for the transgressions haunting my past. The rage at Gray being stolen from this world too early. The rage at

Casimir. At the Abdites. Then I tell him about the words I heard swirling in the air—the way they changed into coherent instructions the moment I gave into the rage.

Erhè akta maht.

Hate. Take. Harm.

Even the memory of it sends a shudder down my spine, and I swear I feel a prickle along the seams of my wielder's mark at the mere thought of them.

I tell him about my thoughts of Draven. How they brought me back to reality, anchoring me in something different than rage. I was lost in a sea of swirling darkness, and Draven was the light. Was the voice calling me back. Demanding I let go.

I don't withhold a single detail from Gray. If there is anyone who will understand—anyone who I can share every ugly thought with, show every disturbing scar without fear of judgement—it is him.

Yet shock ignites my skin and threads along the roots of my bones when he informs me what I thought was only a figment of my imagination—was something I had merely conjured in my desperation—had actually happened. Those were no mere thoughts; they were actions. Draven had *actually* wrapped himself around me and begged for me to let go. Those words I heard? The words I clung to like the stars cling to the night sky? They were real. Uttered by Draven himself in an attempt to bring me back to him.

It's that you live, Lyra. You must live. And if you don't, then I'm coming with you, because I don't want to be in a world where I can't wake up and find you.

I had nearly incinerated him—torn him apart ligament by ligament with the ferocity of my magic. Yet somehow, he still never let me go. The more I erupted, the tighter he held onto me.

No matter what I did, he didn't let go.

My next reply to Gray comes without any real thought.

Is he near? Can I... Can I talk to him?

For whatever reason, a sudden frenzy of nerves overtakes my body. Luckily, Gray's response is quick.

Give me just a few minutes.

A few minutes turns into a lot of minutes, and I am nothing short of an anxious vessel filled with butterflies fluttering about my stomach and chest. I pace the room, attempting to force my attention back to the song I was creating earlier. Yet the task is futile while thoughts of *finally* getting to communicate with Draven send my stomach freefalling.

What will I say? What will he say? Have his feelings changed—does he even still want me like I want him? Everything happened so fast between us after all, like stars slamming together, as if finding what they had unknowingly been searching for.

Does he think I'm a monster after what I did at Bathara?

I shake the thoughts away, blowing out a quivering breath while wringing out my clammy hands. A tiny movement catches my attention from the corner of my eye, and I pivot on my heel, practically diving onto the mattress to grip the parchment.

Draven's handwriting appears at the center of the page, only one word written.

Lyra.

CHAPTER EIGHTEEN

THE LETTERS

Draven,

It's already been three weeks. Where has the time gone? I thought of what I might tell you today since I feel as though I spilled all the ink from my brain already. I considered writing about my training today—I think you'll be impressed with how far both my magic and combat have come. Perhaps even a little aroused. But I don't want to steer my letter in the wrong direction with that thought. Instead, I'll continue telling you about how I almost wrote about the new flowers I am studying, whose petals sparkle like living starlight, or this new drink I tried that sizzles with magic, making one's throat tingle with a popping sensation. I considered writing about Casimir and what I know of his plans, yet decided that would be redundant since I know nothing new from what I last shared with you and Gray. I even thought about writing more descriptions of this place I now find myself living in (I still couldn't tell you anything about its people.)

As I thought about what to write to you—the obvious now being stolen since we've spent three weeks putting a magical quill to not-so-good use yet a practical one—I realize I no longer know what to say. So, today, I decided I will write to you about my dream.

We were surrounded by lavender, collytails, silver leaves, peppermints, and bonaria. You were holding me against your chest, and I was sewing myself up in your arms while the stars danced above our heads. Somehow, there was a symphony playing in the wind, and it swept around us and tickled our skin as it blew through our fingertips. The moon cast glittering light on a nearby waterfall, and everything it kissed, from the dew on the grass all the way to the watery shadows—it all shined. You were stroking my hair, and I was humming us a song. We were peaceful—happy, even. Though, I regret to inform you I saw no rocks flying in the sky.

Would you judge me if I told you I woke up with tears in my eyes?

Lyra

Lyra,

I would never judge you, though I judge the absence of rocks in your dream's sky. As you and I both know, we are doomed to be miserable grouches until that day arrives.

I had a dream as well. It's a recurring dream, actually. We are in a vast field of flowers, and you carry a wicker basket on your hip. There is childlike laughter floating through the air, almost as if the wind itself has recorded and trapped the sound. You walk barefoot on the soil, and I follow you like some helpless fool, admiring you like the first strokes of winter admire the sun. You always turn to me, and when you do, there is a contented smile sweeping your lips. One that is graceful, disarmed—at peace. Like a retired guardsman who needn't bear their armor any longer.

Truthfully, I also woke up with tears in my eyes. Now will you judge me?

Draven

Draven,

I could never.

This might seem random, but I want to tell you about this long, winding path I walked today. It was encased by warm lights shaped like glowing mushrooms, and just off the path, there was a tavern leaking life. I thought about going in—truthfully, it hadn't been the first time I noticed the place—but like all the other times, I did not go. Did not allow myself to associate with the people so willing to follow Casimir. To corrupt their veins and become something differ-ent. But I still heard the music drifting from the open door, swept up on the breeze. It was a fiddle's song, caught some-where between a sad and happy melody. Which leads me into why I am telling you all this.

For reasons I can't really justify, the song reminded me of you. And that got me thinking...

If you plucked the sounds of your soul on the strings of an instrument, what would the song be like? Would the chords be staccato and happy? Or would they be slow and somber, filled with longing and sorrow? Would it be a merry tune? Melancholy? Would it make me want to dance in a field or cry beneath the gaze of the night sky? I want to know your song as you hear it, Draven.

Will you tell it to me?

Lyra

Lyra,

I thought about your question.

My song is more like a symphony, I think. It is filled with the wails of the cello and the swelling notes of the violin. It is not a happy tune. Yet, it is not a hopeless one, either, carrying the cadence of many emotions.

I will tell you what makes it a symphony in all its entirety—its full composition. Truthfully, I've thought about this moment many times, letting you into the deepest parts of me, making you privy to that which I keep in the dark. I know it's odd to write, but it feels nice when I consider you knowing the ugliest parts of me. To know perhaps you might still choose me in spite of them.

So, here goes the ugliness.

My mother and I attempted to run away from House Dalmar once. To forfeit our titles, our wealth. The name we never wanted to carry. We first left Tylderon the morning following my fourteenth birthday, where we stumbled upon a small forgotten town in the countryside named Prith. If I can be wholly truthful with you, Lyra, my heart both lived and died in that city. When I am not dreaming of you, I am probably dreaming of those days. Sometimes, in the quiet, I swear I can still hear the heartbeat of Prith drumming in my ears.

On our first day in the town, my mother and I stumbled upon a small bookshop. We went inside, and we discovered so much more than books. To make a long story quick, we found a family. The bookshop owner's name was Atlas, and he had two daughters, Rhea and Suzumi. They were warm, filled with a type of liveliness I had never experienced in all my life. We shared dinners together. Stories. We spent long nights talking in front of a burning hearth; Atlas stealing glances at my mother, and my mother pretending she didn't notice.

They fell in love, Atlas and my mother. I did as well. Suzumi was fifteen, and I told her things I had never told anyone. In turn, she confided in me.

I was her first kiss; she was my first love.

And she was murdered.

My father discovered where we were hiding after receiving our missive informing him of our plans to renounce our ties to House Dalmar. Finlay told him where to find us after he swore he wouldn't. Though I was able to eventually forgive him, it took me ten years to get there. Kiran still struggles with the choices Finlay made that day. That's why they are constantly at each other's throats.

As you can imagine, my father was not pleased with our new attachments. So, as he does all things he deems a threat or liability, he eliminated the problem entirely. Atlas was murdered. Suzumi was murdered. And my own mother was murdered.

I was there to witness her death, and...

Well, even with the barrier of only writing, I still can't fully bring myself to describe the nature of the deaths I witnessed that day. So, all I will say instead is that it broke something irreparable in me. Something soul deep. I wandered lost for a long time, drinking and fucking and loathing the world. I made terrible decisions. Did terrible things. Yet I got through it, because I realized being Tynan Dalmar's ruthless heir was not my identity; being Lealla Dalmar's son was.

Now, to understand this next portion, I have to tell you something I kept from you. Not because I don't trust you or was scared to share it with you, but because it is such a fragile thing, sometimes it feels like even speaking of it may shatter the glass walls encasing the situation. I have a sister. Her name is Rhea. And yes, if you now recognize the name, it is because she is indeed the other daughter from the bookshop. My father shattered her life as she knew it. He stole her father from her. Her sister. I could not let him steal anything else.

I made a deal with him. A deal he and I still have in place to this very day: so long as he protects and cares for Rhea as if she herself was a Great House Heir, then I will submit to him entirely. Will do exactly as he asks of me, without question.

I've been upholding my end of that bargain for a decade.

I don't regret a single second of it; I love Rhea fiercely and would do anything for her. But right now, that very leash is the thing keeping me from leaving everything behind and traversing the entire world to find you.

No, I don't regret it. But when it comes to you—

comes to securing your own protection—a twisted part of me resents the deal I made. Not Rhea—I could never resent her. In fact, I dream of the day you two can meet. I think my heart might just explode at the sight of it.

Instead, I resent the circumstances surrounding the deal. My father. Society. Power. Wealth.

I resent it all. Every last bit.

So, there it is—my song laid bare for you. Every strum of a chord within me, every changing tune of a note—it all revolves around the same composition.

I am glad to have finally shared it with you, Lyra. To no longer carry the story of another day. Though, I'm sorry for such a long letter. Hopefully you haven't fallen asleep on me. Though I suppose you are a night bird, so perhaps I needn't worry.

Now, if it's alright, I'd like to request something from you in turn: tell me something nobody knows about you. I've already told you of my own selfishness, and as such, I'd like to know things not even Gray Night-enjoy does. Perhaps I'll then boast to him he no longer knows you best.

Simply put, I just want to know you, Lyra.

At your deepest level. To your very core, where your lilac soul rests.

I want to know everything. Will you tell it to me?

Yours,

D x

Draven,

I have spent far too long staring at my blank parchment searching for the right words. I've decided there are no right words. There is nothing I can offer you with my quill that you probably haven't heard before. That will do any sort of justice for describing how my heart aches for your losses. How my stomach churns with disgust at the cruelty of your father. So, instead, I will simply say thank you. For sharing your deepest scars with me. For trusting me to bear them alongside you. As for Rhea? Well... I can't wait to meet her. She must be an amazing woman to have both survived in House Dalmar and put up with your brooding for so many years. (Can you hear the laugh in my words?)

I've decided to put as much consideration into your question as you did mine. So below, please find a small list of facts nobody knows about me. Not even Gray. Not even you, with all those many, many questions you once asked me in between training sessions while resting within the rolling hills of Thanicka.

1. I romanticize the rain.
2. My favorite sound in the world is the high notes of a fiddle.
3. My secret dream is to one day visit the sanctuary and teaching grounds for Gardners in Eden. To see the place where my mother learned and trained.
4. Perhaps my most deeply buried fact of all: I crave the luxury of weakness. I want nothing more than for someone to spot the cracks within me. To savor the fragility of it. Still call it beautiful. The toll of my armor is paid by the weight it

places on my soul, so I simply want to exist in moments where I don't have to bear its heaviness.

And in now knowing that, I will ask you my most hidden question:

If I showed you all my weaknesses, do you think you'd still look at me the same? If the initial sparkle of the defiance, the resilience, the strength you say you saw in me—if it all melted away and you saw the core of a girl who was simply broken and riddled with uncertainties, do you think you'd still be able to love her?

Sometimes I, myself, question whether or not I can.

With all my heart,

L x

Lyra,

It would be the greatest privilege to be privy to your cracks and fractures. I recognize how precious of an exchange it is when one person bleeds in front of another, not attempting to hide the source of their wound. And so I would like you to know you can always bleed in front of me. That you may untether that armor and remove the weight of it from your soul.

As such, allow me to ask you a list of questions—most of which have been plaguing my mind—and provide you with nothing but open space to answer however you please. Because I will never judge your answers; I simply long to be the vessel allowed to help contain them.

I should start by letting you know Gray told me about your nightmares. How they haunt you more nights than not. Are they keeping you awake at night?

Have you been having thoughts of your mother? Of all the cruel memories you were forced to face in the Feargate? Of the events following the Feargate...

Are you feeling your pain? Your grief?

Are you feeling at all?

D x

Draven,

I'm sorry it's taken me a few days to respond. I had tasks I was forced to attend to, and they left me feeling a bit dazed and weak (though you don't need to worry—I am fine.)

The grief lives on within me. I suppose it always will. But I think the true mark of my growth is the thought of that no longer makes me sad. Instead, I find solace in knowing such a thing will always exist—that the kernel of love for my mother was planted so deep inside my bones, nothing could possibly remove the ache of it. Sure, the pain changes shapes and weighs more some days than others, but it is a privilege to love at all, and so it is a privilege to grieve.

I have you to thank for realizing that.

As for my nightmares, they come and they go. Most often, they are no longer of the flames swallowing my mother, but the mass of power I conjured to swallow the lives of others. Of glinting steel slicing through a neck. So yes—those things have been and are haunting me, sometimes even threatening to drown me with guilt for what I've done. Yet I am allowing myself to sit amidst the ugly truth of them. Am feeling the full sting of remorse and grief. It isn't easy, but I am doing it.

I think I have you to thank for that, as well.

Oh, and Draven?

Thank you for allowing me to show you all the parts of me.

Yours,

L

P.S: Gray told you of my nightmares? When did you and he become such friends?

P.P.S: There is that laugh again, can you still hear it?

Lyra,

It happened in a greenhouse, if you can believe it. It seems all my relationships as of late begin there. And yes, I can hear your laugh as clearly as I hear my own heartbeat, distant but there.

The sound is beautiful.

Please know I am still searching for you. From every crooked den to every holy temple, I am doing everything I possibly can to have you in my arms again. To ensure you don't have to feel dazed or weak—for reasons I've decided not to ask. If you wanted me to know, you would have told me. But...

Please, Lyra, just tell me this one more time— Are you alright?

D x

Though Draven waited and waited, a reply never came.

CHAPTER NINETEEN

RHEA

Pleasure wraps around Rhea's skin, caressing her bones in a warm, tingling embrace.

The six-foot-whatever, dark-haired and tattooed third-year on top of her grunts his satisfaction as he rams himself into her. He holds himself upright with one hand against his headboard while his other cups Rhea's breast, his fingers nimbly toying with her peaked nipple.

Rhea alters between closing her eyes and staring up at the ceiling. Satisfaction builds inside her, but it is merely a bodily response—not an emotional one. She is attracted to…. Lyle? Lukas? Luther? Fuck, she forgot his name…. but that is as far as it goes for her. Is as far as it *ever* goes for her.

Leo grips the back of her thigh and hoists her leg over his head, hooking the back of her knee behind his neck. Lucky for him, she happens to be very flexible, and so she doesn't complain when he pushes her knee closer and closer to her chest as his thrusts quicken.

"Fuck," he groans.

Leviticus finds his pleasure, reaching over for a linen rag resting on the table beside his bed as he spills over into the fabric and not inside of her.

A true gentleman, really.

His body slackens with relief after, and he rolls off of her, discarding the sullied rag and laying next to her while panting in breaths. "You didn't finish, did you?"

"No," she answers truthfully.

He shifts onto his side, propping his head up with his fist. "I can change that," he hums, reaching out with his other hand and gliding a finger from Rhea's breast down toward the slope of her stomach.

She feels a microscopic glimmer of pride when she resists the urge to shield her torso with her arms—a sign that all her hard work is paying off. Instead, she musters her best playful smirk. "If that's an offer, then I gladly accept."

He grins wickedly, and before Rhea knows it, he is between her thighs, his tongue teasingly gliding over her swollen clit. At the breathy moan escaping her lips, he adds more pressure to his strokes, integrating his fingers as he sucks and bites her sensitive nerves.

Pleasure finds Rhea quickly, and she erupts in an explosion of ecstasy, gritting her teeth and squeezing her eyes together as she rides out the burst of euphoria for as long as she can.

Maybe Lithaniel is a keeper, after all.

When Rhea reopens her eyes, the knots in her chest feeling temporarily unwound, she sits up and stretches her arms above her head, letting them fall onto Levy's shoulders after. "This was fun."

He chuckles, shaking his head. "Is this the part where you tell me it was a one time thing, though?"

She shrugs, rising from the bed. "Maybe. Maybe not. We'll just have to see what the gods have written for us." She flashes him a mischievous smile and collects her pile of clothes from the floor, using them to shield her exposed body. As she does, she glimpses a cozy thin sweater which looks as though it would swallow her whole, hiding every inch of her.

Perfect.

She points at it. "Do you mind if I wear that out? I promise to give it back." She drizzles her words in honey, adding a small pout in her lip for extra security.

Leon smirks, rising up in his bed and folding his arms across his very broad, very attractive chest. "Alright," he drawls. "You can borrow it if you can answer me one thing."

"And what is that?"

His smirk deepens, and he leans forward to cup his chin in his palm. "What's my name?"

Fuck.

That is the golden question, isn't it?

"Uhm, well… your name is…is…"

He barks a laugh, rearing back to lean against his headboard. "I knew it," he says through laughter. "You *did* forget my name."

Well, there is certainly no denying it now. Rhea shrugs, playing it off as coolly as she can. "Don't take it personally—I'm *really* bad with names."

He runs a hand through his silky hair, his smile filled with a simplicity Rhea envies. "My name is Link. And the next time I see you, I expect you to remember it."

"Alright, *Link*. In exchange for me remembering your name, can I wear your sweater?"

He folds his arms over his chest, his biceps flexing from the movement. "You can," he answers airily.

"Thank you," she chirps back, resting her clothes on the bed and quickly throwing his sweater over her head. It is soft and loose at the neck, caressing her skin like a hug. She draws half her hair back next and plucks her favorite dagger—forged in the style of a hair pin once belonging to her late mother—from her pile of things, stuffing it through her newly secured bun. Rhea regathers her belongings into her arms and heads straight for the door, offering him a parting smirk. "This was fun."

His eyes are bright. "We should do it again sometime."

She snorts a laugh. "What a typical response for me to remember you by." Then, without another word, Rhea slips out the door, quietly pulling it closed behind her.

With nothing but the oversized sweater covering her body, Rhea strides down the corridor, heading back to her bedchamber. She drifts into deep thought as she ponders her plan for the task Tynan assigned to her while being at the academy—locating and transcribing some old book. Yet as she considers the deal they struck, she finds herself thinking about the man himself and her relationship to him instead.

Rhea always wondered why Tynan Dalmar bothered investing in her. Why he put forth his coin, his tutors, his resources, education, training—all the things typically reserved for the children of nobility. For a stint, her young, impressionable mind was convinced he had grown to care about her. And the most twisted part of that was, despite hating him with every fiber of her being, the more Rhea believed the thought to be true, the more she realized she *wanted* it to be. Draven was always gone, occupied with tutors, the other heirs, or one of Tynan's sick lessons. And though he tried desperately to show up for her throughout the years, she still felt lonely. So the more she ached for someone's attention and approval—even someone as twisted as Tynan—the more she fought to receive it.

After she hit puberty and fully came into her body, Tynan introduced her to the world of nobility as a magic-less orphaned girl of some distant relative from across the Arteman Sea. She became known throughout the Erandor Kingdom as his charity project. And when the head of House Hikari—her mother's disgraced noble house —came knocking on Tylderon's door as a result, Tynan held council with him behind closed doors.

The man did not come back after that.

As such, with Rhea's body now deemed somewhat of a "desirable object", as Tynan put it, and with the way her lowborn status resulted in people only disregarding her, she became useful to him. So, she began attending prestigious social events alongside him.

He became philanthropic; she became a spectacle.

Her task was usually a simple one, at least. She was given a target for the night, and she was to get that person abhorrently drunk. Make them comfortable enough to loosen their tongues, then keep them talking. Thankfully, given the nature of Draven and Tynan's arrangement over Rhea, she never had to actually offer her body for information. If, no matter how hard she pushed, the person chose not to speak, she was always instructed to excuse herself politely and waltz away without another word.

Though, since those she spoke with always assumed she was nothing more than a penniless charity case, that seldom happened. They were more than happy to write her off and speak freely—like her lesser mind couldn't possibly grasp the nuances of politics.

They were all self-righteous bastards.

Over time, Rhea began to realize she had been slowly conditioned to rely solely on one man. On his words. His resources. His praise and approval. Some days he would be kind to Rhea, treating her like she was his own daughter. Other days he would reject her, acting as though she was nothing more than a beggar brought in from the street. Repulsive. Dirty. Imperfect.

How cruel it is, to know you hate someone and everything they stand for, yet still long to receive their approval.

Yet this will be the end of all that. The end of her relying on Tynan for anything. The end of watching Draven be forced to bend to Tynan's whims—of watching him live a shackled life because of her. She will fulfill the final task Tynan has given her, freeing both herself and Draven of lives they never wanted in turn. All she has to do is find the item Tynan wants and provide him the knowledge inside.

Simple. Easy. Not at all a big deal or violation of Draven's trust.

Right...?

Rhea sucks in a sharp breath just before slamming into a hard object. She presses her palm to her head and glances up, only to realize it wasn't an object at all, but instead a body. Not just any body —fucking Finlay Fjolla's.

She groans at the sight of him, making to storm past without offering him a word. Yet he sidesteps her, blocking her path.

"What are you doing on the third-year's floor?"

"None of your business."

Finlay narrows his eyes on her. "Actually, it is, seeing as I oversee this aggregate."

She scoffs. "Go fuck yourself."

He snorts. "I'd say the same to you, but it looks like someone already has." His eyes slowly glide along her body, hovering at the hem of Link's sweater as it sways loosely over her knees, moving along to the wad of clothes in her hands next. "Who is the unfortunate bastard?"

She mocks puppy eyes and a pouty lip. "Aw, are you jealous?"

He laughs bitterly and drops his arms. "I just want to know who in my aggregate has such poor standards."

Anger mixed with a bit of hurt lick down Rhea's spine, but she doesn't give him the satisfaction of a reaction. Instead, she cocks her head and sweetly coos, "You shouldn't judge someone based on their sexual preferences, Finlay. For example, somewhere out there in the Three Kingdoms someone has wanted to bed you, and though I find the idea of that entirely indigestible and abhorrent, I would never judge them for their shitty taste in men. So please, don't judge mine, alright?"

"Sleep with whoever you want," he counters with a shrug. "I only judge when a well-raised woman lowers herself to sleep with commoners and lowborns." He threads fingers through the side of his white hair that isn't partially twisted back with small braids. "Seeing as the entirety of my aggregate is composed only of nobility with reputable bloodlines, you have your choice of the lot without any judgment from me."

Rhea picks at her nails. "I must not have put enough, *I don't actually give a fuck*, behind my words. I'm always going to do as I want, whether you judge me for it or not."

"So long as it is in alignment with my rules for Skyborne."

Her eyes narrow. "I'll do it even if you forbid it in blood or threaten to chop my toes off."

Finlay stares at her, his jaw clenching. "It doesn't work like that here, Rhea. I am captain over this aggregate, and as your superior, you are bound to do as I say."

"You can take your 'bound' bullshit and fuck right off." Rhea makes to stride past him, bumping her shoulder into his chest as she goes, but before she can make it two steps, Finlay reaches for her, wrapping his fingers around her wrist.

"Where are you going?"

Rhea whips her head around to glare at him, not hiding the curl in her lip. "None of your damn business." She flicks her eyes down toward the hand still locked around her wrist. "And I suggest you remove that before I slice your fingers off to remove it myself."

With a growl of frustration, he lets go.

Rhea smiles at him as smugly as she possibly can.

"Actually," he counters, his voice brimming with ire and impatience, "it *is* my business, seeing as you and I are supposed to be training together in Skyborne's arena in fifteen minutes."

Rhea curses under her breath. "Of all the assholes in this place, why the hell did they assign me to *you*?"

He meets her stare with equal irritation. "Trust me," he grinds out. "I have already asked myself that question many times. But seeing as I am bound by my duties to this academy, I have no choice. Now go to your chambers, put on some proper clothes, and meet me in our arena. If you are late, I'll make you do hanging sit ups from the highest balcony railing possible."

Rhea almost balks. Almost. But one doesn't live with Tynan Dalmar for ten years and not learn how to mask their reactions. "Why is that the punishment you came up with?"

Finlay snorts like a smug bastard, folding his arms over his chest once more. "Please. Before I left for the academy, you don't think I ever caught on to your fear of heights?"

Faster than a blink, Rhea reaches for the dagger tucked in her hair and lunges toward Finlay, pressing the tip of it against his throat. "Say one more word, and I'll bleed you dry right here and now."

With a cold smirk pressed to his lips and his eyes locked to Rhea's, Finlay steps closer, pressing the tip of the small blade deeper into his neck. "No, you won't."

She moves forward, digging the cool metal deeper, pricking his skin and drawing a small pool of blood. "Wanna make a wager on it?"

Finlay's arrogant smirk stays in place as his gaze drifts over her shoulder. A quick glance back tells her a door has opened. Her evening's entertainment strides out, shirtless.

"Murder a Great House Heir in cold blood while a witness watches," Finlay says, voice low, "and you'll be signing your own death sentence." He glances away, making no effort to remove the dagger pressed to his throat. "Not that I care—you'll deserve whatever happens to you."

Rhea's blood ignites as if suddenly kissed by the sun itself. She drops the blade and takes another challenging step. "Just like my father deserved it, right? Like my sister deserved to be strung up before our eyes? Like Draven's mother deserved to be branded?"

Finlay jerks his gaze back to her. For a fleeting moment, Rhea swears she glimpses a ripple in his eyes. A mixture of pain and regret and something else. Yet just as quickly as she thinks she sees it, it disappears, leaving nothing but the chill residing in his icy gaze.

Before he can say anything, Link approaches them, dipping his chin at Finlay first, whose simmering stare remains fixed on her. "Captain Fjolla." He turns to face Rhea next, holding out her black laced brassiere for her to take. "You left this behind. I figured you'd want it back."

With a sharp breath of frustration, Rhea rips her eyes from Finlay and forces a diplomatic smile to her lips, snatching the item. "Thank you."

He glides a hand through his inky locks. "Not a problem. If your bed gets cold again, you know where to find me." Without another word, Link spins around and strolls back to his room, stuffing a hand into the pocket of his loose, linen pants.

A simple creature, that one.

She feels a brush of skin against her, and she scowls when she realizes it's Finlay pushing past her, his jaw firmly set and lips thin. He continues down the corridor in the direction he was going before she stopped him.

Wait.

He stopped *her.*

Fucking bastard.

She stares at his broad back as if her heated gaze could burn a hole through it.

As if sensing that, Finlay calls out over his shoulder in a rather unenthused tone, "The balconies are waiting for you if you're late."

Her scowl deepens.

Asshole.

Rhea waltzes into the large training room exclusive to the Skyborne members in precisely fifteen minutes. It is filled with lavish swords, spears, daggers, bows—any weapon one could conjure in their mind—and Finlay's aggregate has spared no expense in acquiring the best of them. Skyborne banners hang proudly on every wall, the crisp blues and silvers screaming of self-imposed importance.

She finds His Pompous Royalty located at the far side of the sprawling room, shirtless and running through his own exercises, his wielder's mark on full display to her. Blue-ish-white, sharply-pointed snowflakes undulate across the entirety of his back like a wave, starting thin near his shoulders and growing wider as the mark twirls across the planes of his muscles, until all the snowflakes form a thin, uniform line once more near his hips, either ending there or disappearing behind the seams of his pants. A bejeweled hilt rests comfortably in his palm, the blade of it black and adorned with white markings mirroring the first falls of snow. He swings it forcefully, his toned body flexing as he moves through different positions.

All Rhea can imagine is the tip of it plunging through his chest while she straddles him, pushing the pommel deeper and deeper into his icy heart.

As if sensing her watching him, he stops, glancing over his shoulder at her before dropping his sword to his side. He pushes strands of white hair from his face and swipes the sweat from his brow. Then he strides straight for Rhea, sword still in hand. "What do you want to work on?"

Rhea snorts a laugh, bracing a hand on her exposed hip. "Please. Like there's anything you can help me with. I'm already better than you in combat, Frosty."

"No," he says. "You're not. I've already shown you my magic can overwhelm yours." He cuts her a sharp glare. "Oh, and don't call me Frosty."

"Or what? You'll try to kill me again?" She pouts her bottom lip and shrugs, lifting her hands as she does. "Been there, done that. Still unbothered." A pause. "*Frosty.*"

"I didn't try to kill you," Finlay mutters, rubbing at his forehead.

"No?" Rhea taps a finger to her lips, mocking confusion. "What would you call plunging a thousand dagger-sharp ice shards at me, then? A marriage proposal?"

"Only in your dreams would I ever propose to you." His bitter voice hisses between his clenched teeth.

She frowns. "Really? That's the point you chose to focus on?"

"Fuck off, Rhea. Let's just clock our training hours so we can go our separate ways, alright? I do not want to be here anymore than you do. Believe me, the last thing I'd choose in this world is spending *any* time with you."

The words cause a dull ache to appear in her chest. Not because she cares whether or not *he* wants to spend time with her, but because, despite how much she wishes it didn't, hearing them spoken aloud sends her spiraling through insecurities and past rejections, putting her even more on guard than she already was.

"You're a real special kind of asshole, do you know that?"

"If there was anyone who loves reminding me of it, it certainly is you, Rhea Brooksley."

Hearing her father's surname—*her* surname—falling from his lips sends tendrils of fire lancing up her spine, licking and caressing her every nerve ending until they all burn with rage. "Don't you *dare* say that name."

Finlay blinks, seeming genuinely confused. "What—*your* name?"

"My *father's* name," she hisses. "The name *he* passed on to *me.* Don't. You. Fucking. *Dare.*"

Realization dawns on him, and his expression slackens for a moment as unintelligible emotion flickers in his eyes. Yet the shift in his demeanor lasts only a few seconds before he rebuilds his ice wall and his lips curl into a sneer. "I am so tired of being the scapegoat for your anger. *I* am not the one who made his decisions for him; *he* made his own choices and was forced to face the consequences of them. As did everyone else involved in what happened back then. There are sides to every story, Rhea. So stop pretending like you are even remotely aware of mine."

Yet she barely registers his final sentences. Her brain is stuck on other words. *I am not the one who made his decisions for him; he made his own choices and was forced to face the consequences of them.*

She sees red. Absolute, undiluted, fully-saturated red.

Her fingers curl around the hilts of the sheathed daggers strapped around both her thighs, and she yanks them free, sending each one soaring toward Finlay—one at his heart and the other at the space directly between his eyes. He deflects the dagger soaring toward his face with the blade of his sword and the other with a thick sheet of ice he forms over his heart.

"You are like an insufferable child throwing a tantrum," he hisses. *"Grow up."*

Rhea barks a bitter, cold laugh. "Rich coming from you." Then she charges at him, drawing two more daggers from their holders and positioning them in her palms to strike. She spins on the ball of her foot and attempts to plunge one dagger into his jugular while thrusting the other into his side. Finlay catches her wrist nearest his throat and spins out, avoiding the dagger racing for his side.

"Stop this," he hisses. "We do not need to act like uncivilized barbarians who resort to simply killing each other because of their anger." His chest is pressed against her back, her outstretched arm locked in his hands.

She tilts her chin up just enough to glance back at him. "Whatever do you mean, *Captain?* I am only completing the training hours with you, just as instructed." Her saccharine words drip with honeyed poison.

His grip on her arm tightens. "Rhea..." He almost says her name like a plea.

She isn't sure if he wants to say more. Before she can find out, she uses the dagger in her free hand to make Finlay let go of her, plunging it into the crook of his elbow. As expected, before the blade can actually pierce skin, he drops her and pulls away.

"Why aren't you fighting back, Frosty? Afraid you'll lose to me?"

Finlay doesn't take the bait. "The only thing I'm frightened by is having such an unstable brat at Bathara."

"Stop speaking to me as though I'm still the child you guys left behind at Tylderon. I'm *not*." Rhea charges at him once more, attempting to engage him in combat.

"Then stop acting like you are," he counters, evading the strikes of her daggers with too much ease.

With gritted teeth, Rhea tosses her daggers to the side. She wants his blood on her knuckles instead of the tip of her blades anyways. Finlay huffs. Without peeling his eyes from her, he chucks his sword beside him, lifting his hand and beckoning her forward with two fingers.

"Alright, Rhea. You want a fight? Fine. Let's fight."

She doesn't miss a beat, charging him and throwing a combination of strikes at him that would have made her combat tutor beam with pride. Though he tries to make it look effortless, the dip of his brow and thinning of his lips show Rhea he is struggling to keep track of all her movements. So she puts even more pressure on him, trying to force him to go on the offensive.

Yet he doesn't. He isn't striking back.

Rhea can only chalk that up to him thinking he doesn't *need* to strike back—that she isn't worth the effort in his eyes.

She will make him pay for his arrogance in blood.

She feints, throwing out an arm, and when he brings both his forearms up to defend against the blow, she spins fluidly on the ball of her foot, bringing up her heel and planting it right into the side of his face.

He rears back from the kick, clutching at his nose with his hand. When he pulls his fingers away, blood dribbles from his nostrils, running toward his upper lip in a beautiful stream of crimson. Slowly, he drags the back of his hand across the red stain blemishing his perfect skin, wiping it away as his weighted stare remains locked on her.

"Fight. Back," she bites out.

"This is training. Not an actual battle." He spits blood onto the ground. "I have nothing to prove to you by showing you I can hit you with my fists. It isn't worth it to me—even if Tynan secured you the best training around. I am the Fjolla Heir, not some lowblooded scum."

Anger sends her scattered thoughts ejecting from her lips before she can think better of it. "Stop acting like you're better than me, Finlay. That I'm some charity case Tynan *allowed* to happen, making me *so* privileged to even be in your blessed presence."

He draws his brows together, a wrinkle forming between them. "What? That wasn't the point of what I—"

"Wasn't it?" Her anger and insecurities run away from her. "You spew your nonsense about highborns and lowborns—who deserves what because of their birthright. Well fuck you, and *fuck* birthrights."

Finlay studies her, his brows remaining pinched together. "Birthright establishes political stability. Maintains social order. Creates a hierarchical system that is predictable and upholds responsibility. Without it, the Three Kingdoms would be plunged into chaos."

She scoffs, shaking her head. "Spoken like a true brainwashed noble himself."

"You were raised in House Dalmar," he points out. "Sure, you're only half-blooded, but you were raised in the ways of nobility all the same. Draven, who you claim to love so much, is a noble. Kiran is a noble." He strides toward her, but Rhea doesn't give him a single inch. Instead, she stands her ground and lifts her chin. "You spit on and reject the system which raised you only when it is convenient for you. *That* is your problem, Rhea."

She curls her fingers so tightly into her palms, her nails pierce her skin. "Kiran and Draven don't buy into the senseless bullshit like you do. Even if you weren't responsible for the death of my father and sister, I would still hate you for the way you cling to your foolish ideals and preach them like a gospel given from the gods themselves."

"Kiran and Draven don't bear the weight of their father's expectations like I do," he argues, his voice rising. "They aren't forced to believe in those ideals as I am." Yet he stiffens suddenly, catching his mistake.

Rhea huffs, her upper lip curling while she looks at him. "You're *so* right," she mocks, her low voice sewn from pure disdain. "Draven knows *nothing* of carrying the weight of his father's expectations. Knows not a *single* thing about being pressured into believing in nobility's self-righteous creed." She takes a step toward him, resulting in Finlay tilting his chin down to fully meet her eyes now that they are no more than a finger's length apart. "You want to know the difference between you and Draven, Frosty? He isn't a coward. He doesn't just blindly follow the expectations of a man who never deigned to truly care for him. Instead, he finds every way he can to stand against him. To fight back and rebel. To put the people who matter above the man who doesn't. But you?" Her eyes slowly rake over the entirety of his body, not holding back an inch of the disgust she feels for him. "You are the exact opposite. And that is what makes you a coward. That is what makes you weak."

Finlay flexes his jaw, but says nothing as he holds her scornful glare. Eventually, he flicks his eyes toward the window, where the moon has peaked in the charcoal sky. He slides his gaze back to her, where it lingers a heartbeat longer before he turns away from her.

"Training is over. You are dismissed."

RHEA WANDERS DOWN a green and red lined corridor, begrudgingly shuffling her feet across the scarlet carpet lining the floors, replaying her and Finlay's argument over and over as she imagines all the other words she could have said.

She makes her way deeper into the Elefet wing, burly looking men staring at her unabashedly, watching her with the sort of hungry glint in their eye that makes her skin prick. She glimpses women with seductive eyes and sneered lips watching her curiously as well, their displayed figures cut straight from the male gaze. Rhea hears their hissing whispers when she passes them.

No wonder Draven doesn't like to spend a lot of time in his own damn wing. She wouldn't want to spend time around these people either. But Tynan insists Draven only Select the most ruthless wielders who pass the exams, not wanting to show a glimmer of any weakness within House Dalmar or its heir. No—Draven Dalmar is only allowed to select the strongest. The most barbaric. The most willing to do what needs to be done to achieve their mission. Which is all the more reason for Rhea to fulfill her end of the bargain she made with Tynan.

She rounds a corner and stops short when she finds her brother with a scowl on his face, a woman with a plunging neckline and cropped shirt leaning against him as she attempts to show him her wielder's mark.

Oh, this ought to be good.

Rhea leans her shoulder against the wall she's peering around, folding her arms and crossing her ankles to enjoy the show.

"See, Captain Dalmar?" The girl purrs with a pitchy voice Rhea *knows* is grinding Draven down to his bones. "I swear it's grown longer from last year. I plan to show Master Cahlmon after my Advanced Wielding Techniques class today, but I just wanted your thoughts before I did."

Conveniently for this student—whoever she is—her wielder's mark consists of a small triangle resting at the base of her throat, a line cutting through the upper quadrant of it while ornamental lines punctuated by small dots encase the shape, descending down to a point just above her nearly exposed breasts.

Draven doesn't even glance near it, his simmering stare instead locked on her doe-eyed expression. "I have no thoughts." He takes a retreating step from the busty girl.

"You didn't even look," she pouts.

"I don't need to. I already know I have no thoughts on it nor do I care."

He makes to walk past her, but the girl steps forward and curls her fingers around Draven's annoyingly toned bicep—seriously, Rhea swears he must live to refine his muscles—and presses her chest into him while simultaneously tugging his arm into her as if she intended to hug it. With Draven's shirt being short-sleeved and her shirt cut the way it is, it brings them skin-to-skin.

"But it affects our aggregate," she pleads. "If my mark has truly grown, don't you realize what that means?"

Draven glances back over his shoulder, rage flaring in his eyes. "Remove yourself from my skin before I am forced to remove you myself."

The girl's mouth pops open, and she makes a show of letting go and stepping back. "You're not *listening* to me. Ever since that fucking lowborn whore showed up, you've stopped listening. Stopped caring about your own gods-damn aggregate." There is an undertone of genuine hurt threading through her words.

Draven turns around slowly—scarily so. He faces the girl with a horrifying look so empty, so cold, it sends a chill down Rhea's spine.

"Say that again," he commands, voice low enough to reach the under realm.

"I—I—" The girl flounders for words before she snaps her mouth shut and straightens her spine, lifting her chin to peer up at Draven. "It's true," she says steadily. "Everyone in Elefet is thinking it. Ever since that servant girl showed up for the exams, you've been distracted. And now after she's disappeared? You've been fucking *absent*. You are our *captain*, Draven. You are supposed to command us. Guide us. *Help* us. But frankly? Ever since that lowborn flittered through this place, it seems like you couldn't give two fucks less what happens within our aggregate. What happens to *us*." She slams her palm against her chest, clutching at her heart.

Draven remains expressionless. "I don't." Then he prowls toward the girl, his caged anger palpable.

Rhea blinks against what she thinks she's seeing. Because there is no way something as trivial and minor as this is *actually* causing Draven's veins to turn black—something he normally has on a tight leash.

"Let me be clear," he says, the calm hum of his voice scarier than any creature. "If it ever came down to it, and I was forced to choose between any members of this aggregate or her, I would choose her. No matter the circumstances. No matter the costs. No matter if the fucking stars would plummet from the very sky above our heads. I would choose her. I will *always* choose her."

The girl recedes as though physically slapped. "You would really pick her over us? She is a *lowborn servant*, Draven. And you? You're the gods-damn Dalmar *Heir*. She is beneath you. Is beneath *us*."

"That 'lowborn servant' has overcome more adversity, tragedy, cruelty—fucking *degradation*—than you could ever begin to imagine. Do not stand in front of me and speak as though you understand the strength of a mountain when your weakened spine bends as easily as a blade of trampled grass. That girl? *My* girl, to be clear. Despite everything she faced, she did not break. On even the hardest of fucking days, she did not let this world win." Draven scans the girl—whose eyes now brim with a mixture of hurt and confusion—with a sneer on his lips. "This aggregate is founded on the entirely wrong principles of what true strength is, and I am tired of indulging in its barbarism as if I buy into its fucked up ideology."

Rhea's brows fly up at the intensity of his words—she has never heard Draven speak about anyone like this.

He told Rhea about this girl, Lyra, through their weekly letters. But he never went into too much detail, in fear of their correspondence somehow ever being confiscated. It was overly cautious, of course, because letters written with an Ever-Know Quill fade away within minutes, only being held to the page for as long as the wielder's lakti can support the ink transfer, but even with those short notes he sent about Lyra, despite always coming across absolutely smitten, Rhea never expected to see him like this. At a level that could rival that of his devotion to her—which is saying a lot.

Her lips tug up with a smile at the thought; Draven happy, finally offering his delicate heart to someone. Lyra has no idea how lucky she is to receive it. How much it actually means that he's chosen to give it away.

Draven turns, clearly done with the conversation. Yet the girl reaches out for him again, still not finished, and Draven whirls around once she again presses her skin to his, a snarl on his lips. Rhea practically gulps when she sees black flicker in his eyes.

Oh, shit. Not good. *Not. Good.*

Without really thinking it through, Rhea leaves the corner behind and strides straight toward them. "Well, the tension in this corridor is certainly sharp enough to cut through steel."

Draven glances at her, stiffening. Until he exhales a quiet sigh, and his black veins slowly recede. He arches a brow at her, a question in his now beautifully normal gaze.

"And who are you?" The girl rakes her eyes down Rhea, a sneer pulling at her lips.

"Someone you don't want to fuck with." Rhea flashes her a tight-lipped grin before jerking her chin. "Now go, before Captain Dalmar here does something he regrets." She shoots him a very sharp look, silently letting him know she already saw the black in his eyes and veins.

The corner of his mouth quirks in a microcurve at Rhea's reprimanding. Yet when he turns his attention away from her, his face hardens, and even the smallest sign of warmth slips from his expression. He folds his arms. "You are dismissed," he says to the girl.

"But—"

"*Dismissed,*" he growls. "That's an order from your Captain, Kamina."

Kamina. So that's the girl's name.

Kamina glowers at him in disbelief before turning on her heels and heading in the opposite direction, muttering a string of curses too low for Rhea to fully hear. She stops just before disappearing behind a corner, turning her chin over her shoulder to glare at Draven. "You're going to regret everything you've said today. And when that time comes, I hope you feel like the fool you are for choosing the wrong side."

Draven's stony face and cold gaze offer her nothing in reply. Kamina tears her rage-lined eyes away from the sight of it.

Once she disappears, Rhea lets out a low whistle. "She's a hot-blooded one."

Draven blows out a long breath before turning to face her. "Can you *not* put a target on your back?"

"Whatever do you mean?" Rhea coos in her sweetest voice, fluttering her eyelashes.

He huffs a laugh and rolls his eyes, draping his huge arm over her shoulder while a smirk tips his lips. When Rhea inevitably bends forward from the annoyingly heavy weight, he pushes a knuckle into the top of her head, resulting in her tsking at him and shoving him off her.

"Cut it out," she demands, straightening both herself and her clothes. "I'm not a child anymore."

He cocks his head at that and takes those annoyingly big arms of his and folds them over his equally as annoying big chest. "Says the one pouting like one," he quips, amusement filling his eyes. "Your first training session was with Finlay today. Did you play nice?"

"Fuck no I didn't play nice. I *hate* him, Draven. You know that."

"Rhea," he admonishes.

She and Draven have had this conversation many times, and she has no interest in rehashing the ugly mess of it right now. Just because he was able to forgive Finlay for what he did doesn't mean she has any intentions to do so as well.

Seeming to sense her resolve, he drops his arms back down to his sides and sighs. "Are you at least going to explain to me what you're doing in Elefet's wing?"

"What? I need a reason to visit my dear, doting big brother?"

He huffs, clearly not convinced. He pins her beneath that spine-chilling gaze of his; the one which makes her feel as though he can see down to the very marrow of her bones.

"Fine," she concedes through a sigh. "I need your help with something."

His brows twitch, a small indent forming between them. "What is it? Has Tynan done something? Is he holding anything over your head?"

Well, technically yes.

But Rhea can't let Draven know that.

"No," she answers instead, guilt clotting inside her veins as she is forced to lie to him.

Yet Tynan's instructions were clear: if he is to uphold his end of their agreement, Draven is to not know anything about their bargain. And though Tynan is many things and has plenty of questionable qualities, not upholding his end of a deal has never been one of them. Unfortunately, he is also far too clever to lie to—with eyes and ears in every crevice of every place—and Rhea doesn't want to risk losing out on this opportunity by letting something slip free. She just needs to locate this forgotten tome and scribe the information inside by the Winter Solstice's ball without Draven finding out. Easy. Plus, after some asking around, she has a pretty good idea of where to find the ancient book.

"I want to enter the library."

Draven cocks a brow. "So enter the library."

"No. I want to enter the *library*."

His gaze sharpens at that. "Why?"

"Because I heard it has invaluable books on both nullifying magic *and* my style of combat. I want to grow stronger. Become unbeatable. You already know my aspirations."

It echoes through her like a pledge. *I want to kill Tynan Dalmar with my own two hands.*

Draven eyes her. "You're forbidden from entering."

"I know." She sways and bounces on her toes. "But you're not. I just need you to get me past the Overseer. I can nullify whatever magic blocks me from there on." At his hesitation, Rhea pulls out her sweetest expression and softest voice. "Please."

Draven glides a hand down his face, sighing. "If you get caught, I know nothing." He levels her with a stern gaze. "And I can't help you if there's a hearing with Bathara's Council—they're not exactly fans of mine."

Rhea's lopsided smirk is helpless. "You mean the people in positions of power don't like the super strong magic wielder who doesn't listen to anyone or anything?" She places a hand lightly to her chest. "I am *shocked*."

He rolls his eyes but chuckles. "Come on. I was just about to head toward Castaria's wing anyways, so I'll drop you off on the way."

Rhea follows. As they walk the corridor, down the stairs and through the courtyard, a sharp, unmovable resolve piles in her stomach. She will find this book before the Winter Solstice. She will provide the person who has loved and cared for her almost half his life with the basic right to make his own decisions—to be the force of nature he is in all its glory. To love the woman he has fallen for without restrictions.

And the first step to that begins now.

CHAPTER TWENTY

"Where are we going, exactly?" Gray asks, watching Kiran as he laces his black tunic.

"To a village that lies just north of Dead Man's Cove. Ninmere. We've received reports of a band of rogue wielders terrorizing residents of the town."

"And they're not Abdites?"

"Nope. Just your average group of criminals who use their magic for the wrong reasons."

Gray folds his arms, studying Kiran. "And you've taken a special interest in them because…?"

Kiran sighs, his smirk faltering. "I received a tip surrounding a brewing uprising not long ago, and I have been investigating the claim ever since. If what I've gathered thus far is to be trusted, the leader of this group might hold a big piece of the puzzle."

Gray feels his brows wrinkling at the information. "An uprising? What are they claiming to fight against?"

"I don't know. That is precisely the answer I am hoping to find out today." He finishes his tie enclosure before turning to face Gray. "Normally, you'd be forbidden from accompanying me on such a task, but given the new rules Bathara is adhering to, you can join my team without any resistance. Delightful, isn't it?"

"Unimaginably so," Gray jokes.

Over the passing months, he and Kiran have become close, spending time together training, testing how far he can push his illusionary magic and theorizing with Draven locations Lyra may be. Gray and Draven have also grown to have an understanding, ever since their time together in the greenhouse. They're friendly, even.

Together, they've deduced Lyra must be located somewhere on Erandor's southern border or within the Anatolè Kingdom's territory, based on her description of the sun. They ruled out the Arid Wastelands due to its harsh, barren climate making it largely uninhabitable, and they've now also removed Rivara from their search, not knowing of a single place within the kingdom where the sun shines red. So when Gray isn't attending his classes or mandatory training sessions outside of his private ones—and when Kiran and Draven aren't attending to their obligations as presiding captains—they are normally together, conspiring ways to best search their targeted areas and bring Lyra home.

He even joined Kiran and Draven for a late night drink recently. Draven had just returned from another search—this time toward the southeastern border, near the port city of Halfin—and Gray wanted to hear his report. They had already opened a bottle by the time he arrived, and so the expected brief conversation turned into a nearly all night one. Gray's resulting hangover was brutal, and he soon learned Draven and Kiran are not to be underestimated when it comes to holding their drink. Especially not when Draven is drinking away his frustrations.

Kiran rests a firm hand on Gray's shoulder, his expression shifted. "I will only be saying this to you, Nightenjoy. This mission is layered. And if we succeed and I am able to interrogate the rogue wielders' leader, I may not only glean more insight on the growing uprising, but perhaps information surrounding Lyra as well. While I can't be certain, the man is deeply connected to the skull trade, rumored to be overflowing with powerful secrets." He pauses, eyes hardening. "We cannot fail. I swore to Draven we wouldn't."

Gray holds his stare. "Then we won't."

"Good." Kiran slides his hand from his shoulder.

Gray asks, "Why isn't Draven coming with us?"

"He can't," Kiran says through a sigh. "He's been dispatched with members of his own aggregate elsewhere."

Gray nods. "And who else from Castaria will be accompanying us?"

Kiran doesn't answer, instead slipping back into his usual demeanor, offering him only a mischievous smirk. It tells Gray two things simultaneously. The first is that he probably asked Marcella to join them—a fact which both excites and unnerves Gray, seeing as the more time they spend together, the more Gray is unsure of how to act. He's never been one to consider himself shy with girls. In fact, he's overall been quite bold in his life when it comes to someone he has taken interest in. But with Marcella, it's different. Complicated—even if his feelings, in a sense, are so simple. She is progressing through her stages of grief. Lyra is still missing. And the foundation of Bathara is trembling beneath their very feet as the academy attempts to rebuild. So Gray continues lying to himself, ignoring the flutters of butterfly wings in his stomach when she's near and the acceleration of his pulse when he gazes into Marcella's glittering cobalt eyes.

As if summoned by his thoughts, Kiran's chamber door swings open, and Marcella steps through the threshold. She is dressed in a deep-blue top that laces at her throat and gray pants that flare just slightly around her thighs, tapering at the ankles. Her mane of copper hair is twisted back into a braid, revealing the full depth of her features.

Gray's eyes trail over her, noting every freckle, line, and tiny mark composing her face. His eyes snag on the slope of her lips, but he catches himself and quickly tugs them away—only to drown in the most beautiful sea of blue he's ever seen.

Marcella watches him, an arch in her brow. "What?" she teases. "Surprised Kiran asked me to tag along or something?"

Gray noticed long ago Marcella tends to deflect with humor when she feels vulnerable or judged. Though, why she would feel such a thing right now with him, he can't be certain.

Gray folds his arms over his chest, a smile lifting his lips. "Not in the slightest."

"Good."

Kiran bounces his gaze between the two of them. He clears his throat. "I hear atop of your impressive skills with magic, you are also a skilled tracker."

Marcella plops herself down in a lounging chair. "I am."

"Castles and estates aren't the only places where one can learn things," Gray chimes in, winking at Marcella.

Her eyes crinkle at the corners as a helpless grin sweeps over her lips.

The sight makes Gray's heart squeeze tight in his chest, and for a heartbeat, as their eyes remain gridlocked, he forgets where they are. That they aren't alone.

Marcella clears her throat, pulling her gaze away from him. "Will anyone else from Castaria be joining us?"

Kiran cocks his head, mocking a hollow sort of consideration. "Not exactly."

Right on cue, a knock sounds at the door.

"It's open," Kiran practically sings.

The latch clicks and the hinges squeak as the wood creaks open. Gray realizes then he was correct on the second thing he surmised from Kiran's smirk a moment ago: expect something entirely unexpected.

Nuri, Klytis, and the Nullifier—now known to be Draven's little sister—step through the threshold. Gray tugs at his brows as he glances at Kiran, confused why members of other aggregates are here, then strolls over and outstretches his arm to Klytis. He beams as he embraces Gray, clasping his hand to Gray's outstretched forearm.

"It's good to finally get to you see," Gray says through a small bout of laughter.

Klytis chuckles. "It's almost cruel, isn't it? Being at the academy together but in separate aggregates with no aligning classes."

Gray snorts his disdain for that. "We have so much to catch up on."

Klytis's expression shifts, and though his smile remains on his lips, there is now a solemnness to it. "Indeed, we do."

They drop their arms back down to their sides, and Gray glances at the Nullifier, who is leaning against the wall on the far side of the room, her knee bent as her booted foot is propped up behind her. She is dressed in all black clothing, matching the dark kohl lining her eyes and the color of her half-drawn hair.

He walks over to her and outstretches his hand. "Gray," he offers.

"Rhea." There is a rough quality to her tone, though not exactly in the sound itself. She places her palm in Gray's, and they offer each other a quick shake. When finished, she folds her arms over her chest, a bored expression punctuating her features once more.

Gray studies her for a heartbeat longer, surprised to find someone who has mastered the art of stoicism as well as Draven. Then again, he supposes he is looking at the product of being raised in House Dalmar all the same.

He turns on his heels and finds Nuri and Marcella already engaged in hushed conversation. He strides to them next, inclining his head. "Nuri," he says.

"Gray Nightenjoy," she replies with a level of diplomacy that seems practiced, her Anatolian accent heavy as ever on her tongue.

He forces a civil smile to his lips. That sun pendant he noticed on her neck the first time they met is conveniently gone. Instead, it is replaced with a nondescript gold chain which matches the quality of the gold piercings lining her ears and ringing around her left nostril. Gray does a quick scan for any other notable jewelry or clothes, but there's nothing.

He finds that deeply interesting.

"Is something the matter?" she asks, not taking her eyes off him.

"Not in the slightest," he answers, his tone soft and pleasant. "I was just thinking how grateful I am to have you as our healer again. You were pivotal in our success during the second test of the entrance exam, so it brings me comfort knowing you'll be accompanying us."

Marcella snorts and props her elbow on the arm of the chair, cupping her chin in her palm. "Get a room," she mutters tauntingly.

Nuri huffs an amused laugh. "Kind of you to say."

As he watches her, he reflects on her explosion during the conscription announcement. Naturally, one could easily chalk that up to her being someone who loves her kingdom and refuses to believe it would outright deny such a diplomatic request, but with Nuri, it seemed deeper than that. Like the current of mistrust and scrutiny running through her stems from something different than simple disbelief. She *knows* something. Something specific about the Anatolé Kingdom, leading to her outburst.

Of course, one small thread is not enough to suspect a spider. However, when there are numerous threads all leading to the center of a hidden web, it's logical to then believe a spider is out there somewhere. At face value, there is no reason to suspect Nuri of anything and attribute her outburst to dedication. But when remembering her essence flower—Goldenlight, a flower which has only bloomed for *exceptional*, longstanding magical bloodlines since its conception—and the lavish sun pendant forged in materials far exceeding what a simple merchant's daughter should have access to, Gray finds it perfectly reasonable at this point to have questions about Nuri.

Though he chooses to let all that go for now and focus on their task at hand.

He turns to Kiran. "How were you able to get approval to recruit wielders outside your aggregate? This is a Castaria assignment, meaning it should be fulfilled only by members of Castaria, according to Bathara's rules. How'd you pull it off?"

The corner of Kiran's mouth tugs up. "Bathara is in a very delicate state at the moment, and this is a very delicate mission. I needed wielders I could trust, and so I made personal pleas to all three of their presiding captains. They signed their consent, and once I showed that to Josiah, he signed off as well. A lot more work than I typically like, but it'll be worth it." Kiran glances at Klytis, his smirk shifting into something more like a helpless smile. "Plus, Klytis here is the most experienced aether-wielder Bathara now has. Being that he previously served King Alastair, he has been far across the Three Kingdoms and thus can open more portals than any other aether-wielder here can."

Klytis drags his fingers through his auburn hair—bordering more brown than red—as his pale blue eyes drop to the ground, a twitching smile consuming his lips. "Thanks," he mutters, seeming suddenly shy.

And...

Gray has never known Klytis to be shy with anyone.

Rhea snorts from her side of the room. "I'm surprised my asshole of a captain signed off on me being here."

Though it takes a few seconds, Kiran finally drags his eyes away from Klytis to look at Rhea. "Your captain *is* indeed an asshole, but in the case of you, my dearest, I did not leave him much of a choice. "

Rhea's answering smirk is purely wicked. "And that's why I love you."

Kiran winks at her. "The feeling is entirely mutual." Then, he claps his hands together, skimming his eyes across every face in the room. "Now then, shall we be on our way?"

NINMERE IS a small coastal city built on lush green scattered across undulating hills, the unignorable red mountainous rock of the Burning Bluffs hovering in the western background, the sight at once eerie and magnificent.

Luckily for their group, Klytis has been to Ninmere once before. A few years back, King Alastair was seeking to strike a trade agreement on the mineral resources Ninmere sits upon. According to Klytis, they stayed with the governing lord over the area, which is why he is able to open a portal directly in the heart of the clustered city—with the presiding Lord previously insisting on a full, merry tour.

When they arrive, the sky is an odd mix of gold, blue, and red. Gray guesses it is a result of the radical heat emitted from Illithious

Lake and the Burning Bluffs surrounding it. It leaves the sky to look as though it is fading into a sunset, despite them arriving midday. Truthfully, it's breathtaking and unlike anything Gray has ever seen before.

They raise their hoods on the nondescript cloaks Kiran provided each of them before beginning their trek through the city's cobble-stoned streets. A mix of stone buildings—some built with brown bricks and terracotta roofs while others are carved in smooth beige stone with red-tinted roofs—cluster around the streets. As they walk, they pass a lively market filled with stalls selling fresh seafood, salted fish, jewelry, fruits, and baked goods—the buzz floating from the area a soft tune which seems to be the heartbeat of the city. A peculiar smell of sea salt, fish, and marine wax floats through the streets, and Gray isn't quite sure if he loves it or finds it abhorrent.

Kiran leads them deeper through the city, toward the coastline overlooking Glass Water Gulf, Klytis following him in stride. Nuri and Rhea walk a few paces behind them, and Marcella trails behind them. Gray takes up the rear, casting wary glances as he maintains sharp vigilance of everything around them.

He slams into a body directly in front of him.

"What the—"

Marcella stares up at him, and though her face is covered by hooded shadows, he can still make out her taunting look of disapproval. "Focusing too hard on everything beside you will result in you missing what's directly in front of you."

Gray frowns. "I didn't think I had to watch out for someone from my own team."

"Mistake number one." A pause. And then, "You can let go of me now, Gray."

It takes him a few seconds to process her words. A few pounding heartbeats to realize his hand remains tightened on Marcella's waist, bracketing the dip of her curves while his other hand is curled around her shoulder from his attempt to balance her after their collision. "Oh," he mutters, thankful for his hood now more than ever as heat scorches his cheeks. "Apologies." He removes his hands and clears his throat.

She laughs. "You're fine."

They regard each other, the rhythm of their breaths slowing as the world dims into a quiet lull. He thinks he should say something. Perhaps she feels the same, seeing as her lips crack open then close. Yet before either of them musters any courage, instead only seeming capable of studying the other, shouts erupt in the distance.

"Rogues! The Rogues are here!"

A rotund man with a balding head and long sideburns barrels between Gray and Marcella. Gray grabs him, spinning him around and bracing him by the shoulders. "What's going on?" he asks, trying to calm the hysteric man.

A mix of impatience and urgency flickers in the man's eyes. "Take shelter. Board your windows." His gruff voice is quickened. He does a fast inventory of Gray's body. "Traveler, I suspect. Your inn will know what to do. Get there immediately. The Rogues are moving!"

With that, he shakes off Gray and runs down the street. Not more than a few heartbeats pass before a resounding *boom* echoes through the air as magic clashes against magic.

"Shit," Marcella curses under her breath.

"Come on," Gray says, realizing their group is no longer in sight. "We need to catch up with them."

As they sprint toward the noise, Gray can't help but wonder how they fell so far behind in the first place. It couldn't have been more than a few passing seconds that he and Marcella stopped…

Right?

He shakes his head, frustration coiling in his chest as he is forced to acknowledge his thoughts scatter when he is near Marcella. She is the unbidden Moon and he is the bewitched Tide—her magnetic force capable of pulling him in whichever direction she pleases.

Their sprint leads them to a sprawling stone quay, the buildings now far behind them while the stretch of oceanic water glistens in front of them. A series of fishing boats and sailboats rest docked in the small marina. One such boat finds itself caught in the crossfire as a wielder with a half-shorn head and a tattoo stretching across his cheek slams burning wind magic into its wooden frame in an attempt to deflect Kiran's flames. The flames mostly die in the water, but a small ember catches the cloth sail, spreading up and up as it chews the ship's structure away with fiery teeth. Gray curses under his breath.

They didn't bring a water-wielder or an ice-wielder with them. Not to mention, Marcella's magic would only feed the flames, and Gray's illusions can do nothing to stop the truth of destruction. Nuri is a healer. Klytis an aether-wielder. Rhea *would* have been able to stop the fire if she were able to reach the flames before they made contact with the sailboat, but now that the element has collided with something else, it is no longer magic fueling it. Just pure, reactive science.

"Shit," he mutters again.

Gray quickly assesses everyone's positions. He counts nine rogue wielders, and he doesn't sense any others. Nuri is locked in hand-to-hand combat with a man featuring slimy black hair and a scar marring his left eye, her daggers moving swiftly and efficiently. He remembers when Nuri said she was quite proficient with daggers. She wasn't exaggerating.

Rhea wields dual daggers as well, fighting against two men and one woman at once. By engaging them in combat, she is well within her range to nullify their magic, and Gray can visibly see the frustration and confusion on their faces as they are forced to go blow-for-blow with Rhea while reaching for magic that won't answer.

Klytis has taken on a supporting role a small distance behind the battle, attempting to redirect magic attacks where possible by opening small portals and casting the magic out over the water in the middle of the gulf, away from anyone or anything. Gray suspects he took up the position after the sailboat caught fire.

Which still leaves the matter of the burning ship. If left unattended, the growing blaze will soon spread to the other ships, and a raging inferno their group is incapable of extinguishing will tear across the marina as a result, destroying everything in its wake.

Gray balls his hands at his sides, spotting Kiran last as he battles at the center of the chaos. He fights against a wind-wielder—who, at this point, can reasonably be deemed the strongest of the Rogues—a water-wielder, and a fire-wielder. While wind and water is not an ideal match up for Kiran, from what Gray sees, he is handling himself fine.

It leaves Gray feeling confident in what he's chosen to do.

Marcella takes a quick step, preparing to sprint toward the ongoing battle, but Gray reaches out and grabs her wrist, pulling her back toward him as gently as he can manage. "Wait." At her sharp glare, Gray releases his hold on her and exposes his raised palms.

"I swear to the gods, Gray Nightenjoy, if you just stopped me to spew some bullshit about safety, I—"

"No," Gray interjects, cutting her off, not wanting to waste time. "That's not it in the slightest. I have a plan, but I need your help." His eyes bounce between Marcella and the burning sailboat, the fire becoming an increasing threat to the other ships surrounding it. Time is against him, and it makes him jittery with anticipation.

A wrinkle forms between Marcella's brows, and she traces Gray's line of sight to the burning ship. She shakes her head. "That isn't our priority. The ships can burn for a bit while we neutralize the Rogues before they harm anyone. The ships are on the water, away from buildings *and* pedestrians. This is as straightforward a decision as they come, emphasized in our classes."

Gray shifts on his feet. "From a tactical standpoint, I know you're right, but—"

"—but *nothing*, Gray! We're in our first active assignment, acting as Jurafen would. Don't mess it up. Leave it *alone*."

Gray flexes his jaw. "These people, this city—they are fishermen. It is a *fishing* town, Marcella."

"*So?!*" she asks, eyes wild and voice incredulous.

"So those boats are their livelihoods!" His arm makes a sweeping gesture toward the burning sailboat and the docks awaiting an untimely demise. "If they're destroyed, most of the families residing here will lose their source of income. It will plunge them into poverty, and who knows if they will even be able to scrape together the resources to replace their burned ships. Children will go hungry. Men may result to crime. And who can say how it might affect the trade markets. Is that really what you want?"

Marcella slides her tongue along the grooves of her teeth. Eventually, she darts her narrowed stare to the now burning mast, then at Kiran and the others—who have already rendered two Rogues unconscious, someone already having bound them in magic blocking manacles.

She rubs at her forehead, blowing out a long sigh after. "Tell me what to do."

CHAPTER TWENTY-ONE

MARCELLA

Marcella's feet pound against the quay as she advances. She throws a palm out, sending two thick vines racing toward the wielder's ankles. They slither around the lip of her stained boots like living snakes, and Marcella yanks her arm back, sending the Rogue plummeting to her back and sliding across the stone. Then, Marcella waits as the woman reorients herself. Waits until the woman realizes it was Marcella who forced her to the cold stone.

As anticipated, the rogue wielder is furious. "You dirty bitch."

"Dirty?" Marcella pretends to be offended. "This coming from the one covered in *actual* filth?" She makes her words ooze with condescension.

The woman's face stains a near-tinted purple from her rage. She scrambles to her feet, barely balanced before she is making a fluid motion, dragging loose hands from where the gulf surrounds them and toward the quay stretching between them. Sharp streams of twisting water shoot for Marcella, and she drops down, slamming her palms into the ground. Winding branches curl and twirl over themselves, forming an arched wall which covers her. The water slams into the creaking branches, leaving only tiny droplets to splash against Marcella's cheeks.

She lifts her palms and rises, dropping the wall. The woman glares at her with a curled lip and twisted features, rearing back, preparing for her next strike. Marcella frowns at her for only a second.

Then she turns on her heels and runs in the opposite direction.

The woman seems too stunned by the gesture to chase after her at first, but it isn't long until Marcella hears stomping footsteps and angry shouts echoing after her. "Coward! Fight me like a real woman would. What—can only get your blows in when the person isn't paying attention to you? Hey! HEY!"

Marcella doesn't slow to glance over her shoulder or call back to the enraged Rogue. No. She only stops once she reaches the tiny, glowing red flower carved into the stone, so utterly missable, a person would *really* have to be looking for it. Or simply already know it's there, like Marcella does.

She halts right atop of it, and the flower sizzles and flares beneath her feet before disappearing. A serene portrait is painted behind her of placid water glittering beneath the peculiar sky, bleeding red and gold while still cradling blue hues. It's odd, but in a way, it reminds her of the sunrises she would watch as a small child back home in the Anatolé Kingdom—so, to an extent, its strangeness is also comforting.

The water-wielder halts a few paces in front of the scene, panting for breath. "Nowhere to run now, Coward."

Marcella mocks a cool shrug. "Guess you'll have to try to hit me with one of those pathetic water attacks you wield so poorly."

The Rogue's brows slam together and she jerks her head back, like she can't believe what she's just heard. "You want to say that again... *Coward?*"

Marcella tugs at her lips, her smile sickeningly sweet. "I think once was enough, actually."

The small wielder's mark on the Rogue's wrist—a curling three wing design branching from a central circle—glows blue. She bends her knees and outstretches her arms, performing a series of fluid movements that, under any other circumstance, Marcella would actually find quite pretty. Given the intricacy and precision of them, actually, it's clear this girl has been trained—and by somebody *good*, no less.

Interesting.

The Rogue sends a spiraling torrent of water at Marcella, the thick, crystal-hued streams pelting her with a fierceness capable of cracking stone. And the attacks do not stop coming. No—the Rogue is pissed and her frayed nerves are clearly burning with a personal vendetta from Marcella's taunts and actions. So she continues sending one roaring stream after the other, annihilating Marcella with all she has.

Eventually, the Rogue hunches over her knees and heaves in gasping breaths. Beads of sweat form along her dark brow, and she swipes them away with the back of her hand. A smug smirk curls the corner of her lips when she sees Marcella's body strewn across the stone ground. A smirk that quickly twitches before fading altogether as the sky flickers. Once. Twice.

The illusion Gray weaved over the area fades, taking the image he conjured of Marcella with it, revealing instead an incinerated sailboat whose flames have now been entirely doused by the woman's water magic. Marcella steps out from around the stack of crates and barrels lining the quay's ledge—positioned just perfectly to where the woman can't see her but Gray can—and she smirks at the Rogue, her hand braced—albeit a bit smugly—on her hip. The Rogue's face pales, and she shakes her head as she tries to make sense of what the hell she is seeing.

"But... but you were just—just *there*." She points at the blackened ship, burnt probably to the point of irreparability.

Marcella mocks a perplexed expression, her lips falling into a confused frown. "Now how could I be where that ship is if I'm standing right here? I don't know of any magic that allows a wielder to duplicate themselves. Do you?"

The woman's mouth flounders like a fish. "But...but..."

The sound of metal clasping together *clinks* in the salty air as Kiran snaps the magic-inhibiting manacles on the Rogue's wrist, catching her entirely off guard. "Well played," he drawls wryly, glancing at Marcella with an amused yet proud smile splitting his lips.

She shrugs, feigning indifference. "It was Gray's idea."

He huffs a laugh. "So it was." He guides the girl over to the seated circle of formally captured criminals, shoving her down next to another woman with an admirable amount of gentleness.

Nuri, Klytis, and the new girl who introduced herself as Rhea stride toward her. It looks like all the rogue wielders have been apprehended, and a quick scan over her fellow teammates' bodies reveals a few cuts and bruises, but nothing to be concerned about. She whips her eyes back to the smoking ship, searching. Yet she is unable to find Gray.

She knows he had positioned himself near the bow of the sailboat, claiming it would help him cast a more believable illusion if he were actually central to the image. Naturally, Gray cast the illusion over the area itself, so Marcella was seeing what the Rogue was, but she swore she caught glimpses of his blurry figure once or twice.

Or maybe she was imagining it, just desperate to know he was okay.

As she stares on, tapping her foot, the townspeople slowly trickle out from their hiding places, crowding around to catch glimpses of the aftermath. Most everyone appears tentative—hesitant. Like they are treading on ice, and at any given moment, the smooth surface might crack and plunge them somewhere they don't want to be trapped within.

A woman's shrill voice pierces through the quiet. "Edmund! Guinevere!" She sprints through the crowd, her movements frantic and without a lick of grace. Marcella steps out to meet the hysterical woman, yet she pays her no mind, attempting to barrel through her instead.

A whoosh of wind pushes past Marcella's lips from the impact. Yet she grips the woman by the elbows and attempts to steady her flailing —alongside her own loss of balance.

"Let me go!" The woman demands. "My children are in there! My *children!*"

Marcella's stomach sours. "What?" she asks, her brows furrowing as disbelief, confusion—perhaps even denial—send a chill down her spine. "Where? Your children are where?"

"*There!*" She points at the charcoaled sailboat, ash flakes wafting through the air, punctuating the destruction with a false sense of calm. "My son, Edmund, was teaching his younger sister how to work the sails and steer the ship today. He is twelve, and she is eight. I—I tried to get to them," she explains. Her hands tremble. "But I am a seamstress and was out on a delivery. The family whose home I was in boarded their doors at the announcement of the Rogues, and I..." She stops, physical pain coating her features. "I couldn't get out. Couldn't...couldn't get to them." Tears well in her eyes, but the mother steels her voice in lieu of letting emotion rattle it. "Edmund!" she shouts again. "Guinevere!"

A splintering crack splits the air, and the slow groan of breaking wood echoes cruelly. Marcella turns her chin over shoulder, the move shaky. Disbelieving. She still can't find Gray anywhere on the ship, but she does find the burnt mass collapsing, crashing forward and obliterating the entire front of the boat—loud cracks and creaks booming as profoundly as a thunderclap.

The ship caves in on itself, and Marcella loses her grip on the mother entirely, her body going slack as splintered wood pieces soar through the air while the sailboat caves in on itself from the impact, water immediately flooding the remaining small cradle, weighing it down, down, down as the gulf officially claims the marred boat as its own.

The world pulses then freezes. Her heart skips through its beats, then she swears it just stops trying altogether. She sees no movement. No bodies.

Had Gray been hurt somehow by the Rogue's attacks? No. *No.* There is no way he would have been foolish enough to be hit by an attack he knew was coming. Yet...

Where the hell *is* he? Why can't she find him?

Against every defiant fiber in her body, she sees crimson-stained lips and fading eyes. Feels a growing cold in her palms as words swirl softly in her mind like a lament.

Be happy, Marcella.

She runs her hands through her braided hair. How the hell is she supposed to be happy when misfortune keeps befalling everyone she dares to actually give a shit about?

"Edmund! Guinevere!" The mom barrels toward the sinking boat, and Marcella snaps out of it, running for her and catching the woman by the waist.

There is a full crowd now, everyone watching with somber eyes and thin lips at the display unfolding before them.

"I'm sorry," Marcella murmurs, the emotion pressing against the words not at all faked. "But I can't let you kill yourself by running onto a sinking ship."

The mother whirls around on Marcella. "If my children die," she cries, tears falling steadily down her cheeks while her eyes are punctuated by cold lines. "I may as well already be dead."

Marcella feels a warm prick in her own eyes, and she pulls her bottom lip between her teeth before it can tremble. Her heart, her chest—the entirety of all she is—aches at the thought of facing life without Gray Nightenjoy.

He came into her life like a flash of brilliant light, becoming someone so pivotal, she didn't realize he had become a pillar to her very foundation until he was just stolen away, toppling her world around her. When she wouldn't speak—grief too heavy on her tongue—he came to her room every single day and laid quietly on the bed opposite her so she didn't have to be alone. When she refused food, Gray saw to it that she would eat. At least... *something.* When she was willing to give up, he helped her hold on. When she sobbed over Lyra, over Griff, he held her. When she feared going into classes for the first time, he held her hand. He was there for her.

Since the beginning, from the very first moment their paths crossed, he had *always* shown up for her.

And now he's just—what? *Gone?*

A sob pounds in Marcella's chest, but she refuses to let it out in front of all these people. Instead, she turns her back on the ugly scar sure to permanently mar her heart. She is seconds away from guiding the mother away from the scene, too, but then a series of hushed murmurs and gasps buzz through the quay. One by one, spectators lift stiff fingers, pointing at something behind her. Marcella whips her head over her shoulder, something a lot like hoping blooming in her chest.

A choked gasp escapes her at what she sees.

Gray treads across the dock, onto the base of the stone quay. He is dripping wet, soot-stains still somehow pressed into his tattered clothes. His face looks dirty, though not as dirty as Marcella is sure it was before dipping into the water. A trail of fresh blood rolls down from his temple. But he is alive—beautifully, perfectly, astonishingly *alive*. And perhaps most notable of all—

He is carrying two children.

One is draped loosely over his back, the boy's wounded arms clinging to Gray's neck, while a small girl with red-tinted hair lays unconscious in his arms. She has burn marks on her face, and her lips are a chilly blue. Gray has removed his cloak and wrapped the small girl inside it, but... it doesn't look like it'll be enough.

The mother sprints for Gray, meeting him halfway. She is a frantic mess, seeming to want to check over her son but knowing she needs to attend to her too pale daughter. He hands the child over to her, carefully removing the stirring boy from his back next.

"Guinevere?" the boy rasps beside his unmoving sister. "*Guinevere?*"

The mother begins pressing forcefully against the girl's sternum, but she makes no more than two movements before Nuri rushes to her knees beside the mother.

"I'm a healer, and a student at Bathara," she offers by way of explanation.

The mother blinks furiously, but ultimately nods her head, a small whimper of panic slipping past her lips. "Please," she murmurs. "Save her."

Nuri wastes no time, golden light pouring from her palms. Kiran steps forward, his hood firmly in place, and cups a flickering flame in his palm, hovering it over the girl's body, controlling the temperature with such precision, it does no damage to the child's skin.

A few heart-stuttering minutes pass. Eventually, the girl coughs, her skin flushes, and the burn marks littered across her body fade. Her eyes flutter open, and she sits up, confusion pinching her delicate features. Yet the moment her mother's face enters her focus, the child throws her arms around her mother's neck and nestles into her like safety is a place and she has returned to her haven. Danger cannot touch a child when locked in her mother's arms.

The crowd erupts with claps and cheers, joyous to witness a happy ending in a world filled with cruel, bitter ends. One man with a bushy white mustache waltzes over to Marcella, his quality tunic and trousers telling her he probably holds some position of power within the town. "My dear girl," he says, voice jubilant. "Whoever is that boy, and what in the name of the gods have I just witnessed here?"

Marcella gazes at Gray, who watches the boy, small girl, and their mother reunite in a trembling, tear-stricken embrace, his soft eyes crinkled at the corners. She smiles, the action as genuine and helpless as anything she has experienced since the attack on Bathara.

"His name is Gray Nightenjoy," she says.

Then she tells the man everything.

MARCELLA WATCHES Kiran as he paces in front of the burning hearth, chatter from the front of the modest inn ringing softly in the distance. He glides a hand absently along his jaw as he swims in his thoughts.

After the dizzying spectacle, their group had to reorient their attention back to the captured Rogues. The identified leader—the man Nuri was fighting, with the long black hair and scar marring his eye—was confirmed to have a Skull Trader tattoo hidden on his forearm. Currently, he finds himself bound and kept in the inn's cellar, nothing but a thin bedroll and a pot to keep him company.

Well, until Kiran makes a decision, that is.

The man refuses to talk, and Kiran is growing restless. Desperate, even. He hasn't told Marcella exactly what information he is trying to extract—though based on his stricken features, she suspects it has to do with Casimir Vivaldri or something of the like.

"Gray's illusionary magic would thrive in this scenario," Marcella offers from her nearby tufted chair, attempting to lessen the weight of his decision. "You can make the man see and feel all kinds of things to loosen his tongue, and there would be little risk to it."

Kiran halts his pacing, shooting her an uncharacteristically disparaging look. "Please," he scoffs, though not with malice. "You and I both know the last place Gray Nightenjoy should be anywhere near is a… physically involved…interrogation."

Marcella huffs an absent laugh, not sure if she appreciates or is irritated by the delicate way he attempts to put it. "He might surprise you," Marcella pushes. "I think there's more to him than just noble deeds and moral will." She remembers that first judgment. The way he had grabbed the man later identified as his cousin, Huxley, by the shirt, gold flickering in his eyes. Marcella thought she had imagined it, but later, when Lyra finally discussed all the details with her, what she had seen in that moment was confirmed.

Kiran shakes his head, the curves of his lips tugging up gently. "Well, let's not go out of our way to taint the best of us, hm?" Marcella opens her mouth to speak, but before she can, Kiran raises a silencing hand. "Besides," he continues. "Whatever information the man has, I want to be the only one to hear it. It's just…" he trails off, taking a moment. "I never have been good at this part of gathering intel."

"Let me guess," Marcella quips dryly. "Draven and Finlay were better?"

He laughs. "Much, much better." There is a fondness to his words, which is odd, considering the subject matter.

Still, Marcella feels no need to press the issue, and Kiran clearly has no desire to keep talking about it. So, she reorients her attention to the piece of parchment clasped between his fingers. The parchment which has remained permanently within his grip since receiving it.

She nods toward the item. "What's that?"

He frowns down at the parchment before bringing it up to his face, scanning its contents once more. Marcella thinks this is the third... fourth...no, definitely fifth...time he's done so, his brows heavily wrinkled as he stares at the letter. "It's nothing." His tone betrays him, yet he continues on anyhow. "I sent correspondence to my parents letting them know I was nearby. I was planning to make a stop at my family's home, Emberthorne, before going back to Bathara. But..."

"But...?" Marcella pushes.

The wrinkle in his brow deepens. "But I just received word back from them informing me they are unavailable to take visitors at this time. Including myself."

"And that's odd?" she asks, not having the slightest idea what is and isn't normal for a Great House Heir.

"Very," he replies. Marcella considers probing, but before she gets the chance, Kiran folds the letter neatly and stuffs it into his pocket. "No matter," he says, shaking his head while his brows do a little jump on his forehead. "They are probably just preparing for the upcoming Winter Solstice ball. I'm not sure why, but I've heard Talderine has spared no expense this time around. Supposedly, they are giving it some extravagant theme this year."

"What's the theme?"

He shrugs, shifting back into his usual demeanor. "No one knows yet. They're waiting to make a grand announcement."

"Who's making an announcement?" Rhea strides into the sitting area and plops herself down on the chair adjacent to Kiran, sinking back and immediately propping her feet up on the mahogany table.

"Talderine," Kiran supplies. "We were discussing the upcoming Winter Solstice ball. For whatever reason, it's supposed to be quite the spectacle this year."

Rhea wrinkles her nose, and for a second, Marcella swears she looks like she is going to spit on the ground at the mention.

"I'll take it you're not a fan?" Marcella asks, a small arch notched in her brow.

"Talderine and everyone within its pompous walls can burn in the realms of hell for all I care." Rhea doesn't even look at her when she says it, instead inspecting her black-painted nails. "In fact, Kiran? Care to torch any cities soon?"

"Not particularly," he hums, sitting down on the far end of the long wooden chaise boasting worn beige cushions. He folds one leg over the other, props an elbow up on the circular arm, then rests his cheek lazily against his fist.

Marcella turns her attention back to Rhea, regarding her. Gray had filled Marcella in on Rhea and Draven's background when Marcella was ready to put laxatives in both their food—a method she thought Lyra would appreciate—after watching her and Draven embrace each other like their lives depended on it in front of the entire academy.

Though, looking back on it now, even Marcella had to concede perhaps using the mildly toxic plants she had grown with her flora magic mixed in with a concoction which supposedly made hair fall out was a bit much.

Still, Rhea is different than Marcella imagined. Rough around the edges and jagged as a saw blade, sure, but that's not what's caught her most off guard. It's the glimmers of hatred Marcella catches her randomly showing. A raw, festering vendetta against the world. Yet in spite of that, today, she's also caught glimpses of her softness. Even now, Rhea's stony expression crumbles into something tender and loving as she gazes at Kiran, a small curve tugging at the corner of her mouth.

Truthfully, Marcella hasn't fully decided what she thinks of the Nullifier. She doesn't dislike her by any means—in fact, she finds the girl rather badass and admirable. It's more that she isn't entirely sure what to make of her—if she can *trust* her.

Nuri, Klytis, and Gray come strolling in, Klytis clapping Gray on the shoulder and beaming. "They can't stop talking about you! Do you hear them outside?" He swoons his voice to mimic that of the crowd who gathered in front of the inn once their group's whereabouts had been leaked. "*Lion! Lion!*" Klytis snorts, tapping his fingers against Gray. "Wait until your father hears of this. He's going to smile from ear to bloody ear."

Rhea lifts a dark brow. "Why *lion?*"

Klytis looks positively jovial. "Lion of the Heart. That's what they're calling him."

"That's dumb," she deadpans, returning her attention to her nail beds.

Klytis's mouth pops open right as Nuri sits down on the floor next to Marcella, who barks a laugh at Rhea's quip. One glance at Kiran reveals he is laughing quietly at the comment as well, though his eyes remain glued to the roaring hearth.

Gray sits down next to Kiran, chuckling lightly, and Klytis sits next to him.

Look at that, the team's all here.

Well, not everyone...

Marcella's smile dies, fading as quickly as a shooting star breaking across a horizon. As if noticing her shift in demeanor, Gray sobers from his bout of laughter, tilting his head almost imperceptibly as he studies her.

Marcella can't meet his questioning gaze.

Not after what she realized. Not after feeling the things she did while thinking he had sunk alongside that ship.

Heat stings her cheeks, and she cups her chin in her palm—splaying her fingers across her skin—as she attempts to look bored and hide the forming red mess. She realizes she's missed some of the passing conversation, caught in a web of her own thoughts. By the time she's tuned back in, it seems they are teasing Klytis for something.

"What would you have had me do?" Klytis protests, his tone light-hearted. "Let stray blasts of magic pelt you guys in the face?"

Nuri giggles, shaking her head. Her knees are tucked into her chest, revealing the golden sun stitched into the hem of her tapered pants. "Of course not," she assures him through her soft laughter. "But your motives do not change the fact that Rhea *is* correct—we are forced to stay in this inn tonight because you drained too much of your magical resources by doing so."

Klytis slouches, seeming to nearly fold his arms over his chest but thinking better of it, probably wanting to avoid looking like a pouting child. "A simple *thank you* would have sufficed," he grumbles.

Nuri chuckles while Rhea snorts a laugh. Kiran, finally dragging his gaze back from the fire, scans the scene, as if missing everything that's just transpired. He shakes his head quickly, then lifts his chin before slapping a smile on his face. "Soo," he drawls, a wry and entirely implicating vibrato to the word. "What are the room assignments?"

Rhea cuts him a look. "As Captain over this mission, isn't that for you to decide?"

His smile widens. "I suppose it is, isn't it? How many rooms did my coin secure us?"

"Three," she answers.

"Two beds each?"

"One."

He huffs a laugh. "Fantastic."

Marcella groans, sprawling out in her chair and draping an arm over her eyes.

Kiran spares a taunting, helpless glance at her. "What do you want from me?" he pleads, his tone entirely unserious. "I didn't anticipate staying in Ninmere overnight, and Nightenjoy over there gave all his handy coin to the family whose ship burnt to bits."

Despite herself, Marcella removes her arm from her face and spares a glance at Gray. He looks sheepish at the mention of what he's done, dropping his eyes to his palms. Once he finally looks up, he meets her probing gaze. Marcella feels a sharp jolt lance down her spine at the eye contact. She straightens at the sensation, hiding her sudden movement with a cough.

A mistake, given she also draws the eyes of Kiran, Nuri, Rhea, and Klytis as a result.

From her peripheral, Marcella catches Rhea studying her a moment longer than everyone else, pulling her gaze away slowly. "Yeah, well," she says, eyes redirecting toward Kiran. "Your lack of planning resulted in an unwanted sleepover. His" —she jerks her chin toward Gray— "resulted in a fan club."

Everyone laughs, and any remaining tension melts away. Before, there was a noticeable lack of cohesion with their group. Not that people were stand-offish or acted poorly toward one another. Just hesitant and even a bit guarded, perhaps. Given the nature of everyone's familiar yet divided relationships, their group was made of functioning parts which had yet to come together to make a formidable whole.

But this laughter? Marcella can feel the shift—feel the bond forming between them all, earned and entirely their own. Plus, she must admit—despite the day they've had, this is the best she's felt since Griff's passing and Lyra's capture.

Marcella just hopes this mission was worth whatever information Kiran seeks. She hopes it matters. That maybe even whatever Kiran is able to glean tonight from the criminal band's leader might just lead them back to Lyra. Toward something productive. Something *good*.

Klytis stretches his hands over his head and yawns. "So about those room assignments."

MARCELLA TRUDGES awkwardly from the bathing chamber, wet hair already braided back and her dirty clothes clinging uncomfortably to her now clean body—as begrudging as that is.

Gray halts mid-movement, the thin quilt pulled half back, revealing bland, beige-colored sheets. He wrinkles his nose at her. "Why in god's veins did you put your dirty clothes back on?"

She gapes at him, thinking he surely has to be joking.

He isn't.

"Forgive me for forgetting to pack my best tunic and trousers for this glorious overnight outing I had no idea I'd be taking part in."

He frowns. "You didn't think to pack extra clothes just in case?"

"You *did*?"

For some reason she doesn't understand, the question seems to almost make him sad. Wistful, even. Though it's a fleeting thing, and a soft chuckle soon falls from his lips. Gray drops the quilt and pads to the other side of the modestly sized room, to where the one nonde-script chair is tucked neatly into a small writing desk. Gray unlatches his satchel and rummages inside. Then, he pulls something out and strides back over to her.

"Here," he says, holding out what Marcella soon realizes to be a man's tunic.

"You don't need it?"

He shakes his head, his expression seeming torn between something like a smile and a frown. "I brought an extra."

She eyes him pointedly. "So you didn't just pack spare clothes; you packed spares for your spare as well?"

He huffs a soft laugh. "It's a habit of mine."

"Randomly packing extra shirts is a...habit of yours?"

"Yes. Now do you want the tunic or not?"

Marcella feels a slight flush in her cheeks. She flicks her gaze down to the clean fabric gripped between his fingers, stretched like some offering between them. It looks soft and clean and comfortable and like something she could drown in.

She sighs, conceding. "Yes, please." He hands the large shirt over with humor now glinting in his gaze. Marcella narrows her eyes on him before turning away to strip her sweat-stained clothes off and drape Gray's amber-scented shirt over her body instead. "Why are you looking at me like that?" she asks before changing, her tone at once accusatory and dryly bemused.

"You said please," he answers, his smile annoyingly genuine and heart-stirring.

She scoffs at that. "I am well-mannered, you know."

"Are you?"

"*Yes,*" she hisses.

His smile turns lopsided. "If you say so," he says with a shrug, waltzing back to finish preparing the bed for them to sleep in.

"And suddenly I find myself thinking of ways to punish Kiran for assigning you to be my roommate."

He slides his eyes to her, a sharp curve wedged deep into the corner of his mouth. "I remember a time when you begged for me to be your roommate. How did it go, again? Something like, 'there's always room for a handsome man like you in our chambers' and 'you and I can share a bed.'" He laughs at his own impression of her voice, dropping his eyes back down to the pillows, seeming content with himself at mocking the words Marcella said to him upon their first meeting.

Heat stings Marcella's cheeks. It was different when she made those comments; she didn't know him then, and it was all too easy to make light of his annoyingly handsome features and toned body. It was almost like joking about the obvious shielded her from the ramifications of it—protected her from falling captive to it.

Look at her now, the damned, flush-cheeked fool.

She heads over to the far side of the room and turns her back to Gray, finally stripping off her dirty clothes and draping herself in Gray's blissfully clean tunic. Once finished, she steadies herself and struts right up to him, determined not to show him a lick of the embarrassment she feels. Instead, she braces a hand on her hips and lifts her chin.

"I remember you blushing like a school girl at the mention of sharing a bed with me."

Officially finished with his work on the bed, he turns around slowly, facing Marcella head on. Slowly—unnervingly so, actually—he scans her, his eyes snagging on the hem of his shirt as it hovers above her bare knees. "Yet look at us now," he says, a thick rasp to his voice. "Sharing a bed as if it's nothing at all."

"It is nothing," she confirms, her expression firmly locked to his. "Means nothing."

Yet even as she says the words, the way her chest tightens and stomach somersaults tells her that isn't entirely true.

His eyes—his warm eyes, a swirling mix of earth's finest color pallet—hold her like a caress. "Of course." He makes a gesturing motion to the bed behind him, still not looking away from her. "After you."

Marcella snorts, lifting her chin and folding her arms across her chest, not budging an inch. Gray scoffs—the sound more a laugh than anything else—and shakes his head, amusement brightening his handsome face.

"Must you always be so stubborn?"

"Would I be me if I weren't?"

He grins at that. "Fair point."

He starts unbuckling the leather belt strapped around his hip—that micro grin wedged permanently into the corner of his lips—and Marcella's heart picks up speed in her chest. "What the hell are you doing?"

He arches a taunting brow. "You don't expect me to sleep in all this, do you?" His eyes dart down to his toes—which are still encased in combat boots—before slowly roving up his own body for emphasis. Which results in Marcella scanning his body, too. Which also results in a cluster of butterflies suddenly fluttering about her stomach.

She grits her teeth in annoyance.

He just *had* to be all noble and almost die today, making Marcella painfully aware of feelings she was perfectly content being blissfully unaware of.

She makes an exasperated expression, feigning complete and utter boredom. "I don't care what you sleep in, Nightenjoy, so long as you let me sleep in peace."

"Great," he chirps, tugging his shirt over his head and discarding it somewhere across the room.

In that passing moment, Marcella realizes she is faced with two very contrasting options. One option is to allow her gaze to roam freely and without restraint, snagging on each and every slope of muscle stretching across Gray's sculpted torso. The second option is to deny herself the thing she very much wants to do, instead choosing to look entirely uninterested, not letting her eyes so much as flick down at his exposed chest.

Naturally, she chooses the latter—self-preservation of pride and all.

With her heart now skipping in her chest, she breaks their unending eye contact—putting an end to the seemingly silent challenge—and makes to strut past him, stopping only to drum her fingers against his bare shoulder. "Be sure to wash up before getting into bed, would you? I'd prefer not to be holding my breath from a foul smell all night."

She swears she feels Gray stiffen. Biting down on her growing smile, she drops her hand from his shoulder, slowly letting her finger-tips glide down his skin—a humming sensation overtaking the tips of her fingers as she drags them across his toned bicep. She walks over to the other side of the bed, propping herself up on the thick sheets and nestling beneath the quilted covers.

"Good night," she chirps merrily, driving her provoking knife deeper. "Enjoy your cold bath."

In a nearly imperceptible gesture, he angles his chin over his shoulder, just enough to glance back at Marcella, something indis-cernible glinting in his gaze. Wordlessly, he walks across the floor and again rummages through his satchel, a fist full of fresh clothes clutched between his fingers as he strides into the bathing chambers.

In the downtime of his absence, Marcella tries to fall asleep. She shuts her eyes, conjures image after image of clouds, sheep—all the shit they tell children to visualize when they can't sleep.

It doesn't work. Not even a little.

Her mind, it would seem, is instead too preoccupied with conjuring visuals of all the different ways tonight could go. Imagining what it would be like to feel Gray's skin against hers. Contemplating if she would feel guilty for moving on from Griff so soon. Wondering what Gray would be like in bed. Would he be soft and gentle, like his personality? Or much like the flashes of that hidden anger he keeps on that tight leash of his, does he have a carnal side he keeps locked away? Would his kisses be light and reverent? Or hungry and consuming?

The questions roll through her mind wave after wave, relentless and utterly hypnotizing. Honestly—and to her absolute irritation—she thinks about it so much, she finds the space between her legs throbbing, begging to find out the answers to those demanding questions.

So by the time Gray pads back into the modest room, the smell of freshly used soap wafting through the air, Marcella presses her knees together and her face down into the pillow, cursing her body for getting so riled up over mere thoughts. She then pretends to be in the gentle grips of a peaceful sleep, keeping her shut eyes as still as possible and the rhythm of her breaths as smooth as she can. Through her closed eyelids, she is able to note the distinct dimming in the room as the candlelight winks out completely. She feels movement on the other side of the bed as Gray shifts in beside her.

Marcella's breath catches in her throat at his proximity, and her task of maintaining the illusion of sleep becomes a hell of a lot harder. Because there is something about being covered in a veil of darkness which gives a person courage; that allows them to act uninhibited, as if bravery is bred in dark bedrooms where actions grow bold and defenses wane soft.

She opens her eyes, her vision taking a moment to adjust to the pitch black room. "How was your bath?" she asks with a taunting lilt.

She hears rustling beside her, and Gray turns over on his side. "I thought you were asleep?" He sounds so close.

Too close.

Her throat dries, but she swallows against the sensation. "Can't sleep," she admits.

"Why not?"

"Too many things on my mind."

A slight pause. And then—

"Do you want to talk about it?" His voice is so soft—so filled with genuine concern that something might actually be bothering her, completely unaware that *he* is the source of the many things swarming her thoughts.

Marcella rolls onto her side and lays her cheek on her palms as they press together atop her pillow. She has a sneaking suspicion Gray is laying in a similar position directly next to her. It's hard to explain, exactly, but aside from the obvious sensation of a person being near, there is this current of electricity she can feel passing between them. Similar to the feeling one has when they first meet the eyes of another —that initial jolt. Only, this is unending and far more intense.

"Maybe eventually," she murmurs after a moment, biting her lip sheepishly, feeling like she can drop her guard tonight. Be a softer, more vulnerable version of herself—a version she does not reveal easily.

Maybe it's from the thrill of being in a new place with a man in her bed after going so long without any sort of intimate touch. Maybe it's her having a completely normal human need she wants sated. Or maybe...

Maybe it's more. Maybe it has *always* been more, and Marcella has just been too stubborn to admit that to herself until today.

"Whatever it is you have to say," Gray replies, his voice like a soothing caress to her senses, "I'd like you to know that I *want* to hear it. No matter how heavy, no matter how dark or light or funny or terrible—if it is coming from you, then it has my full interest."

Marcella finds herself stunned at the words, and despite being enshrouded by a thick darkness dulling their visibility to nothing more than a fuzzy shadow—Marcella has never felt so seen.

"I miss my family." She blurts the words softly, completely surprised by her own sudden admission.

Yet Gray doesn't miss a beat. "What are they like?"

She snorts, the sound filled with a thousand memories. "I am the quiet one of my family, believe it or not. The least stubborn, too. My brothers are all thickheaded and filled with more personality than they know what to do with, passed along honestly from our loud mother and hard-headed father. It made life on our farm rather... interesting, to say the least." She smiles, a warmth spreading through her chest that she hasn't been privileged enough to feel lately. "But there was love. In our cooking. Cleaning. Farm work. In the songs we'd sing and constant music we'd play. In everything, there was love."

"Sounds colorful," he says through a quiet laugh. "And wonderful. Will you tell me more about it? Your life before coming to Bathara, I mean."

She blinks, a wrinkle forming between her brows. "You want to hear about all that?"

"I already told you—I want to hear everything."

Her heart squeezes, and a tingling warmth spreads in her chest. Something she's never quite felt before—something exceeding attraction or desire.

"Okay," she whispers.

She tells him everything. About her life growing up in Rolfbear. Her family's struggles with poverty and being incapable of putting nutritious meals on the dinner table when it was at its worst. How—after her magic awakened and she went through and cultivated all the fields in her small farming town—everyone held a banquet in her honor, where the music played on until the sky bled red from an approaching dawn. She tells him about her brothers and how unbelievably protective they are over her. How they were nearly bursting with joy when they took her to the Ardoris Comet Festival. About how her parents cried before she left for Bathara, tears of pride and sorrow mixing together to form a single salty riverbank on their cheeks.

She talks and talks and talks, words surfacing from long forgotten places she didn't even realize still harbored things to say. All the while, Gray listens and asks questions when he wants to know more about something she's told him. In return, she finds herself asking things about him, as well. About his life in Rivara. What it was like growing up as the son of the very famous Sterling Nightenjoy. Gray tells her about the pressure he sometimes feels to be a man as great and well-respected as his father. Tells her about his talented mother and how she is one of the best Gardners in all of Solaya, pure adoration punctuating his every word.

As they converse, without realizing she's doing it, Marcella inches closer and closer to Gray, the edges of her forearms now scraping against his while one of her bent knees brushes against his thigh. Heat courses beneath her skin when she realizes how close their bodies are to being entangled. How appealing the idea of nestling into his side truly is. Truthfully, thinking about it shows her just how badly she wants to be held—held by Gray Nightenjoy, that is. She wants to feel his arms wrap around her while he presses her against his chest. She wants to curl her fingers around his arms and rest her eyes, feeling safe and unguarded.

Most importantly, she wants *him*.

All of him.

Every precious piece.

She swallows against the lump now in her throat, willing her racing heart to still. Silence fills the room as their current line of conversation reaches its natural end. She uses the pause to inch surreptitiously toward him, moving slowly and in small increments, hoping what she's doing won't be quite as noticeable. Though she knows it's *always* noticeable.

Through the expanse of a blackened veil, stretching between them like a mask covering all the unsaid words, she leaps—reaching for him across the illusionary distance.

Slowly—tentatively—her fingers brush against his skin, tracing the outline of his body, rising until she is sure they've found the slope of his jaw. She cups his chin lightly between trembling fingers and swipes her thumb across his stubbly cheek, scooting even closer, until she can practically feel his breath against her lips.

A warm hand lands on the curve of her hip, twitching subtly before splaying its fingers across her side and squeezing tightly, dragging her closer to an unmovable body. Marcella sucks in a quiet yet sharp gasp, pulling her bottom lip between her teeth.

A simple touch should not feel like that.

Like her body is being set ablaze. Like she has just been struck by lightning and her nerve endings have absorbed the electrical shock, sending the sensation cascading down the fabrics of her skin. Her chest tightens with emotion, and she finds herself overwhelmed by a conglomeration of feelings for this person in front of her.

This pure, wholly good, and entirely genuine heart that has always been beating a fingertip's length away from her grasp.

Marcella nestles into the curve of Gray's body, tucking her leg between his, pressing their chests together—which in turn presses other parts of them together, making a throbbing ache appear between her thighs once more. Her nose brushes against his, and Gray finds her effortlessly in the darkness, gently gliding the tips of his fingers from the corner of her temple, down her cheek, until they reach her chin. He pinches it between tender fingertips and tilts it up toward what she can only assume would be his lips. Then he slides that hand down, along the curve of her hips and onto the small of her back. He wraps the entire length of his arm around her waist, swallowing her whole in his embrace as he drags her across the remaining space between them, pressing their hips firmly together.

She melts at the hard bulge she feels waiting for her.

With an undeniable, burning need now coursing through her, she slides her free hand around Gray's neck, toying with the strands of his still semi-wet hair, their chests flush with each other as they remain silent. It's as if they're both scared words will shatter the moment, seemingly both aware of how fragile a thing it is. So Marcella continues to say nothing as she subtly—as covertly as one possibly can in this situation—grinds her hips against him, relishing in the low, breathy groan rattling in the back of Gray's throat as a result. His fingers dig into the skin of her back as he fists at the shirt covering her body—*his* shirt.

Flames dance deep in the pit of her stomach.

She threads her fingers through his hair and tugs, almost tempted to moan from the sequence of passing touches alone. Yet she manages to keep all her noises restrained, not letting a single sound slip past her lips. Instead, she is preoccupied with a consuming thought—

Kiss me. Kiss me. Kiss me.

Marcella—completely consumed by him and lost to the swirling haze filling her mind—seems to lose every semblance of her usual defenses as she accidentally lets the thought spill from her lips.

"Kiss me," she breathes, a thousand other words resting in the cadence of those simple two.

Gray's hand clenches then unclenches against the small of her back. He stills completely. "I...can't."

A heat entirely different from the one she was previously feeling invades her body, and she rears back, the delicate moment officially splintered. "Why?" The question slips out before she can think better of it.

"Because...." He sighs, the sound heavy and loaded and filled with a finality that nearly shatters Marcella's heart. "I can't—"

"You know what?" Marcella interjects, feeling unable to hear his explanation as both embarrassment and self-preservation fuel her scrambling, hollow words. "It's fine." She pulls back from Gray's embrace entirely, rolling away to her side of the bed, putting her back to him as she refurbishes her armor.

She hears the rustling of sheets as he shifts. "Marcella, please. Let me explain. It's not..." Another sigh. "It's not what you think. I want—"

"I mean it, Gray," she again cuts in, a sinking feeling turning leaden in her stomach as her chest carves a hollow hole inside itself. "You owe me nothing because *this* was nothing. Nothing even happened."

"But you wanted it to."

She can't tell if it's meant as a question, a statement, or something else entirely. For whatever reason, it feels like the worst response he could have given her.

Her bottom lip quivers as she feels like the world's biggest fool. Why had she even assumed he feels that way for her? At the end of the day, he's done nothing but be a good friend to her. Key word, *friend*.

The words she whispered while swept up in their hypnotic moment haunt her. *Kiss me.*

Fuck, she was so ignorant for letting her guard down. For getting so swept up in the feelings of being in bed with another person, covered by the shields of darkness. He doesn't feel that way about her. It seems so gods-damn obvious now. Still...

Rejection sucks, and for the life of her, she cannot recall ever feeling it as viscerally as she does in this moment. It stings. Hurts. Rubs her raw, until she feels like she has nothing of worth to give.

"Just go to sleep, Gray." The words tumble hollowly from her lips, barely above a whisper.

"Marcella," he murmurs, reaching a hand out to touch her shoulder. "Please, let me explain."

The touch makes her jerk—makes her stomach flip, but in a way that nearly makes her nauseous. She doesn't want to be touched—not after learning the person she now realizes she truly wants doesn't want her back.

"Go. To. Sleep." She enunciates each word slowly, speaking with a finality that leaves no more room for discussion. He pulls his hand back, the stretching silence uncertain as she wonders if he will or won't say anything else.

If she does or doesn't want him to.

But it seems she was firm enough in her response, because she feels the mattress dip and the sheets rustle as he seems to shift back into his sleeping position, not deigning to say anything else.

And as heaviness clots the air, so different from the buzzing possibilities fluttering through the night-kissed room mere moments ago, a single tear slips free from the corner of her eye, strolling slowly down her cheek until it mingles with the corner of her lips, as if in some cruel, poetic kiss.

It is the only moment of pity Marcella allows herself to have.

"Hello, Kiran. Good of you to join me."

"Hello, Kiran. Good of you to join me."

Kiran strolls into one of Castaria's many private lounges, shocked to find Audwin Fjolla, Finlay's unpleasant and terribly pompous father, sitting perched atop a sprawling blue chair—the finest chair in the room, as it so happens. Meaning he is the one who summoned Kiran from his personal chambers. Interesting. But also particularly annoying, considering the muscular company currently warming his bed, awaiting his—hopefully—timely return. Company he is hoping will also escort him to Erandor's upcoming Winter Solstice ball when he asks. Though he supposes he shouldn't be thinking about that at the moment.

"Audwin," Kiran drawls mildly, taking the seat in front of him. The hearth beside them is lit, crackling and popping in the following silence as Audwin and Kiran regard each other through the dim yellow light.

They never have been the best of friends.

Kiran folds one leg over the other, smiling a politician's smile. "What a surprise it is to see your pale face here at Bathara. Hopefully your unexpected presence within the Borderless Region is due to a desire to finally see your son?"

Audwin smiles tightly. "A natural assumption."

Kiran leans back in his chair. "What other reason is there for you to be within these walls, then?" He pinches his chin between his fingers with a theatric flare. "Better yet... Why summon *me* instead of him? To what do I owe the honor?"

Audwin bites down on his growing scowl. "We need to talk," he says tersely.

Talk.

Kiran nearly laughs at Audwin's approach. Though Kiran must admit he thought he would be afforded a bit more time to strategize with Draven first—who still has not even returned from his own aggregate's mission—or at least tell him the information he uncovered before broaching the subject. Because what Kiran found out during his interrogation with the skull trader? The knowledge he received in that damp, mildewed cellar? It is a weapon.

So until Kiran is able to speak with Draven about all he's uncovered, he will play his hand as he must.

And he always has been quite good at playing cards.

Kiran twirls a lazy hand in the air. "That's all the Heads of the Great Houses seem to want to do these days. Talk, talk, talk." He sighs. "The trouble is, I'm all talked out. Now, I only just returned from a rather grueling mission yesterday, and I find myself exhausted and in need of a bit more rest, so if you'll excuse me." He rises, but before he makes it halfway across the room, Audwin stops him.

"How interesting," he hums, his tone taking a drastic shift—as if he, somehow, has just gained the upper hand. "That mission in Ninmere is exactly what I wish to talk about." Kiran turns slowly to study Audwin, who is smiling like a cat. "Now, *sit.*"

He pushes his tongue into his cheek before gliding it along the grooves of his teeth. Still, he does as Audwin requests and sits back down. "How do you know about Ninmere?"

Audwin snorts, leaning back in his chair. "Everyone in the bloody Three Kingdoms already knows about the mission you headed. Sterling Nightenjoy's son has made quite the name for himself because of it. Genius, really. Save the ships then give coin to the fisherman's family whose ship burned. He'll have the backing of the people for quite some time because of that decision."

"I don't think that's where Nightenjoy's head was at when he made his choice," Kiran counters.

"You don't think?" Audwin asks, ignoring Kiran's dry, pointed tone entirely. "Why else do it, then?"

Kiran sucks on a tooth, annoyance bubbling up and into his chest. Thankfully, he doesn't have to say anything before Audwin speaks again.

"Lion of the Heart," he says slowly, as if trying out the taste of the words. He pauses, tilting his head as if giving the nickname genuine consideration. "Has a nice ring to it, actually. If only my worthless son could have made such a name for himself in as little time as Sterling's son has."

Kiran grinds his teeth. "Get to the point, Audwin. I'm sure you're not here just to swoon over another man's son."

The corner of his lip hooks up. "No, I am not." There is a brief passing silence as Audwin watches Kiran, seeming to look for something within his gaze. Yet Kiran offers him nothing. The curve wedged into the corner of Audwin's mouth deepens. "Why have you been investigating an underground uprising?"

The question enters the space between them so bluntly—so dryly —Kiran only blinks, slightly taken aback by it. "Pardon?"

"You have been tracking the movements of a forming uprising, have you not? Currently, they move stealthily. Within the shadows, gathering followers and supplies."

An uneasy feeling turns in Kiran's stomach. "Gathering followers and supplies for what cause?" he asks carefully.

Audwin smiles. "Exactly the reason I have requested an audience with you. That is precisely what I'd like to know."

"And why do you assume I've found the answer to that question?"

"Because I know you have." He says it so smoothly. So matter-of-factly.

It ignites a quiet anger within Kiran.

"See, I have it on good authority that you captured and interrogated a former Skull Trader. And no ordinary Skull Trader, mind you. No, you captured the great Livinthuis Noxtus."

"Who?" Kiran coos, inspecting his nails as he attempts to keep his face a mask of cool indifference.

Audwin scoffs, shaking his head. "Don't play dumb with me, boy. I have been trained far more extensively than you could ever imagine. You think I am cruel? You think I treat Finlay harshly?" He snorts, the sound nothing short of resentful. "You should have met my own father. But you know what? His brutality made sure I was strong. Capable. And now I am grateful for it, because it turned me into the man I am today."

"Unpleasant?" Kiran drawls with boredom, keeping his eyes intentionally on his nail beds.

"Powerful," Audwin grits back. "Now, start speaking with me truthfully. Tell me everything you know. Every single detail, down to the smallest of descriptions. The smallest motivations."

Kiran hums, contemplating. "You mean details such as where this uprising is pulling their ideologies from? Or better yet, *whom?*"

A heavy stillness overtakes the air. Audwin leans forward, bracing his elbows on his knees, peaking his fingers in front of his lips. His features are much harsher than Finlay's, though the colors filling in their details are one and the same. Bright, aqua-colored eyes. Pure white hair brushing against his broad shoulders, small braids tugging one side of it back past his ear. A sneer that permanently taints otherwise nicely defined lips.

The man before Kiran is everything Finlay strives to be.

Yet he is also everything wrong with that which they've built around themselves. And no matter how hard Finlay tries to pretend he is just like his father, he isn't. He never has been. It is the very reason he was forced to face the wrath of Audwin Fjolla time and time again. Was forced to suffer the cruel bite of rejection as Audwin spit in his son's face and told him he was worthless to him. What child wants to hear that? No matter how twisted their parents are, a child still wants nothing more than to receive their love, and Finlay was denied any part of the feeling once his mother died. It is why he has spent the following years of his life trying to mold himself into his father's image. Be everything Audwin is and wants Finlay to be.

It is because for once in his gods-damn life—though Finlay will never openly admit it to himself or anyone else, for that matter—Kiran knows Finlay just wants to feel loved.

Which is why at the end of the day, even when Kiran hates Finlay with a burning ferocity, he still loves him with an unending dedication which will never waver. Despite the many decisions Finlay incorrectly made, despite the numerous occasions he let Kiran down greater than words can convey, Kiran still loves his brother far deeper than he will ever truly accept.

Audwin clears his throat, snapping him from his wandering thoughts. "Details surrounding the foundations on which this uprising is built is precisely the sort of information I'd like you to share with me."

"And why should I?"

Audwin huffs a condescending laugh and leans back in his chair, keeping the tips of his fingers pressed together. "Because I think you'll find it in your best interest." He reaches into the inside pocket of his lavish white and arctic-blue doublet and pulls out a rolled scroll sealed with black wax. Without removing his eyes from Kiran, he reaches out, passing off the item.

Kiran recognizes the seal encrusted into the wax instantly; it's unmistakable who it belongs to.

"What is this?" he asks, a pointed sharpness punctuating his words.

"It's for you," Audwin replies smoothly. "I was instructed to give it to you before we begin the next part of our discussion."

A feeling of unease winds in his chest as Kiran breaks the wax seal and unrolls the scroll, reading the contents awaiting him inside.

His heart drops into his stomach.

He has lost his game of cards.

A filthy grin twirls Audwin's lips. "Ready to talk now?"

269

CHAPTER TWENTY-THREE

FINLAY

Finlay stands in the back of the ongoing class, his arms folded and patience wearing thin.

Master Asara Strithmore asked Finlay to be a guest lecturer today once she concludes her current lesson. They are diving into the foundations of magic in her class, discussing its different components and functions. Why the hell she's asked Finlay to take up the rear and explain the process of strengthening one's laktî, he hasn't the slightest clue. She could have very well finished that portion of her lecture on her own, or asked any other gods-damn person at this academy.

Truly... *anyone* else.

"The theories regarding where our magic comes from are endless," she explains. "Boundless, even. We believe in what is called the Cycle, a mystical force which recycles and returns all energy—all magic. Yet who or what created it? Whom does it answer to? The gods? Something greater?" She clasps her hands behind her back as she paces at the front of the class, her twin silver braids shifting as she walks. "Though it's hard to prove the conceptual origins of magic itself, there is still much we have since learned and now understand about it. Tell me, who can answer the two broadest categories we use to define wielders?"

A girl with flowing black hair shoots her hand into the air, and Finlay tips his chin with a hint of pride at recognizing her as a newly Selected first year of the Skyborne aggregate. "I can," she chirps.

"Go on, then."

"To make things simple, the Tani has created two distinct magical categories where each different magic type may fall: Conjurers and Elementals."

"Very good," Master Strithmore encourages. She directs her attention away from the girl and to the rest of the class. "And what are Conjurers and Elementals?"

Another hand lifts into the air, and Finlay follows it to find Gray Nightenjoy as the owner. He sits in the back of the classroom, alone at a table meant for three. Finlay can't help but wonder if the lowborn girl he normally spends his time with isn't assigned to this class with him. He also finds it odd that he would choose to sit alone. Frankly, even Finlay is aware of how well-regarded the man is. Certainly plenty of students in this room would love to have him at their tables. Yet he chose to isolate his position in the class.

Interesting.

Gray Nightenjoy is sharp and cunning—alarmingly so. He parades an easy-going, gentle disposition beautifully, as though he isn't always watching and assessing. Finlay supposes Gray has his father, Sterling Nightenjoy, to thank for being so exceptional at it, but all it takes is a concerted moment of watching his shrewd gaze and carefully selected words to recognize he is not someone to be taken lightly.

Truthfully, Finlay is still mildly bitter he didn't choose Skyborne, instead picking Kiran's aggregate, Castaria. He would have made Gray Nightenjoy the first ever nontitled member of his renowned aggregate. It was not something Finlay took lightly either when bidding to Select him. Still, Gray chose Kiran. Because of course he did.

A flash of memories plays through Finlay's mind. He drops his eyes and sighs, the memories giving way to the thought plaguing him incessantly as of late.

How is Finlay supposed to do wrong by Draven once more, even if at the council of Bathara's behest? Just before arriving to this class, he had a meeting with Master Cahlmon regarding the progress in his private search for Lyra. It was a very brief meeting. Very. Finlay has found nothing. No leads. No person with any sort of knowledge about Casimir and Lyra. So, luckily, he had nothing to offer Master Cahlmon, which has bought him the unpurchasable: more time. Yet time does not run on forever. He must make a decision soon, forced to draw his line somewhere.

Forced to decide if he will draw one at all.

Finlay shakes the traveling thoughts from his head, focusing on the present. Master Strithmore, it seems, called on Gray, who is now mid-answer to her question.

"Conjurers are those who create their magic's ability while Elementals are those who pull their magic directly from the resources around them. We know Elemental's laktî matches the frequency of that which it wields, fueling their magic and allowing them to access and create the resources as if they were their own, while less is known about where Conjurers actually pull their magic from."

"Can you provide an example?" she asks.

"Of course," Gray answers. "My own." He turns his palm up to the sky and a bright flash of golden light swells in his palm before a sprawling sunset overtakes the room, casting the walls and windows in a warm mix of red, gold, and pink. It only lasts a moment before Gray curls his fingers back into his palm, erasing the illusion.

Master Strithmore does not remove her eyes from him the entire time. "Exceptional gift," she muses. "It's a shame you refuse to use it on others, from what the other Masters heading your combat classes tell me."

Finlay whips his eyes back to Gray, stunned at that admission. Silently, he chastises Kiran for allowing Gray to get away with such a thing. If Nightenjoy was a member of his aggregate, that would never be acceptable. Ever.

Gray Nightenjoy shrugs. "I don't like to use my magic," he informs Master Strithmore as if that is no strange thing to say at Bathara Academy at all. "In fact, I've always found it rather ironic that I was gifted the magic of illusions. I believe in honor, integrity, and truth, yet I was gifted a magic of deceit and lies—sometimes false truths." He smiles a near poignant smile before chuckling. "The twists of fate are not lost on me."

Master Strithmore hums her consideration. "We do not always get to choose what we are given, though we always get to choose what we do with it. Sometimes inaction is as deplorable as unwanted action itself." Then, without any further words for him, she turns her gaze away from him and back onto the class, pacing once more. "Who can tell me how magic is then divided from those two categories, and how that affects the creation of Jurafen teams?"

The rest of her class continues as they discuss the assigned divisions of offensive magic types and defensive magic types. Most people with Elemental gifts are considered offensive—fire, water, wind, ice. Namely because they are able to wield magical attacks causing mass destruction, should they so choose. Then there are defensive magic types. Annoyingly, Rhea gets brought up as an example, with her nullifying magic being used as the golden standard for defensive magic. They then go on to explain how Bathara uses their evaluations to form balanced teams, taking into account wielders' magics who fall more on one end of the spectrum over the other. Finlay has to fight against his dozing mind more than a few times, given how familiar he is with all this information.

Though his attention is soon claimed when Master Strithmore halts her pacing, squaring her shoulders to her class. "And Abdites? What can you tell me of them?"

"That they're mad lunatics," one girl grumbles near the front of the room, resulting in a bout of snickering laughs.

"Are they?" Master Strithmore questions.

The girl who answered looks stunned at the Master's follow-up question. "Well...yeah."

"And is that all they are?"

The girl's voice dims, a tiny quiver rattling her words now. "I mean, not before they corrupt their magic, no."

"But it is after?"

"Well..." The girl swallows. "In our other classes, we are learning the nature of their corruption. Just what, precisely, the properties are that beckon them into such lunacy. Yet all the Masters say the same thing: once they are corrupted, they might as well be treated the same as dangerous magical beasts. They are lost, vile, and outside the possibility of saving."

"So you believe the corruption in their veins robs them of their human claim? Strip them of the protections all humankind should receive?"

The girl blinks furiously at Master Strithmore, seeming to work out if the question is a trick or not. "Once corrupted, there is nothing human about them."

"And what of the circumstances that may have caused their corruption?"

"What about it?"

"Is that not a factor worth considering?"

"Why would it be? Everything we're taught says once they've become an Abdite, they are beyond saving. Does it really matter what drove them there? They still did it. And Jurafen are still expected to neutralize or detain them, regardless of circumstance."

Master Strithmore folds her hands behind her back, allowing the words to settle over the classroom, giving the students time to process and digest their own thoughts on the conversation. It's her trademark while teaching.

Finlay takes the moment to consider, knowing to the letter the exact answers his father would give. The answers his father would want him to give.

"Thank you for your participation in the conversation, Zyria," she eventually says. Master Strithmore claps her hands together. "Now, I would like to invite Captain Fjolla to the front of the classroom. I've asked him to join us today to give his personal techniques and recommendations for strengthening laktî. Please give him your undivided attention."

Finlay strolls forward, surprised when he glimpses the lowborn girl sitting one chair away from a student hailing from a lesser noble house near the front of the class. She looks elsewhere—like she is physically here, but her mind is not. Though, that is not for him to worry about, nor does he care to contemplate the conditions of someone beneath him. His father warned him against such a thing.

When he reaches Master Strithmore, he straightens his spine and lifts his chin. "Wielders, today I am going to provide you with some training techniques that'll help enhance your laktî's capabilities. You should strive to complete these exercises at least once a day, when—"

Someone clears their throat. Finlay's eyes rove toward the back of the room where the disruptive noise came from, his tongue already preparing its lashing. Yet surprise clamors through him at the sight of The Keeper, Josiah.

"Forgive my interruption," he says, that calm yet captivating voice of his carrying lightly through the room. "But I'm afraid I am in need of both Captain Fjolla and Gray Nightenjoy."

Finlay quickly steals a glance at Gray, finding an equal amount of surprise resting in his expression.

"For what reason?" Master Strithmore questions, the slightest current of irritation brushing against her words.

"I'm not at liberty to discuss such things openly," he says through an easy smile, as inviting as it is diplomatic.

Josiah's warm charm is something that has always astounded Finlay. The authoritative way in which he carries himself, yet the current of calm always surrounding him.

"Very well," she concedes through a sigh. "But know your timing could not have been more inconvenient. Captain Fjolla was just about to provide my class with a small lecture on ways to strengthen their laktî."

"Hopefully he will be gracious enough to return to provide the students with such knowledge another time."

Finlay grunts at that. For the love of the gods, he does *not* want to have to sit through another first-year class again.

"Hopefully," she agrees. She turns her attention onto Finlay and dips her chin at him. "Be on your way then. I'd prefer you not make the Keeper wait longer than he must." She throws a glance at Gray. "You too."

Gray rises, collecting his things and stuffing them into a satchel. As Finlay struts through the center of the class to meet them, he catches the farm girl glancing back at Gray, a flash of some expression Finlay would have preferred not to see.

Truthfully, it makes him scowl—the momentary open display of weakness.

Yet he doesn't have time to think about it further. He reaches Josiah and Gray, and after Josiah jerks his chin, motioning for them to follow him outside the classroom, they wordlessly do as instructed and trail behind the aging, white-haired man until he eventually leads them out the final winding corridor and into an elaborate garden. His *personal* garden, Finlay realizes with no small amount of surprise.

Questions bubble in his throat, but he remains silent, not wanting to speak first.

Josiah stops between a line of terracotta pots where tall and leafy black dahlias flourish and prosper in thick and staggeringly tall bundles. "Congratulations to you both." He reaches into the inside of his light blue tunic and pulls out two rolled up scrolls, each sealed with the Erandor Kingdom's official crest—a castle wedged between two rivers. He places a scroll in each hand, extending them out to Finlay and Gray.

Gray, with a crease in his brow, takes the scroll tentatively. "Why are we being congratulated, exactly?" He breaks the seal and scans the scroll's contents.

Josiah looks to Finlay next, gesturing for him to take his own scroll. He holds the man's blue-eyed gaze a moment longer before reaching for it and unsealing the parchment, scanning the contents as well.

He grimaces first. Then, his lips twist into a bitter scowl as he actively works to not let a long, dissatisfied groan spill from his lips at the instructions awaiting him in his personalized note.

By the fucking gods...

"You both have been cordially invited to this year's Winter Solstice

Ball, held at the beautiful Sagamon castle in Talderine, King Erasmus's home itself."

Finlay knows his expression must look positively bored—he has attended this event more times than he cares to count. Though a flash of surprise does flicker through him at Gray's invitation. He glances at him sidelong, finding it odd that Nightenjoy's expression remains unchanged. Even if anyone with the slightest understanding of political underpinnings would know his invitation is no mere coincidence, with Gray Nightenjoy arguably being one of the most beloved damn figures Erandor Kingdom has right now. Word about what he did in Ninmere for both the town and its people has spread like wildfire.

It's irritating.

Lion of the Heart, they call him. Dumb and impractical, in Finlay's opinion. It doesn't even have a catchy ring to it.

"It seems your recent fame has resulted in you being invited to one of the most prestigious events in Erandor," Finlay muses to Gray.

His resulting smile is slanted. "Indeed."

"You have each been granted leave for the duration of the night. You both have been offered rooms in the castle as well," Josiah informs them. "An aether-wielder will transport your group, and he will return the following sunrise to bring your group back."

"Group?" Gray questions.

"Captain Dalmar, Captain Larking, and Captain Sulien will be joining the two of you for the event as well. Then of course, the dates you each select to accompany you for the evening."

"Some of us don't get to choose who we bring," Finlay mutters under his breath, irritation heating his blood as he again curses the instructions within his scroll. *You must bring Rhea Brooksley as your date.* Signed with his father's very own signet ring and all.

Really...what in god's veins is his father thinking? Why *her*?

"Be that as it may," Josiah replies through a skip of laughter. "You will enjoy the company of a date nonetheless."

"Enjoy is a loose word in this context." Finlay feels his sneer curling his lip.

Josiah ignores him. "Oh, by the way. Huxley Rangard will be

joining you as well. As the son of Lord Rangard, I understand his presence is also expected."

Gray openly grimaces at the information, and Finlay arches a brow at the surprising gesture. "Do you have a problem with a member of my aggregate I should be aware of?"

"None other than my cousin being an unbearably unpleasant ass."

Finlay's brows shoot up. *"Cousin?"*

Gray groans before heaving a frustrated sigh, pinching the bridge of his nose. "Unfortunately." Yet he only seems to sulk in his frustrations a moment, dropping his fingers from his face and resetting his expression into something focused and quizzical. "Josiah?" he asks through a particularly curious lilt.

"Yes?"

"Why are you allowing us leave for the duration of the night? Or perhaps I should instead narrow my question to focus solely on me. It makes sense why Captain Fjolla, Dalmar, and Sulien must attend, seeing as they're the heirs to their Great Houses. Even Captain Larking and Huxley make sense, since their Houses also reside within Erandor's borders and are deeply connected to King Erasmus. Yet I am a nontitled son from the Rivara Kingdom whose name is only circulating because of my recent actions. Actions only stemming from my responsibilities as a future Jurafen." He pauses, as if wanting to emphasize his next point. Finlay's eyes narrow in curious anticipation. "Jurafen answer to no king, and Bathara is politically neutral. Why, then, grant me leave to accept a politically motivated invitation?"

Josiah studies Gray for a long beat, seeming to really consider the question. "There are times where it is necessary to simply show your face. Even for Jurafen. Though having you in attendance is most certainly some political ploy concocted by King Erasmus's advisors for one reason or another, it also holds benefits for Bathara to have you there as well." He steps forward and cups Gray's cheek while something inscrutable swims in his gaze.

Finlay's brows furrow at the intimacy of the moment—Josiah holding Gray's face as if they have known each other far longer than the short time Gray has been here at Bathara. And there is something else about the gesture which catches Finlay's attention. A near-imperceptible sorrow seeming to line the man's eyes as his fingers twitch with an apology. Then again, Josiah has always been one of the few people Finlay has never been very skilled at reading, so he could be off the mark entirely.

"Take someone you care for and enjoy yourself, Gray," Josiah says with a peculiar sternness.

Though he looks hesitant, Gray nods. "I will."

"Good," Josiah murmurs, dropping his hand and stepping back. "That is good." With distant eyes, he draws in a loud breath and claps his hands gently together. "Well then, if you two will excuse me, I have other matters I must attend to. Gray, give your father my regards, would you?" Gray again nods, and Josiah offers each of them a parting smile before turning his back to them and strolling deeper into his sprawling garden.

Gray calls out, stopping him. "Wait." He steps forward and reaches for a small, oblong item clinging to Josiah's shirt. He plucks it from him and holds it up for all to see. "This was stuck to your back."

Josiah gingerly reaches for the stray black dahlia petal and observes it for a long, silent moment. Until he ultimately grinds the velvety thing between his fingertips, scatters the deep maroon pieces to the ground, and strolls away without so much as another word.

CHAPTER TWENTY-FOUR

RHEA

Rhea stares at her reflection in the mirror a moment longer before glancing back at the small gilded table near her bed, where her Ever-Know Quill rests perched on the side, fresh magical ink sizzling into the parchment, sending the cursive scripts of her handwriting.

She's received her instructions from Tynan regarding what she is expected to do this evening. She's also sent all the information she's gathered over the past two weeks to him, hopefully giving him what he wanted. She sure as shit didn't know what to make of all the old texts she transcribed—she didn't understand the language, only copied its characters. Still, she has this gnawing feeling that whatever knowledge she just stole for him will not be used for the greater good nor some neat parlor trick. Truthfully, she feels gods-damn awful about it. It leaves a sour churning in her stomach, clawing at her from the pits of all she's had to swallow to survive.

But this is it. Will *be* it. She just has to get through tonight, following through with Tynan's final request of her. Then, Draven will finally be free of his twisted father, and she will continue on at Bathara without a shadowy threat looming over her at every turn.

She glances back in the mirror, assessing her reflection once more.

Her hair is half-drawn, numerous small winding braids twisting at each side. The silver pieces line her face with a delicate curl framing her makeup-coated features, a blood-red stain punctuating her lips. The dress Tynan sent her for tonight is multicolored, saturated mainly in midnight black with silver glimmers trailing through and dripping in fine jewels, cinched at the waist and featuring a plunging neckline that would have made her father send her to her room years and years ago. Rhea imagines her late older sister, Suzumi, nagging their father in place of her.

"Rhea's grown now," she would have argued on her behalf. "This is the sort of thing women wear to these types of balls."

"*Women*," her father would have countered. "Not my baby girl."

Rhea would have pretended to roll her eyes and groan while Suzumi would have laughed at the two of them.

Gods, she misses them. There are days where it's harder than others, and today…

Today feels like an exceptionally hard day. Probably in part because she feels her mind slipping—feels the claws of her very own monster digging into her. It roars at her as her eyes scan her own reflection, snagging on all the exposed skin. Highlighting all the imperfect places. Noticing bulges where Tynan and her former ladies would have pointed at and said should be flat; where her skin is flawed and how to make it better.

Nights like these, she was always groomed to be perfect, in both appearance and manner. So she was scrutinized inch by every inch, and now she is trained to see herself through those very lenses. To always spot the imperfections. To identify the places where her skin spills over the gown. To be aware of her posture, and the way it affects the visible size of her body.

It's what sent her spiraling into such a bad, harmful place the first time. The core reason she had to fight tooth and nail to pull herself out of a venomous, never-ending pit of terrible thoughts and harmful words to herself.

Yet still, like some sick form of conditioning, her brain wonders those same volatile thoughts.

Do I look small enough right now?

She doesn't think so...

Rhea hisses, squeezing her eyes closed and attempting to shake all those thoughts away. Because fuck that. *Fuck* that. She's not going to let it win. Not tonight.

She reopens her eyes and looks in the mirror again.

She hates that disgust is the first emotion to fill her body at what she sees. She hates that she hates herself despite knowing she is the only person in this world who could ever truly validate her to the point of feeling like she's enough. She hates how much she fucking hates and hates and hates.

Despite the waves of nausea now roiling in her gut, she stares at the image looking back at her. She inhales deeply, trying to steady herself. "You are enough," she says plainly to the reflection. "You are enough," she says again.

Yet for each time she says it, the opposite feels more and more true. It makes her feel all the more broken. As if her wires are crossed, and she is nothing more than a defective doll. Cracked, not up to the standards of her creators. Of those who wish to use her. Play with her.

She tries again.

"I am enough." Her voice quivers now. "I am enough. I am pretty. My body is beautiful, and I am worthy of feeling as such." Tears roll down her cheeks.

Liar. Liar. Liar.

She pinches her teeth into her trembling bottom lip, defiantly holding her stare in the mirror, her eyes scanning the image that reflects three times the weight of what she actually is. "You are beautiful," she whispers. "Your body is fine, Rhea. It's all in your head."

She continues looking at herself, and her lip curls at the image. In this moment, in this gown and with all this makeup that is supposed to make her feel her prettiest, she has never felt so disgusting. It makes her hate what she sees all the more. So she loses the battle against her own reflection, ripping her eyes away from the mirror, on the verge of vomiting as the meal she ate earlier suddenly sits heavy as lead in her stomach.

"*Fuck,*" she hisses under her breath, tears slipping steadily from her eyes now. She swipes at them in anger. "Fuck," she says again, her voice sounding even more pathetic to her ears. "Just be okay," she pleads with herself, the mirror now to her back. "Just get your shit together. You are fine. Your body is fine. It's *fine.*"

The voices pelt her.

Rhea, you look like you've put on some weight. What have you been eating?

Rhea, you're looking a bit thin lately. Are you not eating? Is everything okay?

Ah, my sweet Rhea... I hate I must be the one to relay this to you, but Tynan noticed fat spilling out near your hips in your dress last night, and per his orders, I must now add more cardio to your training, both in the mornings and the evenings.

With hot, blurry tears clouding her vision and a fist squeezing her chest, Rhea looks across the room to her bed. She marches over and jerks the pillow off the thin mattress, clapping it over her mouth and burying her head into it.

She screams until she makes her vocal cords ache as painfully as she does in her heart.

She screams until her throat feels like it's bleeding.

She screams until she feels like she has adequately vocalized the noises in her head.

She buries herself into the pillow, hoping to suffocate herself of all the volatile thoughts hissing at her that she isn't enough—that her body isn't enough. That she isn't pretty enough. Talented enough. Smart enough. Skinny enough. She—

A knock sounds at the door.

Rhea stiffens, dropping the pillow onto the bed and whirling toward the sound. Fuck. Of course he arrives *now.*

She hurries back to the mirror, more tears spilling over her eyes. Hurriedly, her fingertips swipe them all away, and she reaches for a small linen rag, rushing back over to the table beside her bed and dipping it into the water pitcher resting atop it. Then she scurries back and swipes the dark smudges from beneath her eyes and makes quick work of reapplying the powder underneath them, relining her blue gaze after.

"Rhea?" he calls from the other side of the door, his voice sharp and filled with irritation.

She grits her teeth, too many emotions clamoring through her right now to focus on a measly one. "Just a minute," she calls back, a quiver to her voice that makes her scowl at her own inability to pull her shit together.

She finishes with the last of her reapplications—doing the best she can given she has no remaining time—and huffs a breath that puffs out her cheek. She smooths her hair, readjusts her mother's hairpin wedged neatly into the center of her small bun, and she strides for the door. She counts to three silently for good measure, then pulls on the knob—revealing Finlay fucking Fjolla.

He is dressed as lavishly as she expected. A finely crafted arctic-blue, silky brocade jacket lined by silver threads and adorned with fine silver cuffs accentuates his already broad shoulders. The deep-aqua brocade waistcoat highlights his eyes, making them appear brighter and somehow even more lightened in their shade of blue—something Rhea didn't even know was possible. The House Fjolla sigil —an artistic snowflake wearing a crown—is stitched into the breast of his jacket, and his white hair is slicked back, his signature three small braids still tugging at one side of his head, tracing the slope of his ear —a particularly annoying detail, considering Rhea also chose to orna-ment her hair with small braids this evening.

Frankly, he looks positively handsome, and it annoys her down to the marrow of her bones.

He looks ready to snap at her, his eyes hard and mouth already slightly parted, as if he has been waiting for her with preloaded words on his tongue. Yet within a second of her opening the door, his features slacken, melting away at their roughened seams. His eyes trail over her, and something shifts in his expression—softening, even. "Have you been crying?" he asks, his voice surprisingly gentle.

She curls her lip at the question, making her displeasure at the inquiry clear. "What?" she scoffs. "No. Why? Did I mess up my makeup or something? Is this your twisted way of getting your shots in early?"

Through furrowed brows, he doesn't respond right away, choosing instead to watch her intently for a long, silent moment. It makes Rhea uncomfortable, feeling like someone is nearly seeing through her bull-shit. So she reinforces her mask and lifts her chin, finding the willpower to hold his intensely assessing stare.

Finally, he shakes his head, clearing his throat and resetting his expression. "No," he says, his brash tone returning, though notice-ably...different. He sweeps his eyes down the length of her once more, but it is quick and efficient. In the way one does more as an obligation than actual interest. "You look beautiful."

Despite her desire to roll her eyes at the sentence she's sure is entirely forced, she instead manages to find a pretty smile in her arsenal and paint it across her lips. "Thank you. You look... handsome."

He laughs, the sound seeming genuine. "That sentence seemed to pain you more than a dagger wound."

Her next smile comes easily. "It did." She reaches for her mask off her bed before stepping through the threshold and shutting her door, not needing to bring anything else tonight other than her best fabricated laugh and cultivated doe-eyed gaze. "But since I've been instructed to play nice tonight, forbidden from sticking a blade through your heart, it seems I am required to say it none-theless."

Like some psychopath, that sentence makes him grin wider, and Rhea can't detect an ounce of falseness to the gesture. He holds out his arm for her to take. She flicks her eyes down at it, meeting his gaze after with a pointed brow.

"Come on, Rhea," he pleads. "You've said it yourself—we've both been instructed to play nice tonight, so let's just...do it. At least for the evening."

Remaining silent, she simply arches her brow higher.

Finlay heaves a sigh, looking at her imploringly. "Look, for tonight and tonight only, let's agree to a truce, alright? Then, as soon as the sun rises over the horizon, you and I can go back to hating each other once more like tonight never happened."

"And if I refuse?"

He levels her with a knowing look. "We're both under orders, Rhea. No matter what you say or how difficult you try to be, you and I both know we can't be at each other's throats tonight. So, we might as well try to make a pleasant evening of it. Perhaps we'll even enjoy ourselves."

She inspects her nails. "The words you, pleasant, and enjoy have no business being in a sentence together."

He huffs a laugh, shaking his head as if accepting that comment. "Be that as it may," he pushes, motioning once more for her to take his arm. "Let's just try. Who knows, maybe we'll find we actually like each other by the end of the night."

Rhea finally allows her eyes to fall back to his. "Not possible," she deadpans, taking his arm in a way that shows Finlay she isn't happy about it.

"True," he agrees, now leading her down the blue carpeted corridor. "But I think you'll be surprised to learn I can be quite charming."

"The only thing charming about you is when your mouth is shut."

"So you're saying I'm good to look at?"

"I'm saying you're a pompous asshole, and the only time it's possible to forget that is when you're not talking."

He laughs, and Rhea eyes him sidelong, a strange feeling moving about her stomach. Everything about this feels odd. Them talking, him laughing. Still, she has no choice, because though she won't admit it to Finlay, he's right—she does have her orders to fulfill this evening, so she might as well make the best of it.

"What mask have you chosen for the ball?" he asks, jerking his chin toward the silver and black item clutched in her hand, the glittering jewels outlining its edges glinting from the braziers.

She glances down at it with indifference. "Nothing special."

"It matches your hair," he points out.

Rhea snorts at him in slight amusement, slight annoyance. "I'll bet your mask matches your hair, too. It's probably white and blue and caked with gemstones." She taps a finger against her chin. "In fact, I'd wager coin on it." She makes a show of scanning him. "Where is the thing? Come on, might as well show it to me."

He laughs, the sound dry but also... still genuine. "You'll see it once we arrive at the ball."

They round a corner, heading toward the stairwell leading to the main courtyard, where Draven, Kiran, and a few others should be waiting for them to depart for Talderine.

Finlay looks down at Rhea. "Why do you think Tynan and my father are instructing us to go to this ball together, anyways?"

She shrugs, her answer not *entirely* a lie. "Your guess is as good as mine." Sure, she knows the information she is meant to extract from Finlay this evening, but she hasn't the slightest clue what Tynan intends to do with it. "Maybe they want to fix the rift wedged between us?"

He scoffs. "Doubtful." A pause, and then, with a quick sidelong glance at Rhea, he asks, "Think that's possible?"

"Not a fucking chance."

A ghost of a smile haunts his lips.

They reach the winding stairwell at last, and Rhea steps forward, prepared to descend the first step. Yet Finlay gently wraps his fingers around her bare arm and halts her, holding her in place. His grip is surprisingly warm; she had always thought it would be cold as ice.

She glances up at him, a crease forming between her eyes. "What is it?"

He pushes his tongue into his cheek, sliding his jaw side-to-side as he appears to grasp for the words he's stopped her to say. "I just," he begins, snapping his mouth shut almost immediately. His lips thin. Eventually, though, the tight muscles slacken, and he tries again. "In the spirit of our alliance, I just wanted you to know I meant what I said earlier." A pause. "You really do look beautiful tonight, Rhea. Truly. You could bring any man you want to his knees, and I..." His jaw flexes. "I just wanted you to know the compliment was true."

She stares at him, confusion clamoring through her at the kind and seemingly sincere words. How—in spite of who they're coming from—desperately she wanted to hear that. She knows her worth and value stems from her own inner thoughts and feelings, but on the days where she feels too empty to fill her own cup, it's nice to have someone hold the weight temporarily in her place and pour it for her.

It's not a permanent fix, and she knows that. But...it helps.

If only a little.

"Thank you," she murmurs, entirely aware that she has never once in her life taken such a sincere tone with him before.

He nods, and as they descend the stairs together, she is utterly floored by feeling such gratitude toward Finlay Fjolla.

CHAPTER TWENTY-FIVE

GRAY

Gray paces back and forth across the red carpet lining the commons area, biting at the inside of his thumb.

It took him two weeks. Two whole weeks to convince Marcella to come with him to this Winter Solstice ball, and frankly, now that the night is finally here, he's practically a disheveled mess. They haven't spoken much lately. Not that they've been ignoring each other, but things between them have been…different. After their stay in Ninmere, where nothing happened yet everything changed, Marcella has put distance between them. Understandably so. It claws at Gray knowing his actions hurt her, regardless of whether he believed them to be right or not. Though, the more he ponders it, the more he struggles to reconcile what truly would have been the right thing to do.

It's as if the harder he tries to choose correctly given the current circumstances, the more incorrect things become. Like when he approached Marcella only a few days after they got back, determined to explain everything to her and let her know how desperately he ached to know the taste of her that night, but how he feels like, in some illogical way, doing that while Lyra's still being held captive somewhere seems wrong to him. Feels selfish and insensitive. Yet he never got the chance. In his attempt to do the right thing and tell her his reasonings, he only brought sadness upon her, made certain as he had to watch the pain flashing in and out of her eyes at him opening what she's clearly deemed an already closed wound. He only forced her to erect her defenses as she shut down the conversation before it could truly begin, strapping on the armor she now feels she needs to wear around him.

He wishes he could make her see she doesn't need it. Not with him. Yet he fears he drowned a beginning before it could ever truly bloom, ruining their chance at ever being something beautiful together.

Gods, if only she could feel the utterly hypnotic rhythm his heart dances to when she's near. If only she could understand how she haunts his every waking thought and caresses him in his dreams. If he could somehow make her know that he spends every waking second longing for her, pining for her affection, curling his fingers into his palms just so they don't do something foolish like reach out and brush her lips.

The memory of her lips so close to his swirls through his mind, and it's pathetic—how many times he's replayed the moment. He has turned it over, inspected it, reimagined it with an alternative ending. One where he slams his mouth to hers and drinks from it as though he has never known oxygen. A different outcome where he twines fingers through the mane of her hair and pulls, exposing her neck to him so he can place reverent kisses down the slope of it. Where he gives into his burning need for her and bites at her ear before roving lower, lower, lower—

The sound of heels clicking from the nearby stairwell, soon muffled by the plush carpet, snaps Gray from his thoughts. He halts his pacing and drops his thumb from his lips and back down to his side, staring at the figure emerging into the room.

He sees a goddess.

There is no other way to describe the captivatingly beautiful woman standing before him.

She is draped in a deep, royal blue beaded dress that hugs her waist and spills out near her feet. The neckline clutches her throat, and the short sleeves taper inward, cutting into her shoulders and revealing the entirety of the vines and leaves composing her wielder's mark. Her coppery hair is twisted back into an elegant, loose braid, and tendrils frame her delicate features. Her accompanying mask is midnight blue, and it glitters with the same subtle shine as her dress, lined by an ornate silver thread which twists into a design mirroring woven branches, rising into a small peak at the base of her forehead.

Gray stills at the sight of her, and for a moment, he swears his heart ceases to beat in his chest.

Just one look.

One look at her, and he knew he would give her the sun if she asked. He would crumple time with his fists and do away with every moment they wasted, every second he pretended as though he didn't feel a maelstrom of emotions for this beautiful, wild, brilliant girl in front of him. This one look is all it takes for him to realize he has been hopelessly ruined—doomed to never have a chance of feeling so much as a glimmer of the overtaking emotions clamoring in his chest for another person.

She braces a hand on her hip. "Are you just going to stand there staring at me, or are you going to offer me your arm like a proper gentleman and escort me to the meeting spot?"

Gray clears his throat, running fingers through his hair, only to remember it's been styled and he probably shouldn't be doing that. He strides across the room, reaching for her hand and lifting it to his lips as he bends at the waist and presses a tender kiss to the back of it, relishing in the tingling sensation he feels the moment his mouth brushes against her skin.

Marcella snorts at the gesture, pulling her hand back. "Unnecessary chivalry," she chides, mirth gleaming in her bright eyes, accentuated into sparkling cobalt jewels by the mask covering the upper half of her face.

"All the same. Who would I be if not chivalrous?" He clasps his hands behind his back and rolls his shoulders while straightening his spine, mocking excellent posture.

Marcella barks a laugh at him. "Ever the gallant guy," she muses through her tilted grin.

Gray shrugs, smiling like a helpless fool at her. "It's kind of my thing."

"Oh," she laughs, "I know. In fact, everyone in the whole gods-damn Three Kingdoms knows now. It's so much your thing, it's gotten you an invitation to one of Erandor Kingdom's most elite events, *Lion*." She drawls his nickname with a comedic flare, grinning tauntingly at him.

And like a fool, all Gray can do is stare at the work of art that is Marcella Lynderful, mesmerized and hopelessly captivated by her charm—by the charisma dripping from her sharp smiles and playful taunts, helpless to fall prey to her magnetism.

Gods, has he missed seeing and engaging with such treasures. Missed laughing and teasing and bantering with her.

For a time, she holds his gaze—whether in defiance of him or for some other reason, he can't be sure—but her glittering eyes remain connected to his, and embers rise in his chest, heating his skin at the way holding eye contact with her is like being hit by a jolt of lightning. Silence stretches between them, and he feels this overwhelming desire to reach for her. To act like she is his just as he knows he is irrevocably hers. To pretend as though he didn't ruin their chance at something more. He thinks about giving into the overwhelming feeling, too.

But then Marcella sucks in a sharp breath, retreats a barely noticeable step, and cups her elbows with her hands. "Where's your mask?" she asks, a noticeable shift in her tone as the earlier playfulness melts away and her wall erects firmly into place.

The space between them has never felt so distant.

Gray expels the strange mix of pain and longing clenching in his chest on a single breath, determined to make the best of tonight. "I don't have one."

She balks. "It's a masquerade ball, Gray. What do you mean you don't *have* one?"

He grins at her before pressing two fingers together and twirling them in a quick spin. He feels his magic warming in his veins, and at Marcella's arching eyebrows, he knows the illusion has taken effect.

"Can that really last the entire night?" There is both an air of approval and skepticism to her question.

His answering smile brims with confidence. "Definitely. I've strengthened my laktî considerably over these past few months, and the illusion requires such little magic from me, I suspect I could cast it for days, maybe even weeks."

Her lips tilt, and she rests a hand on her hip. "Well, aren't you just something to behold?"

"Yet I still find myself eclipsed by something greater in this moment."

Marcella's cheeks flush with a pink tint, and she playfully shoves his shoulder, tucking a stray strand of coppery hair behind her ear after. "Come on," she drawls, taking Gray's arm and holding onto it in a way that sends his heart skipping. "We have a long night ahead of us."

CHAPTER TWENTY-SIX

DRAVEN

Draven glances back up at the crisp night sky, irritation bubbling in his chest.

"What's taking them so long?" Arden asks from beside him, dressed in a tight-fitted, plunging purple gown that accentuates the warmer hues of her skin.

"Maybe they all did themselves a favor and got lost," he mutters dryly under his breath.

She shoots him a pointed look. "Can you at least try not to be the legendary Draven Dalmar, notorious asshole tonight?"

"Give me one name in attendance of tonight's event that deserves a different side of me."

"Arden Larking, Captain of the Iradine aggregate who just so happens to also be your date for the evening."

At Draven's at once noticeable and passive silence paired with the scowl on his face, her eyes soften, if only a fraction, and she sighs, lightly gripping her slender nose in a way that prevents ruining her carefully done-up face. "I didn't ask for this either, Draven. You know that."

He snorts, the sound devoid of any sympathy. "You certainly didn't help matters either with all your pining and advances over the years."

Her mouth pops open, and she looks uncertain as to whether the sentence makes her angry or pained. "In case you've forgotten, you were the one who brought *me* to *your* bed that night," she hisses at him. "Not the other way around."

He clenches his jaw. "It was a mistake," he says tersely. "I was hurting, and you were there. I regretted it the moment it happened."

She snaps her fingers, and a burst of light appears in front of Draven's gaze, blinding him with a jarring, heat-licked intensity. He winces, pressing his thumb and middle finger against his eyes. She snorts a victorious laugh. "That's for being such a damned asshole." A pause, and her voice drops. "I was only sixteen when I met you for the first time. Did you know that? We met at an event quite like the one we are attending tonight. My father said to me, 'Arden, that is the man you are going to marry someday, and it is going to make you the pride of House Larking.' And so that's what I believed." Her features stiffen, hardening with an anger she seems to be releasing bit by bit. "You were handsome and broody and muscular, and by the gods, you were all the things a sixteen-year-old is captivated by."

Draven arches a brow at her, silently indicating he'd like to know if there is a point to what she's saying. The sharp look she gives him in answer seems to tell him there is.

"I felt all the lust in the world toward you for many years following that," she continues. "My father kept saying to me that we would marry, and it was like a fan to those flames, making me so sure those feelings swirling around inside me were something real and special. Yet you barely glanced in my direction. Even while at Bathara. Even after becoming captains together. And then that night when I found you outside that tavern, I will never forget the moment you finally kissed me. How it was both everything I wanted and nothing like I thought it would be—hollow, empty, and cold. You tasted like sorrow. Then you dragged me into your bed, and..."

Arden drifts off, a moment of silence stretching between them. Draven's previous irritation toward her slowly gives way to regret and even a bit of a pity—though it's a feeling he recognizes no person ever wants from a former sexual partner. Still, he was a world-class asshole for what he did to her, and he knows it. He knew how she had felt about him all those years. He knew he would be crossing a boundary that, once stepped over, couldn't be uncrossed. But he was buzzed and lonely, and she was there, and he took advantage of that.

The stars twinkle overhead, bathing the rolling, shadow-kissed hills in a soft, luminescent glow. The glittering light reflects off the surrounding glassy waters, and the hums of the distant waterfalls lull softly in the background, a calming constant. Everything feels peaceful. Still.

Almost too still—like an omen of sorts.

Arden releases a quiet sigh. "Pining after you for a small time has never been the worst thing. Sleeping with you, only to find myself alone in an empty bed the following morning with a splintered heart, feeling—*knowing*—there was no chance it would ever be fixed by you was not the worst thing. No." She returns her honey-tinted eyes to his, lifting her chin and keeping her voice sturdy, as if she is merely stating facts. "The worst thing that has happened to me is finding myself betrothed to a man who I know will *never* want me. Will never touch me with the tenderness and reverence I deserve. To know I am somehow deemed the villain in his story because of my past affections, as if I *want* to be married to someone who wants nothing to do with me."

Draven steps forward, dropping his voice. "Then help me find a way out of this arrangement."

She scoffs, looking at him incredulous. "You made a gods-damn bargain, Draven. There's nothing I can do. You think me rejecting this proposal will *actually* make it go away?" She snorts, the sound nothing short of bitter. "For whatever reason, our fathers want this, and now they can have it—uniting House Dalmar and House Larking. At long last, darkness will finally merge with the light." At his openly surprised expression, she shakes her head, her dry chuckle not holding the slightest hint of actual joy. "What? You didn't think your father would inform mine of the nature of our arrangement?" Arden shrugs, trying to act like it doesn't bother her, but he can clearly see it does. "It's rather romantic of you, really—to attach your life to someone you care nothing for to save the life of the girl you love."

Love.

What a foreign word that would have been to him a few short months ago. Even if he has still never spoken the word aloud to another person. Not since his mother's passing.

"Maybe there's a way we can both find our happy endings," he counters, his rough voice steadied by an earnest determination.

"Happy endings are for hopeless fools, and I would've thought you of all people would know that."

Draven opens his mouth, but before he gets his chance to respond, Kiran's airy voice carries into the chilly night air.

"Children," he drawls wryly, "we're not already fighting, are we?" His lightened tone carries a hint of both amusement and accusation, his smirk wedged firmly in place. Though it looks...different. Less genuine, perhaps? Or maybe Draven's just imagining it after the conversation he's had.

Kiran is dressed in a fine black, silk shirt paired with a lavish red and black tapestry vest and fitted black trousers. The upper portion of his face is covered in a golden mask adorned with rubies that compliment his red, slicked back hair. The mask is framed by orange and vermillion markings, mimicking the path of flames. A closer look, and Draven can see he imbued some of his fire magic into the outlines of the gold, presumably keeping it at a low enough temperature to prevent the metal from melting while the twirling tendrils flicker constantly in a never ending loop across the top of the glinting thing.

"And if we were?" Arden challenges, the corner of her mouth already finding itself curved into a half smile.

"Well then, I'd feel compelled to point out that's no way to treat each other on the night of your betrothal announcement."

Draven swears under his breath, and Arden hisses.

Kiran shrugs. "It's true."

"Thanks," they retort bitterly in unison.

Draven offers her the smallest of smiles as he meets her sidelong glance, and Arden huffs a small laugh. Only a few more seconds pass before Finlay and Rhea appear, strolling through the pathway lined by juniper trees to the west, the roaring flame torches illuminating them in the distance. Draven braces himself for the inevitable sideway glances and comments Rhea is sure to give him tonight—she doesn't know about the coming announcement yet. No one, save for Kiran, does.

Once they reach them, Draven does a quick sweep over Rhea, making sure she is alright. Though they've never openly spoken about it, he knows she struggles with the image she has of herself. That on the nights of formal events, her struggle intensifies—harms her more physically than most other days. He also knows she has House Dalmar to thank for that.

Just another reason to hate his fucking name.

"You look breathtaking," he says by way of greeting. He slides his eyes to Finlay, a taunting smile tugging at his mouth. "I guess you look pretty decent, too. Even if you don't deserve to be standing within an inch of your date."

Finlay rolls his eyes.

Kiran frowns, bouncing his eyes between the two of them. "What in the forces of nature convinced you two to go to the ball together?" He steps forward, taking Rhea's hand and pressing a light kiss to the back of it. "And Draven is right—you are as radiant as the stars."

Finlay seems to stiffen at the gesture, and Draven swears he sees him take a tiny step closer to Rhea, as if feeling the need to proclaim she is with him for the evening and no one else.

What in god's veins?

"Tynan and Audwin insisted we accompany each other this evening," Rhea answers, oblivious to everything else as she watches Kiran, who has now dropped her hand and stepped back into his original position. "Now where's your date? After Ninmere, I'd have figured you'd ask—"

"I decided to attend the ball alone," Kiran answers before she can finish.

Her eyes narrow on him, yet Draven's eyes narrow on her, still assessing.

Rhea's expression has been carefully crafted to show nothing but annoyance at attending tonight's event with Finlay. Yet there is a small glint in her eye that Draven can't help but notice. Like an extra wick was lit inside her, and the light can't help but flicker behind her gaze. It leaves him wondering what the hell he has missed in the span of a few hours?

Arden snorts, folding her arms. "Consider yourself lucky you had the option," she says to Kiran. "Clearly, not all of us are so fortunate."

Both Finlay and Rhea's brows furrow, their curious gazes shifting between Arden and Draven.

"Are you two also going to the ball together?" Finlay asks, sliding a quick look at Draven.

Draven can pin at least three unspoken questions tacked to that single one.

"So it would seem," is Arden's only reply.

Rhea stares at Draven wearing a frown, clearly unhappy with not knowing about this. But Draven is saved from a lecture or any expectations to elaborate when Gray and Marcella stroll in from the east path.

"Well would you look at that," Kiran drawls. "Everyone's here."

Draven and Gray lock eyes in a way that says they both know everyone is *not* here.

The quickly passing look makes Draven's heart ache, reminding him of his growing madness—of the unspeakable actions he's beginning to consider in his desperation to find Lyra. He has been mildly pacified over the last few weeks after getting to write to her; the letters had been like receiving air in suffocating lungs. The world felt saturated again, and some of the tightness that had been knotted in his chest had loosened with the knowledge Lyra is alive—with getting to hear her words echo in his mind.

The deal he made with his father, all the actions he's been taking—it's all worth it, because writing with her showed him Lyra is *alive*. And from what she's written to both her and Gray, she is decently well cared for. A fact of which both perplexes Draven and leaves him feeling grateful.

Yet those small glimmers of hope were recently snuffed out when her letters suddenly stopped coming. Without warning, she stopped replying. Stopped writing to him. And having to wonder the reasons surrounding that has been eating at his mind and soul for over a week now.

He has managed to get away and discreetly follow three more leads down at the southern borders, yet still...nothing. It is as perplexing as it is frustrating, and Draven isn't sure how many more dead ends he can take. He also can't help but wonder if he weren't juggling his father's orders and threats if he would have found Lyra by now. If he would be able to hold her in his arms and know she is safe.

The guilt presses against him. He knows he is doing his best at managing it all—to give each element his full self while keeping everyone protected. Yet still, he can't help but feel like he is failing his girl by taking so long to find her. To bring her home.

Chattering voices snap Draven from his wandering thoughts.

"I love your dress," Rhea says to Marcella, eyeing her head to toe with appreciation.

"Thanks. My brothers picked it up for me when they were in Lydith recently. They couldn't believe it when I told them I was going to the ever-elite Winter Solstice Ball at the infamous Sagamon Castle. Next thing I know, this dress arrives through aether-mail." She laughs, and her eyes trail the length of Rhea's sparkling black and silver gown in a similar fashion. "Your gown is gorgeous. It fits you like the designer made it with you in mind."

"Unfortunately," she drones, "he did. Tynan had it specially made for tonight's event."

"You know, I haven't met the guy yet and I already loathe him with my entire being. He sounds more dull than the brooding hunk of muscle over there." She jerks her chin at Draven. "And an even more self-righteous asshole than popsicle over here." She jerks her chin at Finlay next.

"I resent that," Finlay mutters stiffly.

"And I'm not dull," Draven deadpans, folding his arms. "I'm stoic. There's a difference."

Rhea bursts with laughter, and despite the blatant insult she just threw Draven's way, he can't help but smile at the sight of her like that. Such a rare sight nowadays—to see her react without inhibition. A fact that will always stain his conscience, knowing it was his father who shaped the careful, guarded, and spiteful woman she's become.

But for now, in this moment, he catches a glimpse of the small, fun-loving ten-year-old girl he met all those years ago back in Príth, who would laugh and brawl and interrogate ceaselessly without a care in the world. The girl who wore her heart on her sleeve.

In that moment, seeing the reflection of Rhea's former happiness brought out so effortlessly by Marcella makes Draven understand why Lyra immediately gravitated toward the flora-wielder. Begins to understand just a bit more the allure that is Marcella Lynderful.

"You do realize you just casually insulted two of the most powerful people in the entire Three Kingdoms?" Arden points out.

Draven watches as Marcella glances at Rhea, who gives her a small nod. Her grin widens. "And do *you* realize you are wearing that dress like it's a crime, Captain Larking?" Though her tone is playful, it isn't mocking.

"Please," Arden says through her answering laugh, trying to play off the compliment like it doesn't mean anything to her. "No need to call me by my title tonight. Just Arden is fine."

The sentence stirs an old, forgotten memory, tucked neatly into a hole in some cobwebbed place within him.

I am just...Draven.

Alright, Just Draven.

The girls say more, and as if on instinct, Draven's eyes wander to Kiran, expecting him to join in with some wry comment. Yet his eyes remain locked on something in the distance, as if he hasn't been paying attention to the passing conversation in the slightest. It seems he, too, has lost himself to his mind.

"Kiran?" Draven asks.

He snaps his eyes away from the landscape, coming back to himself. "Yes?"

"Everything alright?"

Noticing his question, Finlay takes a few steps closer to them, listening for Kiran's answer, though not looking at him as he does—his eyes instead remaining locked on Rhea. Gods, Draven wishes those two would just figure their shit out already. Also…

He seriously has some questions for Finlay after tonight. Because why the hell *does* he keep looking at Rhea like that?

Kiran plasters a wide grin to his face. "I'm always alright when there is endless drink in my future."

Rhea chimes in, "Why *haven't* we left yet? I'm with Kiran—if I'm going to make it through tonight, I need a drink."

Marcella regards her. "You know, you're really growing on me."

"You're not so bad yourself," Rhea replies with a tilted smirk.

Finally speaking for the first time, Gray drones in a flat tone, "We are waiting for my terrible cousin to join us, and we still need the aether-wielder who will be transporting us to arrive."

Rhea eyes him. "And who is your terrible cousin, exactly?"

Right on cue, that slimy prick, Huxley Rangard, strolls down the same path Rhea and Finlay traveled along, his chin lifted high as he struts like he owns the gods-damn world. A low growl rattles in the back of Draven's throat at the sight of him.

Arden steps forward, leaning over and whispering, "I'll take it you're not a fan?"

Draven's grunt is his only confirmation. He doesn't bother to explain that 'not a fan' doesn't begin to cover it. He nearly murdered the little rat all those months ago after overhearing what he said to Lyra during their first judgement.

His magic flares beneath his skin, growing warm and whispering to be released. Draven is not happy with how much effort it takes to silence the hissing pleas of his magic. He rolls his neck side to side.

"Ladies, gentlemen." Huxley bows low at the waist, his jade-colored suit glinting beneath the moonlight. "Captains. It is an honor to be traveling with you this evening."

Kiran rolls his eyes and groans. "For the love of the gods…"

One glance in Gray's direction, and it appears he has assumed a similar demeanor. Truthfully, Draven has never seen Nightenjoy be so openly perturbed by someone before.

Huxley straightens, sparing a quick look at Gray and choosing to ignore him entirely. "I apologize for my tardiness," he simpers. "Shall we be on our way? My father is expecting me, so—"

"All of our fathers are expecting us," Finlay says sharply, cutting him off. "We just need an aether-wielder to travel."

As if summoned, a swirling black and silver portal appears, and the Conscripted aether-wielder, Klytis, steps through. "Everyone ready?"

Gray steps forward, smiling at the man as he extends his arm out to him. "Are you joining us for the entire evening?"

Klytis shakes his head, clasping his hand to Gray's forearm. "I am merely the transportation tonight." Though he says it lightly, there is something loaded in the quality of his words. His eyes temporarily float to Kiran—who is not looking back—before retreating to look at Gray once more. The smile he forms is thin and tight.

"Well then," Finlay says, clapping his hands together with an air of impatience. "Let us finally be on our way."

CHAPTER TWENTY-SEVEN

LYRA

Casimir tosses a beautifully crafted mask down on the desk in front of me.

I frown at it. "What is this?"

"We've been invited to a ball," he says, as if that is any explanation at all.

"You have those around here?"

He doesn't answer my question, instead watching me—studying my expression with unnerving scrutiny.

Things have been tense between Casimir and me lately. Or perhaps I should say more intense than the usual current surging from me to him. Outside of our brief interactions during my training —which he has been leaving to Neilina more and more after what happened, who I've since begun to form quite the kinship with—and him accompanying me to the Astral Chamber while I continue entering the Veil for my training, which has been frustratingly stagnant, seeing as the Veil hasn't shown me anything intelligible since the first time I entered—he and I haven't really spoken much. Not that I'm complaining.

I thought I was going to *actually* attempt to kill him after he stole away the only glimmer of hope I've found since being here.

It had to have been around midnight when he knocked on my door and strolled into my room unannounced. It was a little over two weeks ago. Why he was there or what he wanted from me, I still don't know. But he had wanted to say something, and he wandered into my chamber to say it. I drift briefly into the memory, allowing myself to taste the bitter ashes of it on my tongue as a small fire comes alive in the pit of my stomach.

"What are you doing here?" I asked Casimir, whipping the Ever-Know Quill behind my back as I scurried from my bed.

His brows scrunched together. He had entered the room with a particular softness—something unarmed and almost conciliatory. Yet the air around him shifted—sharpened. "What are you hiding behind your back?"

My heart dropped. "Nothing," I lied, avoiding the urge to grit my teeth. There was no way I could truly hide the Ever-Know Quill—not with his eyes boring into me like that.

He stepped toward me, flicking his eyes to my ruffled bed, where a piece of worn and wrinkled parchment sat half-covered by bedsheets. Something flashed in his eyes, and I was surprised to find hurt at the forefront of it. Yet just as quickly as I thought I saw the emotion, it was gone, instead replaced by a cold rage.

He extended a hand. "Give it to me."

I feigned ignorance. "Give what to you?"

He was in no mood to play games, and the sharpness of his tone and icy threat glinting in his amber eyes said as much. "The magical quill you are hiding behind your back."

It was an act of the resting gods I didn't openly blanch at his correct deduction. Instead, I tucked the quill into the band of my undergarments, annoyed at how useless my nightgown was to me at that moment. I held up my now free hands, exposing my palms to him. "I haven't the faintest clue what you're talking about."

His lips thinned as he seemed to actively check his visibly increasing anger. "This is the final time I will ask you."

I remained silent.

He wielded a strike of air magic so forceful, it thrust my gown up over my face and the quill tumbled from its precarious position against my body and onto the floor. I thrusted the silky fabric back down, rage igniting the blood I could already feel pounding in my ears. "What the hell is your problem?" I snarled.

Ignoring me, he strode to where the Ever-Know Quill laid resting on the hardwood floor, picking it up and examining it closely. After, he curled his fingers around it so tightly, his knuckles paled. "Will we never be enough for you?" he asked, his low voice crackling like the first signs of a coming storm.

I blinked at him, confusion, anger, and irritation all clamoring in my chest. "It has nothing to do with you and everything to do with them. I miss my friends. My home. How you can stand there and pretend it so preposterous I feel that way is beyond me."

"Because I will never understand how you continue to defend the version of your life where you were treated like dirt. We have been good to you. I have been good to you." There was almost a plea in his words. He stomped forward and ripped the parchment from the bed, the last words Draven wrote to me still seared onto the page.

Are you alright?

Casimir stared at it, and his nostrils flared. "And this?" He waved the parchment in the air for emphasis. "This is how you repay all my kindness?"

I saw red.

"What about kidnapping me is kind? What about murdering one of my friends is kind? What about forcing me into the Veil every week, my body feeling wrecked each and every morning after, is kind? Where is the kindness in your plans for genocide and revenge? Tell me, what am I missing?"

Casimir prowled toward me, stopping only when there was a breadth of space between us. "You can say what you will about all the actions I have taken," he murmured so low, I could barely hear the rasping words. "But what you cannot deny is that you have been treated far better and with far more dignity in my home than you ever were in the Three Kingdoms. And you know what makes that fact all the worse? It's that you—as you so love to point out—are a prisoner here. So even as a prisoner in my home, you are treated with more respect than as a citizen in yours."

I held his eyes, my chest heaving with anger. "Get out," I hissed between clenched teeth.

"Gladly," he replied. "But not before I take care of one act of business."

Without averting his gaze from me, he lifted the Ever-Know Quill and snapped it apart into tiny pieces, sprinkling them onto the floor around him. Then, he tore the only piece of parchment I had into scattered ribbons, letting them float to the ground like snowflakes.

My chest practically caved in on itself, and I was overcome with the urge to fall to my knees. Yet I did not let myself show an ounce of weakness in the presence of this fucking monster. Instead, I lifted my chin and let every ounce of loathing I felt for Casimir Vivaldri twist my expression. "I hate you."

"Yeah?" He took one step closer to me, no more than a finger's length between us now. He leaned down, his hardened features set while some inscrutable emotion flickered in his eyes. "Good."

I snap out of the memory, only to find Casimir still watching me. Though, now he looks as though he wants something from me. "Sorry?"

His brows twitch, but he doesn't comment on me spacing out. "I said the ball isn't happening here; it's happening in Talderine."

I jerk out of my chair so forcefully, it falls back with a loud *thud*. "What did you just say?"

He leans against the ledge of the interior greenhouse wall, crossing his ankles and tucking one hand beneath the elbow of his other arm. "See," he says, wagging a lazy finger, "now that is the reaction I was anticipating."

"Don't toy with me," I warn, hope swelling in my chest as a pragmatic counterweight attempts to dilute the feeling.

"I assure you, I am not."

My body sags, and I brace one hand against my work desk. I look at Casimir, narrowing my gaze on him. "How did you receive an invitation to a ball in Talderine? Better yet, how did *we* receive one?"

The gravity of the question rattles through me. It means someone in Talderine knows where Casimir's been hiding. Knows that I'm here with him.

Knows how to reach us.

"Precisely what I'd like to know," he answers with an air of annoyance.

My heart races, trepidation leaking into my veins as I gather the courage to ask my next question, fearful to receive an answer I don't wait to hear. "And are we..." I clear my throat. "Do you intend to accept the invitation?"

He does not answer right away, instead gazing at me intently. Finally, after seconds that feel like years, he glances out the arching greenhouse windows and sighs. "I do." Seeing the hope bloom on my face—plans upon plans forming in my mind about how to escape and get word to Draven or Gray or *somebody* that I'm coming home—Casimir kicks off the wall and strides over to me. "Do not get any ideas, Lyra. I still have plans I need you for. The only reason I am accepting this offer is because—" He stops suddenly, as if chewing on how to explain his reasoning without giving too much of himself away. His jaw flexes. "There was something in that letter which I must follow up with. And though I would *love* to simply attend this masquerade ball alone, the letter's only requirement for my attendance is that you join me for the evening's festivities."

So it's a masquerade ball, huh? That explains the mask he tossed onto my desk.

Still. Who is this person, and why the hell do they want me joining Casimir at some ball in Talderine? While there is no chance I'll be passing up the opportunity, something about this seems....wrong. Orchestrated.

"Do you know who sent the letter?" I ask.

He shakes his head, irritation flickering in his eyes. "Who sent it. How they got it here. How they were capable of learning where *here* even is. All questions I do not have answers to but intend to receive tonight."

"*Tonight?*" I balk.

"Yes," he confirms with a small dip of his chin. "Tonight."

Nerves, hopes, cautions, dreams—they all race through me in a blur, tangling and merging into one incohesive blob of emotion.

"I..." Casimir pauses, face scrunching as his lips purse with thought. Another sigh, and his voice softens. "There are multiple dresses laid out for you in your bedchamber which you may choose from. I remember how poorly it made you feel when I picked out your last dress. Neilina is waiting for you. She volunteered to help attend to you in preparation for this evening. We leave at sunset."

Then he turns and silently exits the greenhouse, leaving me to drown in my thoughts and relish in all my what-if possibilities.

Free.

Perhaps by the end of the night, I can finally be free.

A ripple of seafoam colors my vision, and for a moment, I close my eyes and allow myself to imagine the sensation of being held in arms that will never let go at last.

NEILINA CHATTERS ABOUT, seeming to be excited for my night out with Casimir. Listening to her enthusiasm and seeing the gleam in her eye almost makes me feel guilty.

I can't tell her I don't plan on coming back.

Yet that decision is accompanied by a tinge of melancholy. I will miss Neilina. Through these passing months, she has become a friend. Or perhaps it's better to say she has become something like I imagine having a little sister to be like. No…maybe I should say older sister, because despite our age differences—with me having nearly five years on her after my birthday quietly passed by—she still nags me, speaks to me, and encourages me in all the ways I imagine an older sister would. She is stern, yet kind. Direct and truthful, though not unnecessarily so.

I am convinced watching her and Marcella together would be something to behold.

At the pointed clearing of Neilina's throat, I snap my eyes up to her face using the mirror resting in front of us. "Are you even listening to me?" she asks pointedly, humor glittering in her gray-tinted eyes as her fingers are knotted in my hair.

"Sorry," I mutter. "My head is running in a lot of directions right now."

She offers me a sympathetic look. "Are you nervous to go back?"

My fingers twirl over themselves. "Why would I be nervous?"

"From what Master has told me, your home has not been very kind to you."

I arch a brow. "And what else has *Master* told you about me?" I don't hide the mocking emphasis on Casimir's given title. Neilina just stares at me expectantly, not allowing me to dodge her question. I sigh. "All homes are not without their issues."

She returns to styling my hair—a simple design, we decided, where the shoulder-length strands are curled into soft waves while one side is twisted back elegantly. "Though true that may be, there is a difference between a place with grievances and fundamental classism. You are discarded by them because they deem your blood of little worth, but what gives their blood any more special properties than your own?" She pauses, despite the question being clearly rhetorical. "An abundance of coin—that's what. Which has nothing to do with blood whatsoever."

I watch her through the mirror, surprise and awe filling my features. "Are you sure you're only seventeen?"

She shrugs, a smirk pulling at her lips. "Our education is different here. We're not spoonfed lies purporting the entitlement of one's claim to power over another's. Instead, we're taught to ask questions —to peel back the masks of the regime giving instructions. To ponder: *Why would someone* really *be doing this?*"

"I had no idea," I murmur.

"What?" Neilina asks through a teasing snort. "That we are educated, or that those are the principles on which our education is built?"

"The latter," I assure her through a weak laugh. My eyes study Neilina carefully. "You truly love it here, don't you? Love serving Casimir and don't mind in the slightest that you're an Abd—" I cut myself off, wincing at the use of a term I'm not entirely sure she would find offensive or not.

But I do know it for certain now. I finally glimpsed her wielder's mark while training—a large circle on her forearm encasing an upside down triangle, where inverted waves fill the inside. She's a water-wielder, yet when she wields, the water—though still fluid—is more like a solid than it is a liquid. It was strange to witness, to say the least.

"An Abdite," she finishes for me. "You can say it. It is the title your home has given to wielders like me, after all. Though, we call ourselves *Lahtiuma* here." A long silence stretches as Neilina finishes with my hair and steps back, inspecting her work a final time. Once satisfied, she sits down on the edge of the canopy bed, and I turn in my chair to look at her. "I have left here once before, you know."

Though I don't think she is really asking, I shake my head all the same.

"It was two years ago. I was fifteen, and Master needed to visit your home. He'd been working on something—a cure of sorts, I guess you could say. To erase the corruption from the laktî of those who never wanted it there in the first place. He took myself and three other personal guards with him." She stills, taking a breath as shadows awaken in her eyes. "Some succumbed to the madness quicker than others. They say the stronger the magic, the stronger the resistance. I was the last to slip into it, and… Those voices, their commands…"

I move to sit next to her on the bed, taking her hand in mine. I remain silent, not entirely sure what to say. So, I simply sit there and give her space to remember. To speak freely.

"I'll never forget the feeling—like my consciousness was trapped inside a tiny cage, and anger, hatred, and psychosis became the puppetmaster pulling all my strings. I was aware of myself, yet I simultaneously had no control over myself. I hated it."

I squeeze her hand.

"My point in telling you this is because I want to answer your question—yes, I love it here. The old magic encasing our home keeps the madness away. I am cared for. I am seen and cherished and live without persecution for something I never asked to be. Sure, there *are* wielders who willingly corrupt themselves and give into the forbidden magics. But those of us here? We didn't ask for our fates. And Master? Master found us—*cares* for us. Has worked hard to create a paradise we can live freely within."

My brows furrow as I think of the plan Casimir created. If

everyone is happy here, why bother going through all the trouble of resetting the corruption and classism happening within the Three Kingdoms? Why does he worry about their freedom if they feel entirely uninhibited here? If they can live without their madness, why leave? It sounds like he loves them and they love him, so why not simply stay here, living in peace?

I say as much to Neilina.

A heavy sadness fills her gaze. "Because the magic protecting us here is dying. We can all feel it—random moments where our minds slip. That's why Master was working even more diligently to find a cure for us. Why he brought half our numbers to recover you from that academy, knowing the sacrifice they'd be forced to make."

I'm at a loss for words, my mind trying to process and make sense of what I've just learned. I'm in the middle of considering if the dying magic is a result of the cracking golden statue towering in that temple when Neilina speaks again.

"Is it really so bad to live amongst us in your eyes?"

The question catches me off guard, and I shake my head at the implications encasing it. "No," I answer, surprised to realize just how much I mean it.

"So why are you so eager to leave us behind? To reject this place and all of us within it?" For the first time since I've known her, Neilina finally looks her age—like a young teenager, trying to understand the ways of this world.

"I'm not," I rasp, an unexpected sadness piling in my chest. "It's just…" I sigh. "I have people I love back home. People who love me in return. And… I miss them. In more ways than you could imagine." I chew on my next sentence, attempting to get the message right. "It's not the place I miss—it's the people. The way my life feels more saturated with them in it. It's hard to simply let that go because someone has told you to."

Neilina seems to sit with that thought. Eventually, she nods. "I think Master is beginning to feel that way about you. He's different with you than he is with us. Not kinder or more attentive, but…more illuminated, perhaps?"

For whatever reason, the words bring the slightest flush to my cheeks. I stamp down the sensation immediately. "Why do you call him Master if all of you are free here?" It's a question I've been wondering for some time now.

She laughs softly, a smile I'd almost identify as fond tugging at her lips. "It's our choice to do so. Truthfully, I heard from some of the other personal guards that he loathed the title when it was first given to him many years ago. Yet it helps steady our minds when they slip. By committing to calling him nothing but Master, we program ourselves—our brains—to believe that's true. Because of that, if we ever slip into madness, the fabrics of both our identity and magic take that as fact, and we answer to him instead of the voices."

"That's a lot of trust you've put in him."

She shrugs. "From what I've seen and heard, he's earned it." She slaps her hands to her thighs and rises from the bed. Oddly, she seems lighter. Like that conversation was one she had been sitting on for a while, and now that she's said what she's wanted, she can glide along more easily. "You should consider giving this place a chance," she muses, her cheery voice like a sweet drink to my senses. "I think you might find it'll grow on you—if you let it." Neilina stretches her hand out to me, and I take it with a small huff of laughter.

We're both smiling when she pulls me up from the corner of the bed and escorts me to the wardrobe, where three elegant and incredibly lavish gowns await my attention.

Casimir certainly has a sense of style, I have to give him that.

Neilina glances at me, seeming giddy with anticipation. "Which will you choose? We'll do your eye makeup to match the tones of whichever one you pick."

I chuckle, shaking my head while staring at the dresses. "You do remember I'll have a mask on, right?"

"All the more reason to make sure those pretty, mismatched eyes of yours pop."

Mismatched eyes.

My heart aches, and I'm filled with the gnawing wonderment if going to Talderine is going to be harder than I expect. Will it hurt, being so close yet far from Draven with no way to reach him? No way to let him know how near I am? Will it make the hollow throbbing in my chest only intensify?

What if he's somehow there? It is his home city, after all.

Just as quickly as the thought races through my head, though, I shove it away as wishful thinking. Draven hates Talderine. Hates any sort of formal function. He even told me how much he hates dancing. No. Despite how much I wish it possible, the odds of Draven being at whatever event I'm attending tonight are marginal at best, and I shouldn't waste my energy nor efforts on foolish fantasies that will only grind my heart into smaller broken bits.

I offer Neilina a half-hearted laugh as a reply and study the dresses. Two of them are sleeveless while the other features nude, mesh sleeves, leaving the skin still visible, though blurred with a complimenting layer much like a nice powder to the face. I shift on my feet, my eyes glancing down at the scars running along the length of my left arm before back up at all the glittering fabric.

"I think I'll choose this one," I say, gliding a finger along the gown with mesh sleeves.

Though the sleeves are not the isolated reason for why I pick it. The other dresses are either sparkling with large jewels or overly colorful and attention-seeking. The gown I've chosen feels soft and understated, maintaining an undeniable elegance. It has a plunging v-neckline extending from its sheer, illusion-style bodice, stitched from the same mesh material composing the arms of the dress. It is adorned with delicate, embroidered silver thread work which plunges down to meet the torso of the off-white gown in lavish spirals, spreading along the length of the tulle until it meets the hem, where a latticework of flowers and vines overlap in a remarkably beautiful design.

It will be the nicest article of clothing I've ever worn. The sort of dress I used to notice women wearing during King Alastair's events and envy, glancing down at my sheer pants and skimpy tops and always feeling horribly tawdry in comparison. Now, as I consider slip-ping into such a dress, I'm filled with an unexpected giddiness—near excitement, even.

For the first time in my life, I will simply be a guest at one of these parties, made all the sweeter by knowing I will have the privilege of being hidden by a mask. I will simply be a girl dressed in a beautiful ball gown dancing under the moonlight. Though I highly doubt I'll *actually* be doing any dancing this evening.

Neilina looks to the dress then back at me. She is beaming. "I think it's perfect for you."

CHAPTER TWENTY-EIGHT

LYRA

When I find myself standing in front of Casimir's chamber door, I'm filled with the strangest sense of exhilaration.

I've never been to Talderine, so it is with an odd anticipation I await getting to see it for the first time. I'm also curious to know what event we are attending, who is hosting, and hopefully learn the identity of whoever it is that located Casimir. There are also the other swirling branches of thoughts I have—all the other possibilities that may bloom from tonight.

Freedom.

Just one second of the stars aligning, and I could potentially find a way out of this whole mess. To get away from Casimir and back to Bathara.

Yet the thought is instantly met with the weight of two others. What if he comes for me just like he did last time, murdering more and more people? And why do I feel oddly saddened by the thought of never seeing Neilina again—never giving this place or its people the proper chance it deserved?

The door swings open—my fist hovering midair—and I nearly suck in a gasp at the sight of Casimir. Though, I manage not to—

thank the Mother. I simply lift a brow at him instead. "Shouldn't we be attempting to go unnoticed this evening?"

Even through his mask, I make out his frown. "What do you mean?"

My brows lift higher at his seemingly genuine confusion. "I mean, you are going to draw every eye in the gods-damn room dressed like that. Trust me, I've worked plenty of balls, and I know what type of looks get the most attention." I make a show of sweeping my eyes over him. "And you? You are *definitely* going to get a lot of attention."

He is dressed in a finer suit than anything I've ever seen. The black fabric is like silk, yet...not. Again leading me to wonder for a second time what material his clothes are made from. His fitted tailcoat is adorned with gold embroidery which trails along the outer lengths of the jacket, glittering subtly beneath the light. It whorls until meeting a floral pattern, and I'm struck with the oddest hunch that the design is intentional. His hair is half-drawn, held in place by a leather band the exact shade of his attire, and covering the upper-portion of his face is a sparkling amber and onyx mask, decadently crafted and undeniably beautiful. Leaving me to believe my prior teases of him may actually be correct...

I think he truly *does* love fashion.

He sighs, the sound long and deep in his chest. "Well, there's no time for me to change now, so let's just hope I can slip in, have my meeting, and then we can be on our way."

I scoff a laugh. "I have a sneaking suspicion it won't be that simple."

"Nothing ever is." He nods toward the door, beckoning me inside. "Come on. I'll open the portal from in here."

I stroll inside while Casimir holds the door for me, scanning my surroundings. The room looks practically unchanged from when I last saw it. Almost unnervingly so. His onyx sheets appear to be bunched exactly as they were when I saw them the night after the death ceremony, and the inkwell and parchments scattered along his writing desk against the far wall are in the exact same order as before.

Odd.

I feel Casimir behind me before I see him. Whirling around, I find him watching me, the mask removed from his face and instead clutched between his fingers. He studies me, but not in any way that makes me feel uncomfortable.

"I assumed that would be the dress you chose."

"Oh?" I say through a laugh. "As if you know my tastes in gowns so well?"

He shakes his head, a small curve lifting one side of his mouth. "No," he counters. "I just also thought it was the most fitting for you."

I hum, eyeing him.

"Would you like a drink?" He struts over to the unlit hearth and reaches for a crystal decanter, popping off the glittering top and pouring a light amber liquid into two wide glasses. Wordlessly, he strolls back to me and extends one of them out for me to take.

"I never said yes."

"I know," is his only reply. He stretches the glass out further.

I flick my eyes between him and the drink, releasing a quiet sigh as I decide why the hell not. I take it from his hand and down it all in one gulp, the burning sensation permeating through my body nearly instantly. Casimir watches me, his brow raised.

"What?" I quip. "Never seen a woman down a drink before?"

"No." A light chuckle fills the word. "I most certainly have. It's just...been a long time." He swirls the liquid around his glass, then, in a similar fashion, downs the whole thing in one gulp.

Wordlessly, he reaches to take the glass from my hand—tingling warmth already spreading to my fingertips—and he returns them to the mantle, seemingly deciding to attend to them later. Once he is back in front of me, he locks his gaze onto mine and hums, as if considering something.

"What is it?" I ask.

Still not saying anything, he steps forward and reaches down toward my fingertips. My heart quickens, and my cheeks again flush —though most likely from the potent liquor I just downed.

"Relax," he breathes, seeming to sense how rigid I've become. His fingertips wrap around the mask I've been clutching in my hand all this time, and he takes it into his own hand, holding it up and waving it around in the air as if to say that is all he wanted.

My muscles ease, and though I manage not to hunch in relief, I do exhale a loosening breath. Casimir eyes me a moment longer, then inspects the mask.

"You should put this on now. Once I open the portal, we will step through and at once be met by someone attending to the arrangements I have made. I do not want so much as a glimpse of our identities getting out."

"Arrangements?"

He returns the mask to me, and I pull it over my face while keeping my eyes carefully on him. "Given the distance and nature of this particular trip, it requires a lot of magic from me," he explains. "Since I do not know precisely what we are walking into nor who we are dealing with, I'd like to give myself time to replenish a bit of my magical resources beforehand."

"Alright," I draw out, my expression pinched.

"I'm correct in thinking you've never been to Talderine, yes?"

The wrinkles in my brows deepen. "Yes," I answer, tone tentative. "Well, I guess I mean no—I haven't."

"Perfect."

WE STEP through Casimir's portal and are met by a large, powder-blue carriage featuring two beautiful white-speckled horses.

The wheels and spokes of the carriage are golden, its seats plush and red-leathered. A driver is already propped up in the driver's box, the horses' reins clutched in his white-gloved hands. Two gilded lanterns rest on each side of him, and when he turns toward us, he jumps as if startled.

"Oh!" he squeaks. "I beg pardon. I didn't see you arrive." His accent is funny. A mixture of posh and poverty.

Casimir inclines his head to the man. "We only just got here."

"Ah." The man eyes him for a good moment, seeming to weigh a question in his mind. Whatever it is, though, he doesn't ask. Instead, he shifts, making to get up from his seat to open the carriage door for us.

Casimir stops him. "No need," he says, voice soft. "I have got it."

The man dips his chin and resettles himself back into his seat. "Are your plans still the same for the evening, Lord Christopher?"

Casimir props open the carriage door and extends his hand out to me. "They are."

I step toward him and place my hand in his, glancing at him pointedly. "Lord Christopher?" I ask under my breath, the tiniest laugh caressing my words.

He shrugs, the gesture nearly imperceptible. "I needed a name to use," he whispers back. "Now be quiet about it and do not blow my cover." There is a playful glint resting in his eyes that I haven't seen before, and I can't help but snort a laugh at it. He straightens, his smile showing teeth now. "M'lady," he drawls, inclining his head as he helps me up the step.

I roll my eyes but accept the aid and enter into the carriage. Once he's taken up his seat directly next to me and the carriage door is closed behind us, I regard him with teasing disapproval. "Is all of this really necessary?"

"It is."

"Why?"

"You'll see in just a moment."

The reins snap and there is a *click* of the driver's tongue. The wheels groan as they start their journey along the cobblestone streets, and the horse's hooves *clop* against the rock in a soothing melody. A spicy, woodsy scent floods the carriage, wafting from Casimir. It is peppery and warm, a mixture of musk and vanilla.

I glance at him, studying his features, realizing just how deeply he confuses me as a person. He is soft where he is rough. He is bloodthirsty where he works for peace. He is kind where he is cruel. He cares deeply while not caring for humanity at all. Is optimistic while losing his faith entirely. A man who I'm convinced loves fashion. A man who loves his family; a man who loves nothing.

How can one person be all those things simultaneously?

Catching my attention, Casimir turns his chin to look at me. "What?"

My question comes from seemingly nowhere, unexpected yet demanding. "What are you searching for in the Veil? Why do you have me enter it every week?"

A flash of surprise flickers through his eyes. "What made you think of that?"

"I'm always thinking about it," I answer honestly.

"I see." Casimir studies me for two heartbeats longer, eventually releasing a sigh before propping his elbow up on the small lip of the carriage's interior, resting his cheek upon his closed fist. He glances out the window, and something shifts in his expression. Suddenly, the lines on his face don't look so rough, and his gaze doesn't appear to be hardened like stone. Instead, they fill with a wistful softness, as if he was seeing ghosts of memories out the window.

"Truthfully?" He still isn't looking at me.

"I don't see why you'd lie."

He hums a laugh. "The truth is," he begins, words slow and testing, "I do not even know what I am searching for anymore. A girl. A cure. A god. A weapon. Once, there was so much I sought to know from the Veil, but now…" Another sigh. One which dims his voice. "Now, I am not so sure."

"Why not?"

"Because I am tired." He sounds like he means it. "Because I am ragged and worn from following threads which may never lead me back to a beating heart." A pause. "I think I keep letting you go back into the Veil week after week because I am hoping one of these days you will return with an answer for me. One different from the initial one I was seeking."

I turn the contents of what he's just offered me over in my mind. *A girl. A cure. A god. A weapon.* After all the bits and pieces of information he's given me over the past few months, I think I finally am beginning to understand his narrative.

But just to be sure...

"I don't suppose you'd tell me more than that? As the daughter of a Gardner, I'm particularly interested in hearing more about the part where you're searching for a cure for your family."

He stiffens only a fraction before loosening his muscles. "Let me guess," he says. "Neilina told you?"

I mock a shrug. "She and I have become close—what can I say?"

He huffs softly. "Well, at least you gave one member of my family a chance."

The sentence makes a pang of guilt twist in my stomach. I choose to move past it. "If there's a way to cure them, there's a way around your terrible plan, Casimir. I know you've realized this."

"Just as I am sure you've realized cures are fickle things, and there's no way to guarantee I *can* cure them. You know what I can guarantee?"

"I swear to the gods, if you say murder, I'm jumping out the carriage."

I mean it.

Which I think he reads in my gaze, because a flash of amusement passes through his temporarily bunched eyes before he turns his chin back to the window. "No more talking." He doesn't say it like the other times. There is no malice or bitterness in his words. In fact, they were almost swept up on the breeze of something...eager?

"And why not?" I'm not particularly proud of the haughty way I fold my arms over my chest.

He glances at me sidelong, the corner of his mouth flirting with a smile. "Because if we continue, you will miss the view."

Confusion pinches my features. "What do you mean?"

He jerks his chin to the window. Or perhaps it's better to say to the contents waiting *beyond* it. "Look outside."

I follow his instructions, and...

Awe slams into me, a jolting force. My jaw pops open, and my eyes widen at all the towering spires and glittering lights.

Talderine.

And we're traveling directly through the heart of it.

Canopied stalls framed by warm, golden lights strung up on strings outline the cobblestoned streets. Roasting meats and vegetables waft through the air like a savory blanket while loud chatter fills the skies as peddlers barter with customers. Their gloved hands exchange flowers, exquisite painted canvases, fine jewelry, and fire-blown pottery. Triangular banners inked with Erandor's emblem are draped across buildings, a colorful ceiling over the snow-dusted market. Tangerines are stacked in woven baskets illuminated by lanterns, and there is a lulling melody being plucked on strings from somewhere unseen. I decide the song is a melancholy tune, though I can't quite put my finger on why.

I had always thought Talderine would be an ugly city because it is known to be filled with ugly hearts. Yet I should have known better than to think such thoughts—beautiful things are often crafted to conceal hideous intentions.

There are shops with large windows, arched windows, and stained glass windows. There are terracotta roofs and black-shingled ones. Wooden beams frame some buildings while only glittering stone composes others. Towering spires rise high into the sky above the artisan shops boasting colorful silks, hats, scarves, and shoes. There is a large circular sun dial at the city's center, the blues and golds so bright to the eye, one could mistake it for its very own sun. Lanterns hang around the base of it, casting it in an eternal light, and as I stare at it, I realize my mouth still hasn't closed.

How can something so close to Rivara Kingdom be so vastly different?

Yet once the initial glamour of Talderine's heart fades, my eyes begin to notice what I'm sure their nobility would prefer travelers to miss. Woven between the women dressed in decadent silken gowns and the men clad in artistically crafted trousers are servant girls and errand boys, a blemish in their portrait. Their skin is smudged with dirt, their fingernails scuffed and jagged. The stalls—initially glowing like harnessed light—are filled with tired eyes and gaunt cheeks. The alleyways—nearly hidden by pops of color—cradle scandalously dressed men and women in shadow. They reach out for those passing by with a soft touch and low-lidded gaze, their movements mindless and empty. Do those walking past not see how their bodies vibrate, unable to stave off the bite of the cold in their torn and too thin clothes?

I pull back from the window, then, my mouth finally snapping shut, my lips thinning. From the corner of my eye, I catch Casimir watching me.

"You don't like it," he surmises.

I glance out the window and nearly choke from its ravishing colors. Everything feels framed by a cloying decadence now.

"It's even more beautiful than I imagined." The words are not a lie. "I've never seen a city like it." Which isn't exactly saying much, considering I've only ever lived in Keziah, and—outside the shadows of Rivara—have only traveled through a cursed valley and rolling hills harboring a magical academy.

Well, that and wherever the hell Casimir's home is.

"So why is it you look as though your stomach has suddenly soured?"

I rest my chin in my palm. "Because it didn't take me long to see the weeds hiding amongst the flowers."

My answer seems to rattle him to a mild degree. And at the curious expression filling his gaze and the sudden tightness in his muscles, a realization dawns on me.

"You don't need to replenish your magic, do you?"

A long pause, and then, "No."

"So you arranged the carriage for my sake? So I could see the city? Is that why you confirmed I've never been to Talderine before we left?"

His eyes turn to gaze out the window once more. "Yes."

The answer fills me with confusion. "Why?" I ask. "Why do that for me? A person who is nothing more than a captive to you—a pawn in your plans?"

The following silence is so long, I am able to make out the entirety of a whistled child's song flittering from just outside the carriage. It is so long, I've given up on receiving an answer from him.

But then to my surprise—with that nearly glowing gaze of his still glued to the glass—he murmurs, "Because you are not just a captive to me nor some pawn in my plan. And so… I simply wanted to do something nice for you."

CHAPTER TWENTY-NINE

MARCELLA

Marcella has always known the other half lives differently. She never in her wildest dreams, however, imagined different could be so…well…*different*.

Marvel fills her like wine fills the goblets of every high-ranking noble in Erandor Kingdom as she spins around and takes in her surroundings. She pinches her nails into the heels of her palms just to make sure she is awake—that this isn't all some dream or illusion. She needs to be sure that this is real, and somehow, she is *here*, truly experiencing it.

Moonbeam pillars suspend the lavishly painted ceiling resting overhead, depictions of the Canamae gods, the Four Goddesses, and a few other lesser deities twirling over the dome shape. Their pastel faces reach for a portrait of a kingdom between two rivers, desire and envy present in their eyes. Clustered cylinders of perfectly preserved ice crystals rest suspended in midair, making the sky seem blanketed by a sea of diamonds. Interwoven between the crystals are small orbs of golden, glittering light, illuminating the room like hovering fireflies. The ice crystals refract the light into opulent beams across the ballroom floor while spire-shaped braziers coat everything with warm firelight. Staggering arched windows that crawl to mid-ceiling

—offering glimpses of the stars above—replace what otherwise would be walls, individual balconies accompanying each window set. Moonlight cascades through the glass, pouring through more perfectly placed ice crystals in the shapes of celestial bodies, casting twirling silver shadows of moons, stars, and suns on the black and gold marble floor, clear as glass and subtly reflecting the ballgowns and suits of the dancers it supports.

Marcella has never—*ever*—in her life seen anything like this. So grand. So lavish. Hypnotically beautiful.

She is left uncharacteristically speechless, her lips parted as her masked eyes continue drinking in the ballroom. For the first time in a long time, she feels intimidated—borderline frightened. A fact of which probably isn't made better by her having wandered off alone, leaving everyone she traveled with behind—including Gray. *Especially* Gray.

I don't belong here, she can't help but think as she takes in the decadent ballgowns and expensive masks. Far more exquisite and grand than anything she has on her body.

Bracing herself to face the nobility at Bathara was one thing. She could fight. She could wield magic as easily as she could breathe. She is of the caliber to take their respect—*demand* it, whether they wanted to give it to her or not. That knowledge allowed her to craft a mindset allowing her to tap into the full reservoir of her cockiness and wry humor. There, she could be someone who stood up to the attitudes and treatments of a broken system. There, she felt like she could fight back one sharp word at a time. But here?

Here, she just feels like a poor girl playing dress up in a room she doesn't belong in.

Without realizing, she retreats a step, her hands finding her elbows as she draws into herself. She accidentally bumps into a tall man and splashes his brimming drink onto the floor. He scowls at her, and through the lines of his crimson mask, she sees him scan her gown. He doesn't do anything other than walk away after, but on edge and feeling deeply insecure, Marcella suddenly feels like she has a spotlight on her. Has a sign around her neck that reads, *farmer's daughter*.

She convinces herself that the man somehow knew it was a lowborn's dress. That it is obvious the gown was scraped together by her brothers so she could feel pretty.

She hates the unwelcome feeling of embarrassment and shame as it heats her cheeks. Marcella has always prided herself on being proud of both her parents and how far her family has come. She has always loved talking about her family's farm in Rolfbear. Which is why she is left feeling all the more angry at herself for being insecure about it the moment she steps foot onto nobility's terrain.

She retreats another step. Then another.

She decides she is going to turn back and walk out. Stay outside the castle and simply brave the frigid air until the party is over and she can be taken back to Bathara.

But then he is there, resting a gentle hand on the small of her back and offering her a glass filled with liquid colored like a sunset.

"Parties are no fun when you stand in corners by yourself."

Marcella takes the glass from Gray's hand, silently thankful for both his presence and the aid of alcohol in calming her taut nerves. She downs the thing in one large gulp before pressing the stemmed glass back into Gray's fingers. "They're also no fun sober."

"Well," he says through a laugh. "I think you've just begun your solution to that problem."

Marcella turns, squaring her shoulders to him. He is closer to her than she originally thought.

He smiles, the gesture charming and genuine and everything a smile should be. "Hi, again."

"Hi." She hates the pang in her heart; the way her stomach clenches at the sight of him. His hair is neatly half-drawn, and the deep blue of his suit makes him appear at once regal and handsome, the autumnal colors composing the applique design adding warmth to his eyes while the high collar hugging his neck adds an air of importance to his presence.

Gods, he looks like a Crowned Prince.

"Are you enjoying the ball?"

She snorts. "No. It's not my...thing." Her voice quivers at the end of her sentence, but overall, she does a good job at hiding the maelstrom of thoughts she just drowned in.

He only watches her for a few heartbeats before gliding his chin over his shoulder and scanning the room, making a point to rake his eyes over everything before they find Marcella once more. "Probably for the best. You and that dress outshine everyone here, like a ruby in a sea of coal." He leans forward conspiratorially, his lips grazing the tip of her ear as he whispers, "I wish you could see yourself in that dress through my eyes. I think you'd find your usual smile and confidence would discover you a lot easier."

How did he...?

Marcella's cheeks flush, and for a passing second, she genuinely considers throwing her arms around his neck. That compliment....as silly as it is to admit, she needed it. And he offered it to her as easy as breathing, like he knew exactly what she was desperate for at that moment—reassurance.

Gray Nightenjoy always seems to know.

Marcella's lips part slowly as she feels a reply forming on her tongue when two women waltz by, hanging on each other's arms as they scan their surroundings like young school girls.

"I heard his golden mask extends like wings," the one with the glittering bustier whispers—albeit not well—to the girl next to her.

Quick as a blink, the mask covering Gray's face morphs from gold to navy-blue, the once outstretched corners thinning into something more round and subtle. He takes another step closer to Marcella, leaning forward just enough to give the illusion of intense conversation. She can feel the heat of his body, smell the warm, amber scent of his skin. She does not like how off-balanced it makes her feel.

The women pass, and she tilts her head up at Gray. "Did you just...?"

He rolls his eyes up to the ceiling and groans. "I've been propositioned all night."

Marcella fights against the violent wave of jealousy she feels boiling in her stomach at the words. She reminds herself again that she and Gray are only friends. That she practically offered herself to him on a silver platter, and he rejected her. That he doesn't want her in that way, and she just needs to get over it.

But then, why did he say such things to her? *I wish you could see yourself in that dress through my eyes.*

She fights against her own urge to groan. Why the hell did she ever think she could handle coming here with him tonight? Without a word of explanation, she reaches for Gray's half-filled drink and brings it to her lips, downing it also in one gulp.

Liquid, give her courage.

And perhaps thicker skin to not care so much about being rejected. Maybe also courage to not mind the fluttering in her stomach at Gray's all-too-near proximity. That would be particularly helpful, actually.

As the alcohol caresses her system, her nerves unravel even more —nobles really do have the best drink—and she relishes in the warm blanket of armor now coating her skin. "So," she drawls mildly. "Any propositions you're actually considering?"

He glances at her like she's positively ludicrous for even asking the question. "None in the slightest. I was practically cornered at the drinks table after a man recognized me somehow. Then I was followed as I wandered away from it, people hearing my name and catching on. I was stopped every two steps after." A notably irritated pause. "I've been slipped two parchments with addresses, proposi-tioned to align myself with four noble houses—a bold request I'm not even going to begin unpacking considering they all know I'm a student of Bathara—and asked to attend three towns' council meet-ings." He blows out an exhausted breath. "What good is a mask if it won't hide your identity?"

Marcella knows she should be more sympathetic—she is exhausted just listening to that. Yet she can't help but feel amused by it all, so she pouts her lip at him instead. "Aw, poor Lion," she teases. "It must be hard being the desire of everyone's affections."

He scoffs. "It's not affection that drives them, I assure you."

A light chuckle flows freely from her lips. "Of course it isn't. Really, what did you expect? They invited you here for a reason."

"I know," he groans again. "It's just...different than how I expected it to be."

Marcella can relate—somewhat, at least.

A realization dawns on her then. "You anticipated this though, didn't you? It's the real reason you decided to cast an illusion for your mask. So you could change its appearance when necessary."

He confirms the conjecture with the mix of guilt and mischief brimming in his eyes. He laughs, the sound so soft. "Don't mistake me —I hoped to be wrong about needing to use it."

Marcella shakes her head, a pointed smirk sweeping her lips. "Clever, clever boy."

"I'm beginning to feel less clever by the minute," he grumbles as a counterpoint.

He glances toward the ballroom floor and she takes the free moment to study Gray. Truthfully, this conversation is perhaps the most boyish she has ever seen him behave. She can't recall a time where she's ever heard him grumbling so petulantly. It makes her wonder how often Lyra has seen this side of Gray—if it is a side of himself he usually only reveals to her. How often he chooses to show it. What it means that he is allowing Marcella to see it.

Suddenly—distractingly—she realizes he still hasn't pulled away from her, and their bodies are flirting with the possibility of touching. His chest is no more than a hand's length away from her, and at the thought, she remembers how right it had felt when she was roving her hand along the muscles composing that chest. Then—quite ignorantly, she can admit—her eyes flick to Gray's hand, still cupped around an empty glass. Her body remembers what that hand felt like formed around the curve of her hip next. How electric his touch was to her senses.

She glances at his lips, that hungry curiosity to know how he would kiss her rushing through her once more. Would he be tender, similar to how he always speaks to her? Or would he be ravenous, desperate? Would he—

She clamps down on the line of thought, shaking her head forcefully against the path her mind has wandered to.

Goddess's tears—what is *wrong* with her? Has she suddenly grown fond of masochism or something?

She desperately needs another drink. And to find a way to enjoy this party without Gray Nightenjoy by her side—even if that makes her the world's shittiest date.

Which means…

She needs to find Kiran.

Having arrived at a decision she finally feels good about, she taps Gray's chest—drawing his full attention back onto her—and makes to walk away. "Well, try not to join their ranks by the end of the night, yeah?"

She moves, yet he catches her hand, holding it in place against his chest while his own hand falls flat atop it. "Where are you going?"

"To get another drink."

"I'll come with you."

"No," she responds too quickly. "I" —she clears her throat— "I can escort myself."

Even through the illusion of his mask, she can see the disappointment in his eyes. He drops his voice to nothing more than a soft murmur. "Marcella…" He says it like a question and a plea. A demand and a request.

A thousand other words are wrapped around that one utterance. That one breathy spill of her name from his lips.

"Please, Gray," she whispers back. "Don't."

He still holds her hand in place—his skin warm against hers—and their bodies remain so close, Marcella can feel the sensation of them being pressed together like a phantom touch, a beautiful mirage of that night at the inn.

He steps closer, swallowing that final sliver of space between them. His eyes hold hers in a way that makes her knees feel weak. Yet she does not allow herself to buckle—not even a little. Instead, she lifts her chin to meet his gaze as he stares down at her with so much— *something*—coursing behind his eyes.

Gods, when he looks at her like that, she feels so confused. How can he look at her that way while also not wanting her? Not claiming her for himself with the same amount of passion she can visibly see simmering in his eyes?

What about her is missing for him to actually take her as his?

"Please," he whispers, pressing the unspoken issue further, dropping his forehead to hers. "Just let me explain everything to you." He lifts his thumb to her cheek and sweeps it tenderly across the exposed skin just below her mask. She leans into the touch, realizing her heart both shreds and swells at the tenderness of it. She feels his breath on her lips. "I'm not above begging." They are so closely pressed together that if someone were to walk by, they may have thought Gray and Marcella were two lovers sharing a passionate kiss off the dancefloor, stealing a moment in a crowded room for themselves.

The offer hangs between them like a weight on a balancing scale, waiting to see which way the tides will turn. Marcella wants to know —is practically *desperate* to understand—Gray's reasonings for why he said no to her that night at the inn. And here he is, offering to tell her. It should be so simple: she should say yes, and she should hear what Gray has to say.

Yet feelings are many things, and simple is seldom one of them.

Or maybe feelings are incredibly simple, and it is the vessel making them complicated. Regardless, all Marcella knows is that she *should* hear Gray out, and yet for whatever reason, she just…can't. Call it pride, self-preservation, or sheer ignorance, the truth remains: hearing him say the words aloud will make it all the more real, and Marcella—though cowardly and childish as it is—simply isn't ready to face the full weight of its reality. Especially not right now, at this lavish ball filled with sharp eyes and sharper ears.

So despite the ache cracking her chest apart, she turns away from his touch, stepping back from the warmth of his body and putting space between them once more. "I'm sorry," she rasps. "But I can't justify any reason being good enough for why the person I chose didn't choose me back."

Even through his mask, Marcella can see his face crumble. He reaches for her, a desperation to the movement. "Marcella, *please*…"

She doesn't let him finish before waltzing away, her hand finally coming free of his; her heart aching more and more with each and every step she takes away from him.

And though it hurts, she doesn't let herself stop putting distance between them because she knows her worth. She knows she is deserving of a person who, despite whatever barriers they may face, chooses her first, no matter how difficult that may be.

When she reaches the drink table, she finds herself missing Lyra with an added layer of ferocity. She always had the best advice—always listened without judgment.

Marcella made two friends that felt like forever when entering Bathara. Ones who quickly became as much a part of her heart as anyone she had ever known back home.

Now, she is alone, potentially having lost those two people forever, after already having to say a permanent goodbye to Griff.

There are no words to adequately describe what that knowledge does to her. So she doesn't even try.

Instead, she chooses to drink.

CHAPTER THIRTY

FINLAY

Finlay stares out at the ballroom dance floor, wondering what the ever-loving fuck is *wrong* with him.

Rhea dances with some new prick, his hand clutched far too tightly around her waist as he guides her around the ballroom floor. They glide and twirl, and beneath the spheres of light magic and carefully placed ice crystals—created with his father's ice magic, Finlay is sure—she looks…

Finlay swallows.

Well, she looks like a glittering midnight sky given form.

He can't imagine a more fitting dress for her if he tried.

Still, why the hell *is* he trying? Better yet, why has his stare been fixed intently on the dance floor since the moment she stepped onto it with another man? Or perhaps even more pressing, why has he been watching her with *every* man she has danced with this evening? He's watched every flutter of her eyelashes. Every gentle touch she's placed on shoulders and biceps. Every smile. Every conversation. He's maintained a respectable distance, but he has seen it all—made it a point to keep his eye on her.

The man grips the curve of Rhea's waist with even more vigor, and Finlay balls his hands into fists at his sides. He doesn't know this

335

particular noble she's with. Not from this distance and with the man's mask in place. Though he has every intention of finding out. Finlay may hate Rhea, but she is still *his* date for this evening.

His.

No one else's.

Not tonight, at least.

And the man should show some respect for that.

As the thought enters Finlay's mind, he resolves to *make* the man show respect. To waltz right up and remove his mask, letting the man cower once he realizes he is the Fjolla Heir. To grovel at his feet. Yet just as quickly as the thought enters his mind, it is accompanied by the resulting action it would bring—Rhea scoffing and rolling her eyes at him, not impressed by what he had done in the slightest.

His scowl deepens. Finlay is seconds away from merely turning his back on them, not deigning to give it a further ounce of his energy, but—before the song has even ended—he sees Rhea excuse herself from the dance and head in the direction of the corridor leading to the washroom.

He stares, watching her go, telling himself that whatever caused her steps to be filled with such hurried purpose, it does not concern him. He has no business following her. Has no business even being remotely interested in where she is going.

His feet move before his mind has time to catch up.

He pushes through the crowd with ease, being both taller and broader than nearly every person in attendance tonight. When he finally reaches the corridor, he is surprised to find it empty. With quiet steps, he wanders further into the stone halls. He reaches for his magic, even though he knows it's futile.

A Nullifier's laktî can't be sensed.

Go figure the one person he decides is worth chasing is the one person he cannot find easily.

He has just veered left, entering into a hall lined by portraits of past and present kings, when he feels the distinct kiss of a cool blade pressed against his throat.

He doesn't need magic to tell him who the blade belongs to.

"Do you go anywhere without those bloody daggers?"

"Do you go anywhere without that terrible attitude?"

Finlay huffs, and Rhea drops her blade. When he turns to face her, he soon realizes that for the second time tonight, Rhea looks as though she's been crying.

Why does the thought of that bother him so much?

"You've been crying again."

Like anyone raised by Tynan Dalmar would, she shows no reaction.

Finlay scans her even more closely. Her dress is crumpled at the torso, as if she was hunched over for a time. The delicate black lines previously tracing her softly angular eyes are now smeared at the corners, as though she was attempting to fix it but ran out of time. Her lipstick is smudged, and there is a pointed hollowness to her gaze which leaves Finlay feeling uneasy.

She sheaths her dagger back into the holster hidden beneath her dress, wrapped around her thigh. "Are you spying on me, Finlay?"

"No. Is there a reason I should be spying on you, Rhea?"

She shrugs. "Just trying to figure out why you've followed me here."

"You're my date for this evening." He says it so simply. Like that one small sentence should explain everything.

Even he knows it doesn't. Not in the slightest.

"That doesn't change the fact that I still hate you."

"I know," he agrees. "But it also doesn't change the fact that we agreed on a truce for tonight, and I am both a man of my word and honor."

She rolls her eyes. "Gag me."

To his surprise, a rather crude retort pops into his head, which makes a particular image creep into his mind. He squashes both the thought and the image as quickly as he can. "Must you always be so difficult?" His voice is sharper than he intended, a result of the flustered thought, no doubt.

"Must you always be such an *asshole*?"

Finlay clenches his jaw. "Gods, you act like such a child."

She scoffs, the sound holding nothing but bitter disdain. "Oh, I'll take immaturity over narcissism any day."

He squares his shoulders to her, which results in her taking a step closer to him in challenge. "Fuck you, Rhea." He doesn't know why he is allowing himself to get so angry—so worked up over nothing. But this is how it always goes with her.

Nobody can get under Finlay's skin like Rhea Brooksley can.

"You wish you could," she drawls, the words somehow pulling off the cloying contradiction of being at once seductive and spiteful.

"I assure you," Finlay replies, feeling defensive. "I would *never* lay a single finger on your body."

The words seem to strike her far deeper than Finlay intended. Her bottom lip quivers—*Rhea's* lip quivers—and she recedes a step from him. Then another. And another.

She jerks her chin away from him, putting her back to Finlay as she wordlessly walks in the other direction. There is that hurried purpose in her step again, and he can't help but feel like he just somehow royally screwed up. Said something he should not have said.

Though, with Rhea, he has more of those than he can count, his defensive nature always seeming to get the best of him when she is around. Still, something about the hurt that flashed through her features was...different. Deeper.

It looked as though he had openly slapped her.

Though, Finlay can't work out why. As much as it pains him to admit, he has said far worse to Rhea than, *I would never lay a finger on you.* In fact, in most instances, he can nearly visualize her mocking smirk and pointed, *thank the gods for that*, reply.

What is different about tonight? What battles is she facing that he can't see right now?

Why has Rhea cried twice?

Why does he *care*?

Maybe it is just because they agreed to lay down their weapons tonight. Because they have a truce in place, and Finlay is offering her the respect of treating her as a date should be treated. He is an honorable man, after all.

Yes, that must be it. They are not enemies this evening—they do not have to lean into the simmering hatred they feel for one another. For tonight and tonight only, they can reach for something different than pointed words and sharp expressions.

For yet another time, Finlay's feet move without the consent of his mind.

————

IT IS NOT without considerable effort that Finlay finds Rhea again.

She is sitting on the ground at the very end of a long, winding corridor, her head leaning back against stone. Her hands are folded limply in her lap while her feet are stretched out in front of her, heels kicked off and discarded down the carpet. Her eyes are shut, and thin black trails run parallel down her cheek.

She looks…broken.

Finlay feels something break inside him at the sight.

"Rhea?" He steps toward her, feeling an odd sense of caution in his movements.

She cracks her eyes open, and—

Gods…there is not a sliver of light behind them right now. They are hollow. Empty. So terribly empty.

"I don't have the capacity to deal with you right now, Finlay. Go away." Her voice is devoid of any fluctuation.

"What's wrong with you?"

He meant it honestly. As a genuine question. But it appears his lack of experience in both showing empathy and consoling people shows, because her response leads him to believe he chose the wrong thing to say.

Rhea scoffs, shaking her head, her eyes somehow dimming even further. "So much," she whispers sharply. "Too fucking much, in fact."

Finlay sees two paths diverge before him. He can either wish her luck in her miserable moment of self-pity, loathing—whatever this is. In fact, the voice in his head—his *father's* voice, specifically—tells him he should. That sitting here with someone like Rhea is a complete and utter waste of his time and name.

Yet, there is another voice in Finlay's head—softer and less demanding. Another path he can take.

He knows his decision before he accepts it. He tries to rationalize it to himself while walking over to Rhea and sitting himself down directly beside her. He tells himself that he is doing this for Draven. Because he knows how much she means to him, and he would want someone to be there for her right now.

He does it because he still has so much making up to do.

To Draven. To his own father. Even to Rhea, he supposes. He could drown in the sea of debts he still has to pay for all his wrong choices.

Finlay stretches his legs out, mirroring her position. "Why don't you talk to me about what's going on with you. You've been off all night."

"You don't even know me," she replies, voice dry and flat.

"I've known you for over ten years, Rhea."

"And I've hated you for every single one of them."

"I know," Finlay says, a softness to his voice he's not quite familiar with. "I know you have. But we agreed to a truce tonight long before sitting here, did we not?"

The clipped laugh she ejects from her nostrils tells him she concedes that yes, that much is true.

"Tell me what's going on," he pushes, as gentle as he can manage. "I know I'm not Draven or Kiran—I know I'm unpleasant—but... I swear to you I'll do my best to listen."

Rhea glances at him sidelong. "Unpleasant is an understatement."

"Be that as it may."

Silence stretches between them for a long time. In fact, it sits heavy for so long, Finlay nearly gets up, already internally scolding himself for trying. But just as he presses his palms against his thighs to lift himself off the ground, Rhea sighs.

He can't tell if the sound is resignation or defeat.

"I have this...problem...sometimes. With my body. It started a few years ago, but after many intensive sessions with a holistic healer, I was able to overcome the issue. Yet formal events like this..." She pauses, biting into the inside of her cheek. "Let's just say it stirs up remnants of it."

"Have you seen a healer with magic? Can't they fix whatever the ailment is?"

She shakes her head, turning her chin over her shoulder to stare at the opposite wall. "No. The healers...they can't fix this with magic."

"I see..." he says slowly, his mind already racing to solve a problem he doesn't even yet understand. "What is wrong with you then? Why can't magic help?"

She sighs again, the sound long and deep and filled with a heaviness Finlay knows typically accompanies exhaustion. "The healer Tynan had me see after he found me retching after dinner one night called it 'an affliction of the mind.'"

"But I thought you said the problem was with your body?"

She turns back to glance at him, and he had been right—there is such exhaustion in her eyes. A detached pain that he knows is dangerous.

Why is seeing her like this hurting him so much? His feelings of scorn for her have not changed, and yet...

And yet he finds himself wanting to reach out to her and comfort her. To help mend the wound making her bleed out on the floor right in front of him.

"The problem is my mind's *relationship* to my body. At least, that's what the next healer I had to see said—the holistic one." Her face twists like she's tasted something sour. "Tynan said he couldn't have broken resources, and so, he sought out different healers to inspect me. People who could be discreet. Really just meaning someone who was in the pockets of House Dalmar, but...luckily for me, I ended up with someone who was actually good at what she did. Who truly managed to help me."

Finlay tries so hard to understand. Tries so hard to emulate Kiran's comforting ease or Draven's ability to understand emotions. Yet Finlay has none of that. He lost his mother too young to be shaped into a good man like Draven was by his mother. Never trekked the paths Draven walked to get to where he is emotionally. Finlay doesn't have a supportive household like Kiran does or a sibling who would ravage the world to protect him.

He has never in his life been shown how to comfort or care or love. All he knows is his training. Are the ideals his father instilled in him. His virtues and sense of righteousness.

But what good are those things right now? What do they offer him in the face of something human?

He releases a breath, determined to—in spite of all his many short-comings—be there for Rhea anyway. "What happened to make this appear?"

She scoffs, the sound deeply bitter. "What happened was that I was subjected to scrutiny in House Dalmar at every turn, and no matter what I did, what I looked like, it was never enough. *I* was never enough. So my fucked up mind began to believe I could *never* be enough, while simultaneously still wanting Tynan's approval like some masochistic fool. I despise that man with every ounce of my being, and yet somehow, over all these years, I've been conditioned to depend on his favor and respect. I hate him, but I can't stand it when I feel like *he* hates *me*."

"And so that caused you to view yourself poorly?"

"Not just that," she replies, voice rough like gravel. "I started to hate how I was made. Hated eating. Hated undressing, because any exposure of my body was too much. In turn, I began to love the ache of a hunger pang more than I loved myself. I figured an empty stomach was better than a bloated one." She exposes her palms, staring into them like a lifeline. "But that other healer? The holistic one? She helped me work through all those things.

"It was really, *really* fucking hard—hence why I am so pissed off at feeling so much as a glimmer of it right now—but slowly, she helped me retrain my thoughts. To speak to and view and treat myself differently." Rhea pauses. "At first, she told me I had to learn to love myself more than I loved the other things, and that didn't make sense to me because I thought the problem was so obvious: I didn't love myself—*that* was the issue. And her telling me that in order to get better I had to love myself *more* made me so fucking angry.

"Yet over time, the healer helped me understand that loving myself starts with choosing myself. Spending time with myself. Getting to know my own person. And those things? Those things made sense to me. Were like training tasks I was used to performing. So, like the dutiful trainee Tynan made me to be, I did everything she told me to —was intentional with how I went about it—and in the moments between, like it always seems to happen, love started to appear." Rhea toys with her fingers, dropping her voice. "I owe her my life, truthfully. I probably would have done irreparable damage had it not been for her sessions. Especially if I kept on going how I was."

Finlay drags fingers through his hair, a multitude of feelings clamping down in his chest. "I am so sorry, Rhea. I never knew. I mean—you never came across like you were struggling with something like that. How..." He bites down on his lip, reaching for words that do not answer him easily while also trying really hard not to say the wrong thing. "Does Draven know?"

"No," she whispers, drawing her knees into her chest and folding her arms atop of them.

The weight of that rings through Finlay. "How did Tynan manage to do it? To extinguish your fire? Make you question yourself to the extent where..." He studies her through softened eyes. "Well, where you hurt like this." He almost reaches out to take her hand, feeling like it's the right thing to do.

Almost.

"Would you really like to know how, Frosty?" There's still a bitterness coating her words, but for once, he can tell it's not a blade meant for him. "It's because at every moment, at every turn, my body is deemed an object, put on display like some painting in a king's hall, subject to unsolicited scrutiny by anyone who decides they want to look. Too large. Too small. Too flat. Too wide. Too pale. Not pale enough. Too seductive. Not womanly enough. As a woman, I am the only thing that can be at once everything they asked for while being nothing close to that of their measure. And I am *fool* enough to know this, but still be haunted by all the fucking voices that have told me my body isn't good enough the way it is. That have critiqued me. Told me to lose weight, and then told me I looked too thin once I had."

Tears well in her eyes, but there is nothing sad about them. There is only rage living within the small pool forming along her lower lashes.

"And I am *so* pathetic—such a hopeless, fucking fool—that here I am, sitting on the floor telling Finlay fucking Frosty Fjolla all of this. Evidently I'm so broken, I can't even function properly for one evening."

"You're not broken," Finlay murmurs. "A little cracked, maybe. But never broken."

There is a long stretch of silence.

"Why?" Rhea asks, the sound nothing more than a hollow echo of her usual vigor. Her chin quivers, and she rolls her head back onto the stones once more. Her eyes gaze emptily at the ceiling while her chest falls in on itself from her sighs of defeat. "Why can't I just accept that I am enough as I am?"

Throughout the entirety of the conversation, Finlay has felt something akin to drowning, barely able to tread the surface of the admissions Rhea is offering him. He hasn't known what to say. Hasn't known what to do. Nobody comes to him when they're hurting—they go to people like Kiran. Yet now, for the first time, he feels like he knows what to say. Because that question?

He does know the answer to that question.

Before he can talk himself out of it, he wraps one arm around Rhea's shoulders and tucks her into the crook of his side. To his surprise, she lets him without protest, dropping her head to rest against his shoulder. He leans his cheek against the top of her head, and he traces soothing lines down her arm. "You feel that way because my actions forced you to live in a world where we are taught we must earn our place—our ability to live, to love, and be accepted—instead of simply being told we already belong. That we are enough as we already are."

A quiet, bitter laugh falls from her lips. "Because of Tynan, it feels like the only love I have ever known is conditional."

The statement strikes a chord in Finlay. "Me too. With my own father, I mean." A pause. "It's hard to feel like you're enough when the only proof of love you've ever had is reliant on what you can or cannot give."

"Yes," she agrees, "it is." She stretches her legs out once more, a soft sigh spilling out of her. "There was a time I saw what unconditional love looked like, but I barely remember it anymore."

Knots tangle and wind deep in Finlay's chest, painfully gripping all the spaces he wishes they would not touch. "Rhea?"

"Yes?"

"I don't think I have ever told you I am sorry for the role I played in your father's and sister's death." He swallows against the dryness crippling his throat. "I apologized to Draven, but I never have apologized to you. Not directly, anyways. In a manner which truly counts." His fingers still against her skin. "I am sorry I told Tynan where to find your family. I am sorry I told him about Príth. About your father's bookshop. I just...I had barely turned fourteen, and I..." he trails off, sighing. "Well, let's just suffice it to say I am sorry."

She doesn't respond right away, instead staying silent for long enough to make Finlay want to squirm. "Your apology changes nothing," she says finally, her voice far softer than Finlay is expecting. "And neither does what I've shared with you this evening. I still hate you. I will *always* hate you. Nothing will ever change that." Her words are a blunted blade, no longer sharp enough to slice bone.

For some sick, twisted reason, it forces a small smile to Finlay's lips. "I hate you too."

"Good."

"Good," he confirms.

His fingers resume gliding absently across her skin in reassuring strokes. She continues letting her head rest against him. Together, they continue sitting there on the floor dressed in dazzling formal wear, their legs splayed out in front of them, a tangled mess of jaded hearts and sharp personalities that have softened solely for this moment.

"Finlay?"

"Yes?"

"Thank you. For everything you've done and said tonight. For listening. For being here with me."

The words warm him far more than he cares to admit it. "You're welcome, Rhea."

"But you can *never* tell anyone about this. Not Draven. Not Kiran. No one. When we leave this corridor, things go back to normal, agreed?"

There is a small part of him that wonders if that is even possible. Rhea has been humanized to him now. Has been stripped of her mask, allowing him to see the working components of the heart she keeps so carefully guarded.

Yet he is a Fjolla, and so he has to. Because as much as he can admit that something has stirred inside him by being this close to Rhea and holding her against him, that small stir can never grow into what Finlay suspects it could become.

They are not so fortunate to live in a world of fairytales, where the pauper can marry the prince, and the tortured prince can always find his princess.

And so, as he always does, Finlay will do as he must.

"Agreed."

CHAPTER THIRTY-ONE

RHEA

Rhea cannot explain why she just told Finlay everything. She can't even make sense of it herself. Why the words fell giddy from her lips, happy to be released and given to another person in all their terrible, unfiltered glory. She's never been able to do that before with anyone. Not even Draven.

Of course, she suspects Draven has recognized the pattern by now —a formal event arrives, Rhea is forced to play dress up, and she ends up feeling like a stranger in her own skin, scrutinizing and cursing every flaw, every exposed piece of her body, whether hugged by fabric or put on full display. But she also suspects he still is not the least bit aware of how deeply the claws sank into her. How hard she had to work to not be swallowed by a venomous monster who whispered poison in her ear and showed her illusions in the mirror.

She certainly never told him how bad it had gotten. And she knows Tynan would have never cared enough to make him aware.

In thinking of Tynan, a plea-like hope evades her body as she prays he hasn't noticed her long-term absence from the ball. Hasn't yet discovered her deterioration or been made aware of her momentary slip of weakness.

Gods, the words he would have for her if he has.

As Finlay and Rhea return to the party by each other's side, she can't help but steal a glance at him. After he sat with her on the floor until the ache in her soothed, he escorted her to the washroom and stood watch out front while she fixed her makeup and stitched herself back together. Then, he simply offered her his arm and led her away from that tear-stained corridor, choosing not to comment further. He was...gentle. Kind, even. He treated her with the sort of tenderness she was not expecting, yet deeply appreciated, having just bore to him one of the deepest wounds in her soul.

In the decade Rhea has known Finlay Fjolla, she has never known him to be attentive.

It leaves her feeling confused. Like perhaps there *is* some variation of the future where she doesn't have to hate him for what he did—for telling Tynan that Draven and his mother fled from House Dalmar to have a life at her late father's bookshop with her family in spite of promising Draven he wouldn't, killing her father and sister in turn because of Tynan's resulting outrage.

Of course, it never was directly his fault. The weight of true fault has always fallen on Tynan, and she has always been perfectly aware of that. Yet the small, murmuring voice in her head caresses her broken heart and fans her vindictive flames by humming the *what ifs*. What if Finlay had just kept his promise? What if he never told Tynan where to find them?

Her father, Atlas Brooksley, may have been able to hold her tonight and wipe her tears, while her maternal and fiercely loyal older sister, Suzumi Brooksley, rubbed her back and assured Rhea she was the most beautiful girl in the world.

Of course, Rhea knows she isn't. But she also knows her late sister would have been capable of making her feel like she is, and at the end of the day, isn't that what really matters?

A pang of guilt appears in her chest.

Finlay has always been the easiest target to direct all her hatred—all her boiling spite and anger—toward because she is chained to Tynan, thus leaving Draven at the mercy of all his cruel whims. She has always felt like she couldn't afford to fully develop and acknowledge all the deep hatred she held toward Tynan, because her life was simply too interwoven with his. But Finlay? Oh, she could hate Finlay —could put every ounce of blame on him.

Yet now, for the first time in ten years, she is questioning that. Wondering if Draven has been right all along, and Rhea has been terribly, unforgivably misguided and bitter toward Finlay.

They approach the edges of the ballroom floor right as the current song ends. Within seconds, the strings of the violin sing a happy tune, and Finlay turns to face her. He looks as though he wishes to ask her to dance. In fact, she is *sure* he does by the way his tentative, assessing gaze glances at her, his fingers uncurling from his palm as he hesitantly extends his hand out toward her like a silent offering.

The sound of Audwin Fjolla's voice sends that hand dropping back down like the air between them has become poison.

"Where have you been?" He looks only at Finlay, ignoring Rhea entirely.

Finlay lifts his chin, but she can see by the stiffening of his muscles and subtle flex of his jaw that he wants to wince. "I was occupied with other business, Father."

His lip curls. "What business?"

Even through his crystal-bedecked mask, Rhea can see the coldness in his eyes as he gazes at his son. Not a sliver of warmth or a drop of endearment. Just pure, frigid contempt.

Finlay only steals a second's glance at her before rolling his shoulders back and steadying his voice. "It is related to matters of Bathara, and so I am afraid I cannot discuss it."

Audwin snorts. "What? You are elected onto their council and suddenly you think your worth is greater than mine? That you are afforded a rank which somehow tiers above my own?" He steps closer. "Nobody outranks me or House Fjolla, dear son."

Somehow, Audwin manages to make the word "son" sound reprehensible.

Finlay shakes his head. "No, of course not, Father. Being on Bathara's council is merely a step toward proving I am worthy of bearing my title as House Fjolla's Heir. Of receiving your approval to be Head of the House someday."

Audwin huffs a dry laugh. "That day remains far, far away. I swear, every time I see you, you only appear to be more reprehensible. More of a disappointment."

Finlay—so schooled at keeping his features cool and neutral—looks visibly wounded. For some unexplainable reason, it ignites the fire Rhea's soul permanently carries. The silent rage that is as a part of her as her own blood.

"Maybe your eyes are defective, then, because I think it is *you* who is the real disappointment."

Audwin turns his icy attention onto her, and he cocks his head with predatory grace. "I beg your pardon?"

"*Rhea,*" Finlay hisses under his breath. "*Don't.*"

Rhea doesn't listen. "You don't deserve your son," she continues, in spite of the early death Audwin's cold eyes are promising her. "Just as he never deserved to be born to such a shitty father."

Audwin laughs like she's just told the world's best joke. "And what do you know of fathers, girl? Do not forget I am aware of what happened to yours for his own foolish choices. If that sort of pathetic showing is what you associate with the title, then I can see why you are so misguided in your accusations."

Rhea steps toward the man and bares her teeth. "Do *not* speak of my father."

"Yet you are allowed to speak of mine?"

It comes from Finlay, and Rhea finds her mouth falling open at the realization. He steps away from her, moving to be on the side of Audwin, squaring his shoulders to her as though they are now divided by some invisible boundary.

Audwin's lips twirl like a snake at the sight.

"I fear my kindness this evening has led you to operate under misguided assumptions. My father and I are of House Fjolla, while you, Rhea Brooksley, are nothing more than a commoner made into House Dalmar's charity case. You are only something because Tynan has made you so. Because you are fortunate enough to have Draven's protection. But you mistake those truths as a podium elevating you to House Fjolla's stature, when they do no such thing. It is that blatant disrespect and misplaced sense of self which makes me hate you so viscerally."

At the words, Rhea reminds herself that she, too, hates Finlay. She hates him. She hates him. She *hates* him. And she does not respect his opinion nor care what he and his shitty father think of her.

Even if the stinging burn on her cheeks would say otherwise.

She kicks herself for allowing herself to think that she could feel anything for Finlay Fjolla other than hatred. That there might be a version of him which is redeemable.

She is an ignorant fool for thinking anything of the sort.

She could never—*ever*—feel anything but the deepest, most tortuous form of contempt for him. And she is more than content to stoke those flames inside her belly and burn by them.

She takes two steps forward. Until he is forced to tilt his chin down and she is forced to tilt her chin up. "Fuck. You."

"I'm sure you wish you could," he mutters back, condescension lacing his voice, even if Rhea notices it isn't as thick as all the other times they spoke to each other like this.

Not like she cares.

Audwin claps his hands together, seeming amused by their exchange. He rests a jubilant hand on Finlay's shoulder. Something like awe passes through Finlay's eyes at the touch. "You know, Tynan and I debated whether having you two accompany each other to this ball had been a mistake. Yet he was adamant that we use Rhea to extract information from you. Have her pry out the things you might be keen on withholding, given your ties and feelings of obligation to Captain Dalmar. Tynan was convinced you possess a soft spot for the girl." Audwin huffs a light laugh. "While that man is never wrong, he seems to have been off the mark about this."

Finlay whips his eyes to his father. "Information? What information?"

"Regarding the whereabouts of that low-blooded whore, Lyra Izacalli." He waves a lazy hand in the air. "Though it is not of consequence any longer. Tynan Dalmar is nothing if not a resourceful man."

Rhea blinks at the last part. What the hell does that mean? And why the hell is she even here with Finlay tonight if Tynan already has a potential lead up his sleeve?

Finlay's features twist, seeming too fixated on the former words to notice the latter. "I have told both of you everything I know when requested to. Why would you question that?"

"Because there is a lot I question about you, Finlay. You are well aware of my doubts regarding your competence and value."

If Rhea hadn't been seething, she would almost feel pity for how plainly Audwin speaks the words to his son.

Finlay nods, as if he truly *does* understand. Like he has been so conditioned to believe it, that there are no questions surrounding his father's unequivocal truth.

Audwin sighs, as if he has grown bored with the conversation. "If you will excuse me, I have a guest that will be arriving soon which I must prepare for." He squeezes Finlay's shoulder. "It was nice witnessing you not be a complete disappointment this evening. I will not forget what I have seen here."

Finlay looks like he wants to celebrate the words. Like he's just received something he has tirelessly worked for. Yet the subtle glimmer of disappointment in his eyes says the victory of his endeavors does not taste as sweet as he thought it would. "Thank you, Father," he murmurs.

Audwin dips his chin, and then he is strutting in the opposite direction, toward a different corridor on a different side of the lavish ballroom which Rhea knows will lead to a large chamber where powerful men frequently hold council during events such as this.

When he is gone, Finlay shifts his body toward her but will not meet her eyes.

The fucking coward.

"You were going to use me for information?" He has the audacity to sound hurt.

In truth, she was so preoccupied with her own emotional struggles this evening, she hadn't even had the chance to ask him any questions or create an opening to loosen Finlay's tongue. And then, after what he did for her in the corridor, she resolved to do away with Tynan's request completely. She certainly wasn't going to exploit the vulnerable moment they shared together for Tynan's sake. She doesn't know what his plans are or why he is searching for the woman Draven admires so ardently, but she does know whatever it is, it won't have Draven's best interest in mind. So she decided she would simply report back to Tynan that she was unable to extract any useful information from Finlay, knowing that due to Tynan's agreement with Draven, despite his inevitable irritation at Rhea's failure, he would not be able to act on his disappointment in a way that would cause her irreparable harm.

But Finlay doesn't need to know that.

In truth, she receives a sick form of pleasure at seeing the hurt in his expression after what he just said to her. After he chose his father—*again*—instead of standing on a different side. A better side. And so she twists the knife, allowing him to believe the narrative she thinks will inflict him with an equal harm he just inflicted on her.

She lifts her chin, smoothing her voice into something distant and business-like. "Yes. I was under Tynan's instructions this whole evening."

"And that whole display back in the corridor? That was what? Some sick ploy the two of you concocted to get me to drop my guard so I'd speak more openly with you?"

No. That was real.

"Yes," she answers instead, deciding it's better if he thinks her deepest struggle was all some act anyways. It'll only make her less vulnerable in the end.

Finlay huffs a humorless laugh. "Well, aren't I the fool, then?" His voice has grown so cold. He lifts his eyes from the floor, looking at Rhea with an expression she is not sure what to make of. "Well done, Rhea. You played your part brilliantly, because I was eating everything you showed me back there from the palm of your hand." He drops his voice, and Rhea nearly bristles at the pain lacing his words. "You got me. You win. Congratulations."

She doesn't let herself feel pity because *fuck* him. Fuck him for always making the wrong choice. Fuck him for turning on her so quickly. Fuck him for the part he played in the slaughter of her family. Fuck him for being such an asshole and so lost in his father's morally incorrect ideologies.

And most importantly, fuck him for making her feel like her heart is breaking at the sight of him looking at her like that.

Yet like the self-tormentor she is, she only digs the knife deeper, piercing her own flesh in the process. "Maybe you should stop under-estimating us 'lowborns.'"

"Yeah," he agrees in a loaded whisper. "Perhaps I should."

He walks away, and Rhea lets him, instead turning her back to him and setting her eyes to work so that they may find anyone worthy of distracting her from the strange feeling of hurt twisting in her chest.

She moves toward the first person she sees.

CHAPTER THIRTY-TWO

DRAVEN

Draven wants to be hiding in a corner somewhere, watching the depravity lazily from the shadows.

Yet instead, he is forced to be standing at complete attention, alone with his father on the northern balcony, overlooking the spectacle of colored ballgowns and sleek suits as they whirl around the obsidian dance floor, so glossy, it looks like a sea of glass beneath the partygoers' feet.

"What do you think of the ball?" his father asks from beside him. "King Erasmus went to great lengths to make this year's Winter Solstice celebration extra lavish."

Draven spares him only a quick glance. "And I wonder who has the ear of our King."

Tynan chuckles. "A dangerous thing, wondering."

"Indeed."

Draven grips the balcony's railing with both hands as he scans the ballroom. From his vantage point, he can see Gray Nightenjoy being cornered by two women, one of which is draped in a terribly gaudy dress, looking past them and across the room where the drinks are being served. Draven follows his line of sight and spots Marcella at the beverage table, catching her mid-drink as she throws back an entire flute of wine. He sees Finlay next, looking broody and more miserable than usual as he pretends to be entertaining a conversation with some girl with sleek silver hair. Draven knows his brother well enough to know from his body language he isn't the least bit interested. To Draven's absolute dismay, he finds Rhea at the center of the dance floor, dancing with Huxley fucking Rangard.

What the hell is she thinking?

Draven's grip on the railing tightens as he makes a note mentally to have a conversation with her after this event. To explain to her how deplorable—how absolutely despicable—Huxley Rangard is.

As the memory of what he said to Lyra sweeps through Draven for yet a second time tonight, he finds an intense anger flickering within his chest, causing his magic to stir. Draven rests his eyes and stretches his neck left, then right, willing the hungry thing to still. He doesn't need his father noticing.

"Having troubles, are we?"

Internally, Draven grits his teeth and winces. Externally, however, he shows not even a sliver of a reaction. "I don't know what you mean."

The corner of Tynan's lip curls. "Of course not." He turns his attention back onto the ballroom floor. "How is your wife-to-be this evening? I can't help but notice you have not spent much time with her since arriving."

Draven's stomach churns at the words *wife-to-be*. "Right. Because you always spent so much time with my mother at events like this."

Tynan only hums.

He is dressed in a rather nondescript manner for such a formal celebration—his jacket removed, instead electing only to wear his trousers, black silken waistcoat, and dress shirt. His mask is large and covers most of his face with the outline of a panther. Draven's mask holds a similar design—his father's decision—but in a much more subtle fashion.

"When I announce your engagement to Arden this evening, thus announcing the joining of House Dalmar and House Larking, I expect you to do your part and create a visual display which will please the people of Erandor. Make them support your union."

Draven wants to protest. He wants to fight, yell, scream—do anything to get himself out of a loveless engagement. Yet he can't. Because to do so would be to forsake the future of the person he cares for more deeply than he will ever be adequate enough with words to express.

So he hollows himself out, setting his mind on the bigger picture: continuing his search across the continent for Lyra and building her a secure future to come home to, despite how much it makes his heart cry knowing he can't ever be a part of that future.

But at least he is guaranteeing she will have one. That is all that matters.

Gods, how he misses his sweet girl. How he wishes he could hold her against his chest. Expand on all the words they wrote in their letters face-to-face. What Draven wouldn't give to lay his eyes on her. To see her magically appear through those doors, so he could take her hand in his and ask her to dance like any normal man would ask of the woman he adores. To just...exist with her. Even if it could only last for the duration of a single song.

"As you wish," Draven replies, silencing his deepest desires.

Tynan studies him for a good moment; Draven lets him. Eventually, seemingly amused with some piece of knowledge he decides not to let Draven in on, he says, "I am inclined to believe tonight will be filled with a series of surprising turns. In truth, I think you will really rather enjoy some of them."

Draven tries to mask his accompanying expression at the words, yet he fails, his brows still pinching together as his face scrunches beneath his mask. "Why do you think such a thing?"

"Call it my intuition. Call it a gut feeling. Call it a practical deduction. Truthfully, call it whatever you like—my predicted outcomes won't change."

The words feel like both a warning and a riddle in some way, and Draven knows his father well enough to know he does not say such words without a reason.

He sets the full weight of his attention on Tynan. "What are you scheming? What fucked up plan have you set into motion here tonight?"

Tynan smiles at him.

The sight makes Draven's skin crawl.

"All will be revealed in due time. For now, enjoy this beautiful ball with your beautiful fiancée. Though, perhaps you may find more enjoyment elsewhere this evening. Who knows." He clasps his hands behind his back and shrugs, the gesture practiced. "What you do will be your decision entirely."

Draven narrows his eyes on him. "I know you are trying to tell me something." He takes a step closer to Tynan, keeping his shoulders relaxed and his body language as casual as he can manage, seeing as the entire party can gaze up at the balcony and see them. "For once in your gods–damned life, be man enough to tell me directly what you've done."

His slithering smile broadens. "Now where is the fun in that?" He holds Draven's eyes with delight for a heartbeat longer, until he sighs and turns his back to the party. "I find myself in need of a drink paired with a moment's reprieve." He gives Draven a quick, final glance over his shoulder. "Do enjoy what happens in my absence, will you? Consider it my engagement gift to you."

Before Draven can question what the hell he means further, Tynan strides into the shadows, leaving him alone on the balcony. Draven turns back to face the spread below him, again gripping the railing. This time, though, he allows himself to hunch over slightly, letting just a fraction of the unending exhaustion he feels slip free.

He is lost in his listlessness—barely clinging to the persona he must maintain on this balcony—when the large southern doors push open and a lilac-haired girl wearing a plunging, off-white gown strolls into the room.

Time stills. The music dims, until it fades away entirely, leaving nothing but the ghostly hums of a familiar voice which once wrapped around his skin so sweetly.

For a moment, Draven is paralyzed, transfixed at the sight of the impossible. His brain sifts through the possibilities flashing through his mind, trying to rationalize what he sees before his heart swells with an optimism that will inevitably leave it broken. Until he sees piercing amethyst eyes glance up at the very balcony he is standing on, seeming to glow behind their silver mask filled with twisting vines and adorned with glittering jewels resembling flowers.

He goes rigid, his lips parting in tune to his shock.

"You," he breathes, leaning forward over the balcony to get a better look at her.

Both ecstasy and relief knock the wind from him, acting as a hammer to his weakening knees. His heart tumbles from beneath his ribcage and deep into the pit of his stomach, accelerating like an unfolding avalanche.

He doesn't know how it's possible, but there, strutting through a room of shadows as the only beacon of light, stands his heart. There lies his home. Half his soul. His entire salvation, alive and breathing and so gloriously, brilliantly unharmed.

So for right now, Draven does not try to understand it. Does not attempt to hide the sudden urgency fueling his movements as he pries himself from the balcony's railing and runs down the stairwell, daring any person to stand in his way.

As he moves, he hears echoes of words from long ago—words which embedded themselves into the very materials of his heart, a permanent stitch sewing broken pieces of himself together.

You are not a monster.

Draven runs to her, ready to return home at last.

CHAPTER THIRTY-THREE

LYRA

The carriage ride through Talderine was beautiful, despite the scars I noticed resting beneath the color. Regardless, I appreciate Casimir's attempt at something nice for me. It isn't his fault my eyes seemed to snag on everything wrong instead of everything right. Noticed all the cracks instead of all the jubilance.

I say as much to him as he escorts me up the long, torchlit walkway leading to Sagamon Castle's grand entrance—another terrifyingly beautiful feature of Talderine. The castle is a spread of gray stone and blue shingled spires. It is large and demanding; rough yet elegant. A large banner hangs from the uppermost brattice, boasting Erandor Kingdom's emblem: a castle between two rivers.

"There is no need to apologize," Casimir says. "There was nothing lost. Just as it seems there was nothing gained." There is a slight chuckle accompanying his latter words.

I groan, my guilt expanding in my chest. "I really am sorry."

"Don't be," he assures me right as we reach the two guards standing before the entry doors.

"Names?" the guard to the left demands.

With leisurely movements, Casimir reaches into his jacket and pulls a piece of parchment from the pocket inside. Wordlessly, he hands the parchment off to the guard, who takes it with a slight furrow in his brow. I could be imagining it, but I swear the guard blanches at whatever he reads. That as he gives the parchment back, there is a small tremor in his hand which causes the page to rattle. A coating of fear now glazed over his stiff expression.

He looks to the guard manning the right side of the entry. "Open the doors and let them pass."

The guard does as instructed—pulling down on a large bronze lever—and the doors swing open. Both guards keep their eyes forward as Casimir and I stride into the castle, yet I catch the quick flick of the left guard's eyes as Casimir passes through the threshold.

If Casimir notices, though, his face gives nothing away.

We are barely inside for a second before Casimir drops his bent arm, thus dropping my hand with it. He turns to face me. "I must go to my meeting now. Unfortunately, my instructions are to let you wander and enjoy the party while I am occupied." Even through his mask, I can see the way his gaze sharpens. "Please do not do anything you'd later regret. Or better yet, please do not do anything that will force *me* to do something *I* may come to regret."

I fold my arms. "Your choices are your own to make. What I choose to do should have no bearing on whether or not you regret them."

"And yet they do." He glances in the direction of the noise and chatter, too far in and beyond a stairwell to be visible from our current position. "Please, Lyra."

Why is there a part of me that actually *wants* to respect his wishes? How twisted has my sense of reason become since being gone? I have an opportunity to be free of him—to escape. I will not miss this chance for some newly developed feelings of fondness.

Yet right as the thought rings, I see Neilina's face in my mind and hear her words in my head.

I shake it all away.

"Okay," I lie. "I won't do anything."

Casimir heaves a sigh and glides a hand through his hair. "I do not believe you in the slightest."

361

I smile, the gesture more teasing than anything else. "And yet you have to."

"And yet I have to." He studies me intently before letting a low growl rattle in the back of his throat, seeming more directed at himself than me. "Enjoy the party," he says. He takes only one step away from me before he stops, softening his voice as he again looks at me. "I mean it," he murmurs. "I know you've never been able to be on the other side of an event like this. I truly do want you to enjoy it."

I blink at him, thankful for my mask as I sort through my own feelings at the words. "Thank you."

He only nods before striding off, leaving me alone at the bottom of the stairwell. One which will lead me to another set of doors that will give way to a party I am entirely unsure if I am prepared to face.

At the isolation, a series of thoughts race through my mind. Do I run now? Do I explore the castle, looking for exits? What if the guards stop me at the front doors, questioning me extensively? Erandor Kingdom is known to have antiquated views on women and their autonomy. What if I'm caught by guards patrolling the corridors? Then again, what if I'm not? What if someone I know from Bathara is inside? I could reveal my identity to them, and they could help me. But would I be damning everyone in the ballroom to an early demise in doing so? How far would Casimir go?

It's strange, the way getting to know him over these passing months has changed my approach to that question.

After an exhausting sequence of back-and-forths with my own mind, giving options and walking through their potential outcomes, I arrive at the conclusion that for now, the best course of action is to scope out the party. To remain tucked away in the shadows near the back, my mask firmly in place, and get a feel for both the security and the guests.

As I ascend the stairs leading into the ballroom, the music growing louder and the chatter morphing from a dull hum to a vibrant melody, a final desperate wish floats through my heart—

What if Draven is behind those doors, waiting to greet me?

It is a fool's delusion.

Yet just the mere thought of it—the doors pulling back to reveal Draven standing before me, waiting to take me into his arms and hold me—is enough to make my eyes prick with emotion. Though I need to not allow my mind to run off with hopeful fantasies. Instead, I need to keep my wits about me, because if I am to have any chance of escaping without there being casualties in the process, I can't be caught daydreaming about hopeful, happy endings.

I may be in Draven's home kingdom, in his home city, but I know there is nothing about this place Draven considers home. He does not enjoy social events, and with Bathara being in full swing, I'm sure he is busy attending to his duties as captain of his aggregate, leaving him with no reason to be here.

I steady myself, lifting my chin and rolling my shoulders back, preparing to enter into a room full of people I probably have once served in one capacity or another. Yet I do not allow myself to feel daunted by that, instead emulating the silent arrogance nobility always seems to carry at balls such as these.

I enter the room with my chin held high.

***

MY MOUTH FALLS within moments of entering.

Holy *gods*.

I have seen plenty of lavish balls within King Alastair's hall. Yet I have never seen a ball as extravagant as this before.

Is this what it is always like in Talderine? Is this what comes of celebrations held inside the bounds of a city known for its riches?

As I scan the scene, I am not sure if I am daunted, impressed, repulsed, or astonished. Perhaps all of the above?

I move stealthily near the back wall, my eyes roving up and quickly scanning the numerous balconies. Overwhelmed by the immensity of all that lies before me, my brain lags as it takes in all that it sees. My eyes glaze over a figure that—for whatever reason—causes my heart to skip. Yet by the time I give in to that curious feeling and retrace the spot on the balcony which seemed to make my heart snag, there is nobody up there. Just banners boasting behind the railing. Ones I must have mistook for a person.

I continue walking the perimeter of the room, attempting to process and notice everything I can. My preoccupied steps cause me to bump into someone tall and sturdy.

"Oh," I stammer. "I'm so sorry."

The dark-haired man turns, and I can see through his golden mask that his brown eyes crinkle. "You are entirely fine, I assure you." He tilts his head at me and smiles a rather charming smile, offering me his hand. "Would you care to dance?"

My initial reaction is to refuse, naturally. But then I realize guests probably assume I am of some noble house, disguised by a mask. Casimir certainly gave me a nice enough dress to make people believe I belong to nobility. Nobody knows who I am—why I'm here. Though truthfully, it's not like *I* even know why I'm here. So despite everything, I decide why the hell not. Why not steal a moment of fun and a carefree decision from this night?

I accept his hand and give a small curtsy, thankful for my court training. "I'd love to."

The stranger escorts me to the dancefloor, and a flowing, melodic tune gives way to him and me dancing a graceful waltz together. It is freeing and fun, and I enjoy spinning to the sounds of the stringed instruments—even if I remain stiff and on guard, occupied with other thoughts and worries.

By the time the dance is over, the stranger bows at the waist and I again curtsy. "Thank you for the dance, my Lady."

Lady. Now *that* is new.

I have to fight against the snort threatening to burst from me. "It was a pleasure."

He inclines his head, and then I watch as the kind stranger walks away, feeling grateful for the dance. Though, I'm sure I wasn't a very good partner.

A low voice hums from behind me. "Mind if I'm next?"

I stiffen.

That voice.

I *know* that voice. I dream of that voice. My heart *aches* for that voice.

Slowly, with my stomach plunging into a free fall, I turn around—

And nearly buckle to my knees.

I see night-dark hair tousled with waves longer than I last remember, slicked back yet disorderly, as if he was just running. I see a strong jaw accentuating the sharp lines of a perfectly sculpted face. Bright, mismatched eyes, filled with the most beautiful shades of blue and green known to this world. I inhale the scent of sandalwood and citrus, wrapping around me in the most familiar embrace. He may wear an elegant panther mask, hiding the upper portion of his face, but I would know the details of him anywhere.

"Draven," I breathe.

He strides to me and throws his arms around me, slamming me against his chest as he swallows me whole. My fingers clutch at his shirt, and I press my forehead into his torso, avoiding my mask. He holds me so tightly as he rests his chin atop my head. "You've really come back." Draven's voice trembles. "Is this a dream? Am I dreaming right now?"

I shake my head, tears welling in my eyes, gripping at his shirt and pressing myself into his chest as much as I possibly can, wishing I could somehow meld myself with him to feel close enough. "I'm here," I whisper. "I'm real."

"You're real," he breathes, his arms winding tighter around me, his hands settling on the curve of my waist. "You're here."

He holds me with desperation as the next song begins, colorful fabrics twirling around us like an unfurling rainbow in a crystal sky. People move as if looped in their own timeline. But time stills for Draven and me. They move forward, dancing and spinning and laughing, but we remain frozen—motionless and fragile as a held breath.

My chest follows the rhythm of his, and I melt into him—into his warmth, my mind attempting to process that this is *real*, and Draven is finally holding me in his arms again. I hadn't fully realized my body has been in a ceaseless state of restlessness until it finally calms, not feeling as though it needs to be brave and strong and guarded. I breathe—really *breathe* for the first time.

The air is sweetened by the scent of him. It wraps around my lungs and spreads through the veins of all that I am like a promise of something better. At once, my muscles slacken, my taut nerves finally sleep, and there is silence in my head.

A beautiful silence. Something still and tranquil. And I realize...

The feeling is peace.

Utter, blissful peace.

He pulls back, just enough to catch my eyes. "How is this possible? How did you escape? And what are you doing *here*, at Sagamon of all places?"

I want to give him all the answers he deserves, yet through my peripheral, I am forced to take note of all the eyes we are attracting with our intense display of affection, standing frozen in a sea of dancing people. As the song fades, reaching its end, I hear the whispers as hands cover mouths and people lean in, no doubt attempting to decipher my identity and determine what we're doing—why our conversation looks so fervent.

I pull back from him even further, my body screaming—*begging*—for me to stay wedged in his arms. Yet it is put second to a more pressing voice. A voice that reminds me of what Casimir is capable of. What he might do if he realizes Draven is here and has found me.

I recede a step, my heart breaking just as soon as it started to mend. "We can't...I'm not..." My voice is a raspy mess. "Not here," I try instead. "Too many eyes and ears."

Draven—seeming to understand quicker than I expected him to—lifts a hand and sweeps a thumb along an exposed part of my cheek. "Then just dance with me, Lyra."

"What?" I laugh, almost manically. "After everything, with all there is to say, you just want to... *dance?*"

Even through his mask I can see the tenderness in his eyes as he gazes at me. He splays his fingers across my cheek, cupping my face. "Yes," he murmurs so gently, my knees nearly buckle. "For one moment, for one song, I just want to exist in a world where I am at a ball with a beautiful girl I adore, and she and I dance together while the stars dance alongside us."

"Draven..." I whisper.

The corner of his mouth sweeps up into a soft curve, and he extends his hand to me, bowing at the waist. "May I have this dance?"

With emotion swelling painfully in my chest, I place my hand in his.

The touch is like breaking from beneath the water's surface, inhaling oxygen into deprived lungs that have been drowning and starved. It is firecrackers and starlight. A rainstorm on a withering garden bed.

"You may."

He presses his lips gently to the back of my hand, pulling me into his frame right as the instrumentalists begin playing their next song.

And then we dance.

We dance to the vibrato of the brooding cello as it hums into the soles of our feet. We glide across the marble floor as the legato notes carry the melody guiding our muscles, weightless and everlasting as the wind. Draven presses his palm against the small of my back, splaying his fingers across it before curling them into my dress, bringing me flush against his chest. We hold each other's eyes as we move, lost beneath the weight of all there is to say, paralyzed by the immensity of this moment and the gravity of lost time.

Draven spins me, guiding me back to him after. "You look so beautiful," he murmurs. "Somehow, even more beautiful than the last time I saw you. How is that possible?"

"You can't even see me," I point out through a small laugh. "I have a mask on."

He smiles. "Do you? I hadn't noticed."

I wrinkle my nose with mocking disapproval, which results in Draven's hand flexing against my back. "I think it's your hair," he says. "I like it short. It suits you."

I lift gentle fingers to sweep an escaped strand of his own hair from his forehead. "And your hair is longer now."

The light dims in his eyes. "I haven't had much motivation to maintain personal upkeep lately."

My hand grazes the side of his face tenderly before it falls to rest at his neck, where my fingers twine themselves into those longer strands. "And yet you still manage to draw every eye in the room."

"Second to another."

I bite down on my answering smile, my body a complete mess of feelings—though ones I am capable of navigating, thanks to the help of the man standing before me.

He lifts one hand to cradle the back of my neck. Something shifts in his expression, sharpening, and the air thickens between us. "Lyra, I am so sorry I failed you. That I wasn't able to find you. In every sense of the way, I am sorry."

There is so much raw pain in his voice, it stabs me like a blade.

"Don't," I murmur. "You have *nothing* to be sorry for, Draven. *Nothing.*"

He grunts, the sound sad and distant, pulling his eyes from me. "I will not fail you again. Not when it comes to your safety."

I cup his cheek, guiding his gaze back. "You've never failed me as it stands."

Something inscrutable passes through his eyes. A sort of melancholy I'm not quite sure how to place. "What happened that forced you to stop writing to me?" he asks, seeming to change course.

"Casimir found my—well, Gray's—Ever-Know Quill. He destroyed it so I couldn't write to you any longer."

"I'm going to kill him."

For the first time since knowing Draven, a small echo of doubt flickers through me at his abilities to win such a fight. It would be a battle for the ages—Draven against Casimir. I'd fear for both men's ability to survive, yet I now know Casimir can't die, putting Draven at a terrible, insurmountable disadvantage.

Which again makes me think of what Casimir might do if he discovers Draven and me together.

"I don't want to talk about him." At the question I can already see forming on Draven's lips, I quickly add, "Or the place where he was keeping me. It's still as I said in my letters—I truly don't know where I was." I lower my voice, swiping my fingers across the back of Draven's neck. "I just want to live in this moment with you."

Though foolish it is, which I don't say.

He nods, continuing to guide me across the dancefloor, the sweeping tune guiding our movements clearly being extended for show purposes as four violinists step out to the dancefloor and spread out, resting their mahogany instruments on their shoulders as they move about and continue playing. As they do, glittering, golden light rises from their strings, fluttering up and up until it spreads out in a vast array, mirroring starlight—a trick coordinated with light-wielders, no doubt. The light twinkles against the nearly reflective floor, giving the illusion that everyone on the ballroom floor is encased in stars.

Applause erupts from all the bystanders.

Draven and I merely hold each other's eyes, seeing nothing more beautiful than the sight standing directly in front of the other.

I know I need to tell him Casimir is here. I know I need to explain the circumstances surrounding how the hell it's possible that *I* am here, dancing with him right now. But the second I open that conversation, the second this blissful bubble will burst, and both he and I will be forced to remove ourselves from this fantasy dream and face the sharpness of reality. He will switch into his assessing captain mode, and I will be forced to work through and explain the many things I have seen and experienced and learned over the months I've been away. I will have to make the difficult decision of how to best run away—to escape. To determine *if* I can even escape.

I will not risk innocent lives. Not again. And I certainly will not risk Draven's.

But those are all thoughts and decisions I don't want to deal with until after this song. Because right now, it is just as Draven wished for —a smitten girl and an adoring boy, dancing passionately beneath starlight.

My heart pumps emotion through my veins like blood. I nearly feel drunk on it. On the goodness of this moment. On the recognition of its fragility. There is always something so tender and reverent about fragile things. It makes a person appreciative—desperate to preserve and protect that which is breakable.

"Tell me something I can hold onto once this dream is over."

Draven allows me to see the surprise in his eyes. "What kind of something would you like me to tell you?"

"I don't know if I really care," I murmur. "Tell me anything. About how you've been. About how everyone's been. Tell me your favorite color or tell me what it would be like to wake up in your arms tomorrow. Just tell me…something."

His eyes soften. "Your wish is my command."

Draven leads me into a dip, where he then leans over me and grazes his lips up the full length of my neck. His breath is a warm caress against my skin, and the overwhelming feeling of being touched like that after so long makes the air hitch in my chest. He cradles my neck as he guides me upright, his eyes never leaving mine. There is something new and bright burning behind them now.

Draven lowers his mouth to the tip of my ear, brushing against my skin with a feather-light touch that sends my body hair rising. "If I was privileged enough to wake up with you in my arms, I would lazily trace every inch of your skin as if discovering it for the first time. I would press my lips against your mouth, where I would devour you wholly and without apology. Then I would glide my tongue down your neck, until I reached your breasts, where I would pay homage to their divinity. And as I worshipped your skin, I would slip two fingers inside of you, and I would touch you with more reverence than even a god could dream of receiving. And only when my name is quivering on your lips, when the taste of me on your tongue has made you drunk, only then would I slip myself inside of you, thrusting until you made my back bleed."

A hearth roars to life beneath my skin, flushing what feels like every inch of my body with a pink stain. Draven smiles a crooked, loaded sort of smile at the sight of it.

"I would take my time," he continues against my ear, his desire leaking into every word, making my knees weak and heartbeat erratic. "Not wasting a single second with you, savoring every stroke, every kiss, every moan of pleasure I force from your lips." He tilts his chin toward me, making his lips brush against the skin of my cheek. "I would make your body shatter into a million pieces from pleasure, and then I would spend an eternity admiring every beautiful fragment as I stitched you back together."

He pulls his lips back, finally allowing me to see his eyes again. And the heat waiting for me in his gaze has me sucking my bottom lip between my teeth, and—

"Captain Dalmar," a stern voice calls out from beside us.

The final chords of the extended song harmonize in a concluding swell, then end. The violinists exit the dancefloor, taking my fantasy and desire-laden dreams with them.

Draven doesn't look at the man, instead holding my stare. There is something in his gaze—something frantic, almost. Apologetic. But different from the apology resting in his eyes before. He looks as though he is calculating something—attempting to find a way out.

But a way out of what, exactly, I don't know. Maybe it has something to do with me? With this man?

"Captain Dalmar," the man says again irritably, his low baritone seeming to swallow the room now that the music has paused.

I nearly flinch at the commanding sound, but Draven doesn't bat an eye. Instead, he simply studies me for a few seconds longer, as if trying to memorize every pore on my face. Until he releases a clipped sigh, removes his hands from my body, and steps away from me, turning to face the voice.

I'm not sure if my skin has ever before felt as cold and abandoned as it does the moment Draven drags himself away from me.

"Lord Larking," he says in a mild tone, all the warmth in his gaze fleeting away.

"Your father requests your presence." The man doesn't bother an attempt at sounding cordial, leaving his irritation fully unmasked. He slices a look at me. "You should go on and fetch a drink, Lady. Captain Dalmar here won't be coming back for quite some time, and once he does, I'm afraid his attention will be otherwise occupied."

Okay... whatever the hell *that* means.

And did he just say Lord *Larking*? As in *Captain* Larking's father? Meaning... *Arden*?

Why the hell is *he* fetching Draven for his father?

Something else strikes me. The realization that Draven is being pulled away. I don't know how much longer Casimir's meeting will be —if I have the time to meet with Draven again when his father is finished with him. If I'm honest with myself, I probably already know the truth.

I don't.

A frantic desperation grips me.

"My Lord," I say as sweetly as I can manage. "I'm afraid I must kindly protest the idea of—"

"You get no such say, Lady. I don't know your House, but I know it won't outrank House Dalmar. The Supreme Commander has requested his son for an announcement, and so his son must answer."

Announcement?

I turn to Draven, questions brimming in my eyes. He sees them resting there, and that look of apology intensifies in his own gaze. "I'm sorry," he whispers, reaching a hand out and then dropping it, as if meaning to stroke my cheek but thinking better of it. "Don't move from this spot, okay? And don't remove your mask. I will return to you and explain everything as soon as I can." His lips thin as he continues watching me. "Fuck, Lyra—I am so sorry. I thought I was going to have more time to explain."

The accompanying thought rings loudly in my head: *so did I.*

Still, what is *he* talking about? What does he need to explain to me? And why does he look so broken—so filled with contrition?

Before I can ask any of those questions, though, that gods-forsaken man again speaks. "Captain Dalmar," he pushes. "We must be going now."

Draven grits his teeth, jerking his chin to the man. "Do not speak to me as if you hold some authority over me, Lord Larking. I know I needn't remind you that you *don't.*"

372

The man inclines his head. "My apologies, Captain Dalmar. I merely wish to not upset your father."

My eyes shift between them.

A low growl rattles in Draven's throat before he turns his attention back onto me. His features soften. "Wait for me here," he says again, quiet enough so only I will hear. "It's important, okay? No matter if you hate me. No matter how much you won't understand—promise me you'll wait."

I can't promise you that. I might not have time.

Still, how does he think I could ever hate him? *Why* does he think I'll hate him? What am I missing?

As I stare back at him—still glimpsing echoes of the agony that broke his voice—I surprise myself when I instead answer, "I promise."

Draven nods, content. He turns on his heels and follows Lord Larking in the opposite direction of me, his fingers subtly sweeping across my back before flexing and curling into a rigid fist at his side.

I watch him leave, wondering why I feel like we've just said goodbye to each other. I watch as he disappears behind the crowd. As he goes, I also wonder why my heart hurts.

Why it feels oddly... broken.

CHAPTER THIRTY-FOUR

LYRA

The room falls into an anticipatory quiet.

The sort of quiet which makes a person want to hold the air in their lungs captive. The kind of quiet which has parts. That creates nervous glances and causes feet to shift and a room to stifle.

Tynan Dalmar steps forward on the center balcony overlooking the entirety of the ballroom. Chins tilt up as masked eyes find him like flowers finding their sun. He has their undivided attention—a feat which is rather impressive, when considering this is a room filled with people who all think they are the most important person in the Three Kingdoms.

"My esteemed ladies. My noble gentlemen. On behalf of King Erasmus, I welcome you to this year's Winter Solstice ball."

At the mention of the Erandorian King, I suddenly realize I haven't seen him yet this evening. With a quick glance around the room, I confirm that observation—he isn't here.

Which is considerably odd, seeing as it's the Winter Solstice celebration, and one that is being held in his castle, no less.

"Please rest at ease knowing I do not stand before you as the King's Supreme Commander nor his Master Strategist this evening. I am

374

merely here as a representative for my proud House and as a proud father."

At the words, Draven steps into view, standing directly next to his father's hip. Women erupt in husky whispers at the sight of him, drawn out and filled with *far* too much lust for my liking. Though...I get it.

Even with his mask, he still manages to be breathtaking.

"Tonight, I offer a special treat to you all: an announcement, known only to myself and House Larking. Though one I am eager to share. A reason to celebrate this special evening with even more fervor."

That terribly rude man, Lord Larking, steps into view, his daughter by his side, taking up residence near Tynan's opposite hip.

I stare at them, my brain trying to unravel this puzzle before me.

What is going on?

Tynan reaches for Captain Larking's hand, and then for Draven's. "Tonight I announce to you the official union of House Dalmar with House Larking, given form by both my eldest son—my Heir—and Lord Larking's eldest daughter. Two powerful Houses. Two tremendous wielders. Two esteemed captains at our elite Bathara. One perfect marriage." He places Arden's hand in Draven's, then recedes, leaving only the two of them at the front of the balcony as Lord Larking steps back to join Tynan in the shadows.

Draven's eyes are on me the whole time, his expression veiled by perfectly crafted indifference because it has to be. Because all eyes are on him, including his father's.

Applause erupts through the room. The cello and violin zip to life, plucking nothing but merry tunes that facilitate more merriment. Glasses are raised. Whistles are thrown around. Flowers tumble from the ceiling like colored snowflakes—a celebratory feat which was most certainly planned in advance.

Everyone—at least at surface-level—is filled with joy and excitement for the union as they toast in celebration and cheer with a mixture of awe and pride. The room is happy.

I have never known such misery.

My body has a delayed reaction to the news. At first, my heart refuses to accept it. Instead, my brain attempts damage control, rationalizing and using logic to discern the true nature of what's been said. Yet, it keeps drawing blanks—keeps failing to find the rationale. Because this news—Draven's *engagement*—has just been publicly announced at one of Erandor Kingdom's most prestigious events, in a room filled with its most wealthy, high-ranking citizens. Though perhaps not legally, as far as society is concerned, there is nothing more binding than that.

Which forces me to believe it must be true.

Is it because he thought I'd never return? Did he give up on me, after all? Was it all a lie?

Suddenly, I can't breathe. I back up, up, up—away from the raucous room. Away from the jubilant smiles and cloying cheers. Right as I turn to run away to find fresh air that isn't clotted with saccharine congratulations, I bump right into someone's chest. They catch me, steadying me by my elbows.

"I know I'm handsome, but I fear you've thrown yourself into the wrong man's arms."

I look up to find myself having run into a man with slicked back ruby-red hair paired with a mask concealing mischievous sapphire eyes. He wears a beautiful smirk across his lips.

I throw my arms around him immediately. "Kiran," I breathe.

It's strange how much a heart can manage at once. How, like some clever machine, it can change gears between sadness and happiness without diminishing the presence of either.

He presses his hand against my back, embracing me tenderly. When I pull back from him, I swear I catch that smirk of his falter— see a glimmer of something sad in his eyes. Yet as soon as I think I see it, it has disappeared.

"It's good to see you," he says, the words earnest. Like an older brother would his younger sister, he playfully skips the pad of his thumb across my cheek. "And in one piece, no less."

It's such an absurd thing to say, I laugh. The sound is sad and echoes as though I am on the verge of tears, yet it is a laugh all the same.

Kiran notices, and he sighs. "Before things get...messier," he says, his lips pursing as he looks noticeably on edge all of a sudden. "Please allow me to explain what you've just witnessed on behalf of my dear brother."

I snort, the sound dry and angry and...*fuck*. I'm feeling so many things, I'm not even sure *what* I'm feeling. Well, with one exception: heartbreak. "I doubt explanations will make me feel any better."

"I think this one might, actually. Or, if nothing else, it will help. I have no doubts about that much." My face scrunches, and he brackets my shoulders gently. "It's not what you think it is. Or at least, the reasons surrounding it are probably quite different than you imagine."

"So what is it, then? Because it looks a hell of a lot like the man I offered my heart to is recently engaged to someone else—a fact of which he *never* told me."

"Yes, because you have been so easy to find lately." He says it with the perfect ratio of seriousness to playful sarcasm, rendering a balanced retort I can't decide if I want to laugh at or be mad at. None the less...

Touchè.

"Point taken," I grumble. "But it doesn't make it hurt any less."

"I know," he murmurs. "I know it doesn't." Kiran sucks in a loud sigh, dropping his hands from my shoulders. "I'll do my best to keep all of this as succinct and organized as I can."

He then proceeds to tell me everything.

About Bathara's council's decision to bring me in should they find me. That the Tani wants to try me before their jury. That I would undoubtedly be found guilty, then thrown into Toellor Prison until I am either needed or rotted. He tells me about Tynan's proposition. About his promise to prevent that future from unfolding should Draven marry Arden. He explains until my eyes go wide with shock, then brim with curious tears.

I'm not even sure who the tears are for.

When he is finished, he studies me with a sympathetic gaze. "I know that's a lot of information to take in."

"So…he doesn't want it? Doesn't want a marriage with Arden?"

Kiran's eyes soften. "Between you and me, Lyra—though I suspect it is obvious to anyone with eyes in their sockets—Draven wants nothing, and I do mean *nothing*, but a life with you."

My heart shreds into thin ribbons, too broken and confused to be anything else.

"He's giving his entire life away for me, then." I shake my head against the thought of it. "He is sacrificing everything. For *me*. So that I won't be forced into a prison for the power in my veins and the atrocities I committed that day." Guilt merges forcefully with all the other emotions clamoring in my chest. "I can't let him do that, Kiran. Marriage is—is a place to call home. Is a promise to love unconditionally. It is a *future*. I can't let all of that be written for him by his father. I just…*can't*."

Kiran himself looks slightly conflicted. "What would you propose to stop it?"

"I—I don't know. Something—anything. I just need to be able to think for a moment."

As if in some cruel divine timing, a resounding *BOOM* carries from the distant hall, the floor trembling at our feet along with the sound.

My eyes snap to Kiran. "What the hell was that?"

Something passes in his gaze—something I can't quite place but distinctly know not to be right—and his shoulders fall as he again looks at me. "I wish you had more time to think, Lyra. Gods I wish you did."

Before I can utter a single response to that, the wall adjacent from us explodes, shards of rubble crashing and flying across the ballroom. Men and women alike are knocked unconscious, some questionably injured as huge slabs of rock arc through the sky before crushing limbs while smaller pellets pierce through skin. The crowd shrieks with fright, dispersing like a band of discovered rats.

For a moment, flickers of larger toppling walls invade my mind.

My body twitches, then convulses involuntarily as flashes of Abdites, crimson-stained swords, bloodied lips, corrupted magics, and explosions of power temporarily paralyze me. Yet, once the dust and debris clears from the air, it is not creatures that appear.

It is men with swords and spears and pikes. With magic in their palms—their wielder's marks intact—and shields at their backs.

And they are angry.

"Leave not a soul behind!" a middle-aged man with a gruff beard and calloused body steps forward and declares. "Bring them their reckoning! Show them their justice! Bring forth the uprising!"

Cold dread lances down my spine.

That Abdite from Foreigner's Valley all those months ago, Dridus. Her words sing in my mind to the tune of a child's song.

Up the rising goes forward, she chanted manically that night. It was followed by her strange tune. *Up the rising goes. One by one, until it unfolds. Forward we forge, just like the land before. Time rewind, magic that binds, brother by brother. My brother, oh brother.*

She hadn't been wrong. Dridus had been privy to information surrounding an uprising.

And they are here. Have begun their revolution.

The sea of insurgents echoes the leading man's words like a war cry, fisting their weapons and magic into the air.

"Bring forth the uprising! Down with the noble lines!"

CHAPTER THIRTY-FIVE

LYRA

Everything plunges into uncivilized chaos.

Noblemen and women trample each other in their attempts to flee. Those skilled in combat, talented at wielding their Houses' exceptional magics, fight back. Angry swords are plunged into the backs of the fallen. Daggers are jabbed into thighs and necks. Spears are thrown across the room as carelessly as celebratory ribbons. It leaves the once dazzling, crystal-filled ballroom painted in blood and rubble. And for the second time in my life, I am ensconced in the belly of savagery as a gory battle rages before my eyes.

This time, however, I have control over my magic thanks to Casimir's extensive training.

Fire is the first element to answer my call—an increasingly annoying feature, it would seem. I allow the element to feel at one with my veins, coloring them vermillion beneath my skin while the mark at my back burns in the place where the fire symbol resides. I bend my knees and sway my hands as I gather the force of my attack in my palms.

I let the fire blaze.

It incinerates two archers, one of whom had their arrow notched and directed at me, the other of whom was aiming in the opposite direction.

Nausea roils through me at the sight. For the duration of a blink, I see my mother burnt amongst them.

I drop my palms and demand the fire magic to flee my veins. I do not wish to wield fire; in fact, I want nothing to do with it.

Though, speaking of fire...

I search for Kiran, but can no longer see him. In the midst of the chaos, we were separated. At the initial explosion, he reached for me and shielded me with his body, putting his back between me and the rubble. Yet as the invaders raided the ballroom—shouts from distant guards announcing they had infiltrated the whole of Sagamon Castle —scurrying partygoers frightened for their lives wedged us apart.

Now, I find myself standing in my own corner of the room, fighting against an isolated section of the rebellion. Which leaves me with the question: *why am I fighting them?* But then a jolt of lightning reaches for me—making the air look like a bed of fracturing ice—and suddenly that question doesn't matter. Surviving does.

I spin, pulling at wind that thankfully answers for once, redirecting myself away from the attack with just enough time. It crashes into the floor and ceiling alike, sending even more of the hovering ice crystals plummeting toward the ground, shattering like glass against the marble. Three people with handkerchiefs covering the lower portion of their faces surround me.

"Who are you people?" I ask, my palms raised at the ready.

The one farthest left—a woman with braided hair and worn eyes—unsheathes a broadsword from her back. "We are the uprising. The Reapers of Righteousness. The Restorers of the original ways. We are the Restorationists."

There's a familiarity to the title I can't quite place...

"And what do you want? What are you restoring?"

"She already told you," another woman, located on the right, spits. "The original ways. The ways of old. The ways which these lands were originally founded upon." A pool of glowing blue energy accumulates in her palm, but she doesn't strike. None of the three do.

At the small reprieve, without my consent—now not being the time nor the place—my brain wanders, leaping headfirst into all the stored memories I have of Casimir's journal. They do not come back to me easily, but my mind is relentless in its determination to remember. Small echoes from different passages ring out in my head.

I understand that the discord is growing, and that soon, we will be forced to choose: squelch the uprising and deal with the Restorationists, or choose a path of peace and continue negotiations through the means of compromise;

Magaius does not believe we should concede a single thing to the Restorationists. That they are simply unhappy children, and that one does not reward children's bad behavior;

War is coming.

From what I remember, it was all in regard to the Three King System. I had been shocked to learn there was discourse surrounding the change. Our history books have never told us anything of the sort, instead maintaining the narrative that there was only a peaceful division of power amongst the lands of Solaya *after* The Great Clamaté War—not before. Yet Casimir's account of history renders that version impossible, his timeline of events entirely different.

And that's the other thing. History does not tell us of a group known as the Restorationists. Historians do not mention opposition to the signing of the Three King Accords, nor do they mention an uprising opposing it. Yet Casimir does, and now, standing here before me is a group of rebels claiming the title of a people who allegedly never existed.

I study the group as though they hold all the answers I seek. Perhaps they do. "And what are the ways of old? The ways you seek to restore?"

The figure at the center, not having moved nor spoken since they surrounded me, drops the hood covering his face. The man has skin weathered with age, eyes like a glass of brandy. He is rough, yet he does not appear unkind. "The Three King System was created to facilitate greater aid to both the lower class of people and noble houses. Famine plagued the lands while poverty plagued the pockets. Our realm was in a state of unrest, and there was a need for great change. Yet once the last unitary king died—leaving behind not a single heir—those already positioned for power acted, dividing the lands and creating new borders, realigning politics and economics with the change. For a time, this seemed beneficial. With less to rule over, Kings and Houses could better serve their people. Yet they didn't. Nothing changed for the farmers and the black-smiths and the tradesmen. Somehow, instead, the rich got richer while the poor got poorer." He takes one step toward me. "Do you know why?"

I can't decide if I should answer him or not. Luckily, he continues in spite of my silence.

"It is because all the partitions truly did was give hungry men more power; put boundaries on squabbles, then labeled the division of laws and politics as 'The Great Era of Peace.'" He huffs a cold, dry laugh. "There has been no peace in the forgotten slums. In the forsaken farmlands and within the mining towns.

"Tell me, how is it that nearly all of Erandor suffers from hunger, disease, and economic distress while the rich watch their coffers grow more plentiful? Why do the other kings not intervene? What are we supposed to do if those who are meant to supply the checks and balances do nothing? I'll tell you: we rebel. Because what Solaya needs is not three kings and scheming noble houses—it needs one unitary king. It needs cohesion and prosperity. We are through watching our realm be the backdrop for the insatiable greed of power-crazed men. So instead, we will restore the ways of old whilst seeking to form a new pyramid of government beneath a new king—one which main-tains the necessary checks and balances of power."

I study the man and his companions, monitoring for any signs of a forming attack. "What good will that do?"

The man cocks his head at her. "What good will it hurt? All things here are already broken. Look around" —the man glides his arms in a sweeping gesture, showcasing the saccharine ballroom, so lavish it chokes one with its richness— "this is how they live. How they spend their coffers, content to laugh and drink and fuck. I have two boys, both of whom show bone through their skin. Tell me, girl, do you have the slightest idea how bad the slums have gotten? Just how impoverished the world outside of nobility truly is?"

The question strikes me. Not with offense, but guilt.

No.

I don't.

Though I've felt like a slave to this system, I still lived in a king's estate for nearly the entirety of my life. Then, once I was freed of that, I traversed to Bathara, the most elite academy of any in the realm. Then I was kidnapped, living in a sprawling garden oasis, housed in silken sheets and fine rugs.

I've always condemned nobility. Have always felt the chip on my shoulder from being surrounded by them yet entirely on the outside, forced to bear that truth like a nasty brand they could always exploit. Yet I've lived more closely to them than most. Because of my position with King Alastair, I always had food. A bed. Access to healers. I received a top-notch education from Sterling Nightenjoy, one of the most brilliant men in the entire Three Kingdoms. Was trained in court manners and taught to understand politics.

I was privileged to have a security of sorts, as twisted as that is to think about. I've never had to worry about if I will starve. How to put food on my table. If I will make it past the coming winter. Sure, my life as a night attendant was not a glorious nor particularly safe one, but with its atrocities came comforts that not even I can deny.

No, I haven't the slightest clue what the world outside of nobility is like, and bile burns the back of my throat with that realization. It forces me to wonder: if I do not belong with them, and I do not belong with nobility, where, then, do I actually belong?

The man sees the struggle in my eyes. To my surprise, the roughness framing his movements melts away. "There is more to our cause than wanting conflict," he murmurs. "We want change. We want to be heard. To not be squished under fine leather boots any longer." He sighs, sounding so tired all of a sudden. "Yet the price of freedom is blood. It will *always* be blood." An earnest pause. "I'm tired of my people being the ones bled dry."

The words sound so familiar...

The man reaches his hand out to me, seeming so kind—the gesture so sincere—I'm tempted to offer him my hand.

His head splits from his shoulders before our skin can ever greet one another.

A rogue sheet of ice spins toward the wall like a spiraling boomerang, cutting directly through his neck. His body drops to the ground without so much as a moment's notice. The two women at his side go pale, their eyes bulging with the shock of how quickly their friend was just taken from them.

Suddenly, everyone standing here is reminded that we are in the midst of a battle, not a negotiation's table. There is no talking; only fighting.

The woman with purple energy hovering around her palms brings the heels of her hands together and shoves them forward, sending a biting ripple of purple lightning in my direction. Simultaneously, the woman who was on the man's left spins with her broadsword in hand, a hot, bubbling slice of silver falling away from the blade and sent soaring toward me.

A metal-wielder, then.

Great.

A jolt of terror spikes my nerves as I question my ability to defend myself against both attacks. They are strong and quick—refined and fueled with rage, which, from first-hand experience, always seems to elevate magic. Yet before I even have a chance to pull on any magic to defend myself, a shadow panther leaps over my shoulder and swallows the lightning while a contained ice storm erupts in front of me, freezing the silver and forcing it to *clank* to the ground in solid form before it can reach me.

A quick scan, and I don't see Draven anywhere near me. I don't know how he knew to send his shadow panther for me, but...of course he knew.

He always knows. Always attempts to protect me.

When my gaze pivots in the opposite direction, I find the source of the ice magic that saved me from the molten silver.

It's Finlay.

He watches me from a distance, confusion seeming to pinch his features, notably exposed without a mask. Yet before I have time to even consider his curious expression further, another loose magic attack lances for me from across the room.

This time it's a beam of spiraling fire.

Having just seen Finlay and his ice, I pull without thinking. I connect to his laktî and suck air between my teeth at the immensity of it. I feel the prickle of ice in my veins, and the sparkling substance soars free from my fingertips, stopping the fire in its tracks.

My vision throbs. My back burns as though my skin is being stretched taut. I hear whispers. They louden with each pull of my magic.

I ignore them.

A loosed arrow races toward my heart while a man with a bloodied sword races toward my neck. Yet a figure emerges from a blinking portal, slicing his own sword through the skin of the charging man before he grips me by the shoulders and spins me around. We tumble from the force, and my back hits the floor as the arrow hits the figure's back. It ricochets to the ground, bent at the tip, as though it rammed into a steel wall.

Casimir heaves heavy breaths above me, his face twisted with anger. "Of all the moments Solaya chooses to initiate a rebellion, it *has* to be while we are contained within it."

My temporary shock of all that's just happened ebbs away, snapped from its stupor by Casimir's words. "Where you go, conflict seems to follow." I mean it as a joke, but the tight frown pulling hard at his lips tells me it was received as fact.

He sighs, lifting himself from me and offering a hand. "We are leaving."

I accept his hand and brush off the dust and debris from my ruined dress, glancing where Finlay had just stood only moments ago. The space is now empty. "We need to help," I counter, reverting my attention.

"I have no desire to intervene in the reckoning finally being brought upon nobility."

"You will when I tell you the name of the uprising."

That makes Casimir pause. "What is the name?"

"The Restorationists."

A gallery of emotions pass through Casimir's expression. He seems incapable of deciding which he wants to feel. "The Restorationists?" he repeats. "Are you certain?"

I nod. "They told me themselves."

He looks hesitant, but after a long bout of thought, he shakes his head at whatever he was considering. "This changes nothing. We are going. *Now*."

I consider mentioning that I remember the group from his journal entries—pressing that I know his connection to them—but before I get the chance to say anything, he reaches for my wrist. I jerk away. "Hold on," I protest. "I need a moment to think."

I don't say my echoing thought. *I need a moment to decide.*

"To *think*?" he asks, incredulous. "About what? There is nothing to think about. This is not our fight. We do not need to bleed for anyone in this room."

"That's where you're wrong." The words come out faster than I can think better of it, and Casimir's features harden.

Two members of the uprising charge at us, and with a lazy flick of his wrist, he tosses them across the room with a powerful gust of wind "Lyra." He says my name like a warning, and nothing else.

A conceding sigh breaks from my lips as the weight of diverging choices presses against me. As I am forced to come face-to-face with a realization. An acceptance.

A resignation.

I do not belong with nobility, and I do not fully belong with the commoners, either. I cannot be with Draven, and I cannot attend Bathara any longer. My realm has abandoned me—has *condemned* me. Wishes to imprison me for what I did at Bathara, and frankly, I can't even fault them for it. I lost control, and people suffered.

I no longer have a place in the Three Kingdoms—not without letting Draven suffer a price I refuse to let him pay. He always protects me; now it is my turn to protect him.

The wheels in my mind turn, until it all clicks into place. A potential solution to it all.

Before I can think better of the questionable decision and make a different choice—one that is more selfish, built on optimism and dreams—I square my shoulders to Casimir, steeling my resolve. "I will only go with you on two conditions."

He studies me, frowning. "I think you've forgotten the nature of our relationship."

I huff a sardonic laugh. "Trust me, I haven't forgotten. But I'm thinking...perhaps we could modify our dynamic?"

Casimir clasps his hands, his eyes narrowing on me. "I'm listening."

Here we go.

"I will willingly go with you, *if* you promise to halt your grand plan and work with me to find a cure for your family instead. Perhaps we can cure them of their lakti's corruption ourselves, and there will be no need for you to destroy magic and commit unnecessary genocide against the noble houses."

"The magic protecting my home is dying—what of that?" he counters without thought. "Who is to say we succeed? Who is to say this realm will accept them back if we do? I will not give my family their freedoms back, only to then throw them to the gnashing teeth of poverty and the claws of hunger."

"We can at least try, Casimir. And look around you—an uprising has already started. Perhaps things will change."

Casimir laughs, the low sound haunted and loaded thick with something I can't place. "When order is lost, who will be the one to find it again?"

My brows knit together. "What?"

"Nothing," he says, dismissing it with a wave of his hand. He rolls his shoulders back, setting me in his gaze. "I can make you return with me, you know. I do not have to concede to any of your terms to ensure you come back to my home."

"I know," I agree, my voice surprisingly soft. "But I don't think you want to. I think you're tired of forcing me to do things I don't want to do."

I'm betting on it, I don't say.

His eyes remain glued to mine. "And what has given you that impression?"

"I don't know," I answer, telling the truth. "Yet for some reason, I still believe what I've said to be true all the same."

He studies me for so long, he has to deflect two blasts of magic, send a strike of water spearing toward an archer, and defend against a burly man with a spear. Once he has disarmed and—to my surprise—only knocked the burly man unconscious, he blows out a loaded sigh. "Let's say I agree to your wishes, and I redirect all my efforts to discovering a cure for the corruption in my family's veins—will you then give my home and all its people the proper chance they deserve? Open yourself fully to them? Accept responsibility for their futures, someday caring for and leading them as I have planned?"

I consider his question.

Can I? Truly, without reservation, despite all that Casimir and his kind have done?

Going back is worth it to me, to know Draven can choose a life he pleases. And though I will miss Gray and Marcella more than words can possibly describe, I know I'll also be keeping them safe with my decision. Because I will not let Draven marry someone he doesn't love —thus shackling his whole life—for me. Which means I will never receive the aid of Tynan Dalmar to secure my freedom against Bathara *and* the Tani. Which also means, should I stay in Solaya, I would be a criminal on the run, always looking over my shoulder and covering my tracks. I know Gray Nightenjoy well enough to know he would follow me into the depths of hell—though he would probably try to reason with the flames before they could burn us. And Marcella? Marcella barely needs a reason to pick a fight with nobility. Giving her one—and one I know she would fight tooth and nail to protect—would probably be enough to watch her start her own sort of calamity.

Gods, I love them. I will *miss* them. But I can't drag them into my mess, even knowing they would happily plunge into the abyss with me. If I could change anything about what I must do, it's simply that I wish I could see them one final time, hug them properly, and say goodbye.

Plus, will it truly be so bad to go back? To give the others a chance?

If it's on my terms, perhaps Casimir and I can come to agree on different arrangements. Though honestly, I don't even know what those changes would look like. If we are going to find a cure for the corruption in the Abdites' laktî, then I *should* continue entering the Veil. Not to mention, I wouldn't want to stop my training—not when I'm truly beginning to see improvements in my magic. And thinking of getting to see Neilina again fills me with warmth, makes me happy. If I feel that way about the only person I truly got to know in Casimir's home, whose to say I can't feel that way about the others?

You should consider giving this place a chance, she had mused to me. *I think you might find it'll grow on you—if you let it.*

I lift my chin, my decision made. "I will."

"You swear it?"

"I do."

His eyes hold mine, and shimmering blue whirls around his fore-arm. "Will you swear it with your magic?"

I don't even glance down at the radiant blues caressing his arm in glowing tendrils. "I will, so long as you swear to uphold your end of the agreement, in turn."

He dips his chin—once and concisely. "I will."

With his amber, glowing eyes locked to the icy storm of amethyst riddling my own, we clasp forearms, a jolt of something powerful and consuming invading my senses. I gasp at the overwhelming sensation. Gritting my teeth, I call on the essence of my magic and my magic alone, and I allow it to join Casimir's with the force of something unbreakable.

Once finished, I draw back my hand and examine the small blue mark now twisting along the flesh just below my thumb, near the inner part of my palm. It sparkles almost like a rune would. "It's pretty," I muse. "I'm beginning to collect these sorts of marks like a merchant does his trinkets." As if on instinct, my eyes find the place on my finger where the blood droplet had once been, now diminished and faded thanks to Draven's missive to King Alastair.

Casimir hums, something visibly shifting in his eyes as he inspects his own mark for only a moment. "And what is your second condition?"

I almost laugh at the absurdity of it, following the seriousness of my first. "I need you to fetch me a piece of parchment."

He blinks. "Come again?"

"Parchment," I repeat. "I need a piece. A quill would be ideal, too, but given our current surroundings..." I trail off, my gaze doing a dramatic sweep of the dimming rebellion. The Restorationist's numbers are dwindling, unable to withstand the brute force of trained and generational magic.

"Why do you need parchment?" There is a slight wrinkle bunching his nose.

"Why do most people need parchment? I need to write something."

He makes a face, but still, he turns on his heels, glancing around. "Let me see...ah, as I thought." He bends down to where the rough man with kind eyes lays decapitated on the ground. Attached around his body is a worn brown belt, sheaths woven into the sides. On his left hip is a slender buckled pocket, which Casimir flips up, pulling out a small rolled up parchment.

He hands it to me, and I arch a brow at him. "I'm not even going to ask how you knew that was there."

Casimir shrugs. "You asked for parchment, I delivered it to you. Transaction complete." His eyes sober, growing serious. "Now, we leave in under two minutes. Agreed?"

"Fine," I concede through a drawn out sigh. "Can I borrow your dagger, then?"

He looks at me as though I just asked him to bring me the moon. "What in the realms of Kala *are* you planning to do?"

Wordlessly, I just hold out my hand to him, expectation speaking for me through the slits of my eyes. He holds my stare for a beat, then unsheathes a dagger and puts the hilt in my palm.

"Do not make me regret giving you that."

"We have a newly found agreement, remember?" I taunt, wiggling my thumb. "Why would I try stabbing you now?"

"You tell me," he deadpans, folding his arms and watching from behind as I bend to my knees and spread the parchment across the ground.

There is inked script already covering the front of it, so I turn the sheet over, thankful to find it empty. Then, I prick my thumb with the tip of Casimir's dagger, handing the weapon back to him once finished. With a look of curiosity, he sheaths the dagger once more and refolds his arms as he watches.

Ignoring the weight of his attention, I glide my thumb across the parchment, using my blood to spell out one sentence. Four words. I blow on the blood, hoping it will help it dry more quickly, then I roll the parchment back up.

"Now what do you plan to do with that?" Casimir asks me, skepticism lacing loudly through his voice.

"Have a little faith, would you?"

"You have less than a minute left."

"And patience," I grumble, shooting him a sharp look.

A tiny smile pulls at half of his mouth.

I glance around the room, anxiousness gripping me in a vibrating frenzy. "Come on, come on," I whisper.

Ten seconds. Twenty seconds.

Nothing.

I turn to face Casimir, pointing down near his hip. "Can I borrow that dagger again?"

He narrows his eyes on me. Still, he unsheathes the dagger once more, handing it back to me at the hilt. Before I can think better of my crazy idea—probably more like a deluded theory—I turn it over in my palm and slice the blade against my forearm, drawing a river of blood.

"What the *hell* are you doing?" Casimir snaps.

He steps forward, but I hold out my hand, motioning for him to stop. "Wait," I demand, the hilt of the dagger loose in my palm.

Casimir glances at my wound. "You have cut yourself too deeply. You will lose too much blood if you do not let me help you."

"*Wait*," I say again. "He will come. He *always* comes for me."

"*Who?*" Casimir demands, the word teetering between anger and panic.

I don't answer him.

Because there, appearing from across the room through a cloud of ash and disintegrating magic, I see my heart wrapped in the wings of a nightmare, inky shadow panthers prowling at his side as he rushes toward me.

I watch him come, in all his glorious, ferocious beauty.

"Him."

CHAPTER THIRTY-SIX

DRAVEN

raven sees her, and nothing can stand in his path as he races toward her.

The moment chaos erupted in the ballroom, he had set aside as much of his magic as necessary to constantly sense Lyra—sense the magics of others around her. Though it was the first thought to enter his mind when the slaughter began—a nonnegotiable, as far as he was concerned—he was grateful for the decision the moment his magic flared beneath his skin like a warning bell, resulting in Draven sending one of his panthers far across the grand ballroom with one command: *find her.* Shortly after, he felt an intense explosion of heat surge beneath his skin, seeping into his veins, telling him his panther had swallowed lightning.

Ever since that moment, he has been trying to make his way across the ongoing battle and to Lyra, which was made all the more difficult when her magic had just…disappeared. As if suddenly encased in a barrier.

It is the exact way it happened that terrible fucking day, where his precious girl was stolen from him and she nearly eviscerated herself in her perceived grief. Which means Lyra had not been attending this ball alone. She came with someone. And not just anyone.

She came with *him*.

Casimir Vivaldri.

Draven's suspicions are confirmed when he glimpses the man—monster, creature, *thing*—standing behind her.

What game is he playing at? Why is he here in Erandor? At the Winter Solstice ball, no less. It is a masquerade ball, yes, but to get past the entry guards, he would've had to show a missive boasting the king's seal or some other indisputable form of identification proving his invitation to the event. Who gave that to him? And why would that person bring him *here*? Not to mention why Lyra was forced to attend alongside him? No—not even alongside him. She had been allowed to wander freely, without him.

Why?

Draven at least now understands the urgency and pain he saw swimming in her eyes while they danced. She knew they were on borrowed time. In a way, Draven did too, but his sense of it was entirely different.

Gods damn him for his foolish blindness. For being so willing to live in that momentary fairytale with her, pretending they had reached a happy ending while Lyra remained stuck in the part of the story where she was still trapped in a tower.

Draven shakes his head against his raging mind. He doesn't have time to sulk in his wrongdoings nor properly consider the answers to all his questions. His full focus needs to be on reaching Lyra.

As he nears her, he discovers where the sharp spike of her magic—screaming at him as though she'd just been terribly injured—came from. The very thing that allowed Draven to finally sense past that accursed barrier of Casimir's and find her.

A crimson river runs down her arm, leaking into her half-opened palm. There is a gnarly slice cut into her skin; a dagger's hilt held loosely in her hand. Had she sliced herself to summon him? So he could finally know where to find her? Had she somehow known he was sensing her?

She probably did, his clever girl.

Still...the sight of her dripping blood sends Draven's insides boiling.

Lyra stands apart from Casimir, her bottom lip trapped between her teeth as if to keep it from trembling. Her eyes are on him, just as his are on hers. They do not waver nor break apart. She watches him with a quiet desperation in her gaze, and gods, he just wants to put her in his arms and protect her. Keep her safe.

I am coming. I will always *come for you.*

He wishes he was close enough to say the words to her directly.

Ten marks away from her. Five.

"Lyra!" he shouts once he and his panthers are no more than just a few powerful strides away. He summons too much magic, his chest constricting as those voices he keeps buried surface at the force of his pull. Black flickers in his vision. Ink fills his veins.

Yet before he can direct the storm building within his palms, a glittering portal of silver, white, and blue opens, and Casimir reaches for Lyra, practically tugging her against his chest. Draven just barely catches his passing words to her.

"Time's up," Casimir says.

Then he wraps his arm around her waist and directs her toward the portal. Lyra does not seem to put up much of a fight. In fact, she almost seems as though she's going willingly, leaving Draven to wonder what the hell Casimir has threatened her with.

Lyra's eyes are still on Draven, and it is only when she lifts her opposite hand—the hand not filling with blood—that he even becomes aware of the rolled up parchment's existence.

Draven reaches a hand out to her in return, a sudden desperation clawing his heart and slashing against his chest. His fingertips are so close to grazing her skin.

One mark away.

A lone tear slips down Lyra's cheek as she watches him. "I kept my promise," she whispers. "I waited."

No matter if you hate me. No matter how much you won't understand— promise me you'll wait. It was Draven's last request of her.

Their fingertips graze against each other as Lyra is pulled back into the swirling portal, the dagger clattering to the ground beside her. She passes off the parchment she was holding, sliding it into the rough groove of Draven's palm. As he reaches for her—in a duration that doesn't even last the span of a single heartbeat—he catches the look of resignation as it settles within Lyra's eyes. Like this is simply what her fate must be.

Like hell.

His panthers make a final, despairing effort, their large jaws only closing around open air as the portal blinks shut, taking Casimir Vivaldri and Lyra with it.

They are gone.

For yet a second time, Draven loses her. Has failed her.

Few words can describe the terrible mix of thrashing emotions that slam into Draven and threaten to swallow him whole. Anger. Guilt. Grief. Disappointment in himself. Fury for his own incompetence.

He once told Lyra he doesn't lose, ever.

He was a damned arrogant fool.

A quick glance around the room tells Draven the rebellion's battle has nearly reached its end, casualties on both sides, though significantly lesser for the side of nobility. He calls his panthers back into his veins and stares down at the parchment Lyra handed him. His fingers tighten around it, just needing to hold this piece of her—whatever it may be—for a moment.

Before he has a chance to unfold it, a series of portals open to his right, while Gray and Marcella come sprinting toward Draven from his left. A small band of Jurafen step through the shimmering lights, scanning the scene and assessing where they're needed first.

Draven huffs at the sight.

Convenient they should show themselves near the end, after the true heat of battle has already diminished.

Gray draws Draven's attention. "Did I just see Lyra?" he asks, nearly breathless. "I could have sworn..." He stops, shaking head as confusion ripples across his face. "I thought I saw her just before she disappeared into a portal. She was masked, but I—I would know her anywhere."

"It was her," Draven rasps out.

Guilt weighs heavier on him as he watches Gray process the implications of the confirmation.

"She was here?" he whispers. He sounds gutted. "We were in the same room, and I didn't even notice? I–I should have realized. I should have been paying more attention to my surroundings." His voice is a choked rasp. "Why do I keep failing her?"

Marcella steps forward, resting a gentle hand on his shoulder. She watches him with soft eyes, both their masks removed, leaving their expression open and entirely vulnerable. She offers the same strained look to Draven, quietly acknowledging the magnitude of their negligence.

"We were on the balcony, talking," Gray continues, his eyes distant and filled with a guilt-stricken sorrow which Draven's soul reflects. "Marcella and I... we went outside, talking as though the world is a careless place until the battle began. All while Lyra was here, inside, capable of being protected."

Draven sucks in a quivering breath, trying really hard to keep himself together. "Don't," is all he can manage to say, his clipped tone rough as stone. "Don't play that game with yourself. You are at a masked ball, for the gods' sakes, surrounded by powerful magic. It's what made the strategy so perfect—it would be nearly impossible to know. Don't make yourself suffer."

He doesn't say his next thought aloud.

But I did know, so I should suffer.

Draven sighs, turning his attention back onto the parchment still clutched within his fingers.

Marcella notices, pointing at it. "What is that?"

"Lyra gave it to me." No bother in hiding it.

"Well then why haven't you opened it already?" Her voice is sharp—far sharper than Draven feels capable of managing at this moment. Given the pointedness in her gaze, he suspects it has something to do with the announcement of his engagement to

Arden, a spectacle which already feels as though it happened years ago.

"You *saw* her?" Gray bites out, finally lifting his eyes from the ground. Draven swears he sees them flicker gold. "You were close enough to her to where she could hand you a piece of *parchment,* and you let her *go?*"

"I didn't *let* her do anything," Draven snaps back. "Casimir Vivaldri was with her, and I couldn't attack because he was keeping her as a hostage held in front of him. What the fuck was I supposed to do without risking her harm?" He stretches his neck as his anger brings more magic to the surface of his skin. A quick glance at his veins shows them bleeding black.

Fuck.

He *really* has to get that under control before he loses himself to his magic.

Still, in spite of his anger, as Draven considers that he hadn't just been close enough to receive something from Lyra—that he *danced* with her, held her, whispered thoughts of how he would spend a morning with her—he feels all the more like an ignorant, unforgivable fool.

Gray glares at Draven, and he allows Nightenjoy to see everything within his eyes. The regret. The hurt. The anger and unbearable guilt of his second failure. Gray jerks his chin away from him, seeming to have read everything Draven bared to him with crystal clarity, his lips set in a thin line. He says nothing else.

Draven finds the strength to leash his temper, grinding his jaw against the simmering inside him. He glances down at the parchment, a crease forming between his brows as he slowly unrolls it. There is one sentence written in what looks to be blood at the center of the page. Four words.

Do not marry her.

Draven's knees buckle as all that he is and could ever be threatens to topple while he stares at that one sentence.

Do not marry her.

He didn't even get the chance to explain it to Lyra. To make sure she knows he doesn't love Arden. That he would *never* do that to her; that she is the only being in this world who could ever give Draven's heart form. That he only accepted the terms of the engagement with Lyra's best interests in mind.

As he stares at the blood crusted against the parchment, reading the smeared words over and over again, Draven is sure he is going to be sick.

"What does it say?" Marcella asks, her sharp voice like a spear to Draven's unsteady senses.

He doesn't answer. He just continues staring at the parchment.

It isn't until he hears Rhea's voice that he snaps into himself, if only a small fraction.

"Is everyone okay?" she asks, slowing from her sprint as she reaches them. Her eyes land on him, and she tilts her head. "Are *you* okay? You look like you're going to be sick."

"*I'm* going to be sick if I don't figure out what's on that gods-damn parchment." Marcella lurches forward and rips the page from Draven's hand. He nearly bares his teeth and snarls at her in response.

He has his training from House Dalmar—long since embedded into every fiber of his muscles—to thank for his show of restraint.

She reads the short sentence, dropping her hand limply at her side afterwards. Marcella shakes her head, her lip peeling back as she glares at Draven. "You *fucking* asshole. You coward. You worthless piece of *shit*. *This*" —she waves the parchment madly in the air— "is what Lyra focused on getting to you in her final moments?"

She lunges for him, and to Draven's surprise, it is not Gray who stops her—he merely watches her explode with his arms folded across his chest. He doesn't know the truth of Draven's arrangement either, after all. Draven had only told Kiran the whole of it. Instead, it is Rhea gripping Marcella beneath the arms and lifting, locking her into an uncomfortable hold.

"Calm down," Rhea demands.

"Let *go* of me," Marcella hisses, tilting her chin in an awkward angle as she attempts to glance back at Rhea.

"Not until you *calm down*."

"I will fight back," Marcella grits out, her tone venom. "And I will hurt you."

"I don't doubt you'll try, and I like you all the more for it." Rhea tightens her hold, pressing Marcella's body into an even more uncomfortable position. "But I do not bend and I do not break—you're free to test it if you really want to."

"What in all the realms of hell is going on?" Finlay approaches them, caked in grime and dried blood, his once immaculate suit ruined. His eyes snag on Rhea as he takes in the scene.

"Rhea here is defending her dear brother's actions," Marcella dryly explains.

"What actions?" she asks, seeming genuinely confused.

"He's my brother, too," Finlay grumbles, his eyes again hovering on Rhea a heartbeat too long.

Rhea shoots him an admonishing look, something simmering beneath the surface of her reproachful gaze.

Draven flexes his jaw. This is all too much right now. *Way* too fucking much.

"He stabbed my best friend in the heart," Marcella growls, uncurling her fingers from her free palm as she wiggles against Rhea's hold. "He got himself engaged to some properly bred noblewoman, breaking Lyra's heart, and when she was here, standing directly in front of him, all she cared about was giving him *this*." Marcella waves the parchment as much as she can given the restraint on her movements.

Rhea's face scrunches, and she lets Marcella go, taking the worn page and reading it.

"She wrote it in her own gods-damn blood," Marcella adds for emphasis, readjusting her dress.

Gray steps forward and leans over Rhea's shoulder, peeking at the words and reading along with her. Both their eyes lift from the page and onto Draven. Finlay glances between them all, rolling his eyes and groaning. He pries the parchment from Rhea's hand, as if they were all sharing some delightful secret love letter together.

Draven is about to snap at the sight of it.

His magic presses against the back of his mind, the voices whispering to let them in. For a heartbeat, his vision flickers black. Draven grits his teeth, curling his fingers tightly into the palms of his hand.

Control.

He needs to find his control.

When Finlay drops the parchment, Draven now has four sets of eyes on him, questioning and all filled with their own types of reservations surrounding the announcement of Draven's engagement.

He carves a hand down his face. "I can explain."

"Perhaps it would be better if you let me." Kiran strolls over to their group from the other side of the room with his mask still covering his face. His clothes are largely…intact. Unsullied. Especially when compared to the rest of the group. He stops when he reaches Draven, resting a comforting hand on his shoulder.

Draven has never been so grateful for his brother as he is right now.

Feeling temporarily unable to speak and with a strange, clotting emotion filling his chest, Draven merely nods his confirmation for him to go on.

Kiran squares his shoulders to the group, and he explains everything in Draven's stead. Everyone's eyes round, lips parting as the truth of the situation enters the air between them. As they understand the gravity of Draven's decision.

"Why would the Tani do such a thing?" Marcella asks, caught somewhere between anger and disbelief.

"And Bathara," Rhea adds.

Finlay shifts on his feet—something he usually only does when bearing some form of guilt. Still, Draven doesn't press it right now, chalking it up to whatever the hell is going on between him and Rhea after another hesitant glance in her direction.

"Because the Tani will seek to protect what they know of magic," Gray says, gliding a hand through his messied hair. "Because, even if

Lyra hadn't done what she did at Bathara, they would have found a way to pin her with something else. Found another reason to see her locked in Toellor Prison."

"*Why?*" Marcella demands.

He shakes his head. "Because her magic is virtually immeasurable. Because it is in the interest of the powerful to squash or control what they don't know—what could ultimately rise in power against them."

"And my father could ensure that didn't happen," Draven says, the words bitter on his tongue. "*If* I married Arden."

Rhea scoffs with disgust, folding her arms over her chest. "That is just like Tynan," she mutters. "The exact type of dilemma in choice he loves to create."

"You could have told me," Finlay murmurs. Draven sees real hurt in his eyes. "You told Kiran. I could have known, too. I might've been able to help."

Draven shakes his head. "No," he counters. "My father's mind was set, and as much as it pains me to admit, he is the best choice when handling these sorts of matters. I would give my life away ten times over if it meant Lyra has a secure home to return to."

"But what about *her*," Gray murmurs sharply.

"She would be free," Draven says, flexing his jaw.

"She would also be broken," Gray counters. "What good is freedom if your heart is too broken to enjoy it?"

"And what good is a heart if your surroundings are too bleak to let it be warm?"

The air heats and sharpens around them as neither Gray nor Draven backs down.

Kiran clears his throat, lifting lazy fingers into the air. "May I?"

All eyes snap to him. Draven's brows knit together as he studies his brother. "What is it?"

"I saw Lyra here tonight."

The only person who seems shocked by that news is Rhea.

"She and I chatted," Kiran adds.

Gray and Marcella look like they are about to unravel at their very seams from frustration.

"Is *everyone* an incompetent buffoon?" Marcella gapes with anger. "How is it that *two* all-powerful 'Great House Heirs' saw her, yet did nothing to ensure her safety? To ensure she could stay *home*?"

He shrugs. "Because I told her the truth of Draven's situation, and she told me she couldn't let that happen. That she refused to allow Draven's future to be written by his father. I got the distinct impression she wholly meant it."

There is something odd in Kiran's tone that Draven can't place. And unfortunately, his mind doesn't even have the capacity to attempt to try. It is too focused on the information now brought to light.

"Lyra knows the truth?" he asks, his voice a low, breathless whisper.

Kiran nods. "She does. I told her everything the same as I told them."

Draven isn't sure if he wants to hug his brother or gut punch him for telling her.

Finlay glances down at the parchment still in his hand. He holds it out for Draven to take. "I think that might change the meaning of this note."

Draven holds it in front of him, staring until the words go fuzzy.

Do not marry her.

Was that her way of telling him to be free? Had he interpreted the message all wrong? He had, hadn't he...

Lyra was not just instructing him not to marry Arden as some request or desperate plea—not after Kiran telling her everything, being fully aware of her fate within Solaya. It was her way of telling him he didn't *have* to marry her. A message within the message. That's why there was resignation on her face. Why she seemed to go back with Casimir so willingly, like she wasn't putting up a fight at all.

She doesn't ever plan on coming back.

She thinks to save Draven from a loveless future written by his father, she has to stay away. And even if Draven is wrong, and it truly is Casimir forcing her to remain by his side—he doesn't care. The circumstance doesn't matter to him.

For the first time in a long, blurry haze of uncertainty, Draven has found his clarity.

"I'm going after her," he says, resolve unbreakable as Arellian steel. "Tonight."

"You will do no such thing."

All of them turn at the sound of that too-polished voice.

Tynan stands no more than a few steps away, hands clasped behind his back. He strides to Draven, ignoring the rest of the group entirely.

Draven grits his teeth, pushing his tongue into his cheek as his magic flares in anger just at the sight of the man.

Tynan observes him like an insect in need of dissecting. "I heard what I needed to hear. You will not be going anywhere after that girl. You will not leave Erandor in its time of need, nor will you frolic about like some ignorant fool after your engagement has been publicly announced."

"I will not," Draven growls.

His father assumes his full height. He is a tall man, well-defined though not overly so. Just enough to be intimidating to his enemies and lethal to his foes. "I will not speak my demands again, boy. You will submit. You will obey what I have said. You know the consequences if you don't."

He does. She is standing a small ways across from him, well within the reaches of his protection right now. Is now a student at Bathara, protected—though in a precarious manner—from the clutches of Tynan Dalmar.

Tynan is not a man of errors, but he perhaps made his gravest one the moment he allowed Rhea to attend Bathara Academy. Allowed her to be so close to Draven once more. It will allow him to adapt his plans to include Rhea. To ensure her safety from Tynan.

From the corner of his eyes, Draven sees Gray bend down and pick up a discarded dagger not far from them. He studies it, a peculiar expression pinching his face together. Draven realizes it was the dagger Lyra was holding.

Gray's eyes snap up, something like hope brimming within them.

He gives Draven a silent, exacerbated look. A near pleading look, actually.

Tynan demands the full weight of his attention. "Come," he says. "We need to show face in the aftermath of such destruction and address those who remain."

Draven doesn't budge an inch. "I'm not following you—I will be following after Lyra."

Tynan's face remains eerily expressionless. "In spite of the consequences? You will go, knowing that I *will* seek retribution for your disobedience? Knowing all that I'm capable of?"

Draven catches the underlying implication of his tone. He is referring to the murder of his mother. The murder of a bookshop owner who was like a father to him. To the first girl to ever make Draven experience the flutters of love.

Rhea's family; Draven's family.

All slaughtered by Tynan.

"Fuck you and your threats." Draven spits the words he has so desperately wanted to say for years in his father's face. He does not miss the way Kiran, Finlay, and Rhea all blanch at the sight of it. "I'm done being your lapdog. I'm through with following your orders. Through with House Dalmar. I. Am. *Done.*"

Tynan chuckles, a crooked smile tugging at only a portion of his lips. "Let's say you find her. Where will you go, hm? How long can you hide until the Tani's Shadows find her and haul her away to stand trial?"

Draven remains silent, not deigning to indulge Tynan in the games he so loves to play.

That crooked smile deepens. "You'll be bringing her back to a world that wishes her in chains."

"Then I will build her a better one with my bare hands." Draven's rough voice does not waver. "One where she can laugh freely. Can finally be afforded a life she deserves."

"Sentimentality is not your color." Tynan's upper lip curls. "In fact, I find it rather revolting." He leans forward to whisper in Draven's ear, "And you will only be done when I allow it. Remember that, boy."

Tynan pulls away from him, studying him a few seconds longer, his hands remaining clasped behind his back. His smile morphs into something like a serpent's grin. "Your next actions are your own, blatantly against what I've demanded of you." He lifts his shoulders with calculated measure. "You cannot blame me for what comes next." Tynan turns to Gray, who still holds the recovered dagger between his fingers. "And neither can you, *Lion* of the Heart."

To Gray's credit, he does not flinch beneath the weight of the stare. Not an inch.

Tynan fixes them all with an inscrutable parting look. Then, he simply turns and walks away, heading over to a small huddle filled with a few Jurafen and high-ranked nobles, a few remaining rebels held captive and in chains behind them. Audwin is there as well, not so much as glancing in the direction of Finlay to see if he's alright.

Draven watches them for only a heartbeat longer, feeling in his bones that his father just made a cryptic promise.

He can not find it within himself to care one fucking bit.

He turns his attention to Gray. "Tell me what you've realized."

"This dagger," he answers, stepping closer to Draven and holding it out for them both to inspect. "Where did it come from?"

Draven's throat constricts then bobs as he pictures the oozing slice dripping blood down Lyra's arm. "Lyra had it. I suspect it was Casimir's. Why?"

Marcella steps forward, peeking her head into their conversation, not saying anything, but clearly not wanting to remain in the dark, either.

Gray steals a look at her then reorients his full attention back to the item in his hand. "The material composing the hilt and blade," he muses, gliding a thumb along the camel-brown substance. "It's not found in Solaya."

Draven studies the object more closely. "Is it not just leather and steel?"

"No," Gray answers. "Feel it and take a closer look." Draven does as instructed, and Gray continues on. "I read a book once about the origins of the Arellian trade ports. I wanted to learn more about the history of an Arellian forged sword. Apparently, before creatures overtook what is now known as Creature's Bay, Arellia used to use their ports to travel to and from the Arid Wastelands because only the peculiar sands from the Wastelands could be smelted and forged into such high-quality blades. Yet when the neighboring waters became impassable due to the appearance of the sea creatures, they were no longer able to collect sand from the Wastelands. It's why Arellian blades are so rare nowadays—why they've basically become a myth. Because nobody will risk traveling through the treacherous strip of land passing through the Elwood Forest, and the journey to the Wastelands is now virtually controlled by Halfin's port—a city which is not on good terms with Arellia."

"Get to the point, Gray," Marcella pushes.

"Right," he says. "Sorry. My point being, this blade is most certainly forged like Arellian steel, but you can tell by the folding and the temper line that it is *not* Arellian-made. That, coupled with the leaf fibers composing the grip of the hilt being made from what I believe to be the foreign *Heri* plant, can only mean one thing."

Gray has the full attention of everyone in their group. They blink absently at him.

He sighs. "If this truly *is* Casimir's dagger—which, given the make and materials, I suspect it *has* to be—then they're in the Arid Wastelands. I know it was one of the first places we ruled out as a possibility because we thought it was largely uninhabitable, but that has to be where Casimir has been hiding. I can't be sure how they're surviving the barren climate or where in the Wastelands they're located, but I'd wager it's why Lyra was at such a loss when attempting to decipher where she was being kept. All she could really tell us was that the sun shined differently." He pauses for effect. "The Arid Wasteland's sun is red and pressing—is fabricated and doubled behind a mirage created from the heat. I'm confident it's where he's keeping her; it's the only thing that makes sense."

The revelation washes through Draven like a tidal storm. Meanwhile, Marcella takes Gray's face in her hands and kisses his cheek.

"You're a genius," she says. "A gods-damn, history-loving *genius*."

His cheeks flush, though he says nothing. Instead, he locks his eyes on Draven. "You're going after her?"

He nods. "I am."

"Then I'm coming with you."

For a heartbeat, Draven considers protesting the matter. Until he realizes it would be a futile thing. Plus, he can't really deny Gray the request, considering how much Draven knows he cares for Lyra, as she does him.

"I'm leaving tonight," Draven tells him instead of arguing the matter. "I'm not wasting a single second more than I already have."

Gray nods, not at all daunted. "I have a small pouch of coin on me. We can buy supplies as we go and pay for inns to forge our plan through the nights."

Draven turns to Rhea. "You're coming with me."

She shrugs. "Figured."

Draven almost cracks a smile. Leave it to Rhea to be so nonchalant about defying Tynan's orders, putting both their lives at risk, and traversing to an overheated continent to track down a centuries-old prince and a girl Draven would burn the world for.

"I'm going too." Finlay steps forward, and Draven and Rhea shoot him a curious look at the same moment. Though the nature of their expressions seems to be entirely different.

"Why?" she hisses. "Your presence is not needed. In fact, I'd say it's not even *wanted*."

"I disagree" he shoots back. "You are going to a continent filled with such high temperatures, civilization has all but abandoned it entirely. You know why? Because our bodies are not meant to withstand that level of heat. Are not meant to be encased in such dry air, our throats feel barren and pressed by razor blades. *I* can prevent all of you from overheating. Can secure water and comfort with my ice magic. You will need me if you hope to succeed."

Draven observes his brother. He's right—they would benefit greatly from having him. Yet volunteering to go on a rescue mission for someone not titled nor who is assigned directly to him as a mission is far outside his brother's usual behavior. Why is he willing to help now?

"Who is to say your magic will even work the same there?"

Though Rhea means it as a jab to Finlay, it makes everyone pause. She's also right. There is no guarantee magic will move the same in the Wastelands. Though it changes nothing about Draven's plan to go, it is a consideration nonetheless.

"I will stay," Kiran says, breaking the silence. "And I will monitor the situation here in Solaya. I have a feeling Bathara is not going to take kindly to two of its captains disappearing the moment an uprising against Erandor is brought into the light."

Marcella looks conflicted, but ultimately sighs. "I'll stay, too," she says. "Kiran's right—we need people here to keep an eye on all sides of things."

Draven's eyes slide across all the faces before him. His family. Lyra's best friends. He nods at the lot of them. "Then it's settled."

Marcella turns to Gray, and Draven almost feels the need to turn around and offer them privacy at the heaviness passing between them. At the intimacy of their gazes. She again cups his face with her hands, this time different than the last. Her touch is now tender and soft. Unguarded and without humor. "You bring our girl home," she whispers, the earnest words filled with fight.

Gray drops his forehead to hers, letting his eyes fall momentarily shut. "I will," he promises.

When they pull apart, her eyes—now glassy—linger on Gray for only a moment longer before she redirects them onto Draven. "You too," she says. "Bring her back to us."

Draven does not waver. "I swear to you I will. No matter what."

PART II

THE REFRAIN

CHAPTER THIRTY-SEVEN

FINLAY

Dribblets of disturbed salt water kick up from below and kiss Finlay's cheek.

He stands at the back of the modest ship, leaning against the railing of the quarter deck. His eyes remain attached to the rudder; his thoughts remain attached to the missive he just received from Cahlmon through the Ever-Know Quill.

Good work, Captain Fjolla.
Though I began to have my doubts about your ability to locate the girl given how long it took, I now have faith I made the right choice when entrusting you with this mission.
Send your next correspondence only once you have found her and are settled away from the Wastelands. We will form a rendezvous point from there, where the girl can be discreetly transported to a holding room beneath Bathara while we form our next steps.
As a word of caution, do not mention this to anyone else. Not even Josiah.

Until we pen again.
Cahlmon Orius

413

Finlay sighs.

He has done everything asked of him. He has fulfilled his duties as a Great House Heir. Has acted in accordance with his expectations as a captain at Bathara. He even just received the smallest glimmer of hope that his father might finally be willing to accept him as his son once more. He has done everything he is supposed to. Is on the exact path his mind was set to walk, finally on the cusp of grasping everything he's been working for since his mother's passing.

So why does he feel so terrible?

Behind him, Finlay hears the wooden planks creak and groan beneath booted feet. Draven steps up to the deck's railing, bracing his elbows and leaning forward in a position mirroring Finlay's own. He stares out over the endless stretch of the glittering blue water composing Glass Water Bay, the final obstacle between them and the Arid Wastelands.

"You've been distant."

Finlay huffs weakly. "You've been distracted."

Draven turns to look at him. "And you're deflecting."

Guilt weighs heavily on Finlay's chest. Is he really going to betray Draven's trust again? Though to Finlay the situation is incredibly different from how it was the day he broke his blood oath to his brother—being bound by duty, honor, and *true* obligation—it would still be breaking his trust once more all the same. Trust Draven had not given back to Finlay easily.

They went years—nearly a decade, even—without speaking.

They were the darkest years of Finlay's life, being without him and Kiran. Which was really saying something, when he stops to consider all the heartbreak predating those years.

Finlay's shoulders sag beneath the weight of all his wrong choices —of all the priorities he is beginning to wonder have been misplaced.

He lowers his chin to his stacked arms, and his unbound hair flaps freely against the wind. Finlay battles all the many branching decisions before him. Should he tell Draven the truth of Bathara's council's plans? That they would have him betray Draven and Lyra both, wanting her for their own reasons. Perhaps they want to present her to the Tani themselves. Perhaps they wish to keep her as their own weapon. Perhaps they just want to understand; perhaps they fear what understanding might bring.

What if they run tests on her? It's not unheard of for those in the sciences to study enigmatic laktî. Draven himself would probably have been subjected to such tests if his surname hadn't been Dalmar.

Finlay glances at Draven sidelong. He notices.

"You can tell me what's been bothering you, Finlay. I won't be angry with you."

Not likely.

Yet the opening entices Finlay more to come clean of the truth. To tell Draven everything. Perhaps he already knows—or at least suspects—Finlay is on orders. He's sure Draven's already questioned Finlay's intentions for being with them during this mission instead of attending to his usual duties at Bathara—the decision Finlay normally would make.

He's weighing his choices when Draven speaks again.

"It's about Rhea, isn't it?" He turns from the railing to square his shoulders to Finlay, leaning only one arm against the rounded wood. "I noticed the shift between you two during the ball. Noticed the stolen glances and the way you mindlessly gravitated toward her. Then the falling out. You two were at each other's throats even more than usual when we were securing passage in Halfin. I especially can't help but notice the way you two have been on opposite sides of the ship ever since disembarking from the docks."

Ah, so that is what Draven wants to talk about.

His brother, always so perceptive. Only this time his observations are only half right, his scope sighted on the wrong target, his aim—though true—veering to the harmless animal on his left when really it should have aimed for the predator to his right.

Finlay takes it as his sign to drop the matters of Cahlmon, Bathara, and what he will do once they find Lyra from his mind. Instead, he indulges Draven in this line of conversation.

"And what is it you're implying with what you think you've noticed?"

Draven huffs a laugh. "Don't play dumb with me, Fin. I know what I saw."

Finlay shrugs. "And I am merely asking you to state those observations more clearly."

"Alright. I saw you pining for her in a way I've never seen from you before. I saw you gaze at her with longing in your eyes. I saw the way you moved to her. Saw the way your fingers twitched when they were near her. And then I saw the guilt in your eyes when you avoided her. I saw the panic in your muscles as they tensed when you two stood just inside the same room together. I saw it all, Fin. Or would you like me to go on?"

Finlay, unsure of how to respond—his defensive nature already threatening to claw up his throat—merely keeps his eyes locked on the crystal water in front of them. "So what?" he asks instead. "What does any of that matter? I still hate her, and she hates me." He does not like the new pang those words conjure in his chest.

"I hate to tell you this, but one doesn't look at a person they hate with the same type of expression you use when looking at Rhea."

Finlay scoffs. "Don't be ridiculous."

Draven lifts his exposed palms. "All I've done is point out the way you look at her."

Finlay remains silent, instead letting the sounds of the waves crashing into themselves fill the space between them. Eventually, he sighs. "Can I ask you something?"

He notices the small twitch in Draven's brow. "Of course. You can always ask me anything."

"Given your father and all that he's made you do—the ways he's tried to shape you—how did you not royally fuck everything up with Lyra?"

Flashes of the hurt brimming in Rhea's eyes swim in Finlay's mind.

You, Rhea Brooksley, are nothing more than a commoner made into House Dalmar's charity case.

Why had he said that? Why, whenever his father is near, does Finlay always revert to such cruel behavior?

Draven snorts a laugh. "What? Am I truly such a brooding bastard that you had such little faith in me?"

Finlay chuckles, shaking his head. He can't help but notice there is a distinct sadness echoing in the sound. "If I had little faith in anything, brother, it would be regarding your blatant lack of charm and manners."

Draven's smile broadens before his expression sobers. "It is because I was fortunate enough to have people around me who wanted to mold me into something better than my father. It is because I had an exquisite mother. Because I was blessed to know Atlas Brooksley, who both showed me and told me what love truly is. What it *should* be." His voice softens. "Plus, where I am rough, Lyra is soft. Where I am unkind, she offers kindness. In return, where she closes herself off to the world, I open her up. Where she lacks desire to feel, I remind her of the reasons to. It helps make things easier because we just...work, she and I. And being with her... it's like waking up to a world of color after only seeing muted tones." He huffs a soft laugh, glancing down at his palms. "The world is more beautiful to me when it's painted in lilac."

Different emotions grip Finlay's heart. Guilt. A tinge of jealousy. Happiness for his brother.

"I'll never understand how you did it," he murmurs. "How you managed to carry the weight of all your burdens and still find yourself something as fragile as love."

Draven's mouth quivers as it plays with the makings of a smile. "Neither will I." A sigh. "Though we will see if I can keep it, given all I have left to do. All the many failures I will undoubtedly spend my lifetime trying to make up for."

Finlay understands entirely.

A long stretch of comfortable silence passes between him and his brother as they overlook the water. A golden sun descends beyond the horizon, painting the sky and sea in a kaleidoscope of pastels. As they watch the waves, Finlay supposes he and Draven are lost at their very own seas, drowning in their own ways.

Once all the color has nearly bled from the sky, Draven speaks again. "You will never deserve her, you know." His eyes remain forward, his voice soft.

Finlay nods. "I know."

From the corner of his eye, he catches the small curve of Draven's mouth. "As long as you know, then there's no reason you can't try to be someone who *is* deserving."

A quiet melancholy floats through Finlay. "I could spend the rest of my life trying, and it still wouldn't be enough. She deserves far better than I could ever offer her." A pause. "I will never deserve the affections of someone like Rhea Brooksley. Never."

CHAPTER THIRTY-EIGHT

RHEA

Under the quiet of the stars, Rhea can breathe.

She sways within the clutches of a hammock, suspended by wire between the main mast and the foremast of the rocking ship—sounds of waves lapping at the hull her only companion this late into the night.

Being outside the bounds of Solaya—away from the quick pace of politics and schemes and agendas—Rhea can finally reflect. Reflect on what she's done. On what she might have given Tynan. She thinks about the seemingly insignificant information she scribed to him just before leaving for the party. She wonders what Tynan could possibly want with it—with words from an old tongue she couldn't even decipher. She even takes a moment to consider the guilt gnawing at her conscience. Though she is grateful she didn't extract any information from Finlay the night of the ball, she still worries about the potential role she played in helping Tynan at all. Even if she doesn't allow herself to feel guilty—she can't afford such a luxury as guilt.

As she stares at the stars, swaying in her hammock with her hands tucked behind her head, she thinks of Finlay. Thinks of the hurt that flashed in his eyes when she allowed him to believe her deepest vulnerability was nothing more than a ruse to extract information from him. She thinks of how tenderly he comforted her in that corridor. The way it felt when she rested her head on his shoulder, and he laid his cheek upon her. She thinks of the way his hand never left the small of her back as he escorted her to the nearest washroom so she could freshen up before returning to the party. Thinks of the way he wordlessly guarded the door, watching for any prying eyes, determined to give Rhea the privacy she so desperately sought in that moment. She thinks of the way she pondered what Finlay said to her as she relined the kohl framing her eyes.

It's hard to feel like you're enough when the only proof of love you've ever had is reliant on what you can or cannot give.

She thinks of how the words stirred something of a kinship in her chest for him. How the feelings only intensified when she reflected upon them.

Yes, Rhea thinks and thinks and thinks.

Of the turquoise filling Finlay's eyes, the glistening slate of a frozen river. Of the scent of pine clinging to his skin. Of the small braids he wears, proud and dignified. Of the slope of his shoulders. The curve of his lips. The small, rounded tip of his nose.

She thinks of the way he looked at her when she opened her door for him, standing in her ballgown, her deepest insecurities wrapped around her like a second skin. How he had managed to ease them—just a little—with the smallest of assurances.

You really do look beautiful tonight, Rhea, he had said, looking so uncharacteristically shy.

How is she to reconcile that with the cold and pompous asshole he constantly shows himself to be? With the boy who upturned her world? Who looks down on her and shreds her with his words? Who said such cruel things to her in protection of his father?

You are only something because Tynan has made you so.

But then he had also said, *I am sorry I told Tynan where to find you. I am sorry I told him about Príth. About your father's bookshop.*

Is that truly all Rhea had wanted from him for all these years? An apology? Just the smallest acknowledgement of the part he played in taking something so precious away from her? And now that she finally received it from him...now what? She no longer feels the same sweep of pleasure when visualizing her daggers going through his flesh. So what does that leave her with?

Rhea sighs, the sound loaded and desperate. She decides she prefers to think no longer. Because when she does, despite all the many reasons not to, her mind seems to insist on considering a future where she doesn't hate Finlay Fjolla, despite all he's done.

And Rhea, ever the stubborn thing, has decided that is a future she will not accept. Even in spite of the awakening butterflies that flutter in her stomach when she does.

CHAPTER THIRTY-NINE

LYRA

"Had I known you were so good at cards, I would have never asked you to come to the tavern with me tonight." Neilina frowns at the spread across the table.

I laugh. "I didn't even know I was good at cards."

Ophelia—the tavern's fiddle player—rests her cheek on her fist. "So we've been bested by a complete and total rookie?"

"Are you hustling us, Neilina?" An older man asks, sitting to my right.

Neilina glares at him from across the table. "I've lost too, Jax. For the *third* time. I may be the youngest in this place, but I'm not that ignorant."

"Come on, kid," Ophelia pushes, her melodic voice not at all demanding. "Tell us your tricks."

An outside breeze blows through the small tavern, bringing the floral scents along with it. The night air makes the mint somehow crisper, and the moonlight leaks through the threshold just so, shining upon Ophelia's silver hair. It makes it glow. Makes her look like a goddess of sorts.

My chuckle deepens, and I shake my head, reaching for my mug of ale. It is the freshest tasting alcohol my tongue has ever been blessed

422

enough to taste. Citrus, fermented, and a delightfully tangy aftertaste carrying a bit of zest. I sip, fighting the urge to smack my lips together after. "I don't have any tricks. I just...well, given my history, I had to learn how to read people's intentions. I spent a lot of time learning how to read the words hidden within a person's eyes. Learning their tells, their tics—anything expressive, really."

Jax huffs, shooting Neilina another look. "So you brought a bloody body language expert to a *card* game?"

"Pipe down, Jax. I didn't *know*. She's shit in combat. How was I supposed to know she wouldn't be shit at cards?" Neilina winks at me before fixing her gaze back on him.

They continue bickering. I continue drinking. Eventually, Ophelia grows tired of them, wordlessly getting up from her place at the table and retrieving her fiddle from behind the bar. She begins to play, and the few other occupants of the tavern begin to clap along to her tune. I watch, a smile helplessly splitting my face while my mug hovers in front of my lips.

The ale here really is delicious.

A woman who looks my age approaches me with a skip in her step. She reaches her hand out to me, a silent prompt for me to join her at the center of the wooden floor to dance. Luna is her name.

I've learned so many names over the past two weeks.

I wave my hands and shake my head. "I'm happy to just watch."

She scrunches her nose. "To watch is to wonder. But to dance is to live." Her accent is thick. Thicker than most around Halfaria, the name given to their home. Another name I've learned since opening myself up to this place. "Will you wonder about your life, or will you live it?"

Good question.

"I suppose I'll live it," I say, placing my hand in hers.

Luna beams, tugging me to the center of the floor where she loops her arm through mine and spins me around and around. A fit of laughter pours from me as I attempt to follow along, mirroring the dance moves Luna shows me. I haven't the slightest clue what I'm doing—these are not like the dances found in Rivara's courts—but I enjoy doing it nonetheless.

Finally, after two—okay, maybe three—more pints of ale and another round of dance, I say my goodbyes to everyone and head back to my chambers. The night sky is striking, the silver stars stark against the depthless dark. They sprinkle across the world's ceiling in infinite numbers, on and on and on.

I am so lost in them, I don't notice the person heading in the opposite direction down the same path as me. I bump directly into their chest—surprisingly firm, unmovable. When I pull back, I find Casimir standing before me, his raven hair loose and falling into his face. He wears a loose sweater paired with loose pants that are fitted at the ankles. As always, the fabric looks *so* soft. I lean forward, inspecting it.

"I've been dying to know what this fabric is since the first time I noticed it." I pinch the hem of his shirt between my fingers. "You really have to tell me."

"It's called Spin Silk."

"Spin Silk." The words tumble from my tongue. "Never heard of it." I glide the pad of my thumb along the seam of his shirt. "*Gods* it is soft. I think it's softer than regular silk. I'd commit unspeakable crimes to have this on my body."

"It is," he confirms, a laugh bloating his words. "And more durable. Lyra?"

"Yes?"

"Are you drunk?"

"What? Why would you think such a thing?"

"Because you're petting me."

I freeze midmovement, realizing that I, in fact, *am* petting him. Well, his shirt, at least. I drop my hand and recede a step.

Casimir watches me, a pointed smirk on his lips. "Seems finally giving my home and family a chance has not been all that bad for you."

I nod. "Oh, they're great. I fully admit I was wrong to..." I trail off, not wanting to finish that sentence even with the disarming effects of alcohol.

"Judge them based on what you believed about all Abdites?" he finishes for me, folding his arms smugly. "For assuming you knew the circumstances surrounding their madness? For pretending you were somehow better than them merely because you didn't understand them? For deciding that, because some who share their features have acted with evil, they all must act out of evil. For—"

"*Okay*," I say through a wince, cutting him off. "I get it. I was terrible and judgmental and totally in the wrong. I. Get. It." I sigh, gliding a hand across my cheek. "You know, you're a real buzzkill."

Still, though a buzzkill he may be, he is also right. We finally had the conversation two days after returning back to Halfaria, after I had pressed him with questions about this place, and he had finally given me some concrete answers. For example, the true origins of the people he calls his family.

They are the remaining bloodlines of the original Abdites. Their lineage has been cursed to carry the madness for, well, an undisclosed amount of time, evidently. It is the original members' punishment for the choice they made. For corrupting such a purely sacred thing.

Casimir told me about how he blames himself. How, as the person closest to Magaius, he should have realized what he was doing—what he was planning—sooner.

"And what was he planning?" I asked Casimir that day, concertedly brimming with curiosity.

"To form an army which couldn't be beaten. To form a band of wielders so powerful, no one would dare challenge them nor question their power. An army who would even make the progenitor blood-lines cower."

"Did it work?"

Casimir had considered my question, ultimately shaking his head. "Not in the ways he thought it would."

He didn't elaborate further.

Still, I wasn't ready to let the conversation end there. I pressed, "So there are different kinds of Abdites?"

He had sighed, threading fingers through his hair. "Only in the sense that there are those who never asked to be born of their condition, and those who purposefully sought it out. Everyone here, in Halfaria? They are all the former. Those who still wander and roam in Solaya—who barter, and cheat, and hire themselves for coin; who willingly corrupt themselves for greed, or power, or because they are simply vile creatures—they are of the latter."

"I never knew."

"Of course you didn't. How could you when nobody in Solaya in recent years has ever taken a moment to consider the root of creation for Abdites?"

"It's hard when they seem so alike."

He grew very still at those words. "Tell me, when I say to you that my hatred of humanity stems from it being an unsavable cause—that they are all the same to me—do you not wish to tell me I'm wrong? Do you not wish to protest what I've said?"

"That's different. *We're* different."

"Are you the same as a murderer, then? As a rapist? As a mother who abandoned her children? Who used her last coin on a pipe instead of food for her own offsprings' mouths?"

"What?" I asked, incredulous. "No—no, *of course* not."

"Yet those I have listed still belong to your kind, do they not? Are members of the sick race known as humankind?"

Shame and guilt burned my cheeks. "Yes," I had answered in a near whisper. "They are, despite how much I wish people like them were not."

"Then I think it is now fair to ask that you do not compare the cursed ancestry of my family to the chosen actions of evil men who crave access to powers they should never touch." He paused. "They are victims of cruel circumstances. Just like you were, Lyra."

I had no words for him after that.

The following day, I asked Neilina to take me to the most popular spot in all of Halfaria. She had taken me to a large, glittering pool surrounded by jade sculptures, flowers, and towering trees with leaves far greener than anything I had ever seen before.

Sithraki. Sithraki, they all whispered as I passed.

Until I lifted my chin and finally declared, "I am not *Sithraki*. I am not a Savior. I am… Lyra. And I want to know who you are. So please, come and tell me not as Sithraki, but as one of you."

To my surprise, they did.

Now, after my still occurring training sessions and free days between Veilreading, I have spent every day possible with the people of Halfaria, listening to their stories and hearing about their experiences with the small flickers of madness they must endure as the wards protecting their home begin to fail. I try to offer them my earnest truth in consolation.

"I will try to help make the madness go away," I tell them. I never use the word "cure;" it feels wrong after getting to know them more intimately.

Now, as Casimir observes me through seemingly far too knowing eyes, I'd like to make *him* go away. Cure myself of the infection of his presence.

His smile broadens, as if he knows my exact thoughts and feelings. "You should probably get some sleep," he eventually says. "You have training with Neilina in the morning, and then you and I are to pick up where we left off with our cure experiments in the afternoon."

"You're right," I agree through a sigh. "I probably should sleep." I mock a curtsey, which results in a soft chuckle from him.

As I walk past Casimir, he reaches a hand out and lightly grips my wrist, stopping me.

"You didn't say goodnight."

I snort a laugh. "Did you want me to?"

"It would be nice, considering it is such a lovely night and yours is the last face I'll probably see."

"Fine," I say through a laugh. "Goodnight, Casimir."

His answering smile is…beautiful.

"Goodnight, Lyra."

CHAPTER FORTY

LYRA

"You never did tell me what your meeting was about in Talderine." My tongue hooks up at the corner of my mouth as I pour three drops of a yellow liquid into a cylindrical tube filled with Sartooth roots—an exceptionally useful plant, I've come to find. One which is exclusive to Casimir's home.

From behind me, perched up at his own worktable in the converted greenhouse—now used as a mad scientist lab, for all intents and purposes—Casimir answers, "I was propositioned."

"Propositioned? By *who*?"

"Someone who should not be taken lightly." He sounds vexed as he says it, leading me to believe that whatever meeting transpired, it was not a good one. Or perhaps it's better to say it was not a meeting particularly in Casimir's favor, something I'm sure he has grown unaccustomed to over his centuries of life.

"Okay," I drawl while holding up my tube and squinting to see if the drops will react to the extracted roots. Spoiler: they do not. "And what did this mystery person whose identity you still won't share with me want?"

"You."

My spine stiffens, and I gently set down the reactionless tonic.

"What do you mean 'me?'" I manage to stave off my echoing thought, preventing myself from sounding like a child. *Why does it have to be me someone wants* again?

"I hope you are not actually expecting me to dignify that question with an answer."

I scowl, pushing my tongue into my cheek. "Alright, new question, then." I spin around in my chair to face him. "Why are you just now telling me?"

With his back still to me, he shrugs. "Because it didn't matter. I refused the offer."

"And what did they offer you, exactly?"

Casimir goes very still, glancing at me from over his shoulder. "If I left you behind at the masquerade ball with them, they would provide me with information on someone."

"And that information was...?"

He finally turns away from his work and faces me. "Feeling particularly chatty this afternoon, are we?"

I flash him a smile, choosing not to respond in the hopes it'll give me a better chance of actually getting an answer out of him. I mean really. I have never met someone so unwilling to answer a few simple questions before. Though I suppose my questions when it comes to him are rarely simple. Nor are there only a few of them. Still. Those problems are his fault. Not mine.

Casimir observes me for a good while, eventually huffing a conciliatory laugh. "There was a woman I loved before I became what I am."

"Sitara," I point out, not knowing why he's trying to be discreet about her identity now, given all that I know and have learned from the Veil.

His throat bobs. "Yes," he says stiffly. "In the throes of the Great War, she was also cursed—stolen from me by a god."

I'd hardly call being swooned over by the god of the stars a curse—with being gifted the power of the stars and the Great River of Light and all. But I choose to keep that thought to myself, not wanting to be insensitive. Because if one thing is glaringly apparent right now, it's that he really did love her.

Casimir continues, eyes glued to the floor. "The true cruelty of my immortality is I was meant to live for eternity knowing she was not simply dead, but elsewhere. Accessible, yet not. It is perhaps the cruelest component of the curse placed on me by petty gods: we are meant to never find each other again. Not in life. Not in death. Never."

I feel a sharp pang of sadness in my chest at his admission. "You say it's a curse, so is there not a way to break it?"

He laughs, the sound a dangerous type of hollow. "There is," he answers. "I must hear her song once more. The day I do, my heart will finally resume beating, and my mortality will return."

I chew at my cheek as I study him.

He looks so...tired. Broken and worn. Seeing him like this, it makes me wonder how I ever feared him so viscerally? Right now, he doesn't look capable of harming a fly.

He killed Griff.

My mind screams the sentence at me, not allowing me to forget. I suck in a sharp, loaded breath at the debilitating weight of it.

"So was that the final straw that made you change course for such a destructive path? That caused you to kill and loathe humanity as you do? Because she fell in love with Astralis and didn't love you back?"

There are different types of quiet. Contemplative, comfortable, assessing. This quiet is sharp and electric. It radiates with anger, punctuated by a silent warning which sends one's insides flaring in alarm.

Casimir slowly rises and wordlessly heads for the door. I find myself watching him with a furrow in my brow when he again turns around, his movements stiff. "You want to know why I hate human-ity? It is because they love to spin a narrative. And once that narrative has caught fire, nobody—*no one*—takes the time to understand what lit the flame. If perhaps, the fire should have never burned in the first place."

Then he leaves.

And I am left to wonder what the hell just happened.

WHEN I ENTER my chambers that night, there is a fresh pile of clothes stacked neatly on my bed. Curious, I close the door behind me and beeline straight for it. It is a collection of shirts, pants, undergarments —even some new training clothes.

Nearly all of it is made with Spin Silk.

I graze my fingers over the fine seams, still marveling at how unbelievably soft the material is. I'm sorting through the items, a swell of gratitude in my chest, when I finally notice the small slip of parchment resting directly beside the pile.

Lyra,

Here is your own set of clothes made exclusively from Spin Silk.
Neilina provided me with your updated measurements so they should fit you well.
Hopefully now there is no need to commit any unspeakable crimes to acquire them.
Enjoy,

Casimir x

I'm staring at the parchment when a knock sounds at my door.

"It's open," I call out, still staring at the cursive words.

The wood creaks, and Neilina's head pops through the threshold. "Hi."

"Hi."

She strides in, her stark-white hair adorned with braids while streaks of kohl and purple eyeshadow line her gray eyes. Her clothes look nicer than her usual attire.

I grin crookedly. "Are you going on a date?"

She snorts, swatting at the air. "Don't be ridiculous. Tonight we are celebrating *Rashtah.*"

"What's that?"

"The day we found our paradise. Our home. It's a beautiful celebration. Lots of singing, dancing, eating and drinking. It's a fun time."

"Sounds lovely."

She steps closer to me, her grin growing. "I'm glad you think so, because you'll be joining me. Everyone will be there, so you are no exception. Master was supposed to tell you about it while you two were working in the greenhouse, but seeing as you're not ready, I'm guessing he forgot to mention it?"

I laugh, glancing down at the slip of parchment once more. I set it down on the bed. "I don't think he 'forgot' to do anything."

"Trouble in paradise?"

I shoot her a dagger look, and she lifts her palms, her smile still pressed into her lips. "I was wondering what instigated his foul mood at dinner. Now I have my answer. Though, it's no matter. Master loves *Rashtah*. Between you and me, it's the only time I ever see him let loose a little. Whatever tensions currently exist between you two will be forgotten."

The Spin Silk suddenly rests heavier between my fingertips.

Neilina notices the fabric clutched within my grip. "Oh, good! Brynna finished in time for tonight. Master will be thrilled. He was very adamant she got it done as quickly as she could for you. I wasn't sure if she'd actually be able to do it given her short notice, but magic is a wonder, isn't it?" She inspects the clothes, isolating one item in particular. "You should wear this."

I lift my brows in quiet challenge.

"What?" she drawls. "It's pretty. And the color suits you."

I sigh. "Fine. Give it here."

WITH NEILINA AT THE HELM, it feels as though I blinked and was ready.

She made quick work of my hair, drawing half of it up, interweaving small braids on the side. She chided me until I let her line my eyes with a silver-colored substance I'd never seen before, and then she scolded me when I took too long to put on the backless, light gray dress, decorated with a floral pattern at its hem, rising up into the waist.

She made me feel pretty. Confident.

Now, as she and I approach the staggeringly large bonfire at the center of a beautiful spread of open land ensconced between strange-looking trees crowned with fan-shaped leaves, all I feel is nauseous.

Any time I have ever seen a fire this large, it has always ended in death. My mother. Kiran's wall of flames, where Meiji's life was stolen from him. Even here, where Casimir created a pyre for all the souls lost, and I officially got to offer my mother her proper goodbye.

Gods, I hate the flames.

Yet as I listen to the merriment all around, the strings of humming fiddles and clapping and chirps of cheery tunes, I swallow down the acid threatening to burn my throat. I remind myself not of the tragedies that befell me and others like Meiji, but instead the circumstances surrounding those tragedies. Who—*what*—caused them to occur. The people I'm looking at here? They didn't ask for the hand they were dealt. They couldn't choose the circumstances of their birth. All they can do is make the best of the life they were given.

This is them making the best of it.

You do not let this break you. You do not let them win.

I take a steadying breath, allowing myself to feel and embrace all the many emotions clamoring around inside me. I can still grieve for what I lost, but I can also choose to respect what's been taken from them as well. Both tragedies can be true. Can exist at once, neither less than the other.

Neilina reaches for my arm, interlocking it with her own. She turns her chin over her shoulder to look at me, beaming. "Are you ready to see how the *Lahtuima* celebrate?"

"Yes," I say, grinning back. "I am."

I mean it.

CHAPTER FORTY-ONE

LYRA

"You're wearing your new dress."

I startle at the proximity of Casimir's voice, whirling around to find him no more than an arm's length away from me. After his sudden outburst this afternoon—can I actually call it that when his anger was so contained?—an uneasy feeling tips the comfort I've grown to have around him lately back into that cautionary assessment.

"I am."

"It suits you."

My eyes narrow on him. "Thanks." I reach for an ice necklace that isn't there, still not entirely rid of my habit of reaching for it in moments of discomfort.

Casimir tilts his head, eyes soft yet inquisitive. "What is it you are always reaching for when you're uneasy?"

Truthfully, I'm surprised he waited so long to ask. I know he must have noticed all the other times. "It was a necklace given to me by someone as a token of good luck during Bathara's entrance exams."

"What happened to it?"

I eye him pointedly. "Now who's the chatty one?"

He shrugs, the gesture so much looser than his usual movements.

"*Rashtah* puts me in a good mood. It reminds me of the one good thing I was able to preserve and protect within my existence."

"So it would seem." I sigh. "I burnt the necklace to dust when I lost control of my magic."

He grows quiet, and the air shifts as it suddenly bears three times its weight. "I am sorry, Lyra," he murmurs eventually. "I fear I have not yet said those words to you. As I have grown to know you better, after the decision you made to willingly help search for a cure for my family, well... suffice it to say I am both ashamed and regretful for the barbaric methods I used to achieve my objectives."

"People only listen when something irreparable has been lost, right? Only stop cutting when it bleeds?"

He studies me, tucking a loose strand of my hair behind my ear. "Perhaps I was wrong. Perhaps somehow, despite all the many odds, you make me want to believe things can truly be different."

My throat tightens while my heart picks up in my chest, fluttering like the wings of a tiny bird. Though where those wings intend to take me, I have no idea—my heart still feels anchored elsewhere.

When he pulls back his hand, a glint of something bright catches my eye. Silver buttons. I finally scan Casimir's attire. As expected, he is dressed pristinely.

It makes me laugh.

"What?" he asks, an indent forming between his eyes.

"Nothing," I answer through my incessant giggling, shaking my head.

"You're laughing at me."

"No, I'm not."

"Yes, you are."

I sigh, which makes me laugh harder. "Okay, yes I am."

He folds his arms over his chest. "Why?"

"It's because you are so, 'I hate humanity', yet are clearly obsessed with fashion. I just find those traits to be...at odds with one another." I shrug. "The contrast is funny."

He watches me as though he is genuinely considering what I've just said. Eventually, he frowns. "Your impression of me is terrible."

"Oh, no it is not," I counter. "That is *exactly* what you sound like."

His frown deepens. "That's terrible."

"Tell me about it. Now you see why I was so keen on escaping you for so long." As soon as the words leave my mouth, I stiffen, fearing I might have taken the teasing too far. But Casimir's mouth hooks up into a small smile as he drops his eyes and shakes his head.

He laughs quietly, and the sound makes my own smile broaden. "Yes, if I sound like that, I can see why indeed." He leans forward, reminding me of the lack of space between us this whole time. "Between you and me, though," he whispers to the top of my ear, "I am glad you chose to stay." Casimir draws back, and his amber eyes are the softest I have ever seen them be. They are bright as well, different in the way of their usual peculiar glow. It's like life has slowly leaked back into them.

Gods, it makes him look like a different creature entirely.

Yet the look only lasts a moment as a radiant blue light flickers above our heads. It's dome-shaped and bright, covering the entirety of the night sky, bulging out far past the tree line. I've never noticed it before—never even realized it existed. Which means it must be the wards Casimir and Neilina have been telling me about.

The blue-light makes a zapping sound, blinking in and out of existence. Until it just stops, half the light remaining near the horizon while the ceiling of the dome has entirely disappeared.

Casimir's eyes harden. "Protect yourself," he commands, his voice steel. "I've never seen the top of the wards disappear before, and it won't take long before some people's madness starts slipping into place."

He scans the scene, gritting his teeth. Most everyone has stopped, seeming too stunned or cautious to even move. Hell, some of them don't even look like they're *breathing*.

"I need to go to the temple to fix this." Casimir turns to me. "Are you comfortable staying and making sure they do not harm themselves?"

I nod. "I can handle things until you get back."

"You won't fight them?" His gaze is filled with so much worry. So much conflict.

It makes my heart squeeze to see just how much he truly cares for them.

"No," I promise. "If it comes to it, I will only defend myself. Not attack."

"Let's hope it does not come to that." He throws out his hand, and a blue and white portal opens. He steps through, glancing back at me. "I will be as quick as I can."

"Good luck."

He watches me a moment longer, his eyes lined with concentration as he studies me. Until he wordlessly steps through the portal and disappears, the swirling colors disappearing with him.

I reset my focus on all the people around me. I can't find Neilina. But I do see plenty of other faces I now recognize. Terror swims in their eyes.

The first to succumb is the older man from the tavern, Jax. His chin jerks to me, and he cocks his head at an unnatural angle. He grins a child's grin, skipping over as he sings, "Different you see. Different from me. A magic whose power the gods' eyes can see." He stops just short of reaching me.

"Jax," I warn, my voice low and steady. Slowly, I lift my palms, ready to deflect any strikes of magic should I need to. "Try to stay with me. Your Master is returning the wards to their full strength." Though how he intends to do that, I haven't the slightest idea.

"Master?" he croons. "You are Master's key. Our answer to the locked door. And I mustn't hurt the key."

"Jax," I try again, ignoring the small pang in my chest when hearing those words once more. "What would Master tell you right now?"

This makes him pause as he actually considers the question. Through his thin sweater, I see a green glow, dim at first, but growing brighter. The air around us plunges into a bone-chilling cold. Voices hiss in the air, and they make every hair on my arm stand on end. I recognize them.

Erhé akta maht. Erhé akta maht. Erhé akta maht.

Hate take harm. Hate take harm. Hate take harm.

Jax's eyes glaze over, and his fingertips stretch out in front of him. "Blood is blood, the world is cruel. Risings go up, because Solayans are fools." His breathing turns hiccuped, and an odd, mud-like substance falls from his fingertips.

What is his wielder's mark? What magic of his has been corrupted?

I pull on a stream of water, washing the strange substance away from the ground before it can reach my feet.

Jax pulls at more. "Live. Live. I just want to live. Die. Die. That's all they give." The substance pours more ferociously from his fingers, and I soon realize that it is rotting the ground beneath his feet.

Noted. Definitely don't let the creepy mud touch me.

A girl, Claya, I believe her name is, steps forward, muttering incoherent words under her breath. Then another girl steps forward, joined by another man. Madness lives in all their eyes. The hisses in the air grow louder.

Erhé akta maht. Erhé akta maht. Erhé akta maht.

Hate take harm. Hate take harm. Hate take harm.

My vision throbs. My feet sway. The wielder's mark on my back begins to burn. Yet I don't lose my focus.

Strange warped lights begin to materialize from their skin. As more and more slip, the ramblings begin to sound like a hypnotic chant of sorts, too mumbled and frenzied for the words to be intelligible, but loud enough to sound like buzzing hums.

One by one they raise their hands, and it feels like all I can do is shield myself with a ball of wind. I stretch out my arms and guide my hands in a swooping motion, calling for wind magic and thanking whatever deity *is* around at this point when it answers. Strikes of magic barrel into the cocoon of wind. I can see all the colors ricochet off the shell, some intermixing and twirling alongside the gusts of air.

It's like streaks of color in a storm.

I drop the shield and reassess. There is, well…

More madness. More corrupted magic. And I have less ideas.

Great.

Where the *hell* is Casimir?

A ball of inverted flames soars toward my head. It is quickly doused by a lancing strike of water that is...wrong. Stiff where it should be fluid. Tacky where it should be wet. I whip my eyes over my shoulder and see Neilina. Her chest is heaving, eyes wide and calculating.

She has yet to succumb to the madness, thank the Mother.

We exchange wary glances as the air electrifies with magic, coated by an icy wrongness. The hysteric chantings grow louder, corrupted marks brightening. Until everyone just goes...silent.

It is an eerie stillness that sends every warning inside me flaring.

All the wielders lost to the madness crane their necks back, tipping their head to the stars, and they scream. It is blood-curdling and terrifyingly otherworldly. It is the sound of Merikh's realm given form. The sounds of terror and agony woven together.

I slap my hands over my ears to muffle the pitchy screech. From the corner of my eye, I see Neilina do the same. Just when I am convinced the ear-splitting screams will never end, the blue light flickers once more. Until it fully merges together, reforming the entirety of the dome shape. And then it fades, blending into the star-flecked charcoal sky and the lines of trees once more.

A portal opens, and Casimir appears seconds later.

He is just in time to take the brunt of a barrage of corrupted magics as they fuse together and launch toward me. Casimir barely seems to blink as he erects a wall of solid stone from the ground. It groans and quakes, but it does not give. Not until Casimir drops it.

"Brothers, sisters," he declares, voice strong and booming over everyone. "Remember yourselves, as your Master wishes it."

It takes a moment, but it seems the wards' protective qualities kick in, and those who slipped regain themselves, blinking furiously as their eyes refocus and their lips fall into a frown.

Casimir turns around, looking haggard. A small line of blood falls from his left nostril. Yet he either doesn't notice or chooses not to care, letting it run freely down the slope of his skin until it kisses his lips. He holds me captive in the intensity of his gaze. Like a caged beast almost broken free.

"We're running out of time."

CHAPTER FORTY-TWO

LYRA

The moonlight is my only friend on the shadowy path paved in silver light and stone, punctuated by the silhouettes of hanging leaves and flowers. It guides me forward, beckoning.

After the chaos settled from the temporary slips of madness, Casimir excused himself, and I stayed to help Neilina check on all those who fell prey to their curse of corruption. They were all fine, save for the rattling of their minds and for a scrape here and there, but the celebration no longer felt so celebratory. Therefore, the staggering bonfire was quenched, and the people scattered. Many went to taverns. Some went to their beds. Others went to find peace in the sanctuary of secluded gardens.

I am amongst such a group.

My mind is still racing from what I saw tonight, witnessing the version of the Abdites I am most familiar with, yet feeling as though they couldn't possibly be the same as those I've encountered in the past. I understand them now—what composes them, haunts them, and plagues their identities. And it's as if that knowledge allowed me to see their madness as something entirely different. It no longer frightened me—not in the slightest. Not when I knew the face behind the mask.

Why had nobody taken the time to attempt to cure and rehabilitate Abdites before? Don't get me wrong, I am more than certain there truly are just vile wielders corrupting their magic for all the wrong reasons. But what about the others? I now know the descendants of the original Abdites are all cursed to be born with the corruption already in their veins—a fact of which has been either lost to Solaya through the ages or blatantly ignored—yet we condemned them all the same. Who else have we gotten wrong? Who else was hardly more than a victim of cruel circumstance?

Gods, I *hated* it when people summed up my worth and made judgements about me only by looking at my position with King Alastair and my lack of titles, as if that is all I am and all I could ever be. Yet that is exactly what I did to them.

I want to kick myself for it.

My wandering feet lead me around a corner and to a large basin of glittering water, overflowing from a tiered marble pool cut in a perfect square. It is nestled away in its own crook of the land, surrounded by flowers, vines, and trees. Under the glow of the moon and its accompanying stars, it makes the space look otherworldly. Like it belongs in the Mother Goddess's realm. Perhaps it *was* modeled after the Hanging Gardens, given the design of it.

My eyes snag on something beautiful at the center of it all.

Not a flower. Not a tree or some impeccable sculpture. But Casimir, shirtless and glistening from the water dripping down his exposed back, the water rising up just past his hips. He cups his palms and fills them with water, splashing the substance against his cheeks and running it over his already glossy hair, pushing the strands away from his face. His fingers continue their path, gliding down his head to the back of his neck where they lock into place.

His eyes remain closed, and he stands there, seemingly frozen. His pallid skin looks like the surface of the moon, slightly grey, slightly silver; beautiful nonetheless, regardless of the color the beholder decides it to be. As I gaze at him—my mouth strangely dry and my heartbeat oddly erratic—I can't help but feel like he looks like a fallen angel.

From my angle, he is sideways, allowing me to see his back and the entirety of his right arm. It also allows me to see his wielder's mark for the first time. Winding black lines make a square, where they curve into ornate framing around four magic symbols: fire, ice, shadow, and light. At the very center of his spine rests a large hand with a ball of light glowing from the palm—the mark of a healer. Surrounding the hand are more symbols, some I recognize, others I don't. His mark boasts far more magic types than my own, and all of them glow. My symbols only do so when I wield the respective magic, but on Casimir, each one maintains a soft brilliance, a subtle glittering quality filling the light.

Gods, only one word keeps entering my mind—

Beautiful.

What is wrong with me?

From somewhere down the path, there is a loud rustling noise followed by murmurs as people head off down the eastern veer of the trail. Casimir's eyes snap open. And then they land directly on me, the amber filling them seeming to glow in the dark.

"What are you doing here?"

I shrug. "I couldn't sleep, so I've just been walking."

He lifts a dark brow. "And you decided to come here?"

My nose scrunches, and I make a show of looking around. "Where is 'here,' exactly?"

He shifts in the water, folding his arms and squaring his shoulders to me. "This is my personal bathing pool. The area is actually protected by magic to keep it invisible to wandering eyes and to not let anyone besides myself enter past a certain point." He huffs a laugh, dropping his head and shaking it. "Though I suppose it is attuned to recognize my magic. Seeing as you and I share the same magic…" He trails off, a hint of genuine amusement seeming to rise in his eyes.

I, however, feel mortified.

"So I—uh, just interrupted your bath, basically?"

"For all intents and purposes, yes."

A violent heat floods my cheeks. I am at such a loss for what to do, I nearly slap my hand over my eyes. "Oh, gods, Cas... I am—am *so* sorry. I was just walking around and—and—"

He lifts a hand for me to be silent, and I am *more* than happy to oblige, pressing my lips into a thin line. "You called me Cas."

My cheeks grow even hotter, and I manage a jerky shrug. "Casimir feels like such a formal name sometimes. I like Cas."

His answering smile is soft. It is also so genuine, it makes my stomach clench. "My friends used to call me Cas. I haven't been called that in centuries."

I arch a brow. "You realize you just admitted to being friendless for centuries, right?"

"At this point, is such a fact really secret?"

"No," I agree. "I guess it isn't."

He laughs. "Turn around for a second, would you?"

"Why?" I ask, my eyes narrowing on him.

"Just do it." When I don't, he adds, "Please."

"Fine."

I put my back to him, and I hear the water sloshing as he moves around. Only a handful of seconds pass, with more splashing and sloshing noises filling the crisp air, and then Casimir says, "You can look now."

When I face him once more, confusion pinches my features together. He doesn't look any different. Nothing appears moved. He is even standing in the same spot as before. "What did you just do?"

"Put on undergarments so you can dip your feet in the water. It is warmed by magic. Here—" He points in the direction of one of the small marble lips outlining the pool. "You can sit there, if you'd like."

I study him. Truthfully, soaking my feet in warm water after the night's events sounds divine, but why is he offering his personal bathing pool for me to do so? "Is this a trick?"

"Not at all," he answers, holding up a hand as if he were taking an oath. "Since you're here, I thought it might be nice for us to just...talk. Like friends would."

I laugh softly. "I call you Cas *one* time, and suddenly you think we're friends." I walk over to where he pointed, stripping my feet bare and plunging them beneath the water's surface. I nearly moan at how perfect the water feels against my skin. The sensation *has* to be an effect of the magic. "Soo," I drawl, "how'd it feel?"

When I finally glance up from the pool, I find Casimir's eyes intently locked on me. "How'd what feel?"

"To be called Cas again."

The corner of his mouth lifts. "Warm. Like remembering a pleasant memory."

"All good things," I say through a laugh.

"I'd say so." He glides the tips of his fingers over the clear surface, looking thoughtful. "I am going to be leaving at first light tomorrow. There are some items I need to acquire to help ensure the safety of my family. Though I am traveling far, I shouldn't be gone long. I'll prob-ably return before tomorrow's sunset. Perhaps you'd like to eat dinner together when I do?"

There is a shyness to the question that is almost…endearing. A word I never thought I would use when describing Casimir Vivaldri.

I lean forward, bracing my forearms on my thighs. "What are you offering?"

His smile deepens. "What do you want?"

I tap a finger to my mouth, feigning consideration. "Cake."

"Cake?" he asks, chuckling. "That's it?"

"I guess you could add some meat and pickled cucumbers. But mostly, I want cake. And wine. Oh wait, no—ale. From the tavern Ophelia plays at."

"You know their names now."

I flash him a proud grin. "Every last one of them."

"Impressive."

I twirl my hand and mock a bow, making Casimir laugh. It's a nice sound, his laugh.

A passing silence fills the space between us, and I kick my feet beneath the water. "Cas?" I ask eventually.

His eyes are gleaming. "Yes?"

"Before the Mother Goddess gifted you the abilities of a Binder, what was your magic?"

He chuckles, shaking his head. "Given my history, it will make you laugh from shock. Or make you loathe me further. Truthfully, I'm not sure which is the greater possibility."

"Only one way to find out."

His eyes hold me captive for a heartbeat. Until they look away from me and up to the moon. "I was a healer."

My jaw drops. "*What?*"

"I know," he says through a sigh.

I consider the information. "Is that how I was able to be healed? Because of you?"

"I certainly was a large contributing factor. Though, there were others involved in mending you. Since I had healing magic before the Mother Goddess 'blessed' me, I always hold the ability. Whether there is a healer around or not. I can just amplify my healing by binding to more healers, multiplying my strength. It's why I suspect once you accept the primary magic you wish to wield into your veins, it will always be with you. I think it's a peculiarity of Binders." A sharp look. "Which, don't think I have forgotten about your need to provide me with an answer on that."

I glance up to the sky, mocking preoccupation. "Sorry," I say when I drop my chin to look at him. "Did you say something?"

He snorts a laugh, shaking his head. "You're a child."

"Compared to your age, I definitely am."

"My body is frozen at twenty-seven, you know."

I shrug. He laughs.

"A healer," I muse, my mouth creeping up with a smile. "Who would have thought?"

"It is rather shocking, given everything."

Yet when I take a second to think about it, it really isn't. Well, I mean, sure, it is entirely at odds with the version of the monster who shoved a blade through Griff's chest and confessed to mass murder. But if I attempt to remember him in the early entries of his journal, the man I saw in the visions the Veil gave me, he was an advocate for diplomacy and peace. Constantly was choosing life.

Until he didn't.

My voice drops into a whisper as a flash of his blade ripping through Griff's chest haunts me. "Why'd you do it?"

His voice is soft. "Do what?"

"Murder my friend. Murder other people's friends. Their loved ones."

He tilts his head back and stares at the stars, quiet for a beat. "It was a means to an end."

"But when does the end no longer justify the means?"

"I suppose that depends on who you ask; who is narrating the story." He tips his chin back down, eyes finding me once more. "I did what I had to, just as so many others do. To my people, my actions are heroic. To your people, they are villainous. Tell me, who can say for certain which group is right?"

I cup my cheeks in my palms. "The group who doesn't choose violence. That's who."

"So who should win wars then?"

"Nobody," I mutter. "It's not like anybody truly does anyway."

He studies me before moving through the water in my direction, stopping only once directly in front of me. Moonlight practically glints off the planes of his chest. "Can I ask you something selfish?"

The shift in his tone has me lifting my face from my hands to better meet his gaze. "Alright."

"Will there ever come a day where you won't see me as a monster? Where perhaps you might even understand me and my intentions?"

It catches me off guard. Not so much the question, but more so my answer to it. The fact that I feel compelled to answer him so honestly. Answer him at all, even. "Perhaps."

A look flashes in and out of his eyes. It looks like shock mixed with relief, both merging together with a glimmer of hope—though for what, exactly, I don't know. Yet the weight of it presses upon me all the same.

I resume kicking my feet against the swell of water, glancing away.

"I wanted to be a healer once," I murmur out of nowhere. "When I had no magic and would fantasize about it awakening as a small girl."

My toes graze just above the surface, accidentally splashing water droplets up and across my cheek. Casimir reaches forward and gently swipes them away, the pad of his thumb gentle against my skin. As his fingers pull back, his knuckles graze my cheek. "You would have been good at it."

My lips twitch. "You think so?"

"I do."

He takes a step closer, and I officially have to lift my chin to hold his gaze. We remain like that, holding each other's stares in a silent moment of something I dare not name.

I suck in a breath. "I should probably go to bed."

His eyes do not leave me. "Yes," he agrees. "You probably should. Neilina will be training you in my place tomorrow, and I know what she has planned for you. You'll need rest, trust me."

Yet neither he nor I move. Instead, it feels like we get closer—though of no active action on either of our parts. It's like clouds drifting, swept up on a breeze they have no control over. My knees break apart from each other, and Casimir steps closer to fill the space between them. He towers over me now, his chin tilted down while mine remains lifted to peer up at him. We're so close. The closest we've ever allowed our bodies to be before.

He reaches his hand out slowly—tentatively—and he glides his thumb along my jaw, cupping my face, leaning toward me as he searches my eyes.

The action makes me think of Draven. The way he would cup my face in his hand. How good it felt when his fingers wrapped around my jaw, roving down to the base of my throat. How desperately I wish he could touch me like that again.

Yet I know he can't, because I have to stay away from the kingdoms so he can have his life. I'd rather that than see him forced to marry Arden because of me; to have the rest of his life written out for him with poisoned ink only so I might be free. No matter how much it breaks my heart to know Draven will never hold me again. Will never show me the depth of how good a kiss can be once more.

I know I will have to move on eventually—if there ever *will* be moving on from him—but that is a day still held captive by the long night. Dawn is nowhere close to rising in that horizon. Because... there is just no denying how *right* it had all felt with him. How familiar he seemed to my soul. Like I had already met him. Had already wanted him, at least to some capacity, before I ever even accepted it as fact.

I don't suspect such a gift of feeling is so easy to move on from.

Casimir's face has dropped to be so achingly close to mine. There is a part of me which considers letting whatever is about to happen play out. A part of me which believes I may even enjoy what happens next if I do. Especially when I glance up and see the concerted way Casimir is looking at me right now. Yet I just...can't.

I turn my face away from him, and I swear something withers in his eyes. So sad. So tired.

So broken.

Casimir pulls his hand back, immediately retreating two steps. He stares at the hand that just held my face, curling his fingers into his palm before dropping it down to his side.

I want to say something. The air between us is already so different, all signs of that electric current eradicated entirely. Yet every time I open my mouth, my voice simply doesn't work. My *words* don't work.

Casimir straightens. "Try to finalize your decision on your primary magic during your training with Neilina tomorrow. Play around with different magics. Be honest with yourself and decide which one truly feels right in your veins. At this point, we cannot effectively move forward in your training without your decision."

I nod, the motion stiff. "Alright," I murmur. "I will."

"Good." He smiles tightly at me, and I can't help but to think a smile should not be so sad. "Goodnight then, Lyra."

"Goodnight, Casimir."

CHAPTER FORTY-THREE

GRAY

Gray lets the hot sand funnel through his fingertips while the searing sun presses against his back.

He rises from his bent knee, scanning the open landscape. Red-tinted sand dunes undulate endlessly with pits of rust-colored quartz grains sprinkled in between. The sky is a peculiar shade of maroon, filled with the light of a red sun. Gray blinks against the brightness of it all.

"Well?" Draven steps up next to him. "What do you think?" His words are muffled by the cream headdress covering his face.

Gray considers before answering, his breath warm against his own covering. "There is definitely still magic here. Though it feels... different."

Draven nods. "I feel it, too. Powerful. Fluid. But definitely different."

"Look at that, Frosty," Gray hears Rhea mutter from behind him. "You'll be useful after all."

"And how are you intending to be useful?" Finlay shoots back. "Stabbing sand? Hot air, perhaps?"

She crosses her arms. "If I'm lucky, I'll be stabbing an insufferable, icy prick soon."

450

"Knock it off you two," Draven snaps. "We need to stay focused on what's ahead."

Gray agrees entirely. Though, seeing as he is the odd man out between them all, he allows Draven to do the reprimanding.

Traveling with Rhea, Finlay, and Draven thus far has been...interesting, to say the least. After Klytis arrived at Sagamon Castle and opened a portal for them to enter Halfin, the tension in the air has been drawn taut. For a small stint of time, Gray merely suspected it radiated from his ire with Draven, still mildly upset about the colossal blunder regarding Lyra's security. Yet after their second night in Halfin, while everyone was plagued with nervous energy as they were forced to a standstill as they worked to secure a small crew willing to give them passage to the Arid Wastelands and then wait two weeks at the Wasteland's shoreline for their return—thank the gods for House Fjolla's seemingly endless coffers—Gray soon realized the tension was most certainly being fed by whatever was going on between Finlay and Rhea. It was made all the more clear once they finally found their crew days later and reached the docks, each of them immediately splitting for opposite ends of the modest ship, where they then stayed.

Draven turns to Gray. "What do you think is the best course of action from here? I've been trying to decide, and..." He shakes his head, releasing a sigh. "Well, it's not like we're just going to find her footprints in the sand."

Gray huffs a dry laugh. "Life can never be so easy."

"No," he agrees. "It cannot."

Gray allows all the possibilities to swirl in his mind. As far as he is concerned, given their current situation, he can only see one viable option. "Your ability to sense magic is superior to any wielder I've ever met. Given that plus your familiarity with the feel of Lyra's own magic, I'd say the best recourse from here is to see what you can sense first."

Draven grunts.

"What?" Gray asks, feeling like his plan is perfectly reasonable.

"When you think about it, this is just like the first test in Bathara's entrance exam. Only on a much larger, far more difficult scale."

Now that he mentions it…

"You're right," Gray agrees.

Draven smirks like a smug cat. "Good thing I hold the record for the fastest completion time ever seen in Bathara's history."

Rhea snorts at that.

Gray is tempted to roll his eyes. "I don't know, actually. Marcella may have beat your time if she ventured back to Bathara the moment she found her flower. She only returned so late because she stayed to help Lyra."

Finlay huffs an arrogant laugh. "Had I not taken the time to pay my respects to my home mountains when I was an examinee, nobody would have come close to my time."

"Alright popsicle, you find Draven's lost lover then," Rhea challenges.

Finlay jerks his chin away from her. "I'm not as familiar with her. Therefore, in this instance, I am not the better option. Draven is."

"Aw, would you look at that," Rhea fake pouts. "Frosty here can scrounge up some modesty."

"Would you give it a *rest?*" he hisses.

"Sorry," she chirps, her voice growing brittle. "I forgot my blatant disrespect and misplaced sense of self makes you hate me so viscerally."

He winces, and Gray bounces his eyes between the two of them, thinking that whatever they've got going on, he wants *no* part of it.

"Rhea, stop being antagonizing. And Finlay, stop playing into it." Draven carves a hand down his face. "Gods, I sound like Kiran. How the fuck does he make this sort of thing look so easy?"

"Practice?" Gray offers.

Draven gives him an imploring look. "You have no idea." He squares his shoulders back to the sand dunes. "Now, everyone give me a moment to see what I can sense."

Gray happily obliges, finding his mind snagged on one of his previous thoughts.

Marcella.

A pang of guilt stabs him in the chest. He wishes he could talk to her. Finally explain everything—a feat he was at last about to do when he followed her out to the balcony at the masquerade ball. Yet the uprising attack happened not long after, and he missed his opportunity. Again.

Yet no matter how much he wishes things could be different between them, he stands by his decision. Believes he truly *is* doing the right thing by waiting until Lyra is back home, safe. Though...

Will she really be safe?

Gods, that's another thing he has to consider and work through. Where the hell will they go once they return? What will they do to prevent the Tani from arresting Lyra and putting her on trial? Who knows how long she'll have to be on the run, living a life tucked away in the shadows, constantly looking over her shoulder and covering her tracks.

Regardless, Gray will be there right beside her, not letting her walk that dark path alone for a single second. Though, he knows there will be another set of feet walking with them. And truthfully, having Draven Dalmar on their side—despite his recent lapses—makes Gray feel a lot better, strange as it is to admit.

Yet the complication remains: what will Marcella do? Or better yet, what will Gray do without being able to have Marcella around? He already misses her, and it's only been a couple weeks...

He's certain Marcella will want to go on the run with them, but... That is no life to live, and Marcella has too much she'd be giving up. When they recover Lyra, and Gray eventually speaks with her about the matter—after she's had ample time to recuperate and gather her thoughts—he suspects Lyra will be in full agreement.

Gray is saved from his overload of thoughts when Draven snaps his eyes open and rasps, "Southeast."

"You're sure?"

"I wouldn't have stopped searching if I wasn't."

Gray nods, trusting him. "Then that's where we go."

"FROSTY," Rhea drones, "I need more ice. *Please*."

Finlay twirls his wrist, and a collection of small ice cubes appear in her hand. Rhea immediately reaches beneath her headdress to press them against her neck. She moans at the sensation.

Gray understands entirely. Wishes he himself was in a bathtub filled with ice cubes. They've been wandering the Wastelands for days, and Gray has never quite known a misery such as this.

"Are you still confident about this, brother?" Finlay asks Draven, who walks about three paces ahead of everyone, leading their traveling party.

"Yes. The pull of magic is growing stronger with each passing day. We're close. I know we are."

"That's fine and all, but are you sure you're following the *right* trail?"

Draven stills, cutting a look back at Finlay. "Do you really doubt me?"

"I doubt how much longer everyone can withstand these conditions."

"Then make more ice for everyone," Draven bites out. "It's why you're here, isn't it?"

Gray glances between them, sighing internally. Between the travel, minimal food, and the heat, everyone is on edge and dangerously irritable. That paired with the already abrasive temperaments of both Finlay and Draven has been a recipe for an impending disaster.

"Yes," Finlay agrees, tone clipped. "It is. But there are other factors to consider besides just the heat. Bathing. Food rations. Shall I go on?"

"What you *should* be doing is focusing on keeping everyone cool while keeping your thoughts to yourself."

Rhea steps forward, positioning herself between the two heirs. "And both of you should quit bickering."

"Ironic, coming from you," Finlay says dryly.

"Stop talking to her like that," Draven growls.

Rhea glances between them and sighs, pinching the bridge of her nose. "Look, everyone is sweaty, tired, and probably a little malnourished. The sun is about to set, so let's just call it a day and set up camp for the night. Alright?"

When neither of the two heirs say anything, Gray steps forward. "I think that's a great idea. The farther south we've traveled, the colder the nights have gotten. Rhea's right—it's best we stop now and make camp."

Finlay and Draven hold each other's simmering stares, their tension permeating from their bodies as forcibly as the heat from the Wasteland's red sun. Draven's eyes flicker black.

Rhea and Gray exchange wary glances. Are they really going to make them intervene?

Right as Gray is convinced they *will* have to, Draven pulls his chin away from Finlay and heads off in the direction of a rock formation shaped somewhat like a thumb, squeezing his eyes closed and shaking his head. "Fine," he grumbles.

Nobody speaks for a while after that.

A SMALL FIRE dances within a freshly carved pit of sand at the center of their group's circle. The moon hangs overhead, bright and deeply silver. It seems to swallow the night sky, casting the sands of the Wastelands in an eerie glow. The air has plunged into a bone-chilling cold. It is by far the coldest night they have yet to experience here, and the wariness sits heavy in the air.

They could only travel with so much strapped to their backs, and seeing as their days are spent walking in boiling weather, they didn't think to make space for blankets.

Rhea leans toward the fire, her arms wrapped around her torso. "I wish Kiran was here." Her teeth chatter, the *clacking* noise a reminder of the cruel chill.

Draven studies her. "Rhea, your lips are turning blue."

"I'm fine," she says, waving him off.

Only, she doesn't seem fine. Her body shivers so forcefully, she almost appears to be vibrating, and her chin quivers without a sliver of control.

"The fire isn't big enough," Finlay says, his words sounding stiff. "She needs to be able to sit in front of a larger fire with more heat."

"I know that, Finlay," Draven replies. "But where do you expect the materials for that fire to suddenly appear from? We're lucky enough to have scavenged what we did."

Finlay doesn't answer, instead turning his gaze onto Rhea. His eyes fall with concern, his lips thinning into a tight line.

Gray glances between the two of them, an idea coming to mind. Maybe one that could kill two birds with one stone. "If you're comfortable, Rhea, I think you need to share your bedroll with someone so their body heat can help keep you warm. I think at this point, it's the only viable option to make it through the night."

Finlay stiffens at the words.

"P-pass," she says, voice shaking from the cold.

"Rhea," Draven admonishes. "Gray is right. You need more heat, and the only way to get that right now is through a body."

She wrinkles her nose at him. "I am *not* cuddling on a bedroll with your brooding ass."

"How about his brooding ass?" Gray offers with a tinge of humor, pointing at Finlay.

Rhea only spares Finlay a glance before looking sharply back at Gray. "You're joking, right? I'd sooner freeze to death than share a bedroll with that asshole."

Though he hides it well, Gray does not miss the way Finlay deflates at the words. Though he rebounds quickly, lifting his chin and rebutting, "Thank the gods for that."

"Well," Draven muses, "that just leaves you, Nightenjoy."

Rhea studies Gray, then sighs. "Fine. I guess you're okay."

Gray merely blinks. This...is not how he saw it going. Still...

Though he failed at his attempts to play matchmaker, the point he made remains valid—she needs more body heat. So Gray rises from his place across the fire and repositions himself behind Rhea, wrapping his arms around her and tucking her into his chest.

"Is this alright?" he asks, cautious. "Are you comfortable?"

"I'm fine." It only takes a few minutes before her chin stops trembling and her teeth stop clacking together. She blows out a breath, nestling more comfortably into Gray. "This is…better," she says like an admittance, her voice already steadier. "Thank you."

Gray smiles. "Don't mention it." He glances up, and—

By the gods…

From his right, Draven watches him stern-faced and neutral, as if daring him to try anything funny. From his left…

Gods, on his left, Finlay looks as though his head might explode from all the hot air he is trying to contain. Normally, Gray has to give it to the Fjolla Heir—he can be incredibly hard to read, always seeming to do an excellent job at masking his emotions and reactions. Right now, however, he is failing miserably.

Finlay's lips are pressed into a tight line as he watches them. A vein bulges near his temple, and his hands are clasped tightly together in front of him. He glares at Gray with such intensity, Gray isn't entirely sure Finlay is actually *seeing* anything.

Gray shifts, moving his hand just slightly to be more comfortable, grazing across Rhea's stomach.

"Watch where you put that hand," Finlay snaps.

Against his chest, Gray feels Rhea stiffen just before she turns her chin over her shoulder to look at Finlay. To his surprise, though, she doesn't say anything. Only watches him. Yet Finlay does not return her look, instead jerking his chin away from her to gaze out over the shadowed mounds of sand.

Gray opens his mouth to diffuse some of the tension, yet right as he does, a loud zapping noise sounds in the distance, and a flash of brilliant blue light has everyone snapping their heads to the east.

Across the way, tucked behind a few sand dunes, there appears to be a dome of sorts. It flickers in and out, in and out, the radiant blue light stark against the night sky. Then, it disappears altogether.

Draven scurries to a stand, and the rest of them are not far behind him.

"What the hell was that?" Rhea asks.

Finlay steps toward them, stopping when there is only a sliver of space between his and Rhea's shoulders. He watches the sky through narrowed eyes. "Do you feel that?"

Draven nods. "I do."

Gray feels small pricks of electricity in his veins himself, a small warning bell flaring beneath his skin. Though it isn't very loud, and the connection he feels is not very strong, leaving him to wonder what exactly Finlay and Draven are capable of sensing in this moment.

Silently, they all watch the empty spot on the horizon where the dome had flashed. Until, without warning, the blue light flares brightly once more, seeming to burn like a shooting star. The dome merges together into a cohesive shape before disappearing altogether, not leaving so much as a trace in its wake.

There is a long, pressing silence after that. It's as if words aren't needed, because deep in all their bones, they know.

Draven stares at the blackened horizon. "We're coming, Lyra."

CHAPTER FORTY-FOUR

DRAVEN

Draven crouches down, pressing his fingers into the warm markings grooved deep into the sand.

"There's no doubt about it," Finlay says, bending down beside him, his fingers tracing the humming semi-circle. "This is a ward. And judging from the amount of magic I can sense from it, it is a damn strong one."

Gray pinches his chin. "Do you think it's enchanted to keep whatever is behind the barrier concealed?"

From beside Gray, Rhea snorts. "I certainly don't think there is a random magical dome out here just to protect *sand*."

The corner of Draven's lip quirks up, a much needed reprieve from the onslaught of his other raging emotions. He rises, assessing. "We're going to have to break it."

"I don't suspect that will be easy," Finlay muses, standing upright as well. He rubs at the back of his neck, squinting against the brightness reflecting off the lightened sand around them. His feet tread forward three steps, and he outstretches his hand, uncurling his fingers from his palm and laying it flat against the invisible barrier. Within seconds, his eyes flare and he jerks his hand away. "Correction: I don't think it is *possible*."

459

"It can be done," Draven says, grateful that his voice sounds a hell of a lot more sure than he feels.

"We're powerful, Draven," Finlay says. "But we're no match for whatever old magic this is. I felt it. It is…raw. Charged. There is a thread of something different woven through it. I haven't felt anything quite like it before."

Draven says nothing, instead only folding his arms over his chest.

Finlay flexes his jaw, pushing his tongue into the side of his cheek. "Look, we might have to accept the possibility that this is what you were sensing. Not Lyra. She might not even be behind the ward for all we know."

"She is." Draven steps toward the barrier, a faint shimmer pulsing from its boundary. "We'll have to figure out a way to weaken the magic enough to where you and I can overpower it."

Gray clears his throat, gaining the attention of both Draven and Finlay. With one arm folded over the other, he points to his left. To where Rhea is standing with a hand propped on her hip and a wicked smirk on her face.

"Sounds like you need a Nullifier."

"Alright, so that's the plan. Any questions?"

Rhea lifts her hand, and Draven swallows down the bubble of irritation as it rises up his throat, knowing it is completely unwarranted. The heat, travel, and lack of a full meal has been getting to him. Not to mention everything else wrong with his mind right now.

"Yes, Rhea?" he asks.

"Do I have to be paired with Finlay?"

Draven rubs at the skin above his brow. "Yes."

"Why?"

"Because as soon as you have nullified as much of the barrier as you can, he needs to step in with his magic to take advantage of the weak points."

"But why can't you do that?"

"I will be doing that," he answers tersely. "From the other side of the barrier."

"But—"

"*Rhea*," Draven warns, stretching his neck side to side. "Please."

"Since Draven will be the first one to enter the space and we're not sure what to expect on the other side, I need to be closest to him to shield him with an illusion," Gray offers, his voice far gentler than Draven's had been. "And the ward appears to be too large for all of us to remain localized at one point. If this is going to work, the pairings really are necessary."

Rhea slices Draven with a look, then nods. "Thanks, Gray."

He smiles in return, and Finlay clears his throat, far louder and more aggressive than necessary. Gods, if they were in any other circumstance, Draven would probably laugh at his brother's helplessness.

"If we are going to do this," he muses, voice stiff, "then let us do this without any further delays."

"Agreed," Draven says. He approaches Rhea, resting a hand on her shoulder, squeezing gently. "If anything goes sideways, you run. I don't care what you see. I don't care if I have five blades through my chest. You get the hell out of here, and you keep your nullifying magic armed and surrounding you at all times. Okay?"

She holds his stare, staying quiet.

"Rhea," Draven presses. "Please. I can't have anything happening to you." The strings in his heart tighten, and his mouth curves gently. "Suzumi would rise from the grave just so she could kill me herself if I let you get hurt."

"You don't *let* me do anything." Despite her words, her eyes are soft and filled with nostalgia as she, too, dips into her memories of the past. Of a time where Suzumi was still alive, lecturing both her and Draven when they sparred too roughly. Reprimanding Rhea when she acted too recklessly—which was a lot. "I can't promise you I'll run," she murmurs. "But I promise you I'll be smart."

Draven moves his jaw side-to-side, conceding with a nod.

"She'll be with me," Finlay offers, taking a protective step toward Rhea. "I'll watch out for her."

Draven studies his brother, noticing the way he's positioned himself to Rhea. "I know you will." He sucks in a loud breath, turning to sweep his eyes over everyone. "Okay, then. Let's split up and bring this ward down."

SOUNDS ARE MUFFLED. The world is fading. There are only screams and blood and pain. Memories brought to life, given cruel forms in brandished shadows and crimson light.

"Draven!" he hears a male voice call out to him from somewhere outside himself. "You're losing control. *Draven!*"

But those are not the only voices he hears as his palms are pressed against the barriers of the ward. As his skin burns against the magic of it. As the ancient force imbued into the ward ravages him with cruel visions of a time long ago. Pours venom into his deepest scars. Twists the present with the past, putting Draven in a near state of psychosis.

It is the hums of his magic, eager to welcome him, he hears. Eager that Draven was already vulnerable to their invasion from the slips over the past few months. From how frequently he's been digging deeper and deeper into his well of resources. From already being worn from the intense conditions of traveling the Wastelands. From being desperate.

They sink their claws into him as easily as slicing melted butter, where they hook into place.

More memories eviscerate him. Bodies pinned against a wall, blood trickling down like a shadow. His mother strapped to a table, the word *whore* burned into her skin.

You are my greatest accomplishment, she says.

I am your greatest failure, he thinks.

His father holds a dagger to a small girl's throat as she attempts to hold her sobs in her chest.

On your knees, boy.

I own you now.

I own you now. I own you now.

"*We* own you now," the magic hisses inside his head. "*Become us. Accept us. Let us in—all of us.*"

He doesn't have a choice. He is drowning, forced to stare into a looking glass which only replays for him the deepest forms of his misery.

Come in, Draven thinks, nothing more than a leaf swept up in a hailstorm.

The full weight of his magic presses upon him. It is like an eclipsed sun. Never in all of his years has his magic been such a thing.

He sees Lyra, surrounded in a sea of Abdites. They are back at Bathara, the battle between them raging. Within a blink, she is the version of herself where she is desiccated by her own magic, breaths barely coming, only wet and rattling when they do. He sees his fallen comrades at his feet, blood pooling from their lips, skin curdled and strange from the corrupted magic eating at them. Abdites charge at her. Madness splits the air. He blinks again, and Lyra is whole once more. But the Abdites form a circle around her—they wish to attack. They are the *enemy.*

I can save her this time, Draven thinks.

You can save her this time, his magic agrees, giddy with anticipation.

He will not let the Abdites destroy her again. He will not.

He will save her.

Save her.

Save—

Warmth floods him, and the sensation of Lyra in his arms makes him pause. Sage wafts into his nostrils, and he swears he can feel her thumb gliding across his cheek.

When the world fades black, Draven is smiling.

CHAPTER FORTY-FIVE

RHEA

Rhea stares in horror as Finlay screams and screams, his hands appearing to be stuck within the grips of the ward.

"No! *NO!*" His distant, glazed-over eyes are wide with terror. "Mother… Help! Somebody *help!*"

Rhea grits her teeth, yanking her hands away from the barrier. Whatever the ward is doing to Finlay, her nullifying magic prevented it from happening to her. So how can she now stop it from destroying *him*?

She rests her hands atop his outstretched wrists, pouring her magic over his skin. It isn't enough. Whatever ancient magic this is, Finlay was right—it is powerful. *Very* powerful.

"Fuck," she curses under her breath.

Rhea ducks under Finlay's arms, positioning herself to stand in the small gap between them. She presses her back against his chest, laying her arms over his. Then, she squeezes her eyes closed and brings as much of her magic to the surface as she can, directing it outward to form her own barrier. It covers her and Finlay in a warm, shimmering glow. His breathing eases, his chest no longer heaving. She pushes herself further, a heavy strain pressing against her muscles and lungs, body tiring and screaming to not push any harder.

She never has been one for listening.

She takes more from her well. Demands every last drop of her magic.

She feels Finlay stiffen, then the tickle of his hair against her neck as she assumes he shakes his head in an attempt to come back to himself.

"Rhea," he rasps, sounding confused and alarmed at once. "What—"

"No time," she cuts in, voice painfully tight. "Break...barrier..." Rhea leans forward and slams her palms into the ward, the magic coursing into her with the rush of a drug's high.

Finlay follows her lead, leaning forward to press his chest against her back once more. Together, under the protection of her nullifying abilities, they push every ounce of magic they have into collapsing the ward.

It begins to work.

She creates holes in a concentrated center directly in front of her, the gap slowly expanding like a flame eating at a burning sheet of parchment. Finlay, showing impressive cleverness, takes his magic to the areas Rhea's isn't reaching, capitalizing on the weakening points of the ward, weighing it down and eroding its frame with layers of ice that *clink* and *ting* as they expand up and over the dome.

The ward flickers.

They push harder, knowing that Draven is doing the same on his side. Until the barrier cracks, then shatters completely.

The force of it sends Rhea and Finlay soaring backward. He takes the brunt of the force, holding her tight against his chest as his back slams and skids across the ground.

Rhea groans, her head spinning. "Are you alright?" Her voice sounds like she's just swallowed glass.

"Flourishing," he deadpans.

She sits up. When the world steadies and the stars dim from her eyes, her breath catches in her throat at the sprawling sight before her.

Lush green stretches as far as the eye can see, divided by mosaic walkways and punctuated by a small jungle of trees. There are bushes, vines, and flowers. Glittering streams running beneath stone bridges.

The smell of dewy grass mingling with mint and jasmine now trot through the air.

For a time, Rhea merely marvels at it, stunned. "Are you seeing this?" she asks Finlay. When she turns to face him, still ensconced between his legs, Finlay's eyes are glued to his opened palms. He looks haunted and miserable. Rhea drops her head to catch his attention. "What happened when you tried to break the ward?"

"It tried to break me in return," he answers, his low voice raspy and hollow.

"How?"

"By showing me my deepest regrets. By making me relive and experience my most terrible nightmares. I–I think it must have been a sort of fail-safe woven into the barrier. Like some activated instruction: break the mind of the wielder before it can break you. Cruel, but clever."

Pain fills his face, a blemish marring him.

Rhea isn't sure what to attribute her next gesture to. She is not a particularly kind person nor someone who offers comfort just because someone is feeling sad—sadness lives everywhere, in all things eventually. Yet her hand still reaches out to Finlay's face, cupping his cheek while her thumb glides soothingly across it. "Are you okay?"

His eyes snap up from his palms and onto Rhea. They widen, then crumble. Wordlessly, he shakes his head, and all Rhea can hear for a moment is his scream, the sound like a desperate boy. She knows Finlay's mother died when he was young and that his father blamed him for her death. Though that was as much as she could ever get out of Draven or Kiran—they would never tell her more than that. In the past, she only wanted to know what happened so she could exploit that wound in Finlay. To twist the knife and pour salt into it.

Now, Rhea wishes she knew so she might help him heal it.

"Finlay?" she pushes.

His lips press into a thin line, and he averts his gaze. For a heartbeat, Rhea is convinced he is about to reject her attempt at comforting him, making her feel ignorant and unwanted—something he is so good at doing. In fact, she is so sure of it, she soon realizes she has already braced herself against it, dropping her hand back down to her side as she prepares herself for his blade.

What she actually receives is so much sharper.

As if coming to some silent decision, Finlay reaches for her hand and gently returns it to his cheek. He leans into her palm, closing his eyes and releasing a shuddering breath. When he reopens his eyes, there is something softer swimming amongst the ghosts.

Finlay guides Rhea's hand back down to her lap. Then he wraps his arms around her torso and pulls her into him, putting her back flush against his chest. Silently, he nestles his chin into the crook of her neck, burying his face into her hair and shoulder. He holds onto her like she's his anchor. His protection. He holds her like he'd fall apart and crumble without her in his arms.

Rhea lets him.

She is surprised by how good it feels—letting him hold her.

Yet the warm, swelling feeling is not allowed to live long as a new onyx dome of magic soon flashes into existence, pervading the air and plunging the sky into an unnatural dark. The hairs on Rhea's arms rise from both recognition and terror.

No wielder should be capable of such magic. No person should have that much power.

Yet one person does. One wielder is capable of this. And if he has unleashed his magic in such a horrifying way, that means things have gone terribly, terribly wrong.

"Fuck," Rhea whispers.

Finlay goes slack behind her. "Draven's lost control."

CHAPTER FORTY-SIX

LYRA

Everything happens so fast.

One moment I am training with Neilina—Ophelia and Luna watching with interest from the sidelines of our training yard—and the next…chaos.

Similar to how it was yesterday, the ward started flickering above our heads. Unlike yesterday, however, it just…shattered, breaking into pieces like glass.

It doesn't take long for things to spiral out of control after that.

The air plunges, and Neilina quickly looks to Ophelia and Luna. "Go," she instructs, every bit of her authority leaking into her voice. "Lock yourselves in your home. Chain yourselves to a tree. Do whatever you have to do until we can fix this."

They nod, terror swimming in their eyes as they scurry in the opposite direction.

"What do we do?" I ask her, my heart pounding, blood thrumming in my ears. "Casimir isn't here. And I…" I trail off, the air quivering from my lips. "I'm not sure what to do."

She chews on her cheek while she thinks. "Our advantage today is that everyone isn't congregated in one area for a celebration. If they are at home, they know what they are supposed to do should the wards fail."

"And that is?"

"Lock themselves up by whatever means necessary. Some use chains. Some use carved out areas underground. Some drive nails through their palms and see healers after. They do what they must." She stops, expression shifting. "I only have so long before I succumb to the madness." Her voice tightens. "I need your instructions."

"*Mine?*"

"Yes," she answers with a nod. "Master isn't here, and you are meant to be his successor. Which means right now, we answer to *you*."

I press my palm to my forehead. "I–I don't know. There's a temple, and maybe I can—"

I don't get to finish my sentence. A strike of molten ash streams for me, and Neilina barely erects a wave of her corrupted water in time to stop it.

"Shit," she whispers sharply.

Just across the way, three Abdites stride—no, more like skip—in our direction. One is a man named Lythe. The other two are Ophelia and Luna, their changed eyes telling me they have lost themselves to the madness.

Their skip turns into a sprint, a child's grin splitting their lips. The air is ice on my skin now.

Erhé akta maht. Erhé akta maht. Erhé akta maht.

"Play with me. Dance! Dance!" Luna says, a silver stream, solid yet fluid, falling from her fingertips. She twirls in place, the silver splashing in droplets across trees and grass as she does.

Those spots burn away within an instant.

Ophelia moves her hands as though playing an imaginary fiddle. Her stuttering movements call upon black thorns and venomous vapor which pour from petals resembling candlewax.

Lythe's corrupted magic is more straightforward—he was the one who sent the ball of molten ash soaring toward my head. And he sends another strike. One that is paired with thorn-pricked vapor and flowing silver.

In my desperation, I pull at whatever will come easiest, hating the moment a wall of solid flames is what answers.

"Lyra," Neilina croaks from beside me once the magic has been swallowed and burned, her head twitching. "I can't...can't...hold it back much longer."

Panic seizes me. I don't know what I'm supposed to do. Casimir—we never went over this. I think the–the temple is where I should go. But how do I get there? And what do I even *do* if I can find it? I–I—

The encroaching Abdites rip me from my thoughts.

"Dance! Dance!" Luna sings like a child, twirling closer, arms flaring out around her.

Ophelia's imaginary fiddle playing intensifies, her movements turning aggressive. She shuts her eyes and chants, "A fiddle is true. A fiddle is you. A fiddle will show what you can truly do."

Silver lining? At least the man, Lythe, only has an inverted flame glowing directly between his eyes, stretching out to his temples, not rambling or saying anything cryptic.

In unison, they tilt their heads at me.

Then they attack.

Silver *tings* in the air as it rushes for my feet and shoulders. Black, rotten thorns jut up from the ground like teeth and attempt to swallow me like a living beast. All the while, molten ash rains from the sky in a contained storm over my head. Neilina does her best to help. She throws out solid defenses with her water magic when she can. Yet her movements are becoming jerky, and her twitch is turning into a convulsion. I use every ounce of my training I can, pulling mainly at water, fire, and earth. Flora magic is not going to do much for me right now.

My back starts to tingle, then burns. My vision blurs at the edges, flickering red and black. Yet right when wild desperation tightens in my chest, a terrible noise resembling a heavy creaking door echoes in the sky. It is followed by howling winds, then a low-pitched *BOOM*. It makes everyone stop—even the Abdites. A small dot of darkness appears across the way.

Lythe tilts his head at it, frowning. Until he falls to his knees with widened eyes. "A god! A god! A god!"

Ophelia and Luna both snap their eyes to him, their necks craning.

"God? No gods," Ophelia squeaks. "Gods are locked. Gods are caged."

Luna giggles, her neck cracking further to the side. "Not all the gods, you remember. One escaped."

I wish I could ask them what they mean, but a dull ringing sound hangs in the sky, and that pervasive darkness expands, forming a growing dome shape. My brows furrow at the sight of it.

"*Lyra*," Neilina grits out. "I can't...hold on..." Her eyes go distant, traveling far, far away. Until they snap into focus with something unnatural. She tilts her head at me, grinning. "Lyraaaa," she sings. "Lyyyyraaa."

Fuck.

Not good. *Not* good.

I can't even focus on the approaching tidal wave of darkness, because Neilina directs her magic at me, which catches the attention of Ophelia and Luna, who then turn with giddy smiles, following her lead and resuming their magical attacks once more. It takes all my focus, all my training to dodge and defend against their attacks.

The voices in the air hiss louder.

Erhé akta maht. Erhé akta maht. Erhé akta maht.

Hate take harm. Hate take harm. Hate take harm.

But more noises join those voices, creating a cacophony of sound. It is like metal screeching together, rounded out with a low-pitched drone. The darkness is no longer a blemish on the horizon; it is a consuming beast. The Abdites giggle as it approaches.

"A god," Lythe screeches again. "A god! A god!"

What *in* the gods....

The darkness reaches them, blotting out the sun and stripping away the blue sky completely.

It swallows them whole.

Screams erupt in the air. Hundreds of them, coming together, joining their voices like a choir. They scream and scream, and yet I am instead dropping to my knees, stunned by the feeling of what's around me. I *know* this feeling. I know this darkness. I've...been here before, surrounded by it. It's familiar—like a distant memory caught on the tip of my tongue, nearly accessible yet not. The overwhelming feeling of it leaves me disoriented.

I open my eyes, searching the darkness. There are odd warps of light, glimmering and twinkling against the sea of unending onyx. They are like tiny specks of dying stars. Created and destroyed within the span of a blink. Yet they are unending—infinite. Beautiful. It removes the fright from my skin, replacing it instead with awe.

I've seen this before. Been enveloped like this once. But...

How? Why can't I remember?

Right as I stretch my fingertips out to touch it, the darkness falls from the air like raindrops, disappearing before it can ever hit the ground. The world around me snaps back into focus with blinding color. The sky is filled with deep maroons and pinks. The descending sun burns against my fluttering eyes.

Death fills the air.

Luna, Ophelia, and Lythe lay scattered dead on the ground, their glazed eyes wide while burns litter their skin. Their arms are twisted at strange angles, legs bent awkwardly behind them.

My chest caves in on itself, and nausea roils in my gut. Why? And why am I okay? *Why?*

"Ly...ra..." A choked, wet rasp sounds from behind me.

I whirl around and find Neilina covered in similar burns, blood bubbling—no, *boiling*—from her lips.

"Neilina," I breathe, rushing to her.

Up close, her mangled skin and wet breathing are worse than I initially thought. My bottom lip quivers as I take in the wrecked sight of her.

"I'm here," I rasp, dropping to the ground to cradle her head in my lap. "Stay with me," I say, trying to keep the panic from my voice. Her eyelids flutter closed, and I tap her cheek, holding my growing sob deep in my chest. "Come on, Neilina, stay awake."

She opens her eyes, her dimming expression a mixture of sanity battling against madness. Like she is trapped somewhere between the two.

"You need a healer," I say more for myself than her. With a frenzy bordering the lines of mania, I scan our surroundings, as if one might magically appear. Until I remember who I am—*what* I am.

I am a Binder.

I squeeze my eyes and reach. Like stretching out fingertips to grasp at clouds in the sky, I reach for something my hands can never truly hold.

Nothing answers.

Nothing.

It's as if all the healers suddenly disappeared, their magic inaccessible.

I squeeze my eyes closed and try harder. "Please," I whisper. *"Please."*

But just like the first time, I receive no answer. No swells of magic in my veins. Which means...

There is nothing I can do to save her. Not from this. Not with how bad her injuries are.

Neilina stares up at the forming sunset above our heads. I glance up, too. A wave of disgust rolls through me; how can something so beautiful twirl while gazing down upon something so ugly?

Neilina coughs, spitting up more curdled blood. Then, despite everything, from the crook of my lap, she starts to sing. It is a croakish sound. Melodic and agonizing. A tune of madness and truth. Sorrow and pain.

> *Oh anguished soul, what have we become?*
> *We've forgotten that we are our mothers' sons.*
> *We sow our threads, we pull our weeds–*
> *We have forgotten what it means to bleed.*
>
> *Blood drips from the sky like forgotten dreams;*
> *Of a melody once sang, soft and sweet.*

For once there was a vision of a unified sky,
Now eclipsed by the venom of all who've died.

What am I worth,
But the wills of men?
Why can't I fly?
Why can't this end?

This ballad is iron.
This ballad is stone.
This ballad is what–
I hope you take home:

We are not broken.
We are merely men.
We are all a bit broken—
But we can mend.

"What is that?" I whisper once she's finished, trying not to choke on the sob crawling up my throat.

"It is—" She coughs again, more blood driblets propelling from her lips. "A ballad."

"Does it have a name?"

"A Ballad for the Broken."

"It's beautiful," I murmur so low, I'm unsure if she even hears me.

"So are we. All of us. In all our brokenness."

Time passes in a near incomprehensible warp after that. I hold Neilina in my arms, tracing my fingers absently down her skin. At one point—though I'm not exactly sure when—I begin singing to her as she sang to me. I sing her the lullaby my mother used to hum when I was a small girl, barely old enough to spell my own name. I sing her a folk tune of a woman who enlisted in a battalion of men, determined to fight for her cause. I sing her another ballad about a lover lost at sea.

I sing and hum and cry. Until those wet, rattling breaths no longer echo in the too-still air. Until Neilina's unblinking eyes have lost their sun—open yet unseeing.

Once she's gone, I sit in an eerie silence. A silence that feels odd after filling it with somber music. Eventually, I kiss her forehead and somehow find the strength to detach myself from her, resting her head gently on the ground even though her body will never feel any sort of sensation ever again.

Firelight flashes in my mind.

I have to burn her body.

I'm not sure what Neilina believed—I realize now we never talked about it. But the common held belief is that in order for a soul to find its path to the afterlife, a fire must be lit to guide its way. I—I can't leave her soul trapped. Can't let it wander lost somewhere in the Great Between. So despite feeling the anguished defeat of futility, I again shut my eyes and reach for something I don't actually think will answer. Yet...

It does. Because of *fucking* course it's what answers me.

The connection is weak, the magic barely a hum in my veins, but...

It is there.

Dim tendrils awaken at my fingertips, and before they can fade away into the forming night, I throw the fire at Neilina, tears streaming down my cheeks as my body moves on something superseding my mind. Instinct, perhaps? I can't be sure.

Neilina's body brightens with the glow of vermillion and yellow, and I feel the familiar taste of grief on my tongue.

More flames, I think.

Like an old friend, numbness caresses me, beckoning me toward it.

To feel is to give power, my mind hisses at me. *It will carve you like a blade. Turn away from the fire before you get burned.*

I do no such thing.

I instead pull my trembling lip between my teeth and lift my chin. I stare deep into the face of the flickering glow, not conceding to my grief but not denying it, either. Not this time.

"In Death you walk. In Life I remain. Bound together, yet neither the same. Safe travels, weary soul. For I shall see you soon. But until that day, I'll give you life by remembering you."

I stay to honor her, holding steady while the grief claws at my chest and throat, hot tears spouting from my eyes. I do the same ritual for Ophelia, Luna, and Lythe.

I watch them all burn.

CHAPTER FORTY-SEVEN

LYRA

I wander the mosaic walkway toward the Abdites' living area, my eyes red and swollen, cheeks slicked with tears. My mind is full and hollow at once, leaving me to feel something akin to a carcass. A ghost. Yet right as I round the corner leading to the spread of circular stone buildings, I slam back into myself with a force so jarring, my knees buckle.

A man kneels at the center of the path, his undone headdress covered in sand and something which appears black and sticky. His brown hair is half-drawn. Eyes filled with moss and gold.

"Gray?" I press the heels of my palms into my eyes and rub, convinced that somehow between all the magic and grief, I am hallucinating. Yet when I pull my hands back, he is still there. Only, now he is standing, shoulders squared to me.

"Lyra." He doesn't waste a second, taking long strides to me, pulling me into his chest and consuming me with his arms as he embraces me. His hold tightens as he nestles his cheek against the side of my head. "Thank the gods," he whispers against my temple, pressing a kiss to it after.

As he holds me, it's like everything I have been holding falls free, and before I can even say a word to him, I instead sob into his chest, my fist clutching at his shirt while my knees weaken.

"You're okay," he soothes, cradling the back of my head with one hand and steadying me at the waist with his other. "It's alright. I've got you. I'm here." He drops his voice. "I'm here, Lyra."

I cry until it seems my eyes are no longer capable, my pores tight from all the salt they've just swallowed. I finally pull back from him, my chest tightened to the point of pain. "How is this possible? How—how did you *find* me?"

He studies me with soft eyes. "You left a dagger behind in Talderine, at Sagamon. It was like an Arellian blade, but forged differently. That, paired with the materials on the hilt, allowed me to work out your location pretty quickly."

"Which is?"

"The Arid Wastelands."

Shock rattles me—I never was told where this place is located—but the detail seems so unimportant now.

I choke on a manic, disbelieving laugh. "Only you, Gray Nightenjoy."

His smile is weak, seeming only capable of withstanding a second or two of use. "Lyra," he says, features sobering in a way that frightens me. "I didn't come alone. Draven is here. And his sister. And Captain Fjolla. We worked together to break the ward locking you in." He pauses, lips thinning. "I think there was a sort of mechanism built into it which forced someone attempting to destroy it to hallucinate with their worst nightmares."

My heart stops beating. The air dies in my chest. A terrifying, bone-clattering cold sweeps along my skin and down my spine. There is a gnawing in my gut, like an intuition of sorts.

The screams. There were so many screams in that blanket of darkness.

And suddenly, I *know* what he's about to tell me.

I was wrong before—it seems I am capable of more tears. My eyes are already blurring, warm fluids hot and raw as they brim over my lower lash line. "Tell me."

His face falls, and he pulls his bottom lip between his teeth. "I'm afraid I have to show you."

My brows pinch together, but before I can even get a word out, Gray lifts a trembling hand and twirls his wrist. Everything around us ripples and shatters, taking my surroundings from a garden of dreams to a destruction site of nightmares.

The rounded stone buildings are decimated, rubble strewn about the ground, glass from their domed roofs scattered in the mess. Trees have been knocked over. The mosaic walkways shattered and destroyed, the stone bridges connecting them blown away into the streams they once arched above.

Streams which are now black.

Bodies are littered around me, the condition of them entirely the same as Neilina's had been. I know the names of all of them. Recognize each and every one of their faces. So many unseeing eyes. So many paralyzed lungs.

Are there even any survivors?

"The moment I saw you, I threw up an illusion over everything. I just wanted to have a few seconds reunited without the stain of blood all over it."

My body seems incapable of fully processing what I'm seeing. "Did..." My voice breaks, and I swallow against the tremble in my voice. "Draven did this, didn't he?"

Gray's eyes wander behind my shoulder before refocusing on me. He nods. "Even in his own madness, he was attempting to save you from them."

"*Save* me?"

His eyes fill with confusion. "Yes," he answers, that one word slow and filled with a thousand questions. "They were mad, Lyra. Attacking us with corrupted magic."

"You invaded their *home!*" I shout. "Of *course* they attacked you." My hands ball into fists at my sides. "And they weren't mad," I whisper harshly. "I mean they were, at that moment. But not always."

He looks at me as though I am speaking another language. "I don't understand."

"The wards kept them sane, Gray. This was the one place they could be free—could live without their madness. And you tore that down, ripped it apart at its seams, then blamed them for how they were forced to react."

"I...we..." Gray's eyes again look over my shoulder, prompting me to finally turn around.

"What are you looking—"

My words die in my throat. There, slumped awkwardly against a tree, lies Draven.

I can't even describe the sound that gurgles from my lips. I'm not sure if such an ugly, fractured thing has a name.

I race to him, dropping to my knees by his side. A thin steam permeates from his clothes, with one arm stripped of any fabric completely. His skin nurses veins black as tar. They run through his arm, up his neck, spreading over his jaw and into his eyes.

"Draven," I murmur, the tears now spilling down my cheeks as I trace his veins with my fingertips.

Too much. I'm feeling *way* too much. Anger. Relief. Guilt. Grief.

His eyes flutter, head lolling in my direction. I nearly jerk back at the sight of his black eyes, so different from their usual brightness. Yet they seem to sharpen on my face, if only for a moment. A small smile tips his lips. "I came for you." He sounds tired. Like his mind is in a different world.

"I know," I whisper.

His brows furrow while his eyes fade in and out of focus. "I will always come for you." He reaches a hand out, but it falls short, plopping in his lap instead. He goes unconscious.

I sweep a thumb along his cheek. "I know," I whisper again, this time even quieter than the last.

"His eyes get like that sometimes," Gray offers from behind me. "It's what happened when he fought against Casimir Vivaldri as well. It's like his dark magic swallows him. It's...frightening, honestly."

I'm only halfway listening, my mind snagging on the name he just used.

Oh gods.

Casimir.

As the emotions continue piling in my chest, I can't even discern what they're for. Fear for what Casimir will do? Grief for what he's lost? Guilt because I'm basically the cause of all this? Shame because though my heart is breaking, though I'm staring into atrocity, I still can't help but feel a flutter of warmth at seeing Draven? Which of course leads to more guilt. More shame.

So. Many. Emotions.

"How did this happen?" I ask, dropping my hand from Draven's face and leaning back to put my weight on my heels. My low voice is a broken thing. "Why did he do this?"

"He thought he was protecting you," Gray answers. When I don't respond, he takes a step forward, crouching down beside me and resting a hand on my shoulder. "Tell me what is going on, Lyra."

Two figures suddenly emerge from the southern path. Hope blooms in my chest for all of a second, until I realize it is Finlay Fjolla and a girl I don't recognize. She must be Draven's sister.

I have no warm greetings to offer her.

"We finally found you," Finlay says, assessing the scene with cold vigilance. He merely arches a brow at all the bodies surrounding them. "What in the gods were so many Abdites doing all the way out here?" He asks the question with such detached curiosity. Like these bodies—*people*—are nothing more than curious specimens.

I want to spit fire in his icy face.

Draven's sister studies me, then steps forward and crouches down on the opposite side of Draven. "Is he okay?" She presses two fingers against his neck, feeling his pulse.

"He's fine," Gray answers for me. "Unconscious, but alive."

"We saw him lose control," she murmurs, gazing at her brother through tender eyes. "Well, we saw the consequences of him losing control, I should say."

"We watched his magic..." Finlay stops, searching for a word. "Well, truthfully I'm not even sure what to call it. Was anyone hurt?"

My swollen eyes whip to him. "Look around you," I say, disbelief coating my words. "How can you even ask that?"

He cocks his head at me, frowning. "All I see are Abdites."

I scoff, incredulous and disbelieving. Though, is it really so hard to believe, given what we are taught to think and believe about any and all Abdites?

"Lyra." Gray's voice beckons my attention, providing me with new focus. "Talk to me. What do you know that we don't?"

I shake my head, a weight sinking in my stomach on a repeated loop. "Later," I manage. "But for now, can you just…" I swallow against the swell of emotion in my words. "Can you all just go? Please?"

Gray's face is the only one I'm capable of looking at. It looks conflicted. Is filled with its own sort of pain.

"Please," I say again.

He sighs through his nose, nodding. "Alright," he agrees gently. "We'll take Draven and go up to the northern perimeter. I saw some plants there that might be useful."

Wordlessly, I offer a near imperceptible dip of my chin. Gray looks like he wants to say something else, but making the better choice, he simply does as I ask, collecting Draven with the help of Finlay and heading off in the opposite direction. Draven's sister joins them, glancing at me over her shoulder before she goes.

Her eyes are hardened, but there is empathy in them.

When they finally disappear, I mindlessly rise to my feet. My magic reaches out, happy and eager to sense familiar magics. Powerful magics. It is a feeling entirely at odds with everything else weighing down my muscles and clotting my heartbeats.

Not receiving an answer to the magic I need, I go from house to crumbled house, collecting items that will aid me. I gather a thick, wooden branch. Old cloths. I then pour remaining oils from lamps onto the cloths, tying them onto the branch with strategic knots. Then I find my final item: a matchbox.

When I light my makeshift torch, going from fallen to fallen and kissing them goodbye with flames, I sing the song Neilina sang while bleeding in my lap. I'm not sure why. Yet it pours from my lips, not needing to be understood right now, instead only needing to be felt. To be spoken.

I know she called it a ballad, but as I sing it, I can't help but notice it sounds like a lament.

I pause, allowing myself to stare at the forming river of fires, my chest tight.

Draven said he would burn the world for me, and he did. Here, right before my eyes, a world of its own burns.

The words once felt romantic.

Now they taste like ash and bile on my tongue.

———

NIGHT IS WELL on its way by the time I finish lighting each body on fire.

I searched and searched for survivors. I could not find a single one. It results in a winding string of glowing vermillion scattering like burning stars across the ground. Perhaps it might be poetic to honor death this way, after all. From stardust we came, between the ashes of what burns in the sky. To ashes we return, until we remerge into the stars as nothing but dust.

When I return to the main area from my trek down the southern trail, my body exhausted in so many more ways than one, I find a person kneeling at the center of the many ongoing fires, shoulders hunched and unmoving.

I know within an instant who it is.

I stop at the black-stained stream, dropping my torch into the tainted waters. Then I walk to Casimir, kneeling down beside him.

He does not say anything for a long, long time.

"What happened?" he finally asks, his voice both alarmingly steady and hollow.

I swallow, chewing at my cheek as my eyes watch all the smoke rise into the sky. The cloying smell which should not be familiar to me, but is, swims in the air. "They came for me." I don't elaborate. I know I don't need to.

"I see."

Casimir doesn't move. He just stares silently. Not speaking. Not raging. Just…frozen.

"Casimir, I…" I pause, biting down on my lip, not sure what to say. There is nothing I can say. Still, I try. "I am so sorry. This…this is…"

"This is what it always comes to," he murmurs, still not having moved an inch.

"This is *horrific*," I nearly sob. Tears prick my eyes once more, and I truly wonder how much more my heart can withstand and still beat.

"Yet it always comes to this, doesn't it?" He finally turns to face me.

I am gutted beyond the point of repair at what I see.

Every inch of his composure—every single muscle dictating his movements—shows a sullen acceptance for what's before him. But not his eyes. Gods, no. Confusion, shock, incomprehensible pain—it's all there. His eyes show someone who is beyond that of a broken man; they are of a broken soul. Lost. Forsaken. Beyond repair.

My bottom lip quivers at the sight. Just last night, he and I…we were laughing together. Discussing eating cake at dinner. He was thawing, his eyes warming.

Now he's more frozen than ever before.

"It always comes to this," he murmurs again, more for himself than me. "Murder. Persecution. It did centuries ago, and it continues to do so today. Nothing has changed, and it never will. Humanity is broken. It is flawed beyond repair. Corrupt, self-serving, and only attentive to the side of the narrative that is most comfortable to believe. The side that best serves power."

"Cas…" I reach for him, simply feeling like I want to hold him right now. Gods, he just lost everyone he loves. His entire family. How is someone supposed to reconcile that?

He shakes me off, his expression cold and empty as he refuses my touch. Wordlessly, while still staring at the crackling flames surrounding us, he reaches into his pocket and pulls out a dainty, leather-corded necklace. It has a small amethyst stone carved into the shape of a flower resting at the center. He barely glances in my direction as he slowly takes my hand. Casimir places the necklace in my palm, gently guiding my fingers to close around it.

"To replace the one you lost."

My heart squeezes violently in my chest. "Cas," I croak, all other words feeling lodged in my throat. "I am so sorry. I—"

He holds up his other hand. "Don't," he whispers, the harsh sound entering the world softly. He removes his fingers from mine, dropping them into his lap. "Go," he commands, the instruction a fractured rasp. "I won't come after you again. I have no reason to fight anymore. No need for you. You are…free."

"Please." Tears blur my vision. "I don't want to leave you. Not like this. Not after—"

"*Go*," he demands again, the word still a whisper yet booming through my skull as if shouted.

"Come with me," I say without thinking. I reach for his hand with my free one, and I squeeze, trying to bring him back from the void he's sinking hopelessly into. "Don't stay here alone. Don't isolate yourself from the world for two more centuries. You—you don't deserve that. There is good in you, and you have perspective. I have seen it on more than one occasion." The necklace practically burns against the skin of my palm while my silken training clothes sear the rest of me.

"'Good,'" he scoffs lowly. "What a fickle word." His eyes latch onto me, brutal and unrelenting. "You only now think I am capable of good because you began to understand what I was fighting for. If you had not, you would never deem me or my actions as 'good.'"

I don't let him deter me. "So let's help Solaya understand them too. Understand *you*. People need people. It's how we stay the path. Come *with* me."

His smile quivers on his lips. "I am sorry, darling, but I have bled and burned enough for those kingdoms already. I have no desire to help them understand. My only desire is to watch them choke on their own self-righteousness and burn by their own oil-drenched sins. To destroy each other with their very own hands."

"But—"

"Lyra." His voice is entirely devoid of warmth. Detached from any prior fondness he once used when uttering my name. "If you do not leave now, then my temper will snap, and I will show you how far removed from 'good' I truly am by slaughtering all those within my territory." His already frigid eyes somehow grow colder. "That includes you."

I fight off my tremor, lifting my chin instead. "You don't mean that."

"Test me then, if you are so keen on gambling with your life."

"Cas," I plead, ignorantly reaching for him again.

He jerks away. "*Stop* calling me that. Cas is dead. Cas has *been* dead. I was nothing more than an ignorant fool for allowing myself to forget that."

I make one last effort. My final, pathetic plea. "What if I said I need you? *Want* you in Solaya with me?"

"You don't."

"And if I said I care about you?"

His jaw sets in a hard line. Silently, with slow, rigid movements, he rises from the ground, dusting off his clothes. He only spares me a glance. "Then that was your mistake to make."

He walks deep into the sea of burning flames, disappearing behind the smoke.

PART III

THE BROKEN

CHAPTER FORTY-EIGHT

MARCELLA

"This doesn't make sense!" Marcella slams her fist against the wooden table. "Why is Josiah doing this?"

Kiran stares at the roaring hearth, his expression distant. *He* has been distant, smiling less and less over the passing month. There are dark smudges beneath his dulled eyes, no longer glittering like a sapphire stone but instead cloudy like some knock-off gem. Marcella thinks he may have even lost some weight, judging by the sharpness of his cheekbones and slenderizing of his shoulders.

She remembers him that day between the hills when they were all together, helping Lyra with her training. His body was lean and sculpted with toned muscle. He then used those muscles to make graceful, languid gestures. He had smiled lazily. Enjoyed himself against the expectations of a demanding world.

There is no enjoyment in his features now.

"Kiran?" she presses.

He snaps into focus, tearing his eyes from the hearth. "Sorry?"

Marcella fights against her urge to pinch her nose and sigh. "Why is Josiah mobilizing the Jurafen against the uprising? It's political."

"It's destructive."

"And we're supposed to be neutral!" She squares herself to him. "Let the people of Erandor overthrow their king. He deserves it. As does the King of Rivara. Let their people rebel. Let them fight back. We are not the king's force; we are here to protect magical order."

"They do not simply wish to overthrow their kings. They wish to unite Solaya under one king—one banner—once more."

Marcella snorts. "Maybe that's for the best. Let King Yarum rule it all. Have you not noticed how the Anatolé Kingdom has remained unaffected by all this chaos? How his people do not rebel against him? It is because he is a *good* king. A wise king. Let him have it all."

Kiran rubs at the space between his eyes. "Anatolé has forged its entirely own political system and climate. One that is vastly different from Rivara and Erandor—whose differences in their own laws are marginal, with their rule based on similar structures. To have Anatolé suddenly take over and ask so many people to assimilate to a government entirely different from the one they are used to is asking for more chaos and more civil war."

"So who are the people backing, then? Whose banner do they wish to see at the head of rule?"

Kiran's lips thin. He remains silent.

Marcella's eyes narrow. "You actually know, don't you?"

He bites down on his lip, chin jutting out in the opposite direction. He is saved from having to provide an answer when there is a knock at the door.

"Enter," he says gruffly, so at odds with the usual carelessness filling his words.

A man walks in, boasting Skyborne's colors. Marcella doesn't remember his name, but she does recognize his face. Has seen him around during her classes. He offers Kiran a curt dip of his chin. "Captain Sulien."

"What is it?"

"A missive has arrived for you." The man's eyes shift to Marcella. "And you as well."

"Me?" she asks, surprised.

He nods. "Yes. Both are sealed by House Fjolla's crest and are under strict instruction to be delivered directly to you both. I believe the word 'discreetly' was also used."

Kiran stiffens, looking terrified for the span of a heartbeat. Though just as quickly as it is there, it passes. "Bring it here," he instructs, holding out a stiff hand.

The man struts forward, passing off the envelope to him. He hands Marcella her own sealed envelope next.

Kiran stares at the item. "That is all," he murmurs, seeming distracted. "You can go now."

The man again dips his chin and turns for the door. Marcella stops him.

"Please keep this between us." She does her best to manage a tone that is not demanding but is also not a request. "It is important you do."

The man offers her an affirming look. "It arrived through a trusted network used only by Captain Fjolla. I assure you, your discretion will be maintained."

Marcella allows the words to settle inside her, deciding it will have to be enough. "Thank you."

The man goes, leaving behind a hanging silence.

"Should we open them?" Marcella asks eventually, her voice suddenly seeming two times louder than it was before.

Kiran, still staring at the unopened envelope in his hand, merely nods. Marcella decides that is answer enough and turns the thing over in her hand, inspecting the wax seal only momentarily before breaking it apart and tearing the envelope open. She pulls out three sheets of parchment, recognizing the handwriting on the first page immediately.

Gray.

She reads, clapping a hand over her mouth as she does. A choked sound somewhere between a laugh of disbelief and a cry pours from her lips. "Goddess's tears," she murmurs, awe and excitement and so much more bloating her voice. "They found her. They *actually* found her." A quick glance in Kiran's direction shows he is reading his own missive, his features drawn taut like a bowstring. She continues reading. Once she reaches the end of the first parchment, she pauses, again looking up at Kiran. "They're hiding in the Anatolé Kingdom, safe for now. They are forming their next move, deciding what to do about the Tani and Draven's father."

Kiran remains entirely inscrutable as he only again nods to acknowledge he's heard what she's said. He doesn't even look up from his own reading.

Marcella watches him for a beat longer before she sighs, forcing herself to move on. She tucks the now-read parchment behind the other two and moves onto the next sheet.

Another strangled noise exits her throat within an instant.

The handwriting on this page is different, but she recognizes it as well. It is more bubbly. Features more spacing between the curves of her letters.

This is Lyra's handwriting.

Marcella drops into the chair beside her, her heart fluttering like hummingbird wings.

Then she reads.

She reads about Lyra's desire for Marcella not to follow them to the Anatolé Kingdom, not wanting her to jeopardize herself or her position at Bathara. She reads her request to not use Ever-Know Quills right now, not knowing what the Tani is capable of intercepting. She reads what Lyra learned of Abdites. Of what her time away from home has taught her. She reads of her best friend's heartbreak. Of the new turmoil and conflict in her heart.

By the time Marcella finishes reading, she is surprised to realize a small stream of tears now slicks her cheeks. She presses the tips of her fingers against her salt-filled pores, looking across the room to Kiran, wondering what his missive must contain, given all that filled hers. He is standing at the hearth now, his features even more withdrawn than before. When she glances down at the flames, she's surprised to glimpse remnants of parchment caught aflame, sizzling apart into nothing more than ashen bits. Kiran watches, leaning with his arm draped over the stone mantle. He stares into the glowing space with dull eyes.

He says nothing. Offers her nothing.

So she says nothing more in return.

CHAPTER FORTY-NINE

DRAVEN

Draven stares down at the faded black lines still peeking from his veins, running like poisoned rivers beneath the skin of his forearms. He curls his fingers into his palms, using his nails to bite into his flesh. Eventually, once his eyes sting from staring for so long, he tugs his sleeve back into position and drops his hand down to his side, reverting his attention onto the splintered wooden door before him.

His heart pounds against the skin of his neck, shame already a sour taste on his tongue. Still, he cannot bear the distance any longer, so he musters up the nerve to knock, ready to face his rightful trial.

"Come in."

Draven opens the door and finds Lyra sitting beneath an open window, moonlight bathing her in graceful beauty. Her hair is half pulled back, her clothes loose and ill-fitting to her body. An issue they all have at the moment, having found their makeshift attire hanging on lines as they passed through backwater towns. Draven would have felt bad for taking another's clothing, but Gray always made sure their traveling group left behind at least three times what the items were worth for the owners to find. So at least the scales are balanced.

Lyra studies him with a withdrawn gaze, chewing at her cheek.

Her eyes drop to the ground just before she turns her chin away from him, back to the window. "I'm sorry, but I'm not ready to talk yet."

Draven would be lying if he said his heart doesn't deflate at the greeting. It's what she's said to him the other times he's attempted to talk to her about what he'd done in the Arid Wastelands.

He remembers most of what happened—breaking the ward, being fed his deepest nightmares, attacking the Abdites, fearing their threat to Lyra—though some parts feel more like a distant dream than an actual lived experience. Especially the parts where he remembers voices in his head, a part of him yet not. Voices which he, even now, still hears whispering to him. A voice of one but many.

We own you now.

They've been with him, petting his mind, from the moment his eyes fluttered open. They were already halfway returned to the docks at the northwestern corner of the Wastelands—where their original ship and crew were waiting to take them back to Halfin—when he woke up. He was disoriented at first. Nearly manic. But Lyra caressed his face and soothed him, making sure he knew he was alright—that he was safe.

It was the first and last time she has looked him in the eyes since getting her back. The only affection she has shown him since returning.

Draven approaches her, the floorboard creaking beneath his booted feet. The building they've holed up in is abandoned and barely clinging to life, with its cracked walls, creaky wood, and cobwebbed corners. But it has three stories and is tucked perfectly in the outer perimeter of Anatheima, leaving the loud, off-putting noises and cosmetic issues to be the least of his concerns. The very least.

He stops short of reaching Lyra, making sure to respect her space by not getting too close. "I will wait for as long as I must until you're ready to speak with me again, but" —Draven flexes his jaw— "I just need to make sure the day *will* come. That you won't forever look at me the way you are right now." He knows he sounds pathetic; he has ears, and they can hear the cracks in his voice.

He doesn't care.

Tell me I'm not a monster.

"Please," he murmurs, his hands so desperate to reach for her. "At least give me that."

Lyra does not answer him right away, instead continuing to stare at the moon. Draven sees the rise and fall of her shoulders as she sucks air into her chest, holding onto it like Draven clings to his hope.

Eventually, she turns her chin over her shoulder once more, glancing in his direction. In that moment, Draven knows he's a ghost to her. Her eyes look straight through him. "I think it's best if we just get some sleep. Alone."

Draven wants to push. Wants to apologize for the harm he knows he's caused. He nearly vomited when she told him the truth of those Abdites in the Wastelands. How they were purely innocent people. Collateral to a long-ago war. To power.

Yet he knows he doesn't have the right to do such things. Forgiveness is hers to give, and if she chooses to never offer it to him, such is her right. He will bear both the weight and shame of that, because the stain of blood is on his hands. He has to live with what he's done, despite his motives for doing it.

So no, he does not press his case. Does not try to barter or beg for her to listen. He instead does exactly as she asks, turning and going back to the creaky door. His hand hovers on the doorknob, and he allows himself to glance back at her. She holds her bottom lip between her teeth, eyes fixed with purpose on the twinkling night sky just outside the window.

With a new layer of weighted guilt now lining his gut, Draven tugs on the doorknob and exits the room. The moment the latch clicks behind him, someone kicks off the wall, emerging from the shadows.

Rhea.

"She'll come around."

"You don't even know her. You two have barely spoken a word to each other since meeting."

"But I know you. And I know if she doesn't recognize that what you thought you were doing was for her and her alone, she's a fool."

Draven bites down, flexing his jaw. "Don't say that about her, Rhea."

She closes the distance between them, resting a comforting hand on his arm. "I mean it. You're not a murderer, Draven, and I hate seeing her treat you like one."

He feels the hollowness in his gaze as he turns his chin to meet her eyes. "But I am, aren't I? How many lives have I taken? How many fathers have I robbed from their families?" His hands ball tightly at his sides. "She is right to look at me the way she does."

"You kill out of necessity," Rhea presses. "Only with purpose. You kill to protect the people you love."

"That's what everyone thinks about their own actions." Draven sidesteps Rhea. "If you'll excuse me, I need some time to myself."

CHAPTER FIFTY

LYRA

The sky is duller after Draven leaves the room.

And it was odd, the way my heart felt both lighter and heavier the moment he entered. So odd, the way my heart suffers from the same confusion after he's left. Terribly odd how I was so desperate to see him leave yet now ache insufferably for him not to go—for him to come back.

I know I need to speak with Draven soon. That I can't keep putting off the conversation. It's just…so…difficult to look him in the eyes right now and not see a murderer. To not think of him as the person who just slaughtered the people I'd grown to cherish. People I was beginning to truly know in ways which felt important.

I don't *want* to view him in such a light. In fact, on some level, I understand why he did what he did, and I don't entirely blame him for it. Yet the moment things grow personal, justifications and rationalizations change; the threshold one carries for cruelty suddenly lessens. It shouldn't. But it does. So my mind continues spinning webs of different narratives and thoughts, attempting to thread them together in new, digestible ways. Yet each time I think I've made progress, each time I am convinced I've discovered a path to forgiveness which makes sense, I remember holding Neilina in my lap, and I hear her song in my head.

I can't even bear to steal a glance at Draven after those moments. Those resurfaced images.

With conflict warring in my chest, I heave a sigh and remove myself from the spot I have been glued to for hours, staring absently at the changing skies. I need to talk through everything raging in my mind. All the venom and spite and pain stirring in my heart. Because I can't keep going like this, walking a tightrope between hate and forgiveness, waiting to be blown in a certain direction by some decisive gust of wind. I need to make sense of my thoughts. Decide where I stand; what is forgivable. I need perspective.

I need Gray Nightenjoy.

I FIND him sitting just outside the front door, cross-legged and with his double flute pressed to his lips. He is playing a sweet melody filled with melancholy—with longing. His eyes are shut, his body lost in the sound of his music—his unbound hair and baggy clothes making him appear so liberated and free. Like a traveling minstrel. When he finishes playing, I clap, a broad smile managing to find its way to my lips. Gray snaps his eyes open at the sound, a modest laugh escaping him once he sees it's me.

He rubs at the back of his neck. "How long have you been standing there?"

"Long enough to think what you were playing was beautiful."

Gray leans over, reaching for a silken cloth, and wraps his instrument back up. "It was an Anatolian folk song. It felt fitting, given we are hiding in the outskirts of Anatolé Kingdom's capital city."

"I thought you didn't know any Anatolian folk songs?"

His smile is fragile. "I do now." He doesn't elaborate, instead tucking the cloth into the leather satchel beside him, righting himself after and refocusing on me. "To what do I owe the pleasure?"

An amused smile sweeps over my lips, knowing Gray has probably already read me like one of his books. I extend my hand out to him. "Will you walk with me?"

"It would be my privilege." He takes my hand and rises, offering me his arm with a soft, close-lipped grin. I accept without hesitation, immediately looping my arm through his. At the contact, my fingers dig tightly into his bicep, like if I don't clutch onto him with everything I have, somehow he and I will be separated again while traversing only this small distance, and I will be forced to walk my path alone.

Gray guides me away from our abandoned hideout, down a narrow street leading to a small dirt road encased by stout houses and the occasional tree. Signs of life remain scattered about, lanterns lining the streets, some framing the old doors of older buildings. There are stools and baskets. Lingering sandals and the occasional play toy left on the ground. People are definitely within some of these homes, even if we have yet to see them.

"So," Gray says, bringing my thoughts back to focus, "what has prompted you to invite me on a late-night stroll?"

"It's not that late," I point out. "The moon only just peaked."

"Alright," he drawls with humor. "What has prompted you to want an early-night stroll?"

I snort a laugh, my amusement temporary. "Draven," I answer, voice dropping low.

Gray nods, as though expecting that. "You've been avoiding him."

"I've been trying to decide how I *feel* about him."

"Your feelings for him have changed?"

"No. *Gods* no. That would probably be easier to navigate than this. Instead of not caring for him, my heart *aches* for him. For everything to be alright with us."

"Why isn't it?"

I halt, dragging Gray to a stop with me. I drop his arm and turn to face him. "Because how *can* it be? He...*murdered* an entire group of people. People I was growing to care for. Innocent people who didn't deserve to die. Whose only crime was being born with the wrong veins."

"All to save you," he reminds me, voice stern yet gentle. "All to make sure you were safe." Gray pauses, eyes holding mine. "And he didn't know they were innocent, Lyra. None of us did. None of us *could* have known, because the information was kept from us."

Lead appears in the pit of my stomach. "Would you have done it? Killed an entire population just to save me? Abdites or not."

"In a way," he answers, voice unbearably soft, "I already have. We *both* have. At Bathara. In Foreigner's Valley."

"It feels different now."

"Because you knew better this time," he murmurs. "You knew *them*. We didn't, and so it seemed no different to us. It is for that reason I find it hard to persecute Draven with merciless blame."

My bottom lip quivers, forcing me to trap it between my front teeth. "Then who do I blame? Myself? Solaya? Casimir? Those who wore the mark of an Abdite and acted so terribly, making us fear them all? Tell me who to blame, because...I *have* to blame someone."

Gray is silent for a long time. "Maybe that's the problem. Everyone is always looking for someone to blame instead of trying to understand what broke in the first place. What created the problem."

The words sit heavy between us.

I bracket my hips with my hands and jerk my chin up to the star-laden sky. The silver light blurs and morphs as I press my tongue against my teeth. The musk-scented air is silent around us; the noise inside me is blaring.

"If it counts for anything," Gray continues, "I do think you will feel better if you talk to him."

I drag my eyes down from the sky and onto him. "And say what? That I'm angry at him for trying to save me? That it's hard for me to look at him and not see someone I cared for dying in my lap?" I scoff a bitter laugh. "How can I say that, when he did it *for* me? While also knowing I did something so similar and feeling this way makes me a hypocrite? When I know he *didn't* know any better? That he was just fulfilling his promise to always come for me. To burn the world to ash to save me."

"You can say it because you have a right to feel all those things, despite how conflicting they are. You can say it because if Draven is the man you think he is, then he will not turn away from you nor this conversation. You can say it because it is important to question the way of things after innocent lives are taken. You can say it simply because you want to, Lyra."

I draw in a loud breath through my nose, studying Gray intently. He's changed since I last saw him, despite somehow also being exactly who he has always been. My tense muscles loosen, and I release the death grip on my hips. "I missed you."

He smiles at me, reaching out to swipe his thumb across my cheek. "Likewise."

I lean into his touch, then sigh, expelling the remaining turmoil from my heart alongside the air from my lungs. I will talk to Draven. I will force myself to look at him, to tell him what I feel and to hear his response.

But first...

I loop my arm back through Gray's. "Shall we continue our walk?"

He cocks his head at me, his smile lopsided. "I thought you had an important conversation to get to."

"It can wait a little longer. For now, I'd like to finish our walk, and for you to finish catching me up on everything I've missed since being gone. Starting with how you're adjusting to your new-found fame." I elbow him in the side, chuckling.

When we docked at Halfin, we immediately began covering our tracks, staying in the shadows and sleeping only at sketchy inns known for their participation in illicit activities. We arrived at our decision to hide out in the Anatolé Kingdom while on the boat, but we also soon realized we wouldn't be able to travel there by foot, given the territories we would have to pass through.

Simultaneously, however, we did not trust traveling through any of Bathara's aether-wielders. Not even Klytis—who I still am shocked to know is now at Bathara—if only for his potential implication should anything go wrong. Not to mention, nobody has the slightest idea what the Tani is capable of monitoring. How their infamous Shadows always manage to track and find their targets. So we agreed to use only an aether-wielder who operates in the black markets. Someone who didn't know our identities and who is used to not asking questions.

It took us a few days before we were able to find such a person, and during one of those days in waiting, Gray and I went to the markets to gather some food, where a middle-aged woman from Ninmere recognized him, approaching us and calling him, "Lion of the Heart."

He had a lot of explaining to do after that. Which he did, as we packed our belongings and moved locations.

Gray rubs at the back of his neck with his free hand. "It's only in Erandor, really."

I shoot him a look. "If it's in Erandor, then it's in Rivara too. You know that." I bark a laugh. "I wonder what Sterling will have to say about it when we see him next."

Gray laughs, eyes dropping to the stone beneath our feet. "You know, I was at the Winter Solstice Ball in Talderine. I received a personal invitation and everything. Perks of the new fame, I guess."

My lips part with shock. "You were there? I was, too. I came with..." I pause, my throat tightening at the mention of him. "Casimir."

The flower-shaped amethyst strung on a fine leather cord flickers through my mind. I haven't had the heart to wear it. I barely know what to do with it. Therefore it remains wrapped in a cloth, tucked away in my bag, acting as nothing more than a painful relic.

"I know," Gray says, giving no indication as to whether he noticed my shift when mentioning the First Crowned Prince or not. "From what I gathered, we just missed each other. I think I was on the balcony when you arrived. It's where I was when the attack started."

The uprising attack. Another area where I am needing to be brought up to speed. It was easy to forget about when in Halfaria; it felt worlds away. But now I am back in that world, and with that comes navigating the mess of it. Knowing my place in it all.

A new face now flashes in my mind. An older man I had never known. I hear his carefully laid out reasons echoing in my ears.

Remember the fervent way he spoke for his cause. The realization it forced to dawn within me.

If I do not belong with them, and I do not belong with nobility, where, then, do I actually belong?

"What were you doing on the balcony?" I ask, shaking the thought from my head while my brain pins that line of conversation. Gray and I have discussed enough heavy topics for tonight. We can compare our notes on all that later.

"Talking," he answers, voice softening.

I glance at him pointedly through the sides of my eyes. "Talking to *who?*"

He tries to keep his smile contained. He fails. "Marcella. She was my date for the evening."

Though I try not to, I smile at him in that annoying way people do when they witness someone realizing something they've known for awhile.

Gray steals a quick look at me. "Stop looking at me like that."

"Like what?" I croon mockingly, batting my eyelashes at him.

"Like my smug best friend."

My grin widens. "I am smug, and I am your best friend. How else should I be looking at you?" We turn a corner that provides a partial view of the sprawling palace resting at the heart of Anatheima. Specifically, the tower dwelling in the clouds at the back of it. My eyes linger as I think of King Yarum—what he did for me that day during The Founding celebration.

The sound of Gray's voice has me snapping back to attention, and I make a forceful request to my brain to stop wandering around and *focus.*

"You should look at me like the world's biggest fool."

"Fool? Why?"

"Because," he says through a long-winded sigh, "to make a long story short, Marcella and I shared a bed at an inn during our first mission with Castaria, and she...well, she asked me to kiss her, and I told her I couldn't do that. Things became strained between us after that."

My brows kick up at that information. "Why would you tell her no?"

"Because you were gone, and she was grieving. Kissing your best friend after you had been abducted felt selfish. And then kissing a girl who was only just overcoming her grief for her last lover felt insensitive. I wanted to kiss her, Lyra. Gods, you have no idea how badly I wanted that night alone with her. But...I couldn't take it. Not when every moral voice in my head was telling me it was wrong."

I study him; the way his mouth tightens at the corners and his eyes turn downward. My expression softens. "You should tell those moral voices to be quiet sometimes," I poke lightheartedly, though being entirely serious.

He shakes his head, running his free hand through his hair. "Those voices are who I am, Lyra. Are what define me and my character."

"True," I say, nodding my agreement. "And your unyielding dedication to them makes you one-of-a-kind, Gray Nightenjoy." I tighten my grip on his arm. "But I think part of what makes a great person truly great is having strong morals and knowing when the right time is to bend them. It can be dangerous, building your house with nothing but black and white stones."

He is silent for a beat, considering what I've just said. "Maybe. Though I'm not entirely sure I'm convinced of that."

I laugh. "Fair enough." My head falls to rest against his shoulder, and I allow myself to take a moment to appreciate the warmth of this moment between us, despite the ice storm I've found myself trapped inside since leaving the Wastelands.

I have missed Gray. Have missed talking to my best friend.

Hair falls into my face, and he brushes it away from my eyes. "I like your hair like this by the way. It feels more you."

My answering smile is layered. "King Alastair was the one who always made me keep it long, you know."

"I know," he murmurs, reaching for my hand and sweeping his thumb over the back of it. "I remember when you got those sticky Gardner supplies caught in the ends of it and had to cut some of the length off. You couldn't walk straight when you returned from your summons that day, and you never attempted to cut your hair again after that."

A new heaviness piles in my muscles, but I refuse to let it drown me. Because *fuck* him. Fuck King Alastair and all he made me suffer. I am here despite his cruelty.

I squeeze Gray's arm just a little tighter. "I think I'm going to keep my hair short from now on."

"I think you must," he agrees, smiling. "Though to be clear, I think you could be balder than a babe and still be just as beautiful."

I snort a helpless laugh, ramming my elbow playfully into his side. "Alright, enough of that. Tell me, what else have I missed?"

CHAPTER FIFTY-ONE

LYRA

Night is nearly morning by the time Gray and I finish talking.

We discussed things. We laughed. We cried. We hugged. He told me all that happened at Bathara while I was away, and I told him everything that happened with me in Halfaria. Including my Veilreading abilities. He was shocked—stunned, even—but he also said he wasn't surprised, given everything else I can do.

I did not tell him about my final night with Casimir.

Will there ever come a day where you won't see me as a monster?

Perhaps.

No. I did not tell him anything about that. Of the way Casimir held my face with such gentleness. The way he gazed at me with tender eyes—a look which is difficult to reconcile belonging to him. I also exclude mentioning the necklace he gave me. That is all knowledge for me, and me alone.

I now find myself standing at the foot of a cracked wooden door, staring at the rusted hinges while I debate whether or not I wish to knock. He is probably sleeping. Most likely has already gone to bed. Still, I walked up three flights of stairs and down the moonlit corridor to get here, so might as well knock at least once.

My knuckles lightly tap the wood, barely hard enough to even make a thumping noise.

Draven opens the door within an instant.

It's the first time I've looked at him this closely in a while. His mismatched eyes are punctuated by dark bruises painting the bags beneath them, sunken like craters. His hair is disheveled, his jaw coated with black stubble. Draven's gaze is wild and desperate as it bores into me like a starved child doing its best not to dream. It is also haunted. Fractured.

He steps aside and pulls back the door even more. "Would you like to come in?"

I swallow, my throat already tightening. Wordlessly, I nod and enter the room. Unlike my own, the window in his is broken, a few glass shards remaining scattered beneath its sill. It allows a draft to chill the air, making me shiver with a cold which has layers.

Draven follows behind me, his hands shoved into the pockets of pants that don't fit him quite right. He permanently maintains about three steps of distance between us.

There is nothing but silence for long heartbeats. Until Draven finally says, "You're here."

I release a quiet sigh and turn away from the shattered window, finally facing him. "I am."

"And what should I make of that?"

"That I'm ready to have a conversation."

He nods, the faintest curve tugging at the corner of his mouth. "Talking is good."

My eyes fall to the jagged glass beneath the window. "Maybe not when you hear what I have to say."

"Yet I would like to hear it nonetheless." He glances at a fraying leather chair a few paces away. "Would you like to sit?"

"No. I'd prefer to stand, actually."

He nods, then walks across the room, lifting the chair effortlessly and resting it at the foot of the wall directly across from me. Then he sits down, folding his shoulders in, making him appear smaller in size than he actually is. He braces his elbows on his thighs and peaks his fingers together, watching me intently.

I allow my chaotic, grief-stricken thoughts to flow, not bothering to ease into them with a careful introduction or topic sentence. "There was a girl at Halfaria. She was only seventeen, the youngest member to ever join Casimir's personal guard. Gods, she was so proud of that. She helped me train. Helped do my hair and makeup, even when she didn't have to. She laughed with me. Helped guide me to better understand her people. And then she was taken from me. By you. By your magic." My chin wobbles, and I don't even try to hide it. "She died in my lap, singing of all things. *What am I worth, but the wills of men? Why can't I fly? Why can't this end?*" My voice dims. "That is what she sang with her dying breath."

Draven's jaw is locked tight, hands remaining frozen in front of his lips. "I thought they were mad and corrupted. I thought they *chose* to be that way."

"So killing them all was the only option even if they had? What about searching for a cure? What about rehabilitation?"

He shakes his head, the motion weak and slow. "In the heat of the moment, those alternatives didn't even occur to me. I was drowning beneath my own magic, put on edge by the nightmares the ward showed me." A muscle in his jaw flexes. "And I don't say that as an excuse—it is not an excuse. But it is a factor that played a role in what happened. I assessed a threat, and I acted against it."

"By murdering an entire population of people."

"How is it different from what I did at Foreigner's Valley? At Bathara? What we do as Jurafen?" He doesn't ask in a defensive manner—there is no bite or edge to his words. "How could I have known there were different types of Abdites if I was never given that knowledge before?"

"By remembering they were once people, too. By respecting the sanctity of life, regardless of who it belongs to. By not taking your experience with one person and blanketing it over an entire group." I look up to the ceiling, the words Gray said ringing through me. "But you're right: it is no different than what happened in the valley or at the academy. The only difference is now I know better—knew the people being slaughtered—and so now it *feels* different. Now, it hurts."

Draven watches me, remaining silent, as if sensing I have more to say. He is right; I do.

I pace, all of my many thoughts and emotions stirred up and clattering around inside me. "This very thing is the never ending cycle we've created for ourselves which allows me to understand how Casimir turned into who he is. Makes me understand why he believes there's no hope for humanity. We see differences, and we judge. We don't attempt to understand. To listen. Not really, anyways. We fight and rebel against each other—what we don't know—and we turn our misunderstandings into a perpetual cycle of violence." I halt in the middle of the room, my chest unbearably tight.

"I am sorry, Lyra. Please know how deeply I mean that. Had I known they were different..." He trails off, seeming to stop himself from saying he would have chosen differently. Because the terrifying truth is, if it came down to me or them, he wouldn't have, and we both know it. "It hurts me knowing I hurt people who mattered to you," he finishes instead.

The conversation Casimir and I had in that strange temple in the clouds surfaces in my mind. All that he said about justice, murder— the justification of it. I drop both my eyes and my voice when I muse, "Those lives lost are nothing more than a necessary means to an end, right?"

"I am sorry," he says again, raspy voice soft. "I thought I was saving you."

"But why does saving me mean you must persecute all of them?" I whisper, finally lifting my eyes from the ground to look at him once more.

His face pinches together, and he opens his mouth, but then closes it, lips thinning. "It shouldn't."

Silence lingers between us, heavy and uncomfortable in the way which it should be right now. Draven's head is bowed, hands folded against the tops of his knees.

"Her name was Neilina," I eventually say. "The girl I told you about. That was her name."

He doesn't move, save for the heavy rise and fall of his shoulders. I study him, taking note of the defeated hunch of his frame, the rigidity in his muscles. It pains me to see him like this, but in a way, I am also glad to see it. Not from some twisted sense of malice or pleasure, but because he is capable of feeling guilt and remorse for the loss of innocent lives. For the actions which brought their deaths about. To hurt is to be reminded of our humanness. To show remorse is to acknowledge that something precious was taken.

I go to him, pieces of the thorns in my heart remaining in the shadows behind me. I lower myself slowly to my knees, taking his face in both my hands and bringing his eyes to meet mine.

They are moist and rimmed by an awakening puffy redness.

For a brief second, I flashback to the hills surrounding Bathara, when I was walking with Kiran to meet Draven for training. *Let's just say there was the version of Draven that was supposed to exist, and the one that actually existed, and it was not in alignment with the version his father wanted. Growing up, Draven was soft-hearted, incredibly sharp-witted, quiet, and caring.* That's what Kiran told me that day, and now, watching Draven, I can see the whispers of such a boy. So much so, I almost feel like I may have met him once. Held his face exactly as I am holding Draven's now.

To the world, Draven was made to be hard, jaded, and sharp as a finely-crafted blade—forged in the blazing fires of Tynan Dalmar's will. But as Draven drags his glassy eyes to meet mine, I can see it so clearly. That inside his world, he is someone who wants nothing more than to love and be loved—to live quietly, away from the heat of politics and decisions which erode one's soul. Someone who has suffered great loss and is scared to suffer it for someone he loves again. On the outside, he is ruthless. On the inside, he is frightened.

I can see it so clearly now.

Draven pushes his tongue into his cheek, blinking back unfallen tears. "So you knew their names?" he asks after a passing silence, filled with nothing more than our syncing heartbeats.

Grief claws at my heart, air trapped by a lasso around my lungs. "Every single one of them."

"Will you tell them to me?"

"All of them?"

He nods, the gesture nearly imperceptible.

My chest is so tight, it feels like my sternum may collapse from the weight of my own heart's making. "I will."

I expel some of the weight through my lips, clenching and unclenching my hands at my sides. Then, with a newfound steady calmness I have not felt since leaving the Wastelands, I say their names.

Every last one.

THE SUN CRESTS on the horizon by the time we go to sleep.

There is a bedroll near the wall farthest from the broken window. After hearing every name, after more words and a few more tears, Draven escorts me to that bedroll. My mind and body are a plundered thing, so I do not protest before dropping down onto the thin material. My eyes flutter, tempted to close the moment my head falls against the upper flap. But I hear Draven's feet shuffle, prompting me to force them open a while longer. He is bent at the waist beside me, draping an extra blanket over my body. When he starts to rise, I reach for his hand.

"Sleep beside me."

His throat bobs before he nods. He goes to the corner, gathering a few more tattered blankets. He spreads them on the ground beside me, then strips the combat boots from his feet. He lays down on his pallet, and I lift up the blanket he draped over me, inviting him into its warmth. He nestles beneath the fabric, pressing his firm chest against my back, reaching for me and swallowing my torso with his arms.

Draven drags me back against him, and we become two halves finally finding their whole. It feels like every hollow space between my ribcage and sternum is being gripped by fists, my heart an erratic flutter in my chest. Yet the sensation is so different from all the other times before. This is a swelling inside me which seeks to tear me apart and rebirth me in something new. I can feel it so keenly—the way my heart is already accepting the permanence of such powerful, immovable feelings. The kind which supersedes one's self—becomes bigger than what one's body feels capable of containing, threatening to burst open at any given moment.

They mingle and coalesce with the lingering sadness. With the forgiveness and acceptance I offered Draven at the end of our conversation. Everything isn't suddenly better, but I recognized my two choices as we talked: either I choose to forgive him, or I don't. And after seeing him hold so much remorse, after watching him listen so intently as I told him the names of every lost soul—after considering my own actions at Bathara; my own choices which led me there—I knew which side of the line I was on.

So now as he holds me, as he strokes my skin mindlessly and tightens his other hand around my waist, I am a conglomeration of all that I was, am, and could be. A mess of dissonant feelings. Perhaps what makes me most proud of that statement is the way I know what those feelings are. The fact I have learned how to navigate sitting with them, processing them.

I interlace my fingers with Draven's, squeezing his hand before letting it fall back to rest near the base of my stomach. He shifts to press a kiss to my temple. When he stills, I nestle more securely into the crook of his arm.

Our chests fall into a steady rhythm.

Right as sleep reaches its mystic fingers for me, Draven murmurs against my ear, so softly I nearly don't hear the words, "I am not a good man, but you make me want to be a better one, Lyra."

Emotion swells into my throat. "That admission alone might make you one of the best men I know."

He hums, stroking my hair with his fingers. "You are the best thing I have ever known." The words come out slow and rolled, almost how one speaks while drunk.

They are his final words before sleep claims him.

His fingers still, and I listen to the gentle tune of his breathing. It is my companion into the dreamland, a welcome melody.

And as I drift off, I feel the vital piece missing from me finally click back into place.

———

CHAPTER FIFTY-TWO

FINLAY

Finlay stares down at the ink blot bleeding into the parchment, seeping through the fibers like an infection. The quill is limp in his hand, the sun blinking awake behind him. His breath is shallow and trembling against his lips as he considers and reflects.

Is he really going to send this letter to Master Cahlmon, going against his brother for the second time and betraying his trust by leaking their whereabouts? Is he really going to turn in the girl who Draven has chosen to attach his life to?

Finlay himself doesn't particularly care about her. He doesn't even particularly like her. Yet against all odds, he's grown to respect her over their time of travel. Despite her common blood and lowborn status—a fact of which has been feeling less and less relevant.

Truthfully, it is as though leaving the Wastelands behind and seeking refuge in the Anatolé Kingdom with Lyra Izacalli—hell, with *all* the nontitled lot of them, really, seeing as Draven and Finlay are the only true purebreds—made something shift inside him. As though after everything he's experienced and felt since the Winter Solstice has accumulated into a small seed, the kernel planted deep in his gut, and he can no longer ignore the way it is blossoming.

Or perhaps it wasn't an accumulation at all.

Perhaps it is just one simple thing. One person.

Images of Rhea wrapped in his arms, pressed tightly against his chest, appear in his mind. Images that remind him of the way he nestled into her, haunted and desperate to feel something good after the ward forced him to swallow such searing pain. Images that remind him of how his heart stuttered in his chest while holding her. Of how right it felt to have her in his arms. A moment which they have yet to discuss or acknowledge, instead seeming to pretend like it never happened at all. Still...

He knows what Rhea would say about his decision should he send the letter containing their coordinates. Their plans. She would hate him for it—more than she already does. If he sends this letter, she would never forgive him; he would be truly irredeemable in her eyes. In Draven's, too.

The terrible ache the thought causes in his chest is not lost on him.

Yet he also knows what his father would say to him. What his father would tell him to do. And if news of Finlay being the one to hand deliver Lyra's whereabouts to Bathara ever reached his father, especially after the small nod of approval he received during the masquerade ball, he may finally be welcomed back home. May finally experience what it feels like to have his father look at him with something other than hatred and disdain in his eyes.

But the cost...

Finlay drops his head, the weight of what he must do pressing against his sternum as he sees his paths diverging so clearly from all that he wants. It screams at his instincts. Dismantles every carefully laid stone built into his foundation. He knows better. Knows he should not do what it is he is about to do.

It's hard to feel like you're enough when the only proof of love you've ever had is reliant on what you can or cannot give.

Finlay rights himself, realizing what it is he must remember. He tightens his grip on the shaft of the quill, his features smoothing out with acceptance, his eyes now lined with resolve.

He hunches over the desk, and he writes.

CHAPTER FIFTY-THREE

LYRA

The following days come and go peacefully. Anticlimactically, even.

I'm not sure what I expected, exactly, being on the run as Solaya's arguably most-wanted "criminal," but it certainly wasn't long days spent bathing in a warm sun and nights spent in Draven's arms, unbothered and at ease.

Well, save for the night I realized he might actually still be engaged. That night was a headache. I was tucked into the crook of his side while his sleepy fingers traced my skin, and without warning, I jerked up, accidentally smacking him hard in the nose with the back of my head. Blood streamed over his lips, and he had to tip his head back, pinching the bridge of his nose. Now, I am woman enough to admit my next actions were…petty, at best…but I couldn't help but be incredibly irritated that he had told me *nothing* about Arden, about his engagement, and about the current status of it.

"Are you still engaged?" I asked him out of nowhere, my hand on my hip while I wielded my attitude like a blade.

"What?" he replied, his voice nasally and high-pitched from pinching his nose.

"Are. You. Engaged."

"No," he answered, somehow managing to scoff a soft laugh. "I refused my father's wishes just before I left Sagamon Castle the night of the ball to find you."

"And Arden? Does she know that?"

He shrugged. "I can't be sure what they did or didn't tell her. Though I made my feelings on the engagement very clear from the beginning."

My pettiness knew no bounds that day it would seem, because I lifted my chin and said, "And those were?"

Despite his potentially broken nose, he still managed a smirk. "That my heart and my body will always belong to another."

I smothered my grin, approaching him with a newfound satisfaction. "Oh? And who is she?" I grabbed a scrap of fabric and removed his hand, blotting the blood away. "Sorry, by the way. It was an accident."

Draven laughed. "She is someone you don't want to piss off—she'll break your nose if you do."

"Sounds like a real catch," I chuckled.

His grin turned crooked. "She is."

I flashed him a knowing smirk right before reaching out with my magic, incredibly grateful for all the training I received from Casimir the moment I was able to identify and pull on healing magic. I fixed his nose with a careful wave of my hand, and his eyes had gone round, then heavy-lidded.

"You truly are full of surprises today."

We did not leave our bedroll for the rest of that night. Instead, Draven placed strategic kisses on my lips, down my neck, shoulders, and belly. Until he reached my thighs, where his kisses turned firmer —more desperate. Where he then slowly helped guide them apart, only making teasing strokes and touches over my trousers, driving me to a point of near insanity.

But we did not take it past that, despite the nearly inhumane ache I felt to have his bare body against me, thrusting while I clawed at his skin. We *still* haven't taken it past cruel teases. The walls in our hideout are crumbling and parchment thin, so we decided we would wait for a more suitable place. One where we won't have to muffle our sounds, control our impulses, or worry about splinters from torn-up floorboards pricking our skin.

Which…is probably for the best. I never have imagined my first time with Draven being on a bedroll in a dilapidated building while his sister, my best friend, and Finlay Fjolla hover gods-only-know-where.

That night had been nearly two weeks ago, and it is the outlier to the many other repetitive days. Days which quickly became routine. Days I grew to expect.

So imagine my surprise when Gray and Rhea strut into the lowest level of our hideout, arms filled with fine clothes, some jewelry, and perfume, and drop it all onto the chipped table at the center of the room, scattering it about like uncovered treasure.

"What's this?" I ask, thumbing a piece of dyed fabric.

"Clothes," Rhea answers, her dry sarcasm mindless.

I lift a pointed brow. "I gathered that."

Her eyes rove up from the covered table, seeing my look. She shrugs. "You'll get used to my sarcasm."

That makes me laugh. It also makes me feel oddly warm. Rhea and I have talked a little bit more now, getting to know each other at a basic level, but there is still much I have to learn about her and she about me. Yet I like the idea of getting used to her sharp edges. I especially like the implication of her words. As if to say, *I am not going anywhere, and you're not going anywhere, either.*

"This is an assortment of traditional Anatolian festival clothes," Gray answers, crossing his arms and bumping his shoulder into Rhea in silent reprimanding.

She glances at him sidelong, huffing.

Unlike her and me, Gray and Rhea have spent large amounts of time together since arriving in Anatheima. They get along well—though, it's hard not to get along with Gray. They train together during the day, and they have picked up the habit of playing cards in the evening, after Draven and I have gone off to sleep.

From my peripheral, I glimpse Draven and Finlay coming down

the narrow staircase. They are chattering about something, but cease the conversation once they reach us.

Draven sweeps his eyes across the table. "What's all this?"

Finlay gazes at the contents, choosing to stand directly between Draven and Rhea, remaining quiet while his icy features are stoic as ever.

"Festival attire," I chirp.

"Festival attire?" Draven questions, brows lifting in a curious way. "Is it now?"

My face pinches together, and I turn to study Gray. He is trying too hard to look casual, made evident by the way he won't meet my eyes, scanning the room with a forced leisure.

"What's going on?" I drawl slowly, my gaze bouncing between the two men.

Gray's sweeping smile is filled with excitement while Draven's is helpless and tilted. Yet before either of them can answer, a noise rustles from outside, near the front entrance.

The air in the room immediately changes.

"Everyone stay inside," Gray instructs, his voice dropping low. "I'll cast an illusion and go—"

Before he can finish his sentence, a cloaked figure appears from around a shadowy corner, pressing something cold to my throat while jerking me back against them. They don't feel much taller than me, but from the stern way they handle me, I realize the person behind me is *strong*.

Dread piles in my veins. Is this one of the Shadows? Has the Tani already found me?

Rhea's daggers are out within a second, and Gray, after reaching for a sword he quickly realizes is not there, unfurls his fingers from his palms and stretches his hands out in front of him while golden light pools at their center. Finlay is quick with his ice, trapping the cloaked figure by the feet. It bites at the person's ankles, rising up their calves and to their thighs.

To my surprise, Draven hasn't moved, instead only crossing his arms and tilting his head at the person behind me. He looks...amused?

What the hell?

He holds up a hand to Finlay. "No need for that. You can release her."

Her? How does he know it's a woman when she's cloaked? And why the hell is he telling Finlay to let her go?

I hear more than see the ice as it fractures and splits away, releasing my captor. I feel her adjust behind me, the object—thicker than I once thought—repositioned against my throat.

"Who are you?" Gray demands.

Draven's mouth is twisted with a half-formed smile as he seems to wait with anticipation.

"Show your face," Rhea growls next, shifting on her feet as her eyes dart to Draven, her confusion at his lack of urgency scribbled plainly in her features.

"Alright, alright," a voice I recognize with the utmost familiarity drawls from behind me. "Tough crowd."

The person releases me, then takes a step backward. I whirl around to watch her drop her hood. I see copper hair twisted back in a braid. Bright cobalt eyes. Freckles and a wickedly sharp smirk.

"Marcella," I practically squeal as I launch myself at her. She meets my embrace with an *oomph*, squeezing me back with a bout of laughter. I pull back from our hug, my eyes welling at the sight of her. "What in god's veins are you doing here?" I pause, shoving her shoulder. "And what the hell were you holding to my throat?"

She lifts the item up for everyone to see. "It was a cucumber I found outside. I thought it'd be funny."

My jaw drops, bubbling laughter spilling from my lips. "Only you," I say, shaking my head.

"Only me," she agrees through her grin.

"And as to what you're doing here?" The question comes from Gray, resulting in both Marcella and me swiveling our attention to him.

Someone who doesn't know Gray as well as I do would probably think him mad right now. Would probably assume the accusation in his eyes and the thin, hard line of his lips surely mean he is unhappy about Marcella disregarding the request of my letter to not follow us. To stay at Bathara, safe and without implication.

But I see right through it.

I see the hollowness in his mustered anger. The way he attempts to paint a mask over his face to tell a story which isn't true. I see the softness surrounding the hard line of his lips. The glimmer of joy and relief behind the mirage of irritation in his eyes. I see the way his hands are twitching at his sides, as if they already want to reach for her. The way he is leaning forward, as if his body can't help but gravitate in her direction.

No, he is not mad in the slightest. Though he clearly would like her to believe he is.

"I came because I wanted to." She reaches for my hand and laces her fingers through mine. Her tone leaves no room for argument.

There is a passing silence in the room as everyone seems to process. Until Rhea frowns and asks, "How the hell did you find us?"

"Not to mention how she snuck into our current residence without anyone noticing," Finlay adds, folding his arms, eyes still locked on Marcella.

"To be clear," Draven says, "I knew she was coming hours ago, when I first sensed her magic."

"And you didn't think to say anything to anyone?" Rhea mutters.

He shrugs. "I wanted it to be a surprise for Lyra."

A surprise it is, indeed.

Marcella points at the ceiling, her smile wide and proud. "And I snuck in through the broken window upstairs. I wanted to make a memorable entrance."

"Right," Rhea drawls slowly. "But how the hell did you *find* us? If I'm not mistaken, everyone here agreed not to tell anyone our precise location, outside the exception of telling you and Kiran we were in the Anatolé Kingdom. So how is it you managed to discover our hideout —in Solaya's largest kingdom, no less—in only a couple weeks with nothing to go off of?"

"I tracked you the old fashion way."

"*Tracked* us?" Rhea's jaw nearly comes unhinged. "This far?"

Draven and Finlay exchange wary glances, and I press my lips together to stifle my growing laughter while Gray shakes his head.

"I wouldn't question her tracking abilities," he advises Rhea. "If she says that's how she did it, then believe her."

Rhea lifts a pointed brow. "But you realize how hard that is to believe, right?"

Marcella waggles her eyebrows. "Not if you knew me better." Her eyes snag on the table, then, and she walks over to inspect the clothing. Her excitement suddenly doubles. "Oh! You guys have festival clothing. Does that mean you're going—"

In a flash, a shadow panther appears right in front of her face, its glowing violet eyes making the words die in her throat. "Do not finish that sentence," Draven says. "We haven't told her yet."

Curiosity pouts my lip. "Told me what?"

Draven traces his jaw, sighing. "Nightenjoy? I promised you could be the one to do it."

My eyes whip to Gray, anticipation fueling my rapid heartbeats. "Gray?"

His smile is soft as he picks up a cream two-piece clothing set from the table and brings it to me. "Given everything that's happened since the winter solstice, I don't expect you to have fully realized we're just over two months since its passing."

Gods…has it really already been that long? With everything previously on my mind, now paired with the slow-moving days, I truly wasn't the least bit aware.

"Okay," I drawl, still unsure where this is going. "And that matters because…?"

Gray hands the clothes to me, a peculiar, knowing glint resting in his gaze. "Because we are currently on the outskirts of Anatheima—Anatolé's capital city—just over two months after the winter solstice."

I glance down at the clothes now in my hand, realization dawning on me. "Oh my gods," I breathe, an excitement so sharp rippling through me, I'm almost frightened to feel it. "Oh my gods!" I say again.

Draven steps forward, resting a gentle hand on my lower back. "That's what Gray and Rhea were doing this morning. They went into the market to find appropriate attire so we can all seamlessly blend in with the people of the Golden City."

I shake my head, suddenly in a fever dream. "How did we even afford all of this?"

Finlay spares only a glance in my direction. "You're welcome."

I laugh with disbelief. "You did this for me?"

"It wasn't just for you," he replies, his eyes finding Rhea before quickly darting forward, as if realizing they were looking at something they shouldn't be. His mouth tightens at the corners as he folds his arms over his chest.

And at the observation, I remind myself I don't pry into other people's business.

"I almost can't believe it," I say instead, scanning the many items strewn about on the table.

Marcella steps up to my side and drapes an arm over my shoulder, smiling. Gray steps forward to my other hip and does the same.

"Believe it," he says softly, a wide grin sweeping across his lips. "Because it's happening. Tomorrow, you will finally achieve your life-long wish. You *will* attend the Ardoris Comet Festival."

CHAPTER FIFTY-FOUR

LYRA

Since I was a small girl, I dreamed of the day I would see Anatolé Kingdom's legendary Golden City, also known as the City of Golden Wishes. I lived out stories in my head, imagining the one-of-a-kind comets gliding through the red sky. I fantasized about them. Romanticized them. Anticipated the day I would stride through the glittering streets of the festival, free of a gilded cage and a king who suffocated my autonomy with tightened fists. Yet for all my dreaming—all my many wishes upon the colored stars—I never truly believed the day would come.

Now here it is, unfurling before me, my tedious freedom nothing like what I expected, yet more crisp and rich than I could have ever hoped for it to be.

Children run through the limestone streets, parading flags with trailing ribbons meant to resemble the tails of comets. Music awakens the air, filled by the sounds of jubilant lutes, flutes, fiddles, and more. People draped in colorful fabrics crowd every corner of the capital city, congregating mostly in the main market area, circling around a five-tiered golden fountain spitting sparkling water. In the market square, there are rows and rows of colorful booths, lined by brightly dyed tapestries, colorful trinkets, stained glass artwork, and troves of golden jewelry. They are accompanied by food stalls boasting the mouth-watering smells of savory meats, seasoned vegetables, fluffy bread, and even fine desserts.

I stop at one such booth, my cheeks sore from wearing a beaming smile for hours on end now. Draven leans forward beside me, his arm maintaining the loose hold it's kept around my waist while he inspects the table.

"Two coins for two comets," the older stallman says, his words carrying the melodic long vowels indicative of Anatolian origins.

"What is it?" I ask, not caring I carry the excited tune of a curious child.

Wedged securely into a rectangular tray with small holding spaces, a cone made from what appears to be batter is shaped into a comet's tail, where scoops of sky-colored ice cream round out the shape. It is topped by glimmers of something sparkly, making the cone glitter like the stars themselves.

"Comet's Dust," the man answers.

"We'll take two," Draven says, dropping two coins into the palm of the man's already outstretched hand.

He hands over the cones. "May the Divine guide you this festival. *Sahtalla.*" He positions his thumb at his forehead and curls his fingers inward, leaving out only his pinky, and makes a short gliding motion forward.

Draven extends his thanks and turns to leave, but I linger, the curiosity paired with my desire to soak everything in overtaking all else. "What does *Sahtalla* mean?"

The man scratches at his chin, considering. "It is saying of my people, which makes it hard to translate to common tongue. But it means something like, *You are soul, and so you are love; let the soul water the garden, for the eyes only bring thorns.* It is word we say to kin and strangers alike. It shows respect to the soul of person above all else."

"Am I able to show respect by saying it?"

The man smiles. "You are soul, are you not?"

I beam, then form my fingers exactly as the man had, positioning my thumb right at the center of my forehead. "*Sahtalla*," I say, mirroring the motion he made.

"*Zentati*," he replies. "I see you and your garden."

I dip my chin at the kind man, still smiling as I offer him a small wave as I turn to go. Draven watches me through tender eyes, a deep curve tugging at his lips.

"What?"

"Nothing," he says, eyes glittering. He nods toward the cone in my hand. "You try it first."

I don't take much convincing, immediately licking the ice cream in a way which probably resembles something more like a horse than anything else. The chilled texture melts on my tongue, and it tastes similar to vanilla, but with a richer, nuttier flavor. It tastes like divinity.

My shoulders slacken, and I tip my head back while an obnoxious moan escapes me. "By the gods, this is *delicious*. I've never tasted anything like it before."

Draven's eyes become heavy-lidded, and he reaches his free hand for my waist, tugging me against him. He drops his voice into a low whisper. "I've tasted something better, and hearing you make that noise is making me think of tasting it again. So unless you want that to happen in the shadows of some alleyway, I'm going to have to ask you to not make such noises in front of me until we're alone."

My body catches fire. Yet before I can say anything, I hear a familiar female voice joke from behind me, "Do you two ever keep your hands off each other?"

I turn to see Marcella and Gray approaching us, Marcella's festival outfit now completed with arm jewelry, bangles, and a new headpiece featuring a blood-red gemstone hovering just above her brows. Her copper hair is free and roaring with curls, making her resemble some fierce, warrior goddess. From beside her, in his own boastful display of fine fabrics and gems, Gray looks like royalty. Together, they blend into a visual exuding power and elegance.

They stop just a few steps short of Draven and me, and Marcella rests a hand on her popped hip, a sharp smirk tilting her lips. Draven watches her with his own pointed smirk, a simmering challenge flaring in his eyes as he remains silent, taking a bite out of his own ice cream. His hand remains pointedly planted on the curve of my waist, as if daring her to ask him to remove it.

I roll my eyes and elbow him playfully before turning my attention onto Gray and Marcella. "What took you two so long? I thought you left us to get jewelry?"

Gray folds his arms, throwing his head toward Marcella. "She wanted to compete in an arm wrestling competition."

My brows fly up my forehead. "And?"

Marcella shrugs, inspecting her nails. "I won."

"Of course you did," Draven deadpans.

She snaps her eyes up to him. "Wanna give it a go sometime?"

He again takes a bite out of his ice cream—seriously, has no one taught him you are supposed to *lick* the damn thing, not use your teeth? "You don't actually think you're capable of beating me, right?"

"Never know if you never try."

He studies her. "Alright," he drawls after a moment, eyes crinkling. "How about right now, then?"

She flashes him a wicked grin. "Let's do it, pretty boy."

He snorts, passing off his ice cream to me. "Would you mind holding this for me? I'll only need a moment."

Now it's my turn to laugh. I accept the cone and watch them wander to an empty barrel, where they prop their elbows up on the flattened top and clasp hands, fire dancing in both their gazes. Gray steps forward to stand at my side.

"It feels like so much has changed while I've been away," I muse tenderly to him, my lips twitching at the sight of Draven and Marcella as her tongue pokes out of her mouth and Draven counts down from three.

"How so?"

I chuckle, bringing Draven's ice cream to my lips while mindlessly offering my cone to Gray, who surprisingly accepts and immediately goes in for a taste. "Let me think," I begin, my tone theatric. "You're now known as 'The People's Champion.' Draven and you have become friends, despite the odds. He and Marcella also appear to be friends now. We are traveling with Finlay Fjolla—like *that's* normal—and we've been spending time with Draven's sister, who we didn't even know existed a short while ago, who also happens to be sharper than a blade's edge. Not to mention, here you and I are, walking the streets of Anatheima during the Ardoris Comet Festival, just like we always dreamed of as children." I pause, shaking my head. "I just… gods, it is so hard to reconcile the past with the present sometimes. To accept the good as it comes without overthinking it."

Gray wraps his free arm around my shoulders and pulls me into his side. I rest my head on his shoulder, and he presses a kiss to my temple—his silent answer to everything I've said.

We watch in silence as Marcella's face reddens and twists while she grits her teeth, pushing against Draven's arm with all her might. Draven merely watches her without breaking a sweat, smiling smugly.

It makes me smile in turn. "He seems happier."

Gray nods, a soft laugh escaping him. "It's hard to imagine the version of him we met that day in the valley now, isn't it?"

"Gods," I say through an amused scoff, "you have *no* idea."

A vein bulges in Marcella's neck as she continues pushing against Draven's hold. He's just toying with her now.

My expression softens. "People think him impenetrable and cruel —hard and unfeeling. But that's not him at all. Cruel people do not mourn the innocent lives they took. Unfeeling people do not touch another as he touches me." I watch Draven teasingly smirk at Marcella as he holds her at bay, his eyes crinkled. "Kiran told me once that he was incredibly soft-hearted, and at the time, I found that so hard to believe. But he truly is just that, isn't he? Despite the terrifying magic, despite his hardened exterior—he is nothing more than a soft-hearted boy who loves hard."

Gray glances down at me. "People have a way of surprising you when you offer them a chance to show you their deepest selves."

"Yeah," I murmur, my smile blooming like petals warmed by a pleasant sun. "I suppose they do." I lift my head from his shoulder so that I can meet his eyes. "Speaking of, when are you going to talk to

Marcella? I'm back now, and I think it's safe to say she has grieved how she needed to, so there should be no reason why you haven't told her how you feel yet."

Now it's his turn to grin like a smitten fool. "You're right. Which is precisely why I plan to tell her at sunrise tomorrow."

"Sunrise? Why not tonight, during the comet shower?"

"Because I once told her the sun would shine again for her, and so it only feels right."

I watch him as he gazes at Marcella, his expression filled with the same honest admiration and loyalty as a puppy. I shake my head, laughing quietly to myself. "You are quite the romantic, Gray Night-enjoy. I have to give you that."

"No," he counters, voice soft. "I am simply a man who has decided he can't think of any greater happiness than the one standing right in front of him."

Marcella does not beat Draven in arm wrestling. In fact, of the four times she demands a rematch, she does not even come close to winning over him a single time.

I hope she knows how richly she's still won.

CHAPTER FIFTY-FIVE

LYRA

On and on the celebrations continue. Food stuffs my belly to the point of discomfort. Sweets linger on my taste buds. There is dancing, singing, and clapping. Stomping while strings are plucked with endless tunes. And laughter. So much laughter.

Rhea and Finlay still haven't returned to our group yet. Once we entered the festival's main area, Rhea went off to explore by herself, and Finlay, without a word of instruction or parting, turned immediately to follow her, keeping a few steps' distance between them as he went. Now, as the rest of us wander the streets with only a small amount of time left before the comet shower—Marcella's arm looped through my own while Draven and Gray trail behind us, talking—I can't help but wonder where the two of them are now. What they've gotten themselves into.

I am so lost in that trail of thought, I barely notice the person standing right at the corner of a merchant's stall. I accidentally bump into her, pushing her into the table.

"Oh my gods," I say, immediately dropping Marcella's arm to help the woman. "I am so sorry. Are you alright?"

"I am fine, please do not worry." The woman catches her balance and turns to face me.

My jaw hits the ground.

"Nuri?"

She blinks at the sight of me, staring as though she is gazing at a ghost. Until her eyes go wide as the moon. "Through Saffi's good graces," she breathes. "You're back. You're...*alive*." She embraces me in a hug smelling of rosewater.

When she pulls back, I shake my head. "What are you doing here? Shouldn't you be at Bathara?"

Her lips thin, but before she can answer, Marcella strolls over with a wide grin and pulls her into her own hug. "Nuri! What a pleasant surprise." She draws back, scanning her. "What are you doing here? Why aren't you at Bathara?"

"I could ask the same of you," Nuri replies, stern though not unkind.

Marcella rests her elbow on my shoulder. "Fair play."

Nuri chuckles softly, answering Marcella's question only after Draven and Gray have wandered over to us, both expressing similar sentiments to her. "I am here because of my father," she explains. "Because the Ardoris Festival is very important to us and my people."

Though I try to hide it, I feel my brows twitch at her tone. There is a heaviness filling it. One which typically accompanies responsibility.

"Does Bathara know you left?" Gray asks.

She shakes her head. "No. I'm afraid things there are...changing."

I hear the frown in Draven's voice as he asks, "What do you mean? What's happening at the academy?"

Marcella's expression falls alongside her tone. "They're taking sides in the people's uprising," she whispers.

"*What?*" Gray balks. "How is that possible? Bathara is politically neutral, and the uprising is politically-fueled. We are not meant to take sides. It would defeat the whole purpose of Jurafen."

"Why are you just now telling us this?" Draven asks next, demeanor immediately shifting to that of the feared captain.

"No questions," Nuri interjects, answering in Marcella's place.

"Not here." Her eyes dart left then right before she turns back to the merchant, dropping a handful of coins into the woman's hand. The woman hands her a tied velvet sack the size of a sunflower in turn, and Nuri thanks her before squaring her shoulders back to us. She smiles, the gesture graceful.

It is also forced.

"Would you like to accompany me to the palace?" she asks far louder than necessary. "They are hosting a beautiful viewing party for the comet shower." Her bright green eyes slide to me. "I remember what you said about this festival during the exams. I'd love for you to enjoy the beauty of it as deeply as possible." Her smile widens, at odds with the low fervor caressing her next words. "We can speak more freely there. Can catch up, away from the noise of a crowd."

"When you say *palace*," Marcella begins, "is that as in…"

"As in King Yarum's palace? Yes, that is the one."

Her brows rise to her hairline. "Just how popular a merchant is your father?"

"Let's just say he is a very powerful one, and leave it at that, yes?"

WE ROUND the corner of the final stop on our tour of the Zarinee Palace.

"And this here is The Court of Wishes, the inspiration for the golden fountain resting at our capital's center. Its architecture and design acted as inspiration for the heart of the city, founded by Anatolé's first king, Amir, after his subjects began lining up to make wishes in this very pond." Nuri makes a sweeping gesture of the courtyard, her smile broad and brimming with pride.

I gape at the sprawling sight, marveling at its lavishness and architecture. At the heart of the courtyard is a longitudinal pond sprinkled with pink lotus flowers and lily pads, lined by hedges so impossibly green, they look fake. The crisp, blue waters reflect the staggering north tower—tucked securely behind the north pavilion—with astounding clarity, even catching glimmers of the polygonal shapes and stucco work carved into the gorgeous columns framing the pavilion and galleries.

"This is incredible," Gray muses, examining the geometric tilework running alongside the lower portion of the patio's walls. He tips his head back to marvel at the ornate wooden carvings etched into the pavilion's ceiling next. "You can practically breathe in the long-standing history of these grounds."

"I am happy you like it," Nuri says, clasping her fingers in front of her.

Since the tour began—getting glimpses of entertaining halls, lookout points, gardens, and now this courtyard—Gray has been buzzing like an insect, carrying the wide-eyed wonder of a child. He's asked Nuri a plethora of questions, all of which she has not only had an answer to, but has also seemed to enjoy discussing. Gone was the previous tension from the questions surrounding what Bathara was doing. For Gray, it was replaced by reverence for the history of what had been. Though, the same could not be said for Draven or Marcella, even if they are hiding it well as they trudge along at the back of our small group.

I wander further down the patio, examining all the many details carved into the stone and wood. The designs are beautiful, with their overlapping lines and delicate arches. I am staring at one such design when two guards approach from the opposite direction, flanking a man boasting a mess of curls and distinctly green eyes.

"Make way for His Majesty," the one on the left announces.

I clear the path immediately, my heart kicking in my chest at the sight of King Yarum. Flashes of that night during The Founding celebration flood my mind, and I'm struck with the oddest sense of wonderment if he might remember me. A thought I quickly answer, reminding myself he is a king, and he probably helped me only on a whim of mercy or pity or gods-only-know whatever else.

I drop my head as they pass, only daring to lift it once they are a few paces away. To my surprise, the guards halt as they reach Nuri, where King Yarum steps around them to greet her.

She inclines her head at a deep angle. "Your Majesty."

"Lift your eyes, child." She obeys, and King Yarum grins at her. "*Sahtalla,*" he says, fingers motioning the movement the stallman taught me.

"*Zentati,*" she returns, beaming back at him.

He turns to his two guards. "Leave us." They obey without a second's thought. Once they are gone, King Yarum returns his attention onto Nuri. "Who are your friends?"

She turns to her left first. "This is Gray Nightenjoy, from the Rivara Kingdom. Behind me is Draven Dalmar, from House Dalmar, and Marcella Lynderful, from Rolfbear. Gray and Marcella are fellow students of Bathara, and you already know Captain Dalmar's position."

The boys bow at the waist while Marcella dips her chin. The king motions for them to rise. "It is a pleasure to meet Nuri's friends."

Nuri glances over the king's shoulder, where her eyes latch onto me. "Lyra," she calls out. "Come meet His Majesty."

My palms immediately prick with sweat, and my pulse flutters against my neck. Slowly, my feet step one in front of the other, the action happening on nothing but muscle memory alone. I stop once I reach her hip, my eyes still on the ground as I square my shoulders to the King of Anatolé. For reasons I despise, my cheeks flush from my nerves and anticipation, a dirty feeling coating my skin.

Which is worse: for him to remember me as the mocked night attendant that he took pity on, or for him to not remember me at all?

"Your Majesty," I say, still not lifting my eyes from the ground, hoping the act will be taken as a sign of deference.

"Lift your eyes, child," the king instructs, just as he said to Nuri.

With a slight quake in my knees, I do as he asks, dragging my eyes from the ground to look at him. His features are as warm and kind as I remember them to be. Oddly familiar in a way I still cannot place.

He studies me with as much scrutiny as I expected, though there is nothing unkind in his observations. His sharp green eyes narrow with focus, his brows pinching together as he gazes at me with a look I don't understand at all.

Feeling like my nerves are about to explode, I do the first thing I can think of. "*Sahtalla*," I say, hoping the stallman did not lead me astray by saying this was a respect I could offer the people of this kingdom.

Surprise flashes in his eyes, and he regards me with even sharper interest. "*Zentati*," he replies, voice filled with an airiness I hope is good. His gaze lingers on me for only a moment longer before it moves away, focusing now on the group as a whole.

My shoulders nearly sag once free of the near unbearable weight.

"What brings students of Bathara, and an aggregate captain, no less, into the borders of my kingdom?"

"The Ardoris festival," Draven answers without missing a beat. "We have always wanted to experience the festivities and watch the comets pass."

"Ah," King Yarum muses. "So you are not here to spy on my court?"

"No," Draven says, firm as steel.

"With all due respect, Your Majesty," Marcella begins, voice tentative, "even if we were, surely you don't expect spies to answer that question truthfully?"

The golden jewelry at his neck shifts as he cocks his head. "So should a question not be asked merely because it may solicit a lie?"

Her cheeks stain red. "No, I suppose not."

Nuri speaks next. "These were the fellow examinees I previously spoke of who were assigned to my team for the second test. And Captain Dalmar here was the one who stuck his neck out so Lyra would not be eliminated from the exams. They can be trusted." A pause which carries the weight of unspoken words. "Perhaps they can even help."

Something passes between their silent stares, and I glance to Gray, who is also watching them with concerted interest.

King Yarum scans each and every one of our faces, finding mine last, where he lingers. He straightens, clasping his fingers in front of him. "Come," he says, voice soft. "You all will stay as my guests of honor for the evening, provided with rooms for the night and a good meal."

To my surprise, it is Gray who responds with, "In exchange for?"

King Yarum angles his body just enough to gaze out over the placid courtyard. "In exchange for a conversation which you must agree to enter with open ears and minds."

Draven takes a step forward, fingers brushing against my back. "And if we don't?"

King Yarum's eyes find him. His warm gaze is now swallowed by a stone solemnity that dries out my mouth. "Then my kingdom will burn, and my people along with it."

CHAPTER FIFTY-SIX

"Now that everyone is settled, let us begin." King Yarum presses his fingertips together and leans back in his golden chair.

My eyes scan the faces around the table, a lump already forming in my throat. To my left sits Draven—his fingers draped loosely over my thigh—and to my right is Gray. Marcella is next to him, while Nuri sits on King Yarum's right. There are no guards, no advisors—there is nobody else in this lavish room, dripping with gold and punctuated by red and beige accents. Just us and the cool breeze as it whispers in through the panes of the cracked windows, a kind reprieve to the constant warmth heating Anatheima.

Nuri speaks first. "As you may or may not have noticed, the Erandor and Rivara kingdoms have been taking quiet strides to ostracize the Anatolé Kingdom from the rest of Solaya. It has been a slow game with subtle action. Until Tynan Dalmar publicly announced that the Anatolé Kingdom refused to cooperate with their conscription request to supply more wielders to Bathara. That was the first public move they have made, and it was the moment we realized that what we have seen coming for years is finally upon us: King Erasmus and King Alastair seek to move against us."

Draven shifts forward, bracing his elbows on the smooth granite table. "Why would they seek to move against you? What are they after?"

Nuri's lips thin as she shakes her head. "We do not know. We have sent out our own spies to recover such information, but not even they were able to discover the truth. Resources, territory, greed, power—your guess would be as good as our own."

"So they never actually attempted to broker an agreement with you during Bathara's conscription?" Gray asks.

King Yarum shakes his head. "No. We received no such request."

Gray slides his eyes to Nuri. "That's why you reacted with such an outburst the day of the conscription announcement—you were privy to the truth."

"Yes," Nuri answers. "While I knew my reaction was unwise, I wanted to see if I could rattle them. If I could catch any slip of the tongue, any glimmer of information for why they were saying what they were."

Draven's voice is low and gravelly. "My father does not have slips of the tongue."

Nuri sighs. "I know. Still, I had to try."

Draven nods, as if he does truly understand. "I owe you an apology, Nuri."

Both she and I wear the same confused expression at that.

"What for?" she asks.

"I knew what my father was saying that day was odd—was bullshit, really—and I allowed myself to get so distracted, I never followed up with you like I originally intended. If I had, maybe I could have helped intercept whatever scheme they have planned sooner." Draven's eyes remain on Nuri, but he tightens his grip on my leg with a comforting squeeze. As if to reassure me that I am not the distraction nor should I feel like a burden.

I rest one of my hands atop his, a sharp warmth not a result of the heat in the room spreading through me.

Nuri inclines her head to Draven. "I appreciate the sentiment, Captain Dalmar."

I study Nuri, then, my mind simultaneously wandering back to that night during The Founding celebration. The way I noticed King Alastair and King Erasmus strutting off together in the opposite direction of King Yarum, leaving him behind without so much as a word. The way King Alastair hosted members of Bathara's council without Anatolian emissaries present, despite the clear laws in place protecting such a thing from happening.

I realize, then, that I just might be the only person sitting at this table with such insight. Which ultimately results in a quiet sigh blowing past my lips.

"Just after the most recent Founding celebration, King Alastair hosted members of Bathara's council alongside Erandor emissaries. The Keeper of Bathara, Josiah, was amongst them. I waited on them while they dined. I remember thinking it odd, but at the time, I had no proof for the reasons surrounding their visit outside of idle chatter. Well, that is until…" I glance at Gray, whose keen eyes are watching me with concerted intensity. "…I was introduced to Josiah by Gray, and Josiah himself told me they were there for political matters."

Gray's shoulders visibly wobble. "She's right," he murmurs, face pinching together. "He said it in front of me and I missed the weight of it completely because…well…it's *Josiah*. I've known him since I was a boy. My father trusts him, and my father does not place trust lightly." His brows furrow more deeply. "There must be some sort of reason to justify what he was doing. There *has* to be."

King Yarum and Nuri exchange glances, an entire conversation passing silently between their eyes. He dips his chin at her, and Nuri nods to confirm she understands whatever it is they've just agreed upon.

"We fear Bathara has been compromised."

Gray shakes his head. "That isn't possible."

"I assure you," she counters, tone stern though not unkind, "it is very possible, and it has happened. I partook in the entrance exams only as a means to gather more information for my kingdom—for my people. Since gaining acceptance, I have been acting as a spy for Anatolé, and there is so much they aren't telling us."

The news is a paralyzing venom.

I glance at Draven, whose tight expression remains an impenetrable mask. And outside of the tense downward curve wedged into Gray's lips, his face is also rather unreadable. Yet Marcella? She wears her shock openly and without a shred of shame.

"*How?*" she demands.

Nuri looses a breath, looking for some final confirmation from King Yarum. Subtly, he dips his chin at her. She presses her fingertips against the red granite and stands, rolling her shoulders back and straightening her spine with an authoritative flare. "Because my real name is Nuriella Zareena Calliva, and I am the presiding princess of the Anatolé Kingdom and Heir to the Anatolian throne."

CHAPTER FIFTY-SEVEN

LYRA

"Y̶ou're the missing princess?" Marcella gapes.

"I was never missing—only hiding." Nuri sits back down, and it's as if I'm looking at an entirely different person. Because now knowing the truth of her heritage, it seems so obvious. How the sparkling green of her eyes perfectly matches the shade filling King Yarum's. How their noses slope with the same curve and their skin boasts the same warm color of tree bark under gilded sunlight. She is his spitting image, really.

Though isn't that always the way of things? The truth becomes so unbearably transparent only once it's offered.

"Why?" Draven questions, his attention sharp and palpable in the weighted air.

"Because when Nuriella was only a small child," King Yarum begins, weight shifting forward and sharp eyes discerning everyone's expressions, "I was visited by a very talented Veilreader who sought me out to provide a warning: protect the identity of my daughter, or else both my family and my kingdom shall be stolen from me. She also warned me of a terrible, bloody war. She couldn't be sure when it would arrive, only that it was coming. One of those things could be prevented by hiding Nuriella's identity. One could not. Regardless, I made my choice."

Draven's focus is razor-edged. "Why would a Veilreader do that for you? What did they want from you in return?"

King Yarum's expression softens alongside his voice. "She wanted nothing in return. Her only desire was to warn an old friend. She..." His eyes dim with a melancholic longing. "She was someone I knew well in a past life. Someone I cared for deeply."

"And you trusted her enough to hide this kingdom's princess from your own people without question?" Marcella asks, a dull pointedness to her words.

"I did," he answers without a moment's hesitation. "She was never wrong when she spoke of what the Veil showed her. And she always did so sparingly. When she sought me out to tell me what she saw, I knew it was true. Would come to pass."

"Is Veilreading truly so powerful?" I ask, my words far quieter than I would have liked.

There is that peculiar look in his gaze again when he meets my eyes. "The art of Veilreading is so rare these days, it feels like an extinct practice. But let's suffice it to say that if a war is truly on the horizon, commanders and kings would slaughter towns and villages alike to secure a talented Veilreader for their campaign."

Draven's grip tightens on my knee beneath the table. "Veilreaders don't win wars."

"According to written accounts in our grand library they do," King Yarum counters. "We have an entire shelf filled with old war strategies from past generals and strategists alike located in the Library of Ismene. Our scholars report them all saying the same thing: Veilreaders win wars. More than Diviners. More than Seers. And even more than great strategists. Apparently, the fluid, primordial nature of the Veil is what makes it so powerful. The ability to dip into past, present, or future, should the Veil be willing."

Gray clasps his fingers together, resting them gently on the table. "If this is the case, why aren't Veilreaders at the top of the magical hierarchy? Why aren't they as common as Diviners or Seers?"

"Seers nor Diviners are common," Draven interjects, shooting Gray a stiff look.

Gray waves a hand. "I'm only meaning in reference to the ratio of those with the ability. Not the general magic population."

King Yarum sighs. "So much has been lost to time and neglect about the art of Veilreading. From the texts which do remain—if they are to be trusted—I would call it a safe wager to say current Veil-readers are only able to access about a fraction of what Veilreaders used to be capable of centuries ago."

There is a stretch of silence as this information settles to the knowing parties at the table.

"And if one powerful enough to bend the Veil to their whims came along?" Draven's question is carefully neutral.

"Then may their gift forever remain a secret," King Yarum answers.

"And if they were found out?" Gray asks next, again maintaining a carefully half-interested disposition.

The king's eyes linger on Gray before shifting to Draven, then to me, where they remain. "Then may the gods help them against the greed and ambitions of power-hungry men."

Finding myself—like waking up from a distant dream, realizing I am no longer the helpless night attendant King Yarum once saved—I straighten in my chair and bear the weight of his stare. "Then we must hope if such a person exists, they are never found out. Now, should we turn our attention back to the real pressing matters at hand? You say Bathara is compromised, and you believe the Erandor and Rivara Kingdoms are preparing to move against you. Can you lay out the proof for us?"

I catch the sidelong glance from Draven, his mouth tipping sideways at the found confidence ringing in my voice. His fingers rove higher up my thigh, and it takes every ounce of willpower I have not to slap him for the near unbearable distraction. But it's too late. As his fingers crawl over my skin, the space between my legs already starts to pulse, desperate for him and horrifyingly turned on by the blatant lack of propriety.

Damn my body, reacting to him just the way he wants it to.

Draven's touch becomes firmer as he drags his fingers closer and closer to the ache threatening to swallow me whole. Until the pressure he is placing against the sensitive space on the inside of my thigh nearly splits me, and he hooks two fingers, touching—

I jump, reaching a hand beneath the table to subtly jerk his fingers away from somewhere they most certainly should not be right now, given the serious nature of this conversation.

Now is not the time for foreplay, I want to say to him.

But gods...why did that make it feel so much more thrilling? Make each subtle sweep of his skin hum against me like tiny lightning bolts. For a moment, I'm tempted to let his fingers go and see just how crazy he is—how far he would take this, despite our audience.

At the thought—or perhaps it's better to say the mental visual—heat burns through my cheeks and the core of my stomach alike. Still, somehow I find the strength to keep a hold on his hand, not daring to let it go and wander back to where it simply cannot be. If it did, I fear I wouldn't have the strength to stop him a second time.

So subtle I barely catch it, Draven turns his chin to look at me and winks, that tiny tilted smirk of his wedged firmly at the corner of his mouth. He has a smug gleam in his eyes, telling me he is enjoying teasing me *way* too much right now, given the circumstances.

I tighten my hold on his hand, digging my nails into his skin. A mistake, apparently, because that results in him slyly lifting two fingers, a tendril of his dark magic caressing my thigh in place of his fingertips.

A shudder runs down my spine, but I contain it, instead doing something I know he won't expect. I pull for Marcella's magic, as familiar to me as my own heartbeat at this point. Then I conjure a tiny vine with one large thorn, and I press it against the inside of *his* thigh. The release of his magic paired with the amused, approving lift of his brows is the only reaction he gives.

Truthfully, I want to laugh. I can feel it bubbling in my throat. But I shove it all down, far, far away, instead masking my own expression and offering my full attention to King Yarum.

"Atop of a myriad of other infractions against us, which would swallow too much time explaining, I will instead only inform you of the most pressing one: the most recent attack at Sagamon Castle from the Restorationist rebellion group has been pinned on my kingdom. Somehow, King Erasmus and King Alastair have already come together in a show of solidarity, proclaiming to the masses I am the shadowed backer of the movement. They claim to have evidence strong as iron proving my involvement. Evidence which supposedly shows my hand as the puppetmaster, orchestrating the movements of both their last attack and their most recent."

"There was another attack?" I ask, not having heard a peep of such news. Though I suppose it isn't like we have easy access to information currently.

He dips his chin. "There was. It was specifically targeted on the homes of upper nobility and the towns Great Houses preside over. From what we gather, they are protecting their slums and lower nobility, but are seeking to set fire to their kingdoms from the top down."

The news sits heavy in the air. For me, it is a splash of ice water against my burning senses.

Marcella leans back in her chair, folding her arms over her chest. "Well, *are* you the one orchestrating their movements?"

"I find your question very offensive," Nuri—Nuriella? Princess Nuri?—says, bracing her elbows on the table and leaning forward to shoot Marcella a sharp look.

King Yarum lifts a calming hand. "It is alright," he soothes. "They do not know us as we know ourselves. They have every right to ask their questions, especially considering what we must ask of them."

"And what is that request, exactly?" Draven replies, removing his hand from my leg for the first time to clasp his fingers just below his chin.

Nuri sighs, the sound quiet and tired. "I did not seek out entry into Bathara just to spy. I also went to uncover potential allies. To find wielders we could trust and rally them to our cause."

"Allies?" Gray repeats, a solemn heaviness caressing that one simple word. "You speak as though a war is inevitable despite being in an era of peace for centuries."

King Yarum reaches into his silken crimson robe. He pulls out a thick scroll rolled tightly together, sealed in place with white ribbon. He places it gently on the table, sliding it to the center. "You can choose to believe us, or you can choose to question our claims. The outcome will remain because, I assure you, a war *is* coming. Whether we want it or not. If you need more proof, that scroll holds a detailed record of the actions taken against us, too small to notice when isolated individually but undeniable when listed as a whole. It also outlines the most recent events, including King Alastair's and King Erasmus's claims against me."

"If their objective truly is a war against the Anatolé Kingdom," Draven muses, voice low, "then pinning the blame for the uprising attacks in Erandor on you is an ironclad means to sanction their cause."

King Yarum folds his hands in front of his face, nodding once. "Precisely."

Gray reaches for the scroll and tucks it into his satchel. "Which would also give the King of Rivara cause to come to Erandor's aid. They can move as one under the guise of peace—of justice."

Memories of Casimir flood my mind in a debilitating flash. They knock me unsteady as a pensive grief plays the strings of my heart like a familiar instrument. The discordant chords are his words, the aching melody what he was trying to tell me all along.

The murders of hundreds—thousands, as you say—are suddenly digestible when it is in the name of kings. Done under the guise of sovereignty. Stolen under the protection of Her Majesty, 'Justice' herself.

Again, humanity is proving him correct in the claims I fought so hard to dispute. Because disputing him was what seemed right—how could I claim to be someone who was good while believing what Casimir said was correct? I *had* to believe differently. Otherwise, where would that have left my morals? Where would that have left *me*?

Yet...

Perhaps he was right to believe his plan would be the best course of action...

The space nestled deep within the hollows of my ribcage aches suddenly, rising up and into my breastbone. It forces me to realize, in the most twisted way, I *miss* Casimir. Miss some of the days we spent together. It's strange to think I have fond memories with him—like the night we agreed to eat cake together, or when I bumped into him on my way home from a music-filled tavern.

Will there ever come a day where you won't see me as a monster?

So much has changed since those precariously good days between us. So much death, grief, and pain now branded into the soil of a home which will likely never be a home again—into the skin of a man who can scarcely call himself one anymore.

I wonder how he is doing. If he still seeks a cure for Abdites or continues monitoring the gods' cracking statues. If he is still even in the Wastelands at all or has already fled from the bleeding wound. I am a continent away from Halfaria, and I still see their ghosts. I can't imagine how torturous living in their graveyard would be.

As if sensing my sudden turmoil, Draven's hand finds my leg beneath the table again—this time landing respectably on my knee—and at the steadying presence, I shake all the rampant thoughts from my head, forcing my focus back onto the ongoing conversation.

"So that is the way it is," King Yarum says. "We must call on you for aid because there is no one else who will stand with us against the other kingdoms. All we have are my soldiers and a small intelligence network composed of anonymous sources who feed me information when they can. It is not enough to stand against the might of Erandor's legions as is, let alone their forces combined with Rivara's."

"And you think us four alone can help turn the tide of a brewing war?" I ask.

King Yarum observes me with a show of intent. Then he does the same to Draven. "I think both you and Captain Dalmar are capable of such a thing by yourselves. You two are the strongest wielders on the continent, with magics rivaled by very few." He slides his eyes to Gray next. "And you wield a powerful variation of illusion magic unseen in a wielder for centuries." He finds Marcella last. "And I hear you wield a flora magic so strong, you were the single cause of the sudden flourish and prosperity that befell our people of Rolfbear."

At the impressive display of personal knowledge about them, everyone swivels their gazes to Nuri. She shrugs. "What? I already told you I was both spying and scouting for my kingdom."

King Yarum smiles warmly at his daughter before rising from his chair. "You do not need to make a decision at this moment. Take the night, enjoy the rest of the festival and all the beauty it offers, and we can reconvene in the morning."

He departs from the table and knocks twice against the arched doors at the front of the room. A guard hinges one of the double doors open. Before departing, King Yarum glances back at us a final time. "My kingdom is the only thing standing between those men and tyrannical power. Make no mistake, a defining line is being drawn as we speak, and so you must ask yourselves: which side of it do you wish to stand on?"

King Yarum leaves the room, leaving behind a trove of solemn expressions in his wake.

CHAPTER FIFTY-EIGHT

LYRA

It is a while longer before anyone speaks again.

Eventually, Nuri breaks the pressing silence. "I am sorry I lied to you all. But I hope you can understand now why I had to."

"I always knew you were lying about your identity," Gray replies with a shrug, leaning back in his chair. "I just never suspected you were lying about being the hidden princess of Anatolé."

Marcella and I both open our mouths to scold Gray—to tell him to deflate his ego—but both of us are forced to snap our lips closed because he isn't wrong. That day when we were given our team for the second test, he *had* quizzed Nuri about her heritage. A fact which I had always thought odd, but now makes perfect sense.

Nuri chuckles. "What gave me away?"

Gray smirks at her. "I think you know what gave you away, because the next time I saw you, you removed what exposed you from around your neck."

She nods. "The sun pendant."

"The sun pendant," Gray confirms. "Too lavish and expensive, even for a merchant from Lydith. That paired with your essence flower left

550

me certain there was more to your identity than you were sharing with us."

"You do your Nightenjoy name justice," she says, inclining her head to him.

He tips his head at her in return.

The conversation carries on for a while longer after that. Until servants arrive to escort us all to our rooms for the night, and Nuri excuses herself to prepare for the viewing party being held on the palace's rooftop terrace. Apparently to everyone else in the palace, she is still known as Nuri Calhart, but instead of being the daughter of a Lydith merchant, her alias is as a distant relative of the Queen—who is presently away, attending to her sick mother.

Draven, Gray, Marcella, and I follow the servant showing us to our rooms, walking down the arched corridors with wide eyes. The architecture of the palace is unlike anything I have ever seen, the tilework and stuccowork an artistic masterpiece. My chin is fully lifted into the air, marveling at the designs carved into the wooden ceilings, when I glimpse the sight of a beautiful garden resting beyond a large window.

"What's that?" I ask the servant, pointing in its direction when he turns back to see what I'm inquiring about.

"Ah," the man says. "That is King Yarum's private gardens. It is off-limits to all but him."

"It's beautiful," I murmur, a deep-seated desire to go explore all the flowers and plants tugging at me.

"It is," the man confirms with a smile and eyes which silently tell me to keep moving.

I make it only five more steps before I halt in my tracks.

Draven gazes back at me from over his shoulder, his knowing smirk telling me he fully anticipated my decision. I shrug at him, a half-formed smile tilting my own lips. He winks at me just before elbowing Gray in the side and whispering something. Gray turns back, chuckling the moment he sees me standing at a halt in front of the garden's window. They both face forward and continue to follow the servant. Next thing I know, a perfect replica of me appears, walking beside them in the exact position I was before. A tendril of darkness snakes over the ground next, caressing my cheek in an achingly familiar way right before shooting off down a branching corridor, where a nondescript door rests at the end.

Ah, there's the entrance.

My chest swells when I glance back at Draven and Gray, two distinct pieces of my heart.

Then I follow the thin trail of darkness straight to the hidden door, and I enter the gardens.

THE SMELL IS INTOXICATING.

Vibrant lily and musky moss. Fresh sage and fruity citrus paired with aromatic spices. Roses and the distinct metallic scent of soil. It all tangles into the air, mingling to form one wonderful perfume.

My fingertips glide over lively green leaves, and I rub the velvety petals between them. As I take everything in, all I can think about is how much my mother would have loved this garden. How it mirrors the design of the greenhouse she maintained at King Alastair's estate. Even the plants are similarly located, seeming to be clustered together in the same organizational system she used. The "Three Ms," as she called it. Meal, medicine, and materials.

"Are you a fan of gardens?"

I spin on my heels to find King Yarum standing behind me. "Your Majesty." I immediately incline my head, bowing. "I am so sorry for intruding on your private space."

He chuckles. "It is alright. Something about these gardens always seems to bring wanderers. So" —a pause— "do you like gardens?"

I straighten, rolling my shoulders back. "I do, very much. My mother was a Gardner, so I was raised around them. Taught to under-stand all the power each tiny leaf and pretty petal possesses."

"Ah, spoken like a true admirer." He folds his hands behind his back. "I do remember you, in case you were wondering. From my time I last spent in King Alastair's hall. You served me my drink during the party, yes?"

Despite myself, my cheeks flood with heat. "Yes. That was me."

His smile feels as warm as the rays of a pleasant sun. "I remember you being very brave that night, against all your obstacles."

My lungs stutter.

Brave.

I almost want to laugh at the word choice. When I reflect back on my days as an attendant, I always feel like I was anything but. So cowardly, in fact, I couldn't even face the other night attendants—tell them I was the one supplying them with their sleeping tonics.

"I appreciate the sentiment," I murmur instead. My eyes linger on the spread of greens, whites, and reds before me. "May I ask you something?"

"You may."

"That night... Why did you help me? I've spent more than one sleepless night wondering about it."

He studies me, expression inscrutable. "To be truthful, you reminded me of someone I once knew. Someone I once cared for very much." His laugh is soft and quiet as it blows past his lips. "In complete honesty, when I first laid my eyes on you that night, I thought I was seeing her ghost."

I laugh. "Were you?"

"No," he says through a grin. "I do not believe so. Though I suppose she could be a ghost now. I lost track of her whereabouts many years ago." There is a somber quality to his words.

"I'm sorry," I offer.

"Do not be." He jerks his chin. "Come, walk with me. I will show you this garden's prized possession."

I do as he asks and fall into stride beside him. He guides me down a mosaic trail of colored stones, past a trimmed line of bushes and trees.

"Have you given any more thought to what I have asked of you and your friends?"

"The meeting wasn't that long ago," I point out, a small laugh bloating my words.

"This is true," he agrees. "Yet the mind forms thoughts quickly."

"Also true," I say through more soft laughter. We share a few silent heartbeats before I ask, "I'm assuming you know about what happened at Bathara? My actions, I mean."

"Yes, Nuri has told me. Though you would be surprised by how quiet the academy attempts to keep such information."

"They want to contain the truth of my magic," I say. "Or at least control the narrative surrounding it."

He nods. "I am glad you are aware."

The heaviness of my next words puts unbearable pressure against my sternum. "So then it's safe to presume you are aware that the Tani searches for me? Wishes to hold a trial for my crimes?"

"I am aware."

My face scrunches with my growing thoughts. "Then why ask me to fight in your war, knowing I am a dead woman walking? Or if not dead, a liability at the least. Tani law is greater than man's law. Even in the eyes of war, it must be upheld or the Shadows will come."

"I do not fear the Shadows."

I snort a laugh before I can think better of it, temporarily forgetting I am in the presence of a king. I tighten up my casual behavior. "Sorry," I murmur.

"Do not apologize. I understand why you laugh. But it does not change things. I do not fear the Shadows, but I do fear what war will mean for my people. And your power could change their fates, should you choose to use it for our cause."

A heaviness fills my body, and my lips become too weighted to open, my tongue too burdened to speak.

I really wish people would stop telling me that.

Seeming to sense the sharp shift, King Yarum says no more, instead pointing to our left, where a beautiful wooden trough planter rests, adorned with intricate carvings. A quiet pulse zips down my arms, wrapping along my spine, and I stiffen before trudging forward to the petals.

Energy radiates from them. I can feel it. *Sense* it.

My eyes widen. "Are these essence flowers?"

"They are."

Awe washes through me. "How? How are you managing to *grow* them?"

"We have our ways," he says through a proud smile. "A trademark secret of the Calliva bloodline, I am afraid."

I laugh, staring down at the seemingly half-bloomed flowers. Yet I know the truth of them. Know that if their owner were ever to appear and claim them, they would assume their full glory, blossoming into something remarkable.

It brings a fond memory to my mind's surface, and I grin at the warmth of it. "My mother was given an essence flower once. She said it bloomed the moment it touched her palms."

From the corner of my eye, I swear I glimpse King Yarum go rigid. One heartbeat. Two heartbeats. And then—

"Did she tell you what her flower was or how she came to possess one?"

I shake my head. "No. She always said those details were irrelevant."

"I see," he murmurs, his now-scrunched eyes falling to the ground. He grips the edge of the trough, swaying a bit.

"Are you alright?"

"Fine," he says, waving a stiff hand at me. "I am fine. I have not been sleeping as I should with all my council meetings. An impending declaration of war is not kind to the tired, I am afraid."

I study him with a sharp gnawing in my gut. Yet I don't press him for more—he is a king, after all, and I am merely a lowborn.

"Anything I can do?"

He shakes his head, offering me a smile. The curves twitch at the corners of his mouth, framed by a distinct pensive quality. "No. I will be alright. Please, do not worry." King Yarum brings his eyes to meet mine, then. They hold onto me in that peculiar way—something there beneath the surface of his gaze, even more saturated than it was before.

His sharp gaze now carries a glassy quality, and he blows out a deep sigh, pinching his bottom lip between his teeth. "I am afraid I must be going now," he says, bracketing his hands on his hips. "I...

you..." He sighs again. "Please, enjoy the garden for as long as you like. I will see to it you are not bothered."

"Thank you." I offer him a curtsy.

He lifts his hand. "Please. That is not necessary while you are here."

I reorient myself upright, dipping my chin to acknowledge what he's said. King Yarum lingers for a moment longer. His feet take a tiny step in my direction, hands twitching in front of him. And as he studies me, for a moment, I'm convinced he intends to *hug* me.

Though, he doesn't.

Instead, he rolls his shoulders back and clasps his fingers together, striding off without another word.

I watch him leave with the same feeling I had during The Founding celebration. An intuition of sorts. An unnamable knowing-ness—made all the more confusing considering I actually *know* nothing about this feeling at all.

And just like the last time, it does not part from my bones for a long, long time.

CHAPTER FIFTY-NINE

LYRA

When I eventually find my room—a lovely thin trail of obsidian left behind to guide me—I immediately stride for the double glass doors leading to the room's balcony. My fingers dig into the smooth stone of the ledge, an endless collection of thoughts swarming my mind. I buckle forward, the weight of so many things pressing down on me.

Breathe, I remind myself. *Just breathe.*

I steady my attention to the sun as it falls, the sky morphing into the legendary scarlet rumored to fill the world's ceiling as the comets pass. It can't be long now until they appear, if the books I've read on the festival are correct about the timeline. Which means the viewing party is now well on its way. Yet I have no intentions of joining. Not tonight. Not after everything I've heard and with all these loaded thoughts swirling around in my mind.

I catch the faint sound of quiet footsteps just moments before I feel fingertips grazing the hair from my neck. Gentle lips press against my shoulder, up my neck, and along the length of my jaw. I turn my chin just enough to see Draven studying me through low-lidded eyes.

I smirk at him from over my shoulder, some of the frenzy I felt already melting away. "You know, I should lace your food with something for the stunt you pulled earlier."

He reaches out and brackets my hips, his large hands swallowing them as he drags me backward against his chest. "And here I thought I should be rewarded for the self-restraint I showed."

"You call that self-control?" I ask with mocking pointedness, mindlessly wrapping my hands around his wrists.

His fingertips press deeper into my hipbones. "I do. If you knew even a fraction of the thoughts running through my mind—all the many deplorable things I was thinking of doing to you in that room—then you'd call it that, too."

"Down boy," I tease through a laugh. "We still have to make it to the comet show."

A low growl rattles in the back of his throat. "Mmm, pesky things, those comets." He leans forward, pressing feather-light kisses down the length of my neck. "In case you haven't noticed, there is an entire lavish bedchamber behind us. One that we get all to ourselves tonight. I'm not sure about you, but I've already thought about six different ways I'd like to put it to use."

"Six?"

"Mhm."

I laugh, dropping my head back against the firm panes of his chest. "Someone has quite the imagination."

"Oh," he breathes like a promise, "when it comes to you, my creativity knows no end."

My chuckle deepens before fading in tune to the descending sun. Draven drops his chin to the top of my head, his arms extending to envelope me entirely. We remain like that for a blissful time, together and comfortably silent. When he holds me like this, all the world feels quiet. My mind becomes a placid thing, smooth and glistening like a stream beneath a morning's gilded sun.

It is those feelings of security which allow me to voice the words that have been turning on repeat in my mind. "And when they awaken —chosen by the Cycle to harbor the greatest power of all—the ashes of one great war will stir, giving way to another, and the Chosen will decide the fate of kingdoms, just as the raven himself had."

"The words from the prophecy."

I nod, my eyes remaining glued to the darkening sky. "It's all happening just as the prophecy said it would." A pause carrying the weight of mountains presses against the cooling breeze. "I am not what they need," I murmur. "I shouldn't be the one to decide the fate of kingdoms. I mean, *how* is it even possible for someone like me to hold such responsibility?"

"Someone like you?" he whispers.

I shake my head, sighing. "You know what I mean. I'm not strong enough for this. Not someone capable of deciding the fates of *king-doms* for the gods' sakes. Who am I to decide the futures of so many people?"

With gentle force, Draven spins me around by my hips so I can meet his eyes. "You truly still don't see how special you are, do you? Still don't understand the immeasurable worth you hold both to others and this world?"

My eyes drop to my feet. "I really wish people would stop saying that. I am no one special; just a bastard orphan who—only a few solstices ago—was caged in a tiny world by a cruel king."

Draven grips my chin between his thumb and index finger, tugging it up so my eyes are forced to look at him once more. "You are also the brave girl who escaped that king by outwitting him. Are the courageous wielder who took on Bathara's famed entrance exams without proper training and *passed* through your own resilience and cunning. You are the person who has stood against the largest threat these kingdoms might ever know. Were abducted by him, only to get him to agree to search for a better way before massacring an entire class of people." He dips his chin to catch my eyes. "And all of that is aside from the fact that you are the bearer of the most powerful magic in all of Solaya. No one, not even me, could stand against you if you chose to wield your full power." A pause. "Do you truly still not see all that you are?"

My lips swish side to side in tune to my swaying emotions. "No," I murmur, the answer painfully raw but honest.

I wish I did, my mind whispers. *Yet I just...don't.*

His resulting smile is framed by the lines of melancholy. "Then I will continue being the mirror that attempts to show you."

"That's quite the mirror I have."

"The reflection's better."

A tiny grin blooms on my lips, and I again drop my eyes, this time to Draven's hand, where my fingers toy with this.

Draven watches me, smiling a tilted sort of smile. "You know, I am still *very* eager to see the results of all that training you've told me about."

I blow out a quiet laugh. I appreciate his attempt to move my mind past my worries, but my amusement sobers within an instant, giving way to more weariness and crippling uncertainty as my head remains stuck elsewhere. "Draven?"

"Yes?"

"What could I possibly offer the people of Solaya by getting involved in a brewing war? I do not understand the poor. I do not understand the rich. I–I was in limbo, never belonging to one side, feeling the powerlessness of one and living with the privileges of the other. How can I actually aid them?" I don't voice the echo to my question.

How can I help them when I couldn't even help the people of Halfaria?

"Lyra, not belonging solely to one side makes you the perfect person to harbor the power you do."

"I don't want it," I rasp. The weight of the vomited confession presses against my chest. "And I know that makes me the most selfish person in the entire Three Kingdoms, but even now, I can't bring myself to want such power. To know with utter certainty that answering King Yarum's plea for aid is the right thing for me to do. All I want is freedom, Draven. To run away from these games of power and never look back. I never wanted to be caught between greed and schemes. Politics and tyranny. I'm tired of being other people's pawns."

He observes me, remaining silent. Until he eventually sweeps his thumb along my jaw and whispers, "Wherever you go, I follow. I will not ask you to bleed for these kingdoms any more than you already have." His mouth hooks up at the corner. "But" —a pause— "I will ask you to turn around."

With a crease in my brow, I do as he asks—

And am met with the most beautiful sight I have ever seen.

Against the unfurling bounds of a black-and-reddened sky, where clouds have dispersed and the sun has retreated, a million glowing comets stream like ribbons of blue fire one after the other, transforming the horizon into a canvas of blazing trails of light. I tilt my chin up to marvel at the sight, my jaw open and my eyes wide.

"It's so beautiful," I murmur, gripping my fingers more tightly on the balcony's ledge while I lean forward.

"It is. It's the single most beautiful thing I have ever seen."

When I turn my chin over my shoulder, I find his eyes on me, and I nudge my shoulder into his chest. "I was talking about the comets."

"And I was talking about you."

With a helpless grin now wedged permanently into my lips, I turn back to the seemingly infinite spheres of glittering dust and fire, battling this splitting feeling in my chest. Like my heart is threatening to claw free from its cage of bones just so it may be able to stretch out and combine itself entirely to the man standing next to me.

And gods, it leaves me in such a mess of feelings. Because I am at once carrying the weight of pressure I have no idea how to navigate. Expectations I don't believe I will ever meet. But then I am also holding the lightness of a girl who is being stared at adoringly by a man she holds the deepest affections for. When he looks at me, I feel seen. I feel capable, like maybe—just maybe—I could be all the things I never thought possible. That I am more than the things I am not.

It is a complicated mix of emotions, certainly. Yet through my journey of no longer running and hiding from that which makes me feel—not stunting the progression of grief, love, sadness, and so many other things—I think I finally understand that this life is not so simple to allow us to feel only one thing at a time. I can at once feel happy while feeling sad. I can be at the peak of love's mountain while also carrying the weeds of pain in the gardens of my belly. I can be starlight and darkness. Feel nothing and everything. It does not make me broken to feel so many complicated, messy things simultaneously.

It makes me human.

Draven, now standing shoulder to shoulder with me, turns his chin to look at me. He doesn't say anything, instead only smiling, like a smile is all he needs to express all that he wishes to.

I understand the words of his language perfectly.

He unfurls his fingers from his palm, stretching his hand out to me. My breastbone, ribcage, sternum—every part of me—is so inflated with emotion, I fear I may simply float away and join the comets. Though I don't think an existence amongst such beauty would be the worst thing.

I place my hand in his, where his fingers then close around it. Draven and I turn back to watch the comet show. To stare out over a golden city where a glistening, bejeweled fountain spouts crystal water at the center. Where people wrapped in beautiful colors clap and cheer below us, fire magic arcing through the sky in praise while banners illuminated by light magic and trailed by ribbons are waved in the air. The sounds of music and laughter carry up from the streets, inking their melodies deep into our skin.

"Lyra," Draven muses as he stares up at the sky. "Have you realized it yet?"

I answer him with a questioning look.

There is a raw earnestness brimming in his eyes when he again meets my gaze. Both soft and vulnerable. "Rocks are flying. Does that mean we can finally be happy now?"

Draven's words to me after our first day of training together—a day which now feels like a lifetime ago, where my biggest worries were passing an entrance exam and surviving the brutal training of my brooding mentor—slam into my mind.

Maybe happiness will find us like some phenomenon finding its sky. Maybe when...rocks fly; yes, that's it. You and I can be happy when rocks fly.

I blow out a disbelieving, weighted breath. Tears suddenly well in my awe-stricken eyes as they remain glued to the glowing horizon; streams of red, silver, white, and blue zipping past in endless amounts. "I hope so."

Draven's voice is soft beside me. "Then why are you crying?"

I shake my head. "I'm not." A tiny laugh escapes me. "I mean, I *am*, but I feel like there should be another word for when they're happy tears." I swipe said happiness from my cheeks. "It's just...ever since I was a little girl staring up at Rivara's colored stars, I have wished and dreamed for this exact moment to come true. And now...here it is. More beautiful and perfect than I ever imagined it could be." I swallow back some of my growing emotion. "I hope Gray is watching."

"Do you want me to go get him?"

"No," I answer through a smile. "I suspect he is exactly where he needs to be, just as I am." I glance at Draven sidelong, finding him with crinkled eyes and upturned lips. He slides his arm around my waist, holding me against his side while his palm presses firmly against my hip. I lean into him, feeling bathed by sunlight.

As the comet show continues on, overtaking the sky in the most beautiful display of fiery brilliance—leaving me to question if perhaps a flame can be beautiful after all—I feel the caress of Draven's eyes as he watches me and I watch the sky.

Time presses on, and the comets continue blazing over the horizon like pioneers forging onto a better existence. Eventually, I look to Draven, who is still watching me. I want to say something—to let him know all the many, many things I'm feeling. Yet I realize I have no words. Or perhaps it's best to say I have no better words to express what a simple action can.

So I turn, rising onto my toes.

My lips find Draven's like it is the most natural thing they've ever done.

I kiss him with the weight of a thousand words behind it. I kiss him with the desperation of lost time. I kiss him with the fervent passion of deprived petals soaking in their sunshine, greedy and selfish and utterly dedicated to feeling warmth against their skin. I kiss him in the shades of every color, every emotion.

And Draven kisses me back with equal hunger. Equal passion and need.

He slides his arms across my lower back, drawing me tighter against his chest. His hand roves up until it brackets the back of my neck, where he holds me firmly while kissing me deeper. I can taste the desire on his lips as though it were honey.

Our lips move in perfect synchrony, our tongues pressing and twirling together like the perfect dance partners they are. The kiss is beautiful and emotion-ridden. Slow and toying, like we are the keepers of the universe and nothing is more pressing than us discovering every outline and ridge artistically carved into our lips.

Until it isn't.

The kiss turns frantic—more wanting. It becomes not a thing of tender discovery, but insatiable greed. I drag my fingers into his hair and thread them through the silken strands. I tell him everything without having to say anything at all, not wanting to pull my mouth from his for a single second.

I want him everywhere, all at once.

I just want *him*.

Draven, immediately sensing the shift, hoists me up as though I am light as a falling petal. I wrap my legs around his waist, and he maintains his hold on my neck, his mouth growing more savage as it devours me with sharpened hunger. He strides into the bedroom, and I feel him harden against me just before he lays me gently onto the bed, skillfully keeping his body positioned over me so his lips don't break away from mine as he leans over the mattress. Eventually, he pulls back just enough to gaze at me.

"Tell me what you want, Lyra, and it is yours."

I smile against his mouth. "You were the one who said he has six ideas already lined up." I nip his bottom lip. "Why don't you show me one of them?"

His gaze hazes with desire, and he lowers his lips to trace my neck and jaw. He pulls my ear between his teeth, sucking momentarily as his fingers teasingly graze over an area of me aching with desire. They rove up and up, until they still around my neck, his thumb swiping over my pounding pulse while he leans back and studies me, considering his choice.

An immediate thrill dances over my skin. I rise with an arch in my back, pressing another kiss against his lips. "Just let me have you," I breathe.

Draven's eyes darken. "You can do whatever you want with me, Lyra. My body is yours." He reaches for my hand, slowly guiding it down and down until my palm cups the bulge pressing against his pants. "Because this? This is only for you. Will always be for you, and you alone."

I melt.

My fingers wrap around the hardness of him, and I make toying motions, a smirk tugging my lips up even as they find his. I move my hand to grip Draven's wrist—our lips still pressed together—and glide his fingers beneath my pants. "And this is for you. This is what you do to me."

Draven growls possessively against my mouth. "Let me show you how much that pleases me." He slips one finger inside me, his thumb immediately pressing against my clit. I tip my head back, a small moan breaking free. He chuckles lowly. "I have dreamed of hearing that sound spill from you again. I need to hear more of it. *Much* more of it."

Draven slips another finger inside me, where he then moves with such precision, an immediate heat builds at the base of my stomach. It is dizzying and intoxicating. Euphoric and addicting.

I ride his fingers, letting free any illusion of control. I want this more fervently than anything I have ever wanted before. We've earned this moment for ourselves. And being forced apart, being forced to wait and hold off on touching each other like this—even after being reunited—has sharpened every stroke and touch with an energy so intense, it's all-consuming.

Warmth spreads from the base of my neck all the way to the tips of my toes. The pleasure compiles, turning my nerves and skin into living sparks. Draven's lips crash into mine, taking without apology. His other free hand glides up my shirt to cup my breast, and he pinches my hardened nipple toyingly between his fingers. A choked noise of pleasure rises from my throat and collides with Draven's mouth.

He groans with satisfaction.

Draven slips his fingers free of me and brackets my hips, swallowing me with his arms. He presses another kiss to my lips, this one more gentle. He guides my movements, lifting the shirt from my body and removing my undergarment.

Insecurity suddenly dilutes my pleasure, a frigid bucket of sobriety crashing into me.

My scars are laid bare for his viewing—something which we have not touched on after I indicated I wasn't ready during a night we laid pressed together on a pile of blankets. Sometimes it feels like all I can do just to reveal them to the world, let alone discuss them and their implications.

"Do they hurt?" he asks, voice so gentle. He traces the raised lines over my left arm with his thumb.

"No. I don't feel them at all. Sometimes I almost forget they're there."

He is silent as he studies me, and I now have the overwhelming urge to squirm beneath his concerted gaze. Doubts, criticisms, worries—they all press into my mind, their sharp words pelting my confidence bit by bit.

Until Draven lifts a hand to push hair back from my face and cups my cheek, the depths of the sea cradling me as his eyes hold mine. "You are the most exquisite piece of art I have ever seen." His lips sweep up into a grin. "And I don't just say that because your eyes are like mine now. Though, if you start a trend, I reserve the right to say I did it first."

I laugh softly, my smile now light as a flower. "That's fair enough."

He nips my bottom lip. "Glad we have an understanding."

I lean in to brush the ghost of a kiss over his lips, already feeling those insecurities left behind. Draven always makes me feel as though

I am the center of his universe, beautiful and unbreakable. "I still suggest you get that in writing, though."

He hums. "You really should have been a merchant, you know."

My laugh deepens. His grin grows both wider and more crooked.

In the following silence that passes between us, so, too, does the acknowledgement of the remaining things we have yet to fully discuss. My eyes. My scars. The mark on my thumb from my deal with Casimir—which somehow still remains. It's mostly out of vanity on my part, but I just haven't wanted to talk about those things yet. Eventually, I will discuss them in depth with him—perhaps we'll even work together to find answers to the peculiarities surrounding why both our eyes are now dual-colored and how my wielder's mark seemed to prevent the right side of my body from being littered in scars—but for now? For now, I want to enjoy this blissful night like nothing else exists.

Draven watches me a beat longer before bringing his lips to mine once more, kissing me with the full, dizzying weight of passion and desire. He tells me the story of an entire future in the way his mouth holds mine. Offers me an unbreakable promise which fills my chest with a swell so forceful, I'm convinced my ribs will crack beneath the pressure of it.

I love you, I think as he kisses me. *I knew it before, and I know it now. I love you. I love you. I love you.*

Yet I don't find the courage to say it, instead allowing my lips to remain occupied, using their busyness as an excuse to not voice the words in my head.

Draven pulls back, the heat returning to his eyes. He threads his fingers through my hair, twirling the strands over his knuckles. "Allow me to admire you as all great art should be."

I smirk at him. "Only if you remove an article of clothing."

His lips tilt, and he tugs at the beautifully sewn Anatolian shirt he'd been wearing for the festival, tossing it to the side. My eyes drink in the sight of his beautifully honed body, warm like the muted gold of a rudbeckia flower. "Look at that," I tease. "Turns out you're art, too. A living sculpture, in fact."

Draven chuckles. "Lay down."

"Is that an order, Captain Dalmar?"

He lowers his hands to my thighs, slowly guiding them apart. "It is. And it is also an order when I tell you not to withhold a single sound from me when I worship you. To dig your nails into my skin and drag them down my back while you moan my name." He slowly tugs at my billowing pants, guiding them down my legs and removing them from my ankles, tossing them to the floor. He grips the back of my thighs and tugs me forward so I'm at the edge of the bed.

Draven lowers himself to one knee, and then the next, positioning himself directly between my thighs and pressing a kiss to the inside skin of my left leg, then my right. He kisses the most sensitive part of me through the remaining fabric covering me, his pressure firming in a cruel tease of what's to come.

I tip my head back, a moan already escaping me, and I thread my fingers through his hair, my hips moving with their own mind.

When Draven still doesn't remove the final scrap of fabric between us, instead toying with me using his mouth and idle touches alike, I tighten my hold on his hair, tugging forcefully at the strands. "Don't tease me, Draven. I've waited too long for this."

"Which is why I have no intentions of rushing tonight." Another firm kiss between my thighs. "Still" —a teasing stroke with his finger — "your wish is my command." He slides my undergarment from my hips, exposing me entirely to him. He places a few more featherlight kisses around the area where I throb and pulse for him, ready to explode from the anticipation.

Then he brings his lips to the center of me and allows his tongue free range of my body.

My eyes flutter as a rush of pleasure sweeps over me, a choked gasping noise spilling from my lips.

Draven hums his satisfaction, pulling back to slip two fingers inside me. "This is what fills my dreams when you're not near. What I laid awake at night and fantasized about while you were away, after I learned you were unharmed. I always imagined I found you, and then

I laid you bare before me and showed you how desperately I had ached to feel you."

All I can offer him is my heavy breaths and moans of pleasure. Sheer, utter pleasure.

He brings his mouth back to me, his fingers still stroking in and out. Draven sucks my clit between his lips, dragging his teeth tauntingly over the sensitive nerves.

A heady rush tilts the world around me, and I am a mess of propulsive, humming energy as a heat, consuming and fiery as any other, bubbles in my stomach. My fingers tug at the strands of his silken hair again while my other hand clutches at the blanket beneath me. "Gods, Draven. *Fuck*."

He reaches for the hand I have clutched into the blankets, his tongue still working me into a frenzy. He pries my fingers free of the fabric and instead places them on his shoulder. "What did I tell you? If you clutch onto anything, it will *only* be me."

Fuck.

I dig my nails into his shoulder, squeezing my eyes as my pleasure crescendoes, threatening to erupt in warm waves of pleasure. I sit up, pushing him back, not yet ready to find my finish.

Draven looks at me, a smirk tipping his lips. "Yes?" he croons mockingly.

"Switch positions with me."

"Is that an order?"

"It is."

Draven's smirk widens into something devastatingly beautiful. "You know, I'm not used to being the one taking orders."

"Maybe this will do you some good then."

We shift our positions on the bed, Draven's eyes not breaking from mine for so much as a heartbeat. "Oh, I have a feeling it will do wonders for me."

I undo his pants, taking my time while holding his eyes with mischief in my own. I tug them down his legs and strip them from his ankles, taking care to leave his undergarments in place. Then I begin stroking him over the fabric, just as he did me.

"Oh," he growls, propping himself up with his elbows braced behind him to watch me. "Cruel, cruel woman."

Without breaking our heated eye contact, I lower myself to my knees and kiss the bulge pushing through the fabric, placing a taunting pressure on the hardened shaft I can feel through his undergarment. "You have no idea."

His eyes shudder. "Now who's teasing who?"

"You started this," I point out. My fingers curl around his outline, squeezing him with just enough pressure to send his eyes fluttering. "Want me to keep going?"

"Fuck," he breathes. "*Yes.*"

"Beg me."

The corner of his mouth lifts with a sharp curve. "I need you, Lyra. I want you more viscerally than anything I have ever wanted in my entire life. You are my fantasy turned reality, so please, be good for me and keep going."

Intensely satisfied, I look down to indulge his request, but he leans forward and lifts my chin with the crook of his finger.

"Don't look away from me. I want to see your eyes as you take me with your mouth."

With a challenging smirk now pressed into my lips, I do as he asks and hold eye contact while I finish stripping him bare. I hold his eyes even as my fingers curl around the hard length of him, marveling at every glorious inch, sculpted in a way which has me biting my lip and a flood of heat pooling between my legs. I don't break away from his heated gaze even as I spit on the length of him and my palm before stroking him. Even when a feral, guttural sound rips free of his lips.

Gods, hearing him moan for me is as intoxicating as having his mouth pressed against me.

I bring my lips to his hardened length, first planting gentle kisses along his soft skin, until I finish with a precise flick of my tongue at the tip. Then I swallow him, taking him into my throat and stroking him with my tongue.

Draven reaches out and grabs a fistful of my hair, his head tipping back as he groans, sounding as if he has lost all control of himself.

It is fuel to the growing pleasure fanning the flames coating my skin.

I pump my mouth against him harder, until he eventually sits up and stops me, panting with a wild need in his eyes. Without warning, he lifts me up and turns our positions on the bed, his mouth slamming into mine the moment my back hits the sheets.

By the Mother, there is such savage need behind the kiss. Such insatiable desire. Draven bites my lower lip before bringing his lips down my neck, lowering further to suck on my breast while his hand cups my other. Satisfaction rolls through me, and I dig my nails into his back.

He pulls back and smirks at me. "That's my girl."

Draven centers his body with mine, one hand reaching down to steady his shaft while he positions his other beside my head to hold himself up. He gazes down at me, and his expression shifts. Softens into something less desperate and wild, instead becoming tender. "Just you and me, Lyra." He presses a gentle kiss to my lips. "For this first time, no magic. No gimmicks. Let it just be a man bearing his heart to the woman who owns it."

I reach up and glide the backs of my fingers over his stubble, words evading me. I nod right before reaching up to kiss him, a delicate press of my lips, to show him how much those words mean to me.

Draven holds my eyes a heartbeat longer before entering inside me. The motion is an exchange of energy unlike anything I have ever felt. There is pleasure and need merging with desire, but there is also a tender undercurrent of passion and love. I feel it in every stroke he makes against me. Feel it in the way his fingers caress my skin.

I surrender entirely to him and the overwhelming emotions he forces me to feel, resting my head back and letting my hips roll in perfect rhythm with his. His hand moves to my throat, gripping lightly, and my nails claw at his back, scratching his skin as the swell of him inside me overtakes my ability to do anything else. My eyes flutter closed.

"Look at me, Lyra," he demands, voice firm yet soft. "I want you to look at me."

I do as he asks and meet his gaze, feeling stricken by the emotion he allows me to see within his eyes. The truth of its depth. As he slips in and out of me, making my body feel sensations far too good and consuming for this mortal world, I swear I feel something like a thread being tied between us. An irreversible connection, fused together through the electric current simmering between our locked stares.

It causes the pleasure to build inside me, reaching a point of no return. Draven bites down on his lips and his strokes grow more frantic and rough, pounding into me with a force drawing moan after moan from my throat. I know he is close to the edge, just as I am. I can feel it.

He drops his lips to my ear, his fingers tightening the pressure around my throat. "Come for me."

"Come *with* me." I clasp my fingers behind his neck and lift my hips, rolling them as I suggest a change in position.

He follows my lead perfectly, shifting himself beneath me without making me suffer the loss of him inside me. I sit upright in his lap, his fingers now digging into my hips. I allow my body to fully take over, bringing myself up and down against him, hitting a spot that sends colors and sparks flashing in my vision each time I do.

Draven brings his lips to my peaked nipples, biting and flicking his tongue against them. He braces one hand against my back, his hand reaching up into my hair. It makes me drive myself against him harder.

"That's it, Lyra," he groans, his fingers fisting the strands of my hair as he meets me with his own thrusts. "I can feel you tight against me. Now let go. Let go and come for me."

My pleasure swells into every crevice of my body, leaving no single space of skin or strip of nerve untouched by its warmth. I tip my head back, lost entirely to the frenzy of nearing my orgasm. Draven and I meet in perfect rhythm for a final, glorious thrust, and I officially peak, then topple over the edge.

A heated wave sweeps over me, stroking me with flames of pleasure far more intense than anything I have ever been privileged enough to feel before.

It is only fanned by the sounds of Draven's moan as he whispers, *"Fuck,"* under his breath, also finding his release as he continues to drive into me, allowing me to ride the full wave of my orgasm.

And then we collapse next to each other on the bed, our skin slicked with sweat and chests rising with panted breaths. He reaches out for me and pulls me into his chest. There is an intimacy in having our naked bodies pressed together in this way. One which I feel I will never tire of with him. Will always crave.

Draven kisses my forehead. "I'm going to fantasize about that until the next solstice."

"Fantasize?" I tease. "Why dream of it when you can relive it all over again?"

He hums dreamily, grip tightening on my hips. "Careful," he warns. "My thirst for you knows no end, so if you suggest you want more of this, I'm afraid I'll have to oblige."

"Ah, what a shame." I enunciate each word playfully, my eyes sliding to the open door leading to another chamber I hadn't noticed earlier. "Look at that," I muse, pointing toward it. "There is an attached bathing chamber in this room."

"Look at that," he repeats, nipping at my bottom lip.

"Perhaps we should run a bath and clean ourselves up?"

He chuckles darkly against my mouth. "Your wish is my command."

DRAVEN and I lay in bed, a mess of tangled—though now squeaky clean—limbs. I am nestled into the crook of his arm, and he mindlessly glides his fingers through my semi-wet hair. We are teetering somewhere between the bounds of sleep and conversation, our muscles probably overworked and our bodies humming from all the drawn out pleasure.

I trace mindless circles on his chest, my mind dipping in and out of random thoughts. I voice one such passing thought aloud. "It's strange being in King Yarum's palace."

"It is," he agrees. "Life certainly is an interesting journey."

I hum my agreement. "He saved me once, you know. When I was serving drinks at the most recent Founding celebration. It was hosted in Rivara by King Alastair, and Eri Valenwood tried to make me strip for the entire party. It was King Yarum who prevented it from happening." I pause, laughing. "Well, actually...it was King Yarum paired with a sudden burst of unauthorized magic in the hall. I guess truthfully the display saved me first, and King Yarum just made sure I stayed safe after."

Draven is silent for a long time, his fingers stilling in my hair. For a moment, I think he's fallen asleep. Until his low voice eventually murmurs, "I know."

I scoff a laugh. "What—did Eri Valenwood report it all back to your father or something? Or did King Erasmus return and detail how the King of Anatolé humiliated the Supreme Commander's right hand?"

Another long pause. "I know because I was there."

Time stills.

"What do you mean you were *there*?"

"I mean I was there, attending The Founding celebration in place of my father. I lurked in the shadows all evening, remaining unseen. But... I was there. And I saw the whole exchange."

"You were present that night..." I murmur, my brain trying desperately to reconcile the information. Because as my brain puts the pieces together, the revelation suddenly comes with another—one which makes my heart pound and stomach clench. I lift my chin to find Draven's eyes, my slackened jaw confirming to him what I imagine he already suspects.

I've finally put it all together.

The memory of our conversation when I found him on Bathara's rooftop all that time ago plays through my mind.

Have you been to Rivara?

Many times.

To the king's court in Keziah?

Yup; don't worry, you never saw me.

But does that mean you saw me?

"It was you," I whisper. "You were the source of the unauthorized magic that kept me from having to dance that night. The reason King Yarum was even able to intervene. The reason I was kept safe from Eri." Awe fills my words as the shock of that realization rattles through me. "It was all you."

Draven nods, his expression unreadable. "It was. Well, Kiran helped too. He was the one who lit the fire in front of the stables. We knew we needed another layer of distraction to stand a chance at actually helping you."

"And so that's how the stables managed to go unharmed. Because he was in control of the flames."

"Yes."

I stare at him, the revelation a temporary paralytic. "The touch I felt..."

He again nods, not even needing me to finish my question. "That was me, too. I..." He pauses, biting down on his lip. "It was a selfish gesture, truthfully. I was saying goodbye to you."

"Goodbye? You didn't even know me yet."

He watches me, and gods there is something in his gaze I can't discern. Emotion which appears snagged between regret and an apology. Draven sighs. "Before I even knew you, Lyra, I suspect I saw the truth of you. All it took was a moment of watching you in King Alastair's court for me to recognize the defiance breathing through your eyes and the spirit of a fighter clawing through your chest." He softens his voice. "But you are right—no, we did not know each other."

I can see there is more to the story. Something he isn't telling me. Yet I choose not to comment on that, instead allowing this blissful moment to exist as it is.

My voice is barely above a whisper when I reply, "Those stitched from the same threads will always recognize each other."

"Who said that?"

I laugh. "Marcella." My fingers play with a loose strand of Draven's hair, filled with more tiny curls at the end from the grown-out length. I tuck said curl behind his ear, my fingers gliding across his cheek after. "I can't believe it was you."

His smile is soft. "I'm sorry I didn't tell you sooner."

I snort a breathy laugh. "Given recent circumstances, I suppose I can give you a pass this time."

He chuckles, revealing the rare sight of his dimple. "I appreciate the generosity."

"Just add it to the list of all the many reasons why you're lucky to have me," I tease.

Draven pushes fallen strands of hair from my face, grinning. "Deal." Then he studies me, a sharp yet gentle intensity now simmering in his gaze. "Do you have any idea how much I love you, Lyra?"

The admission awakens my every nerve ending with a buzzing jolt. "You love me?"

Draven tilts his head, mocking consideration. "Mm...maybe not, actually."

I balk. "Maybe *not*?"

He shakes his head teasingly. "Mm-mmm."

"And why is that?"

He smiles, sweeping his thumb along my cheekbone. "Because I do not simply love you, Lyra. I would die for you. I would roam the edges of this world for you. Would lay down my magic and sword. For you, I would dance at every ball, stumble my way through any conversation—for you, I would do it all. Because there is no place, no moment, where I am not thinking of you. I walk outside, and you're all I see. In every flower. In every caress of the breeze. When the sun embraces me, and the moon inspires me—it is you who fills my mind. I cannot just say I love you because that would be far too reductive to express all that I feel for you. I yearn. I grieve. I love. I hope. And it is all for you. Every last piece of it."

"You love me," I whisper, this time not a question at all. The words taste foreign on my tongue, feeling too large and pure for me to process. "Even though I'm a recovering cynic? Am someone who would prefer to spend their days amongst flowers and herbs instead of people? Even though the left side of my body is covered in scars from my actions and" —my words hitch, my chest bloated from feeling so many things at once— "even though I am tainted, having been defiled and belittled in so many ways... you still love me?"

He slides his hand over my cheek, cupping it with such tenderness. "You are my salvation, Lyra. I feel complete when I'm with you, and I feel lost when I'm without you. So, yes... I love you. For your good. For your bad. For the strength you carry in spite of your past. For the kindness you offer others because of it. I love every piece of you, jagged or not."

I hold his adoring gaze, harboring the radiance of stars inside me as I do. "And I love you," I whisper, my throat too clogged with emotion to do anything but. "For all that you are. For all that you continue to be. I love you, Draven. So much."

Draven beams, tugging me closer to him so he can kiss me. And when he does...

Gods.

He kisses me with the delicate beauty of cherry blossoms. With the unending dedication of a sunset, always finding its way back to the horizon. He kisses me in the shades of different colors, with the passions of different musics. And I realize there will never come a time where I could possibly get enough of his lips being pressed against mine. Get enough of him.

He is the steady arms where I go to feel safe. The place I roam to where my worries and doubts may quiet. He is the best kind of good I have ever known. Someone who looks at me and allows me to feel seen at every intrinsic level. A person who holds me when I'm not at my best yet encourages me to get back up again.

I love him. I *choose* him.

And he has chosen to love me in return.

There is something quite beautiful in the simplicity of that, I can't help but decide. Something which feels bigger than us yet entirely controlled by us simultaneously. Oddly, for a brief moment, it makes me think of Meiji.

He would smile at the paint I have brushed onto my canvas, I think.

"I am yours," I breathe onto Draven's lips. "And you are mine."

"Always," he confirms, sweeping his thumb along my cheek once more.

I study him for slow heartbeats, my eyes flicking to the circular scar marring his skin just below his collarbone. For so long I've wanted to ask, and in the face of this cradling security we have offered each other, I know now is the right time to finally do it. "Draven?"

"Yes?"

"Will you tell me how you got that scar?"

I remember when we were together in a moonlit cave, beneath the glowing dyotana and a glistening waterfall surrounded by my favorite flower. I remember how he made me feel and the way he touched me. Yet when I had touched his scar, I also remember the way he receded back into himself, rattled yet clearly not wanting to be.

Draven stiffens, then relaxes. "It was originally a brand mark burned into my skin. Specifically, House Dalmar's sigil. I..." He trails off, his voice sounding tight in his throat. "Well, when I decided I could no longer bear the mark being branded onto me, I disfigured it with my own hot iron, deciding I would much rather have a mangled scar than wear a Dalmar sigil any longer."

My chest tightens. "So when I touched it once..."

"It reminded me of who I once was and what I lost. No one had ever touched my scar before—not even when it was only a brand mark. I couldn't bear it. And if I am being entirely truthful with you, Lyra, it scared me when you did because, for a brief moment, I saw all that I stood to lose. Was temporarily reminded of that pain."

My fingers trace soothing lines down his arm. "I'm sorry."

He shakes his head. "Don't be. Because just as quickly as it was there, it was gone. You know why?"

Now it is I who shakes my head.

The corner of his lip curves gently. "Because I learned the tradeoff to accepting love is accepting pain, and I will feel any pain to have your love."

My heart swells, full from an emotion I have never experienced in all my life. I lean forward to press a gentle kiss to his lips. When I pull back, I trace his features, studying him. "I know you told me a little about your past in your letters, but if you're willing, I want to hear more about it. I would like to know all of it, in all its many forms."

His throat bobs. "Are you sure? It is not a happy story, Lyra, and if I were to tell you everything, there are parts which I think will be quite confusing for you to hear."

"I'm sure," I murmur. "I want to know all of your pieces, in all their light and shadows."

"Alright," he says, lacing his fingers through mine.

Draven then proceeds to tell me the entire composition of his many scars.

And he is right.

My world is not the same after.

CHAPTER SIXTY

RHEA

Rhea's eyes remain glued to the sky until the last comet fades, passing by with a final brilliant flare of light.

It was all perhaps the most beautiful sight she's ever witnessed. It left behind in her something akin to the warmth of a really good dream. Of an optimistic promise. A pleasant afternoon spent underneath a gilded sun. She feels hopeful and dreamlike. Beautiful and philosophical in the way one feels after witnessing something poetic. She feels happy. Peaceful, even.

She feels things she is not afforded to feel often.

"That was pleasant."

Ah, there is a more familiar feeling.

Annoyance.

Rhea drags her eyes from the now dull sky and positions them pointedly on Finlay. "You know what would have made it more pleasant? You not following me around all day like a lost puppy at my heels."

From the moment she left their group's side, Finlay has been her shadow. As she moved through the streets, he was there, three paces behind. When she went to the market stalls, he was there, three paces behind. As she tried new food and chatted with men offering to take

580

her to the alehouses to get a drink, Finlay was there. Though that time he did not maintain his three paces. That time, he strode right up and stood next to her, silently folding his arms over his chest and glaring at the man with the sharpness of an Arellian blade.

Rhea thought it best to just walk away from that one. No point in causing trouble or making a scene at a festival.

She instead chose to leave the bustling, crowded streets behind. She walked away from the food, the stalls, and all the golden accessories and colorful fabrics, finding a remote hill covered in a layer of rare grass, where a large boulder sat overlooking the glittering city.

That is where she chose to watch the comets pass—upon that boulder, with the city lights and merry music nothing but a background feature.

But of course, Finlay followed, three paces behind.

"What was I supposed to do? Leave you to your own devices in a foreign city on the day of its most celebrated festival?" He snorts. "I think not."

Finlay sits with his back against a large cypress tree, one leg stretched out in front of him as he whittles a stick with his dagger. Without his usual stiff attire—instead clad in colorful festival wear—he carries a semblance of normalcy. Even if he's only swaddled himself in nice silks and still bears his signature three braids. Somehow, when Rhea gazes at him right now, Finlay seems like just another person. Someone removed from the stuffy Fjolla name. Someone handsome and capable of caring about another. Someone she doesn't have to hate.

Or maybe Rhea has simply gotten to know him better over these passing months. Has begun to understand him. Has humanized him.

It's hard to feel like you're enough when the only proof of love you've ever had is reliant on what you can or cannot give.

She turns away from him and scowls, not willing to give up her grudge. "I don't need a babysitter. I'm not a child."

Finlay's grunted laugh is his only reply.

"I mean it," Rhea presses, turning back to look at him over her shoulder. "I hate it when you treat me like I'm still the little girl I was when I was brought to House Dalmar."

Finlay pauses his whittling to look up at Rhea. "How would you like me to treat you, then?"

"Treat me as an equal. As a person deserving of your respect."

"Do you care if you have my respect? Is that something you actually want?"

Is it?

Why should she care if she has his respect? He sure as shit doesn't have hers.

Yet the idea of him thinking poorly of her bothers Rhea more deeply than she wishes it did. She thinks poorly of *him*. Thinks he is a pompous asshole who cares far too much about societal hierarchies and rigid traditions. So why should it matter if he holds a similar, unimpressed opinion of her?

For reasons she refuses to consider, it does.

Rhea redirects. "Does the answer to that question even matter to you? Will it change the way you treat me?"

Finlay, having gone notably still while waiting for her answer, returns to his whittling. "No," he says. "It probably would not."

The answer makes Rhea angry.

She slides off the boulder, strutting straight for Finlay. "What do you mean, *it probably would not?*" She deepens her voice to do a spiteful mock impression of him. "Why can't you respect me?"

Finlay glances up, his face a perfectly inscrutable mask. "I never said I didn't."

"Yet you refuse to say you do. Why? What is it about me that is so hard to be open and honest with?"

Finlay laughs. He *laughs*. "You're joking, right?"

Rhea's anger—though irrational as it may be—turns boiling. "No, Finlay. I'm not joking." She pushes her tongue into her cheek, the dam splitting open in her chest, allowing a sea of caged emotions to slip through. "Really—what is it about me that you detest so much? That you find *so* deplorable, you belittle me and mock me and call me a fucking charity case to your father?"

Finlay studies her through narrowed eyes for a long, quiet moment. Eventually, he wordlessly sets his stick and dagger on the ground and braces his weight on his legs to stand. He takes slow, measured steps to Rhea. "Perhaps I should ask the same of you. Why do you continue to hold a grudge against me for something I did at only fourteen? I was a *fucking* child, Rhea—no more than a few years older than you were when they died. And yet you treat me as if I am an irredeemable monster. As if I had any *real* choice the day I told Tynan where to find you all."

Anger, grief, and hatred all clamor together in Rhea's chest. "You want redemption, Frosty? Then tell me what you've done to earn it. Tell me what good you've brought into the world." A purposeful pause. "Oh, wait—you can't. Because you continue to be your father's obedient lapdog, spreading his fucked up ideology about blood supremacy." Stricken by both her anger and grief, Rhea reaches back for the hair pin dagger wedged through her half-drawn bun. She takes the thin blade—sharp as any sword's edge—and presses the tip of it into her forearm. Then she drags it across her skin.

Finlay's face twists with shock. "Rhea, what the hell are you doing?"

A crimson seam appears just below the crook of her elbow, blood already dripping down the length of her arm. "See this blood? Do you see the color of it? It is the same as yours. It is the same as everyone in House Fjolla's has ever fucking been and ever fucking will be. Your blood is no different than mine. Yet you and your highborn father would see to it that people like me and the commoners and the poor-folk in the slums think it is."

He remains silent.

"So tell me, Finlay," she demands while sliding her hair pin back into place with her other arm. "Why. Do. You. *Hate*. Me."

"Hate you," Finlay scoffs so low, Rhea nearly misses it. He takes a step closer. And then another. The space between them has diminished to nothing more than the barriers of their own walls and defenses. "At this point, after everything that's happened between us, can you still truly reduce all I feel to me merely *hating* you?"

"Forgive me—what emotion am I missing? Disgust? Anger? Pity? Perhaps all of them?" She lifts her chin, not allowing any of the turmoil swimming in her chest to leak through the cracks threatening to break her apart. "Please, enlighten me on the spectrum of terrible things I force you to feel when you look at me."

He scoffs a sharp laugh, rubbing his fingers across his forehead before threading them through his hair. "You know nothing of what I feel when I look at you, Rhea. *Nothing.*"

"No? Then why don't you tell me. Tell me all about how hard it is to have someone so low and common in the presence of a great Fjolla." Rhea knows she has officially let her anger get the best of her. That she is being childish in provoking him. Yet she seems unable to stop herself. To get control. The words come out like vomit, a desperate defense to expunge some of the venom from her body.

Finlay lowers his chin to meet her eyes fully. "Do not pretend to understand me."

"I don't understand you. That's my problem. I don't understand you, your actions, or your words in the slightest."

"No?" Finlay studies her with a sharp look in his eye.

Rhea lifts her chin even higher, nearly pressing the tips of their noses together. "*No.*"

She can feel the heat radiating between their skin as they hold each other's stares. They are so close that if anyone were gazing upon them right now, they would probably think they were lovers caught in an intimate moment.

Yet they are not lovers, and there is no intimacy here. She would rather stab one of her daggers through her hand or cut another slice on her arm than be intimate with him.

But if that were entirely true, why does Rhea feel a heat simmering in her stomach as she holds Finlay's eyes which is not attributed to anger? Why is there a quiet fluttering in her chest as she notices with full clarity just how close their bodies are? How Finlay's hair looks silver beneath the moonlight. How the shadows chisel his jaw further and expand the broadness of his already impressive frame. Why, then, do her eyes flick down to Finlay's lips? Why do they remain there for two whole heartbeats?

Finlay notices the shift of her gaze, and his eyes widen before shuddering with a passing expression Rhea isn't entirely sure what to make of.

Is he about to make her feel like a fool for what she's just done? Is he going to gloat? Find a way to boast his highborn greatness because, lo and behold, Rhea is evidently twisted enough to somehow be attracted to him after all, wondering what it would be like for a moment if he kissed her?

Damn it to Merikh's realm and back. Why the hell had she just let herself do that? She is a fool. An absolute fo—

"Fuck it."

Finlay swallows Rhea's face with his hands, his grip tight as he slams his lips into hers. The kiss is not gentle. It is not soft nor testing. It holds a burning furnace behind it, his mouth aggressive and rough with hers.

Finlay threads his fingers through Rhea's hair—narrowly missing her hairpin—and tugs at the strands forcefully.

It draws a moan from Rhea's lips, which forces a growl from Finlay's.

Their tongues clash like dueling swords as their lips devour each other. Rhea lifts her hand to the nape of his neck, where she also grabs a fistful of Finlay's hair. It is soft. Silky, even.

She yanks on it right as she pinches her teeth into Finlay's bottom lip, slowly dragging the grooves of them over his plump skin. Ecstasy coats her skin at the low moan he seems unable to hold back. His hand slides down from her face and over the slope of her breasts to bracket her hip, where he digs his fingers so deep against the curve of her, his nails bite into her, bringing about a dull stinging pain.

Rhea is sick for how much it turns her on.

She plants her palms against Finlay's chest and pushes him backward until his back hits the thick trunk of the cypress tree. She sees him glancing down at her, the uncertainty in his eyes at him being the one pinned against something. Until his mouth hooks up at the corner, and he reverses their positions.

Rhea scowls at him, but Finlay only chuckles. "For once, just do as you're told."

She cocks her head, blinking at him with saccharine sweetness. "And what is it you'd like me to do?"

He growls again, the sound low and deep in his throat. "Whatever I tell you to."

"And will you praise me as a good girl if I do?"

She is still teasing him, her tone nothing short of mocking. Yet Finlay's eyes flare with a desire so palpable, it is like fingers caressing her skin; the pleasure she feels from it hums the same.

He leans in even closer, his breath a warm cloud on her lips. "You, Rhea Brooksley, are anything but a good girl."

"Does it make you want to punish me? Force me to behave?" Rhea's hand roves down to find Finlay perfectly hard for her. The bulge in his trousers is so firm—so swollen—Rhea almost licks her lips. Thankfully, she manages to hold off on that action. Instead, she tightens her grip, molding her fingers around the large shape of him. She taunts him with slow, toying motions.

Finlay's head falls forward, his forehead pressed against the trunk of the tree just over her shoulder. "Fuck, Rhea. Do not do that if you aren't prepared for what happens next."

"And what happens next, Finlay? What are you going to do to make me stop?"

He lifts his head from the tree to look at her, his eyes an inferno so at odds with the usual iciness filling the turquoise color. His lips crash into hers again, somehow even more hungry than before.

Rhea welcomes it, her stomach clenching and unclenching with desire.

Finlay slides his fingers from her clavicle, down the center of her breasts, along the slope of her stomach—Rhea not even flinching when he reaches that part of her body—until they reach the top of her pants, where they still. "Tell me you want me to go further."

Rhea, who is breathless and a mess of delirious heat, only holds his simmering gaze with defiance, not wanting to do as she's been told.

Finlay realizes it instantly. He repositions his fingers to toy with her on the outside of her billowing pants, just as she had done to him. The festival clothes she has on are much thinner than her usual attire, which means she feels every teasing stroke he makes against her in vivid color. "Tell me," he demands against her mouth. "Tell me you want me, Rhea. Tell me, and I will be yours."

He has increased the speed of his fingers as they rub against her, sending blissful shocks of warm heat flooding her entire body. She shuts her eyes and bites her lip, sparks of color popping off behind her closed eyelids.

Gods.

She had no idea he would be so skilled with his fingers.

"Tell me, Rhea."

Heat builds and builds inside her, and crazy though she may be for thinking it—for feeling it—she does want him. Gods, she fucking *wants* Finlay Fjolla. All of him. Every last icy piece.

"I...I want..."

Before she can get the words out, an authoritative voice bellows from only a few marks away, "Fire-wielders, *halt!*"

It is an immediate bucket of water to their senses.

Rhea stiffens, and Finlay's eyes widen before he pulls back from her and crouches low. "Get down," he demands, his hand finding her shoulder and pushing her downward before she even has a chance to do it herself.

She doesn't protest.

They both peek their heads out from around the large cypress tree to assess the scene. The blood drains from Rhea's face at what she sees.

Figures wearing hooded cloaks are lined up in four neat rows stretching from east to west. There are so many of them, they aren't even able to see where the line ends. They can only see where it begins—a few marks east from where Rhea chose to hide away from the bustling city.

A man whose hood is removed stands before the cloaked army, a long, jagged scar marring his cheek. "Wielders, prepare your lakti."

In perfect unison, each person exposes their palms to the sky, an unnatural energy sharpening the air. Lights from the magic accumulating in all the wielders' marks glow against the darkness, and Rhea swears she can smell the distinct scent of burning embers.

"Well, what a sight this is to see."

Finlay goes rigid beside Rhea.

She spins around, fingers already reaching for the dagger sheathed at her ankle.

Audwin Fjolla stands behind them, hands clasped neatly behind his back while his tilted head observes them like caged animals meant for entertainment.

Finlay drops to one knee and bows his head. "Father."

"Hello, Finlay. I wish I could say I'm surprised to find you with this girl at your side, but frankly" —he purses his lip— "I am not in the slightest."

To Rhea's surprise, Finlay ignores the comment. "What are you doing here, father?"

"What does it look like I'm doing, boy? I'm overseeing the start of a gods-damn war."

"War?" Rhea echoes.

Audwin slides his eyes to her, his lips twisting as if he's just tasted something unpleasant. "Please, do not speak unless spoken to. I have no time to explain matters reserved for men to you."

Finlay lifts his head and rises from the ground, his hands balled into fists at his sides. His tone is clipped when he replies, "Fine, then I shall ask you the same question. What do you mean overseeing a *war*?"

Audwin sneers at his son. "Have you truly been so blind? You probably have." He sighs pointedly. "The people are rebelling. Noble houses are turning against each other, pointing fingers and looking to place fault. Our biggest threat has been neutralized—broken—and our next biggest threat, the Anatolé Kingdom, has formally been pinned with the blame. Which means all that is left to do is officially declare war. And this? This is our proclamation."

The man whom Rhea now assumes to be a commander bellows instructions into the air a few paces away from them. "Wielders at the ready. Aim. *Fire!*"

In perfect synchrony, the fire-wielders all pool a large ball of flames into their hands, casting a warm glow in the surrounding dark. There are hundreds of wielders, resulting in hundreds of fireballs. They send them racing into the outer perimeter of the city, shooting their magic in a straight line to start.

Rhea goes slack at the sight of it. "No," she whispers, forced to watch the first line of trees and the same abandoned alleyways their hideout was in erupt in a blaze of light. She stares at the vermillion glow, unable to fully process what she's witnessing. For a moment, everything becomes dreamlike.

Until she realizes...

"Draven!" She moves to sprint, but strong arms grip her waist immediately, pulling her back. Rhea twists her chin over shoulder and snarls like a rabid animal. "Let me *go.*"

"No," Finlay says. "Draven will be fine. I'm not letting you run into a city condemned to burn."

"You should listen to him, girl. He's giving you sound advice." A small flurry of ash sways in the wind, falling down onto Audwin's shoulder. He glances at it, swiping it from his fine clothing like a pesky insect. "Besides, I can't have you running off anyway. I am to deliver you somewhere for a very special game. One which Draven will be in attendance for as well. From what I gather, he may have need of you."

"Fuck you." Rhea spits at Audwin's feet.

With his arms still securely around her waist, Finlay lifts Rhea off the ground and turns, setting her down gently behind him. When he squares his shoulders back to his father, Rhea realizes he's just put himself directly in between her and Audwin.

"You're not taking her."

Audwin laughs. "Are you really going to attempt to defy me now for a girl you just called the Dalmar's charity case mere months ago?"

Rhea sees the way Finlay's muscles tense. Still, he does not relent.

"Whatever plans you've made, leave her out of it. Father, please—I have never asked you for anything, but I am asking you for this."

Audwin frowns. "You have never asked me for anything because you've never been in a position to do so. Because you have always been so incompetent—so *worthless*—you knew to never dare request something from me." He strolls forward, a look of genuine confusion pinching his features. "Truthfully, I don't know why you are attempting to play the savior now. I know you were assigned a private mission by Bathara's council to find Lyra Izacalli yourself. That you have been in close correspondence with Cahlmon Orius, detailing for him Draven's movements. It was a big aid to us, honestly. I was even going to reward you for all you've done. Now, however, I am not feeling so kind."

A jolt colder than ice lances down Rhea's spine. "You betrayed Draven? *Again?*"

Finlay turns to face her. He looks like he wants to reach for her, hands twitching in front of him while a silent plea fills his eyes. He takes a step toward her, but when Rhea mirrors his movements in the opposite direction, he halts. Finlay drops his hands back down to his sides.

His eyes harden. "No. I did not betray him in the end."

"You helped them track us, though? Fed them information?"

He bites down, popping the muscle in his jaw. "It's not that simple, Rhea."

"Isn't it? Because it seems pretty fucking simple to me. Either you helped them, or you didn't."

Finlay glides his tongue over the grooves of his teeth, bracketing his hands on his hips and glancing up at the sky. Until his eyes return to Rhea. "I'm telling you, I didn't betray anybody this time."

It's too late. Rhea's mind is made up the moment ghosts of impaled bodies on bloodied walls scream at her. "It was you," she hisses. "You are the reason this army is here—you told them where to find us, didn't you?" Rhea shoves Finlay's chest. Hard. "It is *always* you. You betrayed Draven—betrayed *me*—for yet another time, you *piece* of shit." She slams her palms into the panes of his chest again. And again.

He doesn't budge an inch. Though he doesn't attempt to stop her, either.

Finlay only shakes his head. "No. I never sent the final letter with our coordinates, Rhea. I thought about it—I *was* in communication with Master Cahlmon for a while—but I never—"

Rhea slaps Finlay across the cheek, the sound echoing ten times louder than its actual decibel. She feels the brokenness splitting her glassy gaze apart deep in the hollows of her ribs. "I hate you," she whispers.

It is the quietest she has ever said the words to him. The softest they've ever spilled from her lips.

It is also the most she has ever meant them.

Finlay does reach for her now. "Rhea..."

Without another word to him, she strides past Finlay, her shoulder clipping him as she goes. "Take me to Draven," she demands, facing Audwin.

"Rhea!" Finlay shouts. He sounds panicked. Desperate, even. "Rhea, listen to me—it's not what you think. I didn't do it this time. Not again. I couldn't do it again. Please. I–I need you to know that. *Rhea!*"

She doesn't stop to listen nor turn to face him. Her eyes instead remain forward, locked on Audwin, who looks at his son. "It's time you come home to Aderwynn Castle. I will expect to find you there when I return."

The thought is sour in Rhea's mind. *You finally got it, Frosty. You get to go home at last.*

Audwin guides her away, leading her to a waiting aether-wielder. And when the aether-wielder calls open his portal, Rhea steps through without hesitation, determined to go to the one person who has been there for her as her only constant. The only true person she could ever put her faith in.

As she does, she pretends those aren't tears slipping past her eyes.

Pretends her heart doesn't feel oddly broken.

She scowls at herself.

Fuck a broken heart.

And fuck Finlay Fjolla.

CHAPTER SIXTY-ONE

MARCELLA

Marcella glances through the sides of her eyes, her lips quirking up as she observes Gray attempting to catch the glittering comet's dust falling from the sky.

He is leaning over the rail of the balcony encasing her room, the dimming sky giving its final bow for the spectacular show it just delivered. Just before the comet shower started, Gray knocked on her door and asked if she'd like to attend the viewing party with him. Marcella had declined—she was exhausted and mentally fatigued from that meeting. She just wanted to watch the comets pass from the comforts of her own room, away from people and pandering. She said as much to Gray, which resulted in him revealing the items he had been hiding behind his back.

"Figured as much," he said to her, raising the double-flute in his left hand before showcasing the bottle of wine he snagged from gods-only-know-where in his right. "I thought I'd bring the music and wine to you, if you'll have me."

Though Marcella hates to admit it, she had smiled at him like a smitten schoolgirl, throwing the door open to let him enter her bedchamber. "Fine. Come on."

Now, Marcella leans against the door's threshold leading out to the balcony, that same smile she has been trying to keep contained creeping upward more and more as she watches him. Eventually, after his tongue hooks up at the corner of his mouth and he seemingly has lost all sense of safety, a laugh bubbles free from her throat.

"You're going to fall over the side if you keep that up." They both have consumed more than one glass of wine, yet Marcella is still sober enough to realize heights and alcohol are never the best combination.

"If I get an entire handful of this comet dust, it will have been worth it." He leans even farther over the ledge, and Marcella's heart rate spikes.

"Seriously, Gray. Be careful."

He pays her no mind, instead focusing only on the glitter as it continues raining down from the sky. He wobbles but steadies himself with his knee, tucking it into the balusters to support his tipping weight.

It makes Marcella's palms clammy. "Alright." She kicks off the threshold and struts for him, wrapping her arms around his waist and tugging him away from the railing. "No more. I don't think watching you fall to your death is a great way to end the festival."

He goes willingly, spinning around in her arms while keeping his cupped hands lifted over their heads. He laughs that perfectly boyish laugh of his. "If you wanted to wrap your arms around me, all you had to do was ask, you know."

Marcella tsks at him and quickly drops her arms, her cheeks flushing. "Please, you wish."

"Every day." He says it like he means it.

She stares at him, confusion once again overtaking all her other emotions. She hates when he says things like that. Acts like his feelings extend as far as hers do for him. "Stop doing that."

His expression pinches. "Doing what?"

"Acting like you care."

He drops his cupped hands to his chest, revealing a pile of sparkling dust that glitters like diamond shavings. Yet he doesn't even look down at all the beauty captured between his palms. His eyes remain only on Marcella. "I do care."

She glides her hands through her hair, her frustration finally boiling over. "Yes, I know, Gray. I get it—you 'care.' But not like how I care. Not in the ways I wish you did."

"You're wrong," he murmurs.

She wants to believe him. More than anything else, she wishes she *was* wrong. But if she truly was, Gray would have kissed her that night at the inn. Would have told her during the masquerade ball she was his or that he was hers or...*something*. Instead, every time they broach the subject, all he does is attempt to begin his explanation for why he didn't kiss her that night. Tries to justify it when instead all Marcella wishes for at this point is for him to tell her how he feels *now*. She doesn't want to be reminded of his rejection; she wants a reason to look beyond it. To receive any sort of validation or affirmation from him that she isn't insane for believing he does feel the same way about her when she catches him watching her, something undeniable always seeming to glimmer within his gaze.

Marcella wants him to tell her his feelings. His *true* feelings, unfiltered and in all their pain or glory. She certainly has no intentions of saying anything to him first, considering the last time she put herself out there, the door was slammed shut in her face.

"If I'm wrong, then tell me *why*," she begs, so much emotion laced within those seven words. "Why am I wrong? What makes the words I'm saying to you untrue?"

Gray glances away, shoulders hunching forward. "I was going to tell you at sunrise."

"Tell me *what* at sunrise?" Marcella wrinkles her nose. "And why sunrise?"

"I thought it would be romantic," he answers through a sigh. Gray's eyes fall to the ground, to the sparkling dust still sitting inside his hands, then to Marcella, where they remain. He takes a step forward. And then another. And another. Until there is so little space between them, Marcella feels her heartbeat changing rhythm.

And *gods*, he is looking at her in that way again. A look screaming of attraction and devotion. Of reverence and admiration. A look so riddled with longing, it makes Marcella's chest clench.

Just say it, she thinks. *Give me something to hold onto.*

It's his final chance. She will never leave this door open for him again if he doesn't.

"Marcella," Gray begins, voice unbearably soft. "I'm sorry I haven't done a better job of navigating all this. That I caused you to doubt how perfect you are. That I allowed you to think for even one second denying you was actually something I would want to do. You..." he trails off. "Gods, Marcella, you are everything to me. Everything I could ever want, and more than anything I could ever dream of being worthy to receive."

He moves forward like he wants to reach out for her, realizing he still has his hands pressed together as they contain the oh-so-rare comet dust. His brows pucker together, and he tsks at it.

It makes Marcella laugh, and she is surprised by the sheer volume of emotion the sound holds as it spills from her.

Gray's eyes find her again. They are so gentle. "Marcella, I—"

He doesn't get to finish his sentence.

"*Gray*," Marcella breathes, pointing out at the brightening horizon.

An army of fireballs arc through the sky in a similar way the comets had. Only, these fires do not leave glittering dust in their wake. They leave a trail of smoke and destruction as they clamor into parts of the palace and houses and buildings. As they land in alleyways and tear up the stoned streets. As they slam into the marble composing the fountain at the heart of the city, shattering it into pieces.

The entire city goes up in flames.

"By the gods," Gray says, horror forcing his words to quiver.

The door leading into Marcella's chamber suddenly slams open, and seven cloaked figures charge in. Marcella whirls around, immediately ready to fight. Yet before she even has time to uncurl her fingers from her palms, an aether-portal blinks open. Three of them appear directly behind Gray within an instant, and one behind her. The figure next to her yanks her arms behind her back at an awkward angle and shoves her down to her knees. She jerks, attempting to position herself in a way that would allow her to use a defensive move to break the hold. Yet the one keeping her in place tightens their grip and increases the angle of her elbows, making it impossible for her to move.

She growls with rage.

"Let her go," Gray snarls.

The three cloaked figures pounce, attempting to get Gray in a similar position Marcella managed to get herself stuck in. But he does not go down easily. He spins out, immediately taking one of the hooded attackers out by kicking in their knee. The person snaps like a twig, dropping to the ground with a loud shout of pain.

The other two charge, reaching to grip his arms and contain him. Gray grits his teeth and holds them off, finally revealing to Marcella the true depth of his strength. They push against Gray, but he pushes back, skidding their heels backward. Until he manages to throw one of the attackers on their back.

Marcella reaches for her magic, attempting to subtly weave her fingers to summon a vine of thorns to help him. Yet nothing comes to her. Her magic feels covered by a blanket. Contained somewhere far, far away. The person holding her wrists together huffs a laugh, as if sensing her trying and failing to use her laktî.

That's when she realizes.

"They have a Nullifier!" she shouts to Gray.

He turns, his gaze sharp as it flicks to her, then the person holding her in place. With rage lining his eyes, he pivots, charging at the final person in front of him. He dodges the punch at his jaw and blocks the accompanying jab to his ribcage before throwing his own sequence of attacks. They land true, forcing the person to hunch forward over themselves.

That's when they pull out the daggers.

Marcella's eyes widen with horror. They have no weapons on them right now. Why would they? They thought they were celebrating a festival.

They were fools.

One of the remaining cloaked figures strides into view, his other companion trailing at his side. "Knock him unconscious, but be sure to keep him alive. You know our orders." His voice is soothing and familiar. Authoritative yet soft.

Marcella realizes who he is the same moment Gray does.

"Josiah," Gray breathes, eyes wide.

Josiah drops his hood, revealing his white hair, tanned skin, and blue eyes, narrowed and colder than they ever were at Bathara.

"No." Gray shakes his head. "No, not you. My father *trusted* you."

"That was his mistake to make."

Gray stiffens. "What does that mean, Josiah?"

Josiah offers him no answer.

"Let me slice him," the man circling Gray says. Gray pivots to watch the hooded figure, palms held carefully in front of him as he tracks his movements.

"No," Josiah says. "We are not allowed to harm him."

"The Commander won't notice a slice."

"I said *no*."

"Then how do you propose I knock him unconscious?"

"Like this."

The cloaked figure at Josiah's side lifts his hand, and a portal again appears within an instant, this time directly behind Gray. The seventh cloaked figure leans out of it, slamming the hilt of their sword into the back of his head. Gray's eyes roll backward as he drops to the ground.

"*No!*" Marcella screams, bucking against the hold on her.

"And that," Josiah says, "is the power the art of distraction can hold."

The two cloaked figures closest to Gray grip him beneath the shoulders and drag him up. Gray's head rolls forward, his body completely slack. The aether-wielder opens another new portal, motioning for his companions to take Gray through.

Panic seizes Marcella with ruthless fury. "Where are you taking him?" she demands. Anger clouds her vision, hot and consuming. She glares at Josiah. "Why did you betray us? *Why?*"

He does not answer her, instead only sliding her a disapproving glance and folding his hands behind his back

"Where are you taking him? *Answer* me!"

They drag Gray through the portal, and Josiah stands at the foot of the swirling black and white magic. "You can release her now. We have what we came for."

The figure holding Marcella lets her go, shoving her backward with disorienting force. She scrambles to catch her feet and stands, eyes frantically darting forward to find them. Despite the two remaining cloaked figures being nearly through the portal, she still runs her short sprint forward in an attempt to reach them. To pass through and follow them to gods-only-know-where.

She does not reach the portal in time.

Instead, it blinks from existence right as her fingertips reach out, a quiet buzz pricking them as she grazes the edges of the aether-magic.

The magic, the hooded attackers, and Gray all disappear.

It leaves Marcella to stand alone on the balcony, nothing but her questions, a mess of scattered glittering comet dust, and a burning city to keep her company.

CHAPTER SIXTY-TWO

DRAVEN

Draven has the love of his life wrapped securely in his arms when he hears the screams and smells the smoke.

Begrudgingly, he pulls his arms away from Lyra, who pries her back from his chest and scurries from bed. They both dress themselves quickly, the air already sharp with warning.

"What do you think is happening?" she asks him.

"I have some guesses."

Draven opens himself to all the magic around him, sensing and searching. He locates exactly what he suspected, atop something which temporarily stills his movements.

That...can't be.

Once he finishes securing his pants, he does not even attempt to find his shirt, instead striding immediately to the glass door leading out to the balcony, throwing back the curtains to reveal the world on the other side.

The city is washed in a sea of raging flames.

The glowing sky is covered in thick plumes of smoke, now painted in a strange sepia color as the silver moonlight, bright vermilion and gold, soot, and debris all mingle together. For a moment, Draven is transported a decade in time. He is standing on a crumbling roof while a bookshop catches fire. The shouts on the streets are not of civilians but of pieces of his heart.

He hears a girl scream, "Father! *Father!*"

Father!

Draven's chest constricts, a fist now gripping his heart with merciless force.

He feels a gentle touch on his back. "Draven," the voice murmurs. So soft. So comforting.

Draven shakes his head and blinks, glancing down to realize his arms are painted with black rivers already. The inky trails crisscross over his chest, rising into his neck. He blows out a breath, dragging his fingers through his disheveled hair while memories swarm him.

Love is a liability. It is a fool's dream that will only ever expose you and make you weak.

I do not tolerate liabilities to House Dalmar.

He knows. Knows exactly who to attribute this to. Knows just what this person loves to do. What they are capable of. In fact, he is *so* well acquainted, he even suspects he most likely knows what is planned for both him, the resilient woman beside him, and gods-only-know whoever else.

You are my greatest accomplishment.

Precautionary measures must be made.

He turns to face the other half of his soul. "Lyra, I need you to listen to me very carefully."

DRAVEN EXITS the palace to find chaos on the burning streets.

Mothers run with children clutched to their chests. Rows of men line the streets passing buckets of water for the smaller fires while water-wielders do what they can to tame the larger, more devastating ones.

But the fireballs do not stop blazing through the sky.

They just keep coming, one after the other.

Bright flashes of changing colors blink in and out over the horizon as different wielders use different magics to contain the destruction. Rivers of water sweep through the sky like graceful snakes. Winds circle and push against the soaring flames. Terrain-wielders erect thin mountain peaks. There are ice crystals and spheres of light and streaks of purple lightning.

Draven struts past it all, his mind only focused on following the trail of magic as familiar to him as his own.

He stops only once he reaches the very edge of the capital city, the orange flames blazing on both sides of the street, chewing away at the buildings. He catches a small tapestry in the shape of a comet fluttering to the ground, ashened and helplessly blown about by the powerful gusts of wind.

A cloaked figure stands just on the other side of it.

Draven's heart sinks in his chest. "What are you doing here?"

"I think you already know," the familiar voice says, not sounding familiar to him at all right now.

Draven bites down so hard, he fears he is going to crack his teeth. He shakes his head, unwilling to believe it. "Tell me this isn't true. Tell me you haven't been working with him."

"I cannot tell you that; it would be a lie."

It all comes together in Draven's mind. "You've been keeping him informed of our movements, haven't you? Told him we were hiding in the Anatolé Kingdom?"

A long pause. And then—

"Yes."

"How did you know we were in Anatheima?"

"I laced an item with my laktî and placed it on Marcella before she left."

"Then you guided them right to us." Draven does not say it like a question. Though he still receives an answer all the same.

"Yes."

Draven grips his hips, tongue pushing into his bottom lip. "It could have been anyone but you," he whispers, emotion squeezing painfully in his chest. "Gods, Kiran, why did it have to be *you* who betrayed us?"

Kiran drops his hood, revealing his face. His ruby hair is half-drawn, but that is about the only familiar feature on him right now. His eyes are dimmed and cold, his lips thinned and stretched tight across his face. Purple stains are smudged into the hollows beneath his eyes, made extra eerie by the shadows flickering over him from the flaming walls encasing the two of them.

"I am sorry, brother."

Draven can't hide the hurt in his voice. "Why?"

Kiran remains silent.

"*Why?*" he presses, feeling oddly on the verge of tears.

Kiran flexes his jaw, eyes falling temporarily to the ground. Until he reorients himself, straightening his shoulders and uncurling his fingers from his palms, outstretching his hands. "I've been ordered to bring you in alive."

"Tell me *why*," Draven demands through clenched teeth.

"I'm sorry," is all Kiran says.

Then he strikes.

He moves with the fluidity of a fox, weaving his hands in a circular motion as he draws his flames to the surface of his skin.

Draven shakes his head at the sight. "Kiran, please... I don't want to hurt you."

He slides a foot back, his flames humming as they wind over his forearms like coiling snakes. It burns the fabric of his cloak, disintegrating the threads, growing so loud, Kiran has to elevate his voice. "I understand you even more now, brother. Finlay, too. Things... change...when you have something you are fighting to protect."

The words strike Draven, but before he can question Kiran further, his brother unleashes a barrage of roaring fire strikes. Draven deflects the attack with a quick succession of sheets of obsidian magic. A low growl rattles in his chest as he slices his hand through the air, bringing down an onyx whip aimed at Kiran's feet.

With perfect grace, Kiran plants his hand to the ground and propels himself into a backward flip, dodging Draven's attack. He slams the heels of his palms together and sends a roaring golden lion carved purely from flames at Draven.

Draven erects a large shadow panther in answer. It leaps from over his shoulder to swallow the lion. Yet before his panther's inky fangs can clash with the lion's vermilion and gold teeth, Kiran releases the magic, leaving nothing but a trail of embers in its wake.

He sends a blast of scorching magic at Draven's chest in place of the lion.

Draven slams his hands into the ground and erects a defensive wall just in time to swallow the force of the heated impact. Yet before he can even recover from the grunt expelling from his lips, he sees tendrils of fire weaving over his head, crossing at different intersecting points.

They form a net of flames.

Draven releases his hold on his obsidian wall; Kiran brings down the blazing net atop him.

Draven swears under his breath and tucks and rolls, barely escaping Kiran's net as it swallows the place he just stood.

"Enough," Draven snarls.

He goes deeper into his magic, summoning his own black flame. He is greeted by the voices.

Welcome. Welcome. We are already with you now. Let us take control again.

For a heartbeat, he squeezes his eyes closed and strains against the sudden instability souring his veins.

"No. *No,*" he replies aloud.

The moment costs him.

Kiran raises his hands to the reddened, glowing sky, summoning more fire and lacing it together like winding knots to form an even bigger net. To create even bigger flames.

His shirt has burned completely from his body, revealing his wielder's mark. It wraps around his forearm, glowing like pure molten lava against his skin. That, paired with the glowing wisps whipping over his shoulders, veils Kiran's eyes in more shadows, making them look like depthless pits.

When he glances back down at Draven, he is unrecognizable. "I don't want to do this," he says, his voice devoid of all the usual qualities making Kiran who he is.

"Then don't," Draven bites out.

Kiran's gaze is solemn—filled with a tortured sadness. It flays Draven's insides to see his normally mischievous brother wear such a look. "He has them, Draven. I have no choice."

With one hand now outstretched, two fingers pressed tightly together while his other hand remains raised to the sky, Kiran simultaneously sends an inferno racing toward Draven's chest while dropping what appears to be a burning cage down on him.

Draven meets the blast head-on with his own whirling black fire, the two magics clashing at the center of the distance between them, a resounding *BOOM* splitting the air at the impact. At the same moment, he throws up his left arm, creating a ceiling of dark magic over his head, keeping the fiery, vermillion cage lodged in the sky, unable to crash down and contain him.

Draven's muscles scream from the exertion. "Who?" he barely manages to bite out. "Who does…he…have?" His voice is strained and rough, coming out as if his throat is gripped by unrelenting fingers.

In a way, he supposes it is. His magic is that ruthless when he is forced to use so much of it, and it rages inside him as a result.

Let us take control.

Let us take control.

LET US!

Draven feels the slipping sensation. Feels himself losing to the voices again. In his mind's eye, he sees flickers of all those Abdites, their burned bodies now the faces of ghosts who will always haunt his dreams. He does not want to allow himself to commit such another atrocity.

Yet he continues to slip.

Farther and farther away he fades.

He is…

Draven sees a lilac angel through the sides of his eyes. It snaps him back into himself, an immediate blanket thrown over those hissing voices, muffling them to a near unintelligible whisper. Lyra sprints toward them, skidding to a halt only a few paces away from Draven.

He is just barely able to see from the odd angle of his body the way

Lyra assesses the scene. Just barely able to catch the way a resolve settles over her, as though she just made some pivotal decision.

Her shoulders relax, and she presses two fingers together with both hands, drawing her arms back in the motion one would use when wielding a bowstring.

A sizzling bow materializes, forged entirely from glimmering flames, an arrow notched within the glowing string. She draws her elbow back with perfect form.

Then she sends a flaming arrow straight for Kiran. And then a second. And a third.

It forces Kiran to drop his magic and deflect the arrows as they race toward him. With a rolling wave of fire, he deflects them into the burning buildings to his right.

For a moment after, there is nothing but still silence and the haunting radiance of a city on fire.

Both Kiran and Draven observe Lyra with no small amount of shock. Draven is sure his brother felt it just as he had—that was no ordinary magical attack.

Her bow and arrow…that *fire*?

It carries the prowess of something which feels primordial. Beyond the power one mortal should contain.

Draven seizes on the temporary shock, refocusing on his brother, knowing there's no time for him to ask Lyra more about what he's just witnessed. "Tell me who he has, Kiran. Tell me who you're fighting to protect."

Kiran bites down on his lip, staring at his open palms as tiny bursts of magic flicker from them. He shakes his head, dropping his hands down to his sides. "He has my family. My father. My mother. My sister. He's managed to capture them all, and he's been holding them hostage ever since."

The blood leeches from Draven's face. "How?"

For a heartbeat, Kiran looks unsteady on his feet. "I don't know. But I guess how he did it doesn't really matter, does it? It doesn't change anything. He still has them at his mercy."

"Why didn't you come to me? I would have helped you."

Kiran blows out a humorless laugh. "While tracking down the love of your life and rescuing her from her own captor? While navigating your own situation with Arden and Rhea and your father? While dealing with Bathara's council down your throat or your aggregate ready to riot against you?"

The last part strikes Draven.

How does Kiran know that?

"Adding that atop everything else was too much, even for you," Kiran says. When Draven opens his mouth to protest, Kiran quickly adds, "Besides, it wouldn't have mattered anyway. He said he'd slit their throats if I told you. If he caught so much as a whisper of you getting involved." A heavy pause. "He meant it, Draven."

Lyra approaches on quiet feet, stopping at Draven's side. She looks at him with answers already in her eyes, anticipating the questions inevitably bound to fill Draven's own gaze. She dips her chin once, the gesture steeled with firm certainty.

It is done, then.

His eyes soften in the way they only ever will for her as he studies Lyra, one last question passing between them. It is his final offering he can give her to reconsider. To back out and change course for a different direction than the one they've set sail for. This is the last time he'll be able to ask her *Are you sure?* before it is too late not to be.

She holds his eyes with the unwavering strength, pulling out two small vials and handing one over for Draven to take.

He glides his fingers over her jaw with his empty hand, the barest twitch of a smile tugging at his mouth.

That's my girl.

Draven turns back to face his brother. "What do you have to do to see them freed?"

Kiran's lips thin even further. "My final task is to bring you in alive."

"And what about Lyra?"

"Her as well, but only if she was with you. If she wasn't, he said he had another assigned to bring her to the drop spot."

Draven's stomach boils.

Who? Who would his vile father send for her?

There is no time to question it. Draven knows the reality of their circumstances. Tynan played his hand perfectly, putting their backs to a stone wall at a dead end alleyway. They were cornered. If Draven refuses his brother, he will then be the reason for the slaughtering of Kiran's family. Yet if Draven complies, going with his brother and bringing Lyra along with him, Draven must gamble on the plans his father has in store for them while maintaining the only option he can at some illusion of Lyra's safety.

His father knows what Draven's logic will be. That she is better off with him, and they are better off with Kiran being the one to take them hostage. His father also knows Draven is well aware he won't stop until he gets what he wants. That, so long as Tynan's eyes are set on her, Lyra is not safe.

It is a lose-lose, and Draven must choose the way in which he tastes defeat.

Which is why all he can do is pray his final gamble pays off, in whatever twisted sense it can.

He glances at Lyra, who again nods at him. "Do it, Draven," she says.

Draven nods in return, eyes falling forward. In perfect unison with Lyra, he uncorks the vial still wedged in his palm and tips his head back, downing the contents in one swallow. Then, holding Kiran's sullen stare, he tosses the glass aside and slowly goes down on one knee, then his other.

Kiran's eyes widen at the sight of it. "Draven," he breathes. "No... not that. Do not...don't go to your knees."

"Too late," Draven murmurs, clasping his hands behind his head. Lyra does the same beside him, keeping her hip to his, her vial also discarded beside her. "We are yours to take."

Kiran watches him with so many warring emotions on his face. "Brother..."

Before Kiran can say anything else, a group of cloaked figures emerges from the shadows. Under the strange glow of unnaturally large flames, they look like wraiths.

Two hooded figures break off and slap manzat manacles on both their wrists. Draven feels the manzat disrupt his laktî instantly, immediately faced with the debilitating effects of being blocked from his magic. One glance at Lyra is all it takes for him to know she feels the same, her eyes widening as her shoulders hunch inward.

One of the cloaked soldiers waltzes right up to him, pulling his attention. They stop only once arm's length away, where they then pull back their hood, revealing black hair woven back into a single, intricate braid.

You're going to regret everything you've said today.

Draven's expression hardens at the sight of a wielder from his aggregate standing before him. A member who attempted to pick a fight with Rhea. Who demanded the sort of attention he will never give another woman who isn't Lyra ever again. "Kamina." He says her name like an accusation. "So it is true, then; Bathara is compromised."

"I told you the time would come where you would regret everything you said to me that day. Regret abandoning us."

Draven holds her spiteful gaze. "I regret nothing."

With a curl in her lip, she unsheathes the sword at her hip and slams the hilt of it against Draven's temple.

The world is blanketed by shadows.

CHAPTER SIXTY-THREE

LYRA

I watch Draven's body slacken, then topple sideways.

His head falls directly into my lap. Perhaps the worst part of that is how my fingers are unable to swipe the loose strands of hair from his resting eyes. How I can't trace his soot-stained skin. Can't offer him the strength and comfort I know he is going to need by giving him the details of everything I just did. By making sure he knows it was completed exactly as he instructed.

Well… sort of.

I may have included my own additions.

The girl who just slammed a hilt into Draven's head turns to me, a pronounced curl pulling her lip back from her teeth. "Well, there she is. The precious whore who ruined the great Draven Dalmar himself." She prowls to stand in front of me, crouching down to coldly lock her eyes with mine. Her fingers tighten around my chin, pinching my skin together. "The girl who single-handedly stole my aggregate's captain away from us. Turned him into something unrecognizable."

Kamina. That was the name Draven said.

I hold her stare with equal resolve. "You can't call someone you've never truly seen unrecognizable."

Kamina scowls, her grip tightening around her sword until her fingers bleed their color away. In a swift motion, she jerks her hand up and slams the sword's hilt into my temples, just like she did with Draven.

And as my eyelids flutter and unconsciousness beckons me, it is the light of the flames which reminds me of what I must do. Steadies me against the encroaching fear of what we're about to face if Draven's assumptions are correct.

My head rolls back, and the final image I see before the darkness claims me is a golden city on fire; King Yarum's palace swallowed by flames.

"LYRA."

The familiar voice is warm to my dreams.

"Lyra."

So familiar. So warm.

"*Lyra!*"

My eyes jerk open. Immediately, I am met by a splitting headache and brazier light. I attempt to scrub at my face, but my hands are heavier than usual and unable to move independently.

That's right. The manzat manacles.

The hole inside me makes itself known. Strange, how I once was able to live without magic so effortlessly. Now, being without it has left me feeling carved hollow by a rusted blade.

"Lyra."

My eyes whip left, finding the voice. Finding Draven.

The blood drains from my face the moment I do.

He is somewhere around nine, maybe ten paces away from me. An onyx chain is wrapped around his waist, secured by a steel bracket mounted into a staggeringly large column behind him. His hands are secured at his torso, the magic-blocking manacles securely placed over his wrists. His eyes are frantic.

Until they meet mine.

They soften, then, in perfect rhythm with his shoulders as they slacken. "You're awake."

Somehow in the midst of all this mess, I still manage a small smile. "Sorry I kept you waiting."

His lips tilt. But just as quickly as the soft moment is there, it leaves. Draven's features sober, his expression growing solemn as his eyes shift to look at something in the distance.

That's when I finally rise, taking in the full magnitude of my surroundings.

The first thing I realize is that, just as Draven does, I have a chain locked around my waist, securing me to my own towering column with no more than two paces of length to move around. The second thing I notice is we seem to be in a sprawling cavernous space of sorts. Only, the obsidian-toned rock is smooth and polished like marble, and the vaulted ceiling—feeling as high as the heavens themselves—is so perfectly ground out, it carries the glistening sheen of sleek glass.

The third thing I notice is Draven and I are not alone.

Directly across from me, secured to his own column, is Gray. Next to him and directly across from Draven is Rhea, her hands and waist also bound.

Gray and I lock eyes. He looks unbearably sad. Like the entire world has been uprooted at his very feet.

Are you okay? he mouths to me, seeming too tired to vocalize the words.

Are you? I mouth back.

He shakes his head only once, eyes falling to the ground.

It hits me then that Draven was right in his suspicions. That this is real and is probably going to happen just how he predicted.

Nausea roils in my stomach. The world blurs for a moment as a rush of blood pounds in my ears. Yet the sound of stone scraping against stone forces me to stay steady on my wobbling feet. To not succumb to my growing nerves.

I will not cower. I will not yield. I will not falter.

The words offer me so much more strength now that I have grieved my mother. Now that I properly feel her spirit within me.

Now that I have looked all my worst fears in the face and smiled back at the dark.

Doors open, and three cloaked figures march in, stopping below a lavish balcony built into the eastward wall. Shortly after, three more figures appear on that very balcony, strutting into the blinking firelight, stopping only once their fingers can curl around the deep onyx railing.

The fear once pounding in my chest morphs to shock before twisting into rage. Absolute rage.

Familiar eyes gaze down at me from the pretty balcony, a cruel, twisted smile twirling a pair of lips. "Hello, pet. Have you missed me?"

I hold those vile eyes, wearing every bit of my disgust as I spit on the ground at my feet.

King Alastair chuckles, shaking his head. "My little birdie grew some wings, and so now she thinks she can fly amongst kings." He mocks a pout. "Oh, dear pet, it's time we clip those pesky wings."

"Is that not the girl who used to dance for us at your parties, Alastair?" King Erasmus leans over the railing, squinting his crow-lined eyes.

King Alastair laughs. "It is. I am honored you remembered, because I did so love it when she danced."

"Do not speak to her with your vile tongues." Draven's words are contained, yet they still echo off the stone walls as if shouted between cupped hands.

"You would dare speak to—"

"Please, Your Highness, forgive my son. I fear he has been insubordinate since a young age. Hence his participation in these games." Tynan, who stands between the two kings, turns his gaze to observe Draven as if he were nothing more than an interesting spectacle.

"Games?" The question comes from Gray.

Tynan turns to look at him, a polished smile on his lips. "Yes, games. And rather riveting ones at that."

"We are not your toys to play with." The quiet rage in Rhea's voice is enough to slice like a blade.

"Ah, but that's just it, isn't it?" Tynan coos. "That is *precisely* what you are. What everyone is to someone else. Toys. Pawns. Tools."

"Spare us your game of titles," Draven spits. "Just tell us what you intend for us to do."

"But titles are part of the game, you see. What titles do you believe you bear? Hero. Sister. Chosen. Monster. What titles will you assume once forced to put all that you believe to the test? Will the hero become the villain? Will the whole become the broken? The broken the savior?" Tynan releases a low laugh as he claps his hands together. "Oh, I cannot wait to see."

"Why us?" Gray asks.

Tynan rapidly clicks his tongue. "Ah, ah, mustn't spoil the game. That will all be revealed during each of your turns."

My eyes narrow on him. He seems almost manic with glee. Every interaction I've had with Tynan Dalmar up until this point has been one where he is poised and in complete control. But right now there is a loose thread in his normally impenetrable exterior, threatening to unwind his careful facade entirely.

"Any volunteers to go first?" Tynan asks.

Gray takes a step forward. "I will."

Tynan laughs in tune with the other two kings, and he glances at each of them. "Did I not tell you this is how it would begin?"

King Erasmus nods with approval. "This is precisely why you are my Master Strategist."

King Alastair laughs—the sort of laugh I grew to recognize meant someone was about to suffer unspeakable pain. It typically accompanied moments where he was delivering his punishment from a summons. When seeking retribution from those who he deemed as doing wrong by him.

The hairs on my arms rise, and a chill sweeps down my spine.

"Let justice be served, then," King Alastair mutters as he turns to sit on one of two glittering silver thrones at the center of the balcony.

Tynan's eyes remain pinned on Gray. "Well, Lion of the Heart." He smiles, splaying his arms wide. "Welcome to the Grand Moral Games."

CHAPTER SIXTY-FOUR

GRAY

Gray watches a hooded guard stick a key into the shackles at his waist and turn the lock free. He notices the guard does not dare remove the manacles from his wrists.

Gray strides to the center of the room, keeping his chin lifted high. He remains there as Tynan Dalmar descends the balcony, striding for him with his hands clasped behind his back and a tight—though deeply authentic—smile tucked into his mouth.

"Lion of the Heart." He says Gray's given title with a low vibrato, moving his hands in tune to the sound before clapping them together. "It is a pleasure to meet you at last."

Gray dips his chin—the gesture tight and filled with distaste. He does not take his eyes away from Tynan Dalmar for a single second. "Supreme Commander."

"Are you ready to play the game?"

"It's not as though I really have a choice."

Tynan grins. "May I be honest with you? I actually created it with you in mind. You were the inspiration who gave this artist his muse."

"Don't play with the boy, Tynan. I am eager to see my justice served."

The corner of Tynan's mouth tightens, but that is the only reaction he allows on his otherwise perfectly polished features. Tynan Dalmar is as smooth and unblemished as the glossy walls surrounding them.

He turns just enough to face King Alastair—the sight of whom fills Gray with a potent, molten rage. The moment the repugnant man strode out onto the balcony, Gray saw flashes in his mind of what he did to Lyra. The way he made her strip nude and bare her body to him only to take a whip to it after.

Gray feels his face twist with his distaste and anger. The thought paired with his worries regarding Marcella and her safety is almost enough to make his exterior crack and crumble. But he is the proud son of Sterling Nightenjoy, who taught him how to always keep his wits about him. So he will not allow blemishes in his exterior. He cannot let his frenzied emotions overtake his ability to think rationally.

"Of course, Your Highness," Tynan says, inclining his head. He squares his shoulders to Gray. "Allow me to explain the rules." His lips part, but before a word breaks free, he pauses, observing Gray through narrowed eyes while a serpent's smile curves his lips. He releases an amused laugh. "Though it seems you've already put most of it together, haven't you?"

"Do not give him anything." The growling voice comes from Draven.

Smooth as silk, Tynan holds up a finger to Gray. "One moment, please." He strolls over to Draven, stopping only once he can gaze into his son's eyes. Draven holds his stare with a curl in his lip.

Tynan slams his fist into Draven's gut, then hooks him in the jaw with his other. "You will have your turn, I assure you. So please, do not interrupt me again."

Draven bows slightly forward at the impact, a small grunt escaping him. Yet within seconds, he stands at full attention, spine straightened and shoulders rolled back. He spits blood at Tynan's feet. "Fuck. You."

Tynan grins like a smug cat. "I can't wait to see if you keep that same bravado when your turn arrives." He strolls away, hands clasped behind his back. "Telamon, would you be so kind as to encase them?"

"As you wish, Commander."

The hooded figure to the left steps forward. He exposes his palms to the sky, raising them up slowly. As he does, a whitish-yellow energy thrums in the air, pooling above the heads of Lyra, Draven, and Rhea. He slams his palms downward, and the energy morphs into a solid rectangular barrier, enclosing them.

Barrier magic.

A sound barrier, judging from the glow of it.

As if similarly curious, Gray glimpses Rhea opening her mouth, her face scrunched as if she is releasing a rage-fueled battle cry.

Yet he hears no sound. No signs of their existence.

"Now that we'll no longer be interrupted, shall we continue?"

Gray says nothing, instead glaring at the man in front of him. He has always known Tynan Dalmar was a cold and calculated man. His father made sure Gray was well aware of the rumors surrounding Tynan's insatiable curiosity for human behavior. Why his appetite made him such a profound Master Strategist. Made sure that Gray was well aware they were not rumors at all.

Yet even knowing such information, Gray still would have never thought he would be *this* cruel. This vile.

Tynan takes Gray's silence as his answer. "We begin at the conception of a meticulously calculated plan. A plan where a continent has been split and power has been trisected and delegated. We begin where kings' ambitions lie. Where the desire for more power roots itself into the powerful." Tynan paces, hands folded neatly behind his back. "But I suspect you've already deduced this, haven't you, Lion?"

Gray remains silent.

"Aw, come now. You must indulge me a little. It is a game after all."

Silence.

"Very well," Tynan sighs. "I suppose the choice to speak or remain silent can be level one of your turn then." He halts, turning to the large stone doors carved into the glistening westward wall. "Bring him out."

The stone groans, and a man with manzat manacles and chains around his feet is escorted into the cavernous room by two more guards wearing light-blue hooded cloaks. He has a small binding over his mouth, preventing him from speaking.

The world tilts, threatening to topple Gray with it. He immediately forces his way forward, but two sets of strong hands grip his shoulders, holding him in place. Gray jerks against the holds, and Tynan grins with delight at the sight.

"Ah, ah, ah. No interfering. Only your choices may determine the outcome of how this goes."

They shove Gray's father to his knees beside Tynan. His face is pallid and bruised, his normally warm eyes sunken and hollow. He has lost the once packed muscle from his bones, and Gray winces at how gaunt his cheeks have become.

How long have they been keeping him here? How long has his father been a prisoner while Gray was completely unaware?

Gray feels his expression slacken with grief. "Father..."

He lifts his eyes from the ground, finding Gray. They may have stolen his health, but they clearly have not stolen his mind. His father looks at him with the same sharp clarity in his gaze he always has.

So much passes between them in that silent look.

An apology. Forgiveness. A warning and a message.

"Alright, Lion. Your first test of the game." Tynan moves to stand behind Sterling, where he presses an onyx dagger into his throat. "Tell me the deductions you've made, or watch me slit your father's throat."

Gray flexes his jaw, grinding his molars against one another.

"Three...two..."

"You are attempting to topple the Anatolé Kingdom and remove the need for a third king," Gray spits, face scrunched by his pain and anger. "The only way you can do this seamlessly is by giving the people a reason to believe Anatolé has become a threat to their lives. To their economy and prosperity. So you and the other two kings have been most likely conspiring for years, carefully sewing the seeds of discord, publicly—though subtly—isolating Erandor and Rivara Kingdom from Anatolé and its culture. You mean to make them believe the people have grown dangerous; their king a tyrant who is thirsty for power. Which is why you stoked the flames of the people's uprising. You allowed them to choke on the lavishness of nobility purposefully with the aid of the other two kings. Then you carefully orchestrated attacks and planted evidence that would allow the blame to be pinned on King Yarum, thus giving viable cause for a declaration of war against them." Gray's lips thin, his expression hardening. "But all you are really doing is ruining centuries of peace for the greed and ambitions of men who only wish to feel the thrill of more power and the hollow satisfaction of more coin in their coffers."

"Do not let him speak of us in such a way," King Alastair growls.

Tynan lifts his hand, as if to silence a king. "All in due time, Your Highness." He drops his dagger from Sterling's throat and steps back. His approving smile makes Gray feel coated in grime. "Very good," he muses. "You almost figured it out as beautifully as your father did."

Gray's gaze jumps to his father, his brows pinching tightly together.

"Oh, yes," Tynan confirms, seeming to read the thoughts in Gray's eyes. "He has known about our plans for years. See" —Tynan tips his dagger to point at Gray's father, then King Alastair— "your father here only became King Alastair's closest advisor to monitor and combat his movements. He was a spy, feeding intel to Bathara in hopes they would be prepared to combat these exact events."

Gray grows very, very cold. "Josiah…"

Tynan's smile broadens, showing the full row of his perfectly polished teeth. "*Commendable.* You truly are Sterling Nightenjoy's son." Tynan paces once more. "Yes, all of that intel he was collecting? All the many actions he was taking to dismantle our plans? He had no idea it was all being rerouted straight back to me by Josiah himself."

The knife wound stabbed into Gray's heart at seeing Josiah lead his capture deepens, more crimson blood seeping free from the slice.

"And I am still not thrilled at being made unaware for such a long time," King Alastair grinds out like a pouting child.

"You now know why my strategist did what he did," King Erasmus soothes. "So please, let him continue." His voice carries an air of titillation. Like he tried to hide his eagerness to watch all that's about to unfold but failed. There is also an expectedness wrapped delicately around his tone. As though he knows something the others do not.

"I must tell you, Lion, your father is quite clever. He is the most cunning man I have ever faced. We tried offering him the titles of nobility? He refused, allowing him to continue to operate independently and maintain a commendable disposition as far as the general public was concerned. The great 'noble' Nightenjoy line, respected and powerful, yet not succumbing to the lure of the corrupted noble class. So we tried to catch him in slips of the tongue or in questionable acts." A pause paired with an amused laugh. "Yet through the years, he stayed cleaner than pure snow and harder to trap than a wry fox."

Gray steals a glance at his father, who has not moved nor altered his neutral expression once. Layers of shock course through Gray as he studies him—he had not known the truth of his father's actions. Yet he knows he cannot allow his shock to stunt him nor let his unsteadiness split him open. Just as his father is doing—who is bruised and malnourished and being humiliated—he, too, must maintain himself.

Tynan shakes his head, feigning exhaustion. "And then you, his son, became known as the people's champion for one spur of the moment act to save a child, spreading the name *Nightenjoy* like wildfire." Tynan stills only a pace away from Gray. He frowns at him. "You realize it, right? How burdensome that is. We can't have the people placing their hopes and dreams in you, and yet… You are beloved by those in the slums. A powerful name of hope in the average common house. You are even a contending name in the lower noble houses, who are convinced someone like you could champion their own causes and bring them to greatness." Tynan rocks back on his heels, groaning as he runs fingers through his hair. "Ohh, the Nightenjoy name. Such a thorn in my side."

"Get *on* with it," King Alastair demands, his patience clearly running out.

Gray does not miss the flicker of anger in Tynan's eyes at the instruction. Yet cool as ice water, he straightens himself. "So here we are, in a game that will prune those two thorns with one swift *clip*. It will also provide King Alastair the retribution he seeks for your father's betrayal." Tynan turns on his heels, clapping his hands together. "Bring out the next one."

The stone again groans open, and it feels like a thousand needles prick Gray's skin the moment he sees his mother being escorted out, bound and chained in the exact way his father is. She is shoved to her knees beside Gray's father, whose eyes widen with pure terror.

He didn't know she was here either.

"Lion of the Heart," Tynan drawls, prowling to stand behind Gray's bound parents. "A name given to you because of your fierce determination to do what's right, guided by a moral compass rumored to always point true." Tynan traces a finger along her jaw, and a fire hotter than anything Gray has ever felt erupts within him. "Let us test the truth of those claims."

Gray catches the quiver of his mother's lip, yet her eyes remain resolved not to cower as they remain only on him. She holds her chin high. His father, however, bucks against his chains, gargled murmurs filling the room as he screams against the binds over his mouth.

Tynan's eyes are glittering now. "Well, Lion, which do you choose to die?"

The life drains from Gray, and he stands still as a statue, seeming incapable of processing what is happening. "What?"

"Choose," Tynan repeats. "Show us where your compass points you. What morals guide your choices when there is no clear right or wrong."

Gray's mind lags, as if unwilling to interpret the words. For a few heartbeats, all he can do is stare with wide eyes and swaying feet at his mother, sweet and gentle as they come, and then his father, who always tries to remain honorable and true. Kind and loyal.

Gray shakes his head. "No." The word trembles violently as it flees from his lips. "I will not play your sadistic game. I will not be your entertainment." He lifts his chin, resolved. "I will *not* choose."

Tynan frowns. "No? Pity."

It happens so fast.

Two seconds—maybe three.

His mother's eyes are on him one moment, and then they are rolling backward as an onyx blade glides over the delicate skin of her throat.

Blood spurts free. Her body tips forward, plummeting down with the weight of a boulder.

From somewhere far away, Gray is remotely aware of the terrible gargling sound tearing free from his throat. Feels the bite of the hard ground as his knees slam into it. He hears a sob and a voice and a word. *Mother. Mother.*

"Mother."

He goes to her, rolling her face-down body over as best he can with the restriction his manacles have on his movements. He presses his fingers against her bleeding neck.

He feels nothing. It is too late.

Her eyes are faded; her muscles forever slackened.

There is so much blood.

He cradles her head to his chest, rocking back and forth. Back and forth. Water droplets drip onto her crimson-stained cheeks. Is the ceiling leaking?

"I'm sorry," he rasps, clutching her more tightly. "I'm so sorry."

"No choice is still a choice." Tynan claps his hands together, the sound an unbearable jolt to Gray's muffled, distorted senses. "Time for the final round."

A voice wails in the back of his mind. *Please. No more.*

The stone again groans, but this time Gray doesn't even look up to see who the guards bring in. His eyes instead remain on his dead mother, his convulsing fingers trying to swipe the pool of blood from her neck for reasons he can't explain while his father chokes out sobs beside him.

It isn't until he hears a tiny, familiar voice squeak out his name that he rips his hollow eyes away from the blood.

"Gray...help me..."

Thestis.

No. Gods, *no.*

He wears the same chains and manacles, yet is able to speak freely, without having anything put over his mouth. His freckle-filled face is tear-stained, his eyes red-rimmed and so puffy they nearly look swollen shut.

Gray can't bear it. He can't bear any more of this.

He leans forward to press a final kiss to his mother's forehead. And then he gently rests her upon the cold ground and rises. He feels a prick of heat, and he looks over his shoulder to where Lyra stands in chains. She thrashes against her hold. Gray can see she is screaming—rioting against this. But of course, they can't hear her, and with her magic contained, she can't stop it either.

Thestis watches her through his swollen eyes before they again land on Gray, where they remain as his bottom lip quivers.

Gray feels his do the same. "Be strong, Thestis," he says, voice no more than a broken rasp. "You must be strong."

Thestis pinches his teeth into his bottom lip and nods.

"You shouldn't coddle the boy," Tynan says, striding to rest a hand on Thestis's shoulder. "He just caused his mother's execution, after all."

"What?"

King Alastair answers in Tynan's place. "He stole gold from my estate. My guards found him hoarding it beneath his bed."

Gray's lips part with his disbelief. "Thestis...why?"

Thestis's eyes remain on the ground. "My Ma couldn't afford my tutor any longer, and you were away. I...I wanted to be like King Isaphus, just like you said. I wanted to be great." He looks up, a fresh stream of tears falling down his cheeks. "We all celebrated you and Lyra's acceptance into Bathara, you know. My Ma even cried. And I just thought, if that was her reaction to you two being accepted, imagine the pride she would feel if I was, too?"

Gray gazes at Thestis, his chest crushed beneath the weight of a mountain. Anger rings through him, and Gray sobers the emotion from his face, steeling his eyes and straightening his trembling lips as he turns his attention onto Tynan. "He is just a child," he growls. "Let him go."

Tynan shrugs. "It's not up to me. It is up to the King of Rivara."

Gray glares at the nefarious king. "Let. Him. *Go.*"

King Alastair smiles. "Actually," he drawls with delight, "that decision is entirely up to you, Gray Nightenjoy. See, it is the beauty of Tynan's game. I have a thieving child who went unpunished because his mother invoked Samsara, and I have an advisor who has been betraying my trust and his kingdom for years. Which to choose? Which to punish?" He mocks a shrug. "I suppose that is for you to decide, isn't it?"

Tynan positions himself directly between Thestis and Gray's father. "Well, Lion—time to choose."

His father—now resigned to a defeated slouch—murmurs muffled words against the binds covering his mouth.

Tynan cocks his head at the sounds. "Hmm. I'm curious—let's see what he has to say." Tynan removes the cloth from his lips.

Gray's father does not waste a moment.

"My son," he says, voice so gentle. So calm. "Let me follow her into the next life."

Gray shakes his head, his chin wobbling in the way it did when he was a child running to find his father after busting his knee open from playing too roughly with Lyra. "I'm sorry," he says, voice so tiny. "I can't be the one to do it. I can't send you there."

"You must."

"Come on, Lion," Tynan coaxes. "You're running out of time."

"Son," he presses. "You know the right choice."

He's right. Gray does.

A sudden calmness he has not yet felt washes through him. In this, he is determined. In this decision, he is sure.

He lifts his chin. "Me."

Tynan narrows his eyes with interest. "Sorry?"

"I choose me. To trade my life in exchange for both of theirs. You said it yourself, I am the greatest thorn in your side. The greatest threat to this new system you wish to create."

Gray's father hangs his head, his shoulders drooping forward. Yet he says nothing. Thestis watches Gray, his teeth still pinched into his bottom lip.

Tynan studies him, tapping the blade of his dagger against his cheek as he thinks. "And this is where your compass points you?"

"It is. To me, this is the only correct path. The only moral answer to this twisted game."

"Ah, the moral answer." Tynan nimbly spins the dagger around his fingers. "How interesting a thought when one considers the basis for which we construct morals. The fickle concepts we use when creating them." He paces behind the dangling lives, again tapping his dagger against his cheek. "Allow me to share my choice with you."

"Your choice doesn't matter, because I have already made mine."

Tynan only hums, loosely waving his dagger in the air. He halts suddenly and grips a fistful of Sterling's hair, jerking his head back to expose his sullen face. "See, here is the face of a man who has *lived*. Who has scars and wrinkles and sunspots to show for his time on this continent." He throws Sterling's head forward and moves to Thestis, gliding—though thankfully not cutting—the dagger down his cheek. "And I think this is the face of someone who has not yet had that opportunity."

Tynan drops the dagger from Thestis's cheek, striding forward to stand in front of Gray. "And when I see your face, I see fires and riots and pitiful ceremonies of people who never knew you but will immortalize you as the champion who could have changed everything but never got his chance. I see one thorn becoming a whole bush. I see a martyr." He clasps his hands, sweeping his eyes along the length of Gray. "I also see a wielder who possesses magic which could be indispensable during war. That could change the tides of battles, should he allow himself to be great. I see a youth who bears the cunning of his father without bearing the weight of his father's age." A pause. "I see a resource far more valuable than both those lives combined."

Gray grinds his teeth. "No life is more valuable than another."

Tynan's eyes flare with the thrill of a hunter catching prey. He spins on his heels, returning to stand behind Gray's father and Thestis. "No? Then explain to me which life to save when choosing between a king or an uneducated servant. Between a skilled war general or a simple foot soldier. An exceptional healer on the battlefield or a mediocre water-wielder."

Gray remains silent.

"Part of growing up, boy, is realizing some lives *are* more important than others. It is the way of this world, and those who use such vacillating things as morals to say otherwise are fools." He places a hand on Thestis's quaking shoulder. "You see, Lion: morality is only a story we tell ourselves to make the choices of this world bearable. It gives an excuse to the inexcusable. It is pretty lies served on silver platters to disguise ugly acts as civilized. Weaponizes barbaric actions to dismantle civilizations when necessary. Morality is a tool. A resource which can be used as effectively as a blade. Nothing more. Nothing less."

"Whatever you believe is yours to believe," Gray says, flexing his jaw. "It changes nothing for me. My choice is and will always be my life for the preservation of theirs."

Tynan studies him. "Very well," he concedes through a sigh. "Come here and assume the boy's position, if you must."

Gray does as instructed, nudging Thestis gently with his elbow. "Go be free," he whispers. "Go be great."

"Gray..."

"Go," Gray says one last time.

Thestis steps back, where he is met by two hooded guards who escort him out of the room. The unbearable weight that's been pressing against Gray's chest eases, if only a little.

"Kneel, boy."

Gray does as instructed.

"My son," his father says from beside him. "Please. *Please.* I am already a dead man without my Azalea. But I will become no more than a lost, withered soul if I am forced to lose you too."

Despite everything, Gray manages to smile at his father. "You have raised me to be good and noble and true. I have lived by my morals, and I will die by them as well."

Tynan flips his dagger and presses the blade to Gray's throat. "Ready?"

Gray lifts his chin, providing Tynan with better access to his neck. "Do it."

His gaze wanders and finds Lyra, her eyes wide as she drops to her knees, shaking her head. He knows this will hurt her—devastate her. But she survived the thought of his death once. She will survive it again. Even if this time it is real, and he won't be coming back.

He continues watching her, deciding he is perfectly content for the other half of his soul to be the final thing he ever sees. The girl he roamed courtyards and explored gardens with. The best friend who stayed up late with him sucking on sweet fruit while they giggled incessantly. The partner who always listened to him as he rambled on about his books and made him feel safe when talking about his passions.

Yes, his view as he goes is not a bad one—even if he wishes he could do more to change the tide for everyone. Wishes he could gaze upon copper hair and cobalt eyes one last time.

He never did confess to his feelings. Never was able to kiss her or hold her in the ways he truly wanted. He never managed to tell her he stays up sometimes through the night, his mind awake with dreams of a future where they both wore rings and he played her music while a child's laughter echoed through the wind.

It had always felt like a promise to him.

"Thank you for playing the game, Lion. You made it as interesting as I hoped you would."

Gray shuts his eyes and sees beautiful copper waves rushing over a cobalt shore.

The dagger digs into his skin.

And then there is the *sssst* sound of a blade slicing a throat. The tangy smell of blood as it pours from a fresh body. The dull *thud* as that bleeding body topples to the ground.

Through the haze of his mind, Gray is dimly aware of everything crashing down around him. Understands the ramifications of yet another Nightenjoy being murdered. Yet when he reopens his eyes, his skin unblemished and whole, he knows he is not the Nightenjoy to follow his mother.

He creaks his chin over his shoulder to find his father's body crumpled forward in a pool of his own blood, King Alastair towering over it, a bloody dagger in his hand and a smile on his lips.

Tynan drops the blade from Gray's throat and steps in front of him. "I told you my choice," he says, words cold as ice. "I always go with my choice."

All Gray can do is stare at the crimson puddle as it expands. As he does, he is surprised by how quiet his mind is. How suddenly his body just...ceases to exist. How soon the beautiful copper filling his mind seeps to crimson before turning wholly black.

The frigid numbness ravages him with the swiftness of a lethal storm overtaking a once sunny sea.

Is this what true pain is? Is this what it tastes like to have rot festering inside you?

Tynan grips his hair and jerks his head back. Whatever he sees in Gray's eyes has him humming with approval. "Good. You've been properly broken, which means you are no longer a threat to me or my plans." A heavy pause. "You will be the people's champion no longer."

He releases his hold on Gray's hair, and his head falls forward as languidly as if his neck has no means to support the heavy thing.

Gray stares at the floor. At the red staining it. As he does, he becomes faintly aware of the way his body slowly collapses inward. The way his head droops more and more. The fact that he should rise to his feet and attempt to help the others. To fight or stand by them. Maybe even try to swipe the dagger dangling from Tynan's hand so carelessly in front of him.

It would be so easy. He could do it if he wanted.

He remains still.

There is not a single part of him left that can find it within itself to dredge up a desire to fight. To want something as petty and trivial as a last ditch effort at useless aid.

No.

He does not wish for anything but oblivion.

Tynan's clap echoes like a thunderstrike. "Now, then. Who's next?"

CHAPTER SIXTY-FIVE

LYRA

I stare in horror at the bloodied mess before me, grief and pain chewing at my barely-healed heart.

"Sterling," I whisper. "Azalea."

All it takes is one heartbeat for a lifetime of memories to ravage me, punching my ribs and sawing at my breastbone with its moments of laughter and shared hugs and warm meals taken together. Yet I have no time to sit with my feelings of anguish or nurse my shredded heart. Tynan has already strode to the center of the room, delivering his grand speech to introduce the next stage of the game.

"That was fun, but I must admit it didn't hold quite the theatrics I had hoped for." He scans each of our faces behind the barriers, his face pinched with consideration. "I think for this next round of the game, we need to up the stakes. Make things…" He trails off, chewing on his next words. "Less boring. None of your morals are as interesting to me as Gray Nightenjoy's. Therefore, the game must be remedied to preserve the thrill." He turns, the movement unnervingly precise. "Telamon, lift the barriers."

The barriers flicker then disappear, taking the incandescent light with them. I immediately find Draven, who stands at the very end of his chain's length with his hands balled into white-knuckled fists. His chest heaves in breaths while his taut lips and narrowed eyes are cold to look at. He glares at Tynan, remaining silent.

Rhea is similarly positioned, yet there is something more questioning in her gaze. Less pointed with direct hatred and instead mixed with something more like confusion, hurt, and anger.

Tynan spares neither of them his attention. "Allow me to introduce round two of the games. While simple in nature, I suspect it'll lead to some rather interesting decisions. See, in approximately two minutes, those stone doors are going to open once more, and this time, an entire band of wielders will enter. Twist? They are all rebels facing a death sentence for their participation in the Restorationist attacks. Yet I've struck a deal with them: should any of them successfully kill one of you, their punishment will be lifted, and they will walk free to their families." Tynan scans our faces, grinning. "Suffice it to say they are *very* motivated."

"And what is our participation in this?" I ask, my chilly voice not wavering. "You did say it was a game, after all. Not a slaughter."

Tynan's smile widens as he looks at me with sharpened interest. It makes my skin crawl and prick with alarm simultaneously. "That is correct. It is indeed a game."

"Yet here we are chained to a wall, blocked from using our magic." I hold up the manacles for emphasis. "That doesn't seem very game-like to me."

"Have no fear. You will not be in chains when the rebels funnel in. You will, however, keep the manzat cuffs around your wrists, though the chain restricting your movements will be cut. There will be no use of magic, from you or the rebels. Only weaponry."

"And how are we to defend ourselves?" Draven's gruff voice has dropped an octave, as if he has put something together I haven't yet.

Tynan delights in the question. "You and you alone will be provided a sword."

His eyes shudder at the answer, as if his nightmare has just been confirmed. "And who's to say I won't take that sword and stab it straight through your throat?"

"You won't. I hold the lives of the two people you care most for in the palms of my hand. Take a blade to me, and they will have three blades taken to them."

"This is a death sentence," Rhea hisses.

Tynan glides to face her. "You have more to work with than the Binder and yet you still complain? I know you have hidden daggers sheathed at your ankles and one strapped to your thigh. The other girl has nothing. No weapons. And I will not be providing her with any, either. Be grateful for what you have, girl. Show gratitude for the mercy I am showing you."

Slowly, the pieces start fusing together, and I begin to understand the true ramifications of this game.

"Let us see what my son does when he must defend the lives of the two people he holds such damning affections for with only one sword. What he does when both halves of his putrid heart are swarmed by criminals fighting to regain their own lives. What choices he will make when the cost of his actions will be the life of one over the other." Tynan strides straight up to Draven, clasping his hands together behind his back. His eyes are glued to the color filling his son's, so different yet so similar. "Which person will he choose to protect with that unwavering ferociousness of his? What will he do if he chooses wrong?" Tynan pauses, his mouth gently curving at one corner. "Sound familiar?"

"Stop it. *Stop.*" Rhea is shaking uncontrollably now. "You promised. Gave me your *word* that if I helped you, you would release your hold over Draven and allow him to finally be free of this."

I watch as Draven's face falls, his eyes looking past his father and onto his sister. "Rhea," he breathes. "What did you do?"

Rhea bites down on her bottom lip. Even from the distance between us, it looks painful. Looks hard enough to draw blood. "I wanted to help you," she says, voice cracking. "It seemed so minor— just some old information in some old tome in the warded area of Bathara's library."

Draven's voice is strained. "The one I helped you gain access to?"

Rhea nods. "If I found the tome and gave Tynan the information held within, he swore to relinquish the promise you made to him when we were children. You were supposed to be *free*, Draven. After all you have done to protect me—all you gave up for me—I was supposed to finally repay you by giving you your life back."

Draven's eyes soften before turning downward. "You have no debt to repay, Rhea. Besides, I told you to never make a deal with the devil —no matter how enticing it looks."

Rhea glares at Tynan. "You *swore* to me. And though you are many things, you have never been one to go back on your word."

Tynan turns just enough to look over his shoulder. "I swore to you that if you upheld your end of the bargain, I would no longer use you to force Draven to submit to *my* will. This decision, you see, is entirely his to make. What I want has nothing to do with the direction of his choices."

Anger flares hotly in Rhea's eyes. "You *snake*. You vile, repulsive—"

Draven lifts his hand to silence her. "So that's why you allowed her to be Conscripted. To be so close to me while knowing you would lose your advantage over me in doing so. It was so she could look for the information you needed, placing her somewhere not even you could freely access."

Tynan's polished, close-lipped smile is his only response.

"What's in the book, Tynan?"

No answer.

Draven steps forward, the chain around his waist clanging loudly as it's stretched taut. "Tell me."

Tynan only continues to smile at his son. "All in due time, boy."

Rhea drops to her knees, seeming on the verge of tears. "Draven... I'm sorry. I thought I was protecting you for once. I—I believed him."

"What did you give him, Rhea? What was in the book?"

She shakes her head, unfurling her fingers and staring absently into her palms. "I don't know. It was in a language I didn't understand. I only copied the text and sent it to Tynan with my Ever-Know Quill." She looks like she might say more, but then she just...doesn't.

Tynan chuckles. "You know, it's not the only important book in my possession these days. And I have found myself doing a lot of interesting reading about the god of the stars as a result." There is a mocking quality to his smile, and while I haven't the slightest clue what he is referencing, whatever it is, it makes Draven's eyes widen with anger and Rhea snap her glassy eyes up at Tynan, lips parting with disbelief.

"You have his book?" Draven seethes, voice sharp enough to cut skin.

Whose book? I think, glancing between them all as some unspoken revelation seems to hit Rhea and Draven simultaneously.

"Let's not rush the grand finale, shall we? All great endings are the sum of their journey, and I still have so much to share with you all."

"Hopefully at a quicker pace," King Alastair chastises, still standing near Gray, who remains on his knees surrounded by the blood and bodies of his parents. His hands are folded in his lap, his body slumped forward in complete resignation. Complete defeat.

Gray...

"Truly, this whole spectacle is taking up so much time, I'm beginning to tire of it." King Alastair turns back to the balcony. "What do you think, Erasmus?"

King Erasmus, who remains resting comfortably on the silver, glittering throne, merely shrugs. "I find it perfectly acceptable entertainment. One must be patient, not rushing their gratification."

King Alastair grunts. "If I didn't know any better, I would think that statement a pointed one."

"Should it have been?"

King Alastair lets out a low growl, directing his festering irritation onto Tynan. "Let's get on with this next round." His eyes slide to me. "I am eager to watch my pet perform."

"Yes," Tynan agrees. "Let us do just that." He finally pulls his loaded gaze from Draven, striding toward me. He reaches out his hand, prompting me to jerk back.

"Don't touch me," I seethe through gritted teeth. I hate how my eyes flick to King Alastair, the face of my scars visible.

Tynan observes me for a quiet heartbeat before dropping his voice to where only I can hear him. "While human nature and its accompanying choices fascinate me to an endless degree, my tastes are not the same as Alastair's." A pause. "You do not have to fear such treatment from me." His words are surprisingly...soft. A twisted authenticity lacing through his claim, as though showing me a shred of kindness.

A fact of which is too odd for my brain to reconcile.

Yet just as quickly as the confusing moment comes, it passes. Tynan straightens himself, glancing back at Alastair. "Shall we play a mini round with the girl first?"

"Oh," King Alastair laughs. "Now *that* would hold my interest."

Tynan hums, his tight smile not seeming as delighted as all his others. "Raise the stake."

A hooded figure steps forward and presses their palm into the ground. There is a shimmer of light, and then a wooden post erects from the rock, leaving behind a low groan as the stone rumbles to make room for it. Wordlessly and without instruction, they fasten iron brackets to the wood, and then another hooded wielder steps forward and uses fire magic to weld metal shackles with the brackets. They tug on them to check the security, the metal echoing loudly in the face of silent anticipation.

From the corner of my eye, I catch King Erasmus leaning forward, bracing his elbows on his knees and gazing over his folded hands. There is a curve wedged deep into the corner of his mouth. His eyes are alight with intrigue.

King Alastair turns to head back to his throne on the balcony. "I cannot wait to watch whatever Commander Dalmar has in store for you. Do put on a good show for us, pet."

Two cloaked guards step forward, halting him.

His face twists. "Out of my way."

The two guards grab his arms and tug him backward instead.

"*Fools.* Unhand me this instant. I am a *king*, for the gods' sake. How dare you touch me. How *dare* you defile me. I...I..." When they slam his back against the stake and jerk his wrists over his head, locking them into the shackles which look like my own, his face turns purple. "Commander. *Commander!*" When Tynan only watches him through a level expression, King Alastair turns his eyes to the balcony. "Erasmus, are you truly going to let—"

His words die in his throat, and the purple flees his skin, leaving behind a face pale as a moonflower.

King Erasmus is standing now, hands gripped on the balcony while a curling smile grips his lips. He says nothing.

Tynan squares his shoulders to me, cool like an evening breeze. "Would you like to hear your choices?"

My eyes remain glued to King Alastair as his expression shifts through a spectrum of emotions. As he seems to call on magic that doesn't answer him.

He is bound so similarly to how my mother once was.

"Yes," I breathe.

Tynan grins. "Lyra Izacalli, you may choose to spare King Alastair's life, and thus spare yourself from participation in the next round of my game, removing considerable burden from Draven. Or you may choose to take King Alastair's life, and thus cement your participation in the next round of my game, almost certainly damning him instead." A loaded pause. "Which do you choose?"

The weight of the decision sits heavy in my stomach. I pry my eyes from King Alastair, who is shouting his objections—the threats slowly morphing into desperate pleas—and I look to Draven. He doesn't say anything. Instead, he simply holds my gaze, understanding already softening his eyes.

The guilt compiles in my stomach, building a tower of thoughts closing around my throat.

I find Rhea next. She is still staring at the ground, something seeming to have broken inside her. If I reject the offer—if I refuse to plunge my hands into a bucket of more blood—I can rewrite the trajectory of the next game. Draven can't truly defend us both against gods-only-know how many condemned—not while they are fighting to regain their own lives—but I can give him the chance to save Rhea. *Truly* save her, without sacrificing a piece of his stitched up heart in the process. Plus, I know the choice my mother would want me to make.

It should be so easy to choose correctly. To make the choice that would make my mother proud and secure the lives of the man I love and the sister he loves in turn. Preserve my own life and mortal soul alike. My conscience.

Yes, I know which choice I should choose.

Yet I don't choose it anyway. Because I remember a certain promise I made to myself the night he stripped me nude and brought a whip to me. I remember the thirst I felt when swearing to take my revenge on him.

I remember it all.

I already have a mountain of blood stained on my hands, so what's another crimson seed in comparison?

In a terrible, twisted way, I now understand what Casimir meant when he said those words to me. There is so much blood now staining me—what does one more vile, malignant person hurt?

I lift my chin. "I want him to burn."

Tynan angles his head. "Oh? By what flame?"

"My own."

"Do elaborate, please."

A curl forms in my lip as I watch King Alastair flail against his shackles. Hear his pathetic words, which only ricochet from my ears. "You know exactly what I mean."

"And why would I remove your shackles? Why risk giving you access to your magic?"

"Because I trust you have enough confidence in your own power to not fear me or my magic. I trust you are clever enough to put precautionary measures in place to ensure I don't use my magic elsewhere."

"You would be correct in those thoughts." A sigh. "Very well. Uncuff the girl and position two blades over my son. One at his throat, one at his side." Tynan fixes me firmly in his gaze. "Try anything, and you will live to regret it."

My curt nod is my only answer.

Within moments, the manzat is removed from my wrists, and Draven has two blades pressed into his body.

I'm sorry, I mouth to him.

He shakes his head, the gesture subtle. There is the faintest of curves ghosting his lips. *Don't be*, he mouths back.

It steadies me in a way I didn't know I needed.

My expression hardens. I stare at King Alastair with nothing but cold resentment, and in his petrified gaze, all I see are the horrified gazes of the other night attendants. The dead look in my mother's eyes as a body grunts on top of her. I see her tied to her own stake. Hear the words, *You do not let this break you. You do not let them win. I love you.* I see my nights spent with strangers tattooed on his skin. See the scars from my lashings grooved into the lines of his face. See the hopes and dreams of a tiny girl be stripped from her just as viciously as her pride and dignity were. I see the freshly spilled blood on the floor next to me. I see a thief, who has stolen future after future. A murderer who has played with life as carelessly as a child tossing aside their toys. I see a monster. A stain. A man who is finally facing his long overdue reckoning.

I see nothing more than a promise being kept.

"Please," he whimpers. The fabric at his crotch darkens. *"Please.* Have mercy for your King."

I summon the pain of every moment—every jagged piece of grief —and channel it into my last look at the man who has done unspeakable harm to my life and others.

"You were never my king."

Fire erupts in my palms, brilliant and with a different hue than I expect. The flame I have conjured—the fire I mold into a flaming bow and arrow—is crystal white and outlined by steel blue. It's hypnotic and alluring. Beauty and power.

It is pure destruction.

I pull back and release the notched arrow from my fiery bow. King Alastair goes up in flames the moment the tip grazes his skin, engulfing all but the stone beneath his feet. His ear-splitting scream echoes off the walls, and the smell of his burnt skin paired with burning wood and melted metal quickly fills the air. The fire is bright. Punctuated by the brilliance of a stunning white flame.

As I watch it dance and listen to the song it provokes, all I can think is—

If I have any regrets, it is only that I did not do more to prolong his suffering.

A guard returns to immediately re-shackle me in the manzat manacles, the sensation of being cut off from my magic as disorienting as it was the first time. As he works, a hooded water-wielder steps forward to extinguish the growing fire.

Their water magic does not work.

The flames do not die.

Tynan laughs. "Remarkable." He presses two fingers together and twirls his hand in a circle. A small onyx tornado woven with crimson seams appears, wrapping around the blazing inferno in a smothering cocoon. When it falls away, all that is left is ash. No bones. No wood or metal. Just ash.

There is only silence in the room at the sight.

Until there is clapping. Slow and deliberate.

King Erasmus is beaming. "Bravo. *Bra-vo!*"

With a crease in my brow, I glance at Draven—who thankfully no longer has blades pressed into his body. His expression mirrors that of my own, gears turning behind his eyes as he seems to tie the threads together in real time.

"Commander Dalmar," King Erasmus continues. "Do take a bow. What a show! What a show!"

"Your plan was to cross Alastair all along." Draven does not say the words like a question.

He receives an answer all the same.

"He was a selfish fool who had sick perversions and cared more for his own gratification than he did his own kingdom." King Erasmus stands tall at the balcony's ledge. "And now with the help of my brilliant strategist, we have reasonably declared war on one kingdom while dethroning the king from another in the midst of an uprising. The continent will be plunged into chaos. The people will need a leader. Will need someone to make order out of the disorderly. And who will they turn to? Whose feet will they lay flowers at and offer troves of their gold to for saving Solaya before it could swallow itself? They will thank m—"

A spear of pure darkness spirals through the air and pierces King Erasmus straight through his heart.

His body topples over the ledge of the balcony, falling straight for the stone ground like a baby bird who hasn't yet learned to fly.

It lands with a dull *thump.*

CHAPTER SIXTY-SIX

LYRA

"I have been waiting to do that for years." Tynan readjusts his silken sleeves, pushing his dark hair back into place.

Silence clings to the room as we all stare at King Erasmus's dead body, momentarily paralyzed by the waves of shock.

It all happened so fast. One minute, alive and beaming. The next, impaled and falling.

Draven's lips thin. "And the truth reveals itself at last."

Tynan turns, a smile twisting his features. One different than before. A little less polished. Less refined. "Oh, come now, Draven." He scoffs a blunt, manic laugh. "Have you no pride for all that I've just accomplished?"

"Accomplished?" I repeat, my disgust a thick coating over the word. "You have accomplished *nothing*. All you have done is incite mass chaos throughout Solaya and murdered two kings while declaring war on the third."

His peculiar smile broadens. "Oh, I have done so much more than that."

The silence sharpens, and Tynan begins to pace.

"See, I have been plotting for a long, long time. Playing a very slow game. Yet along the way, pieces came onto my chess board which did not belong there. But as all strategists do, I pivoted—adapted. Like when I caught wind of a centuries-old prince living as some savior to the surviving bloodlines of the original Abdites. One who was forming a plan that would threaten to topple all my hard work; possessed the power to see it truly done. But then that prince turned up searching for his Chosen, and oh..." He claps his hands together and inhales a theatric breath. "I saw my new path unfold with *glorious* clarity.

"I made sure all eyes turned to that lost prince and the preeminent magic he stole away. The girl who possessed it. I stoked the flames of necessity, adding rotten soil to the gardens of those who sought out justice for the tragedy befalling Bathara Academy. Added to their urgency that we *must* find the girl and bring her back—only so they could condemn her themselves, mind you. And when all eyes were directed elsewhere, *I* moved like a wraith through the shadows, liberated by preoccupations and distractions." He pauses, lip curling. "Well, save for one pair of eyes." Tynan glances at Sterling's lifeless body.

Anger boils in my plummeting stomach.

"In my invisibility, I sowed the seeds of discord. Ensured the poor folk learned of an antiquated opposition forged at the dawn of the Three Kings. Made them determined to restore the old ways of one king. I created the Conscription. Used it to further sway the kings' councils and all the houses of nobility against Anatolé, ensuring all the armies down from the southern borders of Erandor all the way to the northern tip of Rivara would answer to me. My chess board was laid out beautifully for checkmate. Yet two pieces remained that could make their move, ruining my grand game. Casimir Vivaldri and Gray Nightenjoy. But how does one win against someone as powerful as the First Crowned Prince? Someone who has grown to be as beloved by the people as the Nightenjoy boy had? Easy. You break them. Obliterate their will. You shatter them to the point of irreparability."

My eyes find Gray, and a silent sob wails in my chest.

Tynan has done it; he has broken Gray wholly. Because the Gray Nightenjoy I know would not remain bowed on his knees, his head hung in total defeat while all this chaos raged on. The Gray I know would stand toe-to-toe against Tynan, engaging him in a battle of cunning as he slowly dismantled the skewed logic with his silver-plated tongue. The Gray I knew would get up and *fight*.

Yet Gray does not get up at all, instead remaining still as a statue as his blood-matted hair falls forward into his downturned eyes.

And as if the sight of that is not enough to gut me, the memories of Casimir in a similar position fill my mind. His body mirroring a similar defeat as Gray's does now. My mind replays flashes of the brokenness in Casimir's gaze. His resignation to cruelty. To the irreparable flaw of humanity.

But wait...

How had Tynan been the cause of that? That was...was...

I realize it just as Tynan says it.

"It was not easy—I had to be quite clever to remove those two pawns from the board. But even the most perplexing puzzle can be solved if you have all the right pieces. You saw how Nightenjoy's solution came together—he was built upon his morals, and those very morals allowed both his parents to die. But what did I do to ensure Casimir was no longer a threat to me or my plans? How did I break *him*?" He smiles like a scholar stating the labors of their research. "By ensuring the only thing he cared about was stolen from him, of course."

"You had nothing to do with that," Draven says in a tight voice. "I did."

"Didn't I, though? Come now, boy. Surely you must have thought about it? Who sent Casimir Vivaldri his invitation to the masquerade ball? Who ensured he brought Lyra with him, knowing your engagement would be announced that very night? Knowing full and well your distasteful protectiveness would never allow her to slip away for a second time. Who else knew how badly you were struggling to maintain the hold on your magic? Who else understood the capabilities of all that it can truly do—what happens once you lose control of it?" A heavy pause. "Who else could possibly have both the resources and the knowledge to know exactly what those wards would do to your mind once you attempted to break them?"

Though he hides it well, I can see that rattles Draven.

I feel similarly off-kilter.

We have been pawns in Tynan's grand chess match for power this entire time, unknowingly playing into everything exactly as he predicted it.

"And that's only half of it," Tynan hums. "So you see, boy, I had *everything* to do with it."

"Why?" The question does not come from Draven, but from me. Because I feel like I need to know. Need to understand *why*.

Why must men make playgrounds of continents so they can feel powerful? Why must they stomp on the backs of the vulnerable so they can stand a little taller? What is the true appeal of inciting mass chaos—causing such damage to so many lives—only to hold threads of corruptive power used only as food for their egos? The hungry are starved only so the full may be stuffed fuller. And always—*always*—the venomous meal is served on platters of manipulation and carefully adorned tactical lies.

Tynan frowns at me. "Why would I tell you anything about my motivations?"

"Did you not just tell us what you've already done?" I counter.

"Yes," he answers simply. "But detailing my accomplishments is not the same as making you privy to my driving forces. That, dear girl, would be exposing a vulnerability to you. Something of which I will not be doing."

"Then answer me this instead," Draven demands. "You and I both know the Three King System is the better system. So how is it you plan to rule as..." He pauses, his upper lip peeling back. "What do you want? To be called a king? A tyrant? A god?"

Tynan only smiles.

Draven's jaw flexes. "The Three King System is what works—there is no denying that. So how is it you plan to grip the reins of power without redistributing them amongst the borders?"

"King Alastair has no heir, so who should claim power over the Rivara Kingdom? And King Erasmus only has two daughters and never named a successor. His sights were too set on returning Solaya to a land united under one king. So who better to rule than the man who saved the kingdoms from their imminent destruction?"

"Destruction all incited by you."

"Yes. I am tearing everything apart so I can stitch it all back together again. And history will forever remember my name because of it."

Draven's mouth tightens. "The people will never allow it. They will continue rebelling. Most will fight against a unitary rule. You will split the masses, inciting a civil war atop the war you've ignited against kingdoms."

"They will until they won't. All they know right now is something is broken; what they don't know is how to pinpoint what that something is. Not while they are desperate. Are hungry for food. For change. Something better. So I'll continue telling them what to believe the problem is, just as I will tell them how to fix it. And when everyone is warring, squabbling over who is right and who has the better opinion, too distracted by the noise of their own bickering voices, I will shape this realm into exactly what I want it to be. I will have already finished my perfect game before anyone ever realizes they were playing in it."

"You underestimate the intelligence of our realm."

"And you underestimate how powerful weaponizing our differences can be." He splays his arms out as if showcasing some masterpiece on a grand stage. He tips his head back and laughs manically, all previous polish rubbing raw, revealing the true jaggedness beneath. "Just look at what I've done already. I have isolated the Anatolé Kingdom—the only opposing force left who could stop me—by waging a war on its people and land. I played the strings of my instrument so beautifully, I even made it look justified. I made the highest councils and the academy meant to check the balances of Solaya focus on locating a benign girl and a centuries-old prince so I could move freely. I have pitted lower noble houses against upper noble houses. Have turned the slums against an entire system, subtly stirring the discord with such perfection, they fight for an old system they don't even truly understand. You know why? All because I told them what to believe in the packaging they found most desirable. In a way that caressed and soothed those fickle morals people so love to cling to."

"You're a monster." The words—which I know have no effect on him—leave my lips in a hiss before I can stop them.

"Am I? Or are the people so willing to point fingers and condemn that which they don't understand the real monsters? Tell me, which is *truly* worse?"

I don't answer, instead choosing to glare at him with all the disgust my eyes can hold. Hearing all of this—*experiencing* such demoralizing circumstances—it is slowly changing something inside me, as though I am clay being remade by a sculptor's rough hand.

And I am not yet sure what I will be forged into.

All the many conversations Casimir and I had flood through me. My heart beats their words as my veins swallow their meanings.

Justice isn't divine, Lyra; it's inherited. Handed down from generation to generation like bloodstained heirlooms. Chiseled into law by the last man standing.

War is not the cost of what I intend to do; war is the cost of forgetting. So I will make sure they never forget again.

Is this what it was like for Casimir, attempting to stand in the face of good while a world ruined itself, dragging so many innocent lives into the teeth of war and greed?

I had fought and fought against him. Told him he was wrong. That there *was* a better way. That humanity is worth more than the worst parts of itself. Yet in the face of all this...

Is it?

Had he been wrong? Was his plan truly so terrible? Or was it I who had it all backwards?

Tynan claps his hands together. "No more idle chatter. We still have a game to play."

CHAPTER SIXTY-SEVEN

LYRA

It all happens so fast.

The chains linking our manzat cuffs are cut. The holds on our waists are released. We are escorted by the hooded guards to the center of the obsidian room, so odd in the way it both sparkles and swallows light—is this anthracite?—while Draven is given a plain sword.

He turns to eye both Rhea and me after twirling the weapon in his hand, measuring the weight of the steel blade. "Both of you will stay behind me. We don't have to worry about magic since they'll be wearing cuffs like ours, but we do have to worry about being overrun by their numbers. If we get separated for even a moment, it could mean the end for one of you, which is a fate I am not willing to accept. So no matter what happens, no matter what tricks they have up their sleeves, you do not move past me."

"I want to help," I say, drawing the full intensity of his gaze to me. I step forward and take his free hand in mine, squeezing. "Tell me what I can do to help you."

He studies me, lifting his hand from my fingers so he can pinch my chin. "You can stay alive."

Draven lowers his lips to mine and kisses me tenderly. He grips my neck, and I can feel how frightened he truly is in the seams of his mouth. By the way he savors the kiss. How hard he tries to not let his lips turn it into another goodbye.

Somewhere in the back of my mind, nagging from a far away place, I am aware we should not be kissing right now. Not while death clots the air, and Tynan's prying eyes are upon us. Not while Rhea is mute from her defeat, and Gray is still slumped on his knees, no more than a shell of himself. Yet it feels like time, this world, and the inhabitants attempting to conquer it—they all keep tearing us apart, not allowing us to just *be*. To exist as one, together. To have lazy mornings spent in bed discovering each other's bodies, and long nights spent under the stars exploring each other's souls.

And we suspect we will not have such privileges for a while longer.

So I do not rush this kiss; I treasure it. Allow it to dance for as long as our lips need to feel sated.

Draven eventually pulls back, eyes cradling me tenderly for one, final moment. "I love you," he whispers against my lips.

My heart swells. The feeling is temporary.

"I love you."

Draven drops his warm palm from my face and turns to Rhea. "Is it true you have your daggers?"

She doesn't answer.

"Rhea," Draven demands. "*Rhea!* I need you to focus."

Her eyes snap to, and she inhales a sharp, shuddering breath. "Yes," she answers, her voice such a diluted version of the confident and brazen girl I have seen thus far.

"Good. Use them."

The walls around us begin to rattle, shaking the ground violently, nearly rocking me from my feet.

"Ah, good," Tynan says, now returned to his perch on the balcony. "Let the game officially begin."

One by one, the walls encasing us groan as they recede into the ground, exposing a brilliant night sky and a radiant full moon bleeding silver over the shadows. The columns once holding our chains now keep the glistening obsidian ceiling suspended over our heads, the vaulted arches and reflected moonlight creating an odd illusion over the space. It is similar to a house of mirrors, just with less clarity. Yet that is not the element drawing my eye. No.

It is the group of somewhere between twenty, maybe thirty condemned rebels circling around us, swords in each of their waiting hands.

Gods damn it. If only I could use my magic. I would be able to help Draven instead of being nothing but a burden to him.

Should I have never burned King Alastair? Should I have chosen differently?

I already know my answer.

No—he *deserved* to burn.

And despite the bleak fate surrounding us, I can not find it in me to feel a sliver of pity, guilt, or regret.

What does that say about me?

Tynan's voice echoes through the night air. "Begin!"

A roar pierces the night veil as men and women peel their lips back and scream their determination like a promise to the gods. They charge after us, predators collapsing the trap onto their prey. The circle around us narrows as bodies flock to us at all angles.

This is impossible.

Without the use of our magic and with only one sword, we are practically defenseless against this many people.

We are going to die.

"Hey!" Rhea shouts from beside me, despite her hip practically being pressed to mine as Draven stands in front of us, sword at the ready. "Take these." She hands over two pristine daggers and places the hilts in my trembling palms.

"I'm not very skilled with weaponry yet," I confess. "I've been so focused on refining my magic and hand-to-hand combat skills, I haven't practiced much with weapons."

"Well, tonight is a great fucking night to get acquainted with the feel of a dagger in your hand."

Despite the abysmal situation, my lip twitches as I watch a tiny ember respark in her sharpening gaze.

"It's not about blocking," she says hurriedly as the distance between us and death diminishes pace after quickened pace. "It's about redirecting the attack. Remember that."

Quick as a blink, I feel Draven reach one hand back to squeeze my wrist. "You are the most resilient person I have ever known." In spite of the chaos, he is calm. Composed. "You can do this."

I'm glad one of us thinks so.

Seven paces. Six paces. Five paces.

"Rhea," Draven growls, some of that composure slipping. "Stand in front of Lyra, and we will keep her wedged between us."

Four paces.

"If you need me to turn," Draven instructs, "call out for me without hesitation."

Three paces.

"Together?" Rhea asks, glancing back.

Two paces.

"Together," Draven and I agree.

One.

Steel clashes against steel, the high-pitched collision of blades ringing into the air. Rhea moves like water, fluid and graceful, redirecting the glistening tips just as she said to. Draven stands tall with the unmovable force of a rooted oak, not bending against the tidal wave of people. I keep the daggers Rhea gave me firm in my palm, using them to defend against a rogue slice of a blade when it pierces its way through their defenses.

Rhea takes down two condemned fighters, her dagger finding its mark in a neck and then someone's side. I'm not entirely sure how many bodies Draven has littered at his feet, but from my peripheral and a quick glance back, I can see enough to know it's more than a few.

But it's not enough.

The people keep coming, the circle around us pressing in.

Rhea shouts and kicks out, driving a man backward. In the opening, a woman grabs Rhea's leg and pulls. She plummets to the ground, keeping a hold of only one dagger. Her body slides, until it stills, her now dagger-less hand holding form in front of her, her chest heaving.

I glance up to find the dagger lodged into the woman's eye socket, blood spilling down the woman's cheeks like tears.

Was she a mother? A wife? Did she have a family she was fighting to return to?

No.

I can't think about that now. I *can't*. Because the circumstances are clearly set and well outside of our control: either they die, or we do. And I do not plan on dying today.

Silver glints in my peripheral, and I turn just in time to see a blade reflecting the moon as it arcs down for my shoulder. As a reaction, I bring my daggers up, ready to attempt to do *something*, yet before I am forced to, another blade appears, assuming the brunt of the force.

Draven braces his forearm against the length of the blade, swallowing the force of the attack with his body. Within a heartbeat, he parries and thrusts the tip of his sword into the man's stomach, disemboweling him within an instant. "Do *not* touch her."

Two more blades glisten in the night much like the stars, and they swing down on Draven at the same moment. He turns to deflect one, and without thinking but having Rhea's last actions pressed into my mind, I throw my dagger at the charging woman. It nicks her throat and she stills. For a moment, I think I've done nothing but waste a vital weapon.

Until the blood squirts from her neck, and she slaps her hand to where the slice cut deep. She hits the ground within moments.

When I turn around, Draven has neutralized the other fighter, and he has already positioned himself over Rhea to give her time to stand, two swords now in his hand. Cuts are slashed throughout the fabric of Rhea's clothing, and blood drips from her arms and legs.

She avoided a fatal injury, but she was injured while on the ground. That much is certain.

It doesn't stop her from picking up two fallen swords and twirling them around in her hands. Then she moves with swift, brute force, her ability with a blade on par with Draven's, if not better. The black kohl always lining her eyes is smudged while blood mattes her hair and dirt coats her skin. I can't help but think she looks like a goddess of death right now.

The admiration costs me.

I feel a sharp pain slice down my back and then another at my calf. I buckle to my knees, a cry of pain tearing free from my throat. I see the blurry outline of a blade as it plunges down for me, yet the fighter crumbles before it can ever strike true, a blade now protruding through his chest. Draven appears, only one sword in hand, but more fighters keep coming.

There's still so many of them.

One person trips over all the bodies crowding in and falls into me. The man clatters to the ground, yet even that doesn't stop him from attempting to pierce me with his sword. I move with my remaining dagger—the action agonizing from the oozing slice now marring my back—and drive the tip into the crook of his shoulder the same moment his sword is thrust clean through my bicep.

I scream while pain makes my vision pulse with flashing colors.

Is this the fate of humanity? I think in my delirious, pain-induced state. *Are we doomed to forever act with such barbarism?*

Draven bends down and grips the bleeding man roughly, throwing him across the space while my dagger remains wedged into his skin. At the same moment, a woman charges forward and slices clean through his combat boots, her blade reaching the skin of his heels, cutting both tendons. Then she slices with another motion, cutting his calves.

Draven drops instantly.

The woman charges forward, her blade lifted high over her head.

Something beyond instinct overtakes me, propelling my muscles to act with a force superseding what I myself am capable of. I pull the blade free from my arm—so much of my blood spilling free as a result—and I throw myself over Draven's body, driving the steel upward.

It glides straight through the woman's chest.

She sways before tipping backward, landing with a dull *thud*.

"Are you okay?" I ask Draven as I pry myself off him, my vision flickering, my bleeding arm now fully limp at my side.

"Get to Rhea," he says, not deigning to answer me. "Rhea!" he shouts. "I need you." Blood pools around his feet.

Blood pools around my own feet.

So. Much. Blood.

I reach for another discarded sword with my uninjured arm, some small part of my mind reminding me I am supposed to be fighting. Yet my vision is fogging like steamed glass, and my muscles fill with lead, becoming nearly impossible to move.

A body yanks me up from the ground and drags me backward. I feel cool steel positioned at my throat.

"*Lyra,*" Draven's panicked voice cries. He is still flat on his stomach, unable to rise with the wounds splitting his calf muscles and the tendons at his heels. His eyes are ghosts, the whispers of a painful past edging on the precipice of a painful future.

I watch him, my head fuzzy and too heavy to hold upright for much longer.

My heart.

My love.

My person.

An oddly peaceful resignation sweeps over me. Perhaps it's from all the blood loss. Perhaps my body is going into shock. Maybe I've just decided this cruel world isn't worth fighting for any longer.

But if that's true, if there is no reason to fight, why does the man I've given my heart to keep fighting? Why, in spite of not being able to walk, is he finding a way to reach me, even now?

Because he is coming for me.

Because he will always come for me.

With a sword's hilt clutched between his blood-caked fingers, Draven moves one forearm in front of the other, crawling forward on his belly, a trail of blood his shadow. His teeth are bared, resolve and panic blazing in his bloodshot eyes.

The blade digs deeper into my throat.

Why hasn't the person sliced yet?

Draven drags himself forward, inch by slow-moving inch. He crawls to me, unwilling to give up. Further and further and further, he slides over the sticky, crimson lake dividing us.

"Draven…" I murmur at the same moment Rhea's voice echoes through the sky.

"Draven!"

She's been disarmed, a hooded figure clutching her to their chest while positioning a blade at her throat.

Draven glances back. When his eyes return to me, there is now sheer terror muting the resolve once setting them ablaze.

"Well, well," Tynan drawls from the balcony, speaking for the first time since this horrible game began. "Whoever will you choose? What will you do when you can only move—oh, forgive me—*crawl* to one of them?"

Draven grits his teeth, ignoring his father entirely. He positions himself so he can slam the hilt of his sword into the magic-blocking manacles latched around his wrists. He starts with his left hand, slamming the weapon down with so much force, I swear I hear bone crunch. "Fuck. *Fuck!*"

He continues slamming the hilt against the manacles.

They do not budge an inch.

"*Fuck!*" he screams, hysteria now seeming to be the driving force behind his movements.

Though to be fair, it is hard to tell. The world around me is very blurry.

"Too bad," Tynan pouts. "You couldn't even manage to keep one of them protected this time." Tynan lifts his hand, as if to give some signal.

"Choice." Draven growls the word out, somehow quiet and loud all at once.

"Choice?" Tynan echoes. "Please, do elaborate." There is an undercurrent of victory in his voice.

"What's my *choice*? I know you have one for me."

"You're looking at your choice, boy. And it's already been made—you let them both get captured. You've allowed them to both die."

Draven shakes his head, his thin lips stretched with a palpable resentment. "No. I know you have something else for me up your sleeve—a choice which has yet to be offered."

"What gives you that impression?"

"Because having both of them die does nothing for you. So far, each of the choices you've presented has benefited you. Gray Night-enjoy's game was designed to break him so he can no longer be the people's champion. Lyra's game ended with King Alastair's death. So tell me, Tynan: What. Is. My. *Choice*? What have you wagered on happening as a result of this final game?"

Tynan watches Draven for a long, silent moment, a curve wedged deep into the corner of his lips.

I sway on my feet.

"Perhaps there is more Dalmar in you than I thought," Tynan says with approval. "Very well."

He descends from the balcony and strides over, passing by Gray— who still has not moved away from his lifeless parents, his head hung and shoulders slouched forward.

Tynan stops only a few paces short of Draven. "You want a choice, boy? Then allow me to offer it to you."

The stone doors from the remaining walls near the balcony groan open, and a hooded figure carrying an onyx tray with a corked glass vial strides in. They stop at Tynan's side, lowering their head in defer-ence as he plucks the vial from the tray. He only spares the person a glance. "Heal the girl a little, would you? I need her conscious for the finale of these grand games."

"Don't *touch* her," Draven growls through clenched teeth.

Tynan crouches down in front of him, cocking his head at him and frowning. "And are you going to stop me if I do? You can't even stand, boy. Know your place."

The hooded servant approaches me, and a warmth blankets over me. Just enough to remove the blurry haze from my vision and rid some of the heaviness from my swaying head. "Finished, Master." There is something in the croakish voice which strikes a familiar chord.

Tynan points down at Draven. "Now the boy."

The servant does as asked, responding the same way once completed. "Finished, Master." Again, there is something in the cadence of the voice I recognize...

"You are dismissed, then."

The figure exits the room, and Tynan watches me with an antici- patory smirk curling his mouth. He looks back to Draven, who glares at his father as he braces his weight on his sword to rise.

"See this?" Tynan asks, holding up the vial. "This is known as the Drink of Oblivion. It can only be made by a *very* talented Gardner due to its complexities. But once brewed, all it takes is a swig for someone to forget what the creator wishes them to. It's much like your average memory elixir, only three times as potent." Tynan again slides his eyes to me, where they linger a heartbeat too long as he mocks an apolo- getic grin. And then he glances back at where Azalea lays with her lifeless eyes and crimson stains.

Rage flickers through me, a brief but painful swell in my veins as I call on magic that cannot answer. "I will ki—"

The blade at my throat presses deeper, nicking my skin and cutting my words short. The threat in the action is clear: *do not speak unless spoken to.* One glance at Rhea tells me she is simmering beneath the same warning.

"This vial has been brewed specifically for you," Tynan continues, attention now returned to Draven. "If consumed, you will forget everything that has prevented you from being the heir House Dalmar needs. Attachments. Feelings of love and devotion. You will be stripped of your pesky desire to protect. Will be removed of your sentimentali- ties. You will finally be the son I have wanted. Then, you will marry Arden Larking as I have publicly declared, and together, the two of you will create a new heir—a new child born of the light and of the dark."

"And if I refuse?"

"Then the two people you love most will die by the blades currently pressed against their throats at my command. Truthfully, the choice is quite simple: either lose them in life or lose them in memory. Choose the selfish or the selfless." A pause paired with a satisfied grin. "Clever, isn't it?

Draven swipes the vial from Tynan's hand. "Do not stand before me and pretend you've created a choice of great depth. There is nothing clever about pure theatrics. My decision was never in question, and you knew that."

Tynan shrugs, still smiling. "It has been a great show though, hasn't it? It's a shame you won't be able to fully appreciate my final bow any longer."

Draven ignores him. "You swear if I drink this—if I make this choice—you will not kill them?"

"Not tonight at least. Which, given your circumstances, is the best you can hope for."

Draven observes his father, his decision clearly made. He looks at Rhea first. "Do not give into the darkness, Rhea. Do not let your anger swallow you. Do not allow who you are to be lost."

"Draven, don't..." Rhea's voice quivers. "*Please.* I can't...I don't..." She stops. "I don't want to be alone." She is crying now. "Brother, *please.*"

Draven hides it well, but I can see by the stiffness of his shoulders and the way his chin is held a little too steady he is trying hard not to show his devastation. "Find Finlay," he instructs, voice tight. "He will help you navigate all that's to come. He *will* fight to keep you safe, Rhea. Promise me you'll find him."

"No. I'll find Kiran instead."

My stomach drops.

Draven's gaze hardens. "No. Listen to me, Rhea. You find *Finlay.* No one else. Promise me."

"I-I can't. I won't. Draven, he—"

"*Promise me.*"

Rhea jerks her chin away from him, remaining silent.

"*Rhea.*"

"Fine," she whispers, still not looking at him. "I promise."

Draven looks to me next, so many unspoken words spilling over his eyes. How does one say so much in so little time, while not truly being able to say anything at all?

"I love you, Lyra. That can never be rewritten."

Draven uncorks the vial and tips his head back, swallowing the blue contents inside.

My eyes widen with my horror. "No! *No!*" I flail against the hold on me, slicing my neck at the center. It stings and burns, but I don't care.

"You can let her go now," Tynan instructs.

The person releases their hold, and I sprint to Draven, my steps horribly unsteady. As I run, I realize for the first time that the remaining condemned fighters have disappeared. I haven't the slightest idea where they went or how they managed to vanish without me noticing.

Yet I have no time to consider the peculiarity of that. Instead, I only focus on Draven, mounds of dust kicking up and burning my eyes, forcing me to swipe my forming tears away with the back of my hand just before crashing my body into his.

He absorbs the shock of my impact without budging an inch.

I squeeze him, holding onto his waist with wild desperation.

Please hold me back. Please hold me back. Please.

Hold me back.

Draven's hands bracket my shoulders. I pull away to meet his gaze. The gaze I know as intimately as I know my own soul.

Yet there is nothing familiar about the way he looks at me as he pries me off.

He blinks. "Who are you?"

CHAPTER SIXTY-EIGHT

LYRA

Who are you?

I hear the words in my mind again and again as I stare at Draven, my heart squeezing painfully in my chest.

Yet I can't believe it. Not yet. I have to check. I need to be sure of what is truly happening. I refuse to feel anything until I do.

I reach for his hand, sweeping my thumb over his rough, calloused palm. "You don't recognize me?"

"Is there a reason I should?" He looks at me with the same stoic detachment he wore when we first met at Bathara.

"Yes," I murmur. "You should because you love me."

"I love you?" His lip curls, and he recedes a step. "Not possible. I do not wish to love. Ever. Not to mention, I am engaged to another woman."

I take a closer step to him. "No. You did not choose her or that life; you chose *me*."

He blinks at me, eyes narrowing. "And so you chose a monster in turn?"

My chin quivers. Emotion floods my chest. I inch forward another step, lifting my hands to cup his face. "You are not a monster."

His narrowed eyes linger on me, and he wraps his fingers around

657

my wrists. For a moment, I think he may lean forward and do something as foolish as kiss me.

Until he throws my hands away from his face and steps back. "Do not touch me."

Laughter echoes through the night, and Tynan claps his hands together. "It's remarkable what Gardners can do, isn't it?"

I say nothing.

My gaze instead slides to Rhea, the one holding her still keeping a blade at her throat as if she is too much of a wildcard to set free.

But I can see the truth—can recognize the look with sharp clarity.

She has nothing left to offer this fight.

Tynan approaches me, a sharp gleam in his eye. "I must say, I find a poetic irony in all this."

"Go burn in Merikh's realm." I spit at his feet.

"Sorry, but I'm afraid I have a kingdom to conquer and then a continent to run." A smile. "Besides, we have one last game to play. Though I assure you, this one is quick and painless. I'll give you a clue —it's called 'Guess the Name.'"

"I'm done playing your games." My fists clench at my sides. "Have you not taken enough from us already? Are you truly so cruel?"

"Ah, but see, in this game I am not taking. I am *giving* you something. Something I know you will want. Really, you should be thanking me."

"What could you possibly give me that I want? Outside of your son's freedom and your own death."

He chuckles, clasping his hands behind his back. "I can offer you the truth of your heritage."

The shocking weight of that rattles through me. "What?" I breathe before shaking myself free of my daze. "Why?" I demand instead.

"Because, moving forward, I think it will make things very, very interesting."

Uncertainty clings to my skin. Yet it is muted by the overwhelming ache of curiosity. To know what information he has.

It doesn't matter. It changes nothing.

That's what I try to tell myself, anyway. That the truth of my heritage holds no bearing any longer. I am who I am—have lived how I have lived. Why should I care now?

And yet...

I lift my chin. "Tell me."

Tynan smiles with perfect poise. He paces. "From the first moment I heard the surname Izacalli, I knew something was off. And see, that? That piqued my interest. So I investigated. Oh, and what I discovered was *sweet*." He chuckles, shaking his head. "Lyra Izacalli," he hums. "The sole daughter to Railiana Izacalli, a Gardner in servitude to King Alastair. Only, your mother wasn't just a Gardner, was she? She was also a Veilreader, and quite the talented one at that. Do you know the truth of why?"

My heart picks up speed in my chest while fire blazes beneath my skin.

My silence is my answer.

Tynan's smile crawls up at the sight. "It is because Railiana Izacalli wasn't your mother's real name. Railiana *Izavarda* was. She was the lost daughter to the great Izavarda line—a legacy bloodline that, if located inside Erandor Kingdom's borders and not gone extinct alongside its final daughter, would be considered a Great House, right alongside House Sulien, House Fjolla, and my very own House Dalmar."

The world stills for a blurry heartbeat before slamming into me. Glass shards suddenly encase my lungs, and my mind can't seem to fully process those words. As if on reflex, my eyes slide to Draven. He watches the exchange with a perfect mask of indifference.

I shake my head, dragging my eyes away from him.

It...that's...not *possible*. It can't be.

Right?

"This realization certainly leads one to wonder: where, then, did the last part of your surname come from? Personally, I find it a reasonable conclusion to surmise it comes from whomever your father is." Tynan mocks consideration, pressing two fingers to his lips. "Remind me, what is King Yarum's surname?"

The room closes in on itself. The glass shards multiply. My mind tangles in a spider's web.

"Calliva," I answer, breathless. "King Yarum Calliva."

"Ahh." Tynan snaps his fingers "Yes, that's it." He halts his pacing, squaring his shoulders to me. "Lyra Izacalli. Would you like to finally know who your father is?"

I don't answer. I feel incapable of speaking. Hell, simply standing is an act of will at this point.

"Your father," Tynan drawls, eyes bright with delight, "is none other than the great King Yarum Calliva of the Anatolé Kingdom."

Bile burns my throat; I'm going to be sick.

Tynan cocks his head, a frown pulling at his lips. "Do you think he knows about you? Knows he has another daughter out in the world? One with the rumored love of his life, no less." He resumes pacing once more. "You see, I did some digging, and I discovered the most fascinating information. Your mother and father had a secret love affair while he was betrothed to his current wife. It was an arranged marriage, so it's hard to fault him, really. But on the eve of King Yarum's wedding—well, I suppose he was only the Crown Prince at that time—your mother, the final-born Izavarda descendant, simply disappeared, never to be heard from again. Her mysterious vanishing was officially recorded as uncertain circumstances, most likely from unfortunate trafficking or an untraceable murder. Her parents grieved, yet no one questioned it further—made certain by Yarum's father, the former king of that time." He pauses, observing me with a sharp stare. "Do you understand what I'm telling you?"

"Liar." The word flees from my lips less as an accusation and more as a plea.

Tynan chuckles. "I swear to you on the Dalmar name what I tell you is no lie. But if you don't believe me, put the evidence together yourself. Railiana Izavarda. Yarum Calliva. Iza. Calli." He annunciates the final sounds slowly, punctuating each syllable for emphasis. "Put them together and what name does it form?"

Izacalli.

Defined by a name both two and one, born from the ashes of a great love.

Everything tilts, and King Yarum's words to me in his private gardens suddenly take on an entirely different meaning.

You reminded me of someone I once knew; when I first laid my eyes on you that night, I thought I was seeing her ghost.

The reason he saved me during The Founding celebration was because he thought he saw a ghost in me, only...he was *actually* seeing a reflection. He was seeing my mother. He was seeing *me*, the product of them both.

I wobble on my feet.

Tynan watches the truth settle inside me, too indisputable to deny. He grins with unbidden satisfaction and strolls over to me, pinching my chin between his thumb and index finger, lifting it to where I am forced to meet his oceanic eyes.

"Which means you, dear girl, are not only the last member of a legacy bloodline, but you are also a living member of the Anatolé Kingdom's royal bloodline. Perhaps even his only living daughter, if the rumors surrounding the lost princess's fate are to be trusted."

As odd as it is—probably because my mind and body are working so quickly to put a barrier between me and this revelation—a strange relief washes over me by what information Tynan let slip, whether intentionally or not. He still doesn't know the truth about Nuri. Which means the Veilreader—my *mother*, I now suspect—gave King Yarum the correct instructions. Truly helped Nuri evade being identified and targeted.

She saved her life.

Tynan tightens his grip on my face. "You know what that means, girl?"

My upper lip peels back, but I say nothing.

He slides his fingers up, digging them into my cheeks. "It means I suspect you are a Veilreader just like your mother was. And you would be no ordinary reader. No. You would be an *Izavarda* Veilreader." He glares into my eyes like I have materialized a new form. One composed of adorned glass, belonging on a black and white playing board. "Which makes you incredibly useful to me."

"Fuck. You," I bite out, the act of speaking hard with my face pinched between his grip.

I feel it as I hold his eyes—different pieces and elements inside me snapping. Breaking apart and unraveling, shaping itself into something new.

He laughs, the sound sharp. "What—you don't want to serve under a new regime? One of power and grandness? One which will rewrite the course of history as we know it?"

"Fuck your regime. Fuck your power. And *fuck* you. I am through being a pawn in men's games. Through being told who I must serve and what I must want."

"Bold words for someone who has been cowering like a babe for the duration of these games."

"You just drove an arrow through that babe's chest; she exists no longer."

"And suddenly you have no fears?"

I rise to the tips of my toes, holding his stare with matching resolve. "I will *not* cower," I spit, jerking my face free of his grip. "I will not yield. And I certainly won't falter when I end this game of power you insist on playing."

"Cute," he mocks coldly.

My sneer deepens. "You haven't the slightest idea of the monster you've just created."

Yes, it suddenly all makes sense now. How Casimir arrived at his decision. Why he lost his faith—his desire for good and diplomacy. I said there was a better way, but there isn't, is there?

Yes. It's so clear now. Why Draven once told me he trains to never be forced to his knees. Why the depth of one's magic holds such worth within these Three Kingdoms.

Power.

It all comes back to power.

And I was wrong.

Power *is* freedom.

And I only wish to be free.

Tynan smirks. "Oh, I think I'm entirely aware of the many

monsters I've just created." He slides his eyes to Gray, his smirk deepening.

Rage burns my chest. "You know the thing about monsters?"

He arches a polished brow. "Do tell."

"They tend to stop at nothing until they get what they want. At whatever price necessary."

An explosion sounds, snatching our attention. Tynan and I whip our heads to the east, finding flashes of color arcing through the sky.

Fire rains down from the inky clouds, much like it had on Anatolé's capital city.

Yet it is not just fire.

It is water, wind, and terra. There is light magic and—

My heart swells.

Flora magic.

The echoes of pounding hooves suddenly fill the air, and I bring my eyes to Tynan, victory on my lips.

It worked. By the gods it *worked*.

She got my message before I found Draven. The necklace imbued with my laktî.

And she came—actually found us.

She is not alone.

I turn back to Tynan. "You know what I love about chess?" He doesn't answer, and my smile broadens. "I love the way you can swindle your opponents by allowing them to believe you've only made losing moves." My eyes glitter with victory. "Guess what, Tynan? Check *fucking* mate."

A barrage of magic slams into the ground beside us, and a band of wielders appears over the horizon, charging in on horseback, their faces lined with cold fury. Leading the charge is Nuri, her expression written in revenge's bold script. To her left is Marcella, and to her right, to my complete surprise, is Klytis.

They forge ahead with probably somewhere around forty other wielders behind them, most shooting off their magic skillfully while using one hand to keep themselves secured on the reins of their horses.

Tynan scowls, biting down so aggressively on his lip, he draws blood. "You've made one grave mistake, girl."

"I've made more than one, I assure you."

His scowl deepens. "You've forgotten that you no longer have *him*." He thrusts a finger in Draven's direction, who remains standing with his arms folded, his cold expression disinterested.

I straighten my spine and roll my shoulders back. "I will always have him, as he will always have me."

"The sentiment will be your gallows." Tynan turns away, his movements stiff. "Guards! Fighters! Take no prisoners."

The horses close in, and the world around me explodes with color as magics clash against each other. The force of wind barrels into the strength of rock. Fire chews at water, the smoke and steam rising to bloat the sky. Thunder rumbles, shaking the ground at our feet.

"Draven," Tynan growls, his smooth composure fracturing. "Remove the girl from this area and keep her alive. I have need of her."

"As you wish, Father." Draven steps forward, his hands finally leaving the grooves of his biceps. The same hooded guard who released my manacles appears, and he unshackles the manzat from Draven's wrists.

I hear Draven's sharp inhale as the magic floods his veins once more. He shuts his eyes, seeming to brace himself against the weight of it. His veins turn black, running up into his neck. When he reopens his eyes, they appear bloodshot. Only, instead of being red, the lines of his eyes are dark as the night.

Yet in spite of the visual of a living nightmare, my eyes are locked on that key.

I sprint for it.

"You are on a fool's errand," I hear Tynan call out to me as I run.

I don't care. I do not stop.

A lancing spear of ice shoots for me, whipped away by thick green vine coated in thorns. I quickly glance over my shoulder and find Marcella dismounting her horse, sprinting for me. Nuri is not far behind her, daggers in hand, two wielders flanking her sides.

When I reorient my attention forward, I find Draven with tendrils of black snaking over his fingers like a coiling serpent. My throat runs dry, and my knees have a momentary bout of weakness. Yet still, I do not stop running.

For now, this is what I can do, and so I will do it.

I charge on.

Draven lifts a hand as if to send a blast of his magic. Before he can, however, he is tackled to the ground from behind.

"Go!" Rhea shouts. "I'll do what I can."

Draven spins around, pressing Rhea's arms to her side and hoisting her off of him as though she is weightless.

"Draven, *please*," she begs, locked in his grasp. "Don't you recognize me? Don't you remember? Think of The Polished Bookery. Remember Zumi and Atlas and your mother. Nights spent at a dinner table and with books spread out around us."

Draven only blinks at her. "I have no such memories."

And then he throws her aside, discarding her as effortlessly as forgotten scraps, leaving her on the opposite end of the raging battle.

Guilt weighs heavy on me, but I don't allow myself to stop sprinting.

I reach the guard, who lifts an obsidian sheet of rock from the ground and sends it hurling toward me. It is met by an impenetrable wall of darkness.

"You heard my father," Draven growls. "She is *mine* to take."

I don't waste a second of the guard's resulting confusion. I drop to the ground and swipe my leg out, sending the hooded figure toppling backward. And then I swipe the key from their loose grip the moment their back slams into the ground.

With trembling yet still assured fingers, I jerk upright and slam the key into the locks, removing the manacles from my wrists. The power rears into me, and I am temporarily overwhelmed with all the new magics nearby. I can sense them so clearly now, each one like a glowing thread waiting to be plucked.

Casimir was right.

Accepting the flames *had* allowed my magic to advance. I can feel it. As though allowing myself a primary magic has brought order to the chaos.

So I embrace them fully—the flames.

Let the world burn.

Brilliant white erupts in my palms, so at odds with the smoky black pooling in Draven's as he watches me. "Are we really going to do this?" I ask.

I swear I see a whisper of a smile on his lips, a cruel reminder of the way he would look at me. "It's your funeral."

Our magics sound like breaking glass as they collide in the space between us, sparks shooting off as one tries to overwhelm the other. Darkness and radiant white flames twirl and mix, creating an odd reflection of shadows over everyone.

Strangely, it almost looks like starlight.

I grit my teeth, palms stretched out in front of me. The magic surges, yet I breathe through it, remembering everything Casimir taught me.

Breathe. Just breathe.

I pull at more and funnel it against Draven's attack.

The dark magic cedes two paces.

"I'm here," I hear Nuri exhale from behind me. Within a heartbeat, I feel warm hands on my back, healing magic immediately pouring into me.

"The key," I manage to grit out. "Get the key to Rhea, and then Gray."

"Give me thirty more seconds," Nuri counters. "Your wounds are bad, Lyra."

I shake my head. "I don't care. We need to get out of here before Tynan chooses to join the fight."

One Dalmar is hard enough to contend with. Two would be nearly impossible.

"Alright," she says, pulling her hands from me. She grabs the key which remains discarded next to my manacles and sprints for Rhea.

Gods, I hope Rhea knows what to do.

I'm *counting* on the fact that she does.

My muscles groan, and my vision flickers. My laktî hasn't built up enough stamina yet to contend with Draven on this level—to keep holding the force of his magic at bay.

I clench my teeth, and a scream tears free from my throat. I can't hold on much longer. Can't—

The push of Draven's magic against mine suddenly disappears, and my chest sags at the relief. I heave in gasping breaths, my eyes whipping to him instantly.

Mother bless his fiery sister—she did know exactly where she was needed.

Rhea has her arms wrapped around Draven's waist, her teeth gritted as she nullifies his magic. Judging from the strain on her face and the pain glimmering in her eyes, I know she can't hold it for more than a few seconds longer.

It is all we need.

"*Retreat!*" I bellow, as if this small army of wielders came solely at my command. "Fall back and retreat!"

The wielders still mid-movement, the bursts of magic having a temporary lag against the night sky. Yet soon, the word is echoed, passed down between mouths as if it is now the only option available.

Retreat.

Retreat.

Retreat.

I whirl around at a touch on my shoulder. It is Marcella, dirt and soot caked over her face. "Where is Gray?"

"What do you mean? He was right there by his parents." My eyes dart to where Sterling and Azalea remain. But Gray is no longer there. I spin, looking around frantically for him.

I find him in the distance, kicking his heel into a horse's side.

Grief and sorrow latch onto my ribcage like morning dew to grass.

"There," I whisper, pointing in his direction as he gallops off to gods-only-know where.

Gray disappears from our line of sight, behind a cloud of billowing smoke.

"His parents?" Marcella asks quietly, observing the bodies.

"Yes," I murmur. "They are Sterling and Azalea Nightenjoy. I don't have time to explain, but you should know Gray likely blames himself for their deaths. I think it might have shattered something irrevocable in him."

Marcella's eyes widen, then fall. Her lips thin. "I'm going after him. I'm probably the only one who can track him anyway." She turns her gaze to me, filled with layered emotions. Determination. Remorse. Sorrow. Devotion. "I will bring him back to us, Lyra. You have my word."

I nod at her, biting down on my lip, knowing deep in my gut she is the best choice for it. "Go."

She watches me a heartbeat longer, then throws her arms around my neck, squeezing tightly. "Be safe."

I hold her with all I have. "You too."

We pull apart, and Marcella sprints for her horse, mounting with impressive grace. She yells instructions to the mare, turning its reins and making off in the direction Gray went.

I only allow myself a moment to watch her leave.

I sprint to Rhea, throwing out vines before Marcella's magic is out of reach, coiling them around Draven's ankles while his magic is contained, spinning them over his wrists, pinning them away from him.

"I can't..." she chokes when I reach her. "...nullify the magic much longer."

I stretch my hand out to her. "It's okay. Release him and let's go."

Draven squirms against his bindings, one hand already tearing free from my vines. I know I should weave thorns into them—add the extra layer of security. But I just...can't.

"No," Rhea says, keeping her palms outstretched as she funnels her magic over him.

"You must. You aren't safe here."

"*No.* I won't leave him."

I grip her shoulders and drag her back. "I don't want to leave him either, Rhea; this is *killing* me. But we have to. I will explain when we have more time, but for right now, I need you to trust me."

"I barely know you," she hisses, breaking free of my grip. She whirls around on me, and I realize she's lost her hold on Draven's magic. Dark tendrils whip into the air, yet she doesn't so much as turn around. "I'm not leaving my brother."

"*Listen* to me," I seethe back, the lack of time pressing against me. "You trust Draven, right? Well Draven trusts *me*. So I need you to trust me as well, and if you still can't do that, trust Draven's judgement."

Rhea's jaw flexes.

I make one final push. "You know the decision he would want you to make. Know the promise *you* made *him*."

Rhea glances back at him. Draven's upper-half is fully free of my vines, his lower-half alive with a black flame eating away at my magic. Her hands clench at her sides. "Fine," she mutters.

She takes my hand.

We sprint for where Nuri leads the retreat.

Magic clashes and roars around us, guards and wielders alike making their final efforts. Four aether portals are swirling in the air, a mix of glittering silvers, whites, and blacks. I push Rhea to one such portal.

"Go through it," I demand.

She shoots me a warning look, seeming to want to lash out. Yet she swallows her anger instead, eyes finding Draven a final time. He walks toward us at a steady pace, dark magic pouring from him like steam from a hot spring.

"Fuck," she mutters under her breath, hands balled into fists.

Rhea steps through the portal.

I find Nuri next. "You came." The emotion bloating my words is far more loaded than she is capable of understanding.

She nods, acknowledging that which doesn't have time to be spoken. "They have him, Lyra. They captured my father during the raid and are holding him hostage somewhere."

Our father, I correct in my mind.

The weight of that threatens to upend me.

I do not let it.

Instead, I turn back to look at Tynan one last time. He remains where I left him, watching me with that polished smile once more.

He lifts a hand and waves his fingers in goodbye. "I'll be in touch."

I bite down on my anger and swivel my gaze back to Nuri. "We will find him, and we will rescue him. But for now, we must retreat."

She nods. "I know."

I glance over my shoulder at Draven. Black pools in his palms, and he directs his hands at us.

"Go. *Go*."

Nuri watches the remaining wielders as they retreat backwards, battling off the incoming attacks. "See you on the other side, yes?"

"Yes. I'm right behind you."

A spear of dark magic soars through the air, and I pull on terra magic to deflect it with a wall of rock, sending shards of stone flying for Draven's feet after.

Nuri monitors, then nods at me once it seems safe. She disappears behind the glittering silver and black.

I find Klytis next behind two wielders a few paces away. He slides his eyes to me, and I gesture for him to follow into his portal after me.

We need him with us.

Klytis dips his chin with understanding.

I glance back, allowing myself to watch Draven for one heartbeat longer.

Come back to me, my love.

Despite everything, I reach for a slip of parchment tucked into my pocket, pulling it out to read the script.

The world tried to rewrite our story once. We will not let them do it again.

No.

We won't.

I slide the slip of parchment back into place.

Then I step through the portal to face the ashes of an incinerated kingdom and a stirred-up war, revelations wedged beneath my skin and desolate hope clinging to my fingertips.

EPILOGUE

CASIMIR

Some Time After....

A horridly loud crack sounds in the distance.

It comes from the glorified graveyard towering in the clouds. A place mankind remains adamant labeling as a temple merely because it houses the gods. Yet what gives a god its grandeur? Their right to be worshipped as revered deities? Immortality? Power? If so, would Casimir not be a god amongst them?

He does not wish to be anything of the sort. If the gods are the truth of this world, he would prefer to continue with his endless existence swaddled in a lie. Because the gods he has faced—has battled and bled for—are not worth the reverence humanity places upon them. Are not worth their weight in prayers, shrines, and golden offerings.

He knows humanity would be inclined to agree if they ever saw the truth of the bloodlust in their glittering eyes and heard the selfishness in their pretty words.

Power sharper than any mortal could ever comprehend surges, sharpening the air with an intensity so palpable, it pricks even his skin. Casimir knows the gold has officially fractured and split open.

He feels more than hears the tiny voice inside him, warning him as a result.

They are free, my Fallen One.

He knows the words belong to the Mother Goddess. Centuries later, and she still has not fully turned her back on him. Though, she has done nothing to cure him from his sickly disease of immortality, either.

Casimir rests his eyes while sitting atop the bench in his too quiet courtyard. He allows the words which have haunted him for centuries to play through his mind.

But a promise, I can give: another shall come.

One who is defined by a name both two and one, born from the ashes of what the raven desired most, yet never found. And when they awaken—chosen by the Cycle to harbor the greatest power of all—the ashes of one great war will stir, giving way to another, and the Chosen will decide the fate of kingdoms, just as the raven himself had.

It has all finally come to pass.

Lyra Izacalli *will* decide the fate of kingdoms now.

A flicker of sorrow pierces him as he also remembers the warning the prophecy gave. He tried to protect her from it. Tried to forge his interests and desires into a single sharpened blade capable of slicing through each syllable of the prophecy's final cautionary words. He crafted a plan which would not only save his people and allow him to die—it was also supposed to save *her*. Though coldened and cruel he may be now, his final scraps of empathy, pity—whatever to call it—were reserved solely for not wanting her to feel a shred of the pain and heartbreak that led him down his path of spiraling descent.

Should the Chosen fall as the raven fell...

He tried to prevent it. He really did. Yet look where his efforts led him. They brought him straight to the ruination of everything he deigned to finally care for. An obliteration of the final pieces of his withered heart. Pieces he gave to his people, who deserved so, so much better.

He wanted to save them. He wanted to save her.

He failed.

He always seems to fail when trying for good.

Which leaves Casimir no longer knowing his role in all this. He wandered lost for centuries before he reclaimed the bloodlines of the original Abdites as his family. Previously attempted hundreds of ways to end his cursed life in his misery. Now that his only purpose has been stripped from him, what now? For what purpose does he harbor such power? What worth is his immortality?

Perhaps he should still move forward with his plan. To wipe clean the stain of nobility and erase the Cycle of magic. To reset the balancing scales.

Yet...

Is there even a point any longer? Is such a wretched system even worth resetting without having something—someone—to correct it for?

He shuts his eyes again, scrubbing at his face. "I know you would have an answer, my darling," he whispers. "If only you would come back to me. If only I could find you."

There is one thing Casimir can be certain of. The gods *have* awakened—have gone free—and the only currency they know is blood.

A shadow appears over his eyes, the two wielders he sensed long ago now standing over him. Casimir sighs, reorienting himself to sit upright, draping his arm over his thigh and leaning forward to gaze at the strangers with his deadened eyes.

A man stands before him, his long brown hair half-drawn and unruly. He wears an eyepatch, a gnarly gash trailing down from it to mar the base of his cheek. His jaw is coated in stubble, shoulders covered by a black-as-tar cloak.

Casimir blinks, realization dawning on him. "You look different."

The person next to the man drops their hood, revealing a woman with curling, copper hair.

Casimir only spares her a glance, resting his cheek upon his closed fist. "Remind me your name again."

The rough man folds his arms, revealing scarred hands and a cobalt ring. "My name is Gray Nightenjoy. And I have need of you."

ACKNOWLEDGMENTS

It is no exaggeration to say that writing this part of the book somehow always feels amongst the most gratifying.

Firstly, I want to thank every reader who gave the first book in this series a chance. Those who took a risk on a debut from an author they did not know. To everyone who posted about *A Requiem for Fallen Stars*, hyped it, and spread the word to their friends, families, and online communities: my gratitude and appreciation for all of you has no end. Thank you. (And while I could probably fill this entire page listing out many names, I have to give a special shoutout to my girl, Shaelin, @shaelinslibrary. Whenever someone comes up to me and tells me they were influenced to read the book, they're almost always quoting your name as the reason why. You are amazing, and I owe you a truly special, massive thank you.)

Tabatha, I must thank you for your unending patience with me as I unravel the maze in my brain. You always listen intently. Always supply me with thoughtful, well-rounded feedback. You grapple with the story's dilemmas and join me in the weeds as I attempt to sow a rocky garden into something vibrant and alive. I cherish both you and your opinion, and I cannot thank you enough for devoting so much of your time and energy to helping this story become what it is today.

Sharilyn, you are a walking grammar guide. Thank you for fixing my misplaced hyphens and my absent commas. For critiquing questionable word choices and highlighting areas where a sentence can be reworked for stronger impact. Your edits always help elevate the book, and I am eternally grateful for all the effort you put forth in refining my manuscript.

Milleniah, my resident vibes reader and all things pop-culture guru—thank you for being such a monumental pillar and for listening to me while I untangled *A Ballad for the Broken*'s storyline. Thank you for offering invaluable insights and for carrying such enthusiasm for this story and its characters. I appreciate you endlessly.

To my agent, Maddy—thank you for believing in my words, my stories, and my characters. Thank you for choosing to champion them.

To my mother, for being amongst the first to read this story and for being as passionate about its characters as I am—thank you. I love you.

To my husband—thank you for being the shelter to the storms in my mind. For bringing me food when I refuse to leave my computer, and then waking me up with fresh coffee the following morning when I'm groggy because of it. Thank you for letting me ramble. For offering me ideas and feedback when asked. Thank you for being my support and partner in life. I love you. I am thankful for you. I treasure the extraordinary peace you offer me.

And then to you, dearest reader. Again, I must thank you. There is an abundance of amazing books in the world, and so I will never stop being grateful that you chose to read mine. There is no story without you—thank you for letting mine exist.

ABOUT THE AUTHOR

Hazel is simply a lover of words and stories, overflowing with made-up worlds, scenarios, and characters. Ever since she was just a small girl, climbing out of her bedroom window to read on the roof under the stars with her trusted book light in hand (sorry, Mom), she has been enchanted by stories and the art of storytelling.

Hazel lives in Texas with her equally-nerdy husband, her fluffy dog-child, and the two sweetest cats a pet mom could hope for. Aside from writing and consuming far too much caffeine, she enjoys playing sports, watching anime, training exhaustively to become a fierce competitor in the rigorous art of trivia, spending time with her family, and discussing books with her bookish besties.

www.hazelwilkes.com
instagram.com/hazelwilkesauthor

CONTENT WARNINGS

A Ballad for the Broken is a fantasy romance novel set in a fictional world. The story contains mature language, graphic violence, sexually explicit scenes, death of a parent, heavy trauma and grief, mentions of attempted suicide (off page; due to immortality) discussion surrounding past experience with disorderly eating and distorted body image, intense psychological situations, & mass murder.

Readers who may be sensitive to these elements, please read with care.

GLOSSARY

Abdites (Ab-dye-ts): Corrupted wielders lost to the forbidden magics.

Accord of Three Kings: The formal treaty which ended the rule of one sovereign king, recognizing new borders where three new kings may govern their lands by their own laws, so long as they remain in accordance with Tani Law.

Adhara (Ahd-hara): Goddess of love and beauty.

Ahlai (Ah-lay): The Mother Goddess, mother to the Canamae.

Anatheima (An-nah-thee-mah): Capital city of Anatolé Kingdom.

Anatolé Kingdom (An-nah-tahl-lay): The Rising Sun Kingdom.

Algol (Al-goal): God of trickery and deception.

Astralis (Ah-straw-lis): God of the stars and heavens—god of justice.

Araceli (Air-rah-cell-ee): Goddess of health, fertility, and purity.

Ardoris Festival (Are-door-ris): Comet festival hosted yearly in the Anatolé Kingdom.

Bathara Academy (Bah-thaar-rah): Magical academy located in the borderless region— where wielders study to become Jurafen.

Cahlmon Orius (Kahl-mon Oh-rye-yus): Master at Bathara who teaches wielding techniques and magical theory.

Canamae (Con-uh-may): The primary gods, also known as the pillars of the mortal world.

Casimir Vivaldri (Cas-ih-meer Vih-val-dree): Son of the first-ever Rivarian King—the first Crown Prince of Rivara Kingdom.

Dyotana (Dye-oh-tan-nah): Small, translucent caterpillars that live in rock faces, composed of glowing blue bodies that appear almost crystal-like.

Endymion Mountains (En-dim-ee-uhn): Mountain range located in the northwestern region, composed of anthracite.

Erandor Kingdom (Air-en-dor): The Kingdom Between Rivers.

Gardner (Guard-ner): Said to be Ahlai's children, Gardners are similar to apothecaries, but are able to concoct more elaborate potions, tonics, and elixirs using methods only known to themselves.

Great Clamatè War (Claw-mah-tay): A great war which transpired at the dawn of the Three King System, involving gods and mortals alike.

House Dalmar (Dahl-mar): A Great House and Archblood—progenitor bloodline for dark magic. Draven Dalmar is the current heir of this House.

House Fjolla (Fee-olla): A Great House and Archblood—progenitor bloodline for ice magic. Finlay Fjolla is the current heir of this House.

House Sulien (Suh-lee-in): A Great House and Archblood—progenitor bloodline for fire magic. Kiran Sulien is the current heir of this House.

Izavarda Bloodline: An extinct legacy bloodline formally known for their supreme Veil-reading abilities.

Illithious Lake (Ill-lith-ee-ous): A burning lake composed of flames.

Josiah Hartley (Jo-sigh-uh): Keeper of Bathara.

Jurafen: (Jur-ah-fen): Physically fit, strategic, and possess high moral integrity, these are the wielding soldiers of Solaya who vow to protect society from threats of creatures, magic, and man alike—adhere to a strict ethical code and are bound to no king, thus maintaining political neutrality at all times. They answer only to the Keeper, who answers to the Tani.

Keziah (Keh-zee-ah): The capital city of the Rivara Kingdom.

King Alastair (Al-a-star): Presiding king over Rivara Kingdom.

King Erasmus (Ur-az-muhs): Presiding king over Erandor Kingdom.

King Yarum (Yah-rue-mm): Presiding king over Anatolé Kingdom.

Klytis Hilthrop (Kuh-lie-tis): Resident aether-wielder for King Alastair.

Laktî (lock-tee): Substance in a wielder's veins allowing them to harness the properties of magic.

Magaius (Mah-guy-is): Casimir Vivaldri's best friend, as noted in his journal, dating four-hundred and eleven years ago.

Merikh (Mare-ick): God of death and ends; god of war.

Morwenna (More-wen-nah): Goddess of water, known Daughter of the Moon.

Raffir (Rah-fear): God of the harvest and prosperity.

Raima (Ray-muh): Village that House Sulien presides over.

Raun (Rah-un): Sanctioned method to lay claim to a throne. Has only happened twice in record history since the signing of the Accord of Three Kings.

Rivara Kingdom (Rih-var-rah): Kingdom Loved by the Gods.

Saffi (Sah-fee): Goddess of cunning and knowledge.

Sitara: Former friend of Casimir Vivaldri, said to have fallen in love with Astralis and been gifted the power of the stars.

Skull Traders: Underground group known for dealing in knowledge and information through the use of illicit activities.

Solaya (Sol-aye-yah): Name of the continent that houses the Three Kingdoms—Rivara, Erandor, and Anatolé.

Tani (Tahn-nee): Highest order of magical governance. Their laws must be followed by all the Three Kingdoms, without question, as stated in the Accord of Three Kings.

The Cycle: The unknowable power which redistributes the energy all magic possesses. For even the oldest of magic cannot truly die.

Toellor (Toe-lore): Stone prison located within the Spicere Mountains where Abdites are contained.

Tuarana's River Lace (To-ah-rah-nah): A network of braided rivers located in the far northeastern corner of Solaya.

Turely Sea (Too-rel-ee): Northern sea that separates Solaya from the Silver Isle.

Tynan Dalmar (Tie-nen): Head of House Dalmar and Supreme Commander over Erandor's formidable legion—known as the Master Strategist.